YULE-TIDE STORIES

A Collection of Scandinavian and North German Popular Tales and Traditions from the Swedish, Danish, and German

BENJAMIN THORPE

Published by Left of Brain Books

ISBN 978-1-396-31823-8

First Edition

Table of Contents

PREFACE

THE POPULAR TALES AND TRADITIONS, a translation of which is now offered to the Public, are not the fruits of modern imagination, but, as their several collectors and editors inform us, are genuine ancient productions, not a few of them traceable to very remote ages and to the far-distant lands of the East, and the greater number of a date not later than the fifteenth or sixteenth century.[1]

Of the two classes—THE POPULAR TALES and the POPULAR TRADITIONS—contained in this volume, the Tales are undoubtedly the more ancient, and in their nature bear a near resemblance to the Fairy Tales of the Celtic nations, both probably having claim to the same remote origin. They may, therefore, be regarded as property common alike to the European nations, however modelled during the middle ages to harmonize with the superstitions and modes of thinking of the several people among whom they have been naturalized. Thus, while the ground of the texture is the same, the pattern wrought on it alone differs. For the Fairies, the Drakes, the Cluricauns of the Bretons, Welsh, and Irish, we have the Elves, Dwarfs, and Nisser of Scandinavian and North German fiction. These tales are, from their nature, without a definite locality, without date and names of persons. Many of them possess considerable poetic merit, and their moral is invariably excellent.

Of the Swedish Tales, forming the first portion of the collection, the editors thus speak: "We have," say they, "endeavoured to obtain every tale as original and genuine as possible. For this object we have undertaken long

---

[1] Some information on this with reference to the Swedish Tales, may be derived from the Table of Contents, prefixed to the volume, but which is almost equally applicable to the others.

journeys through the several provinces and committed to writing a very considerable number of Popular Stories from the lips of the people. What we have thus collected we have arranged and published free from all arbitrary additions and alterations. That which alone belongs to our province is the external form of the narrative, which, de pending on the various ages and degrees of culture of the narrators, naturally called for some remodelling." To some of these tales those variations are appended that are met with in the several provinces where they are current.

With regard to these Swedish Popular Tales, it will not fail to strike every one familiar with those of Germany, how much more elaborately the Swedish story is told than its German counterpart, as given in the collections of the Brothers Grimm, Bechstein, and others. This circumstance is very remarkable, as involving a degree of mystery not to be solved; for of all those parts of Europe where such tales are extant among the people, Sweden seems to be that in which least of all we should expect to find them so worked out. This observation seems applicable to the Swedish Tales, in all their provincial varieties.

Many of these tales bear evident signs of an origin anterior to the introduction of Christianity into the North, notwithstanding the allusions to the Christian faith occasionally to be found in them, but which are, no doubt, the work of times when heathenism was superseded by the purer faith of the Gospel. Another, and even greater, mystery, is their dissemination among the several nations of Europe, and at a time when communication between countries was beset by obstacles. To solve it we feel ourselves wholly incompetent, and, after all it seems a proposition appertaining to the province of the editor of a series of stories gathered together for the recreation chiefly of juvenile readers at Christmas, or, as our forefathers would have called it, "MERRY YULE-TIDE."

The foregoing observations are to a certain degree applicable to all the Scandinavian Tales, and partially to those also of Germany.

THE POPULAR TRADITIONS, however fabulous their matter, generally refer to persons who are known to have existed, and also to some place, therein differing from the POPULAR TALE. Such Traditions are far from being so worthless as at first sight they may appear. To the inquirer they are important, as affording an insight into the manners, customs, modes of thought, and superstitions of bygone days, points on which history strictly so called is but too generally silent.

With the exception of the Tales from the Swedish, the editor's task has been chiefly limited to the correction of the sheets as they issued from the press.

As many Swedish and Danish names of persons and places occur in the volume, it may be well to observe that the Swedish Å, å and its Danish equivalent Aa, aa, are pronounced as our *a* in *war*, or *oa* in *broad*; g is always hard before *e* and *i*, as in the English words *get*, *give*, and j is pronounced as *y*; the other vowels and the consonants are sounded as in almost every European tongue, and the a final *e* is pronounced as in Mètte, Aasé, etc.

B. T.

THE BIRTH OF THE POPULAR TALE

THERE was a time when there were no Popular Tales and a sad time it was for children; for in their youthful paradise the most beautiful butterfly was wanting. At this time there were also two children of a king, who played together in their father's splendid garden. This garden was full of the choicest flowers; its walks were laid with stones of various colours and gold sand, which vied in brilliancy with the sparkling dew-drops on the flower-beds. In the garden were many cool grottoes, with plashing springs, fountains towering to the sky, beautiful marble statues luxurious seats. In the basins swam gold and silver fish; the most splendid birds fluttered in golden aviaries, while others of the feathery tribe hopped and flew about at full liberty, warbling with sweet voices their delightful melodies. But the two royal children saw these things daily, and were weary of the brilliancy of the stones, the fragrance of the flowers, the fountains and the fishes, which were all so mute, and of the birds, whose song they did not understand. They sat silent together and were sad; they had everything a child could wish for, kind parents, the most costly playthings, the finest clothes, the daintiest food, and liberty to play every day—in the garden: they were sad, although they knew not why, and knew not what it was they longed for.

One day, when the queen, their mother, a beautiful stately dame, with a mild benevolent countenance, approached them, she was grieved to see them so sorrowful; for they only looked at her with a mournful smile, instead of running to her full of boisterous mirth. It afflicted her to know that her children were not happy, as children should and can be, because they yet know no care, and the heaven of childhood is usually a cloudless one.

Seating herself by her children, a boy and a girl, the queen threw one of her full white arms round each of them, and said to them, in a gentle maternal voice, "My dear children, what is it you desire?"

"We don't know, dear mother," answered the boy. "We are so melancholy," said the girl.

"But in the garden, all is so beautiful, and you have everything to give you pleasure. Do you then feel no pleasure?" asked the queen; and the tears stood in her eyes, from which a soul full of goodness beamed.

"What we have does not afford us pleasure enough," answered the girl. "We wish for something, and know not what," added the boy.

The mother was silent and troubled, and thought within herself what children could possibly desire to afford them more delight than a splendid garden, fine clothes, abundance of playthings, and dainty food; but her thoughts busied themselves to no purpose.

"Oh, that I were only a child again!" said she to herself with a soft sigh, "then, perhaps, I might discover what makes children joyful. To comprehend the wishes of a child one must be a child oneself; but I have journeyed too far from the land of childhood, where golden birds fly among the trees of that paradise; birds without feet; because, being never weary, they have no need of earthly rest. Oh, would such a bird but come hither, and bring to my dear children that which would make them happy!"

While the queen was thus wishing, a gloriously beautiful bird was seen floating above her head in the blue heaven, from which there issued a brilliancy like flames of gold or the radiation of a precious gem. It hovered lower and lower, and the queen and the children beheld it. The latter exclaimed only, "Ah! ah!" Their astonishment did not allow them to utter another word.

The bird was beauteous to look upon, as it came floating lower and lower, so glistening, so sparkling, with its vivid rainbow tints, almost blinding the eyesight, and yet fascinating it. It was so beautiful, that the queen and the children slightly shuddered with delight, particularly when they felt the fanning of its wings. Before they were well aware of it, the bird had descended into the lap of the queen and looked on the boy and girl with eyes like the friendly eyes of children; and yet there was in those eyes something that the children could not comprehend, something heterogeneous, appalling; they therefore did not venture to touch the bird. They also observed that this rare, celestial, beautiful creature, had under its bright, variegated pinions, some jet-black feathers, which at a distance were not perceptible. But for a closer survey of the beautiful bird, the children had hardly sufficient time, for it instantly rose again; the footless bird of paradise glistened, flew higher and higher, until it seemed only a many coloured feather swimming in ether, then only a golden streak, and then vanished. During its ascent, the queen and her children looked after it with astonishment. But, oh, wonderful! when mother and children again cast their eyes downwards how were they astonished anew! On the queen's lap lay a golden egg that the bird had laid, which reflected hues of golden green and golden blue, like the most beautiful Labrador feldspar and the finest mother-of-pearl. On beholding it, the children exclaimed with one voice, "See the beautiful egg!" But the mother smiled with pleasure; for she had a presentiment that it must be the jewel that was wanting to her children's happiness that the egg, in its magical coloured shell, must contain a good that should afford to the children what is denied to age, contentment; and allay their longing, their infantine sadness.

But the children could not gaze enough on the wondrous egg, and, in viewing it, soon forgot the bird that had laid it. At first they did not venture to touch it; but the girl at length laid one of her rosy fingers upon it, and suddenly exclaimed, while a deep red overspread her innocent countenance, "The egg is warm!" And then the boy gave it a gentle touch, to feel whether his sister had spoken the truth. At last the mother herself placed her soft white hand on the egg; and then what happened? The shell fell apart, and from it issued a being wonderful to behold. It had wings, yet was not a bird, nor a butterfly, neither a bee, nor a dragonfly; but was something of all these, and altogether not to be described. In a word, it was the party-coloured, winged, glittering delight of childhood, itself a child, the wondrous bird *Imagination*, the *Popular Tale*. And now the mother saw her children no longer sad; for the Tale continued with the children, and they were never weary of it as long as they were children, and it was only after they possessed the Tale that the garden and its flowers, the arbours and the grottoes, the woods and groves, afforded them true pleasure; for the Tale enlivened everything to their great happiness.

The Tale even lent them its wings, and they flew far away in the vast world, and, nevertheless, were at home again as soon as they desired. Those royal children are human beings in their Childhood's paradise, and nature is their beautiful, gentle mother. She wished the wondrous bird Imagination down from heaven, which has such splendid golden feathers, and also some of jet black, and it laid in her lap the golden egg of Fiction.

And as the children contracted an ardent love for the Tale, which sweetened their early days, delighted them with its thousand varying forms and metamorphoses, and flew over every house and hut, over every castle and palace, so was its nature such that even those of maturer age found pleasure in it, provided only that in their riper years they possessed something which they had brought with them from the garden of childhood, a child-like simplicity of heart.

SCANDINAVIAN AND NORTH GERMAN POPULAR TALES AND TRADITIONS

I. SWEDISH.[1]

THE WERWOLF.[2]

From Upland.

THERE was once a king, who ruled over a large kingdom. He was married to a beautiful queen, by whom he had only one child, a daughter. Hence it naturally followed that the little one was to her parents as the apple of their eye, and was dear to them beyond all other things, so that they thought of nothing with such delight as of the pleasure they should have in her when she grew up. But much falls out contrary to expectation; for before the princess was out of her childhood, the queen, her mother, fell sick and died. Now, it is easy to imagine that there was sadness not only in the royal court, but over the whole kingdom, for the queen was greatly beloved by all. The king himself

---

[1] All the Swedish Tales are from the "Svenska Folk-Sagor och Äfventyr, samiads och utgitna af G.O. Hyltén-Cavallius och Geo. Stephens." Stockholm, ii. parts.

[2] Although the belief in the existence of the Werwolf (A. Sax. Werwulf, Fr. Loup-garou) is of remote antiquity throughout all Europe, we have not, in the whole region of popular tradition, met with a counterpart to the story here given.

was so deeply afflicted that he resolved never to marry again but placed all his comfort and joy in the little princess.

In this manner, a considerable time passed on; the young princess grew from day to day taller and fairer, and everything she at any time desired was by her father immediately granted her; many attendants being placed about her, for the sole purpose of being at hand to execute all her commands. Among these there was a woman who had been previously married and had two daughters. She was of an agreeable person, and had a persuasive tongue, so that she well knew how to put her words together; added to all which she was as soft and pliant as silk, but her heart was full of artifices and all kinds of falsehood. No sooner was the queen dead than she began to devise plans how she might become consort to the king, and her daughters be honoured as kings' daughters. With this object she began by winning the affection of the young princess, praised beyond measure all that she said or did, and all her talk ended in declaring how happy they would be if the king would take to himself a new wife. On this subject the conversation oftenest turned both early and late, till at length the princess could not believe otherwise than that all the woman said was true. She therefore asked her what description of wife it was most desirable that the king should select. The woman, in many words, all sweet as honey, answered, "Ill would it become me to give an opinion in such a case, hoping only he may choose for his queen one who will be kind to my little princess. But this I know, that were I so fortunate as to be the object of his choice, I should think only of what might please the princess; and if she wished to wash her hands, one of my daughters should hold the basin, and the other hand her the towel." This and much more she said to the princess, who believed her, as children readily believe all that is told them is true.

Not a day now passed in which the king was free from the solicitations of his daughter, who incessantly besought him to marry the handsome waiting-woman; but he would not. Nevertheless, the princess would not desist from her entreaties, but spoke incessantly precisely as she had been taught by the false waiting-woman. One day, when she was talking in the same strain, the king broke forth: "I see very well that it must at length be as you have resolved, greatly as it is against my wish; but it shall be only on one condition. "What is the condition?" asked the princess, overjoyed. "It is," said the king, "that, as it is for your sake if I marry again, you shall promise me that if at any future time you shall be discontented with your stepmother or your stepsisters, I shall not be troubled with your complaints and grievances." The princess made the promise, and it was settled that the king should marry the waiting-woman and make her queen over all his realm.

As time passed on the king's daughter grew up to be the fairest maid in all the land; while the queen's daughters were as ugly in person as in disposition, so that no one had a good word for them. There could not, therefore, fail of being a number of young princes and knights, from both east and west, coming to demand the young princess; while not one vouchsafed to woo either of the queen's daughters. At this the stepmother was sorely vexed at heart, however she might conceal her feelings, being, to all outward appearance, as smooth and humble as before. Among the suitors there was a king's son from a distant country, who was both young and valorous, and as he passionately loved the princess, she listened to his addresses, and plighted her faith to him in return. The queen observed all this with a jaundiced eye; for she would fain have had the prince marry one of her own daughters, and, therefore, resolved that the young couple should never be united with each other. From that moment her thoughts were solely bent on the destruction both of them and their love.

An opportunity soon offered itself to her; for just at that time intelligence was received that an enemy had invaded the country, so that the king was obliged to take the field. The princess was now soon made to learn what kind of a stepmother she had got; for hardly had the king departed before the queen began to show her true disposition, so that she now was as cruel and malignant as she had previously appeared to be friendly and obliging. Not a day passed on which the princess did not hear maledictions and hard words; nor did the queen's daughters yield to their mother in wickedness. But a lot still more cruel awaited the young prince, the lover of the princess. While engaged in the chase he had lost his way and got separated from his companions. Availing herself of the opportunity, the queen practised on him her wicked arts, and transformed him into a WERWOLF, so that for the remainder of his days he should be a prowler of the forest. When evening drew on and the prince did not appear, his men returned home, and the sorrow may be easily imagined with which the princess was overwhelmed when she was informed how the chase had terminated. She wept and mourned day and night and would not be comforted. But the queen laughed at her affliction and rejoiced in her false heart that everything had turned out so agreeably to her wishes.

As the princess was one day sitting alone in her maiden bower, it entered her mind that she would visit the forest in which the young prince had disappeared. She went, therefore, to her stepmother, and asked permission to go to the wood, that she might for a little while forget her heavy affliction. To her request the queen would hardly give her consent, as she was always more inclined to say no than yes; but the princess besought her so earnestly that at last her stepmother could no longer withhold her permission, only ordering one of her daughters to accompany and keep watch over her. A long dispute now arose between mother and daughters, neither of the stepsisters being willing to go with her, but excusing themselves, and asking what pleasure they could have in following her who did nothing but weep. The matter ended by the queen insisting that one of her daughters should go with the princess, however much it might be against her will. The maidens then strolled away from the palace and reached the forest, where the princess amused herself with wandering among the trees, and listening to the song of the little birds, and thinking on the friend she loved so dearly, and whom she now had lost; the queen's daughter following all the while, with a heart full of rancorous feeling for the princess and her grief.

After having wandered about for some time they came to a small cottage that stood far in the dark forest. At the same moment the princess was seized with a burning thirst and entreated her stepsister to accompany her to the cottage, that she might get a draught of water. At this, the queen's daughter became only more ill-humoured, and said, "Is it not enough that I follow you up and down in the wild wood? Now, because you are a princess, you require me to go into such a filthy nest. No, my foot shall never enter it. If you will go, go alone." The princess took no long time to consider but did as her stepsister said and entered the cabin. In the little apartment she saw an aged woman sitting on a bench, who appeared so stricken with years that her head shook. The princess saluted her, as was her wont, in a friendly tone, with "Good evening, good mother! may I ask you for a little drink of water?" "Yes, and right welcome," answered the old woman. "Who are you that come under my humble roof with so kind a greeting?" The princess told her that she was the king's daughter, and had come out to divert herself, with the hope, in some degree, of forgetting her heavy affliction. "What affliction have you, then?" asked the old woman. "Well may I grieve," answered the princess, and never more feel joyful. I have lost my only friend, and God alone knows whether we shall ever meet again." She then related to the old woman all that had taken place, while the tears flowed from her eyes in such torrents that no one could have refrained from pitying her. When she had concluded, the old woman said, "It is well that you have made your grief known to me; I have experienced much, and can, perhaps, give you some advice. When you go from hence you will see a lily growing in the field. This lily is not like other lilies but has many wonderful properties. Hasten, therefore, to pluck it. If you can do so, all will be well; for then there will come one who will tell you what you are to do." They then parted; the princess having thanked her, continued her walk, and the old woman remained sitting on her bench and shaking her head. But the queen's daughter had been standing during the whole time outside the door, murmuring and fretting that the princess staid so long.

When she came out, she had to hear much chiding from her stepsister, as was to be expected; but to this she gave very little heed, thinking only how she should find the flower of which the old woman had spoken. She therefore proceeded further into the forest, and in the self-same moment her eye fell on a spot where there stood a beautiful white lily in full bloom before her. On seeing it she was so glad, so glad, and instantly ran to gather it, but it vanished on a sudden and appeared again at some distance. The princess was now eager beyond measure, and no longer gave heed to the voice of her stepsister but continued running; though every time she put forth her hand to take the flower it was already away, and immediately afterwards reappeared at a short distance farther off. Thus, it continued for a considerable time, and the princess penetrated further and further into the dense forest, the lily all the while appearing and vanishing, and again showing itself, and every time looking taller and more beautiful than before. In this manner the princess at length came to a high mountain, when on casting her eyes up to the summit, there stood the flower on the very edge, as brilliant and fair as the brightest star. She now began to climb up the mountain, caring for neither the stocks nor the stones that lay in the way, so great was her ardour. When she at length had gained the mountains top, lo! the lily no longer moved, but continued stationary. The princess then stooped and plucked it, and placed it in her bosom, and was so overjoyed that she forgot both stepsister and everything in the world besides.

For a long time, the princess could not sufficiently feast her eyes with the sight of the beautiful flower. It then on a sudden entered her mind, what her stepmother would say, when she returned home, for having staid out so long. She looked about her before returning to the palace, but on casting a glance behind her she saw that the sun had gone down, and that only a strip of day yet tarried on the mountain's summit; while down before her the forest appeared so dark and gloomy, that she did not trust herself to find the way through it. She was now exceedingly weary and exhausted and saw no alternative but that she must remain for the night where she was. Sitting then down on the rock, she placed her hand under her cheek and wept, and thought on her wicked stepmother and stepsisters, and all the bitter words she must hear when she returned home, and on the king, her father, who was absent, and on the beloved of her heart, whom she should never see again; but abundantly as her tears flowed she noticed them not, so absorbing was her affliction. Night now drew on, all was shrouded in darkness, the stars rose and set, but the princess still continued sitting on the same spot, weeping without intermission. While thus sitting, lost in thought, she heard a voice greeting her with "Good evening, fair maiden! Why do you sit here so lonely and sorrowful?" She started and was greatly surprised, as may easily be imagined; and on looking back there stood a little, little old man, who nodded and looked so truly benevolent. She answered, "I may well be sorrowful, and never more be glad. I have lost my best beloved, and have, moreover, missed my path in the forest, so that I am fearful of being devoured by the wild beasts." "Oh," said the old man, "don't be disheartened for that. If you will obey me in all that I say, I will help you." To this the princess readily assented, seeing herself forsaken by the whole world besides. The old man then drew forth a flint and steel, and said, "Fair maiden! now, in the first place, you shall kindle a fire." The king's daughter did as she was desired, gathered moss, twigs, and dry wood, and kindled a fire on the mountain's brow. When she had done this the old man said to her, "Go now further on the mountain, and you will find a pot full of tar: bring it hither." The princess did so. The old man continued: "Now set the pot on the fire." The princess did so. "When, now, the tar begins to boil, said the old man, cast your white lily into the pot." This seemed to the princess a very hard command, and she prayed earnestly that she might retain her lily; but the old man said: "Have you not promised to obey me in all that I desire? Do as I tell you; you will not repent." The princess then, with eyes averted, cast the lily into the boiling pot, although it grieved her to the heart; so dear to her was the beautiful flower.

At the same instant, a hollow roaring was heard from the forest, like the cry of a wild beast, which came nearer and nearer, and passed into a hideous howl, so that the mountain re-echoed on every side. At the same time was heard a cracking and rustling among the trees, the bushes gave way, and the princess beheld a huge gray wolf come rushing out of the forest just opposite to the spot where they were sitting. In her terror she would gladly have fled from it; but the old man said, "Make haste, run to the brow of the mountain, and the moment the wolf comes before you, empty the tar pot over him." The princess, although so terrified that she was hardly conscious of what she did, nevertheless followed the old man's direction, and poured the tar over the wolf, just as he came running towards her. But now a wonderful event took place, for scarcely had she done so when the wolf changed his covering, the great gray skin started off from him, and, instead of a ravenous wild beast, there stood a comely youth with eyes directed towards the brow of the mountain and when the princess had so far recovered from her fright that she could look on him, whom did she behold before her but her own best beloved, who had been transformed into a werewolf!

Now let any one, who can, imagine what the feelings of the princess were at this moment. She stretched out her arms towards him, but could neither speak nor answer, so great were her surprise and joy. But the prince ran up the mountain and embraced her with all the ardour of the truest affection and thanked her for having restored him. Nor did he forget the little old man but thanked him in many kind words for his powerful aid. They then sat down on the mountain-top and conversed lovingly with each other. The prince related how he had been changed into a wolf, and all the privations he had suffered while he had to range about the forest; and the princess recounted to him her sorrow and all the tears she had shed during his absence. Thus, they sat throughout the night, heedless of the passing hour, until the stars began gradually to retire before the daylight, so that the surrounding objects were visible. When the sun had risen, they perceived that a wide road ran from the foot of the hill quite up to the royal palace. Then said the old man, "Fair maiden, turn about. Do you see anything yonder?" "Yes," answered the princess, "I see a horseman on a foaming horse; he rides along the road at full speed." "That," said the old man, "is a messenger from the king, your father. He will follow forth with with his whole army." Now was the princess glad beyond measure and wished instantly to descend to meet her father; but the old man held her back, saying, "Wait: it is yet too soon. Let us first see how things will turn out."

After some time, the sun shone bright, so that its rays fell on the palace down before them. Then said the old man, "Fair maiden, turn about. Do you see anything yonder?" "Yes," answered the princess, "I see many persons coming out of my father's palace, some of whom proceed along the road, while others hasten towards the forest." The old man said, "They are your stepmother's servants. She has sent one party to meet the king and bid him welcome; but the other is going to the forest in search of you." At hearing this the princess was troubled, and was with difficulty induced to remain, but wished to go down to the queen's people: but the old man held her back, saying, "Wait yet a little while; we will first see how things turn out."

For some time, the princess continued with her looks directed towards the road by which the king was to come. Then said the old man again, "Fair maiden, turn about. Do you observe anything yonder?" "Yes," answered the princess, "there is a great stir in my father's palace; and see! now they are busy in hanging the whole palace with black." The old man said, "That is your stepmother and her servants. They wish to make your father believe that you are dead." At this the princess was filled with anxiety, and prayed fervently, saying, "Let me go, let me go, that I may spare my father so great an affliction." But the old man detained her, saying, "No, wait. It is still too soon. We will first see how things turn out."

Again, another interval passed, the sun rose high in the heaven, and the air breathed warm over field and forest; but the royal children and the little old man continued sitting on the mountain where we left them. They now observed a small cloud slowly rising in the horizon, which grew larger and larger, and came nearer and nearer along the road; and as it moved, they saw that it glittered with weapons, and perceived helmets nodding and banners waving, heard the clanking of swords and the neighing of horses, and at length recognised the royal standard. Now it is easy to imagine that the joy of the princess exceeded all bounds, and that she only longed to go and greet her father. But the old man held her back, saying, "Turn about, fair maiden, do you see nothing at the king's palace?" "Yes," answered the princess, "I see my stepmother and my stepsisters coming out clad in deep mourning, and holding white handkerchiefs to their faces, and weeping bitterly." The old man said, "They are now pretending to mourn for your death; but wait a while, we have yet to see how things will turn out."

Some time after, the old man asked again, "Fair maiden, turn about. Do you observe anything yonder? "Yes," answered the princess, "I see them come bearing a black coffin. Now my father orders it to be opened. And see! the queen and her daughters fall on their knees, and my father threatens them with his sword." The old man said, "The king desired to see your corpse, and so your wicked stepmother has been forced to confess the truth." On hearing this, the princess entreated fervently: "Let me go, let me go, that I may console my father in his great affliction. But the old man still detained her, saying, "Attend to my counsel, and stay here a little while. We have not yet seen how everything will terminate."

Another interval passed, and the princess, and the prince, and the little old man, still continued sitting on the mountain. Then said the old man, "Turn about, fair maiden. Do you observe anything yonder?" "Yes," answered the princess, "I see my father, and my stepmother, and my stepsisters, coming this way with all their attendants." The old man continued, "They have now set out in search of you. Go down now and bring the wolfskin which is lying below." The king's daughter did so, and the old man then said, "Place yourself on the brink of the mountain." The princess did so, and at the same moment perceived the queen and her daughters coming along the road just beneath the mountain where they were sitting. "Now," said the old man, "cast the wolfskin straight down." The princess obeyed and cast the wolfskin as the old man had directed. It fell exactly over the wicked queen and her two daughters. But now a wonderful event took place, for hardly had the skin touched the three women than they changed their guise, gave a hideous howl, and were transformed into three fierce werwolves, which at full speed rushed into the wild forest.

Scarcely had this taken place before the king himself with all his men came to the foot of the mountain. When he looked up and beheld the princess, he could not at first believe his eyes, but stood immovable, thinking it was a spectre. The old man then cried, "Fair maiden, hasten now down and gladden the heart of your father." The princess did not wait to be told a second time, but, taking her lover by the hand, was in an instant at the mountain's foot. When they reached the spot where the king was standing, the princess fell on her father's breast and wept for joy; the young prince also wept; even the king himself shed tears, and to everyone present their meeting was a delightful spectacle. Great joy was there and many embracings, and the princess related all she had suffered from her stepmother and stepsisters, and all about her beloved prince, and the little old man who had so kindly assisted them. But when the king turned to thank him, he had already vanished, and no one could ever say either who he was or whither he went.

The king and all his suite now returned to the palace, on their way towards which much was said both about the little old man and what the princess had undergone. On reaching home the king ordered a sumptuous banquet to be prepared, to which he invited all the most distinguished and exalted persons of his kingdom and bestowed his daughter on the young prince; and their nuptials were celebrated with games and rejoicings for many days. And I, too, was at the feastings; and as I rode through the forest, I was met by a wolf with two young ones; they were ravenous and seemed to suffer much. I have since learned that they were no other than the wicked stepmother and her two daughters.

PRINCE HATT UNDER THE EARTH;
OR, THE THREE SINGING LEAVES.[3]

From South Småland.

THERE was once, very, very long ago, a king who had three daughters, all exquisitely beautiful, and much more amiable than other maidens, so that

---

[3] This is a far-famed story. Similar narratives are to be found among the following nations:—

their like was not to be found far or near. But the youngest princess excelled her sisters, not only in beauty, but in goodness of heart, and kindness of disposition. She was, consequently, greatly beloved by all, and the king himself was more fondly attached to her than to either of his other daughters.

---

1. The Norwegians.—See "Asbjörnsen and Moe, Norske Folkeeventyr," Deel ii. No. 42. "Östenfor Sol og Vestenfor Maane."

2. The Danes.—See "Winther, Danske Folkeeventyr," 1st Saml. pp. 20-25. "Prinds Hvidbjörn."

3. The Scotch.—See Chambers, "Popular Rhymes, &c., of Scotland," pp. 75, 76, "The Red Bull of Norroway."

4. The Germans.— *a.* The old poem of "Friedrich von Schwaben," of the 14th century (a pendant to "Partonopeus de Blois," to be spoken of presently), is the oldest form of this story known in Germany. See Neues Jahrbuch für deutsche Sprache, &c., Berlin, 1846, pp. 95-115; also, Massmann, Partonopeus und Melior, Berlin, 1847, pp. 131, 132. *b.* See Grimm, Kinder und Hausmarchen, ii. No. 127. "Der Eisenofen" [Cf. iii. pp. 218-221]. *c.* Also iii. pp. 257, 258. "Die Laus." *d.* See Mullenhoff, Sagen, Marchen und Lieder der Herzogthümer Schleswig, Holstein und Lauenburg. Kiel, 1845, pp. 384, 385. "Vom goldenen Klingel-Klangel." *e.* Also, pp. 385-388. "Der Weisse Wolf." *f.* See Kuhn und Schwartz, Norddeutsche Sagen, Marchen und Gebrauche, Leipsig, 1848, pp. 347-352. "Die Seidenspinnerin."

5. The French.—The Anglo-Norman trouveur, Denis Piramus, from the beginning of the 13th century, in his beautiful poem of "Partonopeus de Blois," employed the same material, but with this difference, that the curious person is a prince, instead of a princess. See G. A. Crapelet, "Partonopeus de Blois, publ. pour la prem fois d'après le MS. de la Bibl. de l'Arsenal, avec trois facsimiles." 2 Vols. 8 vo. Paris, 1834.

6. The Romans.—The oldest known record of this tale is the story of "Pysche et Cupido" in the Metamorphoses of Apuleius [ob. circa A.D. 160]. Bishop Fulgentius, who has given the same story abridged from Apuleius, informs us that it is to be found at full in the writings of a certain Aristophantes. Whether this Aristophantes was earlier or later than Apuleius is nowhere mentioned.

7. The Wallachians.—The beginning is to be found as an introduction to "Die Kaiserstochter und die Füllen" in Schott, Walachische Märchen, Stuttg. und Tubingen, pp. 171-183; and in the same book, pp. 239-246, "Trandafira."

8. The Italians.—See "Basile, Il Pentamerone," i. No. 5; the first part of "Lo Polece;" also ibid. ii. No. 5; "Lo Serpe," and v. No. 3, "Pintosmauto."

9. The Hindus.—See the tale of "Gand' harva." Cf. Wilford's Essay on Vicramáditya and Sativahana, in Asiatic Researches, ix. p. 147, Calcutta edit. A similar story, from oral communication in Calcutta, is given in the Asiatic Journal; a translation of which is to be found in "Das Ausland," Feb. 1843; 2, in Somadevás, Marchensammlung Leipsig, 1843, ii. pp. 194-211; and 3, in Kletke, Marchensaal aller Volker, iii. pp. 30-42. "Des Holzhauers Tochter."

It happened one autumn that there was a fair in a town not far from the king's residence, and the king himself resolved on going to it with his attendants. When on the eve of departure, he asked his daughters what they would like for fairings, it being his constant custom to make them some present on his return home. The two elder princesses began instantly to enumerate precious things of various kinds; one would have this, the other that; but the youngest princess wished for nothing. At this the king was surprised and asked her whether she would not like some ornament or other; but she answered that she had plenty of gold and jewels. When the king, however, would not desist from urging her, she at length said, "There is one thing that I would gladly have, if only I might venture to ask it of my father." "What may that be?" inquired the king. "Say what it is, and if it be in my power, you shall have it." "It is this," said the princess; "I have heard talk of THE THREE SINGING LEAVES, and them I wish to have before anything else in the world." The king laughed at her for making so trifling a request, and at length exclaimed, "I cannot say that you are very covetous, and would rather by much that you asked for some greater gift. You shall, however, have what you desire, though it should cost half my realm." He then bade his daughters farewell and rode away.

When he reached the town where the fair was held, there was assembled a vast multitude of people from all parts of the country; many foreign merchants were also there, displaying their wares in the streets and marketplaces; so that there was no lack of gold and silver, or any other precious things, of which the king made purchases for his two elder daughters. But although he went from booth to booth and inquired of the dealers both from the east and the west, he found no one that could give him any information respecting the three singing leaves, which he had promised to his youngest daughter. At this he was much disappointed, for he would gladly have gratified her as well as his other daughters; but having no alternative, and the evening drawing on, he ordered his horse to be saddled, summoned his attendants, and out of humour proceeded on his way towards his own country.

While riding along absorbed in thought, he suddenly heard sounds, as of harp and other stringed instruments, so exquisitely sweet, that it seemed to him he had never heard the like in his whole life. At this he was greatly astonished, held in his horse, and sat listening, and the longer he listened, the sweeter did the sounds become; but the evening being dark, he was unable to see from whence they proceeded. He did not long deliberate, but rode into a spacious green meadow, from which the tones were heard, and the further he went the clearer and sweeter did they strike upon his ear. Having ridden some distance, he came at length to a hazel-bush, on the top of which were three golden leaves, which moved to and fro, and as they played there came forth a sound such as it would be impossible to describe. The king was now not a little glad, for he was convinced that these were the three singing leaves, of which his daughter had spoken. He was just about to pluck them, but the instant he stretched forth his hand towards them, they withdrew from his grasp, and a powerful voice was heard from under the bush, saying, "Touch not my leaves!" At this the king was somewhat surprised, but soon recovering himself, he asked who it was, and whether he could not purchase the leaves for gold or good words? The voice answered, "I am PRINCE HATT UNDER THE EARTH, and you will not get my leaves either with bad or good, as you desire. Nevertheless, I will propose to you one condition." "What condition is that?" asked the king with eagerness. "It is," answered the voice, "that you promise me the first living thing that you meet, when you return home to your palace." This seemed to the king a singular condition; but he thought on his young daughter, and on his promise, and assented to the prince's proposal. The leaves now no longer withdrew from his touch, and he easily gathered them, and full of joy returned home to his people.

Let us now look into the royal palace. There sat the king's three daughters the whole livelong day, sewing silk on their knee, and talking of nothing but the costly presents their father was to bring them from the fair. On the approach of evening, the youngest princess asked whether they would not go and walk along the road by which their father was to return home. "No," answered the sisters, "why should we do so? It is already late, and the evening dew would spoil our silk-embroidered stockings." But the princess cared little for that, and said:

"If my proposal is not agreeable to you, stay here at home: I will go alone and meet my father." She then put on a cloak and set forth on her way. After she had proceeded a short distance, she heard the tramp of horses, and the noise of people, and the clashing of arms, among all which she could distinguish the sweetest song ever listened to by mortal ears. At this she was overjoyed, for she knew that it was her father, and also that he had got the three singing leaves, as she had requested. She ran to him, sprang up to embrace him, and bade him welcome with great affection. But at the sight of her the king was thunderstruck; for the promise he had given instantly recurred to his memory, and he now saw that he had promised away his own child. For a long time, he could not speak, not even to answer the inquiries made by the princess as to the cause of his sorrow. At length, however, he related to her all that had taken place in connection with the leaves, and that he had promised the first living being he should meet on his return. Now there was lamentation and sorrow such as the like had never before been witnessed, and the king himself grieved more than all the others. The conclusion, however, was, that he returned to the meadow, and left his daughter by the hazel bush, and it seemed to him that he had sustained a calamity that could never be repaired.

We will now let the king ride back with his attendants, and accompany the young princess, who was left sitting weeping by the green hazel-bush. She had not continued there long, before the earth suddenly opened, so that she descended into a spacious apartment beneath its surface. This apartment was not like others that she had seen, but was by far more splendid, ornamented with both gold and silver, and in all manner of ways; but not a living soul was there. The princess now found pleasure in viewing all the beautiful things to be seen in it; and while so engaged, almost forgot her sorrow. When she at length grew weary, she laid herself on a bed, that stood all ready with sheets and coverlet whiter than the driven snow. She had not rested long when the door was opened, and a man entered, who proceeded straight to the bed, bade her welcome with many affectionate words, and said that he was the master of the place, and that he was Prince Hatt. The prince added, that, through the spells of a wicked Troll wife, he might never be seen by any human being, and could therefore come only by night; but that if she would be faithful to him, all would finally be otherwise. He then lay down on the bed and slept by the side of the princess, but rose before daybreak, left his young bride and did not again make his appearance until late in the evening.

Thus did a considerable time pass. The king's daughter sat in the beautiful apartment, and everything she wished for she had; if she was melancholy, she had only to listen to the three singing leaves, and again became cheerful. At the end of nine months, she gave birth to a son, and was now much happier than before, doing nothing throughout the day but caress the little infant, and long after her beloved Prince Hatt.

One evening, it happened that the prince returned home later than usual. On entering, the princess, in a tone of disquietude, asked him where he had been so long. "I come", answered the prince, "from your father's court, and bring you extraordinary tidings. The king is about to marry again, and if it will afford you pleasure, you shall go to the wedding, and take our little son with you." The princess was delighted with the proposal and could not sufficiently thank her consort for his kindness. The prince added, "One thing you must, however, promise me; that you will not allow yourself to be persuaded to violate your faith to me." This the princess promised, and therewith their conversation ended.

On the following morning the princess made preparations with clothes and costly ornaments to go to the wedding. When all was ready there came forth a gilded chariot, in which she seated herself with her little son and was home over hill and dale, and in the twinkling of an eye was at the place of her destination. In the saloon, the wedding guests were already assembled, and the wedding beer was being drunk amid much mirth and revelry. The joy of all at the unexpected entrance of the princess may be easily imagined. The king himself rose from his throne and embraced her with delight, as did his wife, the queen, and both princesses; all went to meet her, and bid her heartily welcome.

When the first greetings were over, the king and queen began inquiring of the princess about various things, but above all the queen was desirous to know about Prince Hatt, who he was, and how he behaved to her. The princess answered very sparingly, so that it was easy to see that she spoke on the subject with reluctance; but the queen's curiosity only rose the higher. When the stepmother would not desist from her interrogations, the king was displeased, and said, "Dearest of my heart, what is all this to us? It is sufficient that my daughter is contented and happy." The queen was then silent; but whenever the king turned his back, she was immediately ready again with her incessant questions.

When the wedding had been celebrated for many days, the princess began to long after home. Instantly the chariot came forth, the king's daughter seated herself in it with her little son, and away they went over hill and dale, until they arrived at the green bush. There she alighted and descended into the underground apartment, and the leaves played so sweetly that it seemed to her far more pleasant beneath the earth than in the king's court. But more delightful still was it in the evening, when Prince Hatt came home, and greeted her lovingly, and told her how his heart's thoughts were constantly on her, both night and day.

After some time passed in this manner the princess gave birth to a second son. She now thought herself yet happier than before, and did little besides playing with her young children, listening to the three singing leaves, and longing for her husband's return when he was absent. One evening the prince returned later than usual. On his entrance the princess asked him where he had been so long. "I come," answered the prince, "from your father's court, and have extraordinary news. Your eldest sister is just on the eve of marriage with the son of a foreign king, and if you desire you shall go to the wedding and take our children with you." This appeared a delightful proposal to the princess, and she could not sufficiently thank him for his kindness. The prince then added, as on the previous occasion, "You must, however, promise me that you will never let yourself be persuaded to violate your faith to me." This she promised.

On the following morning, she made herself ready, as already described, to go to the wedding. The gilded car came forth, and in a few seconds, she found herself in her father's court, where she was welcomed as on the former occasion, and in like manner was questioned by the queen, and to equally little purpose. When the feastings were over, she returned home.

After another period of time had elapsed, the princess gave birth to a third infant, a daughter, and now it seemed to her that she was in the enjoyment of everything that could make her heart glad, and throughout the day did little else than play with her children, listen to the singing leaves, and long for her husband's return. One evening, when the prince returned later than usual, she addressed him with, "Dearest of my heart, where have you been so long? I have been expecting you with fear and anxiety." "I come from your father's court," answered the prince, and have news to tell you. The princess, your second sister, has got a suitor, and is about to be married to the son of a foreign king; and if it will afford you pleasure you shall go home to the wedding, and take all your children with you. At this proposal the princess was greatly delighted and could not enough thank the prince for being at all times ready to afford her pleasure. The prince again made her promise not to violate her faith towards him, as a heavy calamity would else befall them both.

On the following day the princess set forth, as on the former occasions, and, after the first salutations were over, the queen renewed her questions about Prince Hatt; but the princess answered her inquiries very unsatisfactorily. When the queen saw that her stepdaughter was on her guard, she went to work with cunning, as crafty women do not readily desist from that which they have once resolved on. With this object she began to speak in praise of the princess's children, that were playing on the floor; how quick they were, and how fortunate the princess herself was in having such children; that they no doubt took after their father's family, and that Prince Hatt must be a very comely young man. As the maternal heart is always tender, the princess now allowed herself to be deceived by her stepmother's beguiling expressions, and as one word begets another, she at length confessed that she knew not whether the prince was handsome or ugly, for she had never seen him. At this the queen broke forth with great warmth, clasped her hands together, and inveighed bitterly against the prince for concealing anything from his wife. "And," exclaimed she, "I must say that you are very unlike other women in not having satisfied yourself in this matter." The end of the conversation was, as might be expected that the princess, forgetful of her husband's warning, disclosed all that she knew, and asked her stepmothers advice. This was just what the queen had anticipated; she therefore did not allow herself to be long besought but promised to devise some plan before they parted.

So matters stood for a few days; the wedding was over, and the princess began to long after home. When on the eve of departure, her stepmother drew her aside and said, "I will now give you a ring, a flint and steel, and a taper. If you wish to see your husband as he really is, you must rise in the night, strike fire through the ring, and light the taper. Only be mindful that you wake him not out of his sleep." The princess thanked her much for the gift and promised to follow her instructions. She then parted from her relations, seated herself with her three children in the gilded chariot, and in a few seconds was again by the green hush. She alighted and descended; but although the leaves were playing and all was as beautiful and delightful as it had ever been, she found herself ill at ease, for she was so excited that she could think of nothing but what would happen, when she should see her consort in his true shape.

When it was late in the evening and dark, the prince returned according to his custom. There was, it may easily be imagined, great delight at their meeting, and her consort, in terms of the most ardent affection, told her how his heart had been constantly with her during her absence. They then betook themselves to rest, and the prince fell into a deep sleep, which the princess had no sooner observed than she rose, struck the through the ring, as she had been instructed by her stepmother, and softly approached the bed, that she might behold her beloved. But who shall recount in adequate terms the joy she felt at seeing a beautiful young man lying before her. So affected was she that she forgot everything in the world besides only to look on him, and the longer she gazed the more comely did he appear to her, so that she was wholly lost in love. While bending over the prince as he lay sleeping, a hot drop fell from the taper upon his breast, which caused him to move. The princess was now terrified, and was about to extinguish the light, but it was too late, for the prince awoke, rose in a fright, and saw what she had done. At the same instant, the three singing leaves were silent, the beautiful apartment was changed into a cave for serpents and toads, and the prince and princess, with their children, stood there in darkness; but Prince Hatt was—blind.

The princess now repented of her deed, fell down before her consort, and with bitter tears implored his forgiveness for the injury she had done him. The prince answered, "I'll hast thou requited all my love for thee; nevertheless, I will forgive thee, and it now rests with thyself, whether thou wilt accompany thy blind consort, or return to thy father." At these words the princess felt yet more grieved and wept so that her tears trickled down on the earth. She said, "Thou canst never have forgiven me from thy heart, if thou canst ask whether I will go with thee, for I will follow thee as long as I live on earth." Then, taking the prince by the hand, they forsook their home under the green bush, and sad it was to behold how the princess, with her three children and her blind husband, had to seek their way through the wild forest.

After wandering a long distance, they came to a green path which led through the wilderness. Here the prince inquired, "My best beloved, dost thou see anything?" "No," answered the princess, "I see only the forest with its green trees." They proceeded further, and the prince again inquired, "My best beloved, dost thou see anything?" The princess answered as before, "No, I see nothing whatsoever, save the green forest." The prince asked a third time, "My best beloved, dost thou still see nothing?" The princess answered, "Yes; I think I see a large mansion, the roof of which shines like bright copper." The prince said, "Then are we at the house of my eldest sister. Thou shalt go and greet her from me and pray her to take charge of our eldest son and rear him till he has grown up. For myself, I may not come under her roof, nor mayst thou suffer her to come to me hither, for then we must be separated forever." The princess followed her husband's directions, went to the mansion and executed her commission, although it wounded her to the heart to part with her little son. She then took leave of her sister-in-law, with much friendship on both sides. But, gladly as the prince's sister would have gone out to see him, the princess durst not violate her husband's injunction by complying with her desire.

The prince and his consort now resumed their wandering, and journeyed a long way over forests and wastes, till they came to a green path, which led through the wilderness. Here the prince again inquired, "My best beloved, dost thou see anything?" On his inquiring a third time, the princess answered, "Yes; I think I see a large house, the roof of which shines as if it were of silver." The prince said, "Then are we come to my second sister's dwelling. Thou shalt go and greet her from me, and beg her to receive our second son, and rear him till he is grown up; but thou must not allow her to come out to me, for then we must be parted forever." The princess executed her commission as on the previous occasion; and greatly as the prince's sister desired to go out and meet him, the princess durst not act contrary to her husband's injunction by complying with her desire.

The prince and his consort now again resumed their journey, till they found a little green path that led through the forest. Here the prince inquired as before, "My best beloved, dost thou see anything?" On his third inquiry she answered, "Yes, I think I see a large house, the roof of which glitters like bright gold." The prince thereupon said, "We are then come to my youngest sister's dwelling. Thou shalt go in and greet her from me, and pray her to receive our little daughter, and rear her. For myself, I may not go under her roof, nor mayst thou allow her to come out to me, for then we must be parted forever."

The princess followed her husband's directions and met with the kindest reception from the prince's sister and was about to return; but when she had to part from her last child, her heart was ready to burst with grief, and she forgot the prince's injunction and everything besides. Thus did her sister-in-law accompany her, without it ever entering her mind to hinder her. When they joined the prince, his sister could no longer command her feelings, but rushed into his arms and wept bitterly. Prince Hatt, who was now sensible that the princess had broken faith with him, turned pale as death, and exclaimed, "My dearest beloved, this thou shouldst not have done." At the same moment a cloud descended from the sky, and Prince Hatt vanished in the air as a bird fly.

Now, let those who can imagine the sorrow and despair of both. The princess wrung her hands and would not be comforted, for she had lost all that was dear to her in the world, and the grief of the prince's sister was not much less. After having long mingled their tears together, they began to consider how they might again find Prince Hatt, for the princess would not cease from seeking him, even should she wander over all the wide world. The prince's sister said, "I am not able to give you any counsel further than to advise you to go to the great mountain which you see beyond the forest. There dwells an old Troll-wife, named Berta; she is wise on many points, and can most probably afford you some information." The king's daughter said that she would do so and parted from her sister-in-law with great affection, and began her lonely wanderings over hill and dale, field and forest, as the prince's sister had directed her.

When it was so late that she could not proceed further, she perceived a little light glimmering in the field, at the sight of which, forgetting all her fatigue, she continued her way, over stock and stone, until she came to a cave up in the mountain, the entrance of which stood open. Within, she could see where a whole company of Trolls[4], both male and female, were assembled round a fire, most forward of whom sat a very, very old crone. The old woman was ugly of aspect, of diminutive size and bearing deep marks of age. The princess immediately divined that this was old Berta, of whom her sister-in-law had spoken; so, without further consideration she entered the cavern, and greeted

---

[4] A sort of demon or mountain spirite, comprising also the giants and dwarfs.—See Thorpe's Northern Mythology, vol. ii.

her with great humility: "Good evening, dear mother!" At this, all the small Trolls sprang up, and were not a little surprised at seeing a Christian woman; but old Berta, for it was she, with a friendly look, answered, "Good evening again. Who are you that come and greet me so kindly? I have now sat here for five hundred years, but no one before has ever called me 'dear mother.'" The princess then disclosed her errand, asking the old woman whether she could give her any information concerning an enchanted prince, named Prince Hatt under the earth? "No," answered the old woman, "I cannot; but as you did me the honour to call me 'dear mother,' I will, nevertheless, help you, for you must know that I have a sister, who is twice as old as I am, and can probably give you some intelligence." The princess thanked the old woman for her good-will and remained that night in the mountain but on the following day one of Mother Berta's little Trolls was to show her the way.

When the morning came, and the sun had risen in the east, the princess was not slow in making ready for her journey, and one of the little mountain Trolls was to be her guide. When about to bid the old Troll-wife farewell, the old woman said, "May your journey be fortunate I wish you every good, though I do not expect that we shall ever meet again. Nevertheless, as you have done me the honour to call me 'dear mother,' I pray you to accept this spinning wheel as a remembrance. As long as you possess it you will never sniffer want, for it alone spins as much yarn as nine others." The princess thanked her for the present, as she well might, for it was all throughout of pure gold. She then parted from the old woman and went her way as before, wandering over mountains and through deep valleys all the livelong day. Late in the evening they came to a high mountain, on the top of which there glimmered a lightlike a little star. "There," said the little Troll; "I have now shown you the way as I promised, for here dwells my aunt's sister, and it is now time for me to return home." Saying this he started off on his way back; but the princess continued her journey over stock and stone till she found herself up in the mountain, where she saw a cave, the door of which stood open, so that the light of the fire shone red through the darkness.

The princess did not long hesitate but entered the mountain cave, where she again found a great multitude of Trolls, both male and female, sitting round a fire, most forward of whom sat a very, very old woman, who appeared to be mistress over all the others. She was both little and ugly, with a shaking head, and deeply marked by age; hence the princess instantly concluded that she was no other than old Berta's sister. She greeted her and received a welcome similar to that which she had met with from old Berta herself. The old woman could give her no tidings of Prince Hatt but advised her to have recourse to a third sister, who was twice the age of herself. So, she remained in the mountain that night, and when morning dawned, there was a little Troll in readiness to show her the way.

At parting the old woman said, "I wish you all success in your journey, and as you have done me the honour to call me 'dear mother,' I will pray you to accept of this reel as a gift of friendship. As long as you possess it you need suffer no want, for it will of itself wind all the yarn that your wheel can spin." The princess thanked her much for the costly gift, for the reel was not like other reels, but was all of pure gold. They then parted, and the princess wandered as before over hill and dale, till she came to a high mountain, at the top of which a light glimmered like a small star. The little Troll that accompanied her then said, "It is now time for me to return home. My aunt's sister dwells there, up yonder; you can find the way alone." He then ran off. But the princess continued her journey, over stock and stone, till she reached the summit of the mountain, where she found a cave, the entrance to which stood open, so that the fire shone through the coal-black darkness.

On entering she found, as on the former occasions, a multitude of Trolls and a very, very old woman, most ugly of aspect, with an incredibly long nose that came in contact with her chin, and her head, from age, nodding backwards and forwards. Hence the princess easily guessed that this was Berta's eldest sister, and therefore advanced and courteously greeted her with, "Good evening, dear mother." Here, too, the little Trolls all started up, and were greatly surprised at seeing a Christian person. But the old crone, assuming a friendly look, said, "Good evening again; who me you who come hither with so kind a greeting? I have now lived here about two thousand years, but no one till now has ever done me the honour of calling me 'dear mother.'" The princess then told her who she was, and inquired of the old Troll-wife whether she could give her any information concerning an enchanted prince, who was called Prince Hatt under the earth? At this the crone became very thoughtful, and, after long reflection, at length said, "Certainly I have heard speak of Prince Hatt, and can tell you where he is, although there is but little hope that you will ever recover him, for he is enchanted, so that he has forgotten both you and everything else." She added, "But as you did me the honour to call me dear mother, I will help you as well as I can. Stay here tonight, and we will talk together in the morning." This to the princess seemed a good answer; she thanked the old woman with many friendly words and remained that night in the mountain.

When day began to break forth in the east the princess was again ready to set out on her journey. When about to part from the old wife of the mountain, the latter said, "When you go hence, exactly with the sun, you will come at length to a spacious palace. Into this you must enter and do as I will now tell you; for there sojourns the prince your beloved." The old woman then gave her much good counsel, as to how she should conduct herself on all occasions. At length she said, "I wish you now a happy journey, although we shall probably never meet again. Nevertheless, as you did me the honour to call me 'dear mother,' I pray you to accept this purse as a remembrance and the gift of a friend, at the same time holding out to her a silken purse embroidered all over with the ruddiest gold. But it was not with this purse as with other purses; for it had the wonderful property of being always full of silver money, however much were taken out of it. The princess thanked her, as she well might, for the costly gift, and so parted from the old woman of the mountain with many assurances of friendship on both sides.

It came to pass in every respect as the old woman had said; for when the princess had wandered up hill and down dale, through many green woods she came at length to a very, very large palace, that was so exceedingly magnificent that she had never before seen the like. She was now overjoyed at being so near the dearest of her heart, and, without long consideration, went in. On opening the gate, she saw a tall woman advancing towards her, so splendidly attired that the princess immediately believed her to be the Troll-queen who ruled over the palace. On seeing her the Troll instantly exclaimed, "Who art thou, and whence comest thou?" The princess answered, "I am only a poor stranger, who is come hither to seek service. Thou thinkest, then," replied the Troll, "that I have a service for each and all that come hither. No; so instantly go thy way." Saying this the beldam assumed such an angry look that the princess was terrified; but recovering courage, she said in a humble tone, "If it so be, I must be content with what pleases you; nevertheless, I will beg for a few days' shelter, that I may rest after my long wandering." "Well," said the Troll, "that thou mayst have. Thou canst lie in the goose-house, that is just a fitting lodging for such as thou." And thus, it was settled. The Troll-queen went her way; but the princess was to lodge in the goose-house, while resting after her long wanderings.

When the princess had somewhat recovered from her fatigue she did as the old woman of the mountain had instructed her. In the first place she scoured and cleaned and swept in every corner, so as no one has ever seen the like, and then set forth her spinning-wheel, and spun the most beautiful yarn, both of gold and silk then she took her reel and reeled the yarn, and prepared it for weaving, and wove cloth of gold and a beautiful canopy, and covered the room on every side, nor did she cease until the goose house was converted into the noblest apartment in all the palace. When it was finished, she drew forth her silken purse, and went out and bought meat, and mead, and wine, and whatever else was necessary that could be got for money; and boiled, and roasted, and prepared all things for a sumptuous banquet, so that not one of us has probably ever been present at such a magnificent entertainment. When all was in readiness she went up to the palace and requested to speak to the queen. The beldam received her graciously and inquired what her wishes were. The princess said, "My errand is to pray you and your daughter to confer on me the great honour of being my guests this evening." This pleased the Troll-queen amazingly; for she had already heard of the great doings that were going on in the goose-house. She therefore yielded to the princess's request and promised to come at the time appointed.

When the hour arrived for the queen and her daughter to go to the goose-house, they were received in a manner that may well be imagined, and found a banquet awaiting them of the most costly description. While they were sitting at table, and eating and drinking and making merry, the princess took forth her golden spinning wheel, and began to spin. At this the Troll-queen was struck with amazement and thought that it was far more precious than anything she had ever seen. She therefore asked whether she could purchase it. "No," answered the princess, "it is not to be had for money, nor will I make you a present of it nevertheless, you may obtain it on one condition. What may that condition be?" inquired the Troll-queen with great eagerness. The condition is this, that I may sleep to night in the chamber of your beloved. This appeared to the queen a somewhat extraordinary condition, and she deliberated over the proposed bargain for a long time; but being seized with an unconquerable desire to obtain the spinning-wheel, and moreover full of all kinds of guile, she thought she might for once run the risk. Thus, it was agreed that the Troll should have the spinning wheel, and that the princess should sleep one night in the chamber of her own dear Prince Hatt.

The queen then returned to the palace and considered with herself what course she should adopt to prevent the young pair from conversing with each other. For this purpose, she commanded her stepdaughter to place herself clandestinely in the prince's sleeping apartment and listen to all that the strange woman might say during the night. She then filled a cup with mead, into which she put certain potent herbs, and presented it to the prince. But no sooner had he emptied the cup than a deep sleep came over him, so that he sank into a state of unconsciousness, and neither heard nor saw. Seeing this the Troll laughed in her false heart, and conducted the princess to the chamber, according to the agreement, thinking that she was now welcome to talk to the prince as much as she liked.

When the princess was alone with her beloved, she sprang to him, fell on his neck with a heart full of joy, and said how delighted she was to have at length found him. But the prince woke not. At this she was sorely grieved, called him with many expressions of love, told him how she had been wandering over the wide world in search of him; but all to no purpose, the prince returned no answer. The princess could now not think otherwise than that he no longer entertained any affection for her, and therefore fell on her knees before him, prayed his forgiveness for all that she had done to his injury, and wept so bitterly withal that it might have moved a stone to pity. Nevertheless, the prince continued to sleep as before, so potent was the soporific potion. In the meanwhile, the queen's daughter lay and heard every word uttered by the princess, and felt such compassion for the wanderer, that she had not the heart to betray her to her wicked stepmother.

Thus, did the whole night pass. Early in the morning, before break of day, the Troll entered the prince's chamber, to hear all that had taken place. The princess returned to the goose-house, and there sat and wept, so that the tears ran down her cheeks as clear as the clearest pearls. When the Troll-queen learned how her cunning had succeeded, she was so overjoyed that she would gladly have entered into another such a bargain, should it present itself. So, going back to her residence, she did nothing the whole day throughout but spin with the golden spinning-wheel.

When evening drew nigh the princess arose, dried up her tears, and began to prepare for a new banquet that should be much more costly than the preceding one. She then went up to the palace, and invited the queen and her stepdaughter, and found a reception no less gracious than before.

While the princess and her guests were sitting at table, and eating and drinking, and making merry, the princess took forth her reel and began to wind. On seeing it the Troll-queen was struck with surprise and thought it a much more precious thing than anything she had seen before. She therefore asked whether she could purchase it. "No," answered the princess, "it is not to be had either for money or good words. Nevertheless," added she, "I will relinquish it to you on one condition. And what may that condition be?" inquired the beldam eagerly. The condition, answered the princess, "is, that I may sleep another night in the chamber of your beloved." The condition was accepted, and all passed off as on the preceding occasion.

The princess then prepared a third banquet, far more costly than either of the former ones, and while the guests were at table drew forth her silken purse, and showed that it was always full of money, however great the sums that might be taken out of it. This also the Troll—queen obtained, on the condition that the princess should sleep another night in the chamber of her dear Prince Hatt.

The queen then returned to the palace, commanded her stepdaughter to conceal herself, as before, in the prince's sleeping-chamber, and prepared a cup of mead, which she presented to her beloved. As the prince was in the act of taking the cup, he chanced to cast his eyes on the Troll queen's stepdaughter, who by a sign warned him to be on his guard. At the same instant a light as it were burst in upon him, and he called to mind the extraordinary dreams he had had, together with other circumstances. He there fore made a semblance only of drinking and cast the liquor aside while the Troll-queen was looking in another direction then throwing himself back, he appeared to sink into a profound sleep.

When the princess was again alone with Prince Hatt, she fell on his neck with tokens of the most ardent affection and said how heartily delighted she was at seeing him once again. But the prince was so bewildered that he did not understand what she was speaking about and made a semblance of being asleep. At this the princess was sorely afflicted wrung her hands, and with a flow of tears implored his forgiveness for all she might have done to his injury. At the same time, she recounted the story of their former love, and all the miseries she had undergone while seeking him over the wide world; and added that she would now die, as he no longer loved her. After she had thus spoken the prince's memory returned, and he became conscious of all that had happened, and how the wicked Troll had parted him from the beloved of his heart. For some minutes he was unable to utter a word, and it seemed to him that he had waked from a long unpleasant dream. At length he sprang up, clasped the princess to his breast, kissed her, and said that she was the friend he held most dear in the whole world. Now there was joy where but just before there had been weeping and sorrow, and to both the prince and the princess their delight seemed to exceed all the affliction and privation they had suffered during their separation.

While the prince and his beloved consort were thus clasped in each other's embrace, and forgetful of all things in the world besides, the Troll's stepdaughter unexpectedly came forth from her hiding-place and stood before them. On seeing her the princess was terrified, not being able to think otherwise than that their happiness was at an end, and that she would betray them. But the young maiden addressed them in words of kindness, saying: "Be comforted, for I will not betray you, but will aid you to the utmost of my power." She then related to them that she was herself of Christian blood, and that her father was a prince, whom the queen had enchanted, as she had done with Prince Hatt. She added, "It is now long since that my father died of grief, and well would it have been for us all had my wicked stepmother died also; for as long as she lives, we can never look for happiness, neither you nor I."

On hearing this the minds of the prince and princess were greatly relieved, and they thanked the damsel for her good-will. They then sat all three together and consulted how they might get rid of the Troll, it being well known to every one that there is no other way of killing Trolls than by scalding them to death. When they had thus consulted and resolved, the maiden returned to her hiding place, while the prince lay down on the bed and appeared as if sleeping. They had not to wait long, for ere the stars had vanished before the dawn of day the Troll entered the chamber to fetch the princess, and to learn all that had taken place during the night.

Several days now passed, and the princess still continued in the goose-house as before. But in the palace, there was great bustle and tumult; for the queen was to celebrate her marriage with Prince Hatt, and a vast multitude of Trolls were invited to the feastings from both far and near. Immense preparations were now made, and the beldam caused a vast kettle to be brought forth that could hold eighteen oxen at once, so great was its capacity. When the fire was kindled, the oxen slaughtered, and all things in readiness, the Troll sent down to the goose-house, to inquire of the wandering woman how the flesh could best be rendered perfectly tender and well-boiled. The princess did not require asking twice but answered: "It is the custom in my country to have a very powerful fire and to boil the liquor till the kettle is blue at bottom." To the Troll this seemed a good method, and she accordingly ordered the fire to be made three times stronger than before, so that the water bubbled and founted up to the clouds of heaven. After a while the daughter looked to see whether the kettle was yet blue at the bottom; then the princess bent over the brim and looked down into the water, but yet no blue was visible. Thus, did an hour pass, when the queen sent Prince Hatt to look; but he could see no blue. The hag was now angry, and was confident that the kettle must be blue, but that they did not see correctly. She therefore stepped up herself, and looked at the water, which was boiling most furiously; but scarcely had she bent over the edge of the kettle before the prince, seizing her by the heels, cast her headlong into the boiling fluid. So, there was an end of the beldam well befitting so wicked a Troll.

The prince and his beloved consort now took the golden spinning-wheel, the golden reel, and the purse, and many other costly things, and hastily departed from the palace. After a long journeying they at length arrived at a magnificent castle, that lay glittering in the sunshine. In the court of the castle there stood a green bush, from which on drawing near, they heard sweet music, as of harps mingled with the song of birds. Now was the princess right glad, for she recognised the three singing leaves that has been given to her by her father. But infinitely greater still was her joy, when on proceeding she saw her young children, and the prince's sisters, together with a great number of people advancing to meet them, and hailed Prince Hatt as their king and the princess as their queen.

Thus, did they receive the reward of their true love, and lived happy for very many years; and the prince ruled his kingdom with wisdom and vigour, so that a mightier king and a more gracious queen were nowhere to be found. And the three singing leaves never ceased their song, but played day and night, so that a sweeter melody could not be heard and never was any one sorrowful who was not made glad on hearing them. And so is the story told.

THE PRINCESS THAT CAME OUT OF THE WATER.

I. The Beautiful Herd-Girl.

From North Småland.

There was once a king who had an only daughter. She was fair and good, so that she was beloved by all who saw her. The kings consort had also an only daughter; but she was ugly to look upon and of evil disposition, so that no one spoke well of her. At this the queen bore a bitter grudge towards her stepdaughter, which became more manifest on the death of the king, when she put her to all kinds of menial labour. But the poor damsel never complained and was always patient and submissive.

It happened one day that the queen sent her stepdaughter up into the loft to watch corn. While she was sitting and watching, the little fowls of heaven came and flew twittering round the heap of corn, as if they wished to have a few grains. The king's daughter felt compassion for the little creatures, and threw a few grains to them from the heap, saying: "My poor little birds! you are so hungry here is a little corn; peck now quickly, and eat your fill." When the sparrows had eaten, they flew away, perched on the roof, and consulted together how they should reward the damsel for her goodness of heart. One bird said: "I will give, that wherever she treads the ground red roses shall spring up." The second said: "I will give, that she shall become fairer and fairer every day of her life." "And I," added the third, "will give, that every time she laughs, a gold ring shall fall from her mouth." Having thus spoken, they flew away; but all came to pass as the birds had said, and from that day the king's daughter became more lovely than before, so that a more beautiful damsel was not to be found, even if search had been made in seven kingdoms.

When the queen was apprized of all this, she became still more envious than before, and meditated with herself how her own daughter could become as fair as her step sister. With this view, she sent the princess in like manner to watch the corn up in the loft. The damsel went, but in great anger, because so mean an employment had been assigned her. When she had watched a little while the fowls of the air came twittering round the heap of corn, as if they wished to have a few grains. At this the damsel's anger was excited, and, snatching up a broom, she drove away the little birds, saying in her passion: "What do ye want here, ye ugly animals? Can ye not understand that a young lady of rank, such as I am, is not to dirty her hands by giving food to the like of you?" The sparrows then flew away, perched on the roof, and consulted together how they should recompense the princess for her harsh words. One of them said: "I will give, that she grows uglier and uglier every day of her life." The second said, "I will give, that every time she treads on the ground, there shall thistles and thorns spring up." "And I," added the third, "will give, that every time she laughs, toads and frogs shall spring out of her mouth." Having so spoken, they flew their several ways; but all mime to pass as the sparrows had said, and from that day the queen's daughter became uglier and uglier, and more odious in disposition than she had been previously.

The stepmother and her wicked daughter could now no longer endure to see the king's fair daughter before their eyes, and therefore set her to tend cattle in the forest. Thus, the poor damsel had to wander about like other herd girls, while the wicked princess remained with her mother in the royal palace and rejoiced in her false heart that no one could get sight of the king's fair daughter or hear of her beauty.

It happened "one day that the beautiful herd-girl was sitting in the forest knitting a glove, while her cattle were grazing, when some young men came riding by. On seeing the maiden as she sat working so sedulously, they were smitten with her beauty, courteously greeted her, and asked: "Why do you sit here, fair maiden, and knit so diligently?" The king's daughter answered:—

> "I am knitting a glove:—
> I think of getting the king's son of Denmark."

At these words the young men were surprised and prayed the damsel to accompany them to the king's court. But the maiden gave no ear to their entreaties and gave them rings of red gold that they might leave her in peace. On their return they were never weary of telling of the fair herd-girl, whom they had met in the forest, and thus there was much talk about her in the whole palace, both about her beauty and riches.

When the king's young son heard all this, he was seized with a violent desire to see the beautiful maiden and ascertain whether it was all true that the young men had related. He therefore rode out to hunt with his hawks and hounds, and penetrated far into the forest, to the place where the king's daughter sat knitting her glove. The prince approached her, courteously greeted her, and said: "Why sit ye here, fair damsel, and knit so diligently?" The maiden answered:—

> "I am knitting a glove:—
> I think of getting the king's son of Denmark."

On hearing this, the king's son was wonder-struck, and he asked the young maiden whether she would accompany him to his dwelling. The princess laughed at his proposal, and at the instant, a ring of red gold fell from her mouth, and when she rose to go, red roses sprung up in her footsteps. Now was the prince's heart turned towards her, so that he confessed who he was, and asked whether the young maiden would be his consort. The princess answered in the affirmative, and, at the same time, gave him to understand that her descent and lineage were not inferior to his own. They then proceeded together to the royal palace, and the king's daughter became the wife of the prince. Everyone wished her well, but to the king's son, she was dear before all else in the world.

At this news the wicked stepmother was more envious than before and thought of nothing so incessantly as how she should effect her stepdaughter's destruction, and make her own daughter queen in her stead. Just at that time it happened that there was a great war, so that the king's son was obliged to go forth with the army, though the young queen was pregnant and about to be confined in child-bed. Availing herself of this opportunity, the stepmother proceeded to the king's palace, and conducted herself most affably towards everyone. But when the young queen was taken ill, the stepmother treacherously placed her own daughter in the place of the queen and transformed the latter into a little duck that swam in the river outside of the king's palace.

Some time after this, the war was at an end, and the young king returned home, full of longing to see his fair bride again. On entering the sleeping-chamber and finding the ugly stepsister in the bed, he was sorely afflicted, and inquired why his consort was so altered in appearance. The treacherous stepmother, who was instantly ready with an answer, said: "That comes of her illness, and will soon pass over." The king inquired further: "Formerly gold rings fell from her mouth every time my queen laughed, now toads and frogs spring forth; formerly red roses grew in her footsteps, but now only thistles and thorns. What can be the cause of all this?" But the wicked queen was prepared with an answer: "So as she is she will continue, and not otherwise, until the king shall take the blood of a little duck, that swims about in the river. The king asked: "How can I get the blood of the duck?" The stepmother answered: "It must be taken between the increase and the wane." The king now ordered the little duck to be caught, but the bird escaped from all the snares, in whatever manner laid.

On Thursday night, while all were sunk in sleep, the watchmen observed a white form, in all respects resembling the queen, which rose up from the river, and went into the kitchen. The princess had had a little dog, to which she was much attached, called Nappe. On entering the kitchen, she said:—

> "Little Nappe, my dog,
> Hast thou some food to give me tonight?"

"No, indeed I have not, my lady," answered the dog. The king's daughter again said:—

> "Does the Troll Sleep with my dear young prince,
> In the high chamber?"

"Yes, she does so, my lady," answered the dog.

The king's daughter then said: "I will return yet on two Thursday nights, and never again afterwards." She then sighed deeply, went down to the river, and was changed into a little duck, as before.

On the following Thursday night, the same occurrence took place. When the people were gone to rest, the watchmen observed a white form that rose from the river and proceeded to the kitchen. All being greatly surprised at this sight, they went secretly to listen to what she said or did. When she came into the kitchen, she said:—

> "Little Nappe, my dog,
> Hast thou some food to give me tonight?"

"No, indeed I have not, my lady," answered the dog.
The king's daughter then asked:—

> "Does the Troll Sleep with my dear young prince,
> In the high chamber?"

"Yes, she does so, my lady," my lady, said the dog.
The queen continued: "I will yet come again on one Thursday night, and afterwards never more." She then began to weep bitterly, and returned to the river, where she was changed into a little duck, which played about on the water. But when the men perceived all this, it appeared to them as very wonderful, so that they went privately to their lord, and related to him what they had heard and seen. At this intelligence the kings sank into deep reflection, and commanded the watchmen to send him notice when the form should appear for the third time.

On the third Thursday night, when all had retired to rest, the king's daughter again rose from the water, and went to the palace. On entering the kitchen, as was her custom she spoke to her dog, and said:—

> "Little Nappe, my dog,
> Hast thou some food to give me tonight?"

"No, indeed I have not, my lady," answered the dog.
The king's daughter again asked:—

> "Does the Troll sleep with my dear young prince,
> In the high chamber?"

"Yes, she does so, my lady," answered the dog.
The queen then sighed deeply and said: "I shall now never come again," and then began to weep bitterly, and was going out to return to the river. But

the king had been standing behind the door, listening to the conversation; and when the figure was about to depart, he took his silver-bladed knife and wounded her left little finger, so that there came forth three drops of blood. The sorcery was then at an end; the queen awoke as from a dream and said: "Ha! Ha! wast thou standing there?" She then, full of joy, fell on her husband's neck, who bore her up to her chamber.

The young queen now related to her consort all that had passed, and they were overjoyed at seeing each other again. The king then went to the stepmother, who was sitting by her daughter's bed; and the false queen was holding the babe on her arm and feigned to be very weak after her illness. The king on entering greeted the old Troll-wife, and asked: "If any one would destroy my sick queen, and throw her into the river, tell me what would be a fitting reward for her?" The wicked stepmother, not suspecting that her treachery was discovered, instantly answered: "That person would well deserve to be placed in a cask set with spikes and rolled down a mountain." Then was the king filled with anger; he rose up and said: "Thou hast now pronounced thy own doom, and it shall be with thee as thou thyself hast said." So the Troll-wife was placed in a casket set round with spikes, and rolled down the mountain; and her daughter, the false queen, suffered the same punishment. But the king took his right queen and lived with her in peace and happiness. Afterwards I was no longer with them.

II. Lilla Rosa and Long Leda.

From South Småland.

There was once a king and a queen, who had an only daughter. She was called Lilla (Little) Rosa, and was both fair and wise, so that she was much beloved by all who knew her. But after some time, the queen died, and the king took another wife. The new queen also had an only daughter, but she was of a proud disposition and ugly of aspect, so that she acquired the name of Long Leda. Both stepsisters grew up together in the royal court; but everyone who saw them observed a great difference between them.

Both the queen and Long Leda were bitterly envious of Lilla Rosa and did her all the harm in their power. But the king's daughter was at all times gentle and submissive, and willingly performed her tasks, however heavy they might be. At this the queen was still more embittered, and grew more and more malignant, the more Lilla Rosa strove to please her in all things.

It happened one day, as the two princesses were walking in the garden, that they heard the head-gardener speaking to his man and bidding him fetch an axe that had been left among the trees. On hearing this, the queen said that Lilla Rosa should go after the axe. The head-gardener objected and said that so mean an errand was ill-befitting the daughter of a king; but the queen persisted and prevailed.

When Little Rosa came into the wood, as the queen had commanded, she soon found where the axe lay; but three white doves had perched on the haft. So, taking some bread she had brought with her, she crumbled it and held it out to the little doves, saying: "My poor little doves! you must now go away: for I am compelled to carry the axe to my stepmother." The doves ate from the maiden's hand, willingly quitted the haft, and Lilla Rosa took away the axe, as she had been commanded. She had not been gone long when the doves began to converse together, and to consider what reward they should bestow on the young damsel who had been so kind to them. One said: "I will give, that she shall be twice as fair as she now is." The second said: "I, will give, that her hair shall be turned to golden hair." "And I," added the third, "will give, that every time she laughs a ring of red gold shall fall from her mouth." Having thus spoken, the doves flew their respective ways; but all came to pass as they had said. So, when Lilla Rosa came back to her stepmother, all were amazed at her incomparable beauty, at her fine golden locks, and at the red gold rings that fell from her whenever she laughed. But the queen found out all that had taken place, and from that moment entertained a more intense hatred towards her stepdaughter than before.

The wicked stepmother now meditated both day and night only how her own daughter might become as beautiful as Lilla Rosa. To this end she secretly summoned the head-gardener to her presence and told him what he should do. She then went with both princesses to walk in the flower garden, according to her custom. As they passed by the head-gardener, he said that he had left his axe among the trees, and bade his man fetch it; whereupon the queen said that Long Leda should go for the axe. The head-gardener objected to this, as was just, and thought that so mean an errand was ill-befitting a young lady of rank; but the queen persisted and gained her object.

When Long Leda came into the wood, as the queen had ordered, she soon saw where the axe lay; but the three beautiful white doves were again sitting on the haft. On seeing them the evil-disposed damsel could not repress her ill-humour, but cast stones at the birds, cursed them, and said: "Away, ye ugly creatures! you shall not sit here and foul the axe-handle that I am to lay hold of with my white hands." At this address the doves flew away, and Long Leda took the axe, as she had been ordered. But she had not proceeded far on her return, when the doves began to converse together, and to consider what reward they should bestow on the ill-natured damsel for her malice. One of them said "I will give her, that she shall be twice as ugly as she now is." The second said: "I will give, that her hair shall be like a thorn-bush." "And I," added the third, "will give, that a toad shall spring out of her mouth every time she laughs." Having so spoken, the three doves flew their several ways; but all came to pass as they had said. When, therefore, Long Leda returned to her mother, she was wonder-struck at her loathsome aspect, at her hair, which resembled a thorn-bush, and at the toad which issued from her mouth every time she laughed. She was, as might be expected, deeply afflicted at this misfortune, and, it is said, neither she nor her daughter ever laughed from that day.

The stepmother could now no longer endure the sight of Lilla Rosa but strove to injure and destroy her. With this view she secretly called to her a shipmaster, who was going to a far distant land, and promised him a great reward if he would take the king's daughter on board his ship and sink her in the bottom of the sea. Allured by the promised gold, the great root of evil in this world, the shipmaster carried off Lilla Rosa by night, as her stepmother had desired. But when the vessel had put out to sea, and had sailed far away on the raging ocean, a violent storm arose, so that the ship perished, with freight and crew, all except Lilla Rosa, who was borne by the waves until she reached a green isle far out in the sea. Here she long continued without hearing or seeing a single human being, her food consisting of wild berries and roots, which grew in the woods.

One day, while wandering on the seashore, she found the head and leg of a fawn that had been killed by the wild beasts. As the flesh was still fresh, she took the leg and set it on a pole, that the little birds might see it the better, and come and feed upon it. She then lay down on the earth, and slept for a short time, when she was wakened by a sweet song, more beautiful than anything that can be imagined. Lilla Rosa listened to the delightful notes, and thought she was dreaming; for nothing so exquisite had she ever heard before. On looking around her, she saw that the leg which she had laced as food for the little fowls of heaven was changed to a verdant linden, and the fawn's head to a little nightingale sitting on the linden's summit. But every single small leaf of the tree gave forth a sweet sound, so that their tones together composed a wondrous harmony; and the little nightingale sat among them and sang his lay so beautifully, that all who might hear it would certainly have imagined themselves in heaven.

After that day it did not seem to the princess so tedious to dwell alone on the green isle; for whenever she was sad, she had only to go to the musical linden, and her heart became glad. Nevertheless, she could not entirely forget her home, but often sat by the seashore, casting many a longing look over the wide ocean, whose billows roll between land and land.

One day, as Lilla Rosa was, according to her custom, sitting by the sea, she observed a splendid bark sailing towards her. On the deck were many bold mariners, and their captain was a king's son. When the vessel came under the island, and the sailors heard the delightful song that resounded over the water, they thought that it must be an enchanted land, and would instantly put out to sea again. But their Chieftain said that they should not depart until he had ascertained whence the wondrous song proceeded, and his will prevailed. When the king's son came on land and heard the music of the linden and the song of the nightingale, he was singularly affected; for it seemed to him that he had never heard anything so exquisite and fascinating. But still more wonderful did it appear to him, as he proceeded further, when, under the verdant linden, he saw a damsel sitting, whose hair shone like gold, and whose face was as fair as the driven snow. The prince greeted the beautiful maiden and asked whether she ruled over the island. Lilla Rosa answered in the affirmative. The prince again inquired whether she was a sea-damsel or a human being, whereupon she related to him the adventures she had passed through, and how she had been cast by a storm on the uninhabited island; she also informed him of her family and descent. At this, the king's son was highly gratified, and could not sufficiently admire the young maiden's gentleness and beauty. They discoursed long together, and their conversation ended by the prince's proposal that Lilla Rosa should accompany him home and be his queen, to which she gave her consent. They then sailed from the island and arrived in the prince's dominions. But Lilla Rosa took with her the verdant linden and placed it near the royal palace; and the linden-leaves played and the nightingale sang, so that the whole neighbourhood was delighted.

When Lilla Rosa had been married some time, she gave birth to a male child. She then thought of her aged father and sent intelligence to him of all she had undergone; but did not divulge to any one that the queen had been the cause of all her sorrows. At these tidings the old king was overjoyed, as were also his people; for Lilla Rosa was beloved by all. But the queen and Long Leda were sorely vexed that Lilla Rosa was still living and took counsel together how they should effect her destruction.

The false stepmother, then, having prepared herself accordingly, said that she would go and visit Lilla Rosa. On her arrival she was received in the most friendly manner; for the king's daughter was unwilling to bear in remembrance all the evil her stepmother had perpetrated against her, and the queen herself feigned great friendship and spoke many kind words. One evening, the stepmother said to Lilla Rosa that she would make her a present, as a memorial of love and friendship. The stepdaughter, suspecting no treachery, thanked her for the gift, and the queen drew forth a silken sark, every hem of which was embroidered in gold. But the beautiful sark was wickedly enchanted, so that when Lilla Rosa put it on, she was suddenly changed to a goose, that flew through the window, and cast itself into the sea. But as the king's daughter had beautiful golden hair, the goose also had golden feathers. At the same moment the linden ceased its playing, and the song of the nightingale was no longer heard; and the whole palace was overwhelmed with sorrow; but most of all was the consort of Rosa Lilla afflicted, and would not be comforted.

At night, when the moon shone, and the king's fishermen were out at sea, looking after their nets, they observed a beautiful goose with golden feathers, which lay swinging to and fro on the billows. At this sight they greatly wondered, and it appeared to them something miraculous. But one night the beautiful goose swam close to the fishermen's boat and began to converse with them. After greeting them, it said"—

"Good evening, fishers; how are things at home in the royal palace?
    Does my linden play?
    Does my nightingale sing?
    Does my little son weep?
    Does my lord ever make himself merry?"

When the fisherman heard this, and recognised the voice of the queen, he was singularly affected, and answered:—

"At home, in the royal palace, it goes ill:
    Thy linden plays not,
    Thy nightingale sings not,
    Thy son weeps both by night and by day,
    Thy lord never makes himself merry."

The beautiful goose then sighed and appeared deeply afflicted. She said:—

"Poor I!
Who now float on the blue waves,
And never more can be what I have been.
Good night, fisher; I will come twice again, and then never more."

At the same moment the bird disappeared but the fisherman returned home, and recounted to the young king, his master, what he had seen and heard.

Thereupon the king commanded that the golden goose should be caught, and promised the fisherman a great reward, if he executed his commission. The man accordingly prepared his snares and other implements and went out to sea to look after his nets. When the moon had risen, the beautiful golden goose came again swimming on the waves towards his boat. She greeted him, and said:—

"Good evening, fisher; how are things at home in the royal palace?
    Does my linden play?
    Does my nightingale sing?
    Does my little son weep?
    Does my lord ever make himself merry?"

The fisherman answered as before:—

"At home, in the royal palace, it goes ill:
        Thy linden plays not,
        Thy nightingale sings not,
        Thy son weeps both by night and by day,
        Thy lord never makes himself merry."

Then was the beautiful goose sorely grieved, and said:—

"Poor I!
Who now float on the blue waves,
And never more can be what I have been.
Good night, fisher; I will come hither once again, and then never more."

With these words the bird was about to go its way; but the fishermen were prepared, and hastily cast their snares over it. The goose then began to beat with its wings, and screamed mournfully: "Let go quickly, or hold fast! Let go quickly or hold fast!" In the same moment it changed its form, and was changed into serpents, dragons, and other savage creatures. At this sight the fishermen trembled for their lives, and let go the snares, so that the bird escaped. When the king heard the result of their attempt, he was highly displeased, and said, they ought not to have allowed themselves to be frightened by an illusion. He then ordered new and stronger snares to be made ready, in order to catch the golden geese, and forbade the fishermen, on pain of death, to let her escape, when she should next make her appearance.

On the third night, when the moon had risen, the king's fishermen again rowed out to sea to look after their nets. They waited a long while, but no golden goose appeared. At length she came floating on the billows, and swam to their boat, greeting them as before.—

"Good evening, fisher; how are things at home in the royal palace?
        Does my linden play?
        Does my nightingale sing?
        Does my little son weep?
        Does my lord ever make himself merry?"

The fisherman answered:—

"At home, in the royal palace, it goes ill:
　　Thy linden plays not,
　　Thy nightingale sings not,
　　Thy son weeps both by night and by day,
　　Thy lord never makes himself merry."

Then the beautiful goose sighed, and appeared very sorrowful, and said:—

"Poor I!
Who now float on the blue waves,
And never more can be what I have been.
Good night, fishers. Now I come hither never more."

The goose was then about to go, but the fishermen cast their snares and held her fast. The bird then became very unruly, beat violently with its wings, and screamed: "Let go quickly, or hold fast! Let go quickly or hold fast!" It then changed its form, and appeared as serpents, dragons, and other dangerous creatures. But the fishermen, dreading the king's wrath, held the snare firmly and fast, and thus succeeded in catching the golden goose, which they conveyed to the king's palace, where it was closely watched, lest it should escape. But the bird was silent and sullen, and would not speak, so that the king's affliction was even greater than before.

It happened, some time after, that an aged woman, of singular aspect, arrived at the royal palace, and begged to speak with the king. The watch answered, as he was commanded, that the king, in consequence of his sorrow, would not converse with any one. But the woman was extremely urgent, and so gained admittance. When she came before the king, he demanded her errand. She answered: "Sir king, I have been informed that your queen has been transformed into a golden goose, and that you mourn over this great misfortune both night and day. I am now come hither to solve the sorcery and restore your consort to you, provided you will promise to consent to a condition which I shall propose." When the king heard these words, he was exceedingly glad, and asked her what it was she desired. The woman then said: "I have my abode on the declivity of the mountain that lies on the other side of the black river. I now request that you will order a stone wall to be built round the mountain, so that your cattle may not come and annoy me, when they are sent out to graze." This seemed to the king a small request, and he promised readily to grant it however much he might doubt the old woman's ability to keep her word, according to her engagement.

The old woman now began circumstantially to recount all that Lilla Rosa had suffered through her wicked stepmother; but the king found it difficult to give credit to her words, for he could not think that the old queen was so false at heart. The woman then requested to see the beautiful silken sark, which Lilla Rosa had received as a token of affection from her stepmother. The king ordered the sark to be brought, and they then proceeded together to the apartment in which the golden goose was confined. On entering it, the Troll-woman went up to the beautiful geese and drew the garment over it. The sorcery was then at an end, Little Rosa recovered her natural form, and, in place of a golden goose, there stood a beautiful woman with golden locks, as before. At the same instant the linden again began to play, and the nightingale to sing in its summit, so that it was delightful to hear. There was now rejoicing throughout the palace; and the king, seeing that the old woman had told the truth, religiously kept to his promise.

Lilla Rosa and her consort afterwards made preparations to go and visit the king, Rosa's father. On seeing them, the old king was so overjoyed that he seemed to be restored to youth, and the whole kingdom rejoiced with him, for all had heard what a misfortune had befallen the king's daughter. But there was one who was not glad, and that was the queen; for she well knew that her treachery was discovered and her time out. And when the old king was informed of the falsehood and cruelty that his daughter had experienced from her wicked stepmother, he was bitterly exasperated, and doomed the queen to death. But Lilla Rosa interceded for the life of her stepmother, and the king granted her prayer, but placed his consort in a prison tower for the remainder of her days. The queen's daughter, Long Leda, shared the fate of her mother; but the young king and Lilla Rosa returned to their own kingdom. And there the linden plays, and the nightingale, sings; there the prince weeps neither by day nor night: there the king constantly makes himself merry.

III. JUNGFRU SVANHVITA AND JUNGFRU RAFRUMPA.[5]

From Östergötland.

THERE was once a wicked woman, who had two daughters; a daughter of her own and a stepdaughter. Her own daughter was ugly of aspect, and still more ugly of disposition; but the stepdaughter was beautiful in person and of kind disposition, so that all who saw her wished her well. This excited the ill will of her stepmother and stepsister, who were always envious of the defenseless maiden.

It happened one day that the young girl was sent by her stepmother to fetch water from the well. On reaching the brink, she saw a little hand stretched out above the surface of the water, and at the same time a voice was heard, saying: "Maiden fair and gentle, give me thy gold apple, and I will wish thee three good wishes." The maiden felt well disposed towards one that asked so meekly and held forth her gold apple to the little hand. Then stooping over the fountain, she took particular care not to trouble the water while she filled her vessel. When she returned home, the guardian of the well wished that she might become three times more beautiful than she was, that every time she laughed a gold ring might fall out of her mouth, and that red roses might spring wherever she trod on the earth. At the same instant, all that he had wished came to pass; and from that day the maiden was called Jungfru Svanhvita[6], and the fame of her beauty was widely spread over the land.

---

[5] This tale is wide-spread over Europe. We have met with the following versions:

1. In Danish.—See Winther, ut sup. 1st Samling, pp. 102-112. "Svanhvide;" and Anmærkn. ibid. p. 126.

2. In German.—*a.* See Grimm, K. und H. M. i. No. 2. "Brüderchen und Schwesterchen." *b. ibid.* i. No. 13. "Die drei Mannlein im Walde." *c. ibid.* ii. No. 135. "Die Weisse und Schwarze Braut." (Cf. Th. iii. pp. 227, 228.)

3. In Bohemian.—See "Gerle, Volksmarchen der Böhmen," Prag. 1819, ii. No. 5. "Die goldene Ente."

4. In Magyarisu.—See "Mailath, Magyarische Sagen, Marchen und Erzahlungen," 2nd edit. Stuttg. 1837, pp. 209-213 "Die Gaben."

5. In Italian—See Basile, Il Pentamerone, iv. No. 7. "Le Doje Pizzelle."

6. In French.—See Mad. D'Aulnoy, Contes des Fées. " La Rosette."

[6] Jungfru Svanhvita, *i. e.* Maiden Swanwhite.

When the wicked stepmother heard of all this, her malevolence knew no bounds, and she meditated within herself how her own daughter might become as beautiful as Svanhvita. With this object she fished out accurately all that had taken place, and then sent her own daughter in like manner to fetch water. When the evil-hearted maiden came to the well, a little hand was raised above the surface of the water and a voice was heard, saying: "Maiden fair and gentle, give me thy gold apple, and I will wish thee three good wishes." But the crone's daughter was both ugly and avaricious, and never gave anything as a present making therefore a blow at the little hand, she bestowed a malediction on the guardian of the well and answered angrily: "Thou must not think of getting a gold apple from me." Then filling her pail, she troubled the water of the well, and went full of malice on her way homewards. Then was the guardian of the well exasperated and wished her three evil wishes in reward for her malignity. He wished that she might become three times uglier than she already was, that a dead rat might fall out of her mouth every time she laughed, and that fox-tail grass (räf-rumpor) might grow in her footsteps, whenever she trod on the earth. And so it came to pass. From that day the evil-hearted maiden was called in mockery Jungfru Räfrumpa, and great was the talk among people of her extraordinary appearance and disposition. But the crone could not endure that her stepdaughter was fairer than her own daughter; so poor Svanhvita, from that moment, suffered all the wrongs and disgrace that could be inflicted on a stepchild.

Jungfru Svanhvita had a brother who was exceedingly dear to her, and who in return loved her most tenderly. The young man had long since left home and was in the service of a king in a far-distant land. But the other courtiers bore him a grudge on account of the favour shown him by his master, and would gladly effect his fall, if they could find any pretext for ruining him in the estimation of the king.

The young man's enviers kept a close watch on all his actions, and one day presented themselves before the king, saying: "Sir king, we well know that you cannot endure vice and immorality in your servants; therefore have we thought proper not to conceal, that the young foreigner, who is in your service, every morning and evening bends his knee before an idol." When the king heard this, he thought it was malevolence and slander, and gave no credit to it. But the courtiers said, that he could convince himself whether they had told the truth or not. They there upon conducted the king to the young man's apartment and prayed him to look through the key-hole. When the king had looked in, he perceived the young man on his knees before a beautiful picture, and, consequently, could not think otherwise than that all was true that the courtiers had related. The king was now very angry, called the young man before him, and condemned him to death for his great sin. But the young man exculpated himself and said: "Sir king, you must not think that I worship any heathen image: it is my sister's picture, and every morning and evening, I pray to God for her preservation, while she is in the power of a wicked stepmother." The king then desired to see the picture and could not tire of beholding its beauty. He said: "If it is true, as thou sayest, that this is thy sister's likeness, she shall be my queen, and thou thyself shalt go and fetch her. But if thou hast spoken an untruth, thy punishment shall be to be cast to wild beasts, in a lion's den." The king then ordered a vessel to be fitted out in the most sumptuous manner, with crew and precious wares, and sent the young man, in great state, to fetch his fair sister to the royal court.

The young man now sailed far over the ocean, and at length arrived in his native country. Here he executed his commission, as he had been commanded, and afterwards prepared to sail back. Then his stepmother and step sister prayed that they might also accompany them. The young man, feeling averse to their society, denied their request; but Svanhvita interceded for them, and their prayer was granted. When they had put out to sea and were traversing the wide ocean, a violent storm arose, so that the mariners thought the vessel and all in her would go to the bottom. But the young man was of good courage, and mounted on the yard, to see whether he could discern land in any direction. After having looked out from the mast-head, he called to Svanhvita, who was standing on the deck: "Dear sister, I now see land." But it blew so hard that the maiden could not hear his words, and therefore asked her stepmother what her brother had said. The false crone answered "He says we shall never again tread God's green earth, if thou do not cast thy gold casket into the sea." When Svanhvita heard this, she did as it had been told her, and cast her gold casket into the midst of the deep.

Some time after, her brother called to her again: "Svanhvita, it is time that thou arrayest thyself as a bride; for we shall soon arrive." But the maiden did not hear his words, for the violent storm and therefore again inquired of her stepmother what her brother had said. The false beldam now answered: "He says we shall never again tread. God's green earth, if thou dost not cast thyself into the ocean." This Svanhvita thought very extraordinary; but the wicked stepmother, running up to her, suddenly pushed her overboard. The maiden was borne away by the blue waves, and came to the mermaid, who rules over all those that perish by sea[7].

When the young man came down from the mast and inquired whether his sister was attired, the stepmother, with many false words, told him that Svanhvita had fallen into the sea. At this intelligence the young man, together with all the ship's crew, was seized with fear; for they well knew what punishment awaited them, for having so ill-attended to the king's bride. But the false crone devised another deception, saying, they should attire her own daughter as a bride, for then no one would know that Svanhvita had perished. To this proposal the young man refused to accede, but the mariners, fearing for their lives, compelled him to comply. Jungfru Räfrumpa was accordingly attired in the most sumptuous manner, with rings of red gold and a golden girdle but the young man's mind was oppressed with anxiety, and he could not banish from his memory the misfortune that had befallen his sister.

While all this was passing, the vessel reached the land, and the king went down to meet it with all his court and in great state. Precious carpets were spread, and the royal bride was conducted from the ship with much ceremony. But when the king saw Jungfru Räfrumpa, and understood that she was his bride, he was sensible that there was foul play, and was highly incensed. He therefore commanded the young man to be cast to wild beasts in a lion's den, but would not break his royal word, so took the ugly maiden to wife, who thus became queen in her sister's stead.

Jungfru Svanhvita had a little dog, to which she was much attached: its name was Snöhvit (Snowwhite). After its mistress's misfortune, there was no one to take care of the faithful animal, which ran to the king's palace and took refuge in the kitchen, where it lay before the fire. At night, when all had retired to rest, the master-cook observed that the door opened of itself, and a beautiful little duck, fastened with a chain, came into the kitchen. Wherever

---

[7] Here is evidently a trace of the goddess Rân. See Thorpe, Northern Mythology, vx. i. p. 27.

the little bird stept there sprung up the most beautiful roses. The duck then proceeded to the hearth, where the dog was lying, and said:

> "Thou poor little Snöhvit!
> Erst didst thou lie on silken cushions blue,
> Now must thou rest amid the ashes gray.
> And my poor brother! He's in the lion's den.
> Out upon Räfrumpa! She sleeps in my lord's arms."

The duck continued: "Poor I! I will come again two nights more: afterwards I may never see thee again." She then caressed the little dog, and the animal fawned upon her in return. When a short time had passed, the deer again opened of itself, and the little duck went its way.

On the following morning, as soon as it was light, the master-cook took some of the beautiful roses that were strewn about on the floor and laid them round the dishes that were to be served up at the king's table. The king could not enough admire the flowers, and called the master-cook, and asked him whence he had got such beautiful roses. The cook then related what had taken place in the night, and what the duck had said to the little dog. When the king had heard this, he was struck with astonishment, and ordered the master-cook to send him notice when the bird again made its appearance.

The next night the little duck went again up into the kitchen, and spoke with the dog as before, A message was thereupon sent to the king, who came just as the bird had passed out at the door; but all about the kitchen floor there lay splendid roses, that diffused a delicious odour, such as the like had never been experienced. The king now resolved, that if the bird again made its appearance, it should not escape. He therefore posted himself on the watch in the kitchen. After waiting a long while, just as it drew near midnight, the little bird entered, and approaching the dog, as he lay on the hearth, said:

> "Thou poor little Snöhvit!
> Erst didst thou lie on silken cushions blue,
> Now must thou rest amid the ashes gray.
> And my poor brother! He's in the lion's den.
> Out upon Räfrumpa! She sleeps in my lord's arms."

The duck continued: "Poor I! Never shall I see thee more." She then caressed the little dog, and the animal fawned upon her in return. When the bird was about to depart, the king rushed forward and seized it by the foot. It then changed its form and appeared as a hideous dragon; but the king still held fast. It was again transformed, and appeared in the likeness of serpents, wolves, and other ferocious animals but the king did not let go his hold. And now the mermaid pulled hard at the chain but the king, nevertheless held fast, and the chain snapt asunder with a rattling noise. At the same moment there stood a beautiful damsel before him, far fairer than the charming picture. She thanked the king for having rescued her from the power of the mermaid, and he was glad beyond measure, and, clasping the maiden to his bosom, he kissed her and said: "Thee or no one in the world will I have for my queen; and now I see well that thy brother was innocent." He then sent in all haste to the lion's den to see if the young man were still alive; but there he sat sound and well in the midst of the wild beasts, which had not injured him in the slightest degree. At this the king was rejoiced, and also delighted that all had fallen out so well. The brother and sister then related to him how their treacherous stepmother had acted towards them.

As soon as it dawned the king commanded a great feast to be prepared and invited the chief men of the realm to come to the palace. While all were sitting at table and making merry, the king began to relate about the brother and sister, who had been betrayed by their stepmother, and recounted all that had befallen them from beginning to end. When he had finished his recital, the king's men looked at each other, and all were of opinion that it was a most unheard—of tissue of wickedness. Then, turning to his mother-in-law, the king said: "I long to know what punishment a person deserves who would destroy so innocent a life." The false beldam, not perceiving that her own treachery was discovered, answered boldly: "Such a person would well deserve to be boiled in melted lead. Then turning to Jungfru Räfrumpa, the king said: "I also long to hear thy opinion." She answered hastily: "That person would well deserve to be cast into boiling tar." The king in anger then started up from the table and said: "Ye have pronounced judgment on yourselves, and that judgment ye shall undergo." He then commanded the two women to be led to death, according to their own sentence, and there was no one save Svanhvita who asked grace for them. The king afterwards solemnized his marriage with the fair damsel, and everyone was of opinion that a more beautiful queen could nowhere be found. To the young man, her brother, the king gave his own sister; and thus, joy was spread over the whole palace; and if they are not dead, there they live well and happy even until this day.

The story of *The Princess that came out of the Water* is one of the most wide-spread among the popular tales of Sweden and is told with many variations. The editors have had access to the following several versions:—

1. THE GOLD RING AND THE FROG—THE GOLD RING AND THE SERPENT.

From Upland.

THERE was once a man who lost his way in a forest. After wandering about for a long while, without finding a path, he became very disheartened, and sat down on a stone. There came then to him an ugly old hag, who asked him why he was so sad. The man answered that he had lost his way and could not find his road home. The crone thereupon said: "If thou wilt promise to take me to wife, I will show thee the way; otherwise thou wilt never leave this forest alive." In his tribulation, the man promised compliance with her proposal, although it appeared to him a miserable alternative. So, the beldam accompanied him to the town, and became his wife; but she was a Troll-woman and did not allow him many joyful days.

The man had been married previously, and had a daughter by his first wife, who was both good and fair. The crone had also a daughter, who resembled her mother, being both ugly and of evil disposition. Both mother and daughter entertained much envy and hatred towards the man's poor daughter, so that she met with a stepchild's treatment, and was made to suffer much wrong.

It happened one day that the wicked stepmother would take a bath and sent her stepdaughter to see whether all things were in readiness in the bath room. When the damsel approached the spot, she was met by three young maidens, who besought her with great earnestness to bathe them. The stepdaughter answered: "I will readily do so, but you must make haste, that I may not get a scolding from my stepmother." She now bathed the young girls and went her way. After her departure the three maidens consulted together how they should reward the friendly damsel for her kindness. One of them said: "I wish that she may become thrice as fair as she now is." The second said: "I wish that a gold ring may slip on her finger every time she sneezes." "And I," said the third, "wish that every time she sneezes a gold chain may wind itself thrice round her neck." Having so spoken, they went their way.

The husband's daughter now accompanied her stepmother to the bath and attended her while bathing. While so employed she chanced to sneeze, and in the same moment a gold ring fell on the floor, and gaveforth a sound. "What was that?" asked the beldam, snatching up the ring; "this thou hast taken from me." The damsel said nothing, and the stepmother kept the ring. When they had returned to the apartment the damsel sneezed again, and instantly a gold chain twined itself thrice round her neck. "What was that?" again asked the beldam, "that also thou hast taken from me," grasping the beautiful chain, which she likewise kept. But the stepdaughter well knew that the ornaments were a gift from the three maidens.

The crone now meditated how her own daughter might become as beautiful as her stepdaughter. For this purpose, she ordered another bath to be prepared, and sent her own daughter to see whether all were in readiness. When the crone's daughter reached the bath, she was met by the three young damsels, who earnestly prayed her to bathe them; but the ill-nurtured stepdaughter cursed the young maidens and drove them away with harsh words. The three then consulted together how they should reward the ugly creature for her ill-will and malevolence. One of them said: "I wish she may become thrice as ugly as she now is." The second said: "I wish that every time she sneezes a foul frog may come out of her mouth." "And I," added the third, "wish that every time she sneezes a serpent may twist itself three times round her neck." Having so spoken, the three maidens disappeared, and no one has set eyes on them since.

The crone and her daughter now proceeded to the bathroom. On reaching it the girl sneezed, when instantly a foul frog fell on the floor. "Ha what was that?" asked the Troll-wife. The daughter was silent. On returning to their apartment the girl sneezed again, and instantly an ice-cold serpent wound itself thrice round her neck. "Ha! what was that!" exclaimed the woman, while, trembling, she removed the reptile. Thereupon the daughter related to her all that had passed between her and the three little damsels. From that day the Troll-wife and her daughter were much more evil-disposed towards the husband's daughter, and sent her away to the wood to tend cattle, in order that no one might know of her beauty.

It happened one day that some young men were engaged in the chase in the forest, who, when they saw the young herd-girl, as she was tending her cattle, were greatly stricken with her beauty, and insisted on her accompanying them to the king's palace, whether she would or not. The maiden was terrified and promised to give them both gold and other precious things if they would leave her in peace. The young men placed no great reliance on these words; but the herd-girl, stepping aside to a hole she had dug in the sand, took forth both rings and gold chains, which she gave to the huntsmen, who, on seeing all these riches, were yet more wonderstruck; and he who was their chief conceived such a love for the fair maid that it seemed to him he could not live without her. The huntsmen now entreated the herd girl to accompany them to the king's palace, promising she should experience no disgrace or dishonour from them. The damsel then complied with their request and went with them out of the forest. But as they proceeded, she discovered that it was the young king himself who had taken her with him. And the king made love to the fair herd-girl, and made her his queen, and held her dearer than all other things in the world.

When the young king had been married some time, a great war burst out, and he was obliged to take the field. The queen was at this time pregnant. The king sent messengers over all his realm to seek out a midwife who might best attend to his consort during her confinement. At these tidings, the stepmother set out for the royal palace, and was well received. But when the queen fell in childbirth, the Troll-wife, seizing a favourable opportunity, threw her stepdaughter into the sea, and caused her own daughter to act the part of queen in her stead. When the war was ended, and the king returned home, he at once saw that his queen was very unlike her former self; but the false woman was at no loss for an excuse, saying it was a consequence of her illness, and that she would soon be better.

The fair stepdaughter, who had been cast into the sea, was sea taken, and came to the mermaid. After she had been there for some time, she begged the Sea-troll to let her go up to the green earth and see her little son. The mermaid consented; so, the queen went up from the sea, and came late at night to the king's sleeping-chamber. There, sorrowfully bending over the infant's cradle, she said:—

> "God bless thee, dear young son of mine!
> But the king he sleeps in the witch's arms.
> Twice yet again, but never more,
> Shall I thee see."

"Who was that who spoke?" asked the king, starting out of his sleep. "I heard nothing," answered the beldam's daughter, who was acting the part of queen.

The king now commanded the watches, that, if they observed any one coming into the palace by night, they should detain them. Some days now passed; but when Thursday came, the queen again rose out of the sea, and at midnight entered the king's chamber. There again, bending sorrowfully over the infant's cradle, she said:—

> "God bless thee, dear young son of mine!
> But the king he sleeps in the witch's arms.
> Once yet again, but never more,
> Shall I thee see."

"Who was that who spoke?" inquired the king, starting out of his sleep. "I heard nothing," answered the false queen, who was acting the part of queen. But when the watches rushed forward to seize the queen, she disappeared in the ocean.

On the third Thursday night the king himself kept watch, and with him were many priests, clerks, and other learned men. And now, when the queen was in the act of leaving the little prince's cradle, all perceived that she was fastened round the ancle by a heavy iron chain. Seeing this, one of the clerks cast his Bible at the chain, and no sooner had the holy volume touched the links than the sorcery was dissolved, the chain brake, and rushed down into the sea with a great noise and rattling. Thus, was the queen rescued from the sea; and every one can easily conceive the king's delight at having recovered her.

On the following day the king made a great feast, at which were assembled many men of high lineage and degree from all parts of the kingdom. While the guests were sitting at table, and making merry, the king recounted all that had befallen his queen; but no one knew of whom he spoke. Then turning to the old Troll-wife, he said: "What punishment do they deserve who have attempted to destroy so innocent a person!" The crone answered: "They were well worthy to be cast into boiling tar." "Then," said the king, "thou hast pronounced judgment on thyself. So he commanded the witch to be boiled in tar; and her daughter shared the same fate. But the king took again his true wife, with whom he lived happily the rest of his days.

2. THE WREATH.

From South Småland.

THERE was once a man who had two daughters, an own daughter and a stepdaughter. The man's daughter was good-hearted and friendly; but the stepdaughter was ugly and of evil disposition, which was, moreover, fostered by her mother.

One day, the man with his daughter went to the forest to hew wood; but the weather was cold, and it rained hard. When they returned in the evening, the man found he had left his axe behind, whereupon he said to his wife: "My dear, let thy daughter go after the axe, for mine is both weary and wet; she has been the whole day out in the rain." But the woman answered: "Oh, the weather is not so bad but that thy daughter can very well go. If she is wet already, she will bear a shower or two all the better." Thus, the poor stepdaughter was obliged to go, be the weather as it might, to seek after her father's axe.

When she reached the spot where the axe lay, three little doves were sitting on the haft, and looking very sad. The maiden felt pity for the little birds and addressed them kindly: "My poor little doves, fly home to your little dwelling, then you will avoid being out in the rain and getting wet. I must go home with my father's axe, otherwise I shall be chided by my stepmother. Fly now your ways, little doves." Saying this, she took some bread from her evening meal, crumbled it, and gave it to the birds. She then took up the axe and proceeded homewards. But the doves flew to the top of a high tree and consulted together how they should reward the friendly girl for her kindheartedness. One of them said: "I will give her a wreath." The second said: "I will give her birds in it." "And I," added the third, "will give, that no one shall take away the wreath without causing it to wither." Having so spoken, the little doves flew away. When the maiden returned home, she had on her head a wreath of the most beautiful flowers, and among the roses there sat small birds, that sung so delightfully that the like had never been heard.

The stepmother and her daughter could ill brook that the stepdaughter should possess anything so precious; so they took the wreath from her, and set it on the head of the crone's daughter. But no sooner had they so done than the birds were silent, and the flowers shed their leaves. Then the crone sent her own daughter out into the forest, that she might also get a wreath as well as her half-sister. But no sooner had the girl cast her eyes on the three doves, perched on the haft of the axe, than, unable to repress her evil disposition, she screamed: "Ye filthy animals, who has given you permission to sit there and befoul my father's axe? Away, or I will help you." The crone's daughter then took up the axe and went her way. But the doves flew to the top of a high tree and consulted together what reward they should bestow on the girl for her hard words. They agreed that the crone's daughter should never be able to say anything but "Ye filthy animals." And so it came to pass. But from that hour the crone and her daughter could not endure the poor stepdaughter and sought to cause her all the harm and vexation in their power.

It happened one day that the king's son was passing through the forest and caught sight of the maiden with the beautiful wreath and the singing birds. Being smitten with her beauty, he took her with him to the palace, and married her. But the false stepmother, watching her opportunity during the prince's absence, pushed her stepdaughter into the sea, and placed her own daughter in her stead. When the king returned the wreath had disappeared, and the queen could say nothing but "Ye filthy animals!" This to everyone seemed wonderful, and the prince was sorely afflicted thereat.

The queen, who had been cast into the deep, arose thrice from thence, and conversed with her dog. On the first night she went up on the shore, and said:—

> "My little dog, art thou asleep?
> Lies the false Troll-wife in my consort's arms?
> Better was it meant for me."

The second night the same took place. But the third night the prince himself was on the watch and seized his wife just as she was in the act of returning to the sea. She then changed her form, and he came various sorts of animals, both fishes and birds; but the prince, nevertheless, held fast. At last she was changed, as it seemed, into a tar-pot. The prince, then, drawing his sword, cut through the tar-pot, and in the same instant the enchantment was dissolved, and there stood before the prince a fair damsel, having on her head a wreath, in which a number of little birds were singing. Joy and gladness were now diffused over the whole palace, because the prince had recovered his right consort.

On the following day the prince caused a great feast to be prepared. In the midst of the festive mirth he asked the old Troll-beldam what punishment those merited who would deprive a fellow-creature of life. The stepmother answered: "They well deserved to be put in a tun set round with spikes and rolled down a hill." Then said the prince: "Thou hast pronounced judgment on thyself." The crone and her daughter were afterwards rolled to death in a tun set round with spikes; and the prince with his wife lived long and happy.

3. In A. I. Arwidsson's "Läse-och Läro-bok för Ungdom"[8] is given a variation from Ostergöttland, in which this story is combined with that of "The Little Gold Shoe"[9] This version concludes as follows:—

When the stepdaughter (the cinder-girl) had been married some time to the foreign prince, he was obliged to return to his own country; but his consort remained behind with her wicked stepmother, until she had given birth to a child. When the stepdaughter was on the eve of departure, she was persuaded to take the crone's daughter with her as a court attendant. But the base Troll bored a hole in the ship's bottom and transformed her half-sister into a sea snake. When the snake scented the sea air it hastened through the hole, and was received by a Sea-troll, who was the crone's daughter's godmother. The false female then put on her half-sister's likeness, and joined the prince, who received her with great joy. But the stepdaughter's little dog, Locke, was never cheerful afterwards; the little infant wept uninterruptedly; and a weight lay on the prince's mind. The false wife was bad of heart and hated by every one.

---

[8] Stockholm, 1830, Del. i. pp. 19-25.

[9] See the story hereafter.

The little dog lay in a room at the end of the palace, that was occupied by an aged female who nursed the prince's child. One night a loud noise was heard proceeding from the sea, and the old nurse was terrified with the rattling and clank of chains outside the door. Shortly after she heard her former mistress speaking to the little dog, saying:—

> "Locke, my little dog,
> Art thou still alive?"

The dog answered—

> "Yes, I am so, my lady."

The voice continued—

> "Locke, Locke, let me in."

The door was now opened, and the enchanted princess stept in. She asked—

> "Does my little child yet weep?"

Locke answered—

> "Yes, it does so, my lady:"

The princess continued—

> "Does the false Troll yet sleep in my consort's arms?"

Locke answered—

> "Yes, my lady, she does so."

The princess added "I will return home on two Thursday evenings yet, and then never again." The Sea-troll now tugged at the chain, and the princess went back to the ocean.

On the following Thursday night, the prince himself came and listened to his wife's conversation with the little dog. When he observed that all was not as it should be, he consulted one skilled in the magic art. This person instructed him to go on the Sabbath night and harden an axe and a pair of steel gloves in charcoal of the linden and serpent's venom; also to set in the room three vessels, one full of water, one of wine, and the third of milk. The king's son did, in every point, as he had been directed; so when Thursday came, and the princess appeared for the third time, the prince rushed forward, and cut the chain by which she was confined. At the same moment a loud noise was heard out in the sea. But the king's son seized his consort and held her fast with his iron gloves. She was then changed into a sea-serpent, that strove to bite everything near it, and to tear itself loose; but the prince did not let go his hold. He then carried the serpent to the vessel that was filled with water, when a skin fell off from it. He next lifted it into the vessel filled with wine, and a second skin fell off. Lastly, he placed it in the vessel filled with milk, when there stood before him a beautiful princess white as milk, and the king's son recognised his consort who had been enchanted.

Locke was new again cheerful, the little child ceased its weeping, and the weight fell from the mind of the prince. But the false crone's daughter was condemned to be buried alive.

4. According to another version from Ostergöttland, the false stepmother, by her magic art, raised a violent storm, through which the maiden perished in the sea. The Troll afterwards sent her own daughter in another vessel, and she became the prince's bride. But the true bride rose three several nights from the water and sighed:

"Alas! alas! it is so cold in the ocean's depth!"

The third night the king's son was present and conversed with her. About the time of cock-crowing the maiden was about to return to the sea; but the king's son held her fast, notwithstanding her many transformations. The enchantment was then dissolved, and the stepmother and her daughter were condemned to be cast into melted lead.

5. A remarkable though incomplete version from Westmanland relates that the king causes the young man to be cast into a pen of serpents[10]; but his sister, who had been swallowed by the ocean, rose on three Thursday nights from the water, and came to the king's palace, and stopt in the apartment leading to the king's bedchamber, opened her golden casket, combed her long fair hair, and said:

____

[10] Instead of a lion's den, as at p. 52.

"I comb my hair,

And let fall many a tear

My brother lies in the serpents' pen."

On the third night, the king himself was on the watch, and severed the chain by which the damsel was confined. The enchantment was then dissolved, and the king made her his queen.

6. In a version from Upland it is related how the fair maiden laid her head on her stepmother's knee to be combed[11] but the girl having fallen asleep, the false beldam, watching her opportunity, cast her stepdaughter overboard, and placed her own daughter in the other's stead. The story adds, that when the maiden came by night out of the sea to converse with her dog, she sat by the window combing her long hair, from which the most costly pearls fell on the ground. These pearls had attached themselves to the damsel's locks, while she was in the ocean.

7. Another variation from Upland makes the story begin thus:—A stepmother sends both her daughters to the well for water, giving her own daughter a pail, and the stepdaughter a sieve. The continuation accords with the story of "Jungfru Svanhvita and Jungfru Räfrumpa."

8. A version, also from Upland, makes the damsel, who is cast into the sea, to be transformed into a serpent, which the king cuts in three pieces, when it becomes a most beautiful princess. The story concludes by burning the false stepmother and her daughter on a pile.

9. Another version of the story has been given from Upland by the well-known German scholar, H. R. von Schröter, which is mentioned by the Brothers Grimm[12], but is of little value.

10. According to a version from Blekinge, the enchanted maiden rises out of the sea in the form of a little duck, and creeps into the kitchen through a hole. On the third night the king was at hand, and stopped up the hole, so that the bird could not get out. He then seizes the bird, and cuts it in the feet, when three drops of blood come forth, and in the same instant the bird is transformed into a most beautiful female. Her brother is taken unscathed from the lion's den, and the stepmother is burnt for her treachery.

---

[11] Och lat henne löska sig.

[12] Kinder- und Hausmärchen, Th. iii. pp. 406-407.

11. A less interesting and incomplete version from Norrland, makes the stepdaughter to be enchanted by her wicked fostermother, as they are crossing the sea together. Then a little bird sings:—

> "Look not on the billows blue,
>   For then thou wilt turn gray."

But the maiden cannot withstand her longing, and is drawn down in the waves, where she is swallowed up by a monstrous fish. On the day previous to the one fixed for the king's marriage with the false bride, the great fish is caught, and the king recovers his genuine bride.

12. A tradition from Småland relates, that the king's daughter was by shipwreck cast on a mountain, where she was seized by the Mountain Troll. After many entreaties, she at length get permission to go three times to the palace and speak with her little dog. When the third Thursday night came, the king had caused all the crevices and apertures in the apartment to be stepped. He then endeavoured to seize the enchanted maiden; but she became changed to all kinds of animals, and at length into a little sewing-needle which lay glistening on the hearth. The king then taking a thread, drew it hastily through the eye of the needle when the damsel instantly recovered her true form, and the nuptials were solemnized with mirth and pleasure.

THE PALACE THAT STOOD ON GOLDEN PILLARS.[13]

From Westmanland.

THERE was once a peasant, who with his wife lived very, very far in the woods. They had two children, a boy and a girl. They were very poor, all their wealth consisting in a cow and a cat.

---

[13] Of this tale there are the following foreign varieties:—
1. Norwegian—See Asbjörnsen og Moe, et sup. No. 28. "Herrepeer."

This peasant and his wife lived in a state of constant strife with each other, and you might have been sure, that if the old man desired one thing, the old woman always desired another. It happened one day that the old woman had boiled some porridge for supper, and when it was ready and each had received a share, the old man would scrape the not. This the old woman opposed with all her might, asserting that the right of scraping belonged to her, and her only. Hence a desperate quarrel ensued, neither being willing to yield to the other. The end was, that the old woman snatched up the pot and the ladle and ran off, the old man with a whip following close at her heels. And away they went over hill and dale, the old woman first, and the old man close behind her; but our history does not inform us which of the two finally obtained the scraping of the pot.

When a considerable time had elapsed, and no tidings were heard of their parents, the children had no alternative but to go out into the wide world and seek their fortune. So, they resolved on leaving their habitation, and dividing their inheritance. But, as it generally happens, the division was a mighty difficult affair; there being nothing to divide save the cow and the cat, and both being desirous of having the cow. While they were discussing the point, the cat, with a most insinuating mien, approaching the sister, gently rubbed her knee, and mewed: "Take me, take me." So, as the boy would not let go the cow, the girl gave up her pretension and contented herself with the cat. They then parted from each other, the boy with the cow going his way, and the girl with her cat wandering through the wood; but of her and her companion's adventures nothing has been related to me, until they came to a spacious and splendid palace, which lay at some distance before them.

While both travellers were on their way to the beautiful palace, the cat began to converse with his mistress, and said: "If you will follow my advice, it shall bring you luck." The girl, who placed great confidence in her

2. Danish.—A fragment of the story, containing the princess's trial, is given in Andersen's "Eventyr fortalte for Born," 2nd odit., 1st number, pp. 44-44. "Princessen paa Ærten."

3. German.—A similar fragment is to be found in Grimm, K. und H. M. ii. No. 182. "Die Erbsenprobe."

4. Italian.— *a.* See Straparola, Notti piacevoli, xi. 1. *b.* See Basile, Il Pentam. ii. 4. "Gagliuso."

5. French—See Perrault, Contes du Temps passé. Paris, 1697. No. 5. "Le Maitre Chat; ou, le Chat Botté."

companion's prudence, promised to follow his directions. The cat thereupon desired her to take off her old garments, and climb up into a high tree, while he would go to the palace and say, that there was a princess, who had been attacked by robbers and stript both of property and clothes. The girl did, accordingly, threw off her old rags and placed herself in the tree. The cat then went; but the girl sat in a great fright, as to how the matter would turn out.

When the king, who ruled the land, was informed that a foreign princess had suffered such violence, he was exceedingly troubled, and sent his servants to invite her to the palace. The young girl was now abundantly supplied with costly attire, and whatever else she required, and accompanied the royal messengers. On arriving at the palace, all were struck with her beauty and courteous manners; but the king's son paid her the most marked homage and declared that he could not live without her. The queen, however, had her suspicions, and asked the beautiful princess where her residence was. The girl answered as she had been instructed by the cat: "I dwell very far from here, in a castle called Cattenburg."

Still the old queen was not satisfied but resolved with herself to ascertain whether the strange damsel was really a king's daughter or not. For this purpose, she went to the guest-chamber, and made ready a bed for the peasant girl with soft silken bolsters but laid secretly a bean under the sheet; "Because," thought she, "if she is a princess, she cannot fail to notice it." The young girl was then conducted to her apartment with great state. But the cat had observed the queen's stratagem and apprized his mistress of it. In the morning, the old queen entered, and inquired how her guest had passed the night. The girl answered as the cat had instructed her: "Ah, yes, I have slept, for I was very weary after my journey; but it seemed as if I had a large mountain under me. I slept much better in my bed at Cattenburg." The queen new thought that the damsel must have been delicately bred; yet resolved on making one more trial.

On the following evening the queen went again to the guest-chamber, and having prepared the peasant girl's bed as before, laid some peas under the first pillow; and when it was morning, entered and inquired of her guest how she had slept. But, following the cat's instructions, she answered: "Ah, yes, I have slept, for I was very tired; but it seemed as if I had large stones under me. I slept much better in my bed at Cattenburg." The old queen now thought that she had well stood the trial, yet could not entirely dismiss her suspicions, and therefore determined on a third attempt, for the purpose of finding out whether the strange damsel really was of such high birth as she pretended to be.

When the third evening came, the queen went again to the guest-chamber, and, having prepared the bed as before, laid a straw under the second pillow; and when the queen came in the morning and inquired how she had slept, she again answered as the cat had instructed: "Ah, yes, I have slept; for I was very tired; but it seemed as if I had a large tree under me. I was much better served at Cattenburg." The queen now found that there was no sure way of arriving at the truth in this manner, and therefore resolved on keeping watch how the strange damsel conducted herself in other respects.

On the following day the queen sent to her guest a costly dress, embroidered with silk, and with a very, very long train, such as were worn by women of high rank. The peasant girl thanked her for the present and thought no more about it; but the cat, that was close at her elbow, apprized his mistress that the old queen would put her to another trial. When some time had passed, the queen sent to inquire whether the princess would accompany her walk. The peasant girl consented, and they set out. On entering a garden, the court ladies were very fearful lest they should soil their dresses, as it had rained during the night. But the strange damsel continued walking, without heeding whether her long train was being dragged through the mud or not. Whereupon the queen said: "My dear princess, take care of your dress." To which the peasant girl proudly answered: "Oh, there must be more dresses to be had here besides this. I had much better when I was in my castle at Cattenburg." Now the old queen could not think otherwise than that the damsel was accustomed to wear silk-embroidered garments, and thence concluded that she must be a king's daughter; so could no longer entertain any objection to her son's marriage, to which the peasant girl also gave her consent.

It happened one day, as the prince and his beloved were sitting conversing together, that the damsel, on looking through the window, saw her parents come running out of the wood, the old woman first with the pot, and the old man close at her heels with the ladle. At the sight the girl could not contain herself but burst out into a loud laugh. On the prince inquiring why she laughed so heartily, she said, as the cat had instructed her: "I cannot help laughing when I think that your palace stands on stone pillars while mine stands on golden ones." When the prince heard this, he was greatly surprised, and said: "Your thoughts are always dwelling on the beautiful Cattenburg, and you seem to think that all things are better there than with us. We will go and see your splendid palace, let the distance be ever so great." At this the peasant's daughter was so alarmed that she would willingly have sunk into the earth, knowing well that she had not a house, much less a palace. But there being no remedy, she put a good face on the matter, saying that she would consider on what day they should commence their journey.

When she found herself alone, she gave free vent to her trouble, and wept bitterly; for she thought of all the disgrace that would fall on her for her deceit and falsehood. While she thus sat and wept, in walked the sagacious cat, rubbed himself against her knee, and inquired the cause of her sorrow. "I may well be sorrowful," answered the peasant's daughter; "for the king's son says that we shall go to Cattenburg; so now I am like to pay dearly for having followed thy counsel." But the cat bade her be of good cheer, and added, that he would so manage matters, that everything should turn out better than she could imagine; at the same time telling her that the sooner they set out the better. Having had already so many proofs of the cat's wisdom, she followed his instructions, though this time with a heavy heart for she could not free herself from the apprehension that their journey would have an unfortunate termination.

Early on the following morning, the king's son ordered chariots and drivers, and everything besides which he thought necessary for their long journey to Cattenburg. The train then set out. The prince and his betrothed went first in a gilded chariot, attended by a numerous body of knights and squires; while the cat ran foremost of all to show them the way. After travelling for some time, the cat perceived some goatherds driving to the field a large flock of most beautiful goats so going up to the men, he greeted them courteously, saying: "Good day, goatherds! When the king's son rides by and inquires to whom these fine goats belong, you must say they belong to the young princess at Cattenburg, who rides by the prince's side. If you do so, you shall be well rewarded; but if not, I will tear you in pieces." On hearing this the goatherds were much surprised but promised to obey the cat's bidding. He then pursued his way. Shortly after came the king's son riding with all his train. On seeing such beautiful goats feeding in the field, he stopped his chariot, and inquired of the herdsmen to whom they belonged. They answered, as the cat had instructed them: "They belong to the young princess at Cattenburg, who rides by your side." At this the king's son wondered greatly and thought that his betrothed must be a powerful princess; and the peasant girl was not a little glad at heart, and thought that she was not the losing party, when she divided the inheritance with her brother.

They now continued their journey, the cat running foremost. After travelling for some time, they came to where a number of persons were making hay in a pleasant field. These the cat saluted very courteously, saying as before: "Good day, good people! When the king's son comes by and inquires to whom this beautiful meadow belongs, you must answer that it belongs to the princess at Cattenburg, who rides by the prince's side. If you do so, you shall be well rewarded; but if you do not do as I have said, I will tear you to atoms." When the men heard this, they were greatly surprised, and promised to say what the cat desired. The cat then ran on as before. Shortly after came the king's son in his chariot with his whole retinue. On seeing the fertile fields and the number of people, he caused his chariot to stop, and inquired who was the owner of the land. The men, following the cat's instructions, answered: "The fields belong to the young princess at Cattenburg, who rides by your side." The king's son was now yet more surprised, and thought that his bride must be immensely rich, seeing that she owned such beautiful hay-fields.

Resuming their journey, and preceded by the cat, they approached at length a very extensive cornfield, which swarmed with men and women, all busily employed in reaping. Here the cat again ran forth, enjoining and threatening as on the former occasions; so that when the prince came by and inquired to whom the fields belonged, he received an answer similar to the foregoing.

It was now late in the evening, and the prince stopped with his attendants for the purpose of resting during the night. But the cat took no rest, but ran hastily forwards, until he saw a beautiful castle with its towers and battlements and supported by golden pillars. This splendid palace belonged to a fierce giant, who owned the entire neighbouring country; but was at that time absent from home. The cat therefore passed through the castle gate and transformed himself into a large loaf; then stationed himself in the key-hole and awaited the giant's return.

Early in the morning, before the dawn, the frightful giant, who was so huge and heavy that the earth shook under him as he walked, came jogging out of the forest. When he came to the castle gate, he could not open it, because of the great leaf that stuck in the key-hole. Thereupon he became exceedingly angry and cried: "Unlock! Unlock!" To which the cat answered: "Just wait a little, little moment, while I tell my story:

"First they kneaded[14] me as if they would knead me to death."

"Unlock! Unlock!" cried the giant again; but the cat answered as before: "Just wait a little, little moment, while I tell my story:

"First they kneaded me as if they would knead me to death;
Then they floured me as if they would flour me to death;"

"Unlock! Unlock!" vociferated the giant in a towering passion; but the cat repeated: "Just wait a little, little moment, while I tell my story:

"First they kneaded me as if they would knead me to death;
Then they floured me as if they would flour me to death;
Then they pricked me as if they would prick me to death."

The giant was now beside himself with rage and roared out so that the whole castle shook: "Unlock! Unlock!" but the cat was not to be moved, and answered as before: "Just wait a little moment, while I tell my story:

"First they kneaded me as if they would knead me to death
Then they floured me as if they would flour me to death;
Then they pricked me as if they would prick me to death;
Then they baked me as if they would bake me to death."

The giant now felt uneasy and cried out quite gently: "Unlock! Unlock!" but all in vain; the loaf remained quiet in the key-hole as before. At the same moment the cat cried out: "Only see what a beautiful girl is riding up in the sky! As the Troll looked up, the sun had just risen above the forest, at the sight of which he fell back and split into shivers. Such was his end.[15]

---

[14] The original has *bakade* (baked), but as this is inconsistent both with the fourth line, and with the process of bread-making, I have ventured to regard it as an error for knådade (kneaded).

[15] This remnant of the old Eddaic faith seems to vouch for the antiquity of the story. See Thorpe, "Northern Mythology and Traditions," vol. i. p. 8, and vol. ii. p. 9.

The loaf then transformed itself again into a cat and hastened to set everything in order for his guests. After some time, the king's son and his fair young bride arrived with all their train. The cat went out to receive them and bid them welcome to Cattenburg. They were now entertained most sumptuously, and there was wanting neither meat nor drink, nor any costly luxury. The noble castle was full of gold and silver, and all kinds of precious things, such as the like was never seen before or since.

Shortly after the marriage was solemnized between the prince and the fair young maiden; and all who saw her wealth, thought she had good reason for saying I had it otherwise in my castle at Cattenburg. The king's son and the peasant's daughter lived happily together for very many years; but I have never heard how it fared with the cat; though we may almost guess that he wanted for nothing.

1. A version from Upland says, that when the giant returned home at night, and found the castle gate barred, he cried out: "There's riot and revelry in my castle; let me in!" The cat answered. "Thou must not come in before I have told thee how much evil I have suffered:

> "First they sowed me
> Afterwards ground me."

The giant again cried out: "There's riot and revelry in my castle; let me in!" But the cat answered as before: "Thou must not come in before thou knowest what evil I have suffered:

> "First they sowed me,
> Then I grew up,
> Then they mowed me,
> Then they ground me,
> Afterwards thrashed me,
> Then they baked bread of me,
> And then they ate me up."

When the giant was just in the act of peeping, to see whether the loaf was really eaten up, the cat rushed forward on the battlements of the castle wall and reared so awfully that the giant from terror fell backwards and burst.

2. Another variation from Upland makes the country girl to be accompanied by a dog. When she comes to the palace, the queen, desirous of putting her to the proof, the first night lays an apple, the second night a nut, and the third a pea, under the silken bolster. But the girl undergoes the three proofs, and finally marries the king's son.

3. A version from Westergötland differs in its conclusion from the foregoing. It runs thus:

There was once a pair of poor cottagers, who owned nothing in the world but a cow and a dog. They therefore lived in great poverty, and, as is but too often the case, when need crept in, love walked out.

One day a great dispute arose between the husband and wife; for the crone had boiled gruel, and the old man would have milk porridge. After they had quarrelled for about an hour and could not settle their difference, the old woman snatched up the porridge-pot and ran into the forest. The Old man was not slow but ran after her as fast as he was able. Both man and wife now ran with all their might over hill and dale, and never came back; so that their children were finally obliged to think for themselves, to give up their home, and seek their fortune where they best could.

When they came to divide the property between them the boy took the cow; for he was the elder, and the girl must be content with the dog. The brother and sister then parted. The dog's name was *Prisse*, and he was very sagacious, having more understanding than all other dogs. He was, moreover, faithful to his mistress, and attached himself to her both in good and bad fortune; so that she could not but feel convinced she had not got the worse lot of the two.

After some time, the cottager's daughter and her dog came to a large forest, not far from which there was a king's palace, &c.

The story now goes on for a while as the one in the text, excepting that there is no young prince in the way, the young maiden being accompanied by the king on her way to the palace on golden pillars, then continues as follows:

When the morning drew nigh, and all were buried in sleep, the giant came out of the forest and knocked at the castle gate. But the dog had transformed himself into a loaf, and placed himself in the key-hole, so that nothing could slip through. The giant then cried: "Open and let me in!" "No," answered the dog, "thou shalt not come in before thou hast heard how I came to be a loaf:

> "First, they cast me in a grave,
>   Then I grew up as a straw."

"Open and let me in!" vociferated the giant a second time; but the dog did not allow himself to be disconcerted and repeated his words: "Thou must hear how I became a loaf:

> "First, they cast me in a grave,
>   Then I grew up as a straw,
>   Then I became an ear,
>   Then they mowed me."

The giant now waxed monstrously wroth, and screamed: "Open, and let me in!" but the dog continued:

> "First, they cast me in a grave,
>   Then I grew up as a straw,
>   Then I became an ear,
>   Then they mowed me,
>   Then they thrashed me,
>   Then they ground me,
>   Then they kneaded me,
>   Then they pricked me,
>   Then they baked me in the oven."

At that instant the sun rose and shone on the castle. The dog then said: "Turn about, and thou shalt see such a beautiful damsel, who will crown thee with a golden crown." When the giant turned and saw the sun, he fell to the earth and burst, and so there was an end of him.

When the giant was dead, the dog went to his mistress, and, drawing her into a little apartment, in which a flask and a sword were hanging on the wall, said: "I now ask of thee one thing, for all the faithful services I have rendered thee. Thou shalt take this sword and cut off my head. Thou shalt then wash the wound with the water out of this flask: thou wilt then know something thou didst not know before." As the dog was very dear to the cottager's daughter, she was loth to comply with his request, but excused herself as long as she could. But Prisse was importunate, and she could no longer refuse, so cut off his head, and washed the wound with the water from the flask. In one instant the dog changed his form, and there stood before her a comely young prince, far comelier than most kings' sons. The noble youth then clasping her in his arms, betrothed her with red gold rings, that she might be his queen.

When the first transports were over, the prince recounted for what cause he had been enchanted and made to run as a dog. He said: "My father was a mighty king, who ruled over many lands. He was having a palace built and caused a cornerstone to be brought from the mountain in which the giant dwelt. At this the giant was enraged, slew my father, and turned me into a dog, which transformation was to continue until a pure virgin should shed my blood." At this recital the young maiden was overjoyed, for she loved the prince with all her heart.

Preparations were now made for the wedding, &c.

4. In a variation from S. Småland, it is related that there was a peasant family so poor that they were obliged to leave their home and seek their fortune each in a different direction. When they came to divide the property, there was found nothing to divide, save a pot, a pot-ladle, a cow, and a cat. The old man and the old woman quarrelled who should have the pot, and the old woman, snatching it up, ran oil with it into the forest; but the old man seized the ladle and ran after her. Neither of them ever came home again.

In like manner the boy and girl also quarrelled; for both would have the cow. But the cat, approaching the girl, said: "Take me, take me; I will help thee." So the maiden took the cat, and they both proceeded to the king's palace, where the girl begged for employment. The queen asked her what she could do. The girl answered, as she had been instructed by the cat: "I can sew silk." So she was set to sew a coverlet. "Now," said the cat, take a hair from my tail, and use it for a needle." The girl did so and sewed a coverlet such as no one had ever seen the like.

One day the girl saw her parents come running out of the forest, the old woman first, and the old man after, at which she could not refrain from laughing. The king asked her why she laughed so; and the girl, as the cat had instructed her, answered: "I was just thinking how your palace stands on wooden pillars, while mine stands on golden ones." The king thereupon resolved to see the palace that he had heard spoken of, and they set out on the journey.

When they arrived, there was no one at home except the giant's wife. The cat went in, greeted the giantess, and told her she must prepare a great feast; for the giant had invited many guests. The crone did as the cat had said, and they began their preparations. They had now to cut up an ox, and the cat held it while the crone cut; but as she did the work awkwardly, the cat said: "Mother, let me cut, and do you hold." The giantess assented; but no sooner had the cat got hold of the axe than he clove the giantess's skull, and she fell down dead. He then closed the gate, and enticed the giant to look up at the sun; and so he came by his death.

When the giant and giantess were thus disposed of, the cat recovered his right form, and became a handsome prince, who ruled in the beautiful castle. He then caused a sumptuous banquet to be prepared for the king and his young consort and entertained them nobly for many days.

5. In a variation of the story from S. W. Finland, it is related, that after the giant burst, the cat conducted his mistress to a place where there lay a large heap of human bones. He then gave the girl a sithe that had been dipped in milk and rubbed over with whortleberries and dough, at the same time desiring her to cut off his head. The girl did so, and instantly the cat became a handsome prince, with a golden crown on his head. The bones also received life, and became a numerous body of courtiers, knights, and pages. Thus, was the sorcery dissolved, and the young prince solemnized his marriage with the fair maiden.

THE HERD-BOY.

From Upland.

THERE was once a poor herd-boy, who had neither kith nor kin except his stepmother, who was a wicked woman, and hardly allowed him food or clothing. Thus, the poor boy suffered great privation during all the livelong day he had to tend cattle, and scarcely ever got more than a morsel of bread morning and evening.

One day his stepmother had gone out without leaving him any food; he had, therefore, to drive his cattle to the field fasting, and being very hungry, he wept bitterly. But at the approach of noon he dried his tears, and went up on a green hill, where he was in the habit of resting, while the sun was hot in the summer. On this hill it was always cool and dewy under the shady trees; but now he remarked that there was no dew, that the ground was dry, and the grass trampled down. This seemed to him very singular, and he wondered who could have trodden down the green grass. While thus sitting and thinking, he perceived something that lay glittering in the sunshine. Springing up to see what it might be, he found it was a pair of very, very small shoes of the whitest and clearest glass. The boy now felt quite happy again, forgot his hunger, and amused himself the whole day with the little glass shoes.

In the evening, when the sun had sunk behind the forest, the herd-boy called his cattle and drove them to the village. When he had gone some way, he was met by a very little boy, who in a friendly tone greeted him with "Good evening!" "Good evening again," answered the herd-boy. "Hast thou found my shoes, which I lost this morning in the green grass?" asked the little boy. The herd-boy answered: "Yes, I have found them; but, my good little fellow, let me keep them. I intended to give them to my stepmother, and then, perhaps, I should have got a little meat, when I came home." But the boy prayed so earnestly, "Give me back my shoes; another time I will be as kind to thee," that the herd-boy returned him the shoes. The little one then, greatly delighted, gave him a friendly nod, and went springing away.

The herd-boy now collected his cattle together and continued his way homewards. When he reached his dwelling, it was already dark, and his stepmother chided him for returning so late. "There's still some porridge in the pot," said she; "eat now, and pack thyself off to bed, so that thou canst get up in the morning betimes, like other folks." The poor herd-boy durst not return any answer to these hard words, but ate, and then slunk to bed in the hayloft, where he was accustomed to sleep. The whole night he dreamed of nothing but the little boy and his little glass shoes.

Early in the morning, before the sun shone from the east, the boy was waked by his stepmother's voice: "Up with thee, thou sluggard! It is broad day, and the animals are not to stand hungry for thy sloth." He instantly rose, got a bit of bread, and drove the cattle to the pasture.

When he came to the green hill, which was wont to be so cool and shady, he again wondered to see that the dew was all swept from the grass, and the ground dry, even more so than on the preceding day. While he thus sat thinking, he observed something lying in the grass and glittering in the bright sunshine. Springing towards it, he found it was a very, very little red cap set round with small golden bells. At this he was greatly delighted, forgot his hunger, and amused himself all day with the little elegant cap.

In the evening, when the sun had sunk behind the forest, the herd-boy gathered his cattle together, and drove them towards the village. When on his way, he was met by a very little and at the same time, very fair damsel. She greeted him in a friendly tone with "Good evening!" "Good evening again," answered the lad. The damsel then said: "Hast thou found my cap, which I lost this morning in the green grass?" The boy answered: "Yes, I have found it; but let me keep it, my pretty maid. I thought of giving it to my wicked stepmother, and then, perhaps, I shall get a little meat when I go home." But the little damsel entreated so urgently, "Give me back my cap; another time I will be as good to thee," that the lad gave her the little cap, when she appeared highly delighted, gave him a friendly nod, and sprang off.

On his return home, he was received as usual by his cruel stepmother, and dreamed the whole night of the little damsel and her little red cap.

In the morning he was turned out fasting, and on coming to the hill, found it was drier than on either of the preceding days, and that the grass was trodden down in large rings. It then entered his mind all that he had heard of the little *elves*, how in the summer nights they were wont to dance in the dewy grass, and he found that these must be *elfin-rings*, or *elfin-dances*[16]. While sitting absorbed in thought, he chanced to strike his foot against a little bell that lay in the grass, and which gave forth so sweet a sound, that all the cattle came running together, and stood still to listen. Now the boy was delighted and could do nothing but play with the little bell, till he forgot his troubles and the cattle forgot to graze. And so the day passed much more quickly than can be imagined.

---

[16] See Thorpe, Northern Mythology and Traditions, vol i. p. 25.

When it drew towards evening, and the sun was level with the tree-tops, the boy called his cattle and prepared to return home. But let him entice and call them as he might, they were not to be drawn from the pasture, for it was a delightful grassy spot. Then thought the boy to himself, "Perhaps they will pay more heed to the little bell." So, drawing forth the bell, he tingled it as he went along the way. In one moment, the bell-cow came running after him, and was followed by the rest of the herd. At this the boy was overjoyed, for he was well aware what an advantage the little bell would be to him. As he was going on, a very little old man met him, and kindly bade him a good evening. "Good evening again," said the boy. The old man asked: "Hast thou found my little bell, which I lost this morning in the green grass?" The herd-boy answered: "Yes, I have found it." The old man said: "Then give it me back." "No," answered the boy, "I am not so doltish as you may think. The day before yesterday I found two small glass shoes, which a little boy wheedled from me. Yesterday I found a cap, which I gave to a little damsel; and now you come to take from me the little bell, which is so good for calling the cattle. Other finders get a reward for their pains, but I get nothing." The little man then used many fair words, with the view of recovering his bell, but all to no purpose. At last he said: "Give me back the little bell, and I will give thee another, with which thou mayest call thy cattle; thou shalt, moreover, obtain three wishes." These seemed to the boy no unfavourable terms, and he at once agreed to them, adding, "As I may wish whatever I will, I will wish to be a king, and I will wish to have a great palace, and also a very beautiful queen." "Thou hast wished no trifling wishes," said the old man, "but bear well in mind what I now tell thee. Tonight, when all are sleeping, thou shalt go hence, till thou comest to a royal palace, which lies due north. Take this pipe of bone. If thou fallest into trouble, blow it; if thou afterwards fallest into great trouble, blow it again; but if, on a third occasion, thou findest thyself in still greater peril, break the pipe in two, and I will help thee, as I have promised." The boy gave the old man many thanks for his gifts, and the elf king—for it was he—went his way. But the boy bent his steps homewards, rejoicing as he went along, that he should so soon escape from tending cattle for his wicked stepmother.

When he reached the village it was already dark, and his stepmother had been long awaiting his coming. She was in a great rage, so that the poor lad got blows instead of food. "This will not last long," thought the boy, comforting himself with the reflection, as he went up to his hayloft, where he laid himself down and slumbered for a short time. About midnight, long before the cock crew, he arose, slipped out of the house, and began his journey in a northward direction, as the old man had enjoined. He travelled incessantly, over hill and dale, and twice did the sun rise and twice set, while he was still on his way.

Towards evening on the third day he came to a royal palace, which was so spacious that he thought he should never again see the like. He went to the kitchen and asked for employment. "What dost thou know, and what canst thou do?" inquired the master-cook. "I can tend cattle in the pasture," answered the boy. The master-cook said: "The king is in great want of a herd-boy, but it will, no doubt, be with thee as with the others, that every day thou losest one of the herd." The boy answered: "Hitherto I have never lost any beast that I drove to the field." He was then taken into the king's service and tended the king's cattle, but the wolf never got a beast from him, so he was well esteemed by all the king's servants.

One evening, as the herd-boy was driving his cattle home, he observed a beautiful young damsel standing at a window and listening to his song. Though he seemed hardly to notice her, he, nevertheless, felt a glow suffused over him. Some time passed in this manner, the herd-boy being delighted every time he saw the young maiden; though he was still ignorant that she was the king's daughter. It happened one day that the young girl came to him as he was driving the herd to their pasture. She had with her a little snow-white lamb and begged him in a friendly tone to take charge of her lamb and protect it from the wolves in the forest. At this the herd-boy was so confused that he could neither answer nor speak. But he took the lamb with him, and found his greatest pleasure in guarding it, and the animal attached itself to him, as a dog to its master. From that day the herd-boy frequently enjoyed the sight of the fair princess. In the morning, when he drove his cattle to the pasture, she would stand at the window listening to his song; but in the evening, when he returned from the forest, she would descend to caress her little lamb, and say a few friendly words to the herd-boy.

Time rolled on. The herd-boy had grown up into a comely, vigorous young man; and the princess had sprung up and was become the fairest maiden that could be found far or near. Nevertheless, she came every evening, according to her early custom, to caress her lamb. But one day the princess was missing and could nowhere be found. This event caused a great sorrow and commotion in the royal court, for the princess was beloved by everyone but the king and queen, as was natural, grieved the most intensely of all. The king sent forth a proclamation over the whole land, that whosoever should recover his daughter should be rewarded with her hand and half the kingdom. This brought a number of princes, and knights, and warriors from the east and the west. Cased in steel they rode forth with arms and attendants, to seek the lost princess; but few were they that returned from their wanderings, and those that did return brought no tidings of her they went in quest of. The king and queen were now inconsolable and thought that they had sustained an irreparable loss. The herd-boy, as before, drove his cattle to the pasture, but it was in sadness, for the king's fair daughter engrossed his thoughts every day and every hour.

One night in a dream the little elfin king seemed to stand before him and to say: "To the north! to the north! there then wilt find thy queen." At this the young man was so overjoyed that he sprang up, and as he woke, there stood the little man, who nodded to him, and repeated: "To the north! to the north!" He then vanished, leaving the youth in doubt whether or not it was an illusion. As soon as it was day he went to the hall of the palace and requested an audience of the king. At this all the royal servants wondered, and the master-cook said: "Thou hast served for so many years that thou mayest, no doubt, get thy wages increased without speaking to the king himself." But the young man persisted in his request, and let it be, understood that he had something very different in his mind. On entering the royal apartment, the king demanded his errand, when the young man said: "I have served you faithfully for many years, and now desire permission to go and seek for the princess." Hereupon the king grew angry and said: "How canst thou, a herd-boy, think of doing that which no warrior nor prince has been able to accomplish? But the youth answered boldly, that he would either discover the princess or, for her sake, lay down his life. The king then let his anger pass and called to mind the old proverb: *A heart worthy of scarlet often lies under a coarse woollen cloak.* He therefore gave orders that the herd-boy should be equipped with a charger and all things requisite. But the youth said: "I reek not of riding; give me but your word and permission, together with means sufficient." The king then wished him success in his enterprise; but all the boys and other servants in the court laughed at the herd-boy's rash undertaking.

The young man journeyed towards the north, as he had been instructed by the elf-king and proceeded on and on until he could not be far distant from the world's end. When he had thus travelled over mountains and desolate ways, he came at length to a great lake, in the midst of which there was a fair island, and on the island a royal palace, much more spacious than the one from whence he came. He went down to the water's edge and surveyed the palace on every side. While thus viewing it, be perceived a damsel with golden locks standing at one of the windows, and making signs with a silken band, such as the princess's lamb was accustomed to wear. At this sight the young man's heart leaped in his breast; for it rushed into his mind that the damsel could be no other than the princess herself. He now began to consider how he should cross over the water to the great palace; but could hit upon no plan. At last the thought occurred to him that he would make a trial whether the little elves would afford him some assistance; and he took forth his pipe and blew a long-continued strain. He had scarcely ceased, when he heard a voice behind him, saying "Good evening." "Good evening again," answered the youth, turning about; when just before him there stood the little boy whose glass shoes he had found in the grass. "What dost thou wish of me?" asked the elfin boy. The other answered: "I wish thee to convey me across the water to the royal palace." The boy replied: "Place thyself on my back." The youth did so; and at the same instant the boy changed his form and became an immensely huge hawk, that darted through the air, and stopped not until it reached the island, as the young man had requested.

He now went up to the hall of the palace and asked for employment. "What dost thou understand and what canst thou do?" inquired the master-cook. I can take charge of cattle, answered the youth. The master-cook then said: "The giant is just now in great want of a herdsman; but it will, I dare say, be with thee as with the others for if a beast by chance is lost, thy life is forfeited." The youth answered: "This seems to me a hard condition; but I will, nevertheless, agree to it." The master-cook then accepted his service, and he was to commence on the following day.

The young man now drove the giant's cattle, and sung his song, and rang his little bell, as he had formerly done; and the princess sat at her window, and listened, and made signs to him that he should not appear to notice her. In the evening, he drove the herd from the forest, and was met by the giant, who said to him: "Thy life is in the place of any one that may be missing." But not a beast was wanting, let the giant count them as he would. Now the *Tusse*[17] was quite friendly and said: "Thou shalt be my herds man all thy days." He then went down to the lake, loosed his enchanted ship, and rowed thrice round the island, as he was wont to do.

During the giant's absence the princess stationed herself at the window and sang: —

> "Tonight, tonight, thou herdsman bold,
> Goes the cloud from under my star.
> And if thou comest hither, then will I be thine,
> My crown I will gladly give thee."

The young man listened to her song and understood from it that he was to go in the night and deliver the princess. He therefore went away without appearing to notice anything. But when it was late, and all were sunk in deep sleep, he stealthily approached the tower, placed himself before the window, and sang:—

> "Tonight will wait thy herdsman true,
> Will sad stand under thy window;
> And if thou comest down, thou mayest one day be mine,
> While the shadows fall so widely."

The princess whispered: "I am bound with chains of gold, come and break them." The young man now knew no other course than again to blow with his pipe a very long-continued strain; when instantly be heard a voice behind him, saying "Good evening." "Good evening again," answered the youth, looking round; when there stood the little elf-king, from whom he had got the little bell and the pipe. "What wilt thou with me?" inquired the old man. The young man answered: "I beseech you to convey me and the princess hence." The little man said: "Follow me." They then ascended to the maiden's tower:

---

[17] The same as Thurs, one of the old denominations of a giant. See Thorpe, Mythology and Traditions, vol. 1. p. 148.

the castle gate opened spontaneously, and when the old man touched the chain, it burst in fragments. All three then went down to the margin of the lake, when the elf-king sang:—

> "Thou little pike in the water must go,
>   Come, come, hastily!
>   A princess fair on thy back shall ride,
>   And eke a king so mighty."

At the same moment appeared the little damsel, whose cap the herd-boy had found in the grass. She sprang down to the lake and was instantly changed into a large pike that sported about in the water. Then said the elf-king: "Sit ye on the back of the pike. But the princess must not be terrified, let what may happen for then will my power be at an end." Having so said, the old man vanished; but the youth and the fair princess followed his injunctions, and the pike bore them rapidly along through the billows.

While all this was taking place, the giant awoke, looked through the window, and perceived the herd-boy floating on the water together with the young princess. Instantly snatching up his eagle-plumage[18], he flew after them. When the pike heard the clapping of the giant's wings, it dived far down under the surface of the water, whereat the princess was so terrified that she uttered a scream. Then was the elf-king's power at an end, and the giant seized the two fugitives in his talons. On his return to the island, he caused the young herdsman to be cast into a dark dungeon, full fifteen fathoms underground; but the princess was again placed in her tower, and strictly watched, lest she should again attempt to escape.

The youth now lay in the captives' tower and was in deep affliction at finding himself unable to deliver the princess, and, at the same time, having most probably forfeited his own life. The words of the elfin king now occurred to his memory: "If, on a third occasion, thou findest thyself in great peril, break the pipe in two, and I will help thee." As a last resource, therefore, he drew forth the little pipe and broke it in two. At the same moment he heard behind him the words "Good evening." "Good evening again," answered the

---

[18] A complete Eddaic giant. For his prototype, see in Thorpe, "Northern Mythology and Traditions," the stories of Thiassi, Suttung, etc.

youth; and when he looked round there stood the little old man close by him, who asked: "What wilt thou with me?" The young man answered: "I wish to deliver the princess, and to convey her home to her father." The old man then led him through many locked doors and many splendid apartments, till they came to a spacious hall, filled with all kinds of weapons, swords, spears, and axes, of which some shone like polished steel, others like burnished gold. The old man kindled a fire on the hearth and said: "Undress thyself!" The young man did so, and the little man burnt his old garments. He then went to a large iron chest, out of which he took a costly suit of armour, resplendent with the purest gold. "Dress thyself," said he: the young man did so. When he was thus armed from head to foot, the old man bound a sharp sword by his side and said: "It is decreed that the giant shall fall by this sword, and this armour no steel can penetrate." The young herdsman felt quite at ease in the golden armour and moved as gracefully as if he had been a prince of the highest degree. They then returned to the dark dungeon; the youth thanked the elf-king for his timely succour, and they parted from each other.

Till a late hour there was a great bustle and hurrying in the whole palace; for the giant was on that day to celebrate his marriage with the beautiful princess and had invited many of his kin to the feast. The princess was clad in the most sumptuous manner, and decorated with a crown and rings of gold, and other costly ornaments, which had been worn by the giant's mother. The health of the wedded pair was then drunk amid all kinds of rejoicing, and there was no lack of good cheer, both of meat and drink. But the bride wept without intermission, and her tears were so hot that they felt like fire on her cheeks.

When night approached, and the giant was about to conduct his bride to the nuptial chamber, he sent his pages to fetch the young herdsman, who lay in the dungeon. But when they entered the prison, the captive had disappeared, and in his stead, there stood a bold warrior, with sword in hand, and completely armed. At this apparition the young men were frightened and fled; but were followed by the herdsman, who thus ascended to the court of the palace, where the guests were assembled to witness his death. When the giant cast his eyes on the doughty warrior, he was exasperated, and exclaimed: "Out upon thee, thou base Troll!" As he spoke his eyes became so piercing that they saw through the young herdsman's armour; but the youth fearless said: "Here shalt thou strive with me for thy fair bride." The giant was not inclined to stay and was about to withdraw; but the herdsman drew his sword, which blazed like a flame of fire. When the giant recognised the sword, under which he was doomed to fall, he was terror-struck and sank on the earth; but the young herdsman advanced boldly, swung round his sword, and struck a blow so powerful that the giant's head was separated from his carcass. Such was his end.

On witnessing this exploit, the wedding-guests were overcome with fear, and departed, each to his home; but the princess ran forth and thanked the brave herdsman for having saved her. They then proceeded to the water, loosed the giant's enchanted ship, and rowed away from the island. On their arrival at the king's court, there was great joy that the king had recovered his daughter, for whom he had mourned so long. There was afterwards a sumptuous wedding, and the young herdsman obtained the king's fair daughter. They lived happily for very many years and had many beautiful children. The bell and the broken pipe are preserved as memorials, aye even to the present day.

THE PRINCESS ON THE GLASS MOUNTAIN.[19]

From South Småland.

THERE was once a king, who was so devoted to the chase that he knew of no greater pleasure than hunting the beasts of the forest. Early and late he would

---

[19] Similar stories occur among the: 1. Norwegians—See Asbjörnsen og Moe, ut sup. Deel ii. pp. 80-91. "Jomfruen paa Glasbjerget."

2. Germans—*a*. See Vulpius, Ammenmärchen. Weimar, 1791. *b*. Grimm, K. und H. M. ii. No. 136. The first part of the tale of "De Wilde Mann" [Cf. iii. p. 229]. *c*. See Bechstein, Deutsches Marchenbuch, Leipsig, 1848, pp. 65-67. "Hirsedieb." See p. 456.

3. Italians.—See Straparola, Notti piacevoli, V., first part of tale No. 1.

4. Poles—See Woycicki, Polnische Volkssagen und Märchen, Berlin, 1839, iii, No. 5; also p. 156. "Der Glasberg."

stay out in the field with hawk and hound, and always had good success. It nevertheless one day happened that he could start no game, though he sought on all sides from early morn. When evening was drawing on, and he was about to return home with his attendants, he suddenly perceived a dwarf, or "wild man," running before him in the forest. Putting spurs to his horse, the king instantly went in pursuit of him, and caught him. His extraordinary appearance caused no little surprise, for he was little and ugly as a Troll, and his hair resembled shaggy moss. To whatever the king said to him he would return no answer, good or bad. At this the king was angry, and the more so as he was already out of humour, in consequence of his bad luck at the chase. He therefore commanded his followers to keep a strict watch over the wild man, so that he might not escape, and then returned to his palace.

In those times it was an old established custom for the king and his men to hold drinking meetings till a late horn in the night, at which much was said, and still more drunk. As they were sitting at one of these meetings, and making themselves merry, the king, taking up a large horn, said: "What think ye of our sport today? When could it before have been said of us, that we returned home without some game?" The men answered: "It is certainly true as you say, and yet perhaps, there is not so good a sportsman as you to be found in the whole world. You must not, however, complain of our days luck; for you have caught an animal, whose like was never before seen or heard of." This discourse pleased the king exceedingly, and he asked what they thought he had best do with the dwarf. One of the courtiers answered: "You should keep him confined here in the palace, that it may be known far and near what a great hunter you are; provided that you can guard him so that he does not escape; for he is crafty and perverse withal." On hearing this, the king for some time sat silent; then raising the horn, said: "I will do as thou sayest and it shall be through no fault of mine, if the wild man escapes. But this I vow, that if anyone lets him loose, he shall die, even if it be my own son." Having said this, he emptied the horn, so that it was an inviolable oath. But the courtiers cast

---

The latter portion of this tale occurs also in the old Danish ballad (Kjæmpevise) "Brynilds Vise," first printed in "Tragica," Kjobenhaffn, 1657, pp. 35-43; afterwards in "Udvalgte Danske Viser fra Middelalderen," i. pp. 132, 133. Kjob., 1812. The foundation of the story may be traced to the songs and traditions of Sigurd Fafnisbani, how he rode through the fire to Brynhild, Budli's daughter. See the Brynhildarqvida in Sæmund's Edda.

looks of doubt on each other; for they had never before heard the king so speak and could plainly see that the mead had mounted to his head.

On the following morning, when the king awoke, he recollected the vow he had made at the drinking party and accordingly sent for timber and other materials and caused a small house or cage to be constructed close by the royal palace. The cage was formed of large beams, and secured by strong locks and bars, so that no one could break through. In the middle of the wall, there was a little opening or window, for the purpose of conveying food to the prisoner. When all was ready, the king had the wild man brought forth, placed him in the cage, and took the keys himself. There must the dwarf now sit day and night both goers and comers stopping to gaze on him; but no one ever heard him complain, or even utter a single word.

Thus, did a considerable time pass, when war broke out, and the king was obliged to take the field. When on the eve of departure, he said to his queen: "Thou shalt rule over my realm, and I will leave both land and people in thy care. But thou shalt promise me one thing, that thou wilt keep the wild man, so that he escape not while I am absent." The queen promised to do her best both in that and all things besides and the king gave her the keys of the cage. He then pushed his barks from the shore, hoisted sail on the gilded yards, and went far, far away to distant countries; and to whatever place he came, he was there victorious. But the queen stood on the shore, looking after him as long as she could see his pendants waving over the ocean, and then, with her attendants, returned to the palace, there to sit sewing silk on her knee, awaiting her consort's return.

The king and queen had an only child, a prince still of tender age, but who gave good promise of himself. After the king's departure, it one day happened that the boy, in his wanderings about the palace, came to the wild man's cage, and sat down close by it playing with his gold apple. While he was thus amusing himself, his apple chanced to pass through the window of the cage. The wild man instantly came forwards and threw it out. This the boy thought a pleasant pastime and threw his apple in again and the wild man cast it back, and thus they continued for some time. But at length pleasure was turned to sorrow, for the wild man kept the apple and would not throw it back. When neither threats nor prayers were of any avail, the little one burst into tears. Seeing this, the wild man said: "Thy father has acted wickedly towards me, in making me a prisoner, and thou shalt never get thy apple again, unless thou procurest my liberty." The boy answered: "How shall I procure thy liberty? Only give me my gold apple! my gold apple!" "Thou shalt do as I now tell thee," replied the wild man. "Go to the queen, thy mother, and desire her to comb thee. Be on the watch, and steal the keys from her girdle, then come and open the door. Thou canst afterwards restore the keys in the same manner, and no one will be the wiser." In short, the wild man succeeded in persuading the boy, who stole the keys from his mother, ran down to the cage, and let the wild man come out. At parting, the dwarf said: "Here is thy gold apple, as I promised, and thou hast my thanks for allowing me to escape. Another time, when thou art in trouble, I will help thee in return." He then ran off.

When it was known in the royal palace that the wild man had fled, there was a great commotion; the queen sent people on the roads and ways to trace him; but he was away and continued away. Thus, some time passed, and the queen was more and more troubled, for she was in daily expectation of her consort's return. At last she descried his ships come dancing on the waves, and a multitude of people were assembled on the shore to bid him welcome. On landing, his first inquiry was, whether they had taken good care of the wild man; when the queen was obliged to confess what had taken place. At this intelligence the king was highly incensed, and declared he would punish the perpetrator, be he whoever he might. He then caused an investigation to be made throughout the palace and every man's child was called forth to bear witness; but no one knew anything. At last the little prince came forward. On appearing before his father, he said: "I know that I have incurred my father's anger: nevertheless, I cannot conceal the truth; for it was I who let the wild man escape." On hearing this the queen grew deadly pale, and every other with her; for the little prince was the favourite of all. At length the king spoke: "Never shall it be said of me that I broke my vow, even for my own flesh and blood; and thou shalt surely die as thou deservest." Thereupon he gave orders to his men to convey the young prince to the forest, and there slay him; but to bring his heart back, as a proof that his order had been fulfilled.

Now there was sorrow among the people such as the like had never before been experienced; everyone interceded for the young prince, but the king's word was irrevocable. The young men had, therefore, no alternative so taking the prince with them, they set out on their way. When they had penetrated very far into the forest, they met a man driving swine whereupon one of the men said to his companion: "It seems to me not good to lay violent hands on a king's son: let us rather purchase a hog and take its heart; for no one will know it not to be the prince's heart." This to the other seemed wisely said; so they bought a hog of the man, slaughtered it, and took out its heart. They then bade the prince go his way and never return.

The king's son did as they had directed him; he wandered on as far as he was able, and had no other sustenance than the nuts and wild berries, which grew in the forest. When he had thus travelled a long distance, he came to a mountain, on the summit of which stood a lofty fir. He then thought to himself: "I may as well climb up into this fir and see whether there is any path." No sooner said than done. When he reached the top of the tree, and looked on all sides, he discerned a spacious palace lying at a great distance and glittering in the sun. At this sight he was overjoyed, and instantly bent his steps thither. On his way he met with a boy following a plough, with whom he exchanged clothes. Thus, equipped he at length reached the palace, entered it, and asked for employment; so was taken as a herd-boy, to watch the king's cattle. Now he ranged about the forest both late and early; and as time went on he forgot his sorrow, and grew, and became tall and vigorous, so that nowhere was to be found his like.

Our story now turns to the king, to whom the palace be longed. He had been married, and by his queen had an only daughter. She was much fairer than other damsels and was both kind and courteous: so that he might be regarded as fortunate, who should one day possess her. When she had completed her fifteenth winter, she had an innumerable host of suitors, whose number, although she gave each a denial, was constantly increasing; so that the king at length knew not what answer to give them. He one day, therefore, went up to his daughter in her bower, and desired her to make a choice, but she would not. In his anger at her refusal he said: "As thou wilt not thyself make a choice, I will make one for thee, although it may happen not to be altogether to thy liking." He was then going away, but his daughter held him back, and said: "I am well convinced that it must be as you have resolved; nevertheless, you must not imagine that I will accept the first that is offered, as he alone shall possess me, who is able to ride to the top of the high glass mountain fully armed." This the king thought a good idea, and, yielding to his daughter's resolution, he sent a proclamation over the whole kingdom, that whosoever should ride fully armed to the top of the glass mountain, should have the princess to wife.

When the day appointed by the king had arrived, the princess was conducted to the glass mountain with great pomp and splendour. There she sat, the highest of all, on the summit of the mountain, with a golden crown on her head and a golden apple in her hand, and appeared so exquisitely beautiful, that there was no one present who would not joyfully have risked his life for her sake. Close at the mountain's foot were assembled all the suitors on noble horses and with splendid arms, which shone like fire in the sunshine; and from every quarter the people flocked in countless multitudes to witness the spectacle. When all was ready, a signal was given with horns and trumpets, and in the same instant the suitors galloped up the hill one after another. But the mountain was high, and slippery as ice, and was, moreover, exceedingly steep; so that there was no one, who, when he had ascended only a small portion, did not fall headlong to the bottom. It may, therefore, well be imagined there was no lack of broken legs and arms. Hence arose a noise of the neighing of horses, the outcry of people and the crash of armour that was to be heard at a considerable distance.

While all this was passing, the young prince was occupied in tending his cattle. On hearing the tumult and the rattling of arms, he sat on a stone, rested his head on his hand, and wept; for he thought of the beautiful princess, and it passed in his mind how gladly he would have been one of the riders. In the same moment he heard the sound of a footstep, and on looking up, saw the wild man standing before him. "Thanks for the past," said he. "Why sittest thou here lonely and sad?" "I may well be sad," answered the prince. "For thy sake I am a fugitive from my native land, and have now not even a horse and arms, that I might ride to the glass mountain, and contend for the princess." "Oh," said the wild man, "if that's all, a remedy may easily be found. Thou hast helped me, I will now help thee in return." Thereupon taking the prince by the hand, he led him to his cave deep down in the earth and showed a suit of armour hanging on the wall, forged of the hardest steel, and so bright that it shed a bluish light all around. Close by it stood a splendid steed, ready saddled and bridled, scraping the ground with his steel shod hoofs, and champing his bit. The wild man then said to him: "Arm thyself quickly, and ride away, and try thy fortune. I will, in the mean time, tend thy cattle." The prince did not require a second bidding, but instantly armed himself with helm and harness, buckled spurs on his heels, and a sword by his side, and felt as light in his steel panoply as a bird in the air. Then vaulting into the saddle, he gave his horse the rein, and rode at full speed to the mountain.

The princess's suitors had just ceased from their arduous enterprise, in which none had won the prize, though each had well played his part, and were now standing and thinking that another time fortune might be more favourable when on a sudden they see a young knight come riding forth from the verge of the forest directly towards the mountain. He was clad in steel from head to foot with shield on arm and sword in belt and bore himself so nobly in the saddle that it was a pleasure to behold him. All eyes were instantly directed towards the stranger knight, each asking another who he might be, for no one had seen him before. But they had no long time for asking; for scarcely had he emerged from the forest, when, raising himself in the stirrups, and setting spurs to his horse, he darted like an arrow straight up the glass mountain. Nevertheless, he did not reach the summit, but when about half way on the declivity, he suddenly turned his charger and rode down the hill, so that the sparks flew from his horse's hoofs. He then disappeared in the forest as a bird fly. Now, it is easy to imagine, there was a commotion among the assembled multitude, of whom there was not one that was not stricken with wonder at the stranger, who, I hardly need say it, was no other than the prince. At the same time all were unanimous that they had never seen a nobler steed or a more gallant rider. It was, moreover, whispered abroad that such was also the opinion of the princess herself, and that every night she dreamed of nothing but the venturous stranger.

The time had now arrived when the suitors of the princess should make a second trial. As on the first occasion, she was conducted to the glass mountain, the attempt to ascend which by the several competitors was attended with a result similar in every respect to what has been already related.

The prince in the meanwhile was watching his cattle, and silently bewailing his inability to join in the enterprise, when the wild man again appeared before him, who, after listening to his complaints, again conducted him to his subterranean abode, where there hung a suit of armour formed of the brightest silver, close by which stood a snow white steed ready saddled and fully equipped, pawing the ground with his silver-shod hoofs and champing his bit. The prince, following the directions of the wild man, having put on the armour and mounted the horse, galloped away to the glass mountain.

As on the former occasion, the youth drew on him the gaze of everyone present; he was instantly recognized as the knight who had already so distinguished himself; but he allowed them little time for observation, for setting spurs to his horse, he rode with an arrow's speed up the glassy mountain, when, having nearly reached the summit, he made an obeisance to the princess, turned his horse, rapidly rode down again, and again disappeared in the forest.

The same series of events took place a third time, excepting that on this occasion the prince received from the wild man a suit of golden armour, cased in which he, on the third day of trial, rode to the mountain's summit, bowed his knee before the princess, and from her hand received the golden apple. Then casting himself on his horse, he rode at full speed down the mountain, and again disappeared in the forest. Now arose an outcry on the mountain! The whole assemblage raised a shout of joy horns and trumpets were sounded, weapons clashed, and the king caused it to be proclaimed aloud that the stranger knight, in the golden armour, had won the prize. What the princess herself thought on the occasion, we will leave unsaid; though we are told that she turned both pale and red, when she presented the young prince with the golden apple.

All that now remained was to discover the gold-clad knight, for no one knew him. For some time, hopes were cherished that he would appear at court, but he came not. His absence excited the astonishment of all, the princess looked pale and was evidently pining away, the king became impatient, and the suitors murmured every day. When no alternative appeared, the king commanded a great assemblage to be held at his palace, at which every man's son, high or low, should be present, that the princess might choose among them. At this meeting there was not one who did not readily attend, both for the sake of the princess, and in obedience to the king's command, so that there was assembled an innumerable body of people. When all were gathered together, the princess issued from the royal palace in great state, and with her maidens passed among the whole throng; but although she sought in all directions, she found not what she sought. She was already surveying the outermost circle, when suddenly she caught sight of a man who was standing concealed amid the crowd. He wore a broad-brimmed hat, and was wrapped in a large grey cloak, like those worn by herdsmen the hood of which was drawn up over his head, so that no one could discern his countenance. But the princess instantly ran towards him, pulled down his hood, clasped him in her arms and cried: "Here he is! here he is!" At this all the people laughed, for they saw that it was the king's herd-boy, and the king himself exclaimed: "Gracious heaven support me! What a son-in-law am I likely to have!" But the young man, with a perfectly unembarrassed air, said: "Let not that trouble you! You will get as good a king's son, as you yourself are a king". At the same moment he threw aside his cloak, and where were now the laughers, when, in place of the grey herdsman, they saw before them a comely young prince clad in gold from head to foot, and holding in his hand the princess's golden apple! All now recognised in him the youth who had ridden up the glass mountain.

Now, it is easy to imagine, there was joy, the like of which was never known. The prince clasped his beloved in his arms with the most ardent affection and told her of his family and all he had undergone. The king allowed himself no rest, but instantly made preparations for the marriage, to which he invited all the suitors and all the people. A banquet was then given such as has never been heard of before or after. Thus did the prince gain the king's daughter and half the kingdom; and when the feastings had lasted about seven days, the prince took his fair young bride in great state to his father's kingdom, where he was received as may easily be conceived, both the king and the queen weeping for joy at seeing him again. They afterwards lived happily, each in his kingdom. But nothing more was heard of the wild man.

1. In "Runa, En Skrift för Fädemeslandets Fornvänner" utgifven af *Richard Dybeck*, Stockh. 1842, Häft i. p. 7, there is a similar tradition from Westmanland, which tells of a knight who captured an animal, the like of which had never been seen, it being overgrown with moss. It was kept in a tower, and released by the knight's young son, who was playing at ball close by. For this the boy was taken to the forest to be slain but the servants, touched by his lamentations killed a kid in his stead, the heart of which they showed for the boys.

While wandering in the forest he meets with the animal he had liberated, and goes with him into the mountain, where he stays for some years. A proclamation is then sent through the country, that the princess will accept for a husband him who shall be able to ride up a mountain, on which she will one day show herself. The knight's son now gets horse and clothing, and rides away to contend for the princess; but on reaching the middle of the mountain he is struck by a javelin cast from below. He, nevertheless, continues his course, and at length stands before the princess, who gives him a silk handkerchief to bind up his wound, and a day is fixed for the wedding.

When the day arrived, the wonderful animal, ugly as he is, desires to accompany the bridegroom, but contents himself with a place under the table. He there gives him a rusty sword, desiring him to touch him with it, when the old king's memory is drunk. The youth complies with his desire, when, to the astonishment of all, the old king, who, it was thought, had been carried off to the mount[20], rises up. There was afterwards great rejoicing and tumult, and the king himself wishes the young couple joy.

2. According to an Upland version, a king one day lost his way in a forest, where he met with an old man who received him hospitably. The old man was immensely rich in gold and silver, which excited the king's avarice. The old man refuses to tell his name, and the king has him cast into a tower, telling him he should never be released until he disclosed who he was.

Some time after, as the king's son was running about the court, he found a key, with which he opened the tower, and set the old man at liberty. At this the king was bitterly enraged, drove the prince from the country, and forbade him ever to return. On entering the forest, the boy met the old man, who desired him to follow him, which he did. They then took the old man's little gray horse, loaded it with gold and silver, and went to another kingdom. There the prince grew up and became very tall and powerful; and his greatest pleasure was to ride on the gray horse over hill and dale.

It happened that the king who ruled the land had a daughter, who had a vast number of suitors. Her father, therefore, issued a procla0mation, that whoever could ride up the glass mountain and take down a golden crown that was fixed on its summit, should possess the princess. When the prince received this intelligence, he went to the king's court and offered his services as a scullion; but when the suitors were to begin their competition, he ran home, got arms from his foster-father, together with the little gray horse, and rode at full speed up to

---

[20] Berg-tagen (mount-taken) means carried off into a mountain by Trolls, concerning which see Thorpe, "Northern Mythology and Traditions," vol. ii. p. 67.

the mountain's peak. Yet he did not take the golden crown but rode down on the other side and away. On the second day he did the like; on the third day he took the crown, but rode away, so that no one knew who he was.

Some time after, as the princess was sitting in her maiden-bower, the door was opened, and in stept the scullion. He had the golden crown in his hand and told her that he had taken it; but that he was willing to give it back, that the princess might exercise her own free will. This pleased the princess exceedingly, and she prayed her father to assemble all the men of his kingdom together at his court. The king did so.

When they were all assembled, the princess went forward to the scullion, gave him the golden crown, and chose him for her husband. At this there was a great wondering; but the prince, casting off his coarse grey cloak, stood there no longer a scullion, but a powerful king's son. He obtained the princess, and with her half the kingdom.

3. A variation from Gothland omits the introductory part about the wild man, and in its place tells of a poor peasant, whose youngest son was accustomed to sit in the chimney-corner, exposed to the insults of his brothers.

The king who ruled over the country had an only daughter, who had made a vow to marry no one who could not ride up a glass mountain. Whereupon the king issued a proclamation to that effect throughout his kingdom. When the day of trial came, the two elder sons of the peasant mounted their father's old jade and rode off to the glass mount; but the youngest boy might not accompany them, and therefore ran along the road weeping. Here he was met by a little old man, who asked him why he was so sorrowful. The boy told him the cause, when the old man replied: "Wait, I will help thee. Here is a pipe take it and place thyself under that tall pine yonder. When thou blowest in one end of the pipe, there shall come forth a charger with a suit of armour hanging on the pommel of his saddle and when thou blowest in the other end, the whole shall disappear." Hereupon the boy instantly ran to the tree, blew in the pipe, armed himself, and went his way. In passing his brothers, their old nag was so frightened that it ran with its two riders into a ditch, where we will for the present leave them.

The boy then rode on to the glass mountain, where he found an innumerable multitude of people, some with broken legs, others with broken arms, from their attempt to ascend the mountain. He did not, however, allow himself to be frightened, but galloped away, and reached the summit of the mountain, where the princess was sitting. She then threw to him her golden apple, which fastened itself to his knee, and he instantly rode back down the mountain, hastened home to the chimney corner, and found great pleasure in hearing his two brothers relate about a strange prince who had frightened their horse into a ditch.

When the princess had long been waiting in vain for the successful rider, the king sent messengers over his whole kingdom, to ascertain whether any one had a golden apple on his knee. The messengers also came to the peasant's hut. When it was discovered that the youngest son had the apple, there was, it may easily be imagined no small astonishment among them. The messengers desired the boy to accompany them to the king; but he would not, stole out of the hut, blew in his pipe, clad himself in complete armour, and rode alone to the royal palace, where he was instantly recognised, and obtained the princess. But the old peasant and his two elder sons have not recovered from their astonishment to this day.

4. In a version of the story from West Gothland, it is related how a poor peasant boy, as he was digging in a sand-pit, came to a hall, in which he found three horses and three suits of armour, one of silver, another of gold, and the third of precious stones.

The boy afterwards set out to wander about the world, and came at length to a royal palace, where he got employment as a scallion. The king, whose palace it was, had an only daughter, who had been carried away by a Troll, and could appear only on three succesive Thursday evenings, on the summit of a high glass mountain; but if any one could ride up the mountain, and take the golden apple from her hand, she would be released. Hereupon the king, who was in great affliction, sent forth a proclamation, that whosoever would deliver the princess should have her to wife, together with half his kingdom.

When the first Thursday evening arrived, the boy ran to the sand pit, clad himself in the silver armour, and rode half-way up the mountain. On the second Thursday evening he took the golden armour and rode so high that the horse had one fore-foot on the mountain's summit. On the third evening he took the armour of precious stones, rode up to the princess and got the golden apple. He then rode back to the sand-pit.

The king then issued an order that every male throughout the kingdom should appear at his court. The princess goes forth and recognises her deliverer. The scullion casts off his rags and stands in the armour of precious stones. The king gives him his daughter, and half the kingdom.

THE TWO CASKETS.[21]

From South Småland.

THERE was once a crone, who was both old and wicked, which, as we all know, is far from impossible. She had two daughters, one her own, the other a step-daughter. They were as unlike as night and day; for the crone's daughter resembled her mother in every way, while the step-daughter was a perfect *heal-all*[22], so thoroughly good and friendly that she would not hurt a worm. Hence, she was much beloved by all, except her wicked step-mother and step-sister. These did her all the harm they could, and their treatment of her grew worse and worse from day to day, until they at length began to devise how they might get rid of her altogether.

---

[21] The following foreign variations of this story are known to us:—

1. Danish.—Very incomplete in "Winther," ut sup., pp. 36-39. "Den onde Stedmoder."

2. Norwegian.—See Asbjörnsen og Moe, ut sup., No. 15. "Manddatteren og Kjærringdatteren."

3. German.—*a.* See Feen-Marchen, Braunschweig, 1801, p. 1, seqq. "Die belohnte Freigebigkeit." *b.* Grimm, K. und H. M. i. No. 24. "Frau Holle," cf. iii. pp. 42-46. *c.* In a short and more modern form in Busching, "Wochentliche Nachrichten fur Freunde der Geschichte, etc. des Mittelalters," iv. Breslau, 1819, pp. 150-153. "Lohn und Strafe." *d.* Stober, Elsässisches Volksbuchlein. Strassburg, 1842, pp. 113-116. "Die zwei Stiefschwesterlein." *e.* Bechstein, Deutsches Marchenbuch. Leipsig, 1848, pp. 62-64. "Die Goldmaria und die Pechmaria." *f.* Ibid., pp. 179, 180. Fippchen Fappchen. *g. Ibid.,* pp. 219-221. "Der Garten im Brunnen." *h.* Firmenich, "Germaniens Volkerstimmen," ii. Berlin, 1846, p. 45. "E Stickelche." *i. Ibid.,* pp. 224-226. "Das Marchen vom Beenelangmann Beenelangbart." *k.* Abridged and in a Christian garb, in Kuhn und Schwartz, ut sup., pp. 335, 336. "Das Madchen im Paradies."

[22] The plant so called. Sw. läke-blad.

For the sake of a pretext, the crone one day called her daughters, and set them to spin at the brink of the well; when she, whose thread should first break, was, as a punishment, to be thrown into the well. The girls did as their mother desired: they took their spinning-wheels, set themselves by the brink of the well, and began their work. But the crone had not acted impartially between them; for while her own daughter got the finest flax to spin, the stepdaughter got the mere refuse, yet was, nevertheless, required to spin yarn equally fine. It therefore fell out as was to be expected, that, notwithstanding all her care, the stepdaughter's thread was the first to snap asunder. Instantly was the crone in readiness, and, seizing the poor girl by the feet, she cast her headlong into the well, in spite of her prayers, which might have moved a stone to pity. Having so done, the crone returned with her daughter to her dwelling, both overjoyed that at last they had got rid of the stepdaughter, who had so long been an annoyance to them.

But although man proposes, it is God who disposes; and so it was in the present instance; for when the stepdaughter sank to the bottom of the well, the earth opened beneath her, and she found herself in a beautiful meadow, in which the grass grew and the trees flourished as in the upper world, although there was no sun to shine as here. Now, thought she to herself, "What am I to do? I dare not go back to my wicked stepmother, and there is no other in the world that I can turn to. I may as well go forwards and see what course I had best take." She then dried her tears and began to wander across the meadow. When she had gone a little way, she came to an old fence; it was broken and decayed, so that it scarcely hung together, and was all overgrown with old man's beard[23]. The fence addressed her thus: "Dear little maiden, do me no harm, a poor fence, so old and decayed!" "No," answered the girl, "that I certainly will not. Do not be afraid." She then stept over the fence but trod so lightly and carefully that nothing was injured or moved from its place, and afterwards continued her wandering. But the fence, shaking its mossy beard, cast a friendly look after her, and wished all might go well with the considerate maiden.

When she had proceeded a little way further, she came to an oven that stood in the path, full of warm, new-baked bread, one loaf whiter than the other, and a peel lying ready at the oven's mouth. The oven said: "Dear little

---

[23] Geropogon, *clematis?*

maiden, do me no harm, a poor oven! Eat as much as thou wishest, but take nothing with thee, and shove the remainder back into the oven." The girl begged it not to be afraid, for that she would certainly do it no harm. She then took the peel, opened the oven's mouth, drew out a warm, new-baked loaf, and began to eat; but having eaten as much as she required, she shoved in the remainder, closed the door of the oven, and restored the peel to its place; then continued her wandering. The oven cast a friendly look after her and wished that all might go well with her in the world.

After a while, the girl came to a place where a cow was grazing. The cow had a milkpail on her horn, and her udder was so distended that it was easy to see that she had not been milked for a long time. The cow said: "My dear good lass, do me no harm, a poor cow! Milk me and drink as much as thou wilt, but spill none on the ground. Cast the remainder over my hoofs and hang the pail on my horn." The girl thanked her and begged her not to be afraid; for she would certainly do her no harm. She then took the pail, and began to milk, and when she had milked, she drank as much as she required, threw the rest on the cow's hoofs, and hung the pail again upon her horn, just as she had been directed, and then continued her way. The cow cast a friendly look after her, lowed with gladness, and wished that all might go well with the considerate maiden.

When she had proceeded a little way further, she came to a large apple-tree, loaded with the most beautiful fruit, and so weighed down that the boughs were bent to the earth. The tree said to her: "My dear little girl, do me no harm, a poor apple tree! Gather as many of my ripe apples as thou wilt; but take none with thee. Then prop up my branches and bury the remainder at my root." "Thanks," said the girl; "that I will certainly do: only do not be afraid." Thereupon she began plucking some of the ripe fruit, and when she had gathered as many as she wished, she propped up the branches and buried the rest at the tree's root; then continued her wandering. But the apple tree nodded with its green foliage, cast a friendly look after her, and wished that all might go well with the considerate maiden.

When evening was approaching, she came to a gate, by which there sat a very, very old woman, leaning for rest against the gate-post. The maiden approached and greeted her: "Good evening, dear mother!" The old woman answered: "Good evening again! Who art thou that comest and greetest me so kindly?" "I am," answered the girl, only a poor step-child seeking service. The old woman then said: "In that case thou canst well wait a little while and comb me, and we will talk in the meantime." The step-daughter did so, and when she had finished, the old woman said: "As thou didst not think thyself too good to comb me, I will in return tell thee where thou mayest find a service. Only be discreet, and everything will go well with thee." She then showed her the way, gave her much good advice, and they parted from each other; the girl continuing her journey, until she came to a very large dwelling, which she entered, and was received as a servant on the farm, precisely as the old woman had told her.

On the following morning, as soon as it was light, the young girl entered upon her work. She first went to the farm-yard, and on going into the cowhouse, she did not do as many other girls, scream, shout, and scold, but patted the cows on the back, spoke to them kindly, and said: "My poor cows, you must be hungry and almost starved wait, I will give you something to eat." She then fetched hay and straw from the barn, and swept it, and strewed litter, and took care of the cattle in every possible way. When all this was done, she took the milking stool and sat down to milk. And the cows were equally considerate towards her; for whenever she approached them, they lowed with joy; they never kicked the milk out of the pail, or caused her the slightest annoyance, but were quiet and gentle as lambs. It was, in fact, a pleasure to see how the little maid attended to her work, and the cows throve under her care, and became fat and plump, so that there never was a greater abundance of milk, or finer cattle on the farm, either before or since.

When the young girl had seen to her cows, and milked and strained, and collected the milk into the measure, there came round her a whole multitude of cats, both great and small, mewing so earnestly:—

> "Give us a little milk!
> Give us a little milk!"

And she was as kind to the cats as she had been to the cows, and neither snubbed nor beat them, as many others would have done, but stroked them on the back, spoke kindly to them, and said: "My poor little pusses! You are, I dare say, both hungry and thirsty. Wait, I will give you something to drink." Thereupon she took the pail and poured milk for them into their bowl. All the cats then gathered round her, rubbed themselves against her knees, arched their backs, and purred with delight; so that it was a pleasure to see how they caressed the little serving-maid.

When her morning labours were over, the stepdaughter had to sift corn in the barn. While thus employed, there came a numerous flight of sparrows flying into the yard, which, hopping nearer and nearer, perched at length on the threshold of the barn, incessantly twittering:—

> "Give us a little corn!
> Give us a little corn!"

On hearing this she did not do as many others, frighten the sparrows and drive them away, but spoke kindly to them, saying: "My poor little sparrows, that are out the whole day and fare hardly I can well believe you are hungry and starving. Wait, you shall have a little food." Thereupon she took a handful of corn from the heap and scattered it among them; the sparrows all the while hopping about her, and pecking, and fluttering with their wings, and were so glad, just as if they would thank the little maid for being so good to them.

In this manner some time passed, one day like another, and whatever the young girl undertook turned out well. It one day happened that the old woman, to whom the place belonged, sent for her. The step-daughter went, and asked what her mistress's commands were? "I have," answered the old woman, "remarked that thou mindest the cows and does thy other work in a satisfactory manner; I wish, therefore, to see what thou canst do besides. Here is a sieve, and thy first proof shall be to go to the well and bring me the sieve well filled with water, but thou must not spill one single drop by the way." The girl had only to obey, so took the sieve, went to the well, and began taking up water; but as fast as the sieve was full, it was again empty. Seeing she could not execute her mistress's order, she was sorely afflicted, and sat down by the well and wept, and while so doing she saw all the little sparrows flying towards her like a cloud, and perching on the green willow just above her, when each little bird began to twitter and chirp, one shriller than another:—

> "Ashes in sieve,
> Then it will hold!
> Ashes in sieve,
> Then it will hold!"

Now it seemed to her that the sparrows meant to advise her how to act; she therefore ran and fetched ashes and laid them on the bottom of the sieve and behold! she could then carry it full of water without spilling a drop. Having thus done, she returned to the house, and the sparrows flew joyful away. When she appeared before her mistress with the sieve full of water, the old woman was thunderstruck, and asked her: "Who has instructed thee in this? I never imagined thou hadst so much knowledge." But the girl was silent; for she would not betray her little friends.

Some time after, the old woman called the little serving maid again before her, and said, "I will now put thee to another trial. Here are two yarns, one white, the other black. Now thou shalt go to the river, and wash the white yarn till it becomes black, and the black yarn till it becomes white; but they must be ready in the afternoon before sunset." The girl had only to obey, so took the yarns, went to the bank of the river, and began to wash most sedulously; but let her wash and wash as she might, the white yarn continued to be white and the black yarn black, as at first. Seeing she could not fulfil her mistress's order, she was sorely afflicted, and sat down on the bank and wept. Then came a whole flight of birds, like a cloud, and descended among the birches by the river's bank; and all the little sparrows began to twitter and chirp, one shriller than another:—

> "Take the black,
> Turn to the east!
> Take the black,
> Turn to the east!"

Now the girl found that the birds wished to help her a second time, and therefore followed their counsel, took the black yarn turned eastward up the river, and began to wash, and behold! She had scarcely dipt the yarn into the water, when it became whiter than the whitest snow. Having so done, she took the white yarn and was beginning to wash it when the birds sang:—

> "Turn to the west,
> Turn to the west!"

The little maid did as she was told, and turned westward down the river, and began to wash, and behold! She had scarcely dipt the yarn into the water, when it became blacker than the blackest coal. She then returned to the house, and the sparrows flew joyful away. When she appeared before her mistress and had both the yarns with her, the old woman was more astonished than on the former occasion, and again asked her who had instructed her. But the girl was silent; for she would not betray the little sparrows that had helped her.

Again, after a while, the old woman called the little serving maid before her. She went and asked what her mistress's commands were. "I will put thee to another trial," answered the mistress, "and that shall be the last. Here are the two yarns which thou hast washed. Thou shalt now weave a web, but upon which there must be no unevenness or nap, and the whole must be ready this afternoon by sunset." The girl had only to obey; so took the yarn, and prepared it for the web, and began to weave; but the yarn was short and uneven, and brake at every instant, and the longer she worked, the worse it was. Seeing now that she should never execute her mistress's order, she felt greatly afflicted, sat by the loom, resting her head on her hand and weeping bitterly. On a sudden the door opened and in came all the cats, one after another, rubbed themselves against her knee, and asked her why she was so distressed. "I may well weep and be sorrowful," answered she, "for my mistress has ordered me to weave a web, and the whole must be ready this afternoon by sunset; but the yarn is short and brittle, so that I fear it will turn out badly altogether." "Oh," said the cats, "if that's all, that's easily remedied. Thou hast ever been kind to us, so now we will help thee in return." Thereupon they all at once leapt up on the loom and began weaving with a rapidity quite incredible; while the girl sat at the spooling-wheel and spooled as fast as the cats wove. Only a short time had elapsed before the web was ready, and appeared close, and even, and fine, so that nothing could possibly be better. The cats then sprang away, and the little serving-maid went full of joy to her mistress. When the old woman saw the web, she was, indeed, astonished, and asked as before, "Who has instructed thee in this? I never imagined thou hadst so much knowledge." The stepdaughter, nevertheless, made no answer, but continued silent; for she would not betray the friendly cats that had helped her.

When the year was ended and the little maid had served out her time, she prepared to return home. She appeared, therefore, before her mistress, and prayed for her dismissal. The old woman answered that she would give it, although unwilling to part with her. "But," added she, "as thou hast given me satisfaction in all things, I will bestow on thee some reward for thy faithful services. Go, therefore, up into the loft; there thou wilt find several caskets, of which thou mayest take whichever one thou choosest; but do not open it before thou hast set it where thou wishest it to remain." The girl thanked her mistress as was proper and went up to the loft followed by all the cats. On entering, she saw many caskets standing on the floor, some red, some yellow, some blue, and one more elegant than another; but farthest of all there stood a little black casket. While doubting which she should take, for everyone seemed too costly a reward for her little services, all the cats came round her and mowed, and cried out fervently:—

"Take the black!
Take the black!"

She therefore took the black casket and thought herself very handsomely rewarded. She then bade farewell to her mistress, and the cows, and the cats, and all the little sparrows, and there was great sorrow at her departure; after which she set out on the way by which she had come, though nothing is related of her journey until she reached the meadow: there the earth opened before her; she ascended to the upper world, and, on looking about her, she found herself just where we had left her, by the well in her wicked step-mother's yard.

When she entered the room and showed herself to the crone and her daughter, it will easily be imagined what a commotion she caused. The step-mother was at first so overcome with passion that she could not utter a syllable. At length she burst forth: "So, thou art still alive, thou ugly young slut! And I all the while thinking thou wast dead and lying in the well! But such luck was not to be." The young girl told her how she came from the nether world, where she had been in service, and got the little black casket for her year's wages; at the same time asking where she might have a little corner to set it in. At this the crone was almost frantic with rage, drove her out of the room, and said, "So, then, thou thinkest we are to have room in the house for thee and thy wretched trumpery; no, take thyself off to the hen-house, thou young beggar! That's the most fitting place for the like of thee." The young girl obeyed without a murmur, and went immediately to the hen-house, where she scoured and swept in every corner, and at last set her little casket in a place adapted for it. Then at length she resolved on knowing what it contained, and unlocked it, when she beheld something quite different from what she had expected; for it was entirely filled with gold and silver, in girdles and rings, and, in short, everything that was fine and beautiful, the light from which darted up to the roof and along the walls, so that the hen-house became in an instant more brilliant than the most splendid royal saloon. Here upon there rose a great talk and rumouring over the whole neighbourhood, and from all quarters there came persons solely to see the little step-daughter and all her vast riches.

We hardly need mention that the crone and her daughter were ready to die with envy. They could neither eat nor sleep, so great was their vexation; and the mother was already devising how her own daughter might obtain a casket equal in value and splendour to that of her step-daughter. On this she pondered both night and day, and finally concluded that the best course would be to send her own daughter also to serve beneath the earth; "because," thought she, "if my poor stepdaughter has got such a reward, what may my own daughter not expect? It will be, no doubt, both more beautiful and more costly." No sooner said than done. The crone placed her own daughter by the brink of the well to spin refuse, and, when the thread brake, cast her into the well, as she had done with her stepdaughter. All, too, fell out exactly in the same manner; for when the girl sank to the bottom, the earth opened, and she entered into the nether world, and found herself in the green meadow, as already described. She did not long hesitate, but went along the path full of confidence, thinking she should be at no loss, let happen what might.

After wandering for some time, she came first to the old fence, which besought her as it had besought her sister: "Dear little maiden, do me no harm, a poor fence, so old and decayed." But the crone's daughter cared little for the poor old fence's petition, and answered, as might be expected: "Out upon thee for talking so to me! How much dost thou think I care for what an old fence says? Wait an instant, and thou shalt see." Saying this, she pulled the stakes of the fence completely from their fastenings, tore asunder the brushwood it was composed of, scattered the fragments in all directions, and then continued her way at a rapid pace. But the fence shook its grey beard, looked angrily after her, and muttered: "This thou shalt not have done to me for nothing."

The crone's daughter then came to the oven that stood by the way-side, and the oven besought her as it had besought her sister: "Dear little maiden, do me no harm, a poor oven! Eat as much as thou wishest but take nothing with thee, and shove in the remainder. But the wicked girl cared little for the oven's petition and answered as before: "Out upon thee for talking so to me! How much thinkest thou I care for what an old oven says? Just wait a moment, and thou shalt see." Saying this, she wrenched off the door of the oven, scattered the loaves on the earth, broke the peel in shivers, and cast them in all directions; then continued her way as before. But the oven looked angrily after her and muttered: "This thou shalt not have done to me for nothing."

After walking for some time, the crone's daughter came to the spot where the cow was grazing. The cow prayed her: "Dear little maiden, do me no harm, a poor cow! Milk me and drink as much as thou wilt, but spill none on the ground. Cast the remainder on my hoofs and hang the pail upon my horn." But the wicked girl answered as she had answered the others: "Out upon thee for talking so to me! How much thinkest thou I care for what an old cow says to me? Just wait, and thou shalt see." Saying this she took the pail and began to milk and drank as much as she required; but when she had drunk, instead of doing as the cow desired, she did just the contrary, threw out the milk, kicked the pail to pieces, and flung the fragments on every side; then continued her way. But the cow looked angrily after her, shook her horns and bellowed: "This thou shalt not have done to me for nothing."

She came next to the great apple tree. The apple tree besought her: "Dear little maiden, do me no harm, a poor old tree! Gather of my ripe fruit as much as thou wilt but take none with thee. Then prop up my branches and bury the remainder at my root." But the wicked girl answered as before: "Out upon thee for talking so to me! How much thinkest thou I care for what an old apple tree says? Just wait, and thou shalt see." Saying this, she clambered up into the tree, shook down every apple, both ripe and unripe, broke the boughs in pieces and scattered the twigs and leaves in all directions; then continued on her way as before. But the apple tree, shaking its naked top, looked angrily after her, and whispered: "This thou shalt not have done to me for nothing."

It was already the approach of evening when the crone's daughter arrived at the gate where the old woman sat leaning against the gate post. And, it will hardly be believed, she did not vouchsafe to notice her, but passed or: without uttering a word either good or bad. But the old woman asked: "Who art thou that passest without deigning to salute the aged?" The girl answered: "Out upon thee for speaking so to me! As if I had nothing to do but to salute old women!" The old woman said: "What hast thou to do then?" "I am out in search of a place, answered the girl." "Then," said the old woman, thou canst sit a while and comb me, and I will tell thee where thou canst get into service." "I shall comb thee, shall I?" answered the girl; "that would, indeed, be delightful. No! But wait just a moment, and thou shalt see how desirous I am to sit and comb such an old hag as thou." Saying this she slammed the gate so that it resounded in every bar and went her way. But the old woman shook her head, looked angrily after her, and said: "This thou shalt not have done for nothing. Only continue to be as wicked and thou wilt see how it will go with thee in the world."

She then proceeded on her way, and came at last to the mansion, which she entered, and was received as a serving maid on the farm, as her sister had been before her. If now the little stepdaughter had been kind and considerate towards the cows, the crone's daughter was as evil-disposed. She never gave them so much as one friendly word; but the first time she went into the farm, it was as if it were only to beat and curse them and do all kinds of mischief. The cows got no fodder at the regular times, and frequently went without it, and without water; so that there was always something wanting. In short nothing throve under her; the cows became lean and dry. When she went to milk them, they would kick the milk-pail over, and in no one's remembrance was there so little milk and such meagre cattle on the farm.

So it was likewise with the cats. When the crone's daughter had given the morning-fodder, and milked, and strained, and collected the milk into the measure, the poor animals came round her, and mewed, and prayed so earnestly:—

"Give us a little milk!
Give us a little milk!

But she did not do as the little step-sister had done, but chased them away, driving them right and left. The cats in their turn, could not endure her, but the instant they saw her would spit and run round the place, every one into its corner; and never on the farm were there so many mice and rats, either before or since.

When she went to the barn to sift corn, all went on in like manner. The little sparrows came flying into the yard, hopped nearer and nearer, perched on the barn threshold, and twittered:—

"Give us a little corn!
Give us a little corn!"

But she who had given them corn was not the crone's daughter, who chased them away and frightened them whenever she could, and cast stones at them; so that after a time no more little sparrows were to be seen in the yard twittering and rejoicing in God's day; but they flew to the woods, and when they appeared they were dull and shy so that no one had any pleasure in seeing or hearing them.

Thus, a considerable time passed whatever the girl undertook turned out ill, and she was liked by no one, neither persons nor animals, when one day the mistress, to whom the place belonged, called her before her. The girl went and asked what were her mistress's commands. "I have noticed," answered the old woman, "that thou neither takest care of my cows nor dost thy other duties to my satisfaction; nevertheless, I am desirous of knowing whether there may not be something else which thou canst do This, then, shall be thy first proof; thou shalt go to the well and fetch water in a sieve; but thou must not spill a single drop by the way." The girl had only to obey, so, took the sieve, went to the well and began taking up the water; but as fast as the sieve was full it was again empty, and none of the little birds came to her aid as they had come to her sister's. So the crone's daughter had to return as she went. When she came back with the sieve as empty as when she went to fill it, her mistress was displeased, and said: "Ill hast thou attended to my farm, and still worse to other things; nevertheless, I thought there, might be something thou couldst do." They then parted, and so ended their interview this time.

Again, after some time, the old woman summoned the serving-maid before her, and said: "I will now put thee to another trial. Here are two yarns, one white, the other black. Now thou shalt go to the river and wash the white yarn till it becomes black, and the black yarn till it becomes white; but they must be ready in the afternoon before sunset." The girl had only to obey, so took the yarns, went to the bank of the river and began to wash; but let her wash and wash as she might, the white yarn continued to be white and the black yarn black, as at first, and no little sparrows came to instruct her as they had instructed her sister. So the crone's daughter had to return as she went. When she brought back the yarns just as she had received them, her mistress was more displeased than before, and said: "Ill hast thou attended to my farm, and still worse to other things; nevertheless, I thought thou mightest know something." Thus ended the interview, and they parted as before.

When some time had elapsed, the old woman called the serving-maid a third time before her and said: "I will now put thee to a third trial, but it shall be the last. Here are the yarns which thou hadst to wash. Thou shalt now weave them into a web, but in which there shall be neither any unevenness nor knots, and it must be ready by the evening before sunset." The girl had no alternative but to obey, so took the yarns and began to prepare them for weaving as well as she was able, though that is not saying much, and the yarn was, moreover, short, so that the longer she continued the worse it all was, and no cats came to help her as they had helped her sister; therefore when evening drew nigh she had spoiled the whole yarn, which was now only a tangled bunch. On seeing it the mistress was angry and said: "I see plainly that thou art fit for nothing." They then parted from each other.

At the year's end, when the crone's daughter had served her time, she prepared to return home, and went therefore to her mistress to ask her discharge, which was most readily given to her. The old woman added: "Ill hast thou performed thy duties, and little satisfaction hast thou given me in any one thing: nevertheless, I will give also to thee some recompense for thy service. Go therefore up into the loft, where thou wilt find many caskets, of which take whichever thou wilt; but open it not before thou hast set it where thou wishest it to remain." The crone's daughter hardly thanked her for her kindness yet did as she had desired. On entering the loft, she saw many caskets on the floor, one red, one yellow, one blue, and one more beautiful than another; but farthest of all there stood a small black one, precisely as before. "Now," thought she to herself, how shall I just hit on the casket that contains the greatest riches? But, if my sister's little casket contained such precious things, "how much more must there be in this large red one!" So, without further reflection, she took the red casket, then left the place without bidding farewell either to her mistress or any one else; and it may easily be believed there was no one that grieved after her. We are told nothing further about her until she reached the meadow, where the earth opened, so that she ascended through the well, and was in a short time back in the upper world, just as when we there left her.

When she entered the cottage and appeared before her mother, the crone was so overjoyed that, clapping her hands together, she exclaimed: "Well, thou art come at last! That is, indeed, good! And see only what a casket thou hast got, so red and beautiful! That's something very different from the little thing thy sister brought." At all this the crone's daughter was so elated, that she scarcely vouchsafed to notice her mother, but merely asked where she could have a place for her casket. "Ah," said the crone, "that is, indeed, a question! Yet where should we set it but upstairs, where we have the best room in the house." At this suggestion the daughter was well pleased, so they hurried upstairs, thinking only of the wonderful riches they should find in the casket; but its contents proved something very different from gold and other precious things; for, on unlocking it, it was filled with snakes and toads and all kinds of disgusting objects, and a red flame from it ascended to the roof and passed along the walls, so that around all was burning fire, and within a little space the house was laid in ashes, together with the crane and her daughter.

Such was the end of them, nor was it any grief; for they had never been otherwise than wicked. Of the entire house nothing was left unconsumed save only the little hen-house. That was not burnt, and there lived the little stepdaughter, contented and fortunate, all her days. Her casket was afterwards the inheritance of all little, considerate girls, and thence it is that they can always keep themselves neat, however little they may have. And so is the story ended.

THE LITTLE GOLD SHOE.[24]

From North Småland.

THERE was once a king and a queen who had an only daughter, who was dear to them above all things, and no wonder, for she was fair and good, so that there never could be a more amiable child. But after some years had elapsed, the queen fell sick and died, and the king took to himself a new consort, who also had a daughter. But if the first queen was gentle and good, the second was an arrant Troll, both ugly and vicious in all manner of ways, in which respects the daughter was in no wise inferior to her mother. Thus, the king had no great joy in his marriage, and for the little princess it was still worse; early and late she heard nothing but dissensions, and no doubt often experienced the

---

[24] Of this wide-spread story we are acquainted with the following foreign varieties, be des various versions in a dramatic form:—

1. The Norwegians.—See Asbjörnsen og Moe, ut sup., No. 19. The latter part of "Kari Træstak"

2. The Danes.—See Winther, ut sup., pp. 12-17. "De to Kongedottre."

3. The Germans.— *a.* The story is mentioned as early as the 16th century in Rollenhagens Froschmäuseler. *b.* See Büsching, ut sup., i. pp. 137-140, "Ueber die Marchen von Aschenbrodel." *c. Ibid.,* ii. pp. 185-188. "Aschenbrodel." *d.* Grimm, K. und H. M. i. No. 21. "Aschenputtel," Cf. iii. pp. 36-40. *e.* Bechstein, ut sup., pp. 232-235. "Aschenbrödel." *f.* E. M. Arndt, "Marchen und Jugenderinnerungen," ii. Berlin, 1843, pp. 281-320 "Aschenbrodel."

4. The Greeks.—A similar story of Grecian or Egyptian origin, is told of Rhodopis and Psammeticus in Egypt (a. 617, a. c.). See Ælliani Variæ Historiæ, xii. cap. 32, περὶ Ῥοδάπιδος ἑταίρας τύχης (The author lived about A.D. 225.)

5. The Wallachians.—See Schott, ut sup., pp. 100-105. "Die Kaiserstochter Gänsehirtin."

6. The French.— *a.* See Perrault, ut sup., "Cendrillon." *b.* Mad. D'Aulnoy, ut sup., the latter part of the tale of "La Finette."

7. The Italians.—See Basile, Il Pentam. i. 6. "La Gatta Cennerentola."

8. The Welsh.—See Taylor, "Gammer Grethel; or, German Fairy Tales and Popular Stories." London, 1839, p. 332.

9. The Russians.—Cited by Grimm, K. und H. M. iii. p. 40.

10. The Poles.— *a.* Cf. Grimm, ut sup., iii. p. 432. *b.* See Woycicki, ut sup., "Die Eiche und der Schaafpelz."

11. The Servians.—See Büsching, Wöchentl. Nachtrichten, iv. p. 61.

truth of the old saying: that those who have a stepmother have also a stepfather.

Things went on thus for a season, when at last the king also died, and now the young princess had neither kith nor kin in all the wide world, and it may easily be believed that the queen and her daughter did not treat her the better on that account. At the same time, she grew from day to day fairer and fairer, and when she had attained her fifteenth year, a fairer maiden was nowhere to be found. On this account the queen and her daughter bore her a still greater grudge and took good care that no one should know of the princess's beauty. With this object they treated her rather as a peasant girl than as a king's daughter, all works of drudgery being allotted to her; she was never allowed to come forward in the apartments or sit with other people, but her place was always among the ashes on the hearth, close by the mouth of the stove. There she sat covered with rags, raking in the ashes and drinking of former days, while her mother was still living. This was her favourite pastime, and whence she was called in derision the Cinder girl.

After a lapse of time, it one day happened that a rumour was spread over all the country that a foreign prince was coming for the purpose of wooing, and it was also said that he would attend church on the following Sunday. This news caused a great stir; one female thought of herself, another of her daughters, and in the whole kingdom there was not a wench, however poor, who did not entertain the hope of becoming a princess. But in no place was there so much bustle as in the royal palace; there everything was turned upside down and inside out during the whole week; for the queen had not even a thought that her daughter would not be the lucky one. When Sunday at length came, she had her daughter washed and scrubbed till her skin was almost rubbed off, and caused her hair to be combed and curled, and herself tricked out in all sorts of ways both before and behind, so that never was the like seen. She then ordered forth her gilded chariot and made ready to accompany her daughter to church. In like manner did everyone else; for if all could not get the foreign prince, all were at least desirous to see him. But there was one who did not follow with the others, and that was the Cinder-lass: she was ordered to stay at home and sweep, and dress the dinner, and chop pine twigs, and strew the floor, and many other things, which were always her Sunday-work. Poor girl!

When all was in order, and the horses were put to the chariot, and the queen was ready to set out, the daughter thought she would show herself to her stepsister in all her finery and splendour. So with a haughty step and many proud gestures, she proceeded to the chimney-corner, where she stopped, writhed and twisted herself about to the best advantage, and said: "Now, Cinder-wench, what is thy opinion? Am I not elegantly clad? Dost thou see how fine I am? This is somewhat different from thy rags." The other answered that it was so, and in a humble tone asked, whether she also might not sometimes go to the house of God with other folks. At this the queen's daughter, betraying her true disposition, burst forth in a fit of rage: "Heard any one ever the like? The Cinder-wench is also for going to church! I believe thou thinkest to get the young prince! No, stay where thou art, that is more becoming such a beggar-brat as thou." She then went her way, and the sister wept bitterly at her cruel words. But the wicked stepmother did not even allow her to weep in peace; for, like all wicked people, she was always worst on God's holy Sunday; but took a bushel of peas, scattered them about the yard, and said: "I shall teach thee to weep forsooth! Now pick up every single pea, and wash and boil them for dinner and the Lord have mercy on thee, if it is not ready when I return home!" Having given these orders, the queen and her daughter, in full dress, proceeded to church to meet the prince; but the Cinder-girl remained at home picking up peas. That was her pastime.

As the day was now advancing, and the church folks had all set out, the damsel thought it time to begin her Sunday occupations. Taking therefore a pail, she first went to the spring for water. As she was hastening through the field she could not refrain from thinking of former days, how different all was then; and on her wicked stepmother, and on the church, to which she never went, and of the young prince; and as her thoughts thus wandered, she became so sad that she sat down on the earth, resting her cheek on her hand, and wept. As she stooped to draw up water, it happened that a tear rolled down her cheek and fell into the spring. At the same moment there rose to the surface an exceedingly large pike, which asked her why she wept so. "I may well weep and be sorrowful," answered the Cinder-lass; "my stepmother and stepsister are driven out to church, to see the foreign prince, while I am forced to sit at home and pick up peas; and at the same time, I get nothing but maledictions when they come home." "Alas, poor-girl!" said the pike, "thou hast a wicked stepmother. But if thou wilt do as I tell thee, thou shalt go to church as well as the others, and I will do thy work for today." The Cinderlass promised to follow his directions, and the pike continued: "When thou goest now along the path between the birches, thou wilt come to a hollow oak, which stands the highest on the mountain. In that oak thou wilt find a suit of clothes, which thou shalt put on. Thou shalt then saddle the palfrey that stands close by, and ride to church, and sit down on the seat between thy stepmother and stepsister. But thou must not speak to them, for then they would recognise thee; nor must thou wait till the mass is ended but must hasten out and ride back to the oak, and clothe thyself in thy old garments, so that thy stepmother may not remark anything when she returns home."

The Cinder-girl was overjoyed at all this for many a day had passed since she had heard such friendly words. She therefore dried her tears, thanked the pike in the most heartfelt terms, and ran along the path among the birches till she reached the summit of the mountain. On looking into the oak, as the pike had directed her, she saw hanging a dress of the brightest silver, and by the side of the dress there hung a silver saddle and a silver bridle and without there stood a snow-white palfrey, that snorted and neighed and beat with his hoofs, so that the whole mountain trembled. Now it may well be imagined what the damsel's feelings were. She hardly durst look upon the silver garment, it was so exceedingly magnificent, but thought at first that it was all nothing but a dream. Nevertheless, she did as the pike had enjoined her, entered into the oak, divested herself of her old tatters, put on the splendid silver dress, combed her golden locks, and in a short time was transformed from a ragged cinder-girl to the fairest, stateliest damsel that ever rode to court. Having completed her toilet, she saddled her palfrey and proceeded to church, and it seemed when she arrived exactly as if a white silvery cloud had issued from the sky. As she walked up the aisle and seated herself between her stepmother and stepsister, such a brightness shone over the whole church, that all the folks turned about and looked after the stranger, silver-clad lady; but the young prince was so smitten that he could not turn his eyes away from her. There was, in fact, no one that attended to the priest, besides the wicked stepmother and her daughter; for it may be imagined that they thereby strove to conceal their vexation. But in one instant, before anyone was aware, the Cinder-lass suddenly rose from her seat, and hurried out of the church, long before the mass was concluded. Now, it may easily be imagined there was a commotion! The foreign prince instantly followed her, for he was desirous beyond all belief of knowing who she was, as were also the other people; all streamed to the church door, and no one listened more either to text or sermon. But the damsel let nothing detain her and instantly mounted her horse, saying:—

"Light before me!
Darkness after me!"

and so in a twinkling vanished from their sight. While now all were standing gaping and wondering what direction she had taken, she hastened to the oak, divested herself of the elegant silver dress, put on her old tatters, and ran to the royal palace, so that when the queen and her daughter returned, they found neither palfrey nor silver-clad damsel but the peas were boiled, the floor was strewed, and the little Cinder-girl sat down among the ashes, as we have been accustomed to find her.

The queen and her daughter were very far from pleased with what had passed at church, and everyone could easily perceive, both by their words and answers, that things had not proved to their hearts' content. In fact, nothing pleased them, they found fault with and complained of everything; but above all they spoke of a stranger princess who was at church, and who came and departed no one knew whence or whither, ending every conversation with the assurance, that on the next Sunday the queen's daughter should be much finer than the princess. But all this while there was no one that thought of the little Cinder-lass, except to chide and snub her, so that for her the week passed much worse than any preceding one.

As the time drew on it may easily be imagined what hustle and preparations there were in the royal palace, only that the queen's daughter might have everything most fine and costly; nothing being so sumptuous that the queen would not have it yet more so. At length Sunday came, and the queen had her daughter washed and scrubbed till her face was as bright as a May morning[25], combed her hair most curiously, and decorated her both before and behind, so that the like of such finery had never been seen. She then ordered forth her gilded chariot and made ready to drive to church. In like manner did everyone

---

[25] In the original, "blank som en tiggar-krycke," *bright as a beggar's crutch.*

in the royal palace, all being desirous of seeing the foreign prince. The only one that did not go was the Cinder-lass, who, poor young girl! was obliged to stay at home and sweep, and prepare dinner, and chop pine twigs, and strew the floor, and numerous other things, as always formed her employment on Sundays.

When all was in order, and the horses were put to the chariot, the holyday attire examined in every fold, and the queen ready to set out, it occurred to the daughter that she would grant her stepsister the great pleasure of seeing her in all her pomp and finery. She went, therefore, with stately step and many proud gestures to the chimney-corner, where she stopped, twisted and turned herself on every side, that the Cinder-lass might have a complete view of her, and at length said: "Well, what dost thou think? Am I not splendidly clad? Dost thou see how fine I am? This is a little different from thy rags." The stepsister answered, that it was very true, and asked with great humility whether she might not also one day go to church and see the young prince. At this the queen's daughter broke out into a paroxysm of anger: "Well, was the like ever heard? The Cinder-wench will go to church to see the foreign prince! No, stay where thou art, thou beggar-brat, and grope in the ashes; that befits thee far better." She then went her way, and the sister wept bitterly at her cruel words. But the stepmother would not let her even weep in peace, but taking a bushel of groats, she scattered them all over the floor, saying: "I will give thee something else to do than to sit there crying. Pick up now every single grain, and wash them, and boil them for dinner; and the Lord help thee, if they are not ready when I return!" Having given these orders, the queen with her daughter proceeded in full state to church to meet the prince; but the Cinder-lass must sit at home and pick up groats, as her wicked stepmother had ordered. That was her employment.

When the day was so far advanced that all the folk had gone to church, the Cinder-lass began her Sunday occupations. She first of all took a pail and ran to the well to fetch water. As she was hastening across the meadow, she could not refrain from thinking of this and that; of her mother that was dead, how kind and good she had always been, and of her wicked stepmother, and of the church, and of the young prince, whom she should never see again; and while she thus thought she became so sorrowful, that sitting down on a stone and resting her cheek on her hand, she wept bitterly. When leaning forward for the purpose of drawing up water, a tear again rolled down her cheek and fell into the spring. At the same moment, the large pike rose to the surface of the water and asked as before why she sat there weeping so bitterly. "I may well weep and be sad," answered she; "my stepmother and stepsister have driven to church to see the young prince; while I must sit lonely at home and pick up groats, and when the queen returns, I get nothing but chiding and hard words." "Ah!" said the pike, "thou hast a wicked stepmother; but if thou wilt do as I say, thou shalt go to church as well as the others, and I will do thy work, as I did last Sunday." The Cinder-lass thanked the pike for his good will and promised to obey him in everything; and the pike continued: "When thou goest along the path under the birches, thou wilt come to the hollow oak that stands on the mountain. In the oak thou wilt find a garment which thou wilt put on thou wilt then saddle the palfrey, which stands close by, and ride to church, and sit on the seat between thy stepmother and stepsister. But thou must not speak to them, for then they will recognise thee; nor must thou stay till the service is ended, but hasten out and ride back to the oak, and put on thy old garments, so that thy stepmother may not observe anything when she returns home."

The Cinder-lass, on hearing this, was delighted beyond measure; for it ran in her mind that she should see the young prince once again. She therefore dried her tears, returned her best thanks to the pike, and ran along the path under the birches till she reached the summit of the mountain. On looking into the oak, she saw hanging a habit of the purest gold, and together with the habit there also hung a gold saddle with a gold bridle and a gold bit; and all so exceedingly magnificent, that they glittered like fire, when anyone looked on them. Close by without there stood again the snow-white palfrey snorting and neighing, and full of joy, and beating the earth with his hoofs, so that the whole mountain shook. It may now be easily imagined in what state of mind the Cinder-lass found herself; for a long time, she knew not whether she were awake or the whole were only a dream. Nevertheless, she did not forget what the pike had said to her, but went into the oak, cast off her old rags, put on the sumptuous golden garment, combed her golden locks, and was in a short time metamorphosed from a poor ragged cinder-girl to the fairest, stateliest damsel that ever wore a crown of gold. She then saddled her palfrey and rode to church, and it seemed as if a cloud had appeared in the sky with a little star on it. As she proceeded along the aisle and seated herself between the queen and her daughter, such a brightness was spread over the pavement and over the whole church, that all the people turned about on their seats, and gazed only on the stranger damsel. But the prince's heart was so smitten with love that he could not for a moment turn his eyes from her. No one, in fact, attended to the priest, unless it were the wicked stepmother and her daughter. It may be supposed that they thereby strove to conceal their vexation, although they would have rejoiced if the young princess had been a hundred miles off. But while they were thinking over the matter, the Cinder-lass starting suddenly up, hurried out of the church long before the conclusion of the mass. Now, we can well imagine, there was a commotion! The young prince instantly hastened after her; for he was desirous above all things to discover who she was. At the same time all the other people streamed to the church door, and no one cared more either for priest or mass. But they got nothing for their pains; for when the princess came out, she instantly mounted her horse, and said:—

> "Light before me!
> Darkness after me!"

and vanished like lightning from the sight of all. While the prince and all the people were standing gaping, and wondering in what direction she could have taken her course, she hastened back to the oak, put on her old garments, and ran to the royal palace, so that when the queen and her daughter returned, they found the groats boiled and the floor strewed, but neither palfrey nor gold-clad damsel, only the Cinder-girl in her chimney-corner, precisely as they were accustomed to see her.

The queen and her daughter were now even more dissatisfied with their church visit than on the preceding Sunday, and both in their conversation and answers it might be observed that things had not fallen out according to their expectations. Nothing in fact pleased them, neither at home nor abroad, but they found fault with and complained of everything. Above all things they spoke of a strange princess, who was so magnificently clad, always adding how the queen's daughter should be even finer than she. But all the while no one thought of the little Cinder-lass, unless it were to snub and chide her, so that she was always made the object of her stepmother's and stepsister's malignity.

As the time advanced, it is easy to conceive that there were sewing and cutting in the royal palace both early and late, solely that the queen's daughter might appear as fine as possible and however magnificent a thing might be, yet it never was so exquisite that the queen did not require it still more so. At length Sunday came, and the queen caused her daughter to be washed and scrubbed, till she was as bright as a sun, curled her hair after the most tasteful fashion, and decorated her in all manner of ways both before and behind, so that the like of her outfit had never before been seen. She then ordered out her gilded chariot and prepared to ride in it to church. All her people likewise went; for if all could not obtain the foreign prince, yet all were desirous of seeing him. But there was one who was not allowed to accompany them, and that was the Cinder-girl. She must stay at home and sweep, and chop pine twigs, and strew the floor, and many other things, as were now her constant Sunday occupations.

When everything was in order, the horses put to the chariot, the holyday attire examined in every fold, and the queen ready to set out, her daughter thought she would grant her stepsister the happiness of beholding her in all her pomp and finery. With stately step, therefore, and haughty mien she walked to the chimney-corner: there she stopped, twisted and turned herself in every direction, and said at last: "Well, Cinder-wench, what thinkest thou? Am I not sumptuously dressed? Dost thou see how splendid I am? This is something different from thy tatters." Yes, the other answered, it was so, and, with tears in her eyes, asked if she also might not one day go to church and see the young prince. At this the stepsister burst forth in a fit of anger: "Well, was the like ever heard? The Cinder-wench wishes to go with us! I believe thou thinkest to get the young prince! No, stay where thou art, thou beggar-brat! that is more befitting thee." She then took her departure, and her stepsister slowly retired to her chimney-corner, to conceal her tears. But she was not allowed to weep in peace; for the wicked stepmother, who was instantly at hand, took a bushel of meal, cast it out in the middle of the yard, and said: "I will give thee something else to do than to sit there crying; gather up now the meal, every particle of it, and cleanse it, and prepare it for dinner and the Lord help thee if all is not ready when I return home!" Having thus given her orders, she and her daughter rode in full state to church to meet the prince. But the stepdaughter must sit in the yard and gather up meal, as her wicked stepmother had ordered her.

When the time had arrived that the church-folks were all gone, and the Cinder-lass should begin her occupations, she first took a pail and ran to get water from the spring. While thus again tripping over the green meadow, her thoughts began to wander, and she thought of her mother who was dead, and who had always been so kind to her, and of her wicked stepmother, and of the church, which she was never allowed to enter, and her tears began to flow in abundance, like the purest pearls. But most of all it went to her heart when she thought of the young prince, whom she should never again see, and she then became so afflicted, that sitting down on a stone, and resting her cheek on her hand, she gave herself up to despair. As she bent forward to draw the water, a bright tear rolled down her cheek into the spring. At the same instant the great pike again appeared, raised his green head above the surface of the water, and asked her why she wept so bitterly. "I may well weep and be sorrowful, answered the Cinder-lass. My stepmother and stepsister have ridden to church to meet the young prince; but I must sit in the yard and gather up meal, and when the queen comes home, I shall get nothing but maledictions and hard words." "Ah, poor girl!" said the pike, "thou hast a bad stepmother but if thou wilt do as I tell thee, thou shalt go to church like the others, and I will do thy work as I did on the last two Sundays." The Cinder-lass hereupon returned her best thanks to the pike and promised to obey him in all things. The pike continued: "When thou goest along the path under the birches, and comest to the hollow oak, thou wilt there find a habit, which thou shalt put on. Then thou wilt saddle the palfrey that stands close by and ride to church and sit down in the seat between thy stepmother and stepsister. But thou must not speak to them, for then they would recognise thee; nor must thou remain till the mass is over but must hasten out and ride back to the oak, and put on thy old garments, that thy stepmother may observe nothing when she returns."

The Cinder-lass was heartily delighted at this, for her thoughts were on the young prince, although she had never expected to see him again. She therefore dried her tears, returned her warmest thanks to the pike, and hastened along the path under the birches till she reached the summit of the mountain. On looking into the oak, she saw hanging a garment wholly set round with precious stones, close by which there hung a saddle-furniture, which was, in like manner, set with pearls and diamonds from the East; and the whole was so indescribably magnificent that it changed colours and glittered like the brightest rainbow. Close by there stood again the snow-white palfrey, which snorted, and neighed, and was overjoyed, and beat the ground with his hoofs, so that the whole mountain echoed. Now everyone can easily imagine the feelings of the Cinder-lass for a long time she knew not whether it were a reality, or whether the whole was not a delightful dream. She did not, however, forget what the pike had enjoined her, but entered the oak, divested herself of her old tatters, put on the splendid habit set with precious stones; placed a crown of gold on her golden hair, and, within a short time, was metamorphosed from a miserable cinder-girl to the fairest princess that was ever seen in the world. She then saddled her palfrey, mounted it, and rode to church: and it seemed when she entered just as when the sun rises in the heavens through a silvery cloud. As she walked up the aisle and placed herself between the queen and her daughter, such a brilliancy was shed over the whole church that it was illuminated in its remotest corners, and all the people turned about on their seats and looked only on the stranger princess; but the young prince received such a wound in his heart that it seemed to him impossible to live without her. There was, consequently, no one that listened to the priest, unless it were the wicked stepmother and her daughter. It may be imagined that they thereby strove in some degree to conceal their vexation; although they heartily wished the princess a thousand miles off. But while they were thinking over the matter, the Cinder-lass suddenly starting from her seat, hastened out long before the mass was ended. Now, it is easy to imagine there was a commotion! The young prince ran out instantly; for he had resolved within himself that he would discover who she was, let it cost what it might. At the same time all the other church-folks rose from their seats, even the priest himself, who in his hurry forgot both bible and breviary. Just as the princess was passing out at the church-door the prince had caused some tar to be spilt, so that she lost one of her gold shoes, which remained sticking in it; and the prince was so close behind her that she durst not turn round to take it up. She had, therefore, no alternative but to hasten to her palfrey, and say as before:—

"Light before me!
Darkness after me!"

and thus, she vanished from the sight of all. She then rode hastily to the great oak on the mountain; but on turning around she perceived a considerable number of people running in all directions in search of her, and at the same time observed that her stepmother and stepsister were already returning from church. At this she was so terrified that she gave herself no time to change her clothes, out cast her old coarse garments over the sumptuous habit set with precious stones and hurried to the royal palace as speedily as she could. There she placed herself in the chimney-corner, and feigned to be playing with the ashes, according to her custom. The queen and her daughter could therefore observe nothing remarkable; but on their return they found the floor strewed, the porridge boiled, and the Cinder-girl sitting in her usual place, just as they were in the habit of seeing her.

The story now returns to the young prince. When he saw that the princess had escaped from him, he was sorely grieved, for he had resolved either to possess her or no one else in the world. He therefore began to consider how he might again find her. For this purpose, he took the little gold shoe which she had lost at the church door and caused it to be announced over the whole kingdom, that her whom the shoe fitted, and no other, he would take to wife. Now, it may easily be believed that there was a commotion of no trivial kind; for every individual maiden must go and try her luck with the little shoe. But there was no one whom the shoe fitted, and no wonder, for it was so very, very little and delicate, that there probably was never in the world a damsel that trod a more elegant little shoe. It now began to be very doubtful whether the prince would ever find the object of his search again or not; nevertheless, hope did not forsake him, but he sent his followers in every direction to seek and make inquiry, while he himself went about the neighbourhood, both to the east and west, in the hope of fitting the shoe.

While thus wandering he came at length to the royal palace. The queen thereupon immediately caused her young stepdaughter to be shut up in the oven, for she was fearful lest any one should see her extraordinary beauty, but brought forward her own daughter, that she might put on the gold shoe, but all in vain; her foot was, and continued to be, too large, however she might press and pinch it. But the queen was not at a loss; she chopped off her daughter's long heels and clipped her great toes, and thus again brought her forward to try her luck. When the queen's daughter was now again about to try on the gold shoe, there sat a little bird in a tree, which sang:—

> "Chop heel and clip toe!
> In the oven is she whom fits the gold shoe."[26]

"What was that?" inquired the prince, wondering. "Oh!" answered the queen, "it was nothing; it was only the song of a bird." The prince took no further notice of it, the queen's daughter being about to try on the shoe; but the bird did not cease but sang again:—

> "Chop heel and clip toe!
> In the oven is she whom fits the gold shoe."

"What was that the bird sang?" inquired the prince a second time and listened. "Oh!" answered the queen, "it is not worth listening to it was only the twittering of a bird. Away with thee, thou ugly bird!" But it was to no purpose, for hardly had the queen's daughter tried to put on the gold shoe, when the bird in the tree sang for the third time:—

> "Chop heel and clip toe!
> In the oven is she whom fits the gold shoe."

The prince could now easily perceive that there was some trickery at work, and therefore sent his young pages to search the oven, who almost instantly returned with the young stepdaughter, who had been lying concealed there. Now, we may be sure that neither the queen nor her daughter was in the best of humours. They grew pale and red from anger and asked how any one could trouble himself about such a little beggar-brat. But the prince gave no heed to their talk, and ordered the gold shoe to be brought, when lo! it was as if it had grown to the Cinder-lass's little snow-white foot. While they were thus engaged the prince observed that a golden corner peeped out from a hole in her garment. Seeing it, the prince snatched off her old, coarse, gray cloak, and

---

[26] The English nursery tale of Cinderella has:

> "Chiveri, chiveri, chits,
> The maid's in the oven that that shoe fits,"

which seems to prove that both the English and Swedish have reference to a common origin.

at the same instant it was as if a flash of lightning had darted among them; and behold! instead of the ragged Cinder-girl, there stood before them a beautiful princess, the self-same that the prince had seen at church, and the precious stones on her garments glittered like the bright sun, and all who beheld her could not sufficiently admire her wonderful beauty.

At all this, the king's son was so unspeakably rejoiced that he both laughed and wept; but the queen and her daughter did not laugh. He pressed the young damsel to his breast and placed her on his knee and betrothed her with rings of red gold; after which he conducted her with great honour home to his own kingdom and made her his queen. I was present at the, marriage. There the prince tripped in the dance with his fair young bride, and I danced, and all the guests danced with them, all except the queen's daughter. She could not dance, for her mother had cut off her toes. So is my story told.

1. A version from Östergötland[27] relates, that when the queen was going to church, she gave her stepdaughter no food besides a morsel of black bread and a little milk in the cat's saucer. At the same time, she strewed a bushel of peas on the floor, and ordered the Cinder-girl to pick up every pea before the people returned from church.

While the young girl sat weeping, and gathered, and gathered, and wept, she heard a scratching at the door. On opening it there entered a beautiful little white ermine, to which she gave some milk. When the ermine was satisfied, it asked her why she wept, and the Cinder-girl related her whole story. Now, said the ermine, "follow me, and I will help thee." It then blew on the peas, when they immediately flew back of themselves into the measure. The ermine then conducted her to a large oak in the forest, where she found splendid garments, and a palfrey, and little pages, so that she could ride to church in great state and meet the young prince.

The continuation coincides with what is given above, only with the addition, that when the Cinder-girl came to the oak on the third Sunday, the ermine said: "My work is now ended, and I can no longer help thee; but if thou thinkest thou owest me any gratitude, take this knife and thrust it into my heart." The Cinder-girl was loth to reward it so ill for its services; but the

---

[27] Printed in I. Arwidsson's Läse-och Läro-bok för Ungdom. Stockh., 1830. i. pp. 10-25.

ermine besought her earnestly, saying: "Do as I have said; it is my salvation." The damsel then, turning away her eyes, stabbed it to the heart, and at the same instant three drops of blood fell on the field, from which there sprang a comely young prince, who instantly vanished, and was never heard of more.

2. A variation from Gottland makes the stepdaughter go clad in a cloak of crow's feathers, that she might feel shame wherever she might be, and that no one might see how much more beautiful she was than the crone's own daughter. Hence, she was called Krâk-pels, i.e. *Crow-cloak*. At length she received aid from a little old man with whom she had shared her breakfast, and who promised to requite her. He then took her with him to the forest, blew a pipe, and procured her first a habit that shone like the stars in heaven; then one that shone like the moon; and lastly, one that shone like the sun. So Krak-pels went all the three Sundays to church, without being recognised either by her stepmother or stepsister.

When the prince's messenger came to the crone's dwelling, for the purpose of fitting on the little gold shoe, Krak-pels was so frightened that she hid herself in the oven. But there sat a little bird in a tree that sang and betrayed her. She was thus recognised and married to the king's son. The story concludes with the pleasing addition, that she always showed kindness to her wicked stepmother."

3. A version from South Småland tells of a stepdaughter that was called Aske-pjeske, and who had to sit at home and prepare peas, while her stepmother and stepsister went to church to meet a foreign prince. While she sat and wept, there came a little bird, and peeked at the casement, and sang:—

> "Little maiden go to church,
>   I will clean thy peas;
>   I will sweep, and clear, and do all things,
>   Believe me."

At the same moment an eagle came flying, which let fall from his talons a splendid habit. This Aske-pjeske put on and went to church, where everyone was wonder-struck at her great beauty. But the prince was smitten beyond all the others and threw a white silk glove into her lap.

On the following Sunday, she went in the same manner, and the prince threw the other glove to her. On the third Sunday, he cast a golden apple but at every time Aske-pjeske hastened out of the church before the service was over, as has been related above.

When the prince and his attendants came at length to the mansion, to try on the little gold shoe, the crone shut her stepdaughter up in the stable, and chopped off her own daughter's heels and toes but the prince, nevertheless, would not believe that she was the right one. The crone then produced the silk gloves and the golden apple, when the prince could no longer entertain a doubt. At the same moment there came a little bird and peeked on the casement, and sang:—

> "They cut off her heel, they cut off her toe,
>   In the stable is she whom fits the gold shoe."

The stepmother's falsehood was now detected, and the king's son was married to Aske-pjeske.

4. According to another variation from South Småland, the prince allows himself to be misled by the queen's cunning, so that he takes the false damsel with him in his carriage, for the purpose of returning to his own kingdom; but when they had travelled a short distance, they came to a bridge, where a bird was sitting in a tree, which sang:—

> "Chop heel, chop toe;
>   At home sits the damsel in the bathroom and weeps,
>   She whom fits the gold shoe."

The prince now found that he had been deceived, and rode back to the queen's palace, where he found his real beloved in the bath-house, in which she had been shut by her wicked stepmother.

5. A third version from South Småland, called Fröken Skinn-pels Rör i askan, has a long introduction borrowed from the story of De tre Under-skogarne, i.e. *The Three Wonderful Forests*. It tells of a wicked stepmother, who sent her stepdaughter to tend cattle, but gave her no food except a morsel of oatmeal bread. When she had eaten the bread, she sat down under an oak and wept. There then came forth a huge white bear, that asked her why she was so afflicted. The girl told him, as was the truth, that she had been sent out to the field by her wicked stepmother, and that she had no one to look to for help in all the wide world. The bear replied: "If thou wilt be true to me, I will

help thee." To this the maiden consented, and the bear gave her a pipe of gold, in which she was to blow whenever she was desirous of speaking with him.

When some time had passed the young damsel began to long for home. On reaching her stepmother's dwelling she found the crone even worse than before. "So, thou art come back, thou ugly urchin," said she "I thought thou hadst perished with hunger long ago but there is no such good luck." The damsel answered that she had received support from her best friend; so that she had suffered no want. "What friend hast thou had?" inquired the crone. "It is," answered the maiden, "a huge white animal that is called a bear." "Well," replied the crone, "it is fortunate that I have got to know that." She then consulted with her own daughter how they might lay snares and entrap the bear. But when the stepdaughter perceived their design, she went out into the forest, sat down under the oak, and blew in her pipe. Instantly the bear came forth, and the damsel warned him of the crone's design. The bear said: "Have no fear on that account, I shall take care of myself."

One day the bear said: "Thou shalt now go away with me, and then thou wilt escape being longer with thy wicked stepmother. But one thing thou must promise me, that thou wilt obey me in everything that I shall enjoin thee." To this the damsel agreed, and the bear took her on his back, and thus they departed, travelling over hill and dale. At length they came to a very large forest; but this forest was not like other forests, for every, even the smallest, leaf on every tree, was of bright silver, so that it shed light all around. "Now," said the bear, "thou must not touch anything here; for if thou dost, both thou and I will be most unfortunate." And the damsel promised not to touch anything. But when they had reached the middle of the forest, the foliage glittered so beautifully around her, that, forgetting her promise, she broke off a little silver leaf. There upon the bear said: "My love, what hast thou done?" The damsel answered: "I have only broken off a little silver leaf." The bear continued: "That thou shouldst not have done. It is now a chance whether we escape from hence with life." At the same moment, the whole forest was filled with a terrific roaring, and from all sides there streamed forth an innumerable multitude of wild beasts, lions, tigers, and every other kind; and they all went in pursuit of the bear and strove to tear him in pieces. Now the damsel was indeed terrified, and durst not look up, so affrighted was she. But the bear ran with all his might, and the wild beasts after him, so that when at length he came out of the forest he was almost dead with fear and faintness.

Some time after they came to another forest, where every little leaf was of bright gold, so that it glittered all around. Here the same took place as before. At last they entered a third forest, much more extensive than either of the before-mentioned, in which every, even the smallest, leaf was of the brightest diamond, so that it played and sparkled far and wide. There also the damsel could not refrain but broke a diamond leaf from a tree. Instantly there rushed forth an innumerable multitude of wild beasts, and the bear ran, the wild beasts after him, and were so quick upon him that they almost tore him in pieces before he could get out of the forest.

The bear and the damsel now journeyed on gently; for he was both weary and wounded, nor did he utter a single word on the way. At length they came to a clear spring, which flowed out of a mountain, and there they sat to rest. After having rested awhile, the bear said, "Here we must part, for now either thou or I must descend into the fountain." The damsel answered: "In that case it is I that should go down, seeing I have been so disobedient to thee." "No," replied the bear, "that thou, nevertheless, shalt not do but here is a knife; take it and kill me and cast my carcass into the fountain. Afterwards thou shalt clothe thyself in my skin, and go up to the king's palace, and beg to be employed in the court. Every time thou needest help blow in the golden pipe which I gave thee." The damsel durst not do otherwise than obey, and killed the bear, cast his body into the fountain, wrapped herself in his skin wandered with a heart full of sorrow up to the king's palace. There she got employment in the kitchen and sat in the chimney-corner raking the cinders. But every one was struck with wonder at her garb and manners, and called her Fröken Skinnpels rör i askan (Miss Skin-cloak rakes in the ashes).

After this introduction, it is related how the king and the queen and the young prince, together with their court, go to church, and the master-cook is also desirous of going. As he had no one to prepare the king's dinner, he applied to Fröken Skinnpels for assistance. The damsel long excused herself, but finally yielded to his entreaties. So when all the folks were gone their several ways, she took her golden pipe, blew in it, and said: "Up, my little *Pysslings*[28] and prepare

---

[28] See "Northern Mythology and Traditions," vol. ii. p. 94.

a dinner so dainty, that the like was never seen on royal table." Instantly there appeared a numerous swarm of little Pysslings, who began to boil, and roast, and prepare the repast, so as no one ever saw the like. When all was ready the damsel said: "Bring now my silver habit, for I also will go to church." Instantly the Pysslings brought forth the most magnificent of silver habits, and clad Fröken Skinnpels in it, and kept a careful watch over her. She then proceeded to church and seated herself on the bench between the queen and princess. But all the congregation were amazed at her beauty, and the young prince was so smitten that it seemed to him he could not live unless he could possess her.

The continuation and end of the story agree with what is above communicated.

6. A variation from Upland, called "Kråknäbba-pelsen (Crow's nib-cloak), has also a long introduction, composed of originally unconnected fragments. Of these some appear in the introduction to the story of "Rosalill och Långa Leda" (see p. 41), and in the remarks on the same story (Nos. 1 and 2); while others are borrowed from a well-known Troll story of a totally unlike kind[29].

The story treats of a stepdaughter that was sent by her wicked stepmother to tend cattle in the forest without any food. While she was sitting and weeping, a large black ox came to her and said, "If thou wilt do as I say, I will help thee." The girl consented. Then continued the ox: "Shake my ear and hold thy apron under." The girl did so and got as much delicate food as she could eat.

When she returned from the forest, the hag, her stepmother, was still more cruel towards her than before. It happened one day that the crone forgot her axe in the rain and sent her stepdaughter to fetch it. The girl went and found three little doves sitting on the haft of the axe. She spoke to them kindly, caressed them, and gave them food from her hand. The doves then flew up in a tree and consulted together how they should reward her. One of them said: "I wish that every time she speaks, a gold ring may spring out of her mouth." The second said: "I wish she may grow fairer and fairer." The third said: "I wish she may have a king for her husband."

The damsel returned home and was much more beautiful than before; whereupon the crone became envious and sent her own daughter to the forest to fetch the axe. But the crone's daughter cursed the little doves and drove

---

[29] See p. 36.

them away. They again flew into the tree and consulted together how they should reward her ill-usage. One of them said: "I wish that every time she speaks a frog may spring out of her mouth." The second said: "I wish she may grow fouler and fouler every day." The third said: "And I wish that her nose may grow longer and longer." And so it came to pass. She became uglier and uglier, and her nose grew out like a crow's nib, and became so long that she could not open a door. So, she had made a large cloak, which she hung over her nose, to conceal its ugliness.

There was now no good for the stepdaughter in staying at home, so she went to the black ox, and asked his advice. The ox said: Make haste, and take thy sister's crow's nib cloak, then we will depart from hence. The damsel did so, and when they were on their journey the ox said: "Here thou hast a piece of a tree, a bottle, and a stone cast them behind thee, one at a time, when there is need."

After travelling awhile, they perceived the Troll-wife coming after them, and the damsel cast the piece of wood behind her, and there grew up a large forest but the crone returned home for her axe and hewed down the forest. The girl then cast the bottle, and a spacious lake arose but the crone went home for her horn and drank up the whole lake. At last she cast the stone, when a lofty mountain rose up. The crone now went home for her pickaxe, for the purpose of breaking through the mountain; but with her picking and hacking the mountain fell in behind her, and she never came out.

The continuation accords in its chief points with what is related above. The stepdaughter comes to a royal palace, where she gets employment as a stair-sweeper, and rides three Sundays on the back of the ox, and magnificently clad, to church. The third Sunday the prince watches at the door and gets her little shoe. He thereupon issues an order that all the maidens in the whole country should come to the king's palace and try on the shoe, but it does not fit the foot of a single one. A little bird then sings:—

> "In the chimney sits the damsel whom the shoe fits.
> In the chimney sits the damsel whom the shoe fits."

The prince thereupon goes into the kitchen, finds little Kråknäbba-pelsen, and takes her to wife.

On the wedding-day the stepdaughter goes to the meadow to see after the black ox. The ox said: "If thou wilt requite me, take a sword and divide me into three pieces." The damsel did as he desired, although it pierced her to the heart. A comely young prince now started up, who had been enchanted, and could never have recovered the human form without the damsel's aid. Kråknäbba-pelsen's marriage was then celebrated, and with such pomp that it is famed even at the present day.

7. A variation from Upland, called "Kråkskinns-Maja, tells of a wicked queen, who had two daughters of her own and a stepdaughter. When the maidens were grown up, there came a message from a neighbouring king that they should come to his palace; because he was desirous that his son should take one of them to wife. Thereupon the queen's daughters gave their stepsister a soporific potion, because they were envious of her great beauty, and then took their departure. When the damsel awoke, she instantly set out after them, running as fast as she was able.

As the daughters were riding in their magnificent chariot, they observed a little apple come rolling out of a field and crying incessantly: "Oh! Oh! I am freezing." But they had no compassion on the little apple and ordered the driver to give it a lash with his whip, to help it on its way. They then continued their journey, and the apple rolled on and met the stepdaughter. But she did not do as the others had done, but immediately stopped, took up the apple, and warmed it in her bosom. Then said the apple: "Wait until thou art in need, and I will render thee a service in return."

Shortly after there came a little pear rolling into the road, and met the three damsels, when all took place as with the apple; a plum also rolled forth in like manner, crying that it was freezing, and received from the queen's daughters a lash from the whip, but which the stepdaughter warmed in her bosom. Thus did the queen's daughters arrive at the royal palace, and were received with feastings and many tokens of honour; but the stepdaughter sought shelter in a little but by the wayside. She there clad herself in an old cloak, made solely of crow-skins, with a veil before her face, and thus wandered up to the royal palace, and got employment in the kitchen. But the court folks made game of her wonderful appearance, and called her in derision, "Kråkskinns-Maja."

When Sunday came, and all the folks were gone to church, the stepdaughter took forth her apple, and wished for a garment of pure silver. She then said:—

> "Light before me,
> Darkness after me,
> And may no one know whither I go."

And thus, she went to church, where she seated herself between the stepsisters; but they did not recognise her, and the young prince was so smitten with her beauty, that he could not turn his eyes on any other object.

The next Sunday passed in like manner. The stepdaughter took forth her pear, wished for herself a habit of pure gold, and went to church. On the third Sunday she took her plum and clothed herself in a dress wholly of precious stones. As she was hurrying out of church, the young prince ran after her, when she lost one of her gold shoes. But the prince took it up, and issued a proclamation, that no one should be his wife, save her whose foot fitted the little gold shoe.

All the young maidens in the kingdom of whatever degree, must now go to the royal palace and try on the shoe; in doing which they sat behind a curtain, and held forth a foot, each in her turn; but the gold shoe was always too small, till Kråkskinns-Maja came. Now the prince was in no little hurry to put aside the curtain, when lo! There was no longer Kråksinns-Maja, but a beautiful princess entirely clad in precious stones. Thus did the queen's daughters return home with shame, and the prince celebrated his nuptials with the stepdaughter. Such was her reward, because she was discreet and good.

THE BOY THAT STOLE THE GIANT'S TREASURES.

I. THE SWORD, THE GOLDEN FOWLS, THE GOLDEN LANTERN, AND THE GOLDEN HARP.

From South Småland.

THERE was once a poor peasant, who had three sons. The eldest two accompanied their father to field and forest and aided him in his labour; but the youngest lad stayed at home with his mother and helped her in her occupations. Hence, he was slighted by his brothers, who treated him wrongfully whenever they had an opportunity.

After a time, the father and mother died, and the three sons were to divide the inheritance; on which occasion, as may easily be imagined, the elder brothers took for their share all that was of any value, leaving nothing for their young brother. When everything else had been appropriated, there remained only an old split kneading-trough that neither of the two would have. One of the brothers thereupon said, "The old trough is exactly the thing for our young brother, he is so fond of baking and coddling." The lad, as he well might, thought this was but a poor inheritance; but he had no remedy, and from that time he was convinced there was no good to be got by staying at home. So, bidding his brothers farewell, he went out into the world to try his luck. On coming to the water-side he caulked his trough with oakum and so made a little boat of it, using two sticks for oars. He then rowed away.

Having crossed the water, he came to a spacious palace, into which he entered, and demanded to speak with the king. The king said, "What is thy family and thy errand?" The lad answered, "I am a poor peasant's son, who has nothing in the world but an old kneading-trough. I come hither in search of employment." When the king heard this he laughed, and said, "Thou hast, indeed, but a small inheritance; but luck often takes a wonderful turn. The boy was then received among the king's under-servants and was well liked by all for his courage and activity.

We must now relate that the king, to whom the palace belonged, had an only daughter. She was both beautiful and discreet so that her beauty and understanding were the subject of discourse throughout the whole realm, and wooers, from the east and west, came to demand her; but the princess said *nay* to all of them, unless they could bring her, as a bridal present, four precious things that were possessed by a giant on the other side of the water. These were—a golden sword, two gold fowls, a golden lantern, and a harp of gold. Many warriors and sons of kings had gone forth to gain these treasures, but not one had returned, for the giant had seized and eaten them all. This was a cause of grief to the king; he was fearful that his daughter would never get a husband, nor himself a son-in-law, who should inherit his kingdom.

When the lad heard talk of this, he thought to himself that it would be well worth while to make an attempt to win the king's fair daughter so, full of these thoughts, he one day appeared before the king and told his errand, but the king was incensed, and said, "How canst thou, who art a poor peasant, think of performing that which no warrior has hitherto been able to accomplish?" Nevertheless, the boy persisted in his design, and begged for leave to try his luck. When the king saw his resolution, his anger ceased, and he gave him permission, adding, "Thy life is at stake, and I would not willingly lose thee." They then separated.

The lad then went down to the water, found his trough, which he carefully examined on all sides, after which he again rowed over the water, and lay on the watch near the giant's dwelling, where he stayed during the night. In the morning, before it was light, the giant went to his barn and began threshing, so that it resounded through the mountain. On hearing this, the lad gathered a number of small stones into his pouch, crept on to the roof and made a little hole, through which he could look down into the barn. The giant was won't at all times to wear his golden sword by his side, which possessed the extra ordinary property of ringing loudly whenever its owner was angry. While the giant was threshing with might and main, the boy cast a small stone so that it fell on the sword, at which the weapon gave forth a loud clank. "Why dost thou clank?" asked the giant, peevishly: "I am not angry with thee." He resumed his thrashing; but at the same moment the sword clanked again. The giant went on threshing, and the sword clanked for the third time. The giant then lost his patience, unclasped his belt, and cast the sword out at the door of the barn. "Lie there," said he, "until I have done my threshing." The lad, however, did not wait for that, but, creeping down from the roof, he seized the sword, ran to his boat, and rowed across the water. There he concealed his booty and rejoiced that his enterprise had ended so favourably.

The next day the boy filled his scrip with corn, laid a bundle of best in the boat, and again betook himself to the giant's habitation. After lying on the watch for a while he perceived where the giant's three golden fowls were spreading out their wings by the water's edge, so that they glittered beautifully in the bright sunshine. He was instantly at hand, and began softly enticing the birds, at the same time giving them corn from his scrip. All the time they were engaged in eating the lad kept drawing nearer and nearer to the water, till at last all the three golden fowls were assembled in his little boat. He then sprang in himself, and having tied the fowls with the bast, pushed off the boat, and rowed away with all speed, to conceal his booty on the opposite side.

On the third day, the lad put some lumps of salt into his scrip, and again crossed the water. When night drew near, he remarked how the smoke rose from the giants dwelling; and thence concluded that the giant's wife was busied in preparing food; so, creeping up on the roof, he looked down the chimney, and saw where a huge pot was boiling on the fire. Taking then the lumps of salt from his scrip, he let them fall one by one into the pot. He then stole down from the roof and waited to see what would happen.

In a little while, the giantess lifted the pot from the fire poured out the porridge and placed the bowl on the table. The giant was hungry, and instantly began to eat but no sooner had he tasted the porridge and found it was both salt and bitter, than he started up overcome with anger. The crone excused herself, and thought the porridge was good; but the giant bade her taste it herself; he, for his part, would eat no more of her mess. The crone now tasted the porridge, but having so done, grinned most fearfully; for such nauseous stuff she had never before tasted.

The giantess had now no alternative but to boil some fresh porridge for her husband. For this purpose, she took the pail, reached the gold lantern down from the wall, and ran to the well to fetch water. Having set the lantern down on the edge of the well, she stooped forwards to draw up the water, when the lad rushed towards her, and seizing her by the feet, pitched her headlong into the well, and possessed himself of the golden lantern. He then ran off and crossed the water in safety. In the meanwhile, the giant sat wondering why his wife stayed so long away, and at length went in search of her; but nothing of her could he see, only a dull plashing was audible from the well. The giant was now aware that his wife was in the water, and with great difficulty helped her out. "Where is my golden lantern?" was his first question, as soon as the crone began a little to recover herself. "I don't know," answered she, but it seemed to me that some one seized me by the feet and cast me into the well. The giant was highly incensed at this intelligence and said: "Three of my most precious things have now disappeared, and I have nothing left save my gold harp but the thief, whoever he may he, shall not get that. I will secure it under twelve locks."

While this was passing at the giants, the lad was sitting on the opposite side rejoicing that all had turned out so well; but the most difficult task still remained to be performed—to steal the giant's golden harp. He meditated for a long time how this was to be effected; but could hit on no plan, and, therefore, resolved to cross over to the giant's, and there wait for an opportunity.

No sooner said than done. The boy rowed over and stationed himself on the watch. But the giant was now on the look-out, got sight of the boy, and, rushing quickly forth, seized him. "So, I have caught thee at last, thou thief," said the giant, almost bursting with rage. "It is no other than thou who has stolen my sword, my three golden fowls, and my golden lantern." The lad was now terrified, thinking that his last hour has come and he answered meekly: "Let me have my life, dear father; I will never come again." "No," replied the giant, "it shall go with thee as it has gone with the others. No one passes alive out of my hands." The giant then caused the boy to be shut up in a sty, and gave him nuts and milk, that he might grow fat, previous to slaughtering him, and eating him up.

The lad was now a prisoner but ate and drank and made himself comfortable. After some time had passed, the giant was desirous of ascertaining whether he was yet sufficiently fattened: he went, therefore, to the sty, bored a hole in the wall, and ordered the boy to put one of his fingers through. But the lad being aware of his object, instead of a finger, put forth a peg of peeled alder. The giant made an incision in it, so that the red sap dropped from the wood, whence he concluded that the boy must still be very lean, seeing that his flesh was so hard; and therefore caused a larger allowance to be given him of milk and nuts than before.

After another interval had elapsed the giant went again to the sty and ordered the boy to put his finger through the hole in the wall. The lad this time put forth a cabbage stalk, and the giant made a cut in it with his knife. He now thought his captive must be sufficiently plump, as his flesh seemed so soft.

When it was morning, the giant said to his wife Mother, "the boy seems now fat enough; take him, therefore, and bake him in the oven. I will in the meanwhile go and invite our kinsmen to the feast." The crone promised to do as her husband had commanded; so, having made the oven very hot, she laid hold on the boy for the purpose of baking him. "Place thyself on the peel," said the giantess. The boy did so; but when the crone raised the handle of the peel, he contrived to fall off, and thus it happened at least ten times. At length, the crone became angry, and scolded him for his awkwardness; but the boy excused himself by saying that he did not know exactly how to sit. "Wait, I will show thee," said the giantess, placing herself on the peel, with crooked back and drawn up knees. But scarcely had she so done when the boy, seizing hold of the handle, shoved the beldam into the oven and closed the mouth. He then took the crone's fur cloak, stuffed it with straw, and laid it on the bed; seized the giant's great bunch of keys, opened the twelve locks, snatched up the golden harp and hurried down to his boat, which lay concealed among the reeds by the water-side.

When the giant returned home, "Where can my wife be?" thought he to himself, not seeing her anywhere in the house. "Ah, she is no doubt lying down awhile to rest; that I can well imagine." But long as the crone had slept, she, nevertheless, would not wake up, although the guests were every moment expected. So, the giant went to wake her, crying aloud: "Wake up! wake up, mother!" But no one answered. He called a second time, but still without an answer. The giant now lost his temper, and gave the fur cloak a violent shake and now discovered that it was not his old woman, but a bundle of straw over which her clothes had been laid. At this discovery the giant began to suspect mischief and ran off to look after his golden harp. But the bunch of keys was away, the twelve locks had been opened, and the golden harp had also vanished. And when at length he went to the mouth of the oven, to look after his festal repast, lo!—there sat his own wife, baked in the oven and grinning horribly at him.

The giant was now beside himself with grief and rage and rushed out to take vengeance on the author of all this evil. On reaching the water's edge, he saw the boy sitting in his boat, and playing on the harp, the tones of which resounded over the water, and the golden strings glittered beautifully in the bright sunshine. The giant sprang into the water to seize the boy; but finding it too deep, he laid himself down on the shore and began to drink, for the purpose of draining off the water. As he drank with all his might, he caused such a current that the little boat was borne nearer and nearer to the shore; but just as he was in the act of seizing it, he had drunk too much and burst. Such was the end of the giant.

The giant now lay dead on the land; but the boy rowed back over the water with great exultation and glee. On reaching the opposite shore, he combed his golden locks, arrayed himself in costly garments, girded the giants golden sword by his side, took the golden harp in one hand and the golden lantern in the other, enticed the golden fowls after him, and, thus equipped, entered the hall where the king was sitting at table with his courtiers. When the king saw the youth, he was overjoyed at heart, and beheld him with friendly eyes. But the youth, approaching the king's fair daughter, greeted her courteously, and laid the giant's treasures at her feet. There was now great joy throughout the royal palace, that the princess had obtained the giant's treasures, and also a bridegroom so comely and so valorous. The king shortly after caused his daughter's nuptials to be solemnized with great pomp and rejoicing; and when the old king died, the boy was chosen king of the country, and lived there both long and happy. Since that time, I was no longer with them.

1. In "Runa, en Skrift för Fäderneslandets Fornvänner,"[30] there is a popular story (folk-sägen) from Dalsland, the continuation of which is a pendant to the preceding. It runs thus:—

A man had eight sons, the youngest of whom was named Roll. They went out in the world to seek their fortune, and came to a giant's dwelling, where they found no one at home but the giant's wife. The boys besought her to give them a lodging for the night but received for answer: "I will see when father giant comes borne." Shortly after, father giant returned, who granted their request, adding: "It is good, we shall now get a suitor for each of our seven daughters."

In the evening, when all had retired to rest, Roll crept into a corner and listened to the giant and giantess's conversation, from which it appeared that it was their intention to kill the boys as soon as they had fallen asleep. In order to distinguish them from her own children, the giantess had placed caps on the heads of the boys, and bound headcloths round those of the girls. But Roll, stealing out of the corner, placed the caps on the giant's children, and the headcloths on his brothers. So, when the giant rose up in the night to kill the boys, he destroyed his own children instead of them. Roll then waked his brothers and said: "Let us be gone, I have now saved you." He then took the giant's club, by the aid of which a person could pass over running water, and so the boys made their escape.

---

[30] Edited by Richard Dybeck, Stockh., 1843, part iv. p. 33.

When Roll and his brothers had long wandered about, they came to a royal palace. The king who owned it said to Roll: "Get me the giant's golden coverlet, and thou shalt have my youngest daughter." Roll engaged to make the attempt, provided a rope were given him. A rope was given him accordingly, to one end of which be fixed a long book; then, proceeding to the giant's dwelling, he climbed up to the roof, let the rope down through a crack, and so drew up the beautiful gold coverlet. When the giant discovered that his gold coverlet was gone, he called aloud: "Roll hast thou taken my gold coverlet?" Roll answered: "Yes, dear father." He then returned to the king and delivered to him the costly coverlet, according to his engagement.

The king then said to Roll: "Thou must now get me the giant's Yule hog."[31] Roll promised to try. So, taking a pail, he filled it with hog's beans, and enticed the hog with him to the king. The next day he heard the giant calling out: "Roll! hast thou taken my Yule hog?" Roll answered: "Yes, dear father."

The king again said to Roll: "Thou must get me the giant's light, which gives light over seven kingdoms." Roll promised to do his best and proceeded to the giant's. At night the giantess came out to milk the cow and set the light down by side of her. But Roll was at hand, snatched up the light, and was in the act of making his escape over the river, when the giant made his appearance, and seized both Roll and the light.

Roll was now destined to death but just then came the giant's son and asked his father to his birthday feast. The giant excused himself, saying he had something else to do; though at last he went. The giantess, in the meantime, remained, and heated the oven seven times hotter than usual, in order to bake Roll. When the oven was thus heated, the boy said: "Dear mother, do you see the seven stars in the oven?" The giantess peeped in, but in the same moment, Roll pushed her into the oven, and cast a bundle of straw after her.

Roll now hastened down to the water and took boat, followed by the giant and his son. Finding they could not reach him in any other way, they tried to drink up the water. By daybreak there was very little water remaining. Then Roll, pointing to the rising sun, said, "See what a fine young damsel there is yonder!" The giant and his son looked accordingly, and both burst. But Roll returned to the king's palace and obtained his youngest daughter.

---

[31] See "Northern Mythology." ii. p. 50.

2. A version from South Småland, after an introduction, runs thus:—

After Raskargod had delivered his six brothers from the Troll-wife, and conducted them home, he besought his father for leave to go again to the mountain. But the king had a dread of the Trolls, and strictly forbade his son to do them any further harm or annoyance. But the son reeked little of his father's command and resolved on going once more and making sport of the wicked Troll-wife.

Raskargod now set out and arrived at the mountain just as the Troll was busied in washing her linen, which was all bloody from her having cut the throats of her seven daughters in the preceding night. The youth approached her, greeted her, and inquired whether he could assist her in her labour. When the witch saw him again, she suppressed her anger, and gave him many fair words, in order to get him into her power. Raskargod then helped her to wash the clothes. When some time had thus passed, the Troll bade him see to the water in the great kettle, while she went to the forest to fetch wood. Raskargod promised to do what she desired but while the crone was absent, he threw dirt and soot into the kettle, and also sprinkled the clothes with the same. Then taking all of value that he could find, he, with the help of his Troll-staff, crossed the river with all speed.

He had just reached the opposite shore, when the Troll-wife returned from the forest and saw the damage he had done to her wash. Where upon she cried out: "Raskargod, is it thou who hast taken my silver and gold, and spoiled my fine clothes?" Raskargod answered, "Yes, dear mother, I did it." The crone asked, "Art thou coming hither again?" "Yes, to be sure, dear mother," answered the youth. The prince then returned home to his father, but the king being incensed at his disobedience, proscribed him throughout the whole kingdom, so that the prince was obliged to seek an asylum far in a forest, where he found a poor woman who gave him house and home.

Some time having passed thus, the king's son was again seized with a strong desire to pay another visit to the Troll-wife. He therefore set out, and on reaching the mountain, was well received there. One day the Troll said she would go and see her sister, who lived at some distance. She went accordingly, and Raskargod remained behind alone. The prince now began to examine the mountain on every side, until he found a spacious apartment filled with gold, silver, and other precious things. In one apartment he also found a large book, in which were written down the names of the Trolls who were dead and had left riches in their mountains. Raskargod took the great book and everything of value and crossed over the river. Just as he had reached the opposite shore the Troll-wife returned home, and called to him, "Raskargod, is it thou who hast taken my silver and gold?" The king's son answered, "Yes, dear mother, I have." The crone asked: "Art thou coming hither again?" Raskargod replied, "Yes, to be sure, dear mother."

The prince now obtained a ship and men from his father, and sailed to England, where he won the king's daughter. He afterwards fitted out four large ships, with which he sailed away to seek for the mountains that were spoken of in the Troll's book. Thus, he acquired immense wealth. In the last mountain he found an apartment in which the Trolls kept their provisions, of which it is related, that it was not full of food, but of serpents, toads, and other reptiles, which crawled down the mountain, but were unable to go up again.

Raskargod was at length reconciled with his father, and richly rewarded the widow who had given him shelter, and then returned to England, where he betook himself to rest and lives and fares well even to this day.

II. THE GOLDEN LANTERN, THE GOLDEN GOAT, AND THE GOLDEN CLOAK.

THERE was once a poor widow who had three sons. The two elders went out to work for their living. While at home they were of little use, as they seldom complied with their mother's wishes, whatever she might say to them. But the youngest lad always remained at home and assisted the old widow in her daily occupations. Hence, he was much beloved by his mother, but disliked by his brothers, who in mockery gave him the nickname of *Pinkel.*

One day the old widow said to her sons: "You must now go abroad in the world and seek your fortunes while you can. I am no longer able to feed you here at home, now that you are grown up." The lads answered, that they wished for nothing better, since it was contrary to their mother's will that they should remain at home. They then prepared for their departure, and set out on their journey but, after wandering about from place to place, were unable to procure any employment.

After journeying thus for a long time, they came, late one evening, to a vast lake. Far out in the water there was an island, on which there appeared a strong light, as of fire. The lads stopped on shore observing the wondrous light, and thence concluded that there must be human beings in the place. As it was now dark, and the brothers knew not where to find a shelter for the night, they resolved on taking a boat that lay among the reeds, and rowing over to the island to beg a lodging. With this view, they placed themselves in the boat and rowed across. On approaching the island, they perceived a little hut standing at the water's edge; on reaching which they discovered that the bright light, that shone over the neighbourhood, proceeded from a golden lantern, that stood at the door of the hut. In the yard without, a large goat was wandering about, with golden horns, to which small bells were fastened, that gave forth a pleasing sound whenever the animal moved. The brothers wondered much at all this, but most of all at the old crone, who with her daughter inhabited the hut. The crone was both old and ugly, but was sumptuously clad in a pelisse or cloak, worked so artificially with golden threads that it glittered like burnished gold in every hem. The lads saw now very clearly that they had come to no ordinary human being, but to a Troll or Siö-ra[32].

After some deliberation the brothers entered, and saw the crone standing by the fireplace, and stirring with a ladle in a large pot that was boiling on the hearth. They told their story and prayed to be allowed to pass the night there, but the crone answered *no*, at the same time directing them to a royal palace, which lay on the other side of the lake. While speaking she kept looking intently on the youngest boy, as he was standing and casting his eyes over everything in the hut. The crone said to him: "What is thy name, my boy?" The lad answered smartly: "I am called Pinkel." The Troll then said: "Thy brothers can go their way, but thou shalt stay here; for thou appearest to me very crafty, and my mind tells me that I have no good to expect from thee, if thou shouldst stay long at the king's palace." Pinkel now humbly begged to be allowed to accompany his brothers and promised never to cause the crone harm or annoyance. At length he also got leave to depart; after which the brothers hastened to the boat, not a little glad that all three had escaped so well in this adventure.

---

[32] See "Northern Mythology," i. p. 75.

Towards the morning they arrived at a royal palace, larger and more magnificent than anything they had ever seen before. They entered and begged for employment. The eldest two were received as helpers in the royal stables and the youngest was taken as page to the king's young son; and, being a sprightly intelligent lad, he soon won the good will of everyone, and rose from day to day in the king's favour. At this his brothers were sorely nettled, not enduring that he should be preferred to themselves. At length they consulted together how they might compass the fall of their young brother, in the belief that afterwards they should prosper better than before.

They therefore presented themselves one day before the king and gave him an exaggerated account of the beautiful lantern that shed light over both land and water, adding that it will beseemed a king to lack so precious a jewel. On hearing this the king's attention was excited, and he asked: "Where is this lantern to be found, and who can procure it for me?" The brothers answered: "No one can do that unless it be our brother Pinkel. He knows best where the lantern is to be found." The king was now filled with desire to obtain the golden lantern, about which he had heard tell, and commanded the youth to be called. When Pinkel came, the king said: "If thou canst procure me the golden lantern, that shines over land and water, I will make thee the chief man in my whole court." The youth promised to do his best to execute his lord's behest, and the king praised him for his willingness; but the brothers rejoiced at heart; for they well knew it was a perilous undertaking, which could hardly terminate favourably.

Pinkel now prepared a little boat, and, unaccompanied by any one, rowed over to the island inhabited by the Troll crone. When he arrived it was already evening, and the crone was busied in boiling porridge for supper, as was her custom. The youth creeping softly up to the roof, cast from time to time a handful of salt through the chimney, so that it fell down into the pot that was boiling on the hearth. When the porridge was ready, and the crone had begun to eat, she could not conceive what had made it so salt and bitter. She was out of humour, and chided her daughter, thinking that she had put too much salt into the porridge but let her dilute the porridge as she might, it could not be eaten, so salt and bitter was it. She then ordered her daughter to go to the well, that was just at the foot of the hill, and fetch water, in order to prepare fresh porridge. The maiden answered: "How can I go to the well? It is so dark out of doors, that I cannot find the way over the hill." "Then take my gold lantern," said the crone peevishly. The girl took the beautiful gold lantern accordingly and hastened away to fetch the water. But as she stooped to lift the pail, Pinkel, who was on the watch, seized her by the feet, and cast her headlong into the water. He then took the golden lantern and betook himself in all haste to his boat.

In the meantime, the crone was wondering why her daughter stayed out so long, and, at the same moment, chancing to look through the window she saw the light gleaming far out on the water. At this sight she was sorely vexed, and, hurrying down to the shore, cried aloud. "Is that thou, Pinkel?" The youth answered: "Yes, dear mother, it is I." The Troll continued: "Art thou not a great knave?" The lad answered: "Yes, dear mother, I am so." The crone now began to lament and complain, saying: "Ah! what a fool was I to let thee go from me; I might have been sure thou wouldst play me some trick. If thou ever comest hither again, thou shalt not escape." And so the matter rested for that time.

Pinkel now returned to the king's palace, and became the chief person at court, as the king had promised. But when the brothers were informed what complete success he had had in his adventure, they became yet more envious and embittered than before, and often consulted together how they might accomplish the fall of their young brother and gain the king's favour for themselves.

Both brothers went, therefore, a second time before the king, and began relating at full length about the beautiful goat that had horns of the purest gold, from which little gold bells were suspended, which gave forth a pleasing sound, whenever the animal moved. They added, that it will became so rich a king to lack so costly a treasure. On hearing their story, the king was greatly excited, and said: "Where is this goat to be found, and who can procure it for me?" The brothers answered: "That no one can do unless it be our brother Pinkel; for he knows best where the goat is to be found." The king then felt a strong desire to possess the goat with the golden horns, and therefore commanded the youth to appear before him. When Pinkel came, the king said: "Thy brothers have been telling me of a beautiful goat with horns of the purest gold, and little bells fastened to the horns, which ring whenever the animal moves. Now it is my will that thou go and procure for me this goat. If thou art successful, I will make thee lord over a third part of my kingdom." The youth having listened to this speech, promised to execute his lord's commission, if only fortune would befriend him. The king then praised his readiness, and the brothers were glad at heart, believing that Pinkel would not escape this time so well as the first.

Pinkel now made the necessary preparations and rowed to the island where the Troll-wife dwelt. When he reached it, evening was already advanced, and it was dark, so that no one could be aware of his coming, the golden lantern being no longer there, but shedding its light in the royal palace. The youth now deliberated with himself how to get the golden goat; but the task was no easy one for the animal lay every night in the crone's hut. At length it occurred to his mind that there was one method which might probably prove successful, though, nevertheless, sufficiently difficult to carry into effect.

At night, when it was time for the crone and her daughter to go to bed, the girl went as usual to bolt the door. But Pinkel was just outside on the watch and had placed a piece of wood behind the door, so that it would not shut close. The girl stood for a long time trying to lock it, but to no purpose. On perceiving this, the crone thought there was something out of order, and called out, that the door might very well remain unlocked for the night as soon as it was daylight, they could ascertain what was wanting. The girl then left the door ajar and laid herself down to sleep. When the night was a little more advanced, and the crone and her daughter were sunk in deep repose, the youth stole softly into the hut, and approached the goat where he lay stretched out on the hearth. Pinkel now stuffed wool into all the golden bells, lest their sound might betray him then seizing the goat, he bore it off to his boat. When he had reached the middle of the lake, he took the wool out of the goats' ears, and the animal moved so that the bells rang aloud. At the sound the crone awoke, ran down to the water, and cried in an angry tone: "Is that thou, Pinkel?" The youth answered: "Yes, dear mother, it is." The crone said: "Hast thou stolen my gold goat?" The youth answered: "Yes, dear mother, I have." The Troll continued: "Art thou not a big knave?" Pinkel returned for answer: "Yes, I am so, dear mother." Now the beldam began to whine and complain, saying: "Ah! what a simpleton was I for letting thee slip away from me. I well knew thou wouldst play me some trick. But if thou comest hither ever again, thou shalt never go hence."

Pinkel now returned to the king's court and obtained the government of a third part of the kingdom, as the king has promised. But when the brothers heard how the enterprise had succeeded, and also saw the beautiful lantern and the goat with golden horns, which were regarded by everyone as great wonders, they became still more hostile and embittered than ever. They could think of nothing but how they might accomplish his destruction.

They went, therefore, one day again before the king, to whom they gave a most elaborate description of the Troll-crone's fur cloak, that shone like the brightest gold, and was worked with golden threads in every seam. The brothers said, it was more befitting a queen than a Troll to possess such a treasure and added that that alone was wanting to the king's good fortune. When the king heard all this, he became very thoughtful, and said: "Where is this cloak to be found, and who can procure it for me?" The brothers answered: "No one can do that except our brother Pinkel for he knows best where the gold cloak is to be found. The king was thereupon seized with an ardent longing to possess the gold cloak and commanded the youth to be called before him. When Pinkel came, the king said "I have long been aware that thou hast an affection for my young daughter; and thy brothers have been telling me of a beautiful fur cloak, which shines with the reddest gold in every seam. It is, therefore, my will that thou go and procure for me this cloak. If thou art successful, thou shalt be my son-in-law, and after me shalt inherit the kingdom." When the youth heard this, he was glad beyond measure, and promised either to win the young maiden, or perish in the attempt. The king thereupon praised his readiness; but the brothers were delighted in their false hearts, and trusted that that enterprise would prove their brother's destruction.

Pinkel then betook himself to his boat and crossed over to the island inhabited by the Troll-crone. On the way, he anxiously deliberated with himself how he might get possession of the crone's gold cloak; but it appeared to him not very likely that his undertaking would prove successful, seeing that the Troll always wore the cloak upon her. So, after having concerted diverse plans, one more hazardous than another, it occurred to him that he would try one method, which might perhaps succeed, although it was bold and rash.

In pursuance of his scheme be bound a bag under his clothes and walked with trembling step and humble demeanour into the beldam's hut. On perceiving him, the Troll cast on him a savage glance, and said: "Pinkel, is that thou?" The youth answered. "Yes, dear mother, it is." The crone was overjoyed and said: "Although thou art come voluntarily into my power, thou canst not surely hope to escape again from hence, after having played me so many tricks." She then took a large knife and prepared to make an end of poor Pinkel; but the youth, seeing her design, appeared sorely terrified, and said: "If I must need die, I think I might be allowed to choose the manner of my death. I would rather eat myself to death with milk-porridge, than be killed with a knife." The crone thought to herself that the youth had made a bad choice, and therefore promised to comply with his wish. She then set a huge pot on the fire, in which she put a large quantity of porridge. When the mess was ready, she placed it before Pinkel, that he might eat, who for every spoonful of porridge that he put into his mouth, poured two into the bag that was tied under his clothes. At length the crone began to wonder how Pinkel could contrive to swallow such a quantity; but just at the same moment the youth, making a show of being sick to death, sank down from his seat as if he were dead, and unobserved cut a hole in the bag, so that the porridge ran over the floor.

The crone, thinking that Pinkel had burst with the quantity of porridge he had eaten, was not a little glad, clapped her hands together, and ran off to look for her daughter, who was gone to the well. But as the weather was wet and stormy, she first took off her beautiful fur cloak and laid it aside in the hut. Before she could have proceeded far, the youth came to life again, and springing up like lightning, seized on the golden cloak, and ran off at the top of his speed.

Shortly after, the crone perceived Pinkel as he was rowing in his little boat. On seeing him alive again and observing the gold cloak glittering on the surface of the water, she was angry beyond all conception, and ran far cut on the strand, crying: "Is that thou, Pinkel?" The youth answered: "Yes, it is I, dear mother." The crone said: "Hast thou taken my beautiful gold cloak?" Pinkel responded: "Yes, dear mother, I have." The Troll continued: "Art thou not a great knave?" The youth replied: "Yes, I am so, dear mother." The old witch was now almost beside herself, and began to whine and lament, and said: "Ah! how silly was it of me to let thee slip away. I was well assured thou wouldst play me many wicked tricks." They then parted from each other.

The Troll-wife now returned to her hut, and Pinkel crossed the water, and arrived safely at the king's palace; there he delivered the gold cloak, of which everyone said that a more sumptuous garment was never seen nor heard of. The king honourably kept his word with the youth and gave him his young daughter to wife. Pinkel afterwards lived happy and content to the end of his days; but his brothers were and continued to be helpers in the stable as long as they lived.

A version, with slight variations, from Östergötland, relates that the Troll-wife possessed three precious things, a *Gold brand*, a *Gold goat*, and a *Golden coverlet*. For the purpose of getting the gold brand, the boy mounts up to the roof of the crone's hut, and drops stones down the chimney, causing the sparks to fly about all the apartment. When the Troll goes out to ascertain the cause, the boy, who was on the alert, steals the shining brand, and hastily flees across the lake to another country.

To get the golden goat, the boy uses the same stratagem as that related in the preceding story.

When the crone had thus lost both her gold brand and gold goat, she was apprehensive lest she should also lose her beautiful gold coverlet, and, therefore, hid it under her bed. At night the lad stole into the hut, crept under the bed, and began pulling the coverlet softly to him but the Troll-wife waking discovered the thief, and seized him.

The boy is now to be killed, and chooses how he shall die, as in the foregoing story; but the crone, not feeling certain that he is dead, strikes him on the stomach and bursts the bag, so that all the porridge runs out. Thinking that the boy was now killed outright, she runs out in her joy to tell her neighbours all that had passed. But the lad waiting his opportunity, seizes the beautiful coverlet, and flees away over the water to the king's palace, whose daughter he gets for a wife.

III. THE GOLDEN HORSE, THE MOON-LANTERN, AND THE PRINCESS IN THE TROLL'S CAGE.[33]

THERE were once two poor boys, who had neither father nor mother, and were obliged to go about the country begging for a livelihood. In the course of their wandering they came one day to a corn-field, where the grains stood higher than a man. The elder then said: "Let us pluck some cars; we have not yet had any breakfast." The younger brother agreed, and the lads went into the field. They had not been there long before a man met them, he was of large stature and had a fierce countenance. The giant (for such he was) said: "Who has given you leave to pluck ears in my cornfield?" The boys answered: "We thought thou wouldst not be angry with us we were very hungry, and thou hast, nevertheless, an abundance left." The giant now affected great kindness and said: "Neither am I angry; and if ye will follow me home, ye shall eat your fill, and have no need to go about gathering ears of corn." This proposal pleased the elder boy exceedingly; but his brother thought the giant entertained some evil design, and was, therefore, unwilling to place himself in his power. They then consulted with each other. The elder said: "I think we should go with him." "No," answered the younger, "I think it best not." The elder replied: "We can at all events follow him; if we find things pleasant there, we can always go away." The giant now asked whether they would accompany him or not. "Yes, surely," answered the elder brother; and so the two brothers followed the giant home to his dwelling.

On reaching the place, the giant conducted them into a small room, and gave them such entertainment as they had never known before. He then went out and locked the door. The elder boy said: "Was it not clever of me to propose going with the giant? Now we are well off and have no occasion to go about begging." The younger answered: "We have not yet seen how it will all fall out, I am not pleased at our being locked in, and unable to come and go as has been our wont." The elder lad would give no ear to these words, but laid himself

---

[33] This tale occurs in:

1. Norwegian.—See Asbjörnsen og Moe, ut sup., No. 1. "Om Askeladden, som stjal Troldets Solvænder, Sengetæppe Og Guldharpe."

2. English.—In Tabart's Fairy Tales, and elsewhere, under the title of *Jack and the Beanstalk.*

down to sleep, while the younger placed himself on the watch by the door, to discover what was going on outside in the habitation. Several days passed in this manner; the brothers had no lack of food, but were constantly locked in.

One evening, when the boy as usual stood peeping through a cranny in the wall, he saw the giant enter the apartment and ask for food. While he was eating, he inquired of his wife whether the two boys would soon be sufficiently fat. The giantess answered: "One of them is fleshy enough, but the other is only so so." The giant said: "I think they both ought to be fat, provided thou givest them food enough. I will now go and invite our kindred to the feast; thou meanwhile canst kill the two boys, so that they may be eaten tomorrow." When the lad heard this conversation, he went and waked his brother, and told him what he had seen and heard. "What thou sayest cannot be true," said the elder, yet in terror crept close to the wall. When they looked through the opening, the giant had just finished his meal, and called to the maid servant to fetch him water. "Hast thou forgotten," said he, "that I always drink as soon as I have eaten?" The servant-girl excused herself by saying, it was so dark that she could not find the way to the well. "Take my *Moon-lantern*, then," said the giant in a harsh tone. The girl thereupon took from the wall a lantern that shone like the moon at full and went to fetch water. After the giant had quenched his thirst, he began talking again to his wife: "I will now," said he, "saddle my *Golden horse*, and ride to invite our guests. In the meantime, take the boys out, that thou mayest not forget them." He then departed. When the elder boy heard these words, he was mortally terrified, and besought his brother to devise some means of saving their lives. The other answered: "Be of good cheer; I shall, no doubt, hit on some plan."

When the night was a little advanced, the giantess came in to the two boys. She affected to be very friendly and uttered many fair words. "Follow me, little boys," said she, "and ye shall look about the cottage tonight ye shall sleep there." The boys did as she bade them, although the elder was almost dying with fear. The crone now let them go to bed, then laying herself near them, she soon fell into a deep sleep. Towards midnight the younger lad rose up and placed a fire-steel over the giantess's head; for he knew well that steel has power over giants and other Trolls[34], so that if it be laid over them while they are

---

[34] For instances of this virtue in steel, see "Northern Mythology," ii. *passim*.

asleep, they cannot wake before it is daylight. The crone now slept more profoundly and continued sleeping till the following day; but the younger lad waked his brother, and they both stole out of the place, and hastened with all speed from the spot.

Towards dawn they came to a large grange, where they knocked and begged for shelter. The owner of the grange inquired whence they came, seeing that they sought a lodging at so late an hour. The brothers thereupon related their adventure, how with great difficulty they had escaped from the giant. The man received them well, and gave them food, and whatever else they stood in need of. He said: "Few are they who escape with life from the giant's clutches. Take care, therefore, that he does not entice you again. But he has no power as long as you do not pass across the broad ditch that separates our fields." The boys thanked the farmer for his good advice, and promised m all respects to do as he had said.

About noon the giant came riding on his gold horse and stopped close by the broad ditch. His steed had golden hair and was so beautiful that it shone and sparkled whithersoever it went. When the giant saw the two boys, he called to them and asked why they had run away from him, adding, at the same time, a deal of wheedling talk, and saying: "Come back with me, little boys; I will give my gold horse to one of you, and the other shall have a beautiful princess, whom I have in my power." But the boys gave no ear to his talk, and ran off, to wander and beg about the country.

After rambling about a considerable time, they came at length to a spacious royal palace, into which they entered and prayed for employment. The king, to whom the palace belonged, took a liking to the younger lad, on account of his activity, and received him among his pages; but the elder brother went about begging as before. Things continued thus for some time, and the youth was well liked by everyone. When it came to the elder lad's knowledge what good fortune had attended his brother at court, he became extremely jealous, and never rested until he also was taken into the king's service. The younger brother, now become a courtier, interceded for the elder, who was received as a stable-lad. But in proportion as the younger was well spoken of by all, the stable-boy was an object of aversion, on account of his baseness and falsehood. Hence his heart was filled with malice, and he thought of nothing so much as how he might ruin his brother and gain the king's favour for himself.

One day when the king happened to be in the stable viewing his stud, and after he had looked at every horse, he stopped by the one on which he himself was in the habit of riding, and, patting the animal on the flank, said to those about him: "Tell me where in the whole world you have ever seen so excellent a horse as this?" The stable-lad instantly answered: "Sir king, your horse is certainly handsome; but I know of another that by far excels it." The king was now all attention, and asked: "Where is that horse to be seen, and who can obtain it for me?" The lad answered: "I believe no one can obtain it, unless it be my brother; he is likely to know best where it is to be found." The king was now seized with a strong desire to possess the horse, which he had heard so highly praised, and commanded the courtier brother to set out and fetch it. Although the courtier had no great fear, he would, nevertheless, have preferred staying at home. But the stable lad was glad at heart, thinking that his brother would hardly return safe from the journey.

The youth now made his preparations and set forth on his enterprise. When he arrived at the grange, he went in, greeted the farmer courteously, and solicited his good advice as to the course he should take in executing the king's commission. When the farmer recalled to his memory the boy that had escaped from the giant, he received him kindly, and promised him all the assistance in his power. They then held a consultation together, the result of which I will now relate.

In the evening, when the sun had set in the forest, the youth stole forth to the giant's dwelling. He tied a stick to the end of a rope, then cast the stick in through the stable window, by means of which apparatus he climbed up the wall. As soon as he had reached the window, he drew the rope after him, and by its aid descended into the giant's stable. He then saddled the gold horse, opened the door, and hastened away with all speed. On coming to the farmer's house, there was great joy there that his enterprise had been so successful. The young man would not, however, make a long stay there, but, without loss of time, returned to the palace, where the beautiful gold horse excited much admiration, but in no one so great as in the king himself. From that day the young courtier rose higher and higher in the good graces of the king; but the stable-lad was exasperated at his brother's good fortune, and still fostered evil designs against him.

One day the king went to his stable to look at his horses, according to his custom. When he had viewed them all, he stopped by the giant's gold horse, patted it, and said to his men: "Tell me where in the whole world has any one seen such a treasure as this?" The men were of opinion that its like was nowhere to be found. But the guileful stable-lad was at hand, and instantly said: "Sir king, your horse is unquestionably a rare jewel; but I know of another gem, which exceeds it by far in value." At this speech the king was all attention and inquired what he alluded to. The stable-lad then began relating at full about the beautiful lantern, that shone more brightly than the moon in its full. The king then said: "Where is this lantern to be found, and who can procure it for me?" The lad replied: "I believe that no one can procure the lantern for you unless it be my brother. He is likely to know best where it is to be found." The king was now seized with an irresistible desire to possess the moon-lantern, of which he heard so much, and commanded the young courtier to go and obtain it. The young man, although not feeling any great fear, had, nevertheless, rather have stayed where he was. But the stable-lad was glad at heart, thinking that his brother would hardly escape, as he had done on the former occasion.

The youth, having made the necessary preparations, departed on his enterprise. When he reached the farmer's dwelling, he entered, thanked him for his late hospitality, and asked his advice as to how he might obtain the giant's moon-lantern. The farmer gave him a kind reception and promised him all the help in his power. After conversing together for some time, the youth took leave, and proceeded alone to the habitation of the grim giant.

Late in the evening, after it was dusk, the giant returned home from the forest. He had been absent the whole day and was very hungry. When he had finished his supper, the servant-maid had forgotten to fetch water, whereat the giant was displeased, and said: "Hast thou forgotten that I always drink after I have eaten?" The girl excused herself by saying it was so dark that she could not find the way to the well. "Take my moon-lantern, then," roared the giant with angry voice. The woman needed not to be told a second time, but taking the beautiful lantern from the wall, she hurried away to the well. But her journey had a quite unlooked for termination for while she was stooping, the youth, who was close at hand, seizing her by the feet, pitched her head foremost down the mouth of the well. He then took the beautiful lantern, which shone like the moon at full, and ran off in all haste. When he reached the grange, there was great joy that his enterprise had been so successful. The young courtier would not remain there long but started off without delay for the king's palace. Here was great admiration and great wondering at the costly moon-lantern, and the king himself admired it more than any of the others. From that day the young courtier was held in still higher estimation by his master and was looked on as the chief of his servants. But the stable-lad owed him a mortal grudge and was incessantly thinking how he might ruin his brother.

Some time after, the king went again into the stable to look at his horses. After having amused himself with examining them all, he turned to those about him and said: "It would not be an easy task to find a king who owns greater treasures than those which I have. There seems, indeed, nothing wanting." All were of the same opinion; but the guileful stable-lad, who was at hand, immediately said: "Sir king, you possess, it is true, many costly treasures; but I know of one gem that excels them all." On hearing this the king was all amazement, and said: "Of what dost thou speak, and who can procure me that gem?" The stable-lad then began to narrate at full about the beautiful princess that was in the giant's dwelling and concluded his speech by saying: "I cannot obtain the young maiden for you, nor can any one else, save my brother; he best knows where she is to be found." The king had now an unconquerable desire to possess the fair princess, whose beauty he heard praised so highly, and commanded the young courtier to set out and fetch her. Although the youth did not shrink from the undertaking, he would much rather have stayed where he was. But the stable-lad was overjoyed and flattered himself that this would be his brother's last enterprise.

The youth having made the necessary preparations, set out and proceeded to the farmer's abode, as on the former occasions. Having thanked him for his past kindness, he solicited his good counsel as to how he might rescue the king's daughter out of the power of the giant. When they had consulted together, the farmer said: "Your enterprise is difficult, nor do I well see how it can be accomplished; for the princess is confined in an upper apartment, within an enchanted cage. Now it is my advice that you fasten iron wedges in the wall, and by their aid go up to her. It then remains to be seen whether fortune will befriend you." The youth thanked the old man for his advice and promised to follow it. He then bade him farewell and proceeded to the giant's dwelling. The farmer wished him success and awaited his return with anxiety.

In the evening, when it was dark, the youth fixed wedges in the wall, and so ascended to the upper apartment; but the cage, in which the princess was confined, was enchanted, so that no one could open the lock except the person destined by fate to be the maiden's husband. When the princess saw the bold youth, she rejoiced in her heart; and the lock flew back spontaneously, so that he entered the cage. He then related to her the object of his coming and asked whether she was willing to accompany him. She declared herself quite willing, and instantly made herself ready. In descending the wall, the young man held be fast, that she might not fall, at which she was far from evincing any displeasure. They then hastened away and reached the farmer's abode in safety. But the young courtier would make no stay, so bidding the sagacious old man farewell, they proceeded on their way. Thus, they journeyed to the royal palace; but during the journey the youth contracted so violent a passion for the fair maiden, that he felt persuaded it would cause his death, should any one else possess her.

On their arrival there was great joy over the whole palace that the young courtier was safely returned; for he was a favourite with all, excepting his wicked brother, the stable-lad. The king then went to visit the young damsel, and it seemed to him that he had never beheld a more beautiful female. But the instant he began to speak to her, there came the enchanted cage! of which no one could open the lock except him who had rescued the princess out of the giant's power. The king now saw that the maiden was not destined to be his, and therefore commanded a sumptuous marriage to be prepared, and bestowed the princess on the bold young courtier, who had run so great a risk for her sake. When the nuptial festivities had lasted for many days, the king bade them both farewell and sent them, with a numerous retinue, home to the princess's father. Here there was no small joy throughout the whole realm, that the king had recovered his only daughter. The courtier and his wife lived afterwards happily together for very many years. And when the king, the father of the princess, was dead, the young courtier was chosen king over the whole realm. There he lives, according to what I have heard say, and rules the land in prosperity even until this day.

THE BEAUTIFUL PALACE EAST OF THE SUN AND NORTH OF THE EARTH.[35, 36]

From South Småland.

THERE was once a man who dwelt in a forest. Near to his habitation there was a meadow of the finest grass. The man set a high value on this fertile meadow, regarding it as of greater worth than most of his other property. But in the summer mornings, at sunrise, it was often observed that the beautiful grass

---

[35] Kindred stories are met with among the following nations:

1. The Norwegians.—See Absjörnsen og Moe, ut sup., No. 9. "De tre Prindsesseri Hvidtenland;" and No. 27. "Soria Moria Slot."

2. The Danes.—See Molbech, "Udvalgte Eventyr og Fortæl linger, Kjobenh." 1843, pp. 264-270. "Den nedtraadte Ager."

3. The Germans.— *a.* See Grimm, K. und H. M. ii. No. 92. Der König vom goldenen Berg (Cf. iii. pp. 171-174). *b. Ibid.* ii. No. 93. "Die Rabe" (Cf. iii. pp. 174, 175). *c. Ibid.* No. 193. The first part of "Der Trommler." *d.* Cf. the latter part of "Das Wasser des Lebens," in vol. iii. of the same book, p. 184.

4. The Slavonians.—See Kletke, Märchensaal, ii. pp. 41-53. "Die Hexe Corva und ihre Knechte."

5. The Hindus.—*a.* A tale similar in its groundplot, although widely differing in its details, is given in Brockhaus, "Katha Sarit Sagara. Somadevás Märchensammlung. Leipsig, 1843, ii. pp. 7-34. Geschichte des Vidûshaka." [This translation first appeared, together with the original Sanskrit, in Leipsig, 1839.] *b.* See also "Geschichte des Saktivega, Konigs der Vidyadharas," *ibid.* ii. pp. 118, seqq. *c.* Cf. the first part of a similar tale in the 7th fable [Book II.] of Hitopadesa. See Max Müller, "Hitopadesa, cine alte Indische Fabelsammlung, aus dem Sanskrit zum ersten Mal in das Deutsch übersetzt." Leipsig, 1844, pp. 86-88.

6. The Arabians.—*a.* A similar story elaborated into a pseudo historic narrative is to be found in Weil, "Tausend und eine Nacht, Arabische Erzahlungen, zum ersten Male aus dem arabischen Urtext." Stuttgart, 1838, i. pp. 783-880. "Geschichte des Prinzen Kamr essaman und der Prinzessin Bedur." *b.* See *ibid.* ii. Pforzheim, 1842, pp. 311-401. "Gesch. des Hassan aus Bassora und der Prinzessinnen von den Inseln Wak-Wak." *c.* See *ibid.* pp. 572-582. "Gesch. des tragen Abu Muhammed."

7. The Mogols.—See Introduction and conclusion of "Die Krokodillfrosche," in Kletke, Marchensaal, iii. pp. 19-23.

8. The Hebrews.—See Kletke, iii. pp. 45-50. "Die gebrochenen Eide."

[36] There can be no doubt that the idea of this story is derived from the Völund's Saga.— See "Northern Mythology," i. p. 84.

was trodden down, and in the dew, there appeared marks like human footsteps. At this the man sorely vexed, and most desirous to find out who it was that trampled down his grass during the night.

The peasant now considered with himself as to the course he should adopt, in order to get at the knowledge he desired to obtain, and resolved on sending his eldest son to keep watch in the meadow; but somehow or other he had not watched long before he felt very drowsy, and just as midnight drew nigh, he was wrapped in a deep sleep, from which he did not wake until the sun was standing high in the heavens. He then bent his steps towards home, after a fruitless errand; but the grass was trampled down as before.

The following night it was resolved that the peasant's second son should go and keep watch in the meadow. He was not lacking in big words and promised to bring back a good account. But, nevertheless, it fared with him as with his brother; for before he had watched for any length of time, he also felt drowsy and slept, and did not wake before bright daylight. Thus, after a fruitless errand, he likewise returned home, and the grass was trampled down as before.

Seeing that these attempts had, contrary to expectation, proved so vain, the peasant resolved on taking no further steps in the matter, when his youngest son came to him, and begged to be allowed to go to the meadow and keep watch. The father answered: "It is not worth the trouble to let thee go who art so young; for it is not very probable that thou wilt watch better than thy brothers." But the youth said he would try his luck, and so his request was granted. He then proceeded to the meadow, although his father and brothers fancied they could pretty well foresee how his enterprise would terminate.

After lying long on the watch, the lad could see nothing before the hour of matins, when the sun was just about rising. Then he heard on a sudden a noise in the air, as of birds flying, and three doves drew near and descended on the green meadow. After a while the doves laid aside their plumage and became three fair damsels, who immediately began dancing on the verdant field, and danced so delightfully that their feet seemed hardly to touch the grass. The youth was now at no loss to know who it was that trampled on his father's meadow; though he scarcely knew what to think of the young maidens. But among them there was one who appeared to him more beautiful than all other females, and it entered his mind that he would rather possess her than any other in the world. After having for a while thus lain and amused himself with their dancing, he rose and stole away their plumages; then lay down again on the watch to see how the adventure would terminate.

Early in the morning, soon after the sun had risen, the maidens finished their dance, and were preparing to depart; but they could not find their plumages. At this they were seriously alarmed and ran to and fro on the meadow, until they came to the spot where the youth was lying. They asked whether he had taken their plumages, giving him fair words to induce him to deliver them up. The youth answered: "Yes, I have taken them, but I will not restore them except on two conditions." Seeing that their entreaties availed them nothing, the maidens asked what the conditions were, promising to fulfil them. The youth then said: "My first condition is that ye tell me who you are and whence you come." One of them answered: "I am a king's daughter, and these two are my court-attendants. We are from THE PALACE WHICH LIES EAST OF THE SUN AND NORTH OF THE EARTH, whither nothing human may come." The youth continued: "My second condition is, that the king's daughter plights me her honour and faith and fixes a day for our marriage for her and no other in the world will I possess." As the day was now advancing, and the sun already shining on the tops of the trees, the maiden was compelled to submit to this condition. The youth then plighted his troth to the young princess, and they promised to be always faithful to each other. He then gave back the three plumage's, and bade his beloved farewell, who with her companions soared aloft in the air, and pursued their course homewards.

When it was full day, the youth proceeded towards home, where he had to hear a multitude of questions respecting the wonderful things he might have seen or heard during the night. But he spoke very little, saying only that he had fallen asleep, without having discovered anything. For this he was jeered by his brothers, who made a joke of him for having fancied that he could succeed better than they, who were in every respect his superiors.

Some time had now passed, and the day arrived, which the king's daughter had fixed for the marriage. The youth then went to his father and requested him to make preparations for a feast, and to invite all their friends and relations. The father allowed his son to manage all as he thought proper and so a grand feast was prepared with no lack of good cheer. When the hour of midnight drew nigh, and the guests were beginning to be merry, a loud noise was heard on a sudden without the apartment in which they were assembled, and a magnificent chariot approached, drawn by mettlesome horses. In the chariot sat the fair princess clad as a bride, attended by her two court maidens. Now there was great wondering among all the guests, as may easily be imagined. But the young man received his bride with joy and related to the guests his adventure during the night when he was watching his father's meadow. Thereupon the healths of bride and bridegroom were drunk with pleasure and gaiety, and all who saw the young bride pronounced the youth fortunate in having made such a marriage.

Early in the morning, and before dawn, the princess said that she must depart. At this, the bridegroom was grieved, and asked her why she could not grant him yet one short hour of delight. The princess answered "My father, who ruled over the beautiful palace that lies east of the sun and north of the earth was slain by a Troll, by whom I am held in strict captivity, so that I cannot enjoy any liberty, save for a short time at midnight. If I am not back before sunrise, my life is at stake." When the youth had heard this, he would no longer detain his bride, but bade her farewell, adding fervent wishes for her happiness. At her departure the princess gave him a gold ring as a remembrance, and the court-damsels gave him each a gold apple. They then mounted their gilded chariot and drove away with all speed.

From that day the youth enjoyed no rest, he was constantly thinking how he could reach the beautiful palace that lay east of the sun and north of the earth. In this state of mind, he went one day to his father, and prayed to be allowed to travel in search of his bride. The old man told him he might follow his own inclinations; though his journey could hardly be attended with success. The youth then took leave of his relations and departed from home alone.

He journeyed now over mountains and through verdant valleys, over many extensive kingdoms, but could get no tidings of the beautiful palace. One day he came to a very large forest, in which he heard a loud noise, and on drawing near to the spot whence it proceeded, he saw two giants, who were engaged in a violent quarrel. He said to them: "Why do you, two giants, stand here quarrelling with each other?" One of them answered: "Our father is dead, and we have divided the inheritance between us; but here is a pair of boots, which we cannot agree which of us shall have." The youth said: "I will settle your dispute. If you cannot agree, give the boots to me. I am a traveller and have a long way to go." The giant answered: "All that thou sayest may be true; but these are no common boots for whoever has them on can go a hundred miles at every step." When the youth heard this, he was eager to possess such valuable boots, and told the giants it would be much better to make him a present of them, and then they would have nothing to quarrel about. In short, he put his words so well together that the giants thought his advice was good and gave him the boots. The young man then drew on the boots, with which he could go a hundred miles at every step, and travelled further, far away into many strange lands.

After having thus journeyed for some time, he came to another forest, in which he heard another noise and uproar. On advancing, he again saw two giants engaged in a violent altercation. He said: "Why do you, two giants, stand here wrangling with each other?" One of them answered: "Our father is dead, and we are dividing his property, but we cannot agree which of us shall have this cloak." The youth said: "I will settle your dispute. If you cannot agree, give me the cloak. I am a traveller and have a long way to go." The giant answered: "What thou sayest may be very true; but this cloak is not like other cloaks; for whoever puts it on becomes invisible." On hearing this the youth was seized with a strong desire to possess so precious a cloak and said that the giants could not do better than give it to him; for then they would have nothing to quarrel about. This the giants thought excellent advice, and they gave him the cloak. So, the youth got the cloak which rendered him invisible, and pursued his journey far far away into foreign lands.

When he had travelled a considerable time, he came again to a vast forest, in which he heard a great noise and uproar. On advancing, he again saw two giants engaged in a violent dispute. On inquiring why, they stood there wrangling, one of them said: "Our father is dead, and we have been dividing the inheritance. But we cannot settle to which of us this sword shall belong." The youth said: "I will settle your difference. If you cannot agree, make me a present of the sword. I am a traveller and have a long way to go." The giant answered: "What thou sayest may be quite true; but this sword is not like other swords; whoever is touched with its point dies instantly; but if he is touched by the hilt, he immediately returns to life." When the youth heard this, he was seized with a most vehement desire to possess so precious a sword, and told the giants, that if they were wise, they would give it to him for then they would have nothing to quarrel about. This he expressed to such purpose that the giants thought it excellent advice and gave him the sword. The youth then hung the precious sword by his side, drew the hundred-mile boots on his legs, put the wonderful cloak about his shoulders, and seemed to be well equipped for his journey.

One evening, after dark, he found himself in a vast desert, that seemed to have no end. Casting his eyes on every side to discover a lodging for the night, he descried a little light glimmering among the trees. On approaching it, he found it proceeded from a little cot, in which dwelt a very, very, old, old woman who seemed to have seen as many ages of man as others see years. The youth entered, greeted her courteously, and asked whether he could have a shelter for the night. When the old woman heard him speak, she said: "Who art thou that comest and greetest me so kindly? Here have I dwelt while twelve oak forests have grown up and twelve oak forests have withered; but until now no one has ever come who greeted me so kindly." The youth answered: "I am a poor traveller, who am in search of the beautiful palace east of the sun and north of the earth. You can probably direct me to it, dear mother." "No," said she, "that I cannot; but I rule over the beasts of the field; there may perchance be among them one or other that may put thee in the right way." The youth thanked her for her kindness and stayed the night over.

Early in the morning, as the sun was just shining in, the old woman summoned her subjects to assemble. Then came running out of the forest all kinds of beasts, bears, wolves, and foxes, inquiring what their queen's pleasure might be. The old woman said that she wished to know whether there were any among them who knew the way to the beautiful palace east of the sun and north of the earth. Hereupon the beasts held a long consultation, but not one could give any information about the beautiful palace. Thereupon the old dame then said to the youth: "I can give thee no further aid; but many thousand miles from here my sister dwells, who rules over the fishes in the sea; she can, perhaps, give thee the desired information." The youth then bade the old woman farewell, thanked her for her good counsel, and proceeded on his journey.

After travelling a very long way, he again found himself late one evening in a vast desert. On looking about for a shelter, be perceived a little light glimmering among the trees. On approaching it, he found that it issued from a small and very ruinous cottage standing on the seashore, in which sat a very very old woman, who appeared to have lived as many ages of man as others live changes of the moon. The youth stepped in, greeted the old dame from her sister, and asked whether he might stay there that night. When the old woman had heard him speak, she said: "Who art thou that comest hither and greetest me so courteously? I have seen four-and-twenty oak woods grow up, and four-and-twenty wither, but until now no one has ever come hither who greeted me so kindly." The youth answered: "I am a poor traveller in search of the beautiful palace east of the sun and north of the earth, whither no human being may come. You, dear mother, can perhaps direct me in the way." "No," said the old woman, "that I cannot; but I rule over the fishes in the sea, and among them there may probably be one or other that can give thee the information thou desirest." The young man thanked her for her kindness and stayed the night over.

Early in the morning, as soon as it was light, the old dame summoned a meeting of her subjects. Thither came all the fishes of the sea, whales, pike, salmon and flounders and asked what might be their queen's commands. The old woman said, she wished to ascertain whether any among them knew the way to the beautiful palace east of the sun and north of the earth, whither no one may go. The fishes then held a long consultation, the result of which was that not one of them could give any information about the beautiful palace. Thereupon the old dame said to the youth: "Thou seest that I can give thee no further help; but I have another sister, who dwells many many thousand miles from here, and rules over the fowls of the air. Go to her; if she cannot direct thee, there is no one who can." The youth then bade the old woman farewell and resumed his journey.

When he had travelled a very long way further, many many thousand miles, he found himself, late one evening, in a vast desert, that seemed to be boundless. On looking around for a lodging, be perceived a little light glimmering among the trees. On approaching it, he found it proceeded from a small ruinous cottage on a mountain, in which drew dwelt a very very old woman, who seemed to have lived as many ages of man as others live days. The youth entered, greeted the old dame from her sisters, and asked whether he could have a lodging for the night. When the old dame heard him speak, she said: "Who art thou that comest hither with so kind a greeting? Here have I seen eight and forty oak forests grow up, and eight-and-forty wither, but until now no one has ever come who greeted me so kindly." The youth then said: "I am a poor traveller, in search of the beautiful palace east of the sun and north of the earth, whither no human being may come. You, dear mother, can, perhaps, direct me thither." "No," said the old woman, "that I cannot; but as I rule over the birds of the air, perhaps there is one or other among them that can give thee the desired information." The youth thanked the old woman for her kindness and stayed there the night over.

Early in the morning, before the cock had crowed, the old woman summoned her subjects to an assembly. Then came flying all the fowls of heaven, eagles, swans, and hawks and asked what might be their queen's commands. The old woman told them that she had summoned them to assemble, because she wished to learn whether any among them knew the way to the beautiful palace east of the sun and north of the earth. The birds thereupon held a long consultation, the result of which was, that not one could give any information about the beautiful palace. The old dame then appeared vexed, and said: "Are ye all assembled? I do not see the phoenix." She received for answer, that the phoenix was not yet come. After waiting for some time, they saw the beautiful bird come flying through the air, but so fatigued that it could hardly move its wings and sank down on the earth. Now there was joy throughout the assembly that the phoenix had arrived; but the old dame was very angry and demanded to know why it had kept them so long waiting. It was some time before the poor bird could recover itself, and then, in a humble tone, it said: "Be not angry that I have tarried so long; but I have flown a very long way. I have been in a far distant land, at the beautiful palace, which lies east of the sun and north of the earth." On hearing this, the queen was quite appeased, and said: "This must be thy punishment, that thou once again go to the beautiful palace, and take this youth with thee on the journey." The bird thought that this was rather a hard condition; but it had no alternative. The youth then bade the old dame farewell, and seated himself on the bird's back, which then soared aloft, flying over mountains and valleys, over the blue sea and the green forests.

When they had thus journeyed a considerable time the bird said: "Young man, seest thou anything?" "Yes," answered the youth, "I think I perceive a blue cloud far away in the horizon." "That is the country to which we are going," said the bird. They had now travelled a very long way, and evening was coming on, when the phoenix again said: "Young man, seest thou anything?" "Yes," answered the youth, "I see a speck in the blue cloud which glitters brightly, like the sun itself." The bird said: "That is the palace to which we are proceeding." They still continued journeying on, and night was drawing near, when the phoenix said a third time: "Young man, seest thou anything?" "Yes," said the youth, "I see a vast palace resplendent all over with gold and silver." "Now we are arrived," said the bird, descending near the beautiful structure, and setting the youth down on the earth. The youth thanked the bird for his great trouble, which returned through the air to the place whence it had come.

At midnight, when all the Trolls lay in deep sleep, the youth went to the palace gate and knocked; whereupon the princess sent her attendant to inquire who it was that came so late. When the damsel came to the gate, the youth threw to her a golden apple, and prayed for admission. The damsel instantly recognised the apple, and at once knew who had knocked at the gate. She thereupon hastened to her mistress with these glad tidings. But the princess would not believe that her story was true.

The king's daughter now sent her other attendant, and when she came to the gate, the youth threw to her the other golden apple. She also immediately knew her apple again, and full of joy hastened to tell her mistress who it was outside the gate. Still the princess would not believe what they had told her, but went to the gate herself, and asked who it was that had knocked. The youth then handed to her the golden ring which she had given him. Now she knew that her bridegroom was come; she therefore opened the gate and received him with great love and delight, as everyone may easily imagine.

The youth then placing himself by the side of his fair bride, they chatted together all night. At the approach of morning, the king's daughter appeared in deep affliction and said: "We must now part. For the sake of all that is dear to thee, hasten hence before the Trolls wake; else thy life is at stake." Bride and bridegroom then took leave of each other, and the princess let fall many tears. The youth, however, would not flee, but put on his cloak, drew on his hundred-mile boots, girded his precious sword by his side, and prepared him for a contest with the Trolls.

Early in the morning, there was great life and bustle in all the palace. The gates were opened, and the Trolls entered one after another. But the youth stood in the entrance with drawn sword, so that when the Trolls approached, he was quite ready for them, and struck off their heads before they were aware of him. There was, consequently, a bloody game, which was not concluded until every Troll had found his death. When the day was advanced, the king's daughter sent her maidens to get tidings how the contest had ended. They returned with the intelligence that the youth was alive, but that all the Trolls were slain. At this news the fair princess was over joyed; for it now appeared to her that she had overcome all her sorrows.

When the first joy was over, the princess said: "Now our happiness is so great that it can hardly be greater; if only I could get back my relatives." The youth answered: "Show me where they lie buried, and I will see whether I cannot help them." They thereupon went to the spot where the father of the princess and her other relations were laid; when the youth touching each with the hilt of his sword, they were all quickened one after another. When they had thus come again to life, there were great rejoicings in the palace, and all thanked the youth for having restored them. The relations of the princess then took the youth for their king, and the fair maiden was his queen. The youth ruled his realm prosperously and lived to a good old age surrounded by friends. His queen bore him brave sons and fair daughters, and thus they lived in peace and happiness all their days.

Here ends the tale of the beautiful palace east of the sun and north of the earth, from which may be learned the truth of the old adage, that *true love overcomes everything*.

THE GIRL WHO COULD SPIN GOLD FROM CLAY AND LONG STRAW.[37]

From Upland.

THERE was once an old woman who had an only daughter. The lass was good and amiable, and also extremely beautiful; but, at the same time, so indolent, that she would hardly turn her hand to any work. This was a cause of great grief to the mother, who tried all sorts of ways to cure her daughter of so lamentable a failing; but there was no help. The old woman then thought no better plan could be devised than to set her daughter to spin on the roof of their cot, in order that all the world might be witness of her sloth. But her plan brought her no nearer the mark; the girl continued as useless as before.

One day, as the king's son was going to the chase, he rode by the cot, where the old woman dwelt with her daughter. On seeing the fair spinner on the roof, he stopped and inquired why she sat spinning in such an unusual place. The old woman answered: "Aye, she sits there to let all the world see how clever she is. She is so clever that she can spin gold out of clay and long straw." At these words the prince was struck with wonder; for it never occurred to him that the old woman was ironically alluding to her daughter's sloth. He therefore said: "If what you say is true, that the young maiden can spin gold from clay and long straw, she shall no longer sit there, but shall accompany me to my palace and be my consort." The daughter thereupon descended from the roof and accompanied the prince to the royal residence, where, seated in

---

[37] This tale occurs among the following people:

1. The Germans.—*a.* See Grimm, K. und H. M. i. No. 55. "Rumpelstilzchen" (Conf. *ibid.* iii. pp. 97-99). *b.* A similar story is given as a popular tradition in Harrys, Sagen, Märchen und Legenden Niedersachsens, 1st number. Celle, 1840, pp. 16-19. "Zwerge in den Schweckhäuserbergen."

2. The Irish.—The story is mentioned by Taylor, in his "Gammer Grethel," p. 333.

3. The Italians.—See an old, somewhat paraphrastic, tale called "Rosanie," translated into Danish, and first published at Copenhagen, in 1708. Cf. Nyerup, Morskabslæsning, pp. 173-274.

4. The French.—See a part of the story of Ricdin-Ricdon, in the "Tour tenebreuse et les jours lumineux, Contes Anglois tirez d'une ancienne Chronique composee par Richard, surnommé Cœur de Lion, Roy d'Angleterre." Amsterdam, 1708.

her maiden bower, she received a pailful of clay and a bundle of straw, by way of trial, whether she was so skillful as her mother had said.

The poor girl now found herself in a very uncomfortable state, knowing but too well that she could not spin flax much less gold. So, sitting in her chamber, with her head resting on her hand, she wept bitterly. While she was thus sitting, the door was opened, and in walked a very little old man, who was both ugly and deformed. The old man greeted her m a friendly tone and asked why she sat so lonely and afflicted. "I may well be sorrowful," answered the girl; "the king's son has commanded me to spin gold from clay and long straw, and if it be not done before tomorrow's dawn, my life is at stake." The old man then said: "Fair maiden, weep not, I will help thee. Here is a pair of gloves, when thou hast them on thou wilt be able to spin gold. Tomorrow night I will return, when if thou hast not found out my name, thou shalt accompany me home and be my wife." In her despair she agreed to the old man's condition, who then went his way. The maiden now sat and span, and by dawn she had already spun up all the clay and straw, which had become the finest gold it was possible to see.

Great was the joy throughout the whole palace, that the king's son had got a bride who was so skillful and, at the same time, so fair. But the young maiden did nothing but weep, and the more the time advanced the more she wept; for she thought of the frightful dwarf, who was to come and fetch her. When evening drew nigh, the king's son returned from the chase, and went to converse with his bride. Observing that she appeared sorrowful, he strove to divert her in all sorts of ways and said he would tell her of a curious adventure, provided only she would be cheerful. The girl entreated him to let her hear it. Then said the prince: "While rambling about in the forest today, I witnessed an odd sort of thing; I saw a very very little old man dancing round a juniper bush and singing a singular song." "What did he sing?" asked the maiden inquisitively; for she felt sure that the prince had met with the dwarf. "He sang these words" answered the prince:

"I dag skall jag maltet mala,	"Today I the malt shall grind,
I morgon skall mitt bröllop vara.	Tomorrow my wedding shall be.
Och jungfrun sitter I buren och gråter;	And the maided sits in her bower and weeps;

Hon vet inte hvad jag heter.	She knows not what I am called.
Jag heter *Titteli Ture.*	I am called *Titteli Ture.*
Jag heter *Titteli Ture.*"	I am called *Titteli Ture.*"

Was not the maiden now glad? She begged the prince to tell her over and over again what the dwarf had sung. He then repeated the wonderful song, until she had imprinted the old man's name firmly in her memory. She then conversed lovingly with her betrothed, and the prince could not sufficiently praise his young bride's beauty and understanding. But he wondered why she was so overjoyed, being, like everyone else, ignorant of the cause of her past sorrow.

When it was night, and the maiden was sitting alone in her chamber, the door was opened, and the hideous dwarf again entered. On beholding him the girl sprang up and said: "Titteli Ture! Titteli Ture! here are thy gloves." When the dwarf heard his name pronounced, he was furiously angry, and hastened away through the air, taking with him the whole roof of the house.

The fair maiden now laughed to herself and was joyful beyond measure. She then lay down to sleep and slept till the sun shone. The following day her marriage with the young prince was solemnized, and nothing more was ever heard of Titteli Ture.

THE THREE LITTLE CRONES,
EACH WITH SOMETHING BIG.[38]

From Upland.

THERE was once a king's son and a king's daughter who dearly loved each other. The young princess was good and fair, and well spoken of by all, but

---

[38] The following foreign variations of this tale are known to us:—

1. Norwegian.—See Absjörnsen og Moe, ut sup., No. 13. "De tre Mostre."

2. German.—*a.* See Grimm, K. and H. M. i. No. 14. "Die drei Spinnerinnen" (Cf. iii. pp. 25, 26). *b.* Busching, ut sup., i. pp. 355-360. "Die fleissigen Spinnerinnen."

her disposition was more inclined to pleasure and dissipation than to handiworks and domestic occupations. To the old queen this appeared very wrong, who said she would have no one for a daughter-in-law that was not as skilled in such matters as she herself had been in her youth. She therefore opposed the prince's marriage in all sorts of ways.

As the queen would not recall her words, the prince went to her and said it would be well to make a trial whether the princess was not as skillful as the queen herself. This seemed to everyone a very rash proposal seeing that the prince's mother was a very diligent, laborious person, and span and sewed and wove both night and day, so that no one ever saw her like. The prince, however, carried his point; the fair princess was sent into the maidens' bower, and the queen sent her a pound of flax to spin. But the flax was to be spun ere dawn of day, otherwise the damsel was never more to think of the prince for a husband.

When left alone the princess found herself very ill at ease; for she well knew that she could not spin the queen's flax, and yet trembled at the thought of losing the prince, who was so dear to her. She therefore wandered about the apartment and wept, incessantly wept. At this moment, the door was opened very softly, and there stepped in a little little woman of singular appearance and yet more singular manners. The little woman had enormously large feet, at which everyone who saw her must be wonderstruck. She greeted the princess with: "Peace be with you!" "And peace with you!" answered the princess. The old woman then asked: "Why is the fair damsel so sorrowful tonight?" The princess answered: "I may well be sorrowful. The queen has commanded me to spin a pound of flax: if I have not completed it before dawn, I lose the young prince whom I love so dearly." The old woman then said: "Be of good cheer, fair maiden; if there is nothing else, I can help you; but then you must grant me a request which I will name." At these words the princess was overjoyed and asked what it was the Old woman desired. "I am called," she said, "*Storfota-mor*[39] and I require for my aid no other reward than to be present at your wedding. I have not been at a wedding since the queen

---

3. Scotch.—See Chambers's Popular Rhymes, etc., pp. 54, 55. "Whippety Stourie."

4. Italians.—See Basile, Il Pentam, iv. No. 4. "Le sette Cotenelle."

5. French.—See the first part of Madem. L'Heritier's Story of "Ricdin-Ricdon."

[39] Mother Bigfoot.

your mother-in-law stood as bride." The princess readily granted her desire, and they parted. The princess then lay down to sleep but could not close her eyes the whole livelong night.

Early in the morning, before dawn, the door was opened, and the little woman again entered. She approached the king's daughter and handed to her a bundle of yarn, as white as snow and as fine as a cobweb, saying: "See! Such beautiful yarn I have not spun since I span for the queen, when she was about to be married; but that was long, long ago." Having so spoken the little woman disappeared, and the princess fell into a refreshing slumber. But she had not slept long when she was awakened by the old queen, who was standing by her bed, and who asked her whether the flax was all spun. The princess said that it was and handed the yarn to her. The queen must needs appear content, but the princess could not refrain from observing that her apparent satisfaction did not proceed from good-will.

Before the day was over, the queen said she would put the princess to yet another proof. For this purpose, she sent the yarn to the maiden-bower together with a yarn-roll and other implements and ordered the princess to weave it into a web; but which must be ready before sunrise; if not, the damsel must never more think of the young prince.

When the princess was alone, she again felt sad at heart; for she knew that she could not weave the queen's yarn and yet less reconcile herself to the thought of losing the prince to whom she was so dear. She therefore wandered about the apartment and wept bitterly. At that moment the door was opened softly, softly, and in stepped a very little woman, of singular figure and still more singular manners. The little woman had an enormously large hinder part, so that everyone who saw her must be struck with astonishment. She, too, greeted the princess with: "Peace be with you!" and received for answer: "Peace with you!" The old woman said: "Why is the fair damsel so sad and sorrowful?" "I may well be sorrowful," answered the princess. "The queen has commanded me to weave all this yarn into a web; and if I have not completed it by the morning before sunrise, I shall lose the prince, who loves me so dearly. The woman then said: "Be comforted, fair damsel; if it is nothing more, I will help you. But then you must consent to one condition, which I will name to you." At these words the princess was highly delighted and asked what the condition might be. "I am called *Storgumpa-mor*[40] and I desire no other reward than to be at your wedding. I have not been to any wedding since the queen your mother-in-law stood as bride." The king's daughter readily granted this request, and the little woman departed. The princess then lay down to sleep but was unable to close her eyes the whole night.

In the morning, before daybreak, the door was opened, and the little woman entered. She approached the princess and handed to her a web white as snow and close as a skin, so that its like was never seen. The old woman said: "See such even threads I have never woven since I wove for the queen, when she was about to be married; but that was long long ago." The woman then disappeared, and the princess fell into a short slumber, but from which she was roused by the old queen, who stood by her bed, and inquired whether the web was ready. The princess told her that it was and handed to her the beautiful piece of weaving. The queen must now appear content for the second time, but the princess could easily see that she was not so from good-will.

The king's daughter now flattered herself that she should be put to no further trial; but the queen was of a different opinion; for she shortly after sent the web down to the maiden-bower with the message, that the princess should make it into shirts for the prince. The shirts were to be ready before sunrise otherwise the damsel must never hope to have the young prince for a husband.

When the princess was alone, she felt sad at heart; for she knew that she could not sew the queen's web, and yet could not think of losing the king's son, to whom she was so dear. She therefore wandered about the chamber and shed a flood of tears. At this moment, the door was softly, softly opened, and in stepped a very little woman of most extraordinary appearance and still more extraordinary manners. The little woman had an enormously large thumb, so that everyone who saw it must be wonderstruck. She also greeted the princess with: "Peace be with you," and likewise received for answer: "Peace with you." She then asked the young damsel why she was so sad and lonely. "I may well be sad," answered the princess. "The queen has commanded me to make this web into shirts for the king's son; and if I have not finished them tomorrow before sunrise, I shall lose my beloved prince, who holds me so dear." The

______

[40] From stor, *large*, and gunrpa, *nates*.

woman then said: "Be of good cheer fair maiden; if it is nothing more, I can help you. But then you must agree to a condition, which I will mention." At these words the princess was overjoyed and asked the little woman what it was she wished. I am, answered she, "called *Stortumma-mor*[41], and I desire no other reward than that I may be present at your wedding. I have not been at a wedding since the queen your mother-in-law stood as bride. The princess willingly assented to this condition, and the little woman departed. But the princess lay down to sleep and slept so soundly that she did not dream even once of her dear prince.

Early in the morning, before the sun had risen, the door was opened, and the little woman entered. She approached the bed, awakened the princess, and gave her some shirts that were sewed and stitched so curiously that their like was never seen. The old woman said: "See! so beautifully as this I have not sewed since I sewed for the queen, when she was about to stand as bride. But that was long, long ago." With these words the little woman disappeared for the queen was then at the door, being just come to inquire whether the shirts were ready. The king's daughter said that they were and handed her the beautiful work. At the sight of them the queen was so enraged that her eyes flashed with fury. She said: "Well! Take him then. I could never have imagined that thou wast so clever as thou art." She then went her way, slamming the door after her.

The king's son and the king's daughter were now to be united, as the queen had promised, and great preparations were made for the wedding. But the joy of the princess was not without alloy, when she thought of the singular guests that were to be present. When some time had elapsed, and the wedding was being celebrated in the good old fashion, yet not one of the little old women appeared; although the bride looked about in every direction. At length, when it was growing late, and the guests were going to table, the princess discerned the three little women, as they sat in a corner of the dining-hall, at a table by themselves. At the same moment, the king stepped up to them, and inquired who they were, as he had never seen them before. The eldest of the three answered: "I am called *Storfota-mor* and have such large feet because I have been obliged to sit spinning so much in my time." "Oho!" said the king, "if

---

[41] Mother Bigthumb.

such be the consequence, my son's wife shall never spin another thread." Then turning to the second little woman, he inquired the cause of her uncommon appearance. The old woman answered: "I am called *Storgumpa-mor* and am so broad behind because I have been obliged to sit weaving so much in my time." "Oho!" said the king, "then my son's wife shall weave no more." Lastly, turning to the third old woman, he asked her name; when *Stortumma-mor*, rising from her seat, told him that she had got so large a thumb because she had sewed so much in her time. "Oho!" said the king, "then my son's wife shall never sew another stitch." Thus, the fair princess obtained the king's son, and also escaped from spinning, and weaving, and sewing all the rest of her life.

When the wedding was over, the three little women went their way, and no one knew whither they went, nor whence they came. The prince lived happy and content with his consort, and all passed on smoothly and peaceably; only that the princess was not so industrious as her strict mother in-law.

THE THREE DOGS.[42]

From Westergötland.

THERE was once a king who journeyed to a strange land and married a fair queen. After they had been united for some time, the queen gave birth to a daughter. At this event there was great rejoicing both in town and country; for the king was well liked of everyone, on account of his clemency and uprightness. When the child was born, an old woman entered the chamber, of very singular appearance, and no one knew whence she came nor whither she went. The old crone predicted regarding the royal babe and said that it must not come under the open sky until it had completed the age of fifteen; otherwise it was to be feared it would be carried off by the Mountain trolls.

---

[42] The only foreign variety of this story known to us is English. In England an old popular tale is universally known under the name of *Jack the Giant-Killer*, which in its chief features bears a strong resemblance to the one here given.

When the king was informed of this, he treasured the old woman's words in his memory, and set watchers to take care that the young princess did not come under the open sky.

Some time after, the queen brought forth another laughter, at which there was again great rejoicing throughout the kingdom; but the old soothsayer again made her appearance and warned the king not to allow the princess to come under the open sky before she had completed her fifteenth year. Time now passed on, and the queen gave birth to a third daughter, and the old woman came a third time, and predicted regarding this one as she had done with respect to her sisters. This was a cause of great grief to the king; for he loved his children above all things in the world besides. He therefore commanded that the three princesses should be constantly kept under a roof and took every precaution to prevent any one from transgressing his mandates in this particular.

When a considerable time had elapsed, and the royal children had grown up into the fairest maidens that could be seen far or near, a war broke out in the country, and the king their father took the field. One day, while he was absent, engaged in warfare, the three princesses were sitting at the window and admiring how the sun shone on the flowers in the garden, when a strong desire seized them to amuse themselves among the beautiful plants, and they begged permission of their attendants to go for a little while and wander about in the garden. The attendants would not grant their request, for they dreaded the king's anger; but the damsels entreated them so sweetly and fervently, that the men could no longer withstand their prayers, and let them have their will. The princesses were now overjoyed and went in and out of the garden; but their wandering was of no long duration; for before they had thus amused themselves for any length of time, a cloud suddenly descended and bore them away, and every attempt to find them again was fruitless, although search was made in every region of the globe.

There was now great sorrow and lamentation over the whole kingdom, and it is easy to imagine that the king's anguish was extreme, when, on his return, he was informed of what had happened. But, as the proverb says, "What's done can't be undone," so he was forced to let things remain as they were. As therefore no other course could be devised, the king sent forth a proclamation over all his realm, that whosoever should deliver his three daughters out of the power of the Mountain-trolls, should have one of them to wife, and with her half the kingdom. When this announcement became known in the surrounding countries, many youthful champions, with horses and attendants, sallied forth to seek after the three princesses. At the king's court there were at this time two foreign princes, who also started off, to prove whether fortune would befriend them. They armed themselves with corselets and costly weapons and talked amazingly big of how they would never return until they had succeeded in their enterprise.

We will now, for a while, let the two princes wander about seeking, and turn to another quarter. There dwelt at this time a poor widow, far, very far in the wild wood, who had an only son, whose daily employ it was to tend his mother's hogs. While the boy was thus wandering about the fields, he cut himself a pipe to play on, which was his greatest delight; and he played so sweetly, that everyone who heard him was charmed. The youth was tall of stature and stout of heart, and there were few perils before which he would quail.

It happened one day that as the youth was sitting in the forest and playing on his pipe, while his three hogs were busied in grubbing under the pine roots, a very old man came to him, having an ample beard, which reached below his girdle. He had with him a dog, that was both large and strong. When the lad saw the large dog, he thought within himself: "It would be fortunate to have a dog like that as a companion out here in the fields; there would then be no danger." When the old man was aware of what was passing in the youth's mind, he said: "I am come because I wish to exchange my dog for one of thy hogs." The lad was instantly ready for the bargain, and so became possessed of the great dog, giving a grey hog in exchange. The old man then took his departure and on going said: "I feel satisfied that thou wilt be content with the bargain; for this dog is not like other dogs. His name is *Hold*, and whatever thou desirest him to hold he will hold, were it even the fiercest Troll." Thus, they parted, and the youth thought that this time, at all events, fortune was not unfavourable to him.

In the evening the lad called his dog and drove the hogs home from the forest. When the old woman found that her son had given the grey beg for a dog, she was exceedingly angry and gave him a sound beating. But the lad besought her to be content; though to no purpose; for with time the old woman's wrath was rather increased than diminished. Seeing no other course, the boy called to his dog and said "Hold!" Instantly the dog rushed forward, seized the crone, and held her so fast that she could not move; but did her no injury. The old dame was now obliged to promise to be content with what her son had done, and they were again reconciled. Nevertheless, the old woman could not refrain from thinking she had sustained a great injury in losing her fat hog.

On the following day the boy went to the forest with his dog and two hogs. On reaching it he sat down and played on his pipe, as was his custom, and the dog danced to it so artistically, that it was quite wonderful to see. While he was thus sitting, the same old greybeard came again out of the forest, having with him another dog, that was not less than the one before mentioned. When the youth saw the handsome animal, he thought within himself: "It would be well to have a dog like that, as a companion, here out in the fields; there would then be no danger." When the old man was aware of what was passing in his mind, he said: "I am come because I wish to exchange my dog for one of thy hogs." The lad did not waste much time in considering, but closed the bargain; so got the great dog, giving his hog in exchange. The old greybeard then went his way; but when departing, said to the youth: "Verily I think thou wilt be content with our bargain; for this dog is not like other dogs. His name is *Tear*, and whatever thou biddest him tear, he will rend in pieces, were it even the fiercest Troll." They then parted; but the lad was glad at heart and thought he had made a good day's work; though he well knew that his old mother would not be pleased with the transaction.

Towards evening the youth returned home, and his mother was no less angry than on the preceding day. This time, however, she did not venture to beat her son, being afraid of his great dogs. But, as it is wont to happen, that when women have for a length of time been bitterly scolding, they at last resign themselves to patience, so it was in the present instance. The lad and his mother, therefore, made up their difference; though the woman thought she had suffered an injury that could not be repaired in a hurry.

On the third day the youth went to the forest with his hog and his two dogs. Being now full of joy, he sat down on a stump of a tree and played on his pipe, as was his custom and the dogs danced so delightfully that it was a pleasure to look on them. While the lad was thus sitting and enjoying himself, the old greybeard again came forth from the forest. This time he had with him a third dog, as large as either of the two others. When the lad saw the noble animal, he could not help thinking: "It would be well to have such a dog as a companion in the fields; there would then be no danger." The old man then said: "I am come because I wish thee to see my dog; for I well know that thou wouldst gladly possess him." The lad was quite willing, and concluded the bargain, and so got the great dog, giving his last hog in exchange. The old man then went his way, but on going said: "I think thou wilt be content with the bargain; for this dog is not like other dogs. His name is *Quick-ear*, and his sense of hearing is so acute, that he is aware of everything that happens, even if it be many miles distant. Aye, he hears how the trees and the grass in the fields grow."[43] Having thus spoken, they parted in great friendship; and the youth was glad at heart, thinking that now he had nothing to fear in the world.

When evening drew on, and the youth had returned home, his mother was sadly grieved that her son had sold all her property. But the lad entreated her to dismiss her sorrow, adding that he would take care she should sustain no loss; and put his words together so well that the old woman was quite pleased, and thought he spoke sensibly and like a man. When day dawned, the youth went a hunting with his two dogs, and in the evening returned with as much game as he could well carry. He continued hunting for some time, so that his mother's larder was constantly supplied with meat and all kinds of necessaries. He then bade his mother farewell, called his dogs, and said he would wander abroad in the world, and see what fortune would bestow on him.

He now journeyed across mountains and through wild ways, and at length found himself deep in a dark forest. There he met the greybeard, of whom we have already spoken. The youth was very glad to see him again, and greeted him with: "Good day, father. Thanks for our last meeting." The old man answered: "Good day to thee. What road dost thou purpose taking?" The boy replied: "I intend going abroad in the world, to see what turn my fortune will take." Thereupon the old man said: "Pursue thy way onward, and thou wilt come to a royal palace; there thy fortune will change." They then separated. But the youth was mindful of the greybeard's words and continued his course without any delay. Wherever he came to a hostel, he played on his pipe and

---

[43] His ears almost rival those of Heimdall. See "Northern Mythology." i. p. 29.

made his three dogs dance, and never failed to get food and shelter, and whatever else he stood in need of.

When he had travelled for many days, he arrived in a great city, where a vast multitude of people were flocking in the streets. The youth wondered what it all might mean, and at length reached the spot where a royal proclamation was being read, that whosoever should rescue the three princesses from the power of the Mountain-troll, should have one of them, and half the realm besides. The youth was now at no loss for the meaning of what grey beard had said to him. Therefore, calling his dogs, he went on until he reached the palace. Here was little else but mourning and lamentation, from the day on which the king's daughters had disappeared; but the king and queen mourned more than all. The youth now went up to the castle and requested to be admitted to the king and show his dogs. At this the persons of the court were well pleased, thinking it would in some measure alleviate their master's sorrow. The youth was accordingly admitted and exhibited his performances; and when the king had heard his playing and seen how wonderfully his dogs danced, he was so exhilarated that no one had seen him so joyful for seven long years, or since the day that he lost his daughters.

When the dancing was over, the king asked the youth what reward he would have for having afforded them all so delightful an entertainment. The youth answered: "Sir king, I am not come hither to gain goods and gold; but I beg another boon, which is, that you grant me permission to go and seek the three princesses who are in the power of the Mountain-trolls." When the king heard this, his aspect became gloomy, and he said: "Think not that thou canst deliver my daughters. The undertaking is a perilous one and has turned out ill to many who were superior to thee. But if it should so happen that some one releases the princesses, I certainly would not think of forfeiting my word." These words seemed to the youth both royal and straightforward. He then took leave of the king, and commenced his journey, with the resolve to allow himself no rest or quiet, until he had found what he sought.

The youth now travelled through many extensive countries, without meeting with anything remarkable. Whithersoever he went he was attended by his dogs. Quick-ear ran and listened whether anything was to be heard in the neighbourhood; Hold carried the provisions; and Tear, that was the largest and strongest, carried his master, when he was tired with walking. One day

Quick-ear came running at full speed to his master and informed him that he had been near a high mountain and heard one of the king's daughters spinning within it; but that the giant himself was not at home. At this intelligence the youth was delighted, and hastened to the mountain, accompanied by his dogs. When they had reached it, Quick-ear said: "We have no time to lose: the giant is only ten miles off and I already hear his horse's golden shoes ringing over the stones." The youth now ordered his dogs to beat in the door of the mountain, which they did. On entering the mountain, he perceived a fair damsel sitting in the apartment and winding golden thread on a golden spindle. The youth advanced and greeted the beautiful maiden, at which the princess was greatly surprised, and said: "Who art thou who darest to come hither into the giant's hall? For seven long years I have been a captive in the mountain, without ever seeing a human being. For heaven's sake, hasten hence before the Troll's return, or thy life is at stake." But the youth felt no fear and thought he might venture to await the giant's coming.

While they were yet speaking, the giant came riding on his gold-shod horse. On perceiving that the door was open, he became furiously wroth, and roared out, so that the whole mountain trembled: "Who has broken my door?" The youth answered boldly: "I have done it, and I will now break thee likewise. Hold! Hold him; Tear and Quick-ear! Tear him in a thousand pieces." Hardly were the words uttered before the dogs rushed forwards, threw themselves on the giant, and tore him in innumerable fragments. The princess was almost overcome with joy and said: "Heaven be praised! now I am saved." She then fell on her deliverer's neck and kissed him. But the youth would no longer stay there; therefore, saddling the giant's horses, he loaded them with all the gold and treasure he found in the mountain, and hastened away together with the fair young princess.

They now journeyed a long way together, and the youth attended on the princess with decorum and purity of heart, as was due to so exalted a damsel. It happened one day that Quick-ear, having been sent out to get intelligence, came hastily running to his master, and related to him that he had been near a high mountain and heard how another of the king's daughters was sitting in it winding gold thread; but that the giant himself was not at home. With these tidings the youth was well-pleased, and hastened to the mountain, followed by his three dogs. On reaching the mountain, Quick-ear said: "We have no time to waste: the giant is only eight miles off, and I already hear his horse's golden shoes ringing on the stones." The youth instantly ordered his dogs to beat in the door of the mountain, which they did. On entering the mountain, he perceived a fair maiden sitting and winding gold thread on a golden reel. The youth approached and greeted the maiden, at which she was greatly surprised, and said: "Who art thou who darest to come hither, into the giant's hall? During the seven long years that I have dwelt in the mountain, I have not seen a single human being. For heaven's sake, hasten hence before the Troll returns, or thy life is at stake." But the youth told her his errand and thought he could well venture to await the giant's coming.

While they were yet talking, the giant arrived riding on his gold-shod horse and stopped just without the mountain. On perceiving that the door was open, he became furiously wroth, and cried out so that the whole mountain trembled to its very roots: "Who has broken my door?" The youth answered boldly: "I have done it, and now I will break thee also. Hold! hold him; Tear and Quick-ear! tear him in many thousand pieces." Instantly the dogs rushed forwards, threw themselves on the giant, and tore him in as many pieces as are the leaves that fall in autumn. Then was the king's daughter overcome with joy, and she exclaimed: "Heaven be praised! now I am saved." She fell on the young man's neck and kissed him. The youth then conducted the princess to her sister, and it is easy to imagine what joy there was when they met. The youth then took all the precious things that he found in the mountain, loaded with them the giant's gold-shod horses, and departed with the princesses.

They now again travelled a long way, and the young man served the princesses with the decorum and respect due to such high damsels. It happened again that Quick-ear had run out before them to gather intelligence, and came running back to his master, saying that he had been to a high mountain, and heard how the king's third daughter was sitting within it weaving cloth of gold; but the giant himself was not at home. On reaching the spot, Quick-ear said: "Here is no time to lose; for the giant is not more than five miles off. I can plainly hear his horse's golden shoes ringing on the stones." The youth then ordered his dogs to beat in the door of the mountain, which they did. On entering the mountain, he perceived a damsel sitting and weaving cloth of gold. The maiden was so exquisitely beautiful, that the youth thought that so fair a female was not to be found in the whole world. He approached and greeted her, at which the king's daughter was greatly surprised, and said: "Who art thou who darest to come hither, into the giant's hall? For seven long years I have dwelt in this mountain and have never yet seen a human being. For heaven's sake go hence, before the Troll returns, or he will put thee to death." But the youth was stout of heart and said he would willingly risk his life for the lovely princess.

While they were yet talking together, the giant came riding on his gold-shod horse and stepped close by the mountain. On entering and seeing what unbidden guests were come, he was greatly terrified; for he was well aware of the fate that had befallen his brethren. He therefore deemed it advisable to act with caution and guile, seeing that he durst not venture on an open contest. He consequently began with an abundance of fair words and affected to be very smooth and friendly towards the youth. He, moreover, desired the princess to prepare food, that he might show hospitality to the stranger. In fine the Troll so ordered his words that the young man was completely infatuated by his seductive tongue and neglected to be on his guard. He then sat down to table with the giant; but the king's daughter wept in secret, and the dogs were very restless; though no one noticed it.

When the giant and his guest had finished their repast, the youth said: "I have now allayed my hunger; give me also something wherewith I may slacken my thirst." The giant answered: "Up in the mountain there is a spring which runs with the brightest wine; but I have no one who can fetch it." The youth replied: "If that be all, one of my dogs can go up." At these words the giant laughed in his false heart; for he desired nothing so much as that the youth should send away his dogs. The young man then ordered Hold to go to the spring for wine, and the giant gave him a capacious pitcher. The dog went, although, it was easy to see, with no good will. Time crept on and on, but no dog returned.

When a considerable time had passed, the giant said: "I wonder why the dog stays so long away. Perhaps it would be well to let another of your dogs go and help him, as the distance is great and the pitcher heavy." The youth, suspecting no treachery, complied with the giants wish, and ordered Tear to go and find out why Hold did not return. The dog wagged his tail and would not leave his master, but the latter did not observe it, and even drove him away to the spring. The giant now laughed in his sleeve, and the king's daughter wept; the youth, however, did not observe it, but was merry of mood, joked with his host, and entertained not a thought of danger.

A long time again elapsed, but no tidings came either of the dogs or the wine. The giant thereupon said: "I see plainly that your dogs do not do what you order them; else we should not be sitting here thirsting. I think it best that you let Quick-ear go and find out why they do not come back." The youth was stimulated by this speech and ordered his third dog to go in all haste to the spring. Quick ear, however, would not go, but crept whining to his master's feet. The youth then became angry and drove the faithful creature away with violence. The dog was now forced to obey his master and ran in great haste up the mountain; but when he reached the summit, it fared with him as it had with the others: a high wall rose round him, and he was entrapped through the giant's sorcery.

When all the three dogs were away, the giant rose, and, with a changed countenance, seized a bright sword that was hanging on the wall. He said: "Now I will avenge my brothers, and thou shalt instantly die; for thou art in my power. The lad was alarmed and repented having sent away his dogs. He said: "I will not beg for life, seeing that at all events I must die once. But one request I do make that I may repeat my *Pater noster* and play a psalm on my pipe. Such is the usage in our country." The giant complied with this request; but said that he would not wait longer. The youth now fell on his knees, devoutly repeated his *Pater noster*, and began playing on his pipe, so that it resounded over hill and dale. In the same instant the sorcery was dissolved, and the dogs got loose again, and came rushing like a hurricane into the mountain. Instantly the youth started up and cried: "Hold! hold him; Tear and Quick-ear! tear him in a thousand pieces." The dogs then fell on the giant and rent him in innumerable fragments. The youth afterwards took all the precious thing she found in the mountain, harnessed the giant's horses to a gilded chariot, and prepared to depart with the least delay possible.

When the king's daughters were thus found again, there was great joy among them, and they all thanked their deliverer for having saved them from the power of the giant. The youth contracted a strong passion for the youngest princess, and they vowed eternal faith and love to each other. Thus, they travelled on, with mirth and jest and all kinds of pastime; and the youth attended them with the decorum and observance due to such exalted damsels.

During the journey the princesses played with the young man's hair, and each bound her ring in his long locks, as a remembrance.

One day, when they were travelling, they overtook two men, who were journeying in the same direction. The two strangers were clad in tattered garments, their feet were wounded, and from their whole appearance, it was easy to see they had travelled a long way. On seeing them the youth stopped his chariot and inquired who they were and whence they came. The strangers answered, that they were two princes, who had set out in search of the three princesses, who had been carried off by the Mountain-trolls but that their search had been fruitless; so that they now had to wander homewards rather as beggars than as sons of a king. When the youth heard this, he felt pity for the two travellers, and asked them whether they would go with him in the chariot. The princes thanked him warmly for the offer, and they travelled together, and arrived in the country over which the father of the princesses ruled.

When the princes came to know how the youth had saved the three princesses, they were overcome with envy, feeling conscious that their own wanderings had proved quite fruitless. They therefore consulted together how they might get rid of the youth and gain honour and rewards to themselves. In pursuance of their plan, they suddenly assailed their fellow traveller, seized him by the throat, and wounded him in many places. They then threatened the princesses with death, unless they would swear to keep secret what had taken place. The king's daughters, being new in the power of the two princes, durst not refuse compliance with this demand. But they felt great pity for the youth, who for them had risked his life, and the youngest princess mourned for him with all her heart and would know no comfort more.

After this great misdeed, the princes proceeded to the king's palace, and it may easily be conceived what joy there was when the king received back his three daughters. In the meanwhile, the poor youth lay in the forest for dead. But he was not quite forsaken; for his faithful dogs laid themselves by him, protected him with their bodies against the cold, and licked his wounds and ceased not until their master was restored to life. When he had recovered his strength, he recommenced his journey, and, after many hindrances, arrived at the king's palace, where the princesses had their abode.

When the youth entered, he heard a great noise and merry-making over the whole place, and from the royal apartment the sound of stringed instruments.

At this he was greatly surprised and inquired what it meant. The servant answered: "Surely thou must have come from a far distant land, who knowest not that the king has recovered his daughters out of the power of the Mountain-trolls. Today is the marriage of the two elder princesses." The youth then inquired after the youngest princess, whether she was also about to be married, and the servant answered, that she would marry no one, but only wept, although no one knew the cause of her sorrow. At this the youth was overjoyed; for he now felt convinced that his beloved princess was true to him.

The youth now went up into the palace, and caused it to be announced to the king, that a guest had arrived who prayed for permission to increase the mirth by exhibiting his dogs. At this the king was well pleased, and he commanded the stranger to be received in the most hospitable manner. When the youth entered the hall, there was great wondering among the guests at his activity and manly bearing, and all thought they had never seen so bold a youth. But the three princesses instantly recognised him, sprang up from the table, and rushed into his arms. The princes new deemed it no longer advisable to stay where they were; and the princesses related how the youth had rescued them, and everything besides that had befallen them; in confirmation of which, each one looked for and found her ring among his locks.

When the king was informed that the two foreign princes had been guilty of such treachery and baseness, he was exceedingly exasperated, and commanded that they should be driven with ignominy from his palace. But the brave youth was received with great honour, as he well deserved, and on the same day his marriage was solemnized with the king's youngest daughter. After the king's death the youth was chosen ruler over the whole realm and was a valiant king. And there he lives yet with his fair queen and governs prosperously to this day. I was afterwards no longer with them.

1. In a variation from Wermland, the youth's last adventure is related as follows:—

While the youth was sitting with the giant in the mountain, the latter began to relate a fine story of three wonderful curiosities that were to be found in his country. These curiosities were: a spring with *the water of life*, a shrub with *vulnerary leaves*, and a tree with *flowers of strength*. The water of life had such virtue, that all to whom it was given inwardly or applied externally were immediately restored to life, if they were already dead. The vulnerary leaves possessed the power of healing the most dangerous wounds; and the flowers of strength imparted vigour to the weakest. When the youth heard tell of these wonderful things, he was seized with an unconquerable desire to possess them and inquired how he could gratify that desire. The giant answered: "It seems to me advisable that thou shouldst send thy dogs to fetch the three rarities, and I will tell thee where they are to be found." The youth was deceived by this artful talk, and instantly sent away his dogs to fetch the water of life, the vulnerary leaves, and the flowers of strength.

No sooner had the dogs departed, than the giant, rising up, seized his bright sword, saying: "Now thou art in my power, and shalt not escape; for thy dogs are bound in the mountain, and cannot help thee." He was then about to kill the youth; but the latter, taking his pipe, blew so that it resounded over hill and dale. At the same moment the dogs get loose again, rushed into the mountain, and tore the giant in pieces in the twinkling of an eye.

In the following part it is related how the youth was killed by the treacherous princes, and his body cast into a thick wood. But the faithful dogs would not leave their master but watched by him both day and night. When some time had elapsed, one of the dogs said: "I will run and fetch a flask of the water of life; that may probably be of avail." The second said: "I will run for some of the vulnerary leaves and see what they will do." The third said: "And I will run for some of the flowers of strength. The dogs then ran their several ways, and soon returned. They sprinkled their master's body with the water of life, and he was immediately restored to life, though his wounds bled profusely. They next applied some of the fresh leaves to his wounds, which instantly closed and were healed; but the youth was still excessively weak, and scarcely able to move. Finally, they gave him some of the flowers of strength, when he recovered his strength, and was vigorous and healthy as before. When he was completely restored, he hastened away to the king's palace, gained the young princess, and demanded vengeance on those who had so basely murdered him.

2. A version from South Småland, called *Snipp, Snapp, Snorium*, runs thus:—

There was once a miller who had three children, two girls and a boy. When the miller died, and the children divided the property, the daughters took the entire mill, and left their brother nothing but three sheep, that he tended in the forest. As he was one day wandering about, he met an old man, with whom he exchanged a sheep for a dog named *Snipp* on the following day the same old man met him again, when he exchanged another sheep with him for a dog named *Snapp*; and on the third day his third sheep, for a dog named *Snorium*. The three dogs were large and strong, and obedient to their master in everything.

When the lad found there was no good to be done at home, he re solved to go out in the world and seek his fortune. After long wandering he came to a large city, in which the houses were hung with black, and everything betokened some great and universal calamity. The youth took up his quarters with an old fisherman, of whom he inquired the cause of this mourning. The fisherman informed him that there was a huge serpent named *Turenfax*, which inhabited an island out in the ocean that every year a pure maiden must be given him to be devoured; and that the lot had now fallen on the king's only daughter. When the youth had heard this, he formed the resolution of venturing a contest with the serpent, and rescuing the princess, provided fortune would befriend him.

On the appointed day the youth sailed over to the island and awaited whatever might happen. While he was sitting, he saw the young princess drawing near in a boat, accompanied by a number of people. The king's daughter stopped at the foot of the mountain and wept bitterly. The youth then approached her, greeted her courteously, and comforted her to the best of his power. When a short time had passed thus, he said: "Snipp! go to the mountain-cave and see whether the serpent is coming." But the dog returned, wagged his tail, and said that the serpent had not yet made his appearance. When some time had elapsed, the youth said: "Snapp! go to the mountain-cave and see whether the serpent is coming." The dog went, but soon returned without having seen the serpent. After a while the youth said: "Snorium! go to the mountain-cave and see whether the serpent is coming." The dog went, but soon returned trembling violently. The youth could now easily guess that the serpent was approaching, and, consequently, made himself ready for the fight.

As Turenfax came hastening down the mountain, the youth set his dogs Snipp and Snapp on him. A desperate battle then ensued; but the serpent was so strong that the dogs were unable to master him. When the youth observed this, he set on his third dog, Snorium, and new the conflict became even fiercer; but the dogs get the mastery, and the game did not end until Turenfax received his death-wound.

When the serpent was dead the king's daughter thanked her deliverer with many affectionate expressions for her safety and besought him to accompany her to the royal palace. But the youth would try his luck in the world for some time longer, and therefore declined her invitation. It was, however, agreed on between them that the youth should return in a year arid woo the fair maiden. On parting the princess brake her gold chain in three and bound a portion round the neck of each of the dogs. To the young man she gave her ring, and they promised ever to be faithful to each other.

The young man now travelled about in the wide world, as we have said, and the king's daughter returned home. On her way she was met by a courtier, who forced her to make oath that he and no other had slain Turenfax. This courtier was thenceforward looked upon as a most doughty champion and got a promise of the princess. But the maiden would not break her faith to the youth and deferred the marriage from day to day.

When the year was expired, the youth returned from his wandering, and came to the great city. But now the houses were hung with scarlet, and all things seemed to indicate a great and general rejoicing. The youth again took up his quarters with the old fisherman and asked what might be the cause of all the joy. He was informed that a courtier had killed Turenfax and was now about to celebrate his nuptials with the king's fair daughter. No one has heard what the miller's son said on receiving this intelligence; though it may easily be imagined that he was not greatly delighted at it.

When dinner-time came, the youth felt a longing to partake of the king's fare, and his best was at a great loss how this could be brought to pass. But the youth said: "Snipp go up to the palace and bring me a piece of game from the king's table. Fondle the young princess; but strike the false courtier a blow that he may not soon forget." Snipp did as his master had commanded him; he went up to the palace, caressed the fair princess, but struck the courtier a blow that made him black and blue; then, seizing a piece of game, he ran off. Hereupon there arose a great uproar in the hall, and all were filled with wonder, excepting the king's daughter; for she had recognised her gold neck-chain, and thence divined who the dog's master was.

The next day a similar scene was enacted. The youth was inclined to eat some pastry from the king's own table, and the fisherman was at a loss how this could be brought about. But the youth said: "Snapp! go up to the palace and bring me some pastry from the king's table. Fondle the young princess; but strike the false courtier a blow that he may not soon forget." Snapp did as his master had commanded him; he went up to the palace, broke through the sentinels, caressed the fair princess, but struck the false courtier a blow that made him see the sun both in the east and west; then, seizing a piece of pastry, he ran off. Now there was a greater uproar than on the preceding day, and everyone wondered at what had taken place, excepting the king's daughter; for she again recognised her gold neck-chain, whereby she well knew who the dog's master was.

On the third day the youth wished to drink wine from the king's table and sent Snorium to fetch some. Everything now took place as before. The dog burst through the guard, entered the drinking apartment, caressed the princess, but struck the false courtier a blow that sent him tumbling head over heels on the floor then, seizing a flask of wine, he ran off. The king was sorely vexed at all this and sent the courtier with a number of people to seize the stranger who owned the three dogs. The courtier went and came to where the young man dwelt with the poor fisherman. But there another game began; for the youth called to his three dogs: "Snipp! Snapp! Snorium! clear the house." In an instant the dogs rushed forward, and in a twinkling all the king's men lay on the ground.

The youth then caused the courtier to be bound hand and foot and proceeded to the apartment where the king was sitting at table with his men. When he entered, the princess ran to meet him with great affection, and began relating to her father how the courtier had deceived him. When the king heard all this, and recognised his daughter's gold chain and ring, he ordered the courtier to be cast to the three dogs; but the brave youth obtained the princess, and with her half the kingdom.

4. In another version from South Småland, it is related that there was a peasant's son, who tended the cattle of the village in the forest, and who one day met a huntsman mounted on a tall horse and accompanied by three very large dogs. The dogs were far more powerful than other dogs, and were named *Break-iron, Strike-down,* and *Holdfast.* The boy becomes master of the three

dogs; but it is a current story among the maple, that the huntsman, who gave them to him, could be no other than Odin himself.

The youth then bids his employment farewell, and sets out in search of the king's daughter, who has been carried off. In his wanderings he meets with an aged crone, who directs him on the way. But the princess is confined in a large castle, that is well provided with locks and bars; and the lord of the castle has fixed his marriage with the fair damsel to be solemnized within a few days.

The youth is now at a loss how he can gain entrance into the castle. With this object he goes to the warders and asks for employment to procure game for the feast. He is admitted, goes to the forest, and gets an abundance of game. Towards evening he returns, and in the night calls his dog, Break-iron, orders him to clear the way, and so, in spite of doors and bars, reaches the tower in which the princess is confined. The noise wakes the lord of the castle, who comes hurrying to the spot with weapons and attendants. But the youth calls his other two dogs, Strike-down and Hold-fast, and a bloody fight ensues, which ends in the youth's favour, who takes possession of the whole castle.

After the release of the princess the herd-boy sets out on his return to the old king, the damsel's father. On the way he has to engage in combat with a courtier, who would carry off the princess, but the youth is well seconded by his dogs, and comes off victor. The conclusion is the usual one, that the lad gets the king's daughter, and, after his father-in-law's death, becomes ruler over the whole realm.

THE MERMAID.

I. THE KING'S SON AND MESSERIA.

From South Småland.

THERE was once a king and a queen who were childless. At this they were much grieved; for the king desired nothing so fervently as to have an heir to his crown and kingdom; but year after year passed away, and there seemed no hope that his wish should ever be realized.

The queen, the king's consort, found her chief pleasure in sailing about on the sea, whenever the weather permitted. It happened once that her bark suddenly stood still, so that the sailors were unable to move it either backwards or forwards. Now everyone may easily imagine that there was someone in the water, who held the vessel fast. The queen, therefore, went on deck, and demanded who it was that hindered their course, when, from under the keel, a voice was heard, saying: "Never again shalt thou tread the green earth, unless thou wilt give me what thou bearest under thy girdle." To this the queen readily consented, for she knew not that she was pregnant: and then cast her bunch of keys, which hung at her girdle, into the deep. Instantly the bark was again afloat, and began gliding over the billows, until it reached a port in the king's territory.

Some time after, the queen found that she was pregnant. Great joy was thereupon spread over the whole country, and the king was the gladdest of all, that now his fondest wish would be gratified. But the queen was not glad; for she feared within herself that she had unwittingly promised away her own offspring. When the king observed her secret sorrow, he thought it extraordinary, and asked her why she alone was afflicted, while everyone else was full of joy. The queen now imparted to him what had befallen her on her marine excursion. But the king bade her be comforted and cast off her grief, adding that he would take such measures, that the Mermaid should never get their child into her hands.

When the time arrived, the queen gave birth to a boy. The young prince increased in age and strength and became stronger and comelier than all other children. At this the king and queen were rejoiced at heart and regarded the child as the apple of their eye. Thus, passed the time until the prince attained his twelfth year. It then happened that the king received a visit from his brother, who reigned over another kingdom, accompanied by his two sons. The three royal children found their greatest delight in playing together. One day the two stranger princes were amusing themselves with riding in the court before the palace, while their cousin stood within observing their sport; when on a sudden he was seized with an irresistible desire to partake in it. Stealing therefore from his attendants, he ran into the court and mounted on horseback. The youths then went down to the beach to water their horses; but scarcely had the prince's horse touched the water, when it ran out into the sea and disappeared among the billows. The two cousins, on witnessing this disaster, instantly returned to the palace and related what had happened. Now, as it is easy to imagine, there were weeping and sorrow. The king sent his men to seek after the prince; but all their search was vain: the youth was away and remained away.

At the bottom of the ocean the young prince found a green path, which led to a fair palace, that glittered all over with gold and precious stones, so that the like was never seen. In this palace dwelt the Mermaid, who rules over the wind and waves. When the prince entered the palace, the crone looked at him with eyes of benevolence, and said: "Welcome, fair youth! for these twelve years have I been expecting thee. Thou shalt now stay here and be my little page. If thou servest me faithfully and well, thou shalt be allowed to return to thy relations; but if thou doest not as I command thee, thou shalt forfeit thy life." At this speech the youth felt ill at ease for he longed after home and his parents, as is usual with boys of that age; but he was obliged to reconcile himself to his fate and live awhile with the Mermaid in the fair palace at the bottom of the sea.

One day the Mermaid ordered the young prince to appear before her and said to him: "It is time that thou beginnest thy duties, and this shall be thy first trial. Here are two bundles of yarn, one white and one black. Now thou shalt wash the white one black, and the black one white. But the whole must be ready betimes tomorrow, when I wake; otherwise thy life is at stake." The youth then took the two bundles, as the Mermaid had commanded, went down to the beach, and began washing with all his might. But let him do as he would, the white yarn was and would be white, and the black black. When the prince saw that he could not perform his task, he was sadly disheartened, and wept bitterly. In the same moment a young and beautiful maiden appeared before him, who greeted him in a friendly tone, and asked him why he was so afflicted. The prince answered: "I may well be afflicted for the Mermaid has commanded me to wash this white yarn black, and the black yarn white and if I have not done it by the morning, when she wakes, my life is at stake." The damsel then said: "If thou wilt promise to be true to me, I will help thee, and will always be true to thee in return." To this proposal the youth gladly assented; for the maiden was so fair that no one can imagine how fair she was. So, they promised ever to be faithful to each other. The damsel then went to a stone, on which she struck, saying: "Come forth, all my Lady Mother's

Pysslings[44], and help to wash this white yarn black, and the black yarn till it becomes white." At the same moment a whole multitude of little people, or Pysslings, came up, whose number no one could tell; and each Pyssling, taking a little end of thread, began to wash so diligently, so diligently, and did not leave off until the white yarn was washed black, and the black yarn white. When the work was done, the Pysslings crept down under the stone, and no more of them was seen. The young damsel then sat down to converse with the king's son, and related to him that she was a princess, and her name Messeria. She, at the same time, warned him not to let anyone know how they had met with each other.

Early in the morning, before sunrise, the prince went to his mistress, as he had been commanded. As soon as he entered, the Mermaid asked him whether he had executed her orders. The youth answered in the affirmative and showed her the two bundles of yarn. At the sight of them, the Mermaid was greatly astonished, and said: "How has this been accomplished? Hast thou met with any of my daughters?" The youth answered, that he had seen no one; and so, they parted for that time.

Some time after, the Mermaid again ordered the youth to be called before her and said: "I will now put thee to another trial. Here are a barrel of wheat and a barrel of barley mingled together. Thou shalt separate these from each other, so that the barley may be parted from the wheat and the wheat from the barley. But all must be done tomorrow by the time I wake; otherwise thy life is forfeited." So, the youth took the wheat and barley, as he had been commanded, and began picking as well as he could; but let him do as he might, when night approached, he had separated only a very small portion. He was now sadly downcast and wept bitterly, when Messeria on a sudden appeared before him, greeted him kindly, and asked him the cause of his great affliction. The prince answered: "I may well weep and be sad. The Mermaid has commanded me to separate all this grain according to its different kinds, so that the barley be parted from the wheat, and the wheat from the barley. But if I have not done it by tomorrow when she wakes, my life is forfeited." The maiden said: "If thru wilt promise to be true to me, I will help thee, and always be true to thee in return." The prince assured her that he would never love any other in the world; but her

____

[44] See Northern Mythology, ii. p. 94.

only. The damsel then went to a stone, on which she struck, saying: "Come forth, all my Lady Mother's Pysslings, and help to separate the barley from the wheat, and the wheat from the barley. Instantly there came up a countless multitude of Pysslings, each of whom took a grain, and they picked so diligently, so diligently, until all the grain was sorted, the barley by itself, and the wheat by itself. When all was done, the Pysslings crept down again under the stone, and were no more seen. Messeria also went her way; but warned the king's son not to let any one knows how they had met with each other.

Early in the morning, before dawn, the prince appeared before his mistress, as he had been commanded. On seeing him, the Mermaid asked him whether he had performed his task. The youth answered in the affirmative, and showed her the grain separated, each kind by itself. The crone was greatly surprised, and said: "How has this been accomplished? Hast thou met with one of my daughters?" The prince answered that he had not seen any one; and so they parted for that time.

When some time had again passed, the Mermaid sent a message to the young prince. On his appearing before her, she said: "I will now put thee to a third trial. In my stalls there are a hundred oxen, and the stalls have not been cleansed for twenty years. Thou shalt go and cleanse them. If thou hast finished the work by tomorrow, when I wake, I will give thee one of my daughters, and permission to return home to thy kindred. But if thou hast not finished it, thy life is forfeited." The youth then went to the Mermaid's stalls and began throwing and throwing out the dung; but let him toil as he might, it was easy to see that he would never perform his task, as the heap seemed rather to increase than diminish. The prince was now ill at ease and wept bitterly; but on a sudden the beautiful Messeria appeared before him and inquired the cause of his great affliction. The youth answered: "I may well weep and be sorrowful, The Mermaid has ordered me to cleanse the stalls, in which she has a hundred oxen. If I have done it by tomorrow, when she wakes, she will give me one of her daughters; but if I have not done it, my life is forfeited. The damsel said: "If thou wilt promise to be true to me, I will help thee, and always be true to thee in return." The king's son reiterated the assurance, that he would never love any other in all the world. Messeria then went to a large stone, on which she struck, saying: "Come forth, all my Lady Mother's Pysslings, and help to cleanse the Mermaid's stalls." Instantly there came up such a multitude of Pysslings, that the place swarmed with them; and the little men laboured so sedulously and incessantly, that the stalls were soon cleansed. When all was done, the Pysslings crept again under the stone, and were no more seen. But Messeria sat down and conversed with the prince and warned him not to let anyone know that they had met together. She further informed him that the Mermaid's daughters were in reality the children of kings, who had been transformed into all kinds of animals. "But" continued she, "if thou art resolved to be true to me, bear in remembrance that I am changed into a little cat with yellow sides and one of my ears cropped. The youth treasured all this up in his memory and said he would never forget her instructions. They then took a loving farewell of each other.

In the morning betimes, with the first dawn, the prince appeared before his mistress, as he had been ordered. When the Mermaid saw him, she asked him whether he had exe outed her commission. The youth answered "Yes," and they went to the stalls together. On seeing that all was done as she had commanded, she was indeed surprised, and asked how it could be, and whether no one had helped him. The king's son answered that he had seen no one. The Mermaid then said: "If such be the case, I will stand by the word and promise that I have given. Thou shalt choose one of my daughters, and then return home to thy family."

The prince now accompanied the Mermaid, and they came to a spacious saloon, in which he had never before been. The saloon was extremely beautiful, and adorned most sumptuously with gold and silver, and in it was assembled a large collection of animals of all kinds: serpents, toads, lizards, weasels, and others out of number. The Mermaid said to him: "Here thou seest all my daughters; choose now which thou wilt have." But when the youth looked at the ugly animals, he felt painfully embarrassed, and knew not which way to turn, so disgusting did they appear to him. While in this state of anxiety, he chanced to cast his eyes on a little cat, that had yellow sides, and one ear cropped, and walked about the apartment wagging its tail and looking very disconsolate. At the sight of the little animal, the prince instantly thought of what Messeria had told him; therefore, going up to it, he stroked it with his hand, and said: "This I will have, and no other." In a moment the animal changed its form, a fair maiden rose before him, in whom be recognised the beautiful damsel who had helped him. But the Mermaid was greatly disconcerted and said: "Why hast thou chosen her? she was the dearest to me of all my daughters."

When some time had elapsed, the Mermaid sent for the prince, and said: "I will now make preparations for thy marriage; but first thou must go and get wedding clothes for thy young bride. Go, therefore, to my sister and greet her from me, and thou wilt get all that is requisite." When the prince heard that he must go to the Mermaid's sister, he was greatly troubled for he knew that it was a perilous journey; so he sat down and wept bitterly. While he was thus sitting, the fair Messeria came to him and inquired why he was so afflicted. The prince answered: "I may well weep and be afflicted. The Mermaid has commanded me to go to her sister for wedding clothes and I can easily imagine it will be a dangerous journey." Messeria said: "If thou wilt promise to be true to me, I will help thee, and will always be true to thee in return." The king's son again assured her that he would never violate his faith and promise to her. The damsel then continued: "When thou hast travelled for some time, thou wilt come to a gate, which stands on the boundary where the Mermaid's territory ends. The gate is old and heavy; but grease it with the grease out of this grease-horn. Thou wilt next come to two men engaged in hewing an oak by the way-side. They have wooden axes give them these iron ones. Then thou wilt come to two other men who are thrashing. They have iron flails; give them these wooden ones. Afterwards thou wilt come to two eagles, which will swell and threaten when thou approachest them; give them these pieces of meat. At the Mermaid's sister's I have never been; and therefore, cannot counsel thee. Only be cautious and eat nothing." The prince thanked her warmly for her good advice and promised to follow it. He then bade Messeria farewell and set out on his journey.

After travelling for some distance, he came to the gate, as described by Messeria; and, as she had directed him, smeared the hinges, and then continued his journey till he came to the two men, who were hewing the oak. They had wooden axes, but the king's son gave an iron axe to each. He then came to where the two men stood thrashing. They had heavy flails of iron, but the prince gave them wooden flails. Going further, he came to the two eagles, which swelled up, and threatened him as he approached; but the prince gave to each of them a piece of meat, and so, without hindrance, reached the place to which his steps were directed.

When the king's son entered, he went directly to the Mermaid's sister and delivered his message. His reception was the best imaginable; but the crone had a sinister countenance, and the youth could plainly perceive that she did not mean all that she said. She bade him sit down, while she went and prepared the things for the wedding and ordered refreshments to be brought in that he might eat. But the prince, bearing Messeria's injunctions in his memory, would taste no food; but watching his opportunity, concealed it under the couch. When a little time had elapsed, the Mermaid came in, and inquired whether her guest had eaten. The youth answered that he had, at which the ozone laughed in her sleeve, saying:—

"Man's head, where art thou?"

The meat answered:—

"I'm here at the foot of the couch,
I'm here at the foot of the couch."

The youth now felt ill at ease; for he perceived the crone's wickedness; but the Mermaid was angry, sought after the food, and said that the prince should eat of it whether he would or not.

She then went out a second time, and the youth looked about him for a new hiding place. He now thrust the meat into the mouth of the stove, and thus concealed it as well as he could. But ere long the mermaid returned and asked whether he had eaten. The prince answered in the affirmative, and the crone laughed in her false heart, and said:—

"Man's head, where art thou?"

The meat answered:—

"I'm here in the mouth of the stove;
I'm here in the mouth of the stove."

When the Mermaid perceived that the youth was on his guard against her artifices, she became highly exasperated, sought after the meat, and said that the prince should eat of it, or forfeit his life.

She then went away for the third time. The prince was now quite at a loss where to hide the meat; but at length concealed it in his bosom under his clothes. So when the Mermaid, returned, she asked him, as before, whether he had eaten. He answered that he had. Then said the crone:—

"Man's head, where art thou?"

The meat answered:—

"I lie in his bosom,
I lie in his bosom."

Now the Mermaid laughed and said:—

"If thou liest in his breast,
Thou'lt be soon in his maw."

She then gave him many greetings for her sister, and a box containing the things for the wedding, wished him a pleasant journey, and so they parted.

The youth was now on his return, and glad was he, which will seem wonderful to no one. But "it is not wise to cry out hurrah before one has crossed the brook," as the old proverb tells us; for the prince had not got further than to the two eagles, when the crone cried out:—

"Eagles! Tear him in pieces."

He was now dreadfully terrified; but when the eagles saw who it was, they did him no harm, but answered:—

"No, he has given us food,
He has given us food."

So the prince passed by them, and came to where the men were thrashing. The Mermaid then cried out:—

"Thrashers! Beat him to death."

The youth now again trembled for his life but when the men saw who it was, they would not do him any harm, and answered"—

"No, he gave us wooden flails for iron ones,
Wooden flails for iron ones."

Thus, the king's son passed unscathed by the thrashers and came to the men who were hewing the tree. Then the Mermaid cried out:—

"Hewers! Hew him in pieces."

But when the men saw who it was, they did him no injury, saying:—

"No, he gave us iron axes for wooden ones,
Iron axes for wooden ones."

The prince now took to his heels, and ran at full speed till he came to the boundary, when the Mermaid cried:—

"Gate, squeeze him to death."

But the gate answered:—

"No, he has greased me,
He has greased me."

Thus, the youth again entered his mistress's domain, and no one will wonder that he was very tired after such a journey.

When he had rested a while, he continued his journey homewards. While thus travelling along the road, it entered his mind that it might be as well to know what wedding gear was contained in the box; for he thought of his dear Messeria and her warnings and, as is wont to be the case, "youth and wisdom do not accompany each other, the more he pondered the greater grew his curiosity; till at last he could no longer control his inquisitiveness, but opened the lid just, a little at one edge. But a great wonder now met his eyes: for it appeared to him that the box was full of sparks, and a stream of fire issued from the opening; the sparks of which flew in all directions. The prince now repented of his rashness; but it was too late; so that at last he could go neither back nor forwards but sat down and wept bitterly. At length it occurred to him that he would try whether Messeria's Pysslings would help him, and he went to a large stone, struck on it and cried: "Come forth, all my Lady

Mother's little Pysslings, and help me to replace the wedding gear." Instantly there came forth an innumerable multitude of Pysslings, and the little men spread themselves in all directions and ran after the sparks over hill and dale. After a while the whole swarm returned, each having caught a spark, which be replaced in the box. The Pysslings then crept down again under the stone. The king's son now resolved, that another time he would be more cautious and continued his journey to the palace where his mistress dwelt.

When the Mermaid saw him and heard that he had passed through all the dangers, she was greatly astonished, and gave him a kind reception. She then caused the prince's marriage to be celebrated with great state and rejoicings, and all her daughters were present at the feast. But Messeria was the fairest among all the king's daughters, and the bridegroom regarded her as more precious than all the jewels he had seen in the beautiful palace.

When the marriage was concluded, the prince and his fair bride got leave to depart. They bade the Mermaid farewell, heartily wishing never again to set eyes on her. Then placing themselves in a gilded chariot, they travelled over many green plains, till they rose up from the sea not far from the king's palace. Now the youth was seized with a violent longing to see how all things were at home among his kindred. Messeria was opposed to this wish and said it would be better if they first drove to her father, who was likewise a king. But the prince adhered to his determination and prevailed. When about to separate, Messeria received her husband's promise that he would taste no ford during his absence from her but would instantly return. The prince promised to obey her in this and took his departure. But the young bride sat down and wept bitterly for she could well foresee the consequences of his journey.

When the youth entered his father's palace, there were great rejoicings, as it is easy to imagine, but greatest of all was the joy of the king and queen. A sumptuous feast was then prepared, and all wished the prince welcome home. But the youth would neither eat nor drink, saying he must instantly depart. This to the queen seemed very singular, and she would not allow him to go away fasting. So, the prince was at length with many prayers persuaded, and at length prevailed on himself, to taste a peppercorn. From that moment his mind became changed, so that he forgot his fair bride, and all that had passed while he was with the Mermaid. He began then to eat and drink and make merry with his relations. But Messeria sat in the forest till the sun went down, and then, in deep sorrow, betook herself to a little cottage, and begged for shelter of the poor people who dwelt in it.

When some time had elapsed, the king wished his son to marry. The prince had no objection, and set out for another kingdom, to pay his court to a fair young princess. A feast was afterwards prepared, at which the healths of bridegroom and bride were drunk, with all kinds of rejoicings and plays. But the fair Messeria journeyed to the palace and prayed to be received as a waiting-maid. Thus, she passed in and out of the festive hall, and it may easily be imagined that it was with a heavy heart. But she suppressed her tears, and amid the general joy there was no one that noticed her sorrow.

While the wedding was in progress, the table was spread for the guests, and Messeria aided in bringing in the viands. She had with her two doves, that flew to and fro in the hall. When the first course was brought in, she took three grains of wheat and threw them to the doves; but the cock was foremost, and peeked up all the three grains, leaving nothing for his mate. Then said the little dove:—

> "Out upon thee!
> Thou hast served me
> As the king's son served Messeria."

There was now silence in the hall, and the guests were struck with wonder at the little birds. But the bridegroom grew very thoughtful, enticed the doves to him and caressed them.

After some time, another course was set on the table, and Messeria helped to bring in the viands. She again cast three grains of wheat to the doves; but, as on the former occasion, the cook pecked up all the three grains, and left nothing for his mate. Then said the little dove:—

> "Out upon thee!
> Thou hast served me
> As the king's son served Messeria."

Silence again prevailed in the hall, and all the guests listened to the words of the bird; but the prince was singularly affected, and again enticed the little birds and caressed them.

When the third course was brought in, Messeria again cast three grains of wheat to her doves, and the cock was again foremost, and peeked up all the three grains, leaving not one for his mate. Then said the little dove:—

> "Out upon thee!
> Thou hast served me
> As the king's son served Messeria."

Now a deep silence reigned over all the festive hall, and no one knew what to think of this miracle. But when the king's son heard the words of the dove, he awoke as from a dream, and it rushed into his memory how he had rewarded the fair Messeria for all her love. He sprang up from the table, clasped the young serving-maid to his breast, and said that she and no other should be his bride. He then related all the faith and affection that Messeria had proved to him, and everything besides that he had undergone while with the Mermaid.

When the king and queen and the several guests had heard his story, they could hardly recover from their astonishment. The stranger princess was now sent back to her family but Messeria was adorned as a bride, and wedded to the young prince. They lived together for many happy years, virtuously and honourably. But the prince never again forgot the fair Messeria.

II. THE KING'S SON AND THE PRINCESS SINGORRA.[45]

From Skåne.

THERE was once a king who ruled over a powerful kingdom. He was a great warrior, and often lived in the camp, both summer and winter. It happened

---

[45] Similar stories, or stories containing similar features, occur among the following people:

1. The Norwegians.—See Absjörnsen og Moe, ut sup., ii. No. 47. "Mestermo."

2. The Danes—See a Fragment in Winther, ut sup., 1 Samling, pp. 31-35. "Prindsen og Havmanden."

3. The Irish.—See Carleton, "Traits and Stories of the Irish Peasantry." Dublin, 1842, pp. 23-47. "The Three Tasks."

4. The Germans.—*a.* See Feen-Marchen, Braunschweig, 1801, pp. 40, seqq. "Der Riesenwald." *b. Ibid.* pp. 122, seqq. "Die Drei Gürtel." *c.* Grimm, K. und H. M. i. No. 51.

once, when he was at sea, that his bark stood still on the billowy ocean, and could not be made to move in any direction; though no one knew what held the vessel fast. The king thereupon went to the prow, and saw the Mermaid sitting on the waves by the bow of the ship, and now well knew it was she that stopped its course. He addressed her and asked her what she required. The Mermaid answered: "Thou shalt never go hence until thou hast promised me the first living being thou meetest on thy own shore." As the king had no other means of releasing his ship, he agreed to the Mermaid's condition, when the bark was instantly free again, the wind filled the sails and was favourable, until the king again landed in his own country.

The king had an only son, just fifteen years old, a youth of excellent promise. The young prince was fondly attached to his father, and anxiously longed for his return. When he saw the pendant of his parent's ship fluttering in the breeze, he was overjoyed, and ran down to the strand to bid his father welcome. But when the king saw his son, he was sorely grieved; for he remembered the promise he had made to the Mermaid. He, therefore, cast his eyes first on a hog, and then on a goose, that were wandering about on the seashore. On entering his castle, he ordered the hog to be thrown into the sea, which was done.

The next day, a violent storm arose, the sea raged mountains high, and the hog was cast dead on the shore, close by the king's residence. The king now plainly perceived that the Mermaid was angry, and, therefore, ordered the goose to be thrown into the ocean; but the same took place again, a storm arose, and the dead bird was thrown by the waves upon the strand. The king was now

---

"Fundevogel" (Cf. iii. p. 88). *d.* Grimm, i. No. 56. "Der Liebste Roland" (Cf. iii. pp. 99-101). *e. Ibid.* i. No. 79. "Die Wassernix." *f.* ii. No. 113. "De beiden Künigeskinner." *g. Ibid.* ii. No. 186. "Die wahre Braut." *h. Ibid.* ii. No. 193. "Der Trommler." *i.* Kuhn, "Markische Sagen und Marchen." Berlin, 1843, pp. 263-267. "Die Kenigstochter beim Popanz."

5. The Italians.—*a.* See Basile, Il Pentam. ii. No. 7. "La Palomma." *b. Ibid.* iii. No. 9. "Rosella." *c. Ibid.* v. No. 4. The latter part of "Lo Turzo d'Oro."

6. The French.—*a.* See Mad. D'Aulnoy, Contes des Fées; "Gracieuse et Percinet." *b. Ibid.* "L'Oranger et l'Abeille."

7. The Magyars.—See Gaal, "Märchen der Magyaren." Wien, 1822. No. 3. "Dic Gläserne Hacke."

8. The Poles.—See Woycicki, Polnische Volkssagen, iii. No. 10.

9. The Russians.—See Kletke, Marchensaal, ii. pp. 70-79. "Kojata."

sensible that the Mermaid was resolved to have his only son. But the youth was his father's chief delight, who would not lose him for half his kingdom.

But however long the time that elapsed, the king must at last experience the truth of the old proverb, that no one is stronger than his fate. For it happened one day that the youth went down to the strand, to play with other boys of his own age, when suddenly a snow-white hand, with a gold ring on each finger, rose out of the water. The hand seized on the king's son, where he was playing on the shore, and drew him down amid the blue billows. The prince was then conducted through the waters, over many green ways, and rested not until he came to the Mermaid's dwelling. Now we are told that the Mermaid has her abode deep in the bottom of the ocean, and that it is so splendid that it glitters with gold and precious stones, both within and without.

The youth now dwelt in the fair mansion and found there many other royal children. But among the Mermaid's attendants there was a young princess named Singorra. She had resided there for seven long years and possessed much hidden knowledge. The king's son contracted a strong affection for the fair maiden, and they vowed to each other love and faith, as long as they lived in the world.

One day the Mermaid called the youth to her and said: "I have observed that thy inclination is turned to my attendant Singorra. I will, therefore, propose three labours to thee. If thou performest them all, I will bestow on thee the fair maiden, and grant thee permission to return home to thy family. But if thou failest to do what I propose thou shalt stay here and serve me for the rest of thy days." The youth was unable to say much in answer. The Mermaid then led him to a large meadow, that was thickly overgrown with green sea-grass, and said to him: "Thy first labour shall be to mow all this grass, and set it up again, each blade on its root, so that it may thrive and grow as before. But the whole must be done this evening by sunset." Having thus spoken, she went her way, leaving the youth by himself. The prince now began cutting and cutting; but he had not laboured long before he could very well see that he would never get through his task. So, he sat down in the meadow and wept bitterly.

While the youth thus sat weeping, the fair Singorra appeared before him, and asked him why he was so afflicted. The king's son answered: "I cannot but weep. The Mermaid has commanded me to mow the whole meadow and set every blade on its root again. If I have not done it by the time the sun sinks in the forest, I shall lose thee and all the pleasure I have in the world." The maiden replied: "I will help thee, if thou wilt promise to be true to me; for I will never deceive thee." The prince gladly made the promise, adding that he would never break his faith and vow. Singorra then took the sithe, and with it touched the grass, when, in one instant, the whole meadow was mowed, and every little blade of grass fell at once to the ground. She then touched the grass again, and lo! every blade raised itself upon its root, and the meadow was as before. The princess then went her way; but the youth was delighted, and went to his mistress, and announced to her that he had performed the task which she had set him.

The next day, the Mermaid called the youth to her again, and said: "I will give thee another work to perform. In my stable there stand a hundred horses, and it has not been cleansed within the memory of man. Thou shalt now go thither and make it clean. If thou hast done it this evening by sunset, I will stand firm to my promise." Having so spoken, she went her way, and left the youth alone. When he came to the stable, he could very well see that he should never perform the task; and, therefore, sat down and wept bitterly.

He had not sat long, when the fair Singorra appeared before him, and inquired the cause of his sorrow. The king's son answered: "I cannot refrain from weeping. The Mermaid has commanded me to cleanse her stable, if I will not lose thee and every other joy. But the stable must be cleansed this evening by sunset." The maiden said: "I will help thee, if thou wilt promise to be true to me; for thee I will never deceive." The youth gladly made the promise and said he would never love any but her. Thereupon Singorra went to the stable door, took down a gold whip that hung on the wall, and with it struck the horse that stood in the farthest corner. The horse instantly got loose, and began scraping the ground with his hoofs, until the whole stable was clean so that all the hundred horses neighed and stamped for joy. When all was done, the princess went her way; but the youth was delighted, and went to his mistress, to announce to her that he had performed her command.

On the third day, the Mermaid again sent for the king's son, and said: "I will yet assign thee another labour. If thou accomplishest also that, I will adhere to the promise I have given thee; but if thou dost not perform it, thou shalt stay here and serve me all thy days." The prince asked what his mistress required. The Mermaid answered: "In my sty, there are some thousands of swine, and the soil has not been removed for a hundred years. Thou shalt cleanse the pig-sty, and it shall be done this evening by sunset." Having thus spoken, she conducted the prince to a vast pig-sty, wherein lay more swine than any one could count, and the filth rose to a high mount, which no one could traverse, except over a narrow bridge. The Mermaid then went her way and thought for certain that the youth would never complete the task. The prince, too, was of the same mind, and, therefore, sat down with his head in his hand, and wept bitterly.

While he was thus sitting and weeping, the fair Singorra again appeared before him, and inquired the cause of his sorrow. The prince answered: "I may well be sad. The Mermaid has commanded me to cleanse the hog-sty. If I have not finished it before evening, when the sun goes down, I shall lose thee and every other joy." The maiden replied: "Be of good cheer; I will help thee, if thou wilt promise to be true to me; for thee will I never deceive." The king's son gladly said "yes," adding that while he lived, he would never forget her. Singorra then mounted up on the dunghill, and proceeded cautiously over the bridge, until she came to an old grey hog, that lay concealed in the mire. The king's daughter said:—

> "Hog, hog! Make all clean after thee,
> So shalt thou henceforth be free."

And scarcely were the words uttered before the hog sprang up, ran hastily about the sty, poked with his snout, and kicked with his feet, and ceased not until the whole place was as clean as a drawing-room floor. He then went his way, and never returned. The prince was overjoyed and could never sufficiently praise the beautiful damsel for all her aid.

The king's son now again appeared before his mistress and said that he had performed the task she had given him. The Mermaid was ready to burst with anger and resolved that she would try which was the stronger, her craft or the youth's good luck. She therefore concealed her displeasure but, in the morning, at sunrise, she summoned the youth, and told him that he should go to her sister to get necessaries for the wedding; at the same time giving him a box to put them in. But the prince, nevertheless, thought he could perceive from her manner that she did not expect to see him return unscathed from the journey.

When the time for the youth's departure was at hand, the fair Singorra came to him, and said: "I understand that thou art going to the Mermaid's sister, and, if thou doest not as I tell thee, we shall most probably never meet again. Here are two iron knives, two iron-axes, two woollen caps, and two cakes. These thou must take with thee, and dispose of on the way, wherever thou seest occasion. When thou art arrived, be careful where thou sittest. In the Troll's apartment there are five chairs of different colours. If thou sittest on the white chair, thou wilt sink down to the nethermost abyss of the ocean, and never rise again. If thou sittest on the red, thou wilt burn, and never be cool again. If thou sittest on the blue chair, thou wilt be stricken with palsy and sudden death, and we shall never see each other again. If thou sittest on the yellow, thou wilt get consumption, and wilt waste and fade away, and never be well again. But on the black chair thou mayest sit, for on that thou wilt remain unscathed." She then added: "Here is a silken cushion, which thou must lay under the serpent that creeps about the floor. But, above all things, eat no food that is proffered thee; otherwise thou wilt die, and we shall never meet again."

The king's son thanked her fervently for her good counsel and departed from his dear Singorra; and no one will wonder that they parted with heartfelt sorrow on both sides. He then began his journey, but no particulars of his course have reached us, until he came to where two men were occupied in cutting and carving; but they had only one knife, and that by no means a good one, for it was of wood. Now it occurred to the prince what Singorra had told him, so he took forth his iron knives, and gave one to each of the men.

The youth now went on and came to two woodcutters; but their labour proceeded very slowly; for they had only one axe, and that but a poor one, for it was also of wood. Singorra's words now again occurred to the prince, and he gave to each an iron axe. He then continued his journey, and came to two men, who were standing by the way and grinding at a mill, but the wind blew cold, and the men were bareheaded. The prince had pity on them, and gave to each a woollen cap. After travelling a while longer, he came to the castle gate. Here a wolf and a bear rushed forth, and the wolf extended his jaws, and the bear growled, as if they would swallow him up. The youth was, however, in nowise at a loss; but taking a cake, he broke it in halves, and gave the wolf and the bear each a portion. The beasts then crept back into their dens, and left the way free, so that the prince, without any further adventures, arrived at the Troll's habitation.

When the youth entered and appeared before the Troll queen, he greeted her from her sister, and delivered his message. His reception was of the best kind, and the crone promised to furnish the wedding things that were required. She then ordered the white chair to be set and requested the youth to rest himself after his long journey. But the prince, bearing Singorra's caution in his mind, answered that he was not weary. The Troll-queen then ordered the red chair to be set out; but the prince answered, as before, that he was well able to stand. Then the crone ordered the blue chair to be brought; but still the youth would not sit down. And in like manner also with the yellow chair. But as the Troll-queen did not desist from her importunity, the youth walked to the other end of the apartment, sat down on the black chair, and said: "Here I think a little rest may be of service to me." The crone could now plainly see that the prince was on his guard, and it may easily be imagined that she was not a whit the more well disposed on that account.

The Troll-queen now had a sausage brought forth and invited the prince to partake of it, saying he must needs require something after so long a journey. But the youth excused himself by saying that he was not at all hungry; but his excuse availed nothing; for he should eat, whether he would or not. The crone then went away to prepare the things for the wedding; but first said to the serpent that lay in a corner of the room:—

> "Serpent mine!
> Watch thou him."

When now the youth looked about, and perceived the serpent curled up on the floor, he recollected the words of Singorra; so running to the monster, he stroked him with his hand, and laid the silken cushion under his head, with which the serpent seemed well pleased. The prince then withdrew to a comer, hid the sausage under the broom, and returned to his seat.

He had hardly done so before the crone returned and asked whether he had eaten of the food she had given him. The king's son answered that he had. Then said the Troll:—

"Sausage mine!
Where art thou now?"

The sausage answered:—

"Here under the broom,
Here under the broom."

The Troll-queen was now highly displeased, fetched the sausage, and said that the prince should eat it all by the time she returned. She then went out, but first said to the serpent:—

"Serpent mine!
Watch thou him."

While the crone was away, the prince could not, for his life, hit on any place where to hide the foul refection. At last it occurred to him to conceal it in his bosom, under his clothes. A few minutes only had passed when the Troll came in and asked whether he had eaten the food. The youth answered that he had. Then said the Troll-queen:—

"Sausage mine!
Where art thou now?"

The sausage answered:—

"Here, in his breast,
Here, in his breast."

The crone was now quite satisfied, and said:—

"If thou art in his breast,
Thou'lt soon be in his maw."

The king's son then received the box with the requisites for the wedding, took leave of the Troll-queen, and set out for home. But scarcely had he got into the courtyard, before the sausage began to move under his clothes, and became changed into a horrid dragon, that spread its wings, and flew aloft in the air. The youth was terrified and hurried on as fast as he was able. When he came to the castle gate, the crane cried out:—

> "My bear!
> Tear him in a thousand pieces."

The bear instantly rushed forth; but the youth took half a cake and threw it into the animal's mouth. The bear then said:—

> "I was hungry!
> Now I am satisfied,"

and withdrew into his den. But the youth pursued his way till he came to the wolf; when the Troll again cried out:—

> "My wolf!
> Tear him in a thousand pieces."

Instantly the wolf rushed forth with extended jaws; but the king's son took the other half of the cake, and threw it into his mouth. The wolf then retired into his den, saying:—

> "I was hungry!
> Now I am satisfied."

The king's son now thought it advisable not to delay, and therefore began to run with all his speed, and came to where the two men were grinding at the mill. The Troll-queen then cried out:—

> "Millers twain!
> Grind him in a thousand pieces."

But when the millers saw who it was, they refused to do him any harm, and said: "We will not reward good with evil. He gave us woollen caps, when we were standing bareheaded." They then continued to grind without intermission. But the youth ran on till he came to the men who were cutting wood. The crone then again cried out:—

"Wood-cutters twain!
Cut him in a thousand pieces."

But when the cutters saw who it was, they refused to do him any harm, and said: "We will not reward good with evil. We were cutting with a wooden knife, when he gave us iron knives. They then resumed their labour; but the king's son hastened on, and came to where the men were hewing, when the Troll again cried out:—

"Hewers twain!
Hew him in a thousand pieces."

When the hewers saw who it was, they would not do him any harm, and said: "We will not reward good with evil. We had an axe of wood, and he gave us iron ones." The men then went on with their work; but the king's son ran on and stopped not before he reached the Mermaid's abode.

The youth now appeared before his mistress, gave her the wedding things, and rendered an account of his journey. When the Mermaid saw him safe and sound, she was much astonished, and, it was easy to see, not a little angry. In the evening, when people are about to betake themselves to rest, the fair Singorra came to the prince, greeted him with great kindness, and said: "The crone is in a rage, and we must instantly flee from hence, if we value our lives." The prince answered "How is that to be done? We shall never be able to leave the Mermaid' s abode without her consent." The damsel replied: "Be of good cheer; I will devise means, if thou wilt promise to be true to me; for to thee I will never be faithless." The king's son assured her, over and over, that he would never love any other in the world but her. Then said Singorra: "Go down to the stable, and place the golden saddle on the black stallion, and the silver saddle on the black mare. At the hour of midnight, we will flee hence." The prince did as the king's daughter had directed him. But Singorra went to her chamber, rolled some clothes together, and made of them three small dolls, one of which she placed by her bad, one in the middle of the floor, and the third on the threshold. She then cut the little finger of her left hand, let three drops of blood fall on each doll, and said: "Ye shall answer for me when I am away."

At midnight the prince and princess stole down to the stable, mounted their horses, and soon left the Mermaids mansion far behind them. But when the hour of matins drew nigh, and the cocks began to crow, the Mermaid awoke, and called out:—

> "Singorra mine!
> Art thou yet sleeping?"

"No, my lady," answered the puppet, that stood by the bedpost. When some time had elapsed, the Mermaid again called out:—

> "Singorra mine!
> What art thou doing?"

"I am kindling the fire, my lady," answered the puppet that stood in the middle of the floor. After another interval the crone cried a third time:—

> "Singorra mine!
> Does it burn yet?"

"Yes, my lady," answered the third puppet that stood at the threshold. But when daylight approached, the Mermaid herself went to Singorra's chamber, and we can easily conceive that she was far from pleased on finding it empty, and no one in it but the dolls, standing on the floor staring at her. She then ran down to the stable, to see after her horses: but there also she found no comfort, for the black stallion and the black mare were both away; whence the crone could well conclude that the prince and princess had taken their departure.

Her anger now knew no bounds, and she resolved that the two fugitives should not have acted with impunity. She therefore called her serving-man and said: "In all haste saddle my own goat, which goes a hundred miles at a step. Then ride away and seize both little and great!" The servant was instantly ready, saddled the crone's goat, mounted on its back, and rode off, as when the wind skims over the ocean. When Singorra heard the noise and clattering behind her, she at once divined the cause. Turning therefore to the prince, she said: "Dost thou hear that clattering? Now we shall do well to take care of ourselves for the Mermaid's goat is out and after us." She then changed herself and her lover into two little rats, that ran playing along the way. Scarcely had she done this when the Mermaid's man came travelling through the air, so that it resounded around him. On seeing the two rats, he thought within himself: "It can hardly be those that my mistress means. He then rode on, and at length turned back without finding any one or anything. When he came home, the Mermaid was out in her courtyard: she said: "Well, hast thou seen them?" "No," answered the servant, "I saw nothing but a couple of small rats, sporting along the way." "Them thou shouldst have taken," said the mermaid, and was very angry. "Go back now and take both great and small."

The man then mounted again on the swift-footed goat and set off with the speed of lightning. But when Singorra heard the noise behind her, she said to her companion: "Dost thou hear that buzzing? It is best that we take care of ourselves; for the Mermaid's goat is out and after us." She then transformed herself and her lover into two little birds, that flew to and fro in the air. At this moment the serving man came up riding on his goat and passed by like a flash of lightning. When he saw the two birds flying in the air, he thought to himself: "It cannot be those that my mistress means," and rode on; but at length returned without having found anything. When he came home, the Mermaid, who was standing in her courtyard, said: "Well, hast thou seen them?" "No," answered the servant, "I saw nothing but two little birds fluttering about in the air." "Them thou shouldst just have taken," said the Mermaid, highly incensed; "Now go back and take both great and small."

The serving-man now again mounted on the swift-footed goat, and was away like thought. When Singorra heard the noise behind her, she said to the king's son: "Dost thou hear what a buzzing there is? It is advisable that we take care of ourselves; for the Mermaid's goat is again out and after us." She then changed herself and her lover into two trees standing by the wayside; but the trees had no roots. Scarcely had this been done, when the servant came riding up on his goat, and hastened forward with such speed that he caused a whistling through the air. When he saw the two trees, he thought to himself: "They can hardly be what my mistress means," and then rode past them, but at length turned back, after a fruitless errand. When he came home, the Mermaid was again standing out in her courtyard, and questioned him: "Well, hast thou seen them?" "No," answered he, "I saw nothing but two trees standing by the way. They are just what thou shouldst have taken," said the Mermaid. "Did I not command thee to take both small and great?" The crone was now almost beside herself with rage and set off in pursuit of the fugitives.

But Singorra had made good use of the time, so that when the Mermaid drew nigh, both she and the prince were already across the boundary, and she had no longer power over them.

The king's son and the fair Singorra now travelled on, and emerged from the sea not far from the king's palace. When the youth recognised his father's abode, he was seized with an irresistible longing to go and see how all his family were, whether they were yet living. Singorra opposed his wish with all her power; for she could plainly foresee how it would all end. But the youth entreated her so fervently, that she was at length unable to withstand his prayers. It was, therefore, agreed that the prince should go up to the palace; but that Singorra should remain behind and await his return. When on the point of separating, the princess said: "One promise thou must make me, for all the faith and devotion that I have shown to thee. Thou must not speak to any one in thy father's palace; for if thou dost, thou wilt forget the word and promises thou hast given to me." The prince promised accordingly and took his departure. But the princess sat by the wayside and wept; for it seemed to her hard to lose him, whom she held so dear, before everything else in the world.

When the youth came riding to his father's palace, there was great joy among all his kindred, who went out to meet him with gladness of heart. But the prince seemed in a strange state of mind, and would neither speak, nor answer when spoken to but was impatient to ride away again. This appeared very unaccountable to his family; but they could not detain him. When he was in the act of passing through the palace gate, the dogs came rushing towards him barking violently. Now the youth forgot his promise and cried out: "Away! away!" In the same instant his whole mind was changed, so that he forgot his dear Singorra and everything else; and the past appeared to him only as an oppressive dream. He therefore turned back to his family and was by everyone received with heartfelt affection. And there was joy in all the king's palace, and over the whole kingdom, that the king had recovered his only son, who had been so long absent.

We will now return and see how it fared with Singorra, while she sat waiting for her lover. She waited and waited, but no prince appeared. She was now but too well convinced how matters stood and was therefore deeply afflicted so leaving the public road, she went and sat by a little fountain and wept. Towards morning, just as the sun was rising, a young girl came to the spring to fetch water. As she bent forwards and saw the reflection of Singorra's beautiful countenance in the fountain, she was delighted, and felt fully persuaded that it was her own face which she saw. Then clasping her hands together, she exclaimed "What! am I so beautiful? Then am I no longer fit to sit in a but with my blind father." With these words she left her pitcher and ran off. Singorra now took up the pitcher of water, went to the hut to the blind man, and attended him as assiduously as if he had been her father. Nor did the old man think otherwise than that it was his daughter; although it struck him as remarkable that on a sudden her conduct was so altered.

In the meanwhile, a report of the beauty of the old man's daughter was spread about the neighbourhood; it was said that a lovelier female could nowhere be found. This report reached the ears of the courtiers in the royal palace, and they resolved to ascertain whether what was said were true, that the young maiden was as proud as she was fair. They, therefore, agreed that one after another should endeavour to win her good graces, and thought they would at last make good the old saw, that the "dove always looks on while the bow is bending."

When a short time had elapsed, the first courtier thought he would try his luck. He therefore proceeded to the old man's cot, sat down to chat with the fair damsel, and helped her in her household avocations, as young men are won't to do. When it grew late, and people were about retiring to rest, the courtier was loth to depart, and begged for permission to remain the night over. Singorra made semblance to accede to his wish; but at the same moment exclaimed: "Ah! that is true, I have forgotten to shut the shutter, and it will be so cold in the night." The courtier was instantly ready and offered to go in her stead. The maiden thanked him and said: "Tell me when you have hold on the bar." "Well, I am now holding it, answered the courtier. Whereupon the princess cried out:—

> "Bar hold man, and man hold bar,
>   Until the lightsome day."

The courtier was now fast and could not move backwards or forwards; but stood by the shutter pulling and pulling through the whole night. At dawn he became free and sneaked off abashed to the royal palace; and who will wonder that he told no one how ridiculously his enterprise had terminated?

The next evening it was another courtier's turn to try his fortune. He went accordingly to the old man's cot, sat down by the young damsel, and vented forth an abundance of flattering chitchat, as young men are wont to do. When it grew late, and people were retiring to rest, the courtier was unwilling to depart, but begged for permission to stay the night over. The maiden granted his request and seemed very friendly; but on a sudden she exclaimed: "Ah! that is true, I have forgotten to lock the door, and it will be so cold in the night." The courtier was instantly ready and offered to go for her. The maiden thanked him and said: "Tell me when you have hold on the lock." "Well, I am holding it now, answered the courtier. The princess then cried out:—

> "Door bold man, and man hold door,
> Until the lightsome day."

The courtier was now fast at the door and stood there tugging and tugging till daylight. He then got loose and sneaked away abashed home to the palace. But he took particularly good care that no one should know of the ad venture he had in the night.

On the third evening another courtier went to try his luck. He went to the old man's cot, sat down by the young damsel, and extolled her beauty, as females, for the most part, readily listen to the praise of their own charms. The princess affected to hear all this trifling prattle with great pleasure and seemed very friendly. When it grew late, and people were retiring for the night, the courtier would positively not go away, but begged for permission to remain. Singorra yielded to his wish, but on a sudden exclaimed: "Ah! now I recollect that I have not shut the calf in; and that I must not forget." The courtier was instantly ready and offered to do it for her. She thanked him and said: "The calf is difficult to catch; tell me when you have got him fast." "Well, I have got him now, answered the courtier, holding the calf by the tail. The princess then cried out:—

> "Calf hold man, and man hold calf,
> And run over hill, and run over dale,
> Until the lightsome day."

Now a ludicrous race began; the calf bounding over both hill and dale, and the courtier behind him, with his hands fastened to the calf's tail. In this fashion they ran the whole night until sunrise, when the courtier was so weary that he could hardly move. He then returned to the palace and thought it would not greatly redound to his honour, if it were known how his expedition had terminated.

While all this was taking place the king and queen, after consulting with each other, resolved that the prince should marry. The prince willingly acceded to the proposal, departed for a foreign land, and betrothed himself to a fair princess. Preparations were afterwards made for the marriage, and all was pleasure and glee over the whole palace. It one day so happened that the prince was out with his fair young bride and came to the hut where Singorra abode with the old blind man. As they were driving by, the horses became restive, broke the pole, dashed the chariot in pieces, and ran off, so that no one could catch them. Now there was no lack of puzzling and considering how the young couple were to get back to the royal palace; and the three courtiers before-mentioned stared at each other. At length one of them said: "I know where we can get a new pole. If the young lass who dwells in this cottage will lend us the shutter-bar which lies on the roof, I am sure it would do for a pole." Another said: "I know how we can repair the chariot. If the same young girl will lend us the door of her cot, I am certain it would answer the purpose." The third said: "The worst is how to get horses. But if the young lass will lend us her calf, I am pretty sure that he is able to draw the whole chariot, be it ever so heavy." As now no other course seemed to present itself, the prince sent to the young maiden, and begged the loan of the shutter-bar, the cottage door, and the calf. With this request the princess instantly complied, but with the condition that she should be present at the prince's wedding. This he promised her. The bar was now turned into a pole and fitted admirably; the door was likewise placed in the chariot, and also fitted. Last of all the calf was harnessed to the vehicle; and so, the prince and his young bride rode home to the king's palace with pleasure and merriment.

On the day fixed for the wedding, Singorra arrayed herself in a silk-embroidered kirtle, adorned herself with costly ornaments, and proceeded to the palace. Her kirtle was resplendent with red gold at every seam, and she herself so lovely that all were wonderstruck, and thought that she must be the daughter of a king. The wedding guests then sat down to table, and the eyes of all were turned to the stranger damsel, to see how she would act. When a short time had elapsed, Singorra drew forth a box, in which were three little birds and three small gold corns. When the maiden raised the lid, the birds hopped out, and flew over the middle of the table to where the bridegroom was sitting. Two of them had each a gold corn in its mouth; but the third had forgotten its corn. Thereupon the other two birds said to it, "See, thou hast forgotten thy gold corn, as the king's son forgot Singorra." At the same instant there rose as it were a light in the prince's memory, and it rushed into his mind how he had forfeited both truth and honour to his beloved Singorra. He started up from the table, clasped her to his breast, and said: "Thee, or no one in all the world, will I have; for thou art my betrothed."

At this incident great confusion arose in the hall, and the guests looked with surprise at each other. The bridegroom then related all that had taken place from the day on which he was carried off by the mermaid, and what great devotion the young maiden had constantly shown him. The stranger princess was then sent back to her father with great pomp and every mark of honour. But the prince celebrated his marriage with the fair Singorra, the festivities of which lasted many days.

1. In a variation from South Småland, it is related that there was a king and a queen who had no children. On this account the king was sorely grieved and consulted an aged woman who came to the palace. The woman comforted him, saying: "It is well that thou hast no son, for he would be destined to be taken by the Mermaid." But the king would not be content. Then said the fortune-teller: "As thou art so anxious to have a son, know that the queen is pregnant; but be careful not to let the prince go near any water before he is twelve years old, else the Mermaid will have power over him." Having so spoken, the old woman went her way.

It came to pass exactly as the old woman had predicted; for the queen found herself pregnant and gave birth to a son who was called *Anesidei*. The king was overjoyed at this event, and caused a tower to be built, in which the young prince should be reared until he was grown up. When he had attained his twelfth year the king ordered a grand feast to be prepared and fetched his son from the tower with great solemnity. But as the prince was crossing over a bridge, he was changed to a drop of blood, and fell into the water. Thus, the king experienced the truth of the aged crone's prediction.

It is afterwards related how Anesidei came to the Mermaid and met with a beautiful handmaiden named *Meserimei*. This young girl helped him in his tasks, and they vowed to each other eternal faith and affection. When the prince had undergone all the Mermaid's trials, and fetched things for the wedding from her sister, the young couple resolved on taking flight together. Then said Meserimei: "Go and sit on the high stone and call the palfrey on which the crone rode when she was a bride." The prince did so, and returned with the horse, which they both mounted and rode away but the Mermaid, who had observed their flight, went in pursuit of them. When she caught sight of them, she transformed the land before them into a large sea; but Meserimei had skill to turn it again into land. So, the Mermaid was forced to return; but the prince tame up out of the sea, not far from his father's palace.

The conclusion accords with story No. II. The king's son rides to his father's palace; but is persuaded to drink a bowl of milk, and so forgets his beloved and everything that had befallen him. He then courts a fair princess in a foreign land. But Meserimei gets employment in the palace as dairy-maid, and befools the three courtiers, as above related.

At the prince's wedding Meserimei is present, clad in most splendid attire. During dinner she casts three gold pearls on the table for her two doves; but the cock takes all three, and leaves nothing for the hen. The little dove thereupon says: "Out upon thee! thou deceivest thy mate, as Anesidei deceived Meserimei." When the king's son hears this the third time, he wakes as from a dream, and recognises his true betrothed.

2. According to a variation from Roslagen, the young princess is named *Solfålla*. The story has, moreover, the following deviations from the foregoing, No. II.

The prince's second trial consists in his being set to cut down all the trees in the sea-forest and set them on their roots again. The prince and Solfålla then take flight and are pursued first by one of the puppets that is changed into a tap-shaped cloud, and travels through the air. The princess then transforms herself and her lover into two rats, playing by the wayside. The Mermaid now sends the second puppet, in the same form; but Solfålla transforms herself and her lover into a duck and a drake. The Mermaid next sends the third puppet, but to no better purpose; the princess changes herself and bridegroom into two trees, and the puppet passes them unnoticed. At last the Troll herself goes after them and traverses the air like a thick cloud. Solfålla then transforms herself and the prince into a goose and a gander. But the Mermaid perceives her artifice, and transforms herself into a fox, and is on the point of snapping up the goose but at the same instant the sun rises, at which the goose cries out: "Ha! ha! master Reynard, look behind you, there is a beautiful girl coming." The Mermaid turns about, and, on seeing the sun, is split in two through the middle, and so gets her death.

When the prince returns home to the palace, he forgets Solfålla's injunction not to kiss his mother, and so forgets his bride and everything that had befallen him. But the king's daughter takes shelter in a cottage in the forest, and befools the prince, as is above related of the courtiers. The conclusion of the story accords, in other respects, with what is given above.

3. In a variation from South Småland, the prince is named *Flod*, and the princess *Flodina*. They have both been carried off by the Mermaid and agree to escape together. In their flight they are pursued by their mistress but transform themselves first into a thorn bush with a bird in it, then into a church with a priest, and, lastly, into two ducks. When the Mermaid sees the ducks, she lies down to drink the water out of the sea; but drinks too much, and bursts in pieces.

4. A version from Östergötland relates, that there was a queen who encountered a violent storm at sea, and was forced to promise what she carried under her girdle. Shortly after she gave birth to a son, who was named *Tobe*. But hardly was the child born, when the Mermaid assumed an eagle's plumage, flew into the queen's chamber, and carried him off.

Tobe now grew up in the Mermaid's mansion, where he met with a fair young handmaiden, named *Sara*. The children contracted a reciprocal affection and resolved to flee together. Sara then spat on the hearth, on the pile of wood, and in the cellar, bidding them answer for her. She took with her a stone, a brush, and a horsecloth, and so fled with her lover. When the Mermaid was aware of their flight she pursued them in a dense cloud. Sara then cast the stone behind her, which grew to a large mountain, so that the Troll could not pass it, but had to go home for her rock-springer. Tobe and Sara in the meanwhile continued their flight with all speed. But the Mermaid came after them again, when the young maiden threw the brush, and a thick forest sprang up, so that the Troll could not proceed, and now had to go home for her wood-cutter. After a little while she was again after them, when Sara threw the horsecloth, and a large lake arose. The Troll was now obliged to return home for her dog, that was named *Glufsa*. The Troll and Glufsa then lay down to drink the lake dry, but, drinking too much, they both burst.

When Tobe was about to solemnize his marriage with the foreign princess, Sara threw corn to the fowls in the yard; but the cock peeked up all that was thrown; at which the hens cried out: "The cock serves us as Tobe served Sara." The prince instantly recognises his true bride and makes her his queen.

5. In a version from Westergötland, it is told that there was a king's son, named *Andreas*, who had a wicked stepmother. The Troll-wife wished to destroy the young prince, but he was saved by a young maiden, named *Messeria*, and at length fled with her. Before they began their flight the maiden cut herself in the little finger of the left hand, and let three drops of blood fall on the floor, saying that they should answer for her when she was away.

The queen now sent her men to catch the two fugitives; but Messeria formed a little church by the way, transformed the prince into a priest, and herself into the sexton. So, the men, being unable to find them, turned back. The queen then went herself after them; but Messeria formed a lake and changed herself and her lover into two large fishes. When the queen reached the shore the fishes came forth and would swallow her up; for they well knew that if she only got to taste a drop of water, she would have them again in her power.

6. In a very remarkable version from North Småland, the scene of the story is removed from the sea to a hill on land and for the Mermaid we have an ordinary Mountain-troll. The following is an outline of the story. There was once a king's son, who one day in summer was out gathering strawberries, when a Troll came and enticed him into a mount. There he met with a young maiden, who in like manner had been enticed, and had lived seven long years with the Troll crone. The young girl helped the youth to perform his tasks, and they promised ever to love each other.

One day the Troll said to the youth: "Thou shalt go and cleanse my stable, which has not been cleansed these four and twenty years." The youth was at a loss how to proceed, and was so sad, so sad. At this moment the young maiden came to him and said: "Do not weep! If thou wilt promise ever to be faithful to me, I will give thee counsel Mount up on that high stone, and call out:—

> "All mother's shovellers, come forth
> All mother's sweepers, come forth!"

The prince did so, when instantly there came forth a countless multitude of Pysslings, and began to shovel up and sweep, and ceased not until the stable was cleansed.

When that was done, the Troll said: "Here is a bushel of corn. This thou shalt sow in the field; then thou shalt plough and harrow it, and afterwards gather up every grain again. The youth felt completely bewildered, and was so sad, so sad. At this moment the young maiden came to him and said: "Do not weep! If thou wilt promise ever to be faithful to me, I will help thee. Mount up on that high stone, and call out:—

> "All mother's sowers, come forth!
> All mother's ploughers, come forth!
> All mother's harrowers, come forth!
> All mother's gatherers, come forth!"

The prince did so, when instantly there came forth an innumerable swarm of little, little old men, who began to sow, plough, harrow, and gather, and so great was their number that they fought for every single grain. When the corn was all gathered, the prince carried it into the mount: but the young maiden took away three grains, without any one knowing what she purposed doing with them.

Some time after, the Troll-wife said:" I am now going to a wedding. Go, therefore, and fetch my palfrey, on which I rode when I myself went to be married, just four and twenty years since." The prince was row sorely puzzled, for he did not know where to find the Troll's palfrey. At this moment, the young maiden appeared before him, and inquired why he was so sad. The prince answered: "The crone has ordered me to go for her palfrey, on which she rode to be married four and twenty years ago; and I don't know where to find it." The maiden answered: "If thou wilt promise ever to be faithful to me, I will help thee in this, and also in more." The youth made the desired promise. Then said the maiden: "Go first for the bridle, that hangs nearest the door in the stable." The prince did so. The maiden continued: "Here is a loaf when thou comest far, far in the forest, thou must violently shake the bridle, when thou wilt hear a great noise and neighing. Then mount up into the highest tree thou canst see; but when thou art half up the tree, thou must shake the bridle yet more violently, and then hasten up to the very top. The horse will then come running at full speed and will snort and be very untractable. But thou must throw the loaf on his neck, when he will become tame and docile, so that thou mayst catch him, as mother has ordered." The prince thanked her warmly for this good counsel, and they separated for that time.

The prince then went to the forest, having with him the bridle and loaf. When he had proceeded a considerable distance, he shook the bridle violently, and climbed up into the highest tree he could see. Instantly he heard a hideous noise and neighing, so that the whole forest resounded. When he had ascended half-way in the tree, he shook the bridle again yet more violently than before, and climbed, as fast as he could, up to the top of the tree. At the same instant he heard a noise, as if the earth were rent, and the horse came running at full speed, so that the trees and shrubs were broken down wherever he came. The horse was large, and as high as the loftiest pine, and gaped so formidably as if he would swallow the prince at a single mouthful. But the youth did not yield to fear, but was instantly ready, and cast the loaf into his mouth. The animal then became as gentle as a lamb, and patiently waited while the prince put the bridle on him. The youth then vaulted on his back, and rode back to the mount, as the Troll had commanded him.

When the Troll saw that the prince returned safe and sound, she was highly displeased, and meditated in what other manner she might deprive him of life. For this purpose, she commanded her handmaid to kill the youth and bake him, while she herself was absent at the wedding. The maiden promised to do as she was ordered but when the crone was gone the girl made three dolls of cloth, placed them, one at the threshold, one on the hearth, and one by the bed, and commanded them to answer for her. Then she and the youth took all the chattels and gold that were in the mount and fled. When the Troll-wife returned from the wedding she was very tired, and lay down to sleep, and slept the whole twenty-four hours. When she woke, she called to her handmaid: "Dost thou hear, girl? hast thou baked the lad yet?" Then the puppet that was placed at the thresh hold answered: "I am just now heating the oven." The crone then turned around, went to sleep again, and slept another twenty-four hours. When she woke, she again asked "Dost thou hear, girl? hast thou baked the lad yet?" The doll that stood on the hearth answered. "I am now just putting him in. The Troll turned round again, went fast to sleep, and slept for another twenty-four hours. When she woke, she cried out again: "Dost thou hear, girl? is the boy baked yet?" The doll which stood by the bed answered: "Yes, I am just now taking him out." The Troll-wife then rose and went to the maiden's chamber; but when she entered, she saw no one there, except the three rag dolls staring at her.

The crone was now pretty well aware how matters stood and was wroth beyond all bounds. She called her men and ordered them instantly to go in pursuit of the fugitives. Now the king's son and his companion hear a great noise in the air, and the maiden says: "Dost thou hear that noise! Mother has sent all her people after us." She then transformed the prince into a thorn-bush, and herself into a rose growing on it. The men took no notice of the bush and flower but passed by with all speed. When they returned, the crone said: "Well, have you seen anything!" The men answered: "We saw nothing but a little thorn-bush, with a rose in it, that stood by the wayside. The Troll-wife was sorely displeased at this answer and said: "Those are just what you should have taken; I must now go in pursuit of them myself."

The Troll then set out in chase of the fugitives and travelled with such speed that the air whined and whistled. The maiden then said to her companion: "Dost thou hear that hideous din? It is mother herself that is out after us." She then changed herself and her lover into two ducks, and they swam across the lake that lay before them. But when the crone approached and saw them on the opposite side, she laid herself down, and drank up the whole lake. At that moment the sun rose, and the young maiden cried out: "See! what a beautiful damsel is running up yonder." When the crone turned round to look, she split in pieces for, as is well-known, Trolls have not the power of looking at the sun[46].

The prince on his return home, as usual, forgets his bride, and is about to marry a foreign princess. When the wedding-day arrived, the deserted damsel applied for employment as a servant. She had with her a duck and a drake that

---

[46] See "Northern Mythology," i. p. 8, *note*[3].

waddled up and down the festive hall. While the guests were all at table, and all was mirth and glee, the maiden drew forth three grains of corn, and threw them on the floor. Instantly the drake hastened forward and picked up all the three. Thereupon the maiden struck him with her hand, saying: "Out upon thee! That thus castest aside thy mate." When the prince heard these words, he recognised his right bride, and remembered all the fidelity and devotion she had shown him, &c.

THE ENCHANTED TOAD.

From South Småland.

THERE was once a peasant, like many others, who had three sons, but his wife had long been dead. When the two elder lads were somewhat grown up, they went one day to their father, and prayed him to allow them to go from home and get themselves wives. The peasant answered: "It is not becoming that you go about seeking for wives before you have tried your luck in the world. I long to know which of you can earn the handsomest cloth to spread over the table on Yule [Christmas] eve. This proposition was very agreeable to the two brothers and it was, therefore, settled that they should go out in the world, and see which could earn the finest table-cloth. On their departure the peasant gave five shillings to each of them saying it should be for their subsistence until they could procure themselves some employment.

When the two elder sons were on the eve of leaving home, the youngest went to his father, and begged for permission to go and try his fortune. The peasant would not listen to him, but said: "Yes, thou poor little fellow! there are many, forsooth, who will be glad to have thee in their service! It is much better that thou sittest at home in the chimney-corner; that is thy right place." But the boy was urgent, and said: "Father, let me go with them. No one can tell what turns luck may take. It may be that I get on well in the world, though I am little and younger than my brothers." When the old man heard this, he thought to himself: "Well, it may be desirable to get rid of him for some time. Here he is of no use, and he will no doubt, come back before the forest is green again." So the lad got leave to accompany his brothers, and also received five shillings from his father to subsist on during his travels.

The three sons then set out and travelled the whole day. Towards evening they came to an alehouse by the road side, in which a number of travellers and other guests were assembled. The two elder brothers sat down, and ate and drank, and gamed, and made merry, while the youngest lad crept into a corner by himself and would not join the company. When the two brothers had thus got rid of their money, they consulted together how they should continue their course of dissipation. For this object they went to their young brother, and demanded from him his five shillings, telling him he could not do better than return home, and the sooner the better. But the lad refused to give them his money; whereupon the brothers seized and beat him, took his money from him, and drove him out of the alehouse. They then sat down again and ate and drank as before. But the poor boy fled away in the dark night, not knowing whither to direct his steps. He trod many rugged paths, until he was unable to proceed further. Sitting down, therefore, on a little hillock, he wept bitterly until he fell asleep from weariness.

Early in the morning, before the lark had begun his song, the lad awoke and continued his journey. He now wandered over mountains and through deep valleys, heedless in what direction he went, provided only that he could escape from his brothers. After travelling for a long time, he came at length to a green path that led to a mansion. This mansion was so spacious, that he thought it could be no other than a royal palace. The lad did not long hesitate, but entered, and came into many fine apartments, one more sumptuous than another; but not a living soul was there. After wandering about for some time out of one hall into another, he came at last to a room yet more splendid than any of the others. Conspicuous in the place of honour there sat a toad, blacker than the blackest pitch, and so loathsome of aspect that the lad could hardly turn his eyes towards her. The toad inquired who he was, and on what errand he came. He answered, as was the truth: "I am a poor peasant boy and have left home in search of some employment." The toad then said: "Thou hast probably an inclination to stay here with me? I am just now in great want of a lad." The boy expressed his willingness and said that he would gladly serve her. The toad said "Be welcome, then! If thou art faithful to me, it shall be well for thee." The matter was now settled, and the lad assured her that there should be no lack of devotion on his part, provided only that his mistress did not require of him more than he was able to perform.

When all was thus arranged, the lad and the toad went down into the garden that lay around the house, and came to a large bush, of a species that the youth had never before seen. The toad then said: "It shall be thy occupation to cut a branch of this bush every day when the sun is in the heavens. Thou shalt do it on Sunday as well as on Monday, on Yule-day as well as on Midsummer-day; but thou must not cut more branches than one." The boy promised to comply with her wishes in all things. The toad then led him up to a chamber and said: "Here thou shalt henceforward sleep and live. On this table thou will always find meat and drink, when thou art disposed to eat. This bed thou shalt find ready whenever thou art inclined to rest, and in every respect thou shalt enjoy perfect liberty. Only be faithful in what is required of thee. When she had thus spoken, they separated, and the toad hopped away. The lad then went down into the garden, and cut a branch from the bush, and so was at liberty for that day. On the following morning he did the like; so again, on the third, and so throughout the whole year. He fared excellently in the palace, enjoying a super abundance of everything he could wish. Nevertheless, his time seemed long; for the day came and the day went, and he never saw nor heard a human being.

When a year had expired, and the youth had cut the last branch of the bush, the toad came hopping to him, thanked him for his faithful services, and asked him what recompense he wished. The lad answered that he had done very little that deserved a reward and would be quite satisfied with whatever his mistress would be pleased to give him. The toad then said: "I know well enough what thou wouldst like as a remuneration. Thy brothers are gone to earn cloths to spread on their father's table on Yule-eve. But I will give thee a cloth, the like of which they will hardly find, even if they search over twelve kingdoms." With these words she gave the youth a tablecloth whiter than snow, and so fine that it could not be matched. The lad was now overjoyed, thanked his mistress in many expressions of gratitude, bade her farewell, and prepared, with great joy of heart, to return home to his father.

The youth now set out on his journey and travelled the whole day without meeting with any adventure. Late in the evening he perceived a light, towards which he bent his course, in expectation of finding shelter for the night. On reaching the spot he at once recognised the alehouse in which he had left his brothers, and on entering, lo! there sat the two peasant youths in the midst of cups and jugs, eating and drinking, and making merry. As the lad no longer cherished any recollection of the wrong, he had suffered at their hands, he felt glad to meet with his brothers, and went and greeted them affectionately. He then inquired how they had sped since they last saw each other, and whether they had succeeded in getting a cloth to lay upon their father's Yule-table. The brothers answered in the affirmative and said that all had turned out well. Each then produced his cloths, but the cloths were both torn and worn. "Now," said the lad, "wait, and you shall see another sort of thing." He then spread out the cloth given him by the toad, when all the guests in the hostel could never cease admiring the fineness of the texture. But the two brothers could ill brook that their youngest brother should possess a thing so costly. They therefore took the beautiful cloth from him by force and gave him their old ones in return. All the three then returned home to their father. When Yule-eve came, and the youths spread their cloth on the table, the old man was delighted, and could not sufficiently rejoice at their good fortune. The two brothers then began to praise themselves and talked largely of all the great things they had performed. But the youngest lad was taciturn and said very little. He was neither heard nor believed, let him recount what he might.

When the two elder brothers had remained at home over Yule-tide they went one day to their father, and begged for permission to go and get themselves wives. But the old man answered as before: "It does not become you to go about looking for wives before you have further tried your luck in the world. I long to see which of you can earn the handsomest drinking cup to set on the table on Yule-eve." On their departure the old man gave to each of them five shillings as before.

When they had left home the youngest boy went to his father and asked for permission to go again and try his luck. The father at first refused his consent, but at length yielded to the lad's entreaties, thinking to himself he would no doubt come back before the forest was in leaf. So, he got his five shillings and departed.

In the same alehouse the lad found his older brothers eating, drinking, and gambling, and was, in like manner, plundered by them. He then wandered forth and directed his steps to the palace of his late mistress. When the toad perceived him, she returned a friendly answer to his greeting, and asked the object of his coming. He answered: "I am come again to offer my services, if you require them." The toad replied: "Be welcome, I am just now in great need of a servant. If thou wilt serve me well, thy reward shall not be small. The toad then took forth a bundle of short threads, gave them to the youth, and said: "This shall be thy employment; thou shalt tie a thread round every branch of the bush that thou hadst to cut last year. But thou must tie a thread every day the sun is in the heavens, and thou must do so as well on Sunday as on Monday, as well on Yule-day as on Midsummer-day. Thou must not tie many threads, but only one." His treatment in the palace was then such as we have already described.

When the year was at an end, and the youth had bound the last thread round the last branch, the little toad came again hopping to him, thanked him for his faithful services, and asked what recompense he wished. He answered, as before, that he had done little to deserve a recompense, and would be quite content with whatever his mistress might think proper to give him. Thereupon the toad said: "I know well what reward thou wishest above all. Thy brothers are gone to earn a drinking cup to set on their father's table on Yule-eve; but I will give thee a cup, the like of which is hardly to be found." With these words she gave the youth a drinking vessel which was of fine silver, gilt within and without; thirteen masters had set their marks on it; the workmanship was, moreover, so curious and elaborate, that its like was not to be found, even if twelve kingdoms were to be searched through. The youth returned, thanks for the costly gift, as it was well worth, and with great joy of heart prepared to return home.

After travelling the whole day, he came late in the evening within sight of the same alehouse or hostel of which we have already spoken. He would have taken another direction, but a rapid river prevented him from going by any other road and be required shelter for the night. On entering the alehouse, he found his brothers sitting amid cups and jugs, just as when be last parted from them and the treatment he met with at their bands was a perfect repetition of that already described.

When the three brothers had been at home till Yule was past, the two elder ones went again to their father and asked his permission to set out in search of wives. The old man readily granted their request, thinking that his sons were now grown up and well-experienced in all things. He added, "I long to see which of you brings the fairest bride to the village by Yule-eve." Each then having received his five shillings, they set out on their journey.

When they were about to leave home, the youngest son went to his father, and begged to be allowed to accompany his brothers. The old man would not listen to him, but said: "Thou poor stripling, dost thou think there is any one who will have thee for a husband? Better is it for thee to sit at home and rake in the ashes that is the right place for thee." The youth was not, however, to be diverted from his purpose, but said to his father: "Father, let me go with them; no one can tell what will turn up. It may perchance go well with me, although I am little and younger than my brothers." However, the youth might have expressed himself, the old man at last thought: "Well, it may be as well to let him go for a time, he will no doubt come back when pressed by want." Thus, the youth got permission to accompany his brothers, and, on parting from his father, received, like each of them, his five shillings.

The three brothers then set out on their wanderings, and in the evening came to the inn of which we have more than once spoken, and there the same scene is repeated that has been already described. The elder brothers plunder the youngest and thrust him out of the house. After long travelling, he resolves to bend his way again to the palace where he enjoyed so much ease and comfort. He had hardly entertained the thought before he again found himself on the green path, and after proceeding a little further, the palace stood conspicuous before him. He was now overjoyed, and on reaching his destination entered boldly into the beautiful saloon, in which his mistress was in the habit of sitting. She received him graciously and asked the object of his coming. He told her that he came to offer his services, if she had need of them. The toad replied: "Thou art welcome, for I am in great want of a servant. If thou servest me faithfully, thy reward shall be greater than thou now thinkest." The youth assured her that there should be no lack of fidelity on his part, provided she did not require more than he could perform. The toad said: "Thy work shall be neither laborious nor tedious. It shall be thy employment to gather up the branches thou hast cut and tied and lay them together in a heap in the courtyard. But thou shalt take up a branch every day that the sun is in the heavens, and thou shalt do so as well on Wednesday as on Thursday, as well on Yule-day as on Midsummer-day; and thou must not take up many branches together, but a single one only. When the year is at an end, and thou hast gathered up the last ranch, thou shalt set fire to the heap and withdraw a while to thy chamber. Then go down and sweep well round the pile, that every branch may be consumed. If then thou observest anything in the fire, take it out and preserve it." The youth promised to comply accurately with his mistress's directions. She thereupon, as before, conducted him to his chamber, and went hopping away. The lad then went down into the garden, fetched a branch that he had previously cut and tied, carried it to the vacant spot where he purposed erecting the pile, and was afterwards free for the rest of the day. On the following morning he did the like, and also on the third morning, and so on through the whole year. In the palace he enjoyed every comfort, and grew up into a tall, comely young man. But his hours were passed in solitude, for be neither saw nor heard a human being, and he often thought how his brothers were probably taking home their brides, while he had not one.

When the year had run its course and the youth had gathered up the last branch and laid it with the others, he did as the toad had ordered him, set fire to the heap, and withdrew for a while to his chamber. He then returned and swept round the heap, that all the branches, great and small, might be burnt to ashes. While thus occupied, behold! there rose from the midst of the fire a damsel exquisitively beautiful; she was whiter than snow, and her hair hung down to her feet and covered her like a mantle. When the youth perceived the fair damsel, he ran in all haste and snatched her out of the flames. The young maiden then fell on his neck, overcome with joy, and thanked him for having saved her. She was the most lovely and the richest daughter of a king in all the wide world, and had been enchanted by a Troll, who had transformed her into a loathsome toad.

At the same moment a great agitation and noise arose in the palace, and the court was filled with courtiers, knights, and high-born dames, all of whom had, in like manner, been enchanted. All now came forward and greeted their queen as well as the brave youth who had released them. But the princess, not to lose time, ordered horses to be put instantly to her gilded chariot, and made preparations for immediate departure. She then caused the peasant's son to be clothed in silk and rich scarlet, gave him arms and other equipments, such as might beseem a prince's son; and thus was the poor peasant lad transformed into as noble and stately a youth as ever girded a sword to his side. When everything was ready for the journey, the king's daughter said: "I can well believe that thy thoughts are turned to thy brothers, who are directing their steps towards home together with their brides. We will, therefore, travel to thy father, that he may also know what kind of bride thou hast earned for thyself." With all this the youth was as much bewildered as if he had fallen from the clouds; but there was no time for reflection he, therefore, immediately stepped into the gilded chariot, and in great state and with a numerous retinue they departed to visit the old peasant in his cottage.

After travelling for some time, they came to the hostel by the wayside, and the youth naturally felt a strong desire to know whether his brothers, as usual, still made it their quarters. He therefore caused the chariot to stop and stepped into the house. On opening the door, he saw his brothers sitting amid cups and jugs, eating and drinking and making merry. Each of the brothers had with him his betrothed bride, whose persons were of the homeliest cast. When the youth had seen all this, he hastened away without having been recognised, and returning to his bride in the gilded chariot, proceeded on his journey. But the guests in the hostel wondered exceedingly who the great prince might be whom they had just seen.

The youth and his fair bride now travelled on to the old peasant's cottage, at which they did not arrive until late in the evening. They entered and begged to have house-room for the night; but the old man answered, as was the truth, that he was expecting his three sons with their brides, and had, moreover, only a very small cottage, that was ill-calculated to receive persons of such high condition. But the king's daughter said that she would be mistress in the present case, and the old peasant could not gainsay her will. She then ordered a sumptuous Yule-feast to be prepared and sent her pages out into the neighbourhood to invite guests to the entertainment. When the evening was far advanced and the feast was ready, the two elder sons arrived with their brides; and no one will be disposed to wonder that the old man was not particularly delighted with his daughters-in-law. While they were sitting at table, the king's daughter asked the old man whence he had procured so fine a cloth and such a beautiful drinking-cup. The old peasant answered: "My two elder sons were out and received them in recompense for their services." Whereupon the princess said: "No, thy elder sons have earned neither the one nor the other; but if thou wilt know the truth, it is thy youngest son who has earned them; and here you see the fellow both of the cloth and cup." When she had thus spoken, the youth rose from the table, fell on his father's neck, and all might now see that the stranger prince was no other than the old peasant's youngest son, the little lad, who had formerly been so despised by his kindred. When the old man recognised his son, and at the same time, heard all that had taken place, he was stricken with amazement, and could scarcely believe his own eyes and ears. But the two elder sons stood with shame and ignominy before their father and the numerous guests; and their treachery and falsehood became in later times a by-word in the whole neighbourhood.

The youth and the beautiful princess now allowed the guests to drink to their happy union, and there was such a Yule-feast as had not been seen within the memory of man. But when Yule was over, the bride and bridegroom returned to their kingdom, and took the old peasant with them. And the youth became king over the whole realm and lived with his fair queen in love and concord.

THE PRINCESS IN THE CAVERN.[47]

From South Småland.

THERE was once, in very old times, a king who had an only daughter. The young princess was of a very kind disposition and beautiful in person, so that she won the heart of everyone who saw her. When she was grown up, there were many princes and noble youths that sought her hand and affection, and among them was the son of a powerful king from a distant kingdom. He often conversed with the fair maiden, and the youthful pair mutually agreed to possess each other.

In the meanwhile, it happened that a war broke out, and the enemy invaded the country with a large army. Finding himself unable to withstand so great a force, the king caused a cavern to be excavated in the middle of an

---

[47] A similar story occurs among the Danes. See Molbech, ut. sup., pp. 82-92. "Pigeu i Museskindspelsen." See p. 375.

extensive forest, in which he might place his daughter, remote from the perils of warfare. He provided her abundantly with the necessaries of life, and gave her for company a female attendant, also a dog, and a cock, to enable them to distinguish one day from another. The king then prepared for the contest, and the young prince made himself ready to accompany him. But when the hour of separation came, the prince and princess were sorely afflicted, and conversed long with each other. The princess said: "My mind tells me that we shall not soon meet again; I will therefore make one request which thou must not refuse. Thou shalt promise never to marry any one who cannot wash the spots out of this handkerchief and finish the weaving of this gold-web." With these words she handed the prince a handkerchief, and a web that was curiously worked in gold and silk. The prince received them, saying that he never would forget her request. They then parted from each other, and the princess was consigned to the cavern; but the prince and the king went forth to defend the country against the foe.

The armies met and a desperate conflict ensued; but fortune was unfavourable to the king, who fell gloriously in defence of his kingdom; and the young prince returned to his own country. The enemy then overran the whole land with plunder and slaughter, burnt the royal palace, and harried around it both far and near. The foe at length departed, leaving the land little better than a desert. But no one knew what was become of the king's daughter, whether she was dead or had fallen into the hands of the enemy.

In the meanwhile, the princess and her servant still remained in the cavern, and employed their time in gold embroidery, expecting the king's return. But one day went and another came, and yet he did not come to release them from their prison. And thus passed seven long years. Their provisions were now at an end, so that they had no longer wherewith to sustain life, and were compelled to kill the cock; but from that day they no longer had the means of knowing how the time passed, and their lot appeared harder than ever. Shortly after, the servant died of grief and hunger, and the king's daughter was left alone in the dark cave. In her distress she knew not what course to adopt. At last she took a knife, and began scraping and chipping the roof without intermission, and to such good purpose that at length she made an opening in the top, and on the third day emerged from the cave in which she had been confined so long.

The princess then attired herself in her attendant's clothes, called her dog, and set out to wander in the desert. After long journeying, without meeting with a human being, she perceived a smoke rising among the trees, and at length came to where an aged man was burning charcoal in the forest. The princess approached the coal-burner, and begged of him a little food, saying that she would gladly assist him in his labour. The man gave her a morsel of bread, and she helped him to burn coal. While talking together, the young damsel inquired what had taken place in the country, and the old man informed her of the death of the king, and of all that had occurred during the last seven years. At this narrative the princess was sadly afflicted, and it entered her thoughts "they have few friends who reckon many green graves."

When a short time had elapsed, and the coal was burnt, the old man told her that he required no further help and advised her to seek for service up at the king's palace, especially as he could well see that she was not accustomed to hard labour. Thus, the princess again commenced her wanderings; but nothing is recorded of her course before she came to a great water; not knowing how to pass which, she sat down on the margin and wept. While she thus sat a large wolf came running out of the forest, and said:

> "Give me thy hound,
> Then thou shalt cross over wave and ground."

The king's daughter, much as it grieved her, yet durst not deny the wolf's demand, but gave him the dog. When he had satisfied his hunger, he said:—

> "On my back set thee,
> The waves shall not wet thee."

The princess instantly placed herself on his back, and he conveyed her across the lake to the opposite shore. By the water's edge there stood a fair royal palace, of which the king's son, who in former days had plighted his faith to the princess, was lord and master.

We must now relate that, while the princess was shut up in the cavern, the king had died, and the prince had succeeded to the throne after his father. When some years had passed the king's, lieges besought him to choose himself a queen; but he was deaf to their entreaties, for he thought unceasingly on the fair maiden whom he had betrothed in his youth. Thus, seven long years passed on, and not the slightest intelligence could be obtained of the princess. The prince then concluded that she could be no longer living, and therefore, after a consultation with his chief men, he issued a proclamation that she should be his queen who could finish the princess's gold web and wash the stains from her handkerchief. When this was known in various countries, there came maidens from the east and west, all eager to win the youthful king; but there was no one so skillful as to be able to fulfil the conditions. At this juncture there came also a young female of rank, who was in like manner desirous of trying her luck. To this lady the princess went, and begged to be taken into her service, calling herself Åsa. She was taken accordingly as a waiting-maid to the stranger damsel; but there was no one in all the king's court that rightly knew who she was.

The princess's mistress had now to complete the king's web, but it was with her as with the others, she was incapable of proceeding with the curious texture. At this the damsel was severely mortified and knew not well how to act. It happened, however, one day, while she was absent, that the disguised princess sat down at the loom and wove a long piece. At her return the damsel, perceiving that the work was progressing, was well pleased, and wondered who had been helping her. The king's daughter would not at first confess what she had done but was at last obliged to acknowledge the truth. At this the damsel was highly delighted, and she set the princess to work at the web; but no one knew that it was the servant who worked in the place of her mistress.

The rumour was now current throughout the palace that the stranger damsel was completing the curious web. There was, consequently, much talk about the king's marriage, and he himself went to the damsel's apartment to see how the trial proceeded. But whenever the king entered the weaving was always at a stand, and no one was sitting at the loom. This seemed to the king somewhat singular, and he one day asked the stranger damsel why she never wove while he was present. She excused herself, and cunningly said: "Sir, I am too bashful to be able to work while you are looking on." The king let himself be satisfied with this answer, and in a short time the web was completed.

The stranger damsel was now to wash the stains from the princess's handkerchief, but in the second task was as unsuccessful as in the first, for the more she washed the darker were the spots. The work was, however, performed by the princess under circumstances precisely similar to those already related in the case of the web. On the king's inquiry why, the washing was always at a stand while he was present, the damsel answered with deceit: "Sir king, I cannot wash linen while I must have red gold rings on my fingers." The king, as before, let himself be contented with this answer, and in a short time the spots were all washed out of the handkerchief. Thus, the stranger damsel fulfilled both conditions.

When all this became known, great joy prevailed throughout the land, and preparations on a grand scale were made for the king's marriage. But on the very day fixed for the ceremony the bride fell suddenly ill, so that she was unable to ride to church with the company. As she would not let it be known to any one that she was sick, she spoke secretly with her waiting-maid, and besought her to ride as bride in her stead. The young princess consented and was accordingly clad in a bridal dress and adorned with red gold rings; but no one knew that it was the waiting-maid that rode in her mistress's stead. The wedding guests then set out in great state with music and other rejoicings, as was the usage in days of yore. But the princess mourned in secret, and her heart was heavy, when she had to ride as bride with him in whom in earlier days was centered her confidence and love.

The bridal company now proceeded on their way. The bride rode on her palfrey, with a red gold crown but pallid cheek, and the bridegroom rode next to her, little suspecting the sorrow of her heart. When they had ridden a while, they came to a bridge, of which it was foretold that it would break down if crossed by a bride who was not of royal lineage. The princess thereupon said:—

> "Stand firm, thou bridge wide!
> Two noble king's children over thee ride."

"What sayest thou, my bride?" inquired the king. "Oh, nothing of consequence," answered the bride; "I was talking to Åsa, my waiting-maid."

They rode on till they came to the spot where the palace that had been the abode of the princess's father had stood. But the dwelling had been burnt, and weeds sprung up from the heap of ruins. Thereupon said the princess:—

> "Here only thorns and thistles grow,
> Where whilom gold was wont to glow.
> Here litter now the neat and swine,
> Where once I serv'd both mead and wine."

"What sayest thou, my bride?" again inquired the king. "Oh, nothing of consequence," answered the bride; "I was speaking to Åsa, my waiting-maid."

Proceeding further they came to a noble lime-tree, and the princess said:—

> "Here art thou still, thou aged tree!
> Beneath thy shade my love once pledged his faith
> to me."

The king again asked: "What sayest thou, my bride?" But the bride answered as before, "Oh, nothing of consequence; I was only talking to Åsa, my waiting-maid."

Proceeding still further the princess noticed a pair of doves flying and said:—

> "Here with thy mate thou shap'st thy flight,
> While I my true love lose tonight."

"What sayest thou, my bride?" asked the bridegroom, listening to her words. "Oh, nothing of consequence, answered the bride; "I was only talking to Åsa, my waiting-maid."

When they had again ridden for some time, they came to the cavern in the gloomy forest. While riding along, the king requested his young bride to relate to him some story. The princess, sighing deeply, said:—

> "Seven tedious years in the dark cave I pin'd,
> Stories and riddles there pass'd from my mind.
> Much ill, too, befell me,
> I've help'd to burn coal,
> Much ill have I suffer'd,
> On a wolf I have ridden.
> Today as a bride I go,
> In my mistress's stead."

"What is that thou art saying, my bride?" asked the king, again in a tone of surprise. The bride answered, "Oh nothing of consequence; I was only talking to Åsa, my waiting-maid."

They had now reached the church, in which the marriage was to be solemnized, when the princess said:—

> "Here *Mary* was I named, the *Rose and Star*,
>   Now I am *Åsa* call'd, *my waiting-maid.*"

The wedding party then entered the church in procession and in great state, according to ancient custom. First walked pipers, and fiddlers and kettle-drummers, and other musicians; then came the bridemen and the knights of the court, and last of all the bride with her young attendants. The bridal couple were now seated on the "sponsal seat," and the marriage ceremony was performed with great solemnity, as was fitting a royal pair; but no one thought otherwise than that it was the stranger maiden who was united to the king.

When the bridal mass was read, and the king had exchanged rings with the princess, he drew forth a silver girdle and put it round her waist; but the girdle had a lock so artificial and intricate that no one could open it except the king himself. The company then returned to the palace, and the health of the married pair was drunk amid mirth, and dancing and revelry, and all kinds of pastime. But the princess hastened to the female apartments, and exchanged clothes with her mistress, so that no one could know that it was the waiting-maid who had ridden in the place of the stranger damsel.

When it verged towards evening, and the king sat chatting with his young bride, as new married folks are in the habit of doing, he said: "Tell me, my love, what didst thou say when we were riding over the bridge? I should much like to know." At this the face of the damsel grew blood-red, for she knew not what answer to make; but recovering herself she said, "I have entirely forgotten what it was, but I will ask Åsa, my waiting-maid." She then went away to the waiting-maid and inquired of her what she had said on the bridge. She then returned to the bridegroom and said: "Well, now I remember: I said:—

> "Stand firm, thou bridge wide!
>   Two noble king's children over thee ride."

"Why didst thou say so?" asked the king; but the bride returned no answer.

A little while after, the king again said: "Tell me, my love, what didst thou say when we came to the old king's palace? I long much to know." The damsel felt a second time greatly embarrassed; but recovering herself she said: "That too I have entirely forgotten, but I will ask Åsa, my waiting-maid." So saying she went to the waiting-maid and asked what she had said at the old king's palace. She then returned to the bridegroom, and said: "Yes, now I remember what I said:—

> "Here only thorns and thistles grow,
> Where whilom gold was wont to glow.
> Here litter now the neat and swine,
> Where once I serv'd both mead and wine."

"Why didst thou say so?" asked the king; but the bride returned no answer.

Another while passed, when the king again said: "Tell me, my love, what didst thou say as we rode past the linden tree? I am very desirous of knowing." But the bride was unable to answer until she had inquired of Asa, her waiting-maid. When she came back, she said: "My words were:—

> "Here art thou still, thou aged tree!
> Beneath thy shade my love once pledged his faith to me."

"Why didst thou say so?" asked the bridegroom; but the bride answered not.

All this appeared to the king very singular, yet he desisted not from asking what it was she had said on various occasions during their ride; though not one of his inquiries could she answer, but must go and ask Åsa, her waiting-maid. It was now waxing late, and the new married couple were about to retire, when the king said: "Tell me, my love, what thou hast done with the girdle that I gave thee when we were leaving church?" "What girdle?" asked the bride, growing deadly pale, "I must have given it to Asa, my waiting-maid." The waiting-maid was sent for, and on her appearing, lo! she had the girdle round her body, the lock of which was so intricate that no one save the king could open it. The stranger damsel now seeing that her falsehood was exposed, went out, and full of anger left the palace. But the king recognised his genuine bride, and the princess recounted to him all that had befallen her during the long period of their separation. Great was now the delight of the guests, and the king thought himself well recompensed for all his sorrows.

The pair were then conducted to the nuptial chamber, preceded by youths and young maidens bearing wax-lights, according to the ancient custom of our forefathers. When the king and his fair consort retired for the night, the assembled company began singing the old ballad:—

> "The lights all extinguish,
> Clasp thy bride to thy breast."

And there was joy over both town and country, that they were now united who had so long loved each other. Afterwards, I was no longer with them.

1. According to another version from South Småland, a king's son was in love with a princess, but the king, her father, opposed their attachment, and concealed his daughter in a cavern. Whereupon the prince raised an army, and invaded the king's territory, for the purpose of taking the princess by force. Not being able to find her, he burned the royal palace, and carried off only the princess's embroidery frame. He then made a vow, that no one should be his consort, unless she could finish the embroidery that the king's daughter had begun.

When the princess and her waiting-maid had been seven long years in the cavern, their provisions were exhausted. Thereupon the princess said to her attendant: "Either thou shalt die for me, or I will die for thee." The attendant answered: "I will gladly die for you." When the princess had nothing more to live on, she began to tear away the roof, and, on the third day, emerged from the cavern. In the forest she met with some coal-burners, who directed her to the king's palace. On coming to the sea-shore, she there saw a bear standing, that said:—

> "If thou wilt not name my name[48],
> Thou shalt sit on my back, and I'll bear thee across."

Thus the princess crossed the strait, and got into service at the royal palace, as waiting-maid to the stranger damsel, and helped her to embroider her bridal dress, as required by the king's son.

The story then proceeds nearly as the foregoing, until they come to the church, when the prince takes forth a pair of gloves and a gold apple, which he presents to his young bride, on her promise never to part with them except to him alone. The guests then return home, and the stranger damsel steps into the place of the princess. At night the prince inquires after the gloves and gold

---

[48] See "Northern Mythology," ii. p. 83.

apple, when the waiting maid runs behind her mistress, and hands her the things. But the king's son perceiving her artifice, seizes the hand, in which is the gold apple, and says: "Thee, and no other, will I have for my queen." The king's daughter then relates her adventures, and the stranger damsel returns to the place whence she came.

2. Another version from South Småland tells of a princess named *Clara*, who is confined in a mountain by a wicked stepmother; but is at length released by a wolf, who conveys her out through a cleft. The remainder nearly resembles the story as given in the text.

THE HERD-BOY AND THE GIANT.

I. THE BOY WHO CONTENDED WITH THE GIANT IN EATING.

From South Småland.

THERE was once a boy who tended goats. One day, when wandering about in the forest, he came to a giant's dwelling, when the giant, hearing a noise and outcry in his neighbourhood, came out to see what was the matter. Now the giant being of a vast stature and fierce aspect, the boy was terrified, and ran away as fast as he was able.

In the evening, when the lad returned with his goats from the pasture, his mother was occupied in curdling. Taking a piece of the new-made cheese, he rolled it in the embers, and put it into his wallet. On the following morning he went, as was his custom, to the pasture, and again approached the giant's abode. When the giant heard the noise of the boy and his goats, he was angry, and rising up, seized a huge piece of granite, which he squeezed in his hand so that the fragments flew about in all directions. The giant then said: "If thou ever comest here again, making an uproar, I will crumple thee as small as I now squeeze this stone." The boy, however, did not allow himself to be frightened, but made a sham also to seize a stone, though he only grasped his cheese that had been rolled in the ashes, and which be pressed till the whey ran out between his fingers, and dripped down on the ground. The boy then said: "If thou dost not take thyself away, and leave me in peace, I will squeeze thee as I now squeeze the water out of this stone." When the giant found that the lad was so strong, he was frightened, and went into his hut. And thus, the boy and the giant separated for that time.

On the third day they met again in the forest, and the boy asked whether they should make another trial of strength. The giant consented, and the boy said: "Father, I think it will be a good trial, if one of us can cast your axe so high, that it does not fall down again." The giant thought it would. They now commenced the trial, and the giant threw first. He hurled the axe up with great force, so that it rose high in the air; but let him try as he might, it always fell down again. Then said the boy: "Father, I did not think you had so little strength. Wait a moment, and you shall see a better throw." The boy then swung his arm to and fro, as if to cast with the greater force; but, at the same time, very cleverly let the axe slide down into the wallet that he had on his back. The artifice escaped the notice of the giant, who continued expecting and expecting to see the axe come down again, but no axe appeared. "Now," thought he to himself, "this boy must be amazingly strong, although he appears so little and weak." They then again separated, each going his own way.

Shortly after, the giant and the herd-boy met again, and the giant asked the boy whether he would enter his service. The boy consented, left his goats in the forest, and accompanied the giant to the latter's habitation.

It is related that the giant and the boy set out for the purpose of felling an oak in the forest. When they reached the spot, the giant asked the boy whether he would hold or fell. "I will hold," said the boy, but added that he was unable to reach the top. The giant then grasped the tree and bent it to the ground; but no sooner had the boy taken fast hold of it, than the tree rebounded; and threw the lad high up in the air, so that the giant could hardly follow him with his eyes. The giant stood long wondering in what direction the boy had taken his flight; then taking up his axe, began to hew. In a little while the boy came limping up; for he had escaped with difficulty. The giant asked him why he did not hold; while the boy, who appeared as if nothing had happened, in return, asked the giant whether he would venture to make such a spring as he had just made. The giant answered in the negative, and the boy then said: "If you will not venture to do that, you may both hold and fell yourself." The giant let this answer content him and felled the oak himself.

When the tree was to be carried home, the giant said to the boy: "If thou wilt bear the top-end, I will bear the root." "No, father," answered the boy, "do you bear the top-end, I am able enough to bear the other." The giant consented and raised the smaller end of the oak upon his shoulder; but the boy, who was behind, called to him to poise the tree better by moving it more forwards. The giant did so, and thus got the whole trunk in equilibrium on his shoulder. But the boy, leaped up on the tree, and hid himself among the boughs, so that the giant could not see him. The giant now began his march, thinking that the boy was all the while at the other end. When they had thus proceeded for some distance, the giant thought it was very hard labour, and groaned piteously. "Art thou not yet tired?" said he to the boy. "No, not in the least," answered the boy. "Surely father is not tired with such a trifle." The giant was unwilling to acknowledge that such was the case and continued on his way. When they reached home, the giant was half-dead from fatigue. He threw the tree down; but the boy had in the meanwhile leaped off and appeared as if bearing the larger end of the oak. "Art thou not yet tired?" asked the giant. The boy answered: "Oh, father must not think that so little tires me. The trunk does not seem to me heavier than I could have borne by myself."

Another time the giant said: "As soon as it is daylight; we will go out and thrash." "Now I," answered the boy, "think it better to thrash before daybreak, before we eat our breakfast." The giant acquiesced, and went and fetched two flails, one of which he took for himself. When they were about to begin thrashing, the boy was unable to lift his flail, it was so large and heavy. He therefore took up a stick, and beat on the floor, while the giant thrashed. This escaped the giant's notice, and so they continued until daylight. "Now," said the boy, "let us go home to breakfast." "Yes," answered the giant, "for I think we have had a stiff job of it."

Some time after, the giant set his boy to plough, and, at the same time, said: "When the dog comes, then must loose the oxen and put them in the stall to which he will lead the way." The lad promised to do so; but when the oxen were loosed, the giant's dog crept in under the foundation of a building to which there was no door. The giant's object was to ascertain whether his boy was strong enough to lift up the house alone and place the oxen in their stalls. The boy, after having long considered what was to be done, at length resolved on slaughtering the animals, and casting their carcasses in through the window. When he returned home, the giant asked him whether the oxen were in their stalls. "Yes," answered the boy, "I got them in although I divided them."

The giant now began to harbour apprehensions and consulted with his wife how they should make away with the boy. The crone said: "It is my advice that you take your club and kill him tonight while he is asleep." This the giant thought very sound advice and promised to follow it. But the boy was on the watch, and listening to their conversation; therefore, when evening came, he laid a churn in the bed, and hid himself behind the door. At midnight the giant rose, seized his club, and beat on the churn so that the cream that was in it was sprinkled over his face. He then went to his wife, and laughing said: "Ha, ha, ha! I have struck him so that his brains flew high up on the wall." The crone was pleased at this intelligence, praised her husband's boldness, and thought they might now sleep in quiet, seeing they had no longer cause to fear the mischievous boy.

Scarcely, however, was it light, when the boy crept out of his hiding place, went in, and bade the giant-folk good morning. At this apparition the giant was naturally struck with amazement. "What," said he, "art then not yet dead? I thought I struck thee dead with my club." The boy answered: "I rather believe I felt in the night as if a flea had bitten me."

In the evening, when the giant and his boy were about to sup, the crone placed a large dish of porridge before them. "That would be excellent, said the boy, if we were to try which could eat the most, father or I." The giant was ready for the trial, and they began to eat with all their might. But the boy was crafty: he had tied his wallet before his chest, and for every spoonful that entered his month, he let two fall into the wallet. When the giant had despatched seven bowls of porridge, he had taken his fill, and sat puffing and blowing, and unable to swallow another spoonful; but the boy continued with just as much good will as when he began. The giant asked him how it was, that he who was so little could eat so much. The boy answered: "Father, I will soon show you. When I have eaten as much as I can contain, I slit up my stomach, and then I can take in as much again." Saying these words, he took a knife and ripped up the wallet, so that the porridge ran out. The giant thought this a capital plan, and that he would do the like. But when he stuck the knife in his stomach, the blood began to flow, and the end of the matter was, that it proved his death.

When the giant was dead, the boy took all the chattels that were in the house and went his way in the night. And so ends the story of the crafty herd-boy and the doltish giant.

According to another version of this story, also from South Småland, when the giant and the boy are to try which is the stronger, the giant hurled a stone high up in the air; but the stone constantly came down again; while the boy threw up a bird, which he had caught and carried in his cap. When the bird flew away and did not return, the giant thought that the boy's throw had reached the clouds, and thence concluded that the lad must be the stronger of the two.

II. The Boy that let the Giant's Child Fall into the Well.[49]

THERE were once a giant and a giantess who dwelt in a forest. Round about their habitation there were fruitful fields, so that the giant's cattle were always

---

[49] This very ancient story is wide-spread both in and out of Scandinavia. It occurs, with greater or less variations, among the following people:

1. The Lapps.—See Læstadius, Fortsättning af Journalen öfver Missions-Resori Lappmarken, 1828-1832. Stockh. 1833, pp. 464, 465. *Ibid.* pp. 460-464. See also Nilsson, Skandinaviska Nordens Ur-Invanare. Stockh. 1843, cap. iv. § 4. p. 31.

2. The Norwegians. —See Absjörnsen og Moe, ut sup., i. No. 6. "Askeladden, som kapaad med Troldet."

3. The English.—A part of the story is to be found in the old popular tale of *Jack the Giant-killer*, given in Tabart's Fairy Tales, London, 1818; and in many other English collections.

4. The Germans.—*a.* See Büsching, ut sup., pp. 124-127. "Der Schneider und der Riese." See also Grimm, K. und H. M. ii. N o. 183. *b.* Some features of this story have also found admission into that of "Das tapfere Schneiderlein," given in Grimm, i. No. 20. *c.* See also Kuhn, Markische Sagen, pp. 289-294.

5. The Servians.—See Büsching, ut sup., iv. p. 104, in remarks to the story of "Der Bartlose und der Knabe."

6. The Persians.—See the tale of Ameen of Ispahân and the Ghool, in Sir John Malcolm's Sketches of Persia.

Kindred animal fables of high antiquity, and with the same leading features, exist among

in good condition; while the people in the neighbouring parts had poor and scanty pasture. This vexed them, and they sometimes let their cattle graze on the giant's land; the consequence was, that the giant, who was of an exceedingly fierce and cruel disposition, frequently attacked the herdsmen and slew them.

Not far from the giant's abode, there dwelt a poor woman who had an only son. He was little and weakly, but very cunning and daring. One day the boy requested his mother to make three cheeses. The woman did as he requested. When the cheeses were ready, the boy rolled them in the ashes, so that they appeared gray and far from tempting. At this the mother was angry and chided him for having wasted the bounties of heaven. But the boy begged her to make herself easy; for she could not know what he had in mind.

Early in the morning the boy went to the forest with his mother's cattle and drove them on to the giant's land. Here he wandered about without hindrance, as long as the sun was up. Towards evening he collected his cattle and prepared to return home; but in the meanwhile, the giant had become aware of his visit, and now came with great strides towards him. The giant was highly incensed, and looked so terrific, that the boy, in spite of all his boldness, was not a little frightened. "What art thou doing here in my pasture?" cried the giant. The boy answered, that he came to find food for his cattle. The giant said: "Take thyself away this instant, else I will crush thee as I now crush this stone." Saying this the giant snatched up a large gray stone that was lying on the ground and squeezed it so that it flew in a thousand shivers. The boy said: "Thou art very strong; but I am no less so, although I am small of growth." He then took one of his cheeses and squeezed it so that the water ran out. On seeing this, the giant was all astonishment, and thought there must be some deception at bottom. He, therefore, took up another stone, and squeezed it into small fragments; but the boy took another cheese, and pressed the water from it as before. This game was played a third time, and the boy pressed the water out of the third cheese. "Well," said the giant, "I had no idea thou wast so strong. Follow me to my dwelling, and serve me faithfully, and I will give thee three bushels of gold. But if thou dost not please me, I will cut three broad

---

7. The Italians.—See in Straparola, Notti piacevoli, the fable of the Ass and the Lion.

8. The Hindus.—See the fable of the Goat and the Lion, translated from the Pancha Tantra, in Sir J. Malcolm's Sketches.

strips out of thy back." The boy answered: "These seem to me very fair conditions; but I must now drive my cattle into the town." So, they agreed to meet on the following day, and thus their interview concluded for that time.

On the following day, the boy went to the forest and met the giant according to agreement. Thence they proceeded to the giant's abode. But the giant's wife was so large and fierce, that the boy stood in greater fear of her than of the giant himself.

When a short time had elapsed, the giant and his boy went to the forest to cut wood; and the giant said: "As thou art so strong thou canst carry my axe." Now the axe was uncommonly large and heavy, so that the boy could hardly lift it: he, therefore, said: "It is better that you carry the axe yourself, then I can go first and show the way." In this the giant acquiesced, and they set out. On reaching the place, the giant stopped by a large tree, and said: "As thou art so strong, thou canst strike the first blow, and I will strike the second." "No," answered the boy, "I am not accustomed to fell with so small an axe. You can strike the first stroke, and I will strike the next." The giant let himself be content with this arrangement, took up the axe, and struck a powerful stroke close at the root; and so effectual was it, that the tree fell on the earth with a loud crash. Thus, the boy escaped, for that time, giving a proof of his strength.

The tree was now to be carried home, and the giant asked the boy whether he would bear it at the top-end or at the root. The boy said he would bear it at the top. The giant then lifted the tree upon his shoulder, but the boy cried out that he should carry it more forward. The giant did so, and thus got the whole trunk in equilibrium on his shoulder. The boy then jumped up and hid himself among the boughs of the tree. When they reached home, the giant was very tired; but the boy said he thought it quite a light job.

On the following day, the giant said he would go out, and that the boy could remain at home and help the giantess to churn. So she brought out a churn full of milk; but the churn was so large that the boy could hardly lift the churning staff. He said, therefore, to the woman: "Mother, this seems a light sort of job; but I should be glad if you would just show me how to set about it." The giantess did as he desired, and began to churn, while the boy stood looking on. At this moment the giant's child began to cry, and the crone said: "Do thou take the young one with thee to the well and wash her clean: I will churn while thou art away." The boy went, but without in the least hurrying himself; and on reaching the well, at which he was to wash the child, who was somewhat less than himself, it so happened that the child rolled into the water and was drowned. The boy thought this mishap was of no great consequence; but, at the same time, was of opinion that thenceforth it might be as well not to remain longer with the giant-folk.

When the boy returned, the giantess had finished the churning. "Thou hast stayed a long time said she; but what hast thou done with the child?" The boy answered: "As soon as I had washed her, she ran into the forest to meet her father." "Very well," replied the woman, "they will then soon come home together."

Towards evening the giant returned from the forest and was very tired. The crone, on seeing him approach, called to him: "Father, what hast thou done with the child?" The giant answered: "I have seen no child." The giantess, on hearing this, was frightened, and began to cry and lament. The boy proposed that he and the giant should go to the wood in search of the infant, and they set out accordingly; but after looking in every direction, it is needless to say that they did not find it.

After wandering about for a long time, they came to the boundary of the giant's land. The boy then said: "Father, I am now not far from home. Give me leave to go to my mother, who expects me. Tomorrow I will come again and help you to search." The giant answered: "Thou mayest go, as thou hast served me so faithfully; but come back soon." Saying this he took forth three bushels of gold, which he gave to the boy, in reward for his services. The boy thanked him and said that next time he would serve him still better.

The giant and the herd-boy now went different ways. The boy returned to his mother and gave her all the gold he had earned; so that from that day they were rich and fortunate. But the giant wandered about in the forest seeking his child.

II. NORWEGIAN.[1]

GRIMSBORK.

THERE was once a couple of rich people who had twelve sons, the youngest of whom, when he was grown up, would remain no longer at home, but would go and seek his fortune in the wide world. His parents strove to convince him that he was very well off at home, and might well remain with them; but he could not rest, and persisted in his determination to seek his fortune abroad; and so they were obliged to consent. After travelling a long way, he came to a royal palace, where he offered to serve, and was taken into employment.

The king's daughter had been carried off into a mountain by a Troll, and the king had no other child; therefore both he and the whole country were in great affliction; and the king had promised his daughter with half his kingdom to whomsoever would deliver her from the power of the Troll but there was no one who could, although there were not wanting many to make the trial. When the youth had been a year or more in the king's service, he wished to go and see his parents but on reaching home he found both of them dead, and that his brothers had divided all their property among themselves, so that there was nothing left for him. "Shall I alone inherit nothing after my parents?" asked the youth. "Who could think that thou wast still alive, who hast been idly wandering all this time about the world?" replied the brothers: "But there are twelve mares grazing on the heath; if thou wilt have them for thy share, thou canst take them. The youth was well pleased to hear this; so, having thanked them he immediately went to the heath, where the mares were feeding. On approaching them he found that every mare had a sucking colt, and one of them had a large cream-coloured (borket) colt which was so fat, and in such high condition, that it actually shone. "Thou art a beautiful young colt," said the youth. "Yes," replied the colt, "and if thou will kill the other

---

colts and let me suck all the mares for a year, thou shalt see how large and beautiful I shall then be." The youth did so, he killed the eleven colts and then returned home. In the following year he went again to look after the mares and the colt; the latter had grown so fat that its skin shone bright and glossy, and it was so large that the youth could hardly mount it, and the mares had each got a colt again. "Thou saidst truly that I should not be the loser, if I would let thee suck all the twelve mares," said the youth to the one-year-old colt, "but now thou art so big thou must come with me." "No, I must stay a year longer; kill all the twelve colts, and let me suck the mares this year also, and then by the summer thou shalt see how large and beautiful I shall be." The youth did so, and when he came up to the heath in the following year, and looked after the colt and the mares, he found they had each again a young colt, but the cream-coloured colt was so big that the youth could not reach up to his neck, when he wanted to feel how fat he was, and he shone so bright that one could see oneself in his skin. Large and beautiful thou wast last year, my colt, but this year thou art still more beautiful, said the youth, "the like of such a horse cannot be found in the king's palace; and now then must come with me." "No," replied the colt again, "here I must stay for another year, and if thou wilt kill all the twelve colts, and let me suck the mares, thou shalt see what I look like next summer." The youth did as he was told, he killed all the young colts and then returned home.

But when he went the next year to look after the cream-coloured colt and the mares, he was quite astonished. So tall and big he never thought a horse could grow, for he was obliged to kneel down to enable the youth to mount him; and was so fat and glossy that his hide looked like a mirror. And now the colt was not unwilling to go with the youth; therefore, having mounted him, he rode home to his brothers, who clasped their hands together and crossed themselves, for such a horse they had never seen or even heard speak of before. "If you will get me the best shoes that are to be had, and the finest saddle and bridle for my horse, you shall have all the mares that are on the heath, together with their twelve colts," said the youth; for this year they had each again got a colt. This offer the brothers willingly accepted; so, the horse got such shoes that the stones flew in fragments high in the air when the youth rode over the mountain-heaths; and such a gilded saddle and bridle he had that they glittered and shone at a great distance. "Now let us journey to the royal palace," said

Grimsbork, for that was his name; "but remember well to demand of the king a good stable and good fodder for me." This the youth promised he would not forget to do; he rode away, and it can easily be imagined that, mounted on such a horse, it was not long before he arrived at the king's palace.

When he reached it, the king, who was standing on the steps, stared and looked at him as he came riding along. "Well!" said he, "such a horse and such a rider I have never seen before in all my days;" and when the youth asked whether he could be taken into the royal service, the king was so glad that he was ready to dance and skip as he stood on the steps, and said, that might easily be. "But good stable room and food enough for my horse I must have," said the youth. The king promised he should have as much hay and oats as Grimsbork could eat; and the knights were obliged to lead their horses out of the stable, that Grimsbork might stand alone and have plenty of room.

But it soon happened that all the others in the royal service grew jealous of the youth, and if they could, they would have done him all kinds of mischief. At length they told the king that the youth had said he could, if he chose, release his daughter from the power of the Troll, who had taken her into the mountain so long ago. Instantly the king called him into his presence and told him what he had heard; how he had boasted of what he could do, and that now he should do it. To whomsoever could accomplish the adventure, he was aware that he had promised both his daughter and the half of his kingdom, and this promise he would justly and honourably fulfil; but if he failed in the attempt, he should be slain. The youth denied having so said, but it availed nothing, for the king turned a deaf ear to him, and so he had no alternative but to make the trial. He then went down into the stable musing and sorrowful. On Grimsbork asking why he was so dejected, the youth related all that had passed, and said he knew not what course to pursue; for as to recovering the princess that was utterly impossible "Oh, that may easily be done." said Grimsbork, "I will help you, but you must first let me be well shod; you must require twenty pounds of iron and twelve pounds of steel to make my shoes; one smith to forge, and another to fix them on." The youth did accordingly and met with no refusal: he obtained the iron and steel and the smiths, so that Grimsbork was shod in the highest perfection, and the youth galloped forth from the royal courtyard followed by clouds of dust. But on reaching the mountain, into which the princess had been taken, the difficulty was how to climb up the precipice which led to the entrance; for it was from top to bottom as perpendicular as the wall of a room, and as slippery as a pane of glass. The first time the youth attempted the ascent, he had proceeded but a little way when Grimsbork slipped with both his fore feet, and down they fell with a noise like thunder over the heath. At his next attempt he ascended a little higher, but one of his forefeet slipped, and down they came with a crash like that of an earthquake. At the third trial, Grimsbork said: "Now, we must strive our utmost;" and so saying, he rushed up so that the stones flew about them up to the very sky. At length they reached the top, and the youth, at full gallop, rode into the mountain, snatched up the king's daughter, placed her on the pommel of his saddle, and was away again before it occurred to the Troll to move from the spot. Thus, was the princess rescued.

When the youth returned to the royal palace, the king was delighted to have his daughter back again, as can be easily imagined but however that might or might not be, all who were in the palace had so represented matters to the king, that he was, nevertheless, angry with the youth. "Many thanks for rescuing my daughter," said the king to him as he entered the palace and was about going away again. "She ought now to be *mine* as well as *yours*, for you are no doubt a man of your word," said the youth. "Right," said the king, "have her thou shalt, as I have promised but thou must first get the sun to shine in the court of the royal palace." Now, there was a large high mountain just outside the windows, which cast its shadow, so that the sun could not shine in. "That was not in our agreement," answered the youth; "but as no prayers will avail, I must do my best; for the princess I am resolved to have." He then went down again, and told Grimsbork what the king required; and Grimsbork thought it might be accomplished but he must have new shoes, for which there must be twenty pounds of iron and twelve pounds of steel, besides two smiths, one to forge the shoes, the other to nail them on; and then they would soon cause the sun to shine in the palace court. When the youth requested these things, he got them immediately; for the king was ashamed to refuse them. So Grimsbork got new and fitting shoes under him. The youth now mounted his horse and was soon on the road again; and at each spring that Grimsbork made, the mountain sank fifteen ells into the earth, and so they continued till the king could see no more of the mountain.

When the youth returned to the royal palace, he asked the king whether the princess should now belong to him for now he was sure that the sun shone into the palace. But the courtiers had again excited the king against him, so that he answered that the youth should have the princess, and that he never had any other thought, but that he must first procure her as fine a bride's horse as he had a bride groom's. The youth answered, that the king had never before mentioned any such condition, and he thought he had now well earned the princess; but the king was not to be moved, and said, "if the youth could not also accomplish this adventure, he should lose his life into the bargain." He then went down again into the stable dejected and sorrowful, as may well be imagined; here he informed Grimsbork that the king had commanded him to get for the princess as fine a bride's horse as he had a bridegroom's if not, that he should forfeit his life but that is not so easy a task," added be, "for the like of thee is not in the whole world." "Oh yes! there is a match to me," answered Grimsbork, "but it will not be an easy matter to get it, as it is in hell, but we must make the trial. Now, do you go up to the king and request new shoes for me, for which I must again have twenty pounds of iron and twelve pounds of steel, and two smiths, the one to forge the shoes, the other to fix them on; and be very careful that the crooks are made very sharp. We must also have with us twelve barrels of rye, and twelve barrels of barley, and twelve slaughtered oxen; and all the twelve ox-hides must have twelve hundred spikes in each. All this we must have, also a barrel filled with tar." The youth then went to the king and demanded all that Grimsbork required, and which the king thought it would be a shame to refuse; he therefore got all that he wanted.

He now mounted Grimsbork and rode out of the palace yard, and when he had ridden a long long way, over mountains and heaths, Grimsbork asked: "Do you hear anything?" "Yes, there is such a terrible clatter in the air that I feel almost afraid," said the youth. "That is," answered Grimsbork, "all the wild birds of the forest; they have been sent out for the purpose of stopping us; but out a hole in the corn-sacks, they will then be so busied with the corn, that they will quite forget us." The youth did so; he cut a hole in the sacks, so that the rye and barley ran out on all sides. Then all the wild birds that were in the forest came flocking in such numbers, that they quite darkened the sun; but as soon as they saw the corn, they could not refrain from it, but darted down and began to peek the barley and rye, and at last to fight with each other;

and they did no harm either to the youth or to Grimsbork, whom they entirely forgot.

The youth now rode on again a long long way, over hill and dale, over mountains and wastes, when Grimsbork began to listen again, and then asked the youth if he heard anything? "Yes, I hear such a roaring in the forest from all sides, I am beginning to be quite terrified," said he. "Those are all the wild beasts that are in the forest," replied Grimsbork; "they are sent out to stop us, but throw out the twelve carcasses, they will then have something to employ them, and so forget us." The youth threw out the oxen, and then all the wild beasts of the forest, bears, wolves, lions, and all sorts of terrific animals, as soon as they saw the carcasses of the oxen, began to fight for them; so that their blood flowed in torrents, and they quite forgot the youth and Grimsbork.

The youth now rode a long long while again; it was many many miles; for it may easily be imagined that Grimsbork did not proceed slowly; he then began to neigh. "Do you hear anything?" said he. "Yes, I hear something like a young colt neighing gently far far away," replied the youth. "That is a full-grown colt," nevertheless said Grimsbork. "The reason you hear it so faintly is, because it is so far away." They then journeyed on a good way, when Grimsbork neighed again. "Do you hear anything?" asked he. "Yes, I hear plainly a neighing as of a full-grown home," answered the youth. "Well, now you must hear it once again," said Grimsbork, "and then you will say there is no lack of strength in it."

When they had proceeded some miles, Grimsbork neighed a third time; but before he could ask whether the youth heard anything, there was such a neighing on the heath, that he thought both mountain and hills would have burst asunder. "Now it is here," cried Grimsbork. "Make haste and throw the ox-hides with the spikes in them over me, throw the tar-barrel over the field, and then climb up into the large pine-tree there. When it comes it will spout fire out of both its nostrils, and that will set fire to the tar barrels. Then take notice: if the flames ascend, I shall win, but if they fall, I shall lose. If you see that I shall win, then throw the bridle—you must take it off from me—over the horse, and it will become gentle." Just as the youth had thrown the hides with the spikes in them over Grimsbork, and the tar-barrel over the field, and had himself climbed up into the pine-tree, there came a horse, from which there issued such a heat that the tar-barrel was set on fire; and it fought with

Grimsbork, so that the stones flew up to the very sky. They bit and struck with their forefeet and with their hind feet; and the youth looked first at them, and then at the tar-barrel, when at length the flames rose, for wherever the other horse bit and kicked, he found only the hide with the spikes, and was, consequently, obliged to yield. When the youth saw this, he lost no time in descending from the tree and throwing the bridle over it; and it then became so gentle, that one might guide it with a thread. This horse was also cream-coloured, and so like Grimsbork, that no one could have distinguished the one from the other. The youth mounted the horse that he had caught, and rode back to the king's palace, and Grimsbork ran loose by the side of him.

When they arrived, the king was standing out in the court. "Can you now tell me which is the horse I have caught, and which is the one I had before?" said the youth. "If you cannot, then I think your daughter belongs to me." The king went and examined them above and below, before and behind, but there was not a hair's difference between them. "No," replied the king, "I cannot see any difference in them; and since thou hast procured my daughter so beautiful a bridal horse, thou shalt surely have her. But one trial we must yet make and see how that will succeed. She shall hide herself twice, and afterwards thou shalt hide thyself twice; if thou canst find her each time that she is hidden, and she cannot find thee in thy hiding place, then thou shalt have the princess." "Neither is that in our agreement," said the youth; "but we will make the trial since it may not be otherwise." The king's daughter was to be the first to hide herself.

She transformed herself into a duck and went and swam in the water that was outside the royal palace. But the youth merely went into the stable and asked Grimsbork what had become of her. "Oh! you have only to take your gun and go down to the pond and take aim at the duck which is swimming about there," said Grimsbork, "and she will soon come forth again." The youth took his gun accordingly and went down to the water. "I will shoot that duck," said he, levelling his piece. "No, no! dear friend, do not shoot, it is I," said the princess; so, he found her that time. The next time the princess changed herself into a loaf, and placed herself on a table among four others, and so alike were all the loaves that no one could see any difference between them. The youth went down into the stable again and told Grimsbork that the princess had hidden herself a second time, and that he knew not what had become of her. "Oh!" said he, take and sharpen a large bread-knife, and pretend to cut right through the third loaf on the left hand of the four loaves, which lie on the kitchen table in the royal palace, and then she will soon come forth. The youth went into the kitchen and began to sharpen the largest bread-knife he could find, took hold of the third loaf on the left-hand side, and set the knife against it, as if he would cut it in two. "I will have a slice off this loaf," said he. "No, no! dear friend, do not cut, for it is I," said the princess, and so he found her the second time.

Now it was his turn to hide himself, but Grimsbork had given him such good advice that he was not to be found again. First, he turned himself into a hornet and concealed himself in Grimsbork's left nostril; the princess hunted and looked about everywhere, both high and low, and then went into Grimsbork's stall, but he began to bite and kick about so that she durst not venture nearer. "As I cannot find you, you must come forth of yourself," said she; and immediately the youth stood before her in the stable. The second time, Grimsbork also told him into what he should turn himself. This time he became a lump of earth and put himself between the hoof and the shoe of Grimsbork's left forefoot. The king's daughter searched and searched again, both inside and outside of the palace; at last she came into the stable and proceeded to Grimsbork's stall. This time he allowed her to come quite close up to him, and she looked and looked both up and down; but she could not see under Grimsbork's feet, he stood too firm on his legs for her to attempt that; and 'so she could not find the youth. "You must come forth again of yourself," said the princess, "for I cannot find you." And at the same moment the youth stood by her side in the stable.

"And now you are mine," said he to the princess; "for now you can see," said he to the king, "that so it is to be."

"If it is to be so," replied the king, "then let it be so."

There was great preparation made for the wedding, and the youth mounted Grimsbork, and the king's daughter the other cream-coloured horse, and you may well believe they were not long on the, way to the church.

GUDBRAND OF THE MOUNTAIN-SIDE.

THERE was once a man named Gudbrand, who had a farm, which lay on the side of a mountain, whence he was called Gudbrand of the Mountain-side. He and his wife lived in such harmony together and were so well-matched, that whatever the husband did, seemed to the wife so well done, that it could not be done better; let him therefore act as he might, she was equally well pleased.

They owned a plot of ground and had a hundred dollars lying at the bottom of a chest, and in the stall two fine cows. One day the woman said to Gudbrand: "I think we might as well drive one of the cows to town and sell it; we should then have a little pocket-money for such respectable persons as we are, ought to have a few skillings in hand as well as others. The hundred dollars at the bottom of the chest we had better not touch; but I do not see why we should keep more than one cow; besides, we shall be somewhat the gainers; for instead of two cows, I shall have only one to milk and look after."

These words Gudbrand thought both just and reasonable; so, he immediately took the cow and went to the town in order to sell it; but when he came there, he could not find any one who wanted to buy a cow. "Well!" thought Gudbrand, "I can go home again with my cow; I have both stall and collar for her, and it is no farther to go backwards than forwards. So, saying, he began wandering home again.

When he had gone a little way, he met a man who had a horse he wished to sell, and Gudbrand thought it better to have a horse than a cow, so be exchanged with the man. Going a little further still, he met a man driving a fat pig before him; and thinking it better to have a fat pig than a horse, he made an exchange with him also. A little further on, he met a man with a goat. "A goat," thought he, "is always better to have than a pig; so, he made an exchange with the owner of the goat. He now walked on for an hour, when he met a man with a sheep; with him be ex hanged his goat; "for," thought he, "it is always better to have a sheep than a goat." After walking some way again, meeting a man with a goose, he changed away his sheep for the goose; then going on a long long way, he met a man with a cock, and thought to himself, "It is better to have a cock than a goose," and so gave his goose for the cock. Having walked on till the day was far gone, and beginning to feel hungry, he sold the cock for twelve skillings, and bought some food; "for," thought he, "it is better to support life than to carry back the cock." After this he continued his way homeward till he reached the house of his nearest neighbour, where he called in.

"How have matters gone with you in town?" asked the neighbour.

"Oh!" answered Gudbrand, "but so, so I cannot boast of my luck, neither can I exactly complain of it." He then began to relate all that he had done from first to last.

"You'll meet with a warm reception when you get home to your wife," said his neighbour. "God help you, I would not be in your place."

"I think things might have been much worse," said Gudbrand; "but whether they are good or bad, I have such a gentle wife, that she will never say a word, let me do what I may."

"Yes, that I know," answered his neighbour; "but I do not think she will be so gentle in this instance."

"Shall we lay a wager?" said Gudbrand of the Mountain side. "I have got a hundred dollars in my chest at home, will you venture the like sum." "Yes, I will," replied the neighbour, and they wagered accordingly, and remained till evening drew on, when they set out together for Gudbrand's house; having agreed that the neighbour should stand outside and listen, while Gudbrand went in to meet his wife.

"Good evening," said Gudbrand.

"Good evening," said his wife, "thank God thou art there."

Yes, there he was. His wife then began asking him how he had fared in the town. "So, so," said Gudbrand; "I have not got much to boast of; for when I reached the town there was no one who would buy the cow, so I changed it for a horse." "Many thanks for that," said his wife, we are such respectable people, that we ought to ride to church as well as others; and if we can afford to keep a horse, we may certainly have one. Go and put the horse in the stable, children."

"Oh," said Gudbrand, "but I have not got the horse for as I went along the road, I exchanged the horse for a pig."

"Well," said the woman, "that is just what I should have done myself; I thank thee for that, I can now have pork and bacon in my house to offer anybody when they come to see me. What should we have done with a horse? People would only have said, we were grown too proud to walk to church. Go, children, and put the pig in."

"But I have not brought the pig with me," said Gudbrand; "for when I had gone a little further on, I exchanged it for a milch goat."

"How admirably thou dost everything," exclaimed his wife. "What should we have done with a pig; people would only have said that we eat up everything we own. Yes, now that I have a goat, I can get both milk and cheese and still keep my goat. Go and tie up the goat, children."

"No," said Gudbrand, "I have not brought home the goat; for when I came a little further on, I changed the goat for a fine sheep."

"Well," cried the woman, "thou hast done everything just as I could wish; just as if I had been there myself. What should we have done with a goat? I must have climbed up the mountains, and wandered through the valleys, to bring it home in the evening. With a sheep I shall have wool and clothing in the house, with food into the bargain. So go, children, and put the sheep into the field."

"But I have not got the sheep," said Gudbrand; "for as I went a little further, I changed it away for a goose."

"Many, many thanks for that," said his wife. "What should I have done with a sheep? For I have neither a spinning-wheel nor a distaff; nor have I much desire to toil and labour to make clothes; we can purchase clothing as we have done hitherto; now I shall have roast goose, which I have often longed for; and then I can make a little pillow of the feathers. Go and bring in the goose, children."

"But I have not got the goose," said Gudbrand; "as I came on a little further, I changed it away for a cock."

"Heaven only knows how thou couldst think of all this," exclaimed his wife, "it is just as if I had managed it all myself; a cock! that is just as good as if thou hadst bought an eight-day clock; for as the cock crows every morning at four o'clock, we can be stirring betimes. What should I have done with a goose? I do not know how to dress a goose, and my pillow I can stuff with moss. Go and fetch in the cock, children."

"But I have not brought the cock home with me," said Gudbrand; "for when I had gone a long long way, I became so hungry that I was obliged to sell the cock for twelve skillings to keep me alive."

"Well! thank God thou didst so," exclaimed his wife; "whatever thou dost, thou always dost just as I could wish to have it done. What should we have done with a cock? We are our own masters, we can lie as long as we like in the morning. God be praised I have got thee here safe again, and as then always dost everything so right, we want neither a cock, nor a goose, nor a pig, nor a sheep, nor a cow."

Hereupon Gudbrand opened the door: "Have I won your hundred dollars?" asked he of his neighbour, who was obliged to confess that he had.

THE MASTER-THIEF.

THERE was once a peasant who had three sons. He had no inheritance to leave them, nothing to employ them upon; in fact, he knew not what to do with them; he therefore said to them, that they might turn to whatever they had most inclination for, and go whithersoever they pleased, and that he would accompany them on the road, which he did. He went with them till they came to a place where three roads met, when each took a different one. Their father bade them farewell and returned home. What became of the two elder, I could never learn, but the youngest travelled far and wide.

One night, as he was going through a large wood, he was overtaken by very dreadful weather; it blew and snowed so violently that he could hardly keep his eyes open; and on a sudden he became quite bewildered and could find neither road nor path: as he proceeded, he at length saw a light shining far in the wood. This spot he thought he would endeavour to reach; and after walking on for some time he did so. It was a large building, and the fire was burning up so briskly within, that he knew the inmates could not yet have retired to rest. He went in and there saw a woman busied in household occupations. "Good evening," said the youth. "Good evening again," said the woman. "Oh! it is such terrible weather out tonight," said the youth. "It is so," answered the woman. "Can I have shelter and sleep here tonight?" asked the youth. "It would not be safe for you to lie here, answered the woman, for if the people should find you when they come home, they would kill both you and me." "What kind of people then are they that dwell here?" asked the youth. "Oh, they are robbers and the like," said the woman; "they stole me away when I was little and have kept me to be their housekeeper." "I think I will stay and sleep here notwithstanding," said the youth: "for be it as it may, I will not go out again in such weather at night time. It will be the worse for you," replied the woman.

The youth then lay down on a bed that stood in the room, but he did not dare to sleep. Just at the same moment the robbers returned, and the woman told them that a strange youth had come, and that she could not get rid of him.

"Does he appear to have money?" asked the robber "Money! the poor wretch!" said the woman. "He has hardly clothes to his back." The robbers now began to whisper together, as to what would be the best to do with him, whether they should kill him or not. In the meantime, the youth rose up and began talking to them, and asked them whether they wanted a servant, for he would be very glad to serve them. "Yes," said they, "if thou art inclined to follow our trade, we will take thee into our service." "It's all one," said the youth, "whatever trade it is, for when I left home, I got leave of my father to take to whatever I would." "Hast thou then any inclination to steal?" asked the robber. "Yes," answered the youth; for that was a trade he thought he could soon learn.

Now at a little distance from them there lived a man who had three oxen, one of which he was going to take to the next town to sell; and this had come to the knowledge of the thieves: so they told the youth that if he could manage to steal the ox on the road, so that the man should not know it, nor do him any harm, he should then be allowed to enter their service. Well, the youth set out, taking with him a handsome shoe that was standing there: this he laid in the road where he knew the man would pass with his ox, and then went and hid himself in the wood behind a bush. As the man came along, he immediately perceived the shoe. "That is a capital shoe," said he; "if I only had the fellow to it, I would take it home with me, I should then perhaps, bring my old woman for once into a good humour;" for his wife was so ill-tempered and so cross-grained that the intervals between each beating she gave him were far from long. But thinking within himself that he could do nothing with one shoe, if he had not the fellow to it, he continued his way and let the shoe remain. The youth then took up the shoe and ran with it as fast as he could through the wood to get before the man; and then placed the shoe in the road again, where he knew the man would pass. When he approached with his ox, he was vexed with himself, because he had been so foolish as to leave the fellow shoe behind, instead of taking it with him. "I must run back again and pick it up," said he to himself, while tying his ox to a paling; then I shall have a pair of excellent shoes for my old woman, and, perhaps, she will for once be in a good humour.

So, he went back, looking and looking on all sides after the shoe, but no shoe could he find, and was at length obliged to return with the one he had. In the meantime, the youth had taken the ox and hurried off with it. When the man came back and found that his ox was gone, he began to cry, and run about as if he had lost his senses; for he knew that his wife would almost kill him when she found that he had lost the ox. So, he thought he would go home and take the other ox, and drive that to the town to sell, and get a good price for it, and not let his wife know anything about the other. This he did; he went back, and, without his wife's knowledge, took another of the oxen and went to town with it: but the thieves got scent of this also, and said to the youth, that if he could drive off this one also, without the man knowing it, and without his doing him any harm, then he should be one of them. This, thought the youth, can be no very difficult matter.

And now he took with him a rope, put it under his arms and hung himself up across the road where the man would pass. As he approached with the ox, and saw this object hanging there, he was somewhat frightened. "Ah! what must have been thy sorrow, who hast hung thyself up there?" said he; "well, thou must hang there for me, I cannot blow life into thee again." And so, he trudged on his way with his ox. The youth got down from the tree, ran through a footpath, got the start of the man, and hung himself again in his way. "Truly thou hast been sad of heart to hang thyself there! or is it only a spectre that I see. Well! thou must hang there for me, whether thou art a ghost or whatever thou art," said he and continued his way with his ox. The youth did again exactly as he had done on the two former occasions; he sprang out of the tree, ran through the wood by a footpath, and again hung himself before him in the middle of the road. When the man saw this again, he said to himself: "This is sad indeed! can all the three have been so miserable that they have hung themselves? No, I cannot believe it is anything else than an apparition before me. But now I will know it for certain. If the other two are still hanging, then it is really so; but if they are not hanging there, it is a diabolical delusion before me." So, saying he tied up the ox and ran back to see if there were really any one hanging. While he was peering among all the trees, the youth sprang down, took the ox, and went off with it. When the man returned and found that his ox was gone, it is easy to imagine that he was almost frantic; he cried and raged, but at length became more composed, and thought to himself: "There is nothing else to be done than to go home and fetch the third ox, so that the old woman may know nothing of the matter. He went home accordingly, took his last ox and set out again, his wife knowing nothing about it. "And now I must try," said he, to get so much the more money for it." But the thieves had got knowledge of this also and said to the youth that if he could steal this ox as he had done the other two, he should be master over them all.

So, the youth left them, and hastened into the wood; and when the man came along with his ox, he set up a lowing exactly like that of a large ox in the forest. When the man heard this he was delighted, for he thought he recognised the voice of his lost cattle, and now hoped he should find them both again; so, he tied up the third ox, and ran into the wood to look after the others. In the meantime, the youth rode off with the ox. When the man came back, and found that that was also gone, his lamentation and rage knew no bounds, and for several days he did not dare to go home, being fearful that his wife would kill him outright. Nor were the thieves very well pleased at being obliged to say that the youth was master over them all.

They therefore agreed together to devise something that should be beyond his power, and all went out leaving him at home alone.

As soon as they had left the house, the first thing he did was to drive the oxen out into the road, so that they might find their way back to the man from whom he had taken them; and glad was he to see them again. He next took all the horses belonging to the robbers and loaded them with everything he could find of value, as gold, silver, costly clothes, and other precious things. Then bidding the woman give his greeting and thanks to the thieves and tell them that he was going to travel, and that they would find it a difficult matter to catch him again, he left the dwelling.

After wandering for some time, he got into the road he was in when he first came to the thieves. When he arrived near to the place where his father dwelt, he dressed himself in a general's uniform, which he found among the things he had taken from the thieves, and then rode into the yard like some great personage. He walked into the house and asked if he could have a lodging there. "No, certainly not; how can I let any part of my house to such a great personage?" said the father; "I have hardly clothes enough to lie upon myself, and bad enough they are." "You have always been hard," said the youth, "and so you are still, as you will not give your son house-room." "Are you my son?" asked the man. "What! do you not know me again?" replied the youth. He then knew him again. "But what hast thou been doing that thou couldst become such a fine spark in so short a time?" said the man. "I will tell you," answered the youth. "You told me I might betake myself to anything I pleased, so I went apprentice to some thieves and robbers; I have now served my time out and am become a Master-thief."

Close to his father's house there lived an Amtman[2], who had a large farm and so much money that he knew not how to count it. He had also a daughter, who was both neat and pretty. The Master-thief had set his heart upon this young girl and told his father that he must go to the Amtman and demand his daughter for him. "If he inquires of what trade I, am, say I am a Master-thief," said the youth.

"I think thou hast lost thy wits," replied his father; "for in thy senses thou canst not be, to think of such folly." But the youth said he should and must go to the Amtman and demand his daughter; there was no alternative.

"No, I dare not go to the Amtman, who is so rich and has so much money, and be thy spokesman," said the man; "no, that I cannot do." The Master-thief said there was no other resource, he should go whether he would or not; and if he did not go by fair means he should by foul. But the father still persisting in his refusal, the son followed, threatening to beat him with a stout birchen-cudgel, so that he ran in tears into the Amtman's house, "Well, my friend, what is thy business?" said the Amtman. He began telling him how that he had three sons, who had all left home in one day, and how he gave them leave to travel in whatever direction they liked, and also to betake themselves to whatever trade they preferred; "and now" added he, wringing his hands and weeping bitterly, "the youngest is come back, and has forced me

---

[2] A superior revenue officer, having jurisdiction in certain cases; the district over which his authority extends is called an *Amt.*

by threats to come to you, and ask you to give him your daughter, and to tell you that he is a Master-thief."

"Make yourself quite easy on that score, my friend," said the Amtman laughing, "and tell him from me that he must first give some proof of his mastership. If he can steal the meat off the spit in my kitchen on Sunday, while all are watching it, he shall have my daughter." The man did so, and the youth said that would be an easy thing to do. He then got three live hares, put them into a sack, dressed himself in some old rags, and appeared so miserable and pitiable that it was quite painful to look at him, and thus equipped, stole into the passage on the Sunday forenoon, like any other beggar, with his sack. The Amtman himself and all the household were in the kitchen watching the meat as it roasted. At this moment the youth let a bare slip out of the bag, which darted forth and ran round the yard. "Oh! look, there's a hare," exclaimed those in the kitchen, running out to catch it. The Amtman had also seen it. "Let it run," said he, "it is of no use to think of catching a hare running." Ere long the youth let out the second, and the people in the kitchen seeing it and believing it to be the same, would run out again in the hope of catching it; but the Amtman said it was to no purpose. A little while after the youth let the third hare out of the sack, which ran forth about the yard the people in the kitchen saw this one also and thinking it must be the same they had seen before wanted to go out and catch it. That is truly a noble hare, said the Amtman, "come, let us see if we cannot catch it." He then ran out, all the rest following, the bare before and they after, according to approved custom. In the meantime, the Master-thief got the roast meat and ran off with it; and where the Amtman got his roast for dinner I know not; but this I know, he did not get roast hare for his dinner, although he ran till he was both hot and weary.

The priest came to dinner as usual, and when the Amtman related to him the trick the Master-thief had played him, he jeered him beyond all moderation: "I do not think it possible that I could ever be fooled by such a fellow," said the priest. "I will advise you to be on your guard," replied the Amtman, "perhaps he will be with you before you know a word of the matter." But the priest stuck to his opinion and laughed at the Amtman for having been so easily duped.

In the afternoon the Master-thief came and demanded the Amtman's daughter, according to his promise. "You must first give a few more proofs of your mastership," said the Amtman, and entered into a friendly chat with him; "for what you did today was no great affair. But could you not play the priest a good trick, for he sits laughing at me for being made a fool of by such a fellow." That will be no difficult matter," said the youth. He then dressed himself out like a bird, wrapped a large white sheet about him, got a couple of goose-wings, which he fastened to his back, and then crept up into a large plane-tree which stood in the priest's garden. In the evening, when the priest came home, the youth began to cry, "Sir Lars! Sir Lars!" for that was the priest's name. "Who calls me?" asked the priest. "I am an angel sent from heaven, to announce to you that for your righteous life you shall be carried up alive into heaven," said the Master-thief. "You must be prepared for the journey by next Monday evening, for then I will return and take you away in a sack; all your gold and silver, and what you possess of this world's vanity, you must collect in a heap in your large parlour."

Sir Lars fell on his knees and thanked the angel, and on the Sunday following he preached a farewell sermon, in which he said that an angel sent from heaven had appeared to him in the large plane tree, and announced to him that on account of his righteous life he should be taken up to heaven without dying, and made such an afflicting address to the congregation, that every one, both old and young, wept.

On the Monday, the Master-thief appeared again as an angel, and the priest fell on his knees, and returned thanks previous to being put into the sack; and when he was well in, the Master-thief pulled and hauled him over stock and stone. "Oh! oh!" cried the priest in the sack, "where are you taking me to?" "This is the narrow way which leads to the kingdom of heaven," said the Master-thief, dragging him on till he almost killed him. At length he threw him into the Amtman's goose-house, and the geese began to hiss and peek at him, so that he was more dead than alive. "Oh! Oh! Where am I now?" said the priest. "Now you are in purgatory, for the purpose of being purged and purified for everlasting life, said the Master-thief, and went his way, taking with him all the gold, silver, and valuables which the priest had collected together in his large parlour. The next morning, when the maid came into the goose-house to let out the geese, she heard the priest in the sack wailing and lamenting bitterly. "In the name of Jesus who are you, and what do you want?" said she. "Oh!" cried the priest, "if thou art an angel from heaven, let me out and allow me to go back to earth again, for here it is worse than hell itself; little devils are pinching me with tongs." "God mend us!" said the girl, helping the priest out of the sack, "I am no angel. I tend the Amtman's geese, and they are the little devils that have been pecking you, father!" "Oh! this is the work of the Master-thief. Oh! my gold and silver, and all my fine clothes!" cried the priest, and ran home, lamenting so wofully, that the girl thought he had lost his senses.

When the Amtman heard what had befallen the priest, how he had been on the narrow road and in purgatory, he laughed himself almost to death; but when the Master-thief came and demanded his daughter, according to his promise, the Amtman began a friendly chat with him, saying: "You must first give me a better sample of what you can do, and then I can judge what you are fit for. I have twelve horses in the stable; I will put a man on each horse, and if you can steal away the horses from under them, I will then see what I can do for you." "That can be done," said the Master-thief, "if I were but certain of getting your daughter." "Well! if you can do that, I will do my best," said the Amtman.

Hereupon the Master-thief went to a shop and bought two bottles of brandy. He then made a soporific drink and put it into one of the bottles, the other he kept full of brandy. He next hired eleven men to conceal themselves at night behind the Amtman's premises. For money and fair words, he borrowed a petticoat and jacket of an old woman, took a staff in his hand and a bag on his back, and as evening approached limped on towards the Amtman's stables. When he came there the men were all busied in watering their horses for the night. "What in the devil's name dost thou want here?" said one of the men to the old crone as she stopped at the door. "Oh! oh! oh! it is so cold that a poor creature is almost frozen to death," and she shivered and shook all over. "Oh! if I can only get leave to sit inside the stable-door," said she. "Thou shalt get the devil sooner; pack thyself off at once, for if the Amtman finds thee here we shall be made to smart," said one of them. "The poor old cripple!" said another, who seemed to feel some compassion for her sufferings "let the old woman sit there, she can do no harm surely." The rest said they would not have her there; but while they were quarrelling and attending to their horses, she stole further and further into the stable, and placed herself behind the door. By and by no one took any more notice of her.

As the night advanced the men thought it rather cold to sit so still on their horses. "Oh! oh! oh! it is infernally cold," said one of them, swinging his arms about to keep himself warm. "I am so cold that I shiver again," said another. "If one had only a little tobacco," said a third. One of them had a small quantity, which he divided with his comrades, there was not much for each; this helped them but for a short time, and then they were as cold as ever. "Oh! oh! oh!" said another, shaking himself. "Oh! Oh! Oh!" said the old woman, shivering so that her teeth chattered in her head. She then took up the bottle containing pure brandy, and her hands trembled so that the liquor might be heard in the flask, as well as every gulp when she applied it to her mouth. "What hast thou got in the bottle, old crone?" said one of the men. "Only a little drop of brandy, my son," said she. "Brandy! what brandy! let me have a drop." "Let me have a drop," cried all the twelve at once. "Oh, I have got so little," said the old woman, "there is hardly enough for each to wet his mouth." But they must and would have it. So, taking the flask containing the soporific draught she raised it to the mouth of the first man; she trembled no more, but guided the bottle, so that everyone got as much as he desired, and the twelfth man had scarcely finished drinking before the first sat snoring. Thereupon the Master-thief threw away his tatters, and gently lifting each man off his horse set him across the partition between the stalls; then calling in his own eleven men they rode full gallop upon the twelve horses to the Amtman's.

The following morning, when the Amtman went to look after his men some were beginning to awake; some were striking the partitions with their spurs, so that the splinters flew about; some had fallen down, while others remained sitting like fools. "Oh! oh!" said the Amtman, "I can see very well who has been here; but you are a set of miserable varlets, who could sit here and let the Master-thief steal the horses from under you!" So, they all got a sound cudgelling for not having kept a better watch. In the course of the day the Master-thief came and related what he had done, and demanded the Amtman s daughter, according to his promise. But the Amtman chatted with him as before, gave him a hundred dollars, and told him he must do something still better. "Do you think," said he, "that you could steal my horse from under me while I am out riding on it?" "Yes, that is possible," said the Master-thief. "But shall I then have your daughter?" Yes, he would see what he could do, and appointed a day when he would ride out on the esplanade.

The Master-thief lost no time in getting an old worn-out horse, made a rope of osier and broom twigs, bought an old cart and a large cask. He then told a toothless old woman that he would give her ten dollars, if she would place herself in the cask and hold her mouth open over the bung hole, in which he would put his finger—no harm should befall her he would only drive her a little way,—and if he took his finger out of the hole more than once, she should have another ten dollars. He then dressed himself out in some rags, sooted his face, put on a wig and a beard of goat's hair, so that no one could recognise him; and in this disguise proceeded to the place where the Amtman had already been riding a long time. As he approached, he went so slowly and so gently that he seemed hardly to move from the spot; he crept and crept on, then stood quite still, then crept on a little again; and made so miserable a figure, that the Amtman could not possibly imagine that he was the Master-thief. On riding close up to him he asked him whether he had seen any one skulking about in the wood. "No," answered the man, he had seen no such person.

"Hear now," said the Amtman, "if thou wilt ride into the wood and look well about, whether thou canst find some one lurking there, I will lend thee my horse and thou shalt have a good drink-money for thy trouble." "No. that I cannot," said the man, "for I am going to a wedding with this cask of mead, which I have been to fetch; the bung has fallen out on the way, and so I must hold my finger in the hole all the time." "Do thou only ride off," said the Amtman, "I will take care of both the horse and the cask." After much persuasion he consented but begged the Amtman to take great care and be quick in putting his finger into the bung-hole the instant he drew his own out. The Amtman promised he would do the best he could, and the Master-thief mounted his horse and rode off. Time went on, and it grew later and later, but no one came back at length the Amtman grew weary of holding his finger in the bung-hole and drew it out. "Now I shall have ten dollars more," cried the old crone in the cask; the Amtman was now at no loss to perceive how matters stood and returned home accordingly but he had not proceeded far before one of his men met him with his horse; for the Master-thief had been to his house with it.

The next day he came to the Amtman and demanded his daughter according to promise. The Amtman chatted with him again, gave him two hundred dollars, and said he must yet make one more trial; if he succeeded, he should positively have her.

The Master-thief was not unwilling but must first hear what it was to be. "Do you think that you can steal the sheet off our bed and the shift off my wife?" said the Amtman. "That shall be done," said the Master-thief, "if I shall really then have your daughter."

When night came on, the Master-thief went to the gallows and cut down a thief that was hanging on it, laid him across his back and carried him away. He then got a long ladder, which he placed against the Amtman's window, mounted it, and popped the dead man up and down, exactly as if it were someone outside peeping in at the window. "There is the Master-thief, wife," said the Amtman, jogging his wife. "Now I will shoot him," added he, taking up a gun he had laid by the side of the bed. "Oh! no, do not do that," said his wife. "You yourself induced him to come." "But I will shoot him, not withstanding," said he, and lay aiming and aiming. But at one moment the man's head was popped up, so that he could see a little of it, the next it was away again; at length he got a good aim, fired, and the body fell heavily, so that the earth resounded. The Master-thief descended as quickly as he could.

"Although I am the chief authority here," said the Amtman, "yet people will talk about it, if they see the dead body, and it would be a very unpleasant affair; so, I think it will be better for me to go and bury it." "Do what you think best, husband," said his wife. The Amtman rose, went down stairs, and no sooner was he gone than the Master-thief rushed into the room, and ran up to the wife. "Well, husband," said she, for she thought it was he, "have you quite done now? "Yes, I have put him into a hole," answered he, "and raked a little earth over, just to conceal the body; but it is such dreadful weather out, I can do it better another time give me the sheet to dry myself with, for the body was so bloody, that I am quite wet and dirty." This he got. "You must also let me have your shift," said he, "for the sheet is not enough, I find." "Oh! yes, certainly." But now he recollected he had not fastened the door, and that he must go down and do it, before he came to bed again; and so off he went with both shift and sheet.

Some time after the right Amtman came. "How long you have been fastening the door," husband, said his spouse: "what have you done with the sheet and my shift, which you had to dry the blood on you?" said she. "The Devil take him," cried he, "has he managed this also?"

The next day the Master-thief came and demanded the Amtman's daughter, as he had promised, and he durst not refuse him any longer. He gave him not only his daughter, but also a great deal of money, for he was afraid that the Master-thief would steal the eyes out of his head if he did not.

The Master-thief lived afterwards well and happy; whether he stole any more I cannot say; but if he did, it was only for his own amusement.

ALL THINK THEIR OWN OFFSPRING THE BEST.

As a fowler one day went into the wood he was met by a snipe, who accosted him with: "Dear friend, do not shoot my young ones." "Which me they?" asked the sportsman. "The most beautiful that fly in the wood are mine," answered the snipe.

As the man returned, he held in his hand a whole bundle of snipes that he had brought down with his gun "Alas! alas!" cried the old snipe, "why did you shoot my young ones?" "Were they yours?" asked the sportsman; "I shot the ugliest I could find." "Ah! so," answered the snipe, "do you not know that all think their own children the most beautiful."

THE BEAR AND THE FOX.

I. WHY THE BEAR HAS A STUMP TAIL.

A BEAR once met a fox sneaking alone with a bundle of fish he had stolen. "Where did you get that from?" asked the bear.

"I have been out angling, Mr. Bruin," answered the fox.

The bear then had a great wish to learn to angle and asked the fox to tell him how he should manage. "It is a very simple art for you," replied the fox, "and is soon learnt; you need only go out on the ice and make a hole, then put your tail down in it, and there hold it for a good long time. You must not mind if it smarts a little, for that will be a sign that the fishes bite. The longer you can hold it under the ice the more fish you will catch and then you must give it a sudden jerk up."

The bear did as the fox had instructed him and held his tail a long long while down in the hole he had made in the ice, until it was completely frozen fast; he then gave a sudden jerk and jerked his tail quite off, so from that day to this he goes with a stump tail.

II. The Fox cheats the Bear out of his Christmas Fare.

A BEAR and a fox had once upon a time bought between them a tub of butter, which they intended to keep till Christmas, and, therefore, hid it under a thick bush of pine. They then went to a little distance and lay down on a sunny bank to sleep. When they had lain some time, the fox started up and cried out: "Yes," and ran away towards the butter-tub, out of which he ate a good third part. When he returned the bear asked him where he had been, as he looked so greasy about the mouth. He said: "What do you think of my being invited to a christening?" "Oh, indeed! what is the name of the child?" asked the bear. "*Begun upon*," answered the fox.

Thereupon they lay down to sleep again. In a little while the fox sprang up again and cried out: "Yes," and ran to the butter-tub. This time he also ate a good portion. When he came back, and the bear again asked where he had been, he answered: "Oh, would you believe it, I have again been invited to a christening." "What is the name of the child?" asked the bear. "*Half-eaten*," answered the fox.

The bear thought that was a strange name; though he did not wonder long about it but gave a gape and went to sleep again: they had not lain long when the same took place as before, the fox sprang up and cried out: "Yes," and ran to the butter-tub and this time he ate the remainder. When he came back, he had been once more to a christening, and when the bear inquired the name of the child, he answered, "*Licked to the bottom!*" They now lay down and slept a long time.

At length they agreed to go and look after their butter, and when they found it all eaten up, the bear accused the fox, and the fox accused the bear, of having eaten it. One said that the other must have been to the butter-tub while he slept.

"Well! well!" said Reynard, we shall soon see which of us two has stolen the butter. "Let us both now lie down on this sunny bank, and the one whose tail is the greasiest when we wake, must be the one who has stolen it." The bear was willing to undergo the ordeal; so, feeling conscious of his innocence, and that he had not even tasted the butter, he lay down to have a good sound sleep in the sun. But Reynard, instead of sleeping, crept softly to the butter-tub, and got a little that still remained between the staves then sneaking gently back to the bear, he rubbed his tail with it, and lay down to sleep as if nothing had happened. When they both woke, the sun had melted the butter on the bear's tail, so that he was proved to be the one that had eaten the butter.

THERE IS NO FEAR FOR THOSE WITH WHOM ALL WOMEN ARE IN LOVE.

ONCE on a time there were three brothers: how it happened I cannot exactly say, but each had his wish granted, that they should obtain whatever they desired. The elder two did not reflect long; they wished that every time they put their hand in their pocket, they might find money; "for," said they, "if any one only has as much money as he desires, he may always get forward in the world." But the youngest wished what was still better; he wished that all the women who merely looked at him should fall in love with him and this, as you shall hear was better than both money and chattels. When each had wished his wish, the two elders determined to travel and see the world, and the youngest begged that he might go with them but this they would not allow on any account. "Wherever we go we shall be received as counts and princes," said they; "but thou, a poor starveling, who hast nothing and gettest nothing, how canst thou suppose that any one will care about thee?" "But you might, nevertheless, let me go with you," said the lad; "perhaps a tit-bit might sometimes fall to my share, if I am in the train of such great lords."

At length they agreed to take him, provided he would be their servant, otherwise they would not listen to his going. After travelling a whole day, they came to a hostel, into which the two brothers who had money entered, and called for fish and roast meat, brandy and mead, and everything that was dainty; while the younger poor lad was obliged to remain outside and take care of the things belonging to the grand strangers. But as he walked to and fro, hovering about the yard, the hostess, happening to look through the window, saw the servant of the two visitors, and so comely a young fellow she thought her eyes had never before he held. She looked at him, and looked again, and the longer she looked the handsomer she thought the youth appeared to her "What in the devil's name is it that you stand in the window staring and gaping at?" asked her husband. "I think it would be better if you saw to the roasting of the pig than standing there idling; you see what people we have got in the house today," added he. "Oh! what care I for your fine trumpery," answered the woman, "if they do not like to stay, they can go back to where they came from; but come hither and you shall see one who is walking about in the yard! Such a handsome young man I have never before seen in all my life. If you do not object, we will ask him in, and regale him a little, for he does not seem to be over-fed, poor fellow!" "Have you lost the little sense you had?" said her husband; and was so angry that his eyes darted fire; "out with you into the kitchen, and don't stand here gazing at young fellows!" So, having no choice, the woman went into the kitchen to prepare the dinner. She was not allowed longer to look at the comely youth; nor did she dare to regale him; but as soon as she had put the pig on the spit, she feigned some errand out in the yard, and gave the lad a pair of scissors, which had the property, that a person only by clipping in the air with them could cut out the most beautiful clothes of velvet, and silk, and other costly materials, that any one could see. "These you shall have," said the woman, "because you are so handsome."

When the two brothers had eaten all they desired, they resumed their journey, and the youngest stood again behind the carriage as their servant. After travelling some time, they came to another inn. Here the brothers went in; but the youngest, who had no money, they would not have with them; he was to stand outside again, and take care of all that belonged to them; "And if thou art asked whose servant, thou art," said they, "thou must answer that we are two foreign princes." It happened this time, also, just as before. While the youth was loitering about in the yard, the hostess came to the window and saw him, and immediately became as much in love with him as the other had been. She looked and looked at him and thought she could never be tired of looking at him. Just then her husband passed through the room with something the two princes had ordered. "Don't stand there staring like a cow at a barn-door, but take this, and come out into the kitchen and look to your fish-kettle, woman," said her husband; "you see what kind of people we have got in the house today, I suppose." "What care I for your high-flying gentry," answered the woman; "if they do not like what they find here, they can eat what they have brought with them. But come hither, and you shall see something; such a handsome lad as he is, who is out in the yard, have I never seen before in all my life. If you think as I do, you will ask him in and regale him a little, for he seems to need it, poor fellow! oh, he is so handsome!" said the woman. "Much sense you never had, and the little you have seems to have left you, as far as I can see," said the man, who was more angry than the last-mentioned host, at the same time driving his wife away. "Into the kitchen with you, and don't stand here gazing after the young chaps," added he. So she was obliged to look to her fish-kettle, and durst not regale the young man, for fear of her husband; but as she was standing by the fire, she pretended to want something in the yard, and then gave the lad a cloth which possessed the property, that no sooner was it spread than it was covered with every delicacy that could be imagined. "This you shall have," said the woman, "because you are so handsome."

As soon as the two brothers had eaten and drunk of all that was brought to them, and had paid exorbitantly, they took their departure, and the youngest stood behind the carriage. When they had travelled till they felt hungry again, they stopped at another inn, and called for everything of the best and dearest that could be thought of. "For we are two kings travelling," said they, "and money with us is like grass." When the host heard that, there was such a roasting and frying that the fumes reached their next neighbours, and the host did not know what he should devise for the two kings; but the youngest was obliged to stand outside and take care of everything that was in the carriage; and things went here as in the two cases before mentioned; the hostess came to the window, she saw the servant standing by the carriage, and such a comely, beautiful youth she had never seen before in all her life. She looked and looked, and the longer she looked at him, the more comely did he appear to her. The landlord came running through the room with something the two kings had ordered and was not greatly pleased at seeing his wife standing staring out of the window. "Don't you know better than to stand staring there, when we have such persons in the house said he. "Away! into the kitchen, and take care of your cream-custards, and that instantly." "Oh! there is no great hurry for that," answered his wife; "if they won't stay till the custards are made, they may go again. But come hither and you shall see something; such a handsome lad I have never before seen as the one standing down there in the yard. If you are of the same mind as I am, we will ask him in and regale him a little for he looks as if he really wanted it: and so comely he is!" "A runner after the men you have always been, and are so still," said her husband, who was in such a passion that he knew not on which leg to stand: "but if you do not directly go to your porridge-pot, I shall see to get a pair of legs under you."

His wife was therefore obliged to hurry out into the kitchen as fast as she could; for she well knew her husband was not to be trifled with; yet she managed to get down into the yard and gave the youth a tap. "When you turn this tap," said she, "you will get all sorts of excellent drinks, mead, and wine, and brandy. This you shall have, because you are so handsome."

When the two brothers had eaten and drunk as much as they would, they left the inn, and their brother stood up again behind the carriage as their servant; so they drove a long long way till they came to a king's palace; and the elder brothers announced themselves as two emperor' sons, and as they had abundance of money, and were so splendidly attired that they could be seen at a great distance, they received a hearty welcome, and were invited to remain at the palace; and the king was at a loss how to make enough of them. But the youngest, who wore the same rags he had on when he left home, and who had not a penny in his pocket, was seized by the watch at the royal palace, and carried out to an island, to which all beggars and idiots who came to the palace were conveyed by order of the king, that they might not disturb the gaiety of the court, going about so tattered and filthy; and they had no more food brought to them than would just support life. The two brothers, who saw the guard row out with their younger brother to the island, were glad that they had got rid of him, and thought no more of the matter. But no sooner had he come to the island, than taking his scissors, he began to cut in the air, and thus cut out the most beautiful clothes any one could wish to see, of silk and velvet, so that the poor idiots on the island had finer clothes than the king and all the court. The youth then took out his cloth and spread it, when the idiots got food also; and such a feast as had never been seen in the king's palace was served that day on the fools' island. "You must also be thirsty," said the youth, taking out his tap, which he just turned a little, and gave the idiots something to drink; such mead and such beer the king himself never tasted in all his born days.

Now when those who brought food out to the fools and beggars on the island came rowing with cold porridge and whey (such was the food allowed to the poor creatures), they would not touch it, which greatly surprised those from the king's palace; but still more astonished were they on looking at the idiots, who were all so splendidly attired that they believed they were emperors and popes, and that they had rowed out to a wrong island; but on looking more attentively, they found that they were right. It now immediately struck them that it must be the lad whom they had rowed out the day before, who had supplied all this finery and luxury to the poor idiots on the isle; and on their return to the king's palace, they were not slow in telling how the lad whom they had rowed out on the previous day had dressed up all the fools there so magnificently and sumptuously that they could hardly stand. "The porridge and whey we brought with us," said they, "they would not even taste, so grand are they become." One of them had found out also, that the lad had a pair of scissors, with which he had cut out the clothes. "When he raises the scissors," said he, "and cuts in the air, he cuts through silk and velvet." When the princess heard this, she had neither peace nor rest until she saw the youth and the scissors that cut silk and velvet out of the air; the scissors, thought she, would be worth having, for with them she could have as much finery as she desired. She then entreated the king so long, that at length he sent a messenger after the lad who owned the scissors. When, he came to the palace, the princess asked him if it were true that he possessed such a pair of scissors, and if he would sell them to her. "Yes, I have such a pair," answered he, "but I will not sell them." He then took the scissors out of his pocket, and began cutting in the air, so that pieces of silk and velvet flew about in every direction. "Oh thou must sell them to me," said the princess; "thou mayst ask what thou wilt for them; but have them I must." No, sell them he would not for any price, for such a pair of scissors he could never hope to get again, said he; and while they stood conversing about the scissors, the princess looked more and more at the youth, and thought, like the innkeepers' wives, that so comely a young man she had never before seen. So, she began again to bargain for the scissors, and begged and prayed of him to sell them to her; he might ask for them as many hundred dollars as he would, if he would only let her have them. "No, sell them I will not," said the youth; "but I will do what is the same. If I may lie on the floor close to the door in the princess's bedroom tonight, she shall have the scissors. I shall not harm her; but if she has any fear, she can have two men to keep guard in the room." To this proposal the princess assented; provided only she could get the scissors, she was content; so, the youth lay on the floor in the princess's chamber, and two men kept watch there. But the princess did not get much sleep, for whenever she shut her eyes, she thought she must open them again to look at the youth once more, and thus she continued the whole night; so that she had no sooner closed her eyes than they opened to look at him again, so comely did he appear to her.

The next morning the youth was rowed back to the island of fools. But when they brought porridge and whey from the king's palace, there was no one who would taste it on that day either, to the great astonishment of those who brought it. One of them, however, ferreted out, that the lad who owned the scissors had also a cloth, which he needed only to spread out, when it was covered with the best of everything that could be wished. When the man returned to the king's palace, it was not long before he related all this. "Such roast meats," said he, "and such cream-porridge as he had seen in the fools' island, the like had never been in the king's kitchen." When the princess heard this, she prayed and begged of the king so earnestly, that he was obliged to send a messenger to the island to fetch the lad who owned the cloth, and so he came again to the palace. The princess now wished to have the cloth from him and offered him gold and green woods for it: but the youth would on no account part with it for any price. "But if I may be allowed to lie on the bench at the foot of the princess's bed tonight, then she shall have my cloth," said the youth. "I shall not harm her; but if she is afraid, she can set four men in the chamber to watch." To these conditions the princess assented. The youth lay on the bench before the princess, and four men kept watch. If the princess had but little sleep the night before, she had still less this night; she could hardly close her eyes and could not abstain from looking at the comely youth the whole night, and the night even appeared to her too short.

In the morning the youth was again rowed out to the fools' island, although it was against the princess's wish, so happy was she with him; but prayers were in vain, he was obliged to depart. When the porridge and the whey were brought to the poor idiots on the following day there was not one of them that would look at it. At this the men from the palace were not so much surprised, but they wondered that none of them were thirsty. One, however, of the king's messengers found out, that the lad, who owned the scissors and the cloth, had also a tap which possessed the property, by turning it a little, of giving forth the finest drinks imaginable. On his return to the palace, he was no less loquacious than his comrades had been on the two former occasions; he related at full length about the tap, and how easy it was to get all sorts of liquors from it. "The like of the beer and mead was not tasted in the king's palace." said he, "it was sweeter than either honey or syrup." When the princess heard this, she was instantly wishing to have the tap, and had no objection to come to an agreement with the owner of it. She therefore went to the king and prayed him to send a messenger to the isle for the youth who owned the scissors and the cloth, as he had still one thing that was worth possessing; and when the king heard that it was a tap that had the property of producing the best beer and the best wine any one could drink, by only turning it, you may believe it was not long before he sent a messenger after it.

When the youth came to the palace, the princess asked him if it were true that he had such a tap. "Yes," answered he, "I have it in my waistcoat pocket." But when the princess desired that he should sell it to her, he said, as on the former occasions, that sell it he would not even if she offered him the half of the kingdom. "But," added he, "if I am allowed to sleep at the foot of her bed outside the quilt tonight, she shall then have the tap. I shall not harm her; but if she has any fear, she can set eight men to watch in her room." "Oh, no, there is no need for that," said the princess, knowing him now so well. And so, the youth lay at the bed-foot. If she had little sleep, the two previous nights, she had still less this one; she could not once close her eyes, but the whole time continued gazing on the youth who lay before her at the foot of the bed.

When she rose in the morning, and they were about to row the lad out again to the fools' island, she begged them to wait a little while, and then ran to the king and earnestly besought him to let her have the youth for a husband, saying, that he was so dear to her, that if she did not have him, she should die. "Well," answered the king, "if that is the case, thou mayst have him; for he who possesses such things is as rich as thou art."

Thus, the youngest brother was married to the princess and got the half of the kingdom the other half he was to have when the king died. Everything turned out well for him; but his brothers, who had always treated him so ill, he sent out to the fools' island. "There they can remain," said he, "till they have found out who has the least want he who has a pocket full of money, or he who is beloved by all the women."

It did not help them much, I imagine, to jingle money in their pockets on the fools' island: and if their brother has not taken them away from thence, they still wander about, eating cold porridge and drinking whey from that day to this.

THE THREE SISTERS WHO WERE ENTRAPPED INTO A MOUNTAIN.

THERE was once an old widow who lived far from any inhabited spot, under a mountain-ridge, with her three daughters. She was so poor that all she possessed was a hen, and this was as dear to her as the apple of her eye; she petted and fondled it from morning till night. But one day it so happened, that the hen was missing. The woman looked everywhere about her room, but the hen was away, and remained away. "Thou must go out and search for our hen," said the woman to her eldest daughter, "for have it back again we must, even if we have to get it out of the mountain." So, the daughter went in search of the hen. She went about in all directions, and searched and coaxed, yet no hen could she find; but all at once she heard a voice from a mountain-side saying:—

> "The hen trips in the mountain!
> The hen trips in the mountain."

She went naturally to see whence it proceeded; but just as she came to the spot, she fell through a trap-door, far far down into a vault under the earth. Here she walked through many rooms, everyone more beautiful than the other; but in the last a great ugly Troll came to her and asked her if she would be his wife. "No," she answered, she would not on any account, she would go back again directly, and look after her hen which had wandered away. On hearing this, the Troll was so angry, that he seized her and wrung her head off, and then threw her head and body down into a cellar.

The mother in the meantime sat at home expecting and expecting, but no daughter came back. After waiting a long time, and neither hearing nor seeing anything more of her, she said to the second daughter, that she must go out and look after her sister, and at the same time "coax back the hen."

Now the second daughter went out, and it happened to her just as it had to her sister; she looked and looked about, and all at once, she also heard a voice from a mountain-side say:—

> "The hen trips in the mountain!
> The hen trips in the mountain!"

This she thought very strange, and she would go and see whence it proceeded, and so she fell also through the trap door, deep deep down into the vault. Here she went through all the rooms, and in the innermost the Troll came to her and asked if she would be his wife. "No," she would not on any account, she would go up again instantly and search for her hen, which had gone astray. Thereupon the Troll was so exasperated that, catching hold of her, he wrung her head off and threw both head and body into the cellar.

When the mother had waited a long time for the other daughter, and no daughter was to be seen or heard of, she said to the youngest: "Now thou must set out and seek after thy sisters. Bad enough it was that the hen strayed away, but worse will it be, if we cannot find thy sisters again, and the hen thou canst also coax back at the same time." So, the youngest was now to go out; she went in all directions, and looked and coaxed, but she neither saw the hen nor her sisters. After wandering about for some time, she came at length to the mountain-side and heard the same voice saying:—

> "The hen trips in the mountain!
> The hen trips in the mountain!"

This seemed to her extraordinary, but she would go and see whence it came, and so she also fell through the trap door deep deep down into the vault. Here she went through many rooms everyone finer than the other; but she was not terrified and gave herself time to look at this and at that, and then cast her eyes on the trap-door to the cellar; on looking down she immediately saw her two sisters, who lay there dead. Just as she had shut the trap-door again, the Troll came to her. "Wilt thou be my wife?" asked the Troll. "Yes, willingly," said the girl, for she saw well enough how it had fared with her sisters. When the Troll heard this, he gave her splendid clothes, the most beautiful she could wish for, and everything she desired, so delighted was he that somebody would be his mate.

When she had been there some time, she was one day more sad and silent than usual; whereupon the Troll asked her what it was that grieved her. "Oh!" answered she, "it is because I cannot go home again to my mother, I am sure she both hungers and thirsts, and she has no one with her." "Thou canst not be allowed to go to her," said the Troll, "but put some food in a sack, and I will carry it to her. For this she thanked him, and would do so, she said; but at the bottom of the sack she stuffed in a great deal of gold and silver, and then laid a little food on the top, telling the Troll the sack was ready, but that he must on no account look into it; and he promised that he would not. As soon as the Troll was gone, she watched him through a little hole there was in the door. When he had carried it some way, he said: "This sack is so heavy, I will see what is in it," and was just about to untie the strings, when the girl cried out: "I see you, I see you." "What sharp eyes thou hast got in thy head," said the Troll, and durst not repeat the attempt. On reaching the place where the widow dwelt, he threw the sack in through the door of the room, saying: "There's food for thee from thy daughter, she wants for nothing."

When the young girl had been for some time in the mountain, it happened one day that a goat fell through the trap-door. "Who sent for thee, thou long-bearded beast!" said the Troll, and fell into a violent passion; so, seizing the goat, he wrung its head off, and threw it into the cellar. "Oh! why did you do that?" said the girl; "he might have been some amusement to me down here." "Thou needst not put on such a fast-day face," said the Troll, "I can soon put life into the goat again." Saying this he took a flask, which hung against the wall, set the goat's head on again, rubbed it with what was in the flask, and the animal was as sound as ever. "Ha, ha!" thought the girl, "that flask is worth something." When she had been some time longer with the Troll, and he was one day gone out, she took the eldest of her sisters, set her head on, and rubbed her with what was in the flask, just as she had seen the Troll do with the goat, and her sister came instantly to life again. The girl then put her into a sack with a little food at the top; and as soon as the Troll came home, she said to him: "Dear friend, you must go again to my mother, and carry her a little food; I am sure she both hungers and thirsts, poor thing! and she is so lonely; but do not look into the sack." He promised to take the sack, and also that he would not look into it. When he had gone some distance, he thought the sack very heavy, and going on a little further, he said: "This sack is so heavy, I must see what is in it; for of whatever her eyes may be made, I am sure she can't see me now." But just as he was going to untie the sack, the girl who was in it cried out: "I can see you, I can see you." "What sharp eyes thou must have in thy head," said the Troll for he thought it was the girl in the mountain that spoke, and therefore did not dare to look again, but carried it as fast as he could to the mother; and when he came to the door, he threw it inside, saying: "There is some food for thee from thy daughter, she wants for nothing."

Some time after this the girl in the mountain performed a like operation on her second sister; she set her head on again, rubbed her with what was in the flask, and put her into a sack; but this time she put as much gold and silver into the sack as it would hold, and only a very little food on the top. "Dear friend," said she to the Troll, "you must go home again to my mother with a little more food, but do not look into the sack." The Troll was quite willing to please her and promised he would not look into the sack. But when he had gone a good way, the sack was so insufferably heavy that he was obliged to sit down and rest awhile, being quite unable to carry it any further; so he thought he would untie the string and look into it; but the girl in the sack called out: "I can see you, I can see you!" "Then thou must have sharp eyes indeed, in thy head," said the Troll quite frightened, and taking up the sack, made all the haste he could to the mother's. When he came to the door of the room, he threw it in, saying: "There is some food from thy daughter for thee, she is in want of nothing."

When the young girl had been some time longer in the mountain, the Troll having occasion one day to go out, she pretended to be ill and sick, and complained. "It is of no use that you come home before twelve o'clock," said she to the Troll, "for I feel so sick and ill that I cannot get the dinner ready before that time;" so the Troll promised he would not come back.

When the Troll was gone, she stuffed her clothes out with straw, and set the straw girl in the chimney-corner with a ladle in her hand, so that she looked exactly as if she were standing there herself. She then stole home clandestinely, and took with her a gamekeeper, whom she met, to be at home with her mother. When the clock struck twelve, the Troll returned. "Give me something to eat," said he to the straw girl; but she made him no answer.

"Give me something to eat, I say," said the Troll again; "for I am hungry." But still there was no answer.

"Give me something to eat," screamed the Troll a third time: "I advise thee to do so, I say dost thou hear? Otherwise I will try to wake thee."

But the girl stood stock still, whereupon he became so furious, that he gave her a kick that made the straw fly about in all directions. On seeing that, he found there was something wrong, and began to look about, and at last went down into the cellar; but both the girl's sisters were gone, and he was now at no loss to know how all this had happened.

"Ah thou shalt pay dearly for this," said he, taking the road to her mother's house but when he came to the door, the gamekeeper fired, and the Troll durst not venture in, for he believed that it thundered[3]; so he turned about to go home with all possible speed, but just as he got to the trap door, the sun rose, and the Troll burst[4].

There is plenty of gold and silver still in the mountain, if one only knew how to find the trap-door.

THE WIDOW'S SON.

THERE was once a very very poor woman who had only one son. She toiled for him till he was old enough to be confirmed by the priest, when she told him, that she could support him no longer, but that he must go out in the

---

[3] See "Northern Mythology," ii. p. 152.

[4] Ibid. i. p. 8, *note*[3].

world and gain his own livelihood. So, the youth set out, and, after wandering about for a day or two, he met a stranger. "Whither art thou going?" asked the man. "I am going out in the world to see if I can get an employment," answered the youth. "Wilt thou serve me?" "Yes, just as well serve you as anybody else," answered the youth. "Thou shalt be well cared for with me," said the man, "thou shalt only be my companion, and do little or nothing besides." So, the youth resided with him, had plenty to eat and drink, and very little or nothing to do; but he never saw a living person in the man's house.

One day his master said to him: "I am going to travel, and shall be absent eight days, during that time thou wilt be here alone; but thou must not go into either of these four rooms; if thou dost I will kill thee when I return." The youth answered that he would not. When the man had been away three or four days, the youth could no longer refrain, but went into one of the rooms. He looked around, but saw nothing except a shelf over the door, with a whip made of briar on it. "This was well worth forbidding me so, strictly from seeing," thought the youth. When the eight days had passed, the man came home again. "Thou hast not, I hope, been into any of the rooms," said he. "No, I have not," answered the youth. "That I shall soon be able to see," said the man, going into the room the youth had entered. "But thou hast been in," said he, "and now thou shalt die." The youth cried and entreated to be forgiven, so that he escaped with his life, but had a severe beating; when that was over, they were as good friends as before.

Some time after this, the man took another journey; this time he would be away a fortnight, but first forbade the youth again from going into any of the rooms he had not already been in; but the one he had previously entered he might enter again. This time all took place just as before, the only difference being that the youth abstained for eight days before he entered the forbidden rooms. In one apartment he found only a shelf over the door, on which lay a huge stone and a water-bottle. "This is also something to be in such fear about," thought the youth again. When the man came home, he asked whether he had been in any of the rooms. "No, he had not," was the answer. "I shall soon see," said the man; and when he found that the youth had, nevertheless, been in, he said: "Now I will no longer spare thee, thou shalt die." But the youth cried and implored that his life might be spared, and thus again escaped with a beating; but this time he got as much as could be laid on him.

When he had recovered from the effect of this beating he lived as well as ever, and he and the man were good friends as before.

Some time after this, the man again made a journey, and now he was to be three weeks absent; he warned the youth anew not to enter the third room; if he did, he must at once prepare to die. At the end of a fortnight, the youth had no longer any command over himself, and stole in; but here he saw nothing save a trap-door in the floor. He lifted it up and looked through; there stood a large copper kettle that boiled and bubbled, yet he could see no fire under it. "I should like to know if it is hot," thought the youth, dipping his finger down into it; but when he drew it up again, he found that all his finger was gilt. He scraped it and washed it, but the gilding was not to be removed; so he tied a rag over it, and when the man returned and asked him what was the matter with his finger, he answered, he had cut it badly. But the man, tearing the rag off, at once saw what ailed his finger. At first, he was going to kill the youth, but as he cried and begged again, he merely beat him so that he was obliged to lie in bed for three days. The man then took a pot down from the wall and rubbed him with what it contained, so that the youth was as well as before.

After some time, the man made another journey, and said he should not return for a month. He then told the youth that if he went into the fourth room, he must not think for a moment that his life would be spared. One, two, even three weeks the youth refrained from entering the forbidden room; but then having no longer any command over himself he stole in. There stood a large black horse in a stall, with a trough of burning embers at its head and a basket of hay at its tail. The youth thought this was cruel, and, therefore, changed their position, putting the basket of hay by the horse's head. The horse thereupon said: "As you have so kind a disposition that you enable me to get food, I will save you: should the Troll return and find you here, he will kill you. Now you must go up into the chamber above this and take one of the suits of armour that hang there: but on no account take one that is bright; on the contrary, select the most rusty you can see, and take that; choose also a sword and saddle in like manner." The youth did so, but he found the whole very heavy for him to carry. When he came back the horse said, that now he should strip and wash himself well in the kettle, which stood boiling in the next apartment. "I feel afraid," thought the youth, but, nevertheless, did so. When he had washed himself, he became comely and plump, and as red and white as milk and blood, and much stronger than before. "Are you sensible of any change?" asked the horse. "Yes," answered the youth. "Try to lift me." said the horse. Aye that he could and brandished the sword with ease. Now lay the saddle on me," said the horse, "put on the armour, and take the whip of thorn, the stone, and the water-flask, and the pot with ointment, and then we will set out."

When the youth had mounted the horse, it started off at a rapid rate. After riding some time, the horse said: "I think I hear a noise; look round, can you see anything?" "A great many are coming after us, certainly a score at least," answered the youth. "Ah! that is the Troll," said the horse, "he is coming with all his companions."

They travelled for a time until their pursuers were gaining on them. "Throw now the thorn whip over your shoulder," said the horse, "but throw it far away from me." The youth did so, and at the same moment there sprang up a large thick wood of briars. The youth now rode on a long way, while the Troll was obliged to go home for something wherewith to hew a road through the wood. After some time, the horse again said: "Look back, can you see anything now?" "Yes, a whole multitude of people," said the youth, "like a church-congregation." "That is the Troll, now he has got more with him; throw out now the large stone but throw it far from me."

When the youth had done what the horse desired, there arose a large stone mountain behind them. So, the Troll was obliged to go home after something with which to bore through the mountain; and while he was thus employed, the youth rode on a considerable way. But now the horse again bade him look back; he then saw a multitude like a whole army, they were so bright that they glittered in the sun. "Well, that is the Troll with all his friends," said the horse. "Now throw the water-bottle behind you but take good care to spill nothing on me!" The youth did so, but notwithstanding his caution, he happened to spill a drop on the horse's loins. Immediately there rose a vast lake, and the spilling of the few drops caused the horse to stand far out in the water; nevertheless, be at last swam to the shore. When the Trolls came to the water, they lay down to drink it all up, and they gulped and gulped it down till they burst. "Now we are quit of them," said the horse.

When they had travelled on a very long way they came to a green plain in a wood. "Take off your armour now," said the horse, "and put on your rags only, lift my saddle off and let me go loose, and hang everything up in that large hollow linden; make yourself then a wig of pine-moss, go to the royal palace which lies close by, and there ask for employment. When you desire to see me, come to this spot, shake the bridle, and I will instantly be with you."

The youth did as the horse told him; and when he put on the moss wig, he became so pale and miserable to look at, that no one would have recognised him. On reaching the palace, he only asked if he might serve in the kitchen to carry wood and water to the cook; but the cook-maid asked him, why he wore such an ugly wig? "Take it off," said she, "I will not have anybody here so frightful." "That I cannot," answered the youth; "for I am not very clean in the head." "Dost thou think then that I will have thee in the kitchen, if such be the case?" said she; "go to the master of the horse, thou art fittest to carry muck from the stables." When the master of the horse told him to take off his wig, he got the same answer, so he refused to have him. "Thou canst go to the gardener," said he, thou art only fit to go and dig the ground. The gardener allowed him to remain, but none of the servants would sleep with him, so he was obliged to sleep alone under the stairs of the summer-house, which stood upon pillars and had a high staircase, under which he laid a quantity of moss for a bed, and there lay as well as he could.

When he had been some time in the royal palace, it happened one morning, just at sunrise, that the youth had taken off his moss wig and was standing washing himself and appeared so handsome it was a pleasure to look on him. The princess saw from her window this comely gardener and thought she had never before seen any one so handsome. She then asked the gardener why he lay out there under the stairs. "Because none of the other servants will lie with him," answered the gardener. "Let him come this evening and lie by the door in my room," said the princess; "they cannot refuse after that to let him sleep in the house."

The gardener told this to the youth. "Dost thou think I will do so?" said he. "If I do, all will say there is something between me and the princess." "Thou hast reason, forsooth, to fear such a suspicion," replied the gardener, "such a fine comely lad as thou art." "Well, if she has commanded it, I suppose I must comply," said the youth. In going upstairs that evening, he stamped and made such a noise that they were obliged to beg of him to go more gently lest it might come to the king's knowledge when within the chamber, he lay down and began immediately to snore. The princess then said to her waiting maid: "Go gently and pull off his moss wig." Creeping softly towards him, she was about to snatch it, but he held it fast with both hands, and said she should not have it. He then lay down again and began to snore. The princess again made a sign to the maid, and this time she snatched his wig off. There he lay so beautifully red and white, just as the princess had seen him in the morning sun. After this the youth slept every night in the princess's chamber.

But it was not long before the king heard that the garden-lad slept every night in the princess's chamber, at which he became so angry that he almost resolved on putting him to death. This, however, he did not do, but cast him into prison, and his daughter he confined to her room, not allowing her to go out, either by day or night. Her tears and prayers for herself and the youth were unheeded by the king, who only became the more incensed against her.

Some time after this, there arose a war and disturbances in the country, and the king was obliged to take arms and defend himself against another king, who threatened to deprive him of his throne. When the youth heard this, he begged the gaoler would go to the king for him and propose to let him have armour and a sword and allow him to follow to the war. All the courtiers laughed, when the gaoler made known his errand to the king. They begged he might have some old trumpery for armour, that they might enjoy the sport of seeing the poor creature in the war. He got the armour and also an old jade of a horse, which limped on three legs, dragging the fourth after it.

Thus, they all marched forth against the enemy, but they had not gone far from the royal palace before the youth stuck fast with his old jade in a swamp. Here he sat beating and calling to the jade, "Hie! Wilt thou go? Hie! Wilt thou go?" This amused all the others, who laughed and jeered as they passed. But no sooner were they all gone, than, running to the linden, he put on his own armour, and shook the bridle, and immediately the horse appeared, and said: "Do thou do thy best and I will do mine."

When the youth arrived on the field, the battle had already begun, and the king was hardly pressed but just at that moment the youth put the enemy to flight. The king and his attendants wondered who it could be that came to their help; but no one had been near enough to him to speak to him, and when the battle was over, he was away. When they returned, the youth was still sitting fast in the swamp, beating and calling to his three-legged jade. They laughed as they passed, and said: "Only look, yonder sits the fool yet."

The next day when they marched out, the youth was still sitting there, and they again laughed and jeered at him, but no sooner had they all passed by than he ran again to the linden, and everything took place as on the previous day. Everyone wondered who the stranger warrior was who had fought for them, but no one approached him so near that he could speak to him of course no one ever imagined that it was the youth.

When they returned in the evening and saw him and his old jade still sticking fast in the swamp, they again made a jest of him one shot an arrow at him and wounded him in the leg, and he began to cry and moan so that it was sad to hear, whereupon the king threw him his handkerchief that he might bind it about his leg. When they marched forth the third morning there sat the youth calling to his horse, "Hie! Wilt thou go? Hie! Wilt thou go?" "No, no! he will stay there till he starves," said the king's men as they passed by, and laughed so heartily at him that they nearly fell from their horses. When they had all passed, he again ran to the linden, and came to the battle just at the right moment. That day he killed the enemy's king, and thus the war was at an end.

When the fighting was over, the king observed his handkerchief tied round the leg of the strange warrior, and by this be easily knew him. They received him with great joy and carried him with them up to the royal palace, and the princess, who saw them from her window, was so delighted no one could tell. "There comes my beloved also," said she. He then took the pot of ointment and rubbed his leg, and afterwards all the wounded, so that they were all well again in a moment.

After this the king gave him the princess to wife. On the day of his marriage he went down into the stable to see the horse, and found him dull, hanging his ears and refusing to eat. When the young king—for he was now king, having obtained the half of the realm—spoke to him and asked him what he wanted, the horse said: "I have now helped thee forward in the world, and I will live no longer; thou must take thy sword, and cut my head off." "No, that I will not do," said the young king, "thou shalt have whatever thou wilt, and always live without working." "If thou wilt not do as I say," answered the horse, "I shall find a way of killing thee." The king was then obliged to slay him; but when he raised the sword to give the stroke, he was so distressed that he turned his face away; but no sooner had he struck his head off than there stood before him a handsome prince in the place of the horse.

"Whence in the name of Heaven didst thou come?" asked the king. "It was I who was the horse," answered the prince. "Formerly I was king of the country whose sovereign you slew yesterday; it was he who cast over me a horse's semblance and sold me to the Troll." As he is killed, I shall recover my kingdom, and you and I shall be neighbouring kings; but we will never go to war with each other.

Neither did they; they were friends as long as they lived, and the one came often to visit the other.

LILLEKORT.

THERE was once a couple of poor people, who lived in a wretched but where there was nothing but squalid misery, so that they had neither food nor fire. But if they had a scanty supply of other things, they were blessed with abundance of children, and every year they added one to the number. They were now just expecting another, at which the good man was so angry that he went about grumbling and muttering, saying that he saw it was quite possible to have more than enough of these God's gifts; and when the time came for the woman's delivery he went to the forest for wood, having no wish to see the new squaller; he should hear him soon enough, he said, when he screamed for food.

When the man was gone, the woman gave birth to a fine boy, who had no sooner come into the world than he looked about the room. "Oh, dear mother," said he, "give me some of my brother's old clothes and food for a couple of days, and I will go out in the world and seek my fortune, for I see you have children enough without me." "Lord preserve thee, thou poor little creature," said the mother, "thou art too young as yet, that will never do." But the boy persisted in his resolution and begged and prayed until the mother was obliged to give him some old rags and a little food in a bundle, and away he went to seek his fortune in the wide world, cheerful and happy. He had scarcely left the house when the woman gave birth to another son, who also looked round and said: "Oh, dear mother, give me some of my brother's old clothes and food for a couple of days, and I will go out in the world and find my twin brother, for you have children enough without us." "Lord preserve thee, thou poor little creature," said the mother, "thou art too young as yet, that will never do." But it was to no purpose, the child begged and prayed so long that at last he got some old tatters and some food in a cloth and set out boldly in the world to find his twin brother. When the younger had gone some way, he perceived his brother at a distance before him, and called out to him to stop. "Wait a little," said he, "thou art getting along as if thou wast paid for it; thou shouldst have seen thy youngest brother at all events before going out into the world." The elder brother stopped and looked back, and when the younger had joined him, and told him how it was that he was his brother, he added, "but now let us sit down, and see what provisions our mother has given us;" and they did so.

When they had wandered on a little further, they came to a stream that flowed through a green meadow; and here the younger proposed that they should give each other a name for having left home in such a hùrry there was no time for it, "so we had better do it here," said he. "What wilt thou be called?" said the elder. "My name shall be Lillekort," answered the other and what wilt thou be called "I will be named King Lavring," answered the elder. So, they baptized each other, and then pursued their journey. When they had walked on for some time, they came to a cross-road, and here they agreed to part, so that each might take his own course. This they did, but they had not gone far when they met each other again. Here they parted anew, each taking a different road; but in a little while they unexpectedly met again, and thus it happened three times. They now agreed that they would go in opposite directions, one to the east and the other to the west. "But shouldst thou ever fall into any danger or misfortune," said the elder, "then call to me three times and I will come and help thee; but thou must not call upon me until thou art in the greatest need." "We shall not meet again so soon then, I think," said Lillekort. They then took leave of each other, Lillekort taking the road to the east, and King Lavring to the west.

When Lillekort had walked on for some time alone, he met a very old humpbacked woman who had but one eye this Lillekort snatched out. "Oh, oh!" cried the old woman, "what has become of my eye? What will you give me for an eye?" said Lillekort. "I will give you a sword of such a quality that it can overcome a whole army, be it ever so great," answered the woman. "Good! hand it here," said Lillekort. The old woman gave him the sword and got her eye again. Lillekort then went on, and after wandering for some time, he met another very old crook backed woman, who also had only one eye this too, Lillekort stole before the old woman was aware. "Oh, oh! what has become of my eye?" cried the hag. "What will you give me for an eye?" said Lillekort. "I will give you a ship which can go both in fresh water and in salt, over mountains and deep valleys," answered the old woman. "Good! hand it here," said Lillekort. The old crone then gave him a little tiny ship, so small that he could put it into his pocket, and so she got her eye again, and they went their several ways. After wandering on for a long while, he met, for the third time, a very old hunchbacked woman, who had but one eye; this also Lillekort stole, and when the old crone screamed, and cried, and asked what had become of her eye, Lillekort said: "What will you give me for an eye?" "I will give you the art to brew a hundred lasts of malt in one brewing." So for that art the old woman got her eye again, and each went their several ways.

When Lillekort had gone a little further, he thought it was worth while making a trial of his ship; so taking it out of his pocket, he first placed one foot in it, and then the other; but no sooner had he put one leg in, than it became much larger, and when he stood upright with both legs in, it became as large as a ship that sails on the sea. Lillekort then said: "Go through fresh water and salt water, over mountains and through deep valleys, and do not stop till thou comest to the king's palace." And away flew the ship, as swift as a bird in the air, till it came quite near to the king's palace, and there it stopped. In the window of the palace persons were standing and watching Lillekort as he approached and were all so astonished that they ran out to see who it could be that came travelling through the air in a ship. But while the people were running down from the royal palace, Lillekort had stepped out of his ship and put it into his pocket; for no sooner had he stepped out, than it became as small as when the old woman gave it to him; so that there was nothing to be seen save a little ragged urchin standing on the shore. The king asked him whence he came. But the boy said, he did not know, neither did he know how he came there, but supplicated most earnestly to be taken into the king's service, saying, that if there were nothing else, he could do, he could carry wood and water for the cook-maid; and so, he got leave to remain. When

Lillekort came up to the palace, he saw that the whole was hung with black, both inside and out, even the walls and roof: he asked the cook what it meant. "I will tell thee," answered the girl. "The king's daughter has been promised to three Trolls, and next Thursday evening one of them will come to fetch her. The knight Röd has undertaken to rescue her, but God knows whether he will be able; so, thou canst well imagine there is sorrow and misery enough here." When Thursday evening came, the knight Röd conducted the princess down to the sea-shore (for there she was to meet the Troll), and he was to remain to protect her; but he did not do much harm to the Troll, I trow, for no sooner had the princess seated herself on the shore, than the knight crept up into a large tree, which stood near, and concealed himself as well as he could among the branches. The princess wept, and earnestly implored him not to leave her, but the knight cared little for that: "It is better that one perishes than two," said he.

In the meantime, Lillekort entreated the cook to let him go for a little while down to the sea-shore. "What wilt thou do there?" said the maid; "thou hast nothing to do there." "Yes, that may be, but do let me go, dear friend," said Lillekort, "I would so gladly go and play a little with the other children." "Well, go then," said the cook; "but take care thou dost not stay beyond the time when the pot for supper is to be hung over the fire, and the meat put on the spit; and bring in with thee a good supply of wood for the kitchen again!" Yes, all this Lillekort promised to do, and then ran down to the sea-shore.

Just as he came to the spot where the king's daughter sat, the Troll approached with an appalling noise, so that it seemed to roar and thunder around him. He was so large and bulky that he was terrible to look on and had five heads. "Fire," screamed the Troll. "Fire again," said Lillekort. "Canst thou fight?" cried the Troll. "If I cannot, I can learn," answered Lillekort. Hereupon the Troll threw at him a large thick iron bar, which he had in his hand, so that the earth flew five yards up in the air. "Hui!" said Lillekort, "that was something certainly! Thou shalt now see a stroke from me." So saying, he grasped the sword, which the hunchbacked crone had given him, and struck the Troll so that all his five heads flew over the sands. When the princess saw that she was saved, she was so happy, that she knew not what to do, she danced and jumped about for joy. "Now sleep a little in my lap," said she to Lillekort and while he lay she drew a gold garment over him.

It was not long before the knight Röd came down from the tree, who on seeing there was no danger to be feared, threatened the princess, until she was obliged to promise that she would say it was he who had saved her; for if she did not, he told her he would kill her. He then took out the Troll's tongue and lungs, and put them into his handkerchief, and conducted the princess back to the palace where great honour was shown him. The king did not know how to make enough of him and placed him on his right hand at table. Lillekort went first out to the Troll's ship and brought away a number of gold and silver hoops with him, and then ran back to the royal palace. When the cookmaid saw all the gold and silver she was frightened, and said: "My dear friend Lillekort, where didst thou get all this gold and silver from?" for she feared that he had not come by it honestly. "Oh!" answered Lillekort, "I was at home for a short time, and these hoops fell off from some pails, so I brought them with me for you." When the maid heard they were for her, she asked no further questions about them, but thanked Lillekort, and all was right again.

The next Thursday night everything happened just as on the preceding one. Everybody was in grief and mourning; but the knight Rod said, that as he had delivered the king's daughter from one Troll, he made no doubt he could free her from another and conducted her down to the sea-shore. But he did not do much harm to the Troll; for when the time came that the Troll might be expected, he said as before: "It is better for one to perish than two," and as before crept up into the tree. Lillekort now again begged the cookmaid to give him leave to go down to the sea-shore for a little while. "What wilt thou do there?" asked the cook. "Oh! do pray let me go," said Lillekort, "I would so gladly go and play with the other children down there." So, he got leave to go, but must first promise that he would be back in time to turn the spit and bring with him a bundle of wood. Scarcely had Lillekort reached the sea shore, when the Troll came with an appalling noise, so that it seemed to roar and storm around him. He was twice as large as the first Troll and had ten heads. "Fire," screamed the Troll. "Fire again," said Lillekort. "Canst thou fight?" cried the Troll. "If I cannot, I can learn," answered Lillekort. The Troll then struck at him with his iron staff (it was much larger than that with which the first Troll was armed), so that the ground flew up ten ells in the air. "Hui!" said Lillekort, "that was something certainly! Thou shalt now see a stroke from me; so saying, be grasped the sword and struck the Troll so effectively that all his ten heads rolled over the sands.

The king's daughter said again to him: "Sleep a little while in my lap;" and while Lillekort lay there, she drew a silver garment over him. No sooner did the knight Röd perceive that there was no further danger, than he crept out of the tree, and threatened the princess until she was obliged to promise again, that she would say it was he who had rescued her. He then took the tongue and lungs of the Troll, put them into his handkerchief and conducted the king's daughter back to the palace. There was now joy and pleasure, as may easily be imagined, and the king was at a loss how he should show the knight Röd sufficient honour and respect.

Lillekort again took with him a bundle of gold and silver hoops from the Troll's ship, and when he returned to the royal palace, the cookmaid clasped her hands in astonishment, and wondered where he had got all that gold and silver from but Lillekort answered, that he had been home for a little while; and that it was the hoops which had fallen off some pails, and these he had taken with him for her.

On the third Thursday evening, things went on precisely as they had done on the two former occasions. The whole palace was hung with black, and everyone was in sorrow and mourning; but the knight Röd said, he did not see so much to be anxious about, for as he had rescued the king's daughter from two Trolls, there was little doubt that he could also save her from the third. He then led her down to the seashore, but when the time for the Troll's approach drew near, he crept up into the tree again and hid himself. The princess wept and entreated him to remain with her, but to no purpose; he thought as before, that it was better for one to perish than two.

In the evening, Lillekort again asked leave to go down to the sea-shore. "What wilt thou do there?" said the cook maid but he entreated so long that at last he was permitted to go; but was first made to promise that he would be back in the kitchen again when the spit was to be turned. Scarcely had he reached the shore when the Troll came with a thundering and rattling much louder than on either of the former occasions. He was far, far larger than either of the others, and had fifteen heads. "Fire," screamed the Troll. "Fire again," said Lillekort. "Canst thou fight?" cried the Troll. "If I cannot, I can learn," answered Lillekort. "I will teach thee," bellowed the Troll, and struck at him with his iron-bar, so that the earth flew up fifteen ells in the air. "Hui!" said Lillekort, "that was something certainly! now thou shalt see a stroke from me." At the same moment, he grasped his sword and dealt the Troll such a blow, that all the fifteen heads rolled over the sands.

Thus, was the princess saved, and she thanked and blessed Lillekort for having preserved and delivered her from the Troll. Sleep a little while in my lap, said she; and while he lay there, she drew a dress of brass over him. "But how shall we manage," added she, "to make it publicly known that thou art the person who hast saved me?" "I will tell you," replied Lillekort. "When the knight Röd has conducted you home again and declared himself to be the person who has saved you, he will, as you know, have both you and the half of the kingdom. But when on your wedding day, they ask you whom you will have to serve you with wine, answer. "I will have the youth in the kitchen, who carries wood and water for the cookmaid; then while I am pouring out the wine, I will spill a drop on Röd's plate, but none on yours; he will be angry and strike me; and this I will do three times. The third time you must say: 'Shame on thee who strikest my beloved it is he who preserved me, and him will I have.'" Hereupon Lillekort ran back to the kitchen, but not until he had been on board the Troll's ship and taken a quantity of gold and silver and other precious things, from which he likewise gave the cook a whole armful of gold and silver hoops.

No sooner did the knight Röd see that all danger was over, than he came down from the tree, and again threatened the princess, until she was obliged to promise she would say he had saved her. He then conducted her back to the king's palace; and if there had not been honour enough paid to him before, there was more than enough now: the king thought of nothing but how he should exalt him who had saved his daughter from the three Trolls. It was now, he said, a matter of course that he should have his daughter and the half of the kingdom.

On the wedding-day, the princess requested she might have the youth from the kitchen, who carried wood and water for the cook, to serve her with wine at the wedding feast. "But what can you want with that black, ragged lad?" said the knight Röd. The princess answered, that she would have him and no one else. So at last she got permission; and everything took place just as it had been settled between Lillekort and the king's daughter: he spilt a drop on the knight's plate, but none on hers, and each time the knight Rod was angry and struck him; at the first blow all the rags which he wore in the kitchen fell off from Lillekort; at the second the brass dress fell off; and at the third, the silver dress, so that he stood in a gold dress, so bright and beautiful that it was quite dazzling. Then the king's daughter said: "Shame upon thee for striking my beloved! He has saved me, and him will I have." The knight Röd swore and declared that it was he who had saved her. "Then," said the king, "he who has saved my daughter must have some proof to show." The knight, on hearing this, ran directly to fetch his handkerchief containing the lungs and tongue, and Lillekort fetched all the gold, and silver, and diamonds, and other precious things which he had taken from the Troll's ships; and each laid his spoils before the king. "He who has such precious things as gold, and silver, and diamonds," said the king, "must have been the one who killed the Trolls; for such things are not to be gained from others." So the knight Röd was thrown into a den of snakes, and Lillekort was to have the princess with half the kingdom.

One day as the king and Lillekort were taking a walk together, the latter asked the king if he had never had any other children. "Yes," answered the king, "I had another daughter, but she was carried away by a Troll, because there was no one who could save her. One of my daughters and the half of my kingdom thou art to have; but if thou canst recover her whom the Troll has taken, thou shalt have her also, and the other half of my kingdom." "I will make the trial," said Lillekort; "but for that," continued he, "I must have an iron chain five hundred ells long, also five hundred men, and provisions for them, all for fifteen weeks for I must go far out to sea." Well, that he might have, but the king was apprehensive that he had no ship large enough to carry all these things. "I have a ship myself, said Lillekort, taking the ship which, the old woman had given him, out of his pocket. The king laughed at him, and thought he was joking; but Lillekort only begged he might have what he requested, and then the king should see. All was now brought to him, and Lillekort ordered the chain to be placed first in the ship but there was no one able to lift it, and there was not room in the little tiny ship for many at once. Lillekort then took hold of one end of the chain, and laid some links in the ship, when it began to get larger and larger, and at length it grew to such a size that not only the chain but the five hundred men and all the provisions together with Lillekort, had abundance of room in it. Go now over salt water and fresh water, over hill and dale and stop not until thou comest to the place where the king's daughter is, said Lillekort to the ship; and instantly it sailed away so that it piped and whistled around it. When they had thus sailed far far away, the ship stopped in the midst of the ocean. "Now we are arrived," said Lillekort; "but now it behoves us to consider how we shall get from hence." He then took the chain and fastened one end of it round his body. "I must now go down to the bottom of the sea," said he, "but when I pull the chain, to signify that I wish to come up again, you must all pull as one man, or you will all perish as well as myself." Hereupon he plunged into the water, and a yellow whirlpool surrounded him. He sank and sank, and at length came to the bottom there he saw a large mountain with a door in it, by which he entered. When he was come into the mountain, he saw the princess; she was sitting at work but when she looked at Lillekort, she clasped her hands together and exclaimed: "God be praised! I have not seen a Christian man since I came here. I am come to rescue you," said Lillekort. "Ah! thou wilt not succeed," replied the king's daughter, "thou wilt never succeed; for should the Troll see thee, he will take thy life." "It is well you mention him," said Lillekort. "Where is he? I am anxious to see him." The kings daughter then told him, that the Troll was gone out in search of someone who could brew a hundred lasts of malt in one brewing, because he was to have a great feast, and a less quantity would not suffice. "That I can do," answered Lillekort.

"If only the Troll were not of so hasty a temper, I could tell him that," replied the princess; "but he is so ferocious, that I fear he will tear thee in pieces the moment he comes in and sees thee; but I must devise some expedient: thou canst hide thyself in this closet, then we shall see what is to be done." Lillekort did so, and scarcely had he crept in the closet and concealed himself, before the Troll returned. "Hui! here is a smell of Christian blood," cried he. "There flew a bird over the roof with the bone of a Christian man in its beak, and dropped it down the chimney," answered the princess. "I threw it away as soon as I could; but I suppose it is that you smell. Yes, that must be it," said the Troll. The princess then asked him, if he had found any one who could brew a hundred lasts of malt at one brewing. "No; there is no one who can do it," replied the Troll. "Just now there was one here who said he could do it," said the king's daughter. "Then why didst thou not detain him? thou who art always so shrewd, for thou knewest very well that I wanted such a person," answered the Troll. "Nor did I let him go," replied the king's daughter; "but you are always so hasty that I thought it best to shut him up in the closet; so, if you have not got any one else, here he is." "Let him come in," said the Troll. When Lillekort came in, the Troll asked him, "if it were true that he could brew a hundred lasts of malt at one brewing?" "Yes," replied Lillekort. "It is well that I have met with thee," said the Troll so begin directly, "but Lord have mercy on thee, if thou dost not brew the beer strong." "Oh, don't be alarmed on that score," answered Lillekort, and immediately set to work. "But I must have many more Trolls to carry the liquor," said Lillekort; "for these I have got are but poor hands." He then got so many that the place swarmed, and the brewing went on well. When the wort was ready, they must all taste it, first the Troll himself, and afterwards the others; but Lillekort had brewed it so strong that no sooner had they drunk of it than they fell down dead like so many flies. At last there was no one left there but a miserable old woman, who lay behind the stove. "Oh poor thing," said Lillekort, "thou must have a drink of the beer as well as the rest;" and so he went and brought her a jugful from the bottom of the vat, and gave it to her, and then she was disposed of as well as the rest. As he stood looking about, he cast his eyes on a large chest: this he filled with gold and silver, then binding the chain round it, and also round himself and the princess, he pulled with all his strength. Hereupon the crew raised them safely up. When Lillekort was again in the ship, he said: "Go through salt water and fresh water, over hill and dale, and stop not before thou comest to the king's palace." Immediately the ship sailed away, so that the yellow billows foamed around it. When those in the palace saw the ship approaching, they were not slow in going out to meet it with song and music and received Lillekort with great joy; but the happiest of all was the king, who now had got his other daughter back again. But Lillekort was ill at ease, as both the princesses would have him for a husband, and he would have her alone whom he had first saved, which was the youngest. He often walked about pondering what he should do to possess the one of his choice; yet would not willingly offend the other. One day as he went hither and thither thinking about it, it occurred to him, that if he only had his brother, King Lavring, with him, who was so like himself, that no one in the palace could distinguish the one from the other, he could have the elder princess with the half of the kingdom, while for himself the other half would be amply sufficient. No sooner had he thought upon this plan than he went outside of the palace and called upon King Lavring. But no King Lauring came. He called again and a little louder, but no, still no one came. He then cried a third time with all his strength, and there stood his brother before him. "I said that thou shouldst not call on me before thou wast in the greatest difficulty," said he to Lillekort, "and here is not so much as a fly that can hurt thee;" hereupon he began beating him so that Lillekort rolled about the field.

"Oh, shame upon thee to strike me," said Lillekort, "I who have won first one king's daughter and the half of the kingdom, and then another daughter with the other half of the realm, and now thought of giving thee one of the princesses and of dividing the kingdom with thee—dost thou think it just to strike me thus?" When King Lavring heard this, he begged forgiveness of his brother, and immediately they were good friends again, as before.

"Thou knowest," said Lillekort, "that we are so alike that no one can distinguish the one from the other. Change clothes with me, and go up to the palace, and the princesses will think it is I. The one who kisses thee first thou shalt have, and I will take the other." For he well knew that the elder was the stronger, and so could easily guess how it would be. This King Lavring was quite willing to do; he changed clothes with his brother and went up to the palace. When he entered the princesses' apartment, they thought it was Lillekort, and both ran at the same moment towards him but the elder, who was the larger and stronger, pushed her sister aside, threw her arms round King Lavring's neck and kissed him. Thus, he obtained the elder daughter of the king, and Lillekort the younger.

One can well imagine that there was such a wedding, that it was heard of and talked of over seven kingdoms.

THE THREE AUNTS.

THERE was once a poor man who lived in a hut far away in the forest and supported himself on the game. He had an only daughter, who was very beautiful, and as her mother was dead and she was grown up, she said she would go out in the world and seek her own living. "It is true, my child," said her father, "that thou hast learnt nothing with me but to pluck and roast birds; but it is, nevertheless, well that thou shouldst earn thy bread." The young girl therefore went in search of work, and when she had gone some way she came to the royal palace. There she remained, and the queen took such a liking to her that the other servants became quite jealous; they, therefore, contrived to tell the queen that the girl had boasted she could spin a pound of flax in twenty-four hours, knowing that the queen was very fond of all kinds of handiwork. "Well, if thou hast said it, thou shalt do it," said the queen to her. "But I will give thee a little longer time to do it in." The poor girl was afraid of saying she never had spun, but only begged she might have a room to herself. This was allowed, and the flax and spinning-wheel were carried up to it. Here she sat and cried and was so unhappy she knew not what to do; she placed herself by the wheel and twisted and twirled at it without knowing how to use it: she had never even seen a spinning-wheel before.

But as she so sat, there came an old woman into the room. "What's the matter, my child?" said she. "Oh," answered the young girl, "it is of no use that I tell you, for I am sure you cannot help me!" "That thou dost not know," said the crone. "It might happen, however, that I could help thee." "I may as well tell her," thought the girl; and so she related to her, how her fellow-servants had reported that she had said she could spin a pound of flax in twenty four hours. "And poor I," added she, "have never before in all my life seen a spinning-wheel; so far am I from being able to spin so much in one day." "Well, never mind," said the woman, "if thou wilt call me Aunt on thy wedding day, I will spin for thee, and thou canst lie down to sleep." That the young girl was quite willing to do and went to bed.

In the morning when she woke, all the flax was spun and lying on the table and was so fine and delicate that no one had ever seen such even and beautiful thread. The queen was delighted with the beautiful thread she had now got, and on that account felt more attached to the young girl than before. But the other servants were still more jealous of her and told the queen she had boasted that in twenty-four hours she could weave all the thread she had spun. The queen again answered: "If she had said that, she should do it but if it were not done within the exact time, she would allow her a little longer." The poor girl durst not say no, but begged she might have a room to herself, and then she would do her best. Now she again sat crying and lamenting, and knew not what to do, when another old woman came in, and asked: "What ails thee, my child?" The girl would not at first say, but at length told her what made her so sorrowful. "Well," answered the crone, "provided thou wilt call me Aunt upon thy wedding day I will weave for thee, and thou canst go to sleep." The young girl willingly agreed to do so and went to bed.

When she awoke the piece of linen lay on the table woven, as fine and beautiful as it could be. The girl took it down to the queen, who was so delighted with the beautiful web which she had got, that she was fonder than ever of the young girl. At this the others were so exasperated that they thought of nothing but how they could injure her.

At length they told the queen, that she had boasted she could make the piece of linen into shirts in twenty-four hours. The girl was afraid to say she could not sew; and all took place as before: she was again put into a room alone, where she sat crying and unhappy. Now came another old woman to her, who promised to sew for her if she would call her Aunt upon her wedding day. This the young girl consented to do; she then did as the woman had desired her and lay down to sleep. In the morning when she woke, she found that the linen was all made into shirts lying on the table, so beautiful that no one had ever seen the like; and they were all marked and completely finished. When the queen saw them, she was so delighted with the work, that she clasped her hands together: "Such beautiful work," said she, "I have never owned nor seen before." And from that time, she was as fond of the young girl as if she had been her own child. "If thou wouldst like to marry the prince, thou shalt have him," said she to the maiden, "for thou wilt never need to put out anything to be made, as thou canst both spin and weave and sew everything for thyself." As the young girl was very handsome, and the prince loved her, the wedding took place directly. Just as the prince was seated at the bridal table with her, an old woman entered who had an enormously long nose; it was certainly three ells long.

The bride rose from the table, curtsied, and said to her "Good day, Aunt." "Is that my bride's aunt?" asked the prince. "Yes, she is." "Then she must sit down at the table with us," said he; though both the prince and the rest of the company thought it very disagreeable to sit at table with such a person.

At the same moment, another very ugly old woman came in she was so thick and broad behind that she could hardly squeeze herself through the door. Immediately the bride rose, and saluted her with a "Good day, Aunt;" and the prince asked again if she were his bride's aunt. They both answered "Yes:" the prince then said, if that were the case, she must also take a place at the table with them.

She had hardly seated herself before there came in a third ugly old crone, whose eyes were as large as plates, and so red and running that it was shocking to look at. The bride rose again and said: "Good day, Aunt;" and the prince asked her also to sit down at table; but he was not well pleased and thought within himself: "The Lord preserve me from my bride's aunts." After a short time, he could not help asking: "How it came to pass that his bride, who was so beautiful, should have such ugly and deformed aunts." "That I will tell you," replied one of them. "I was as comely as your bride when at her age, but the reason of my having so long a nose is that I constantly and always sat jogging and nodding over the spinning-wheel, till my nose is become the length you see it." "And I," said the second, "ever since I was quite little, have sat upon the weaver's bench rocking to and fro therefore am I become so broad and swelled as you see me." The third one said: "Ever since I was very young, I have sat poring over my work both night and day, therefore have my eyes become so red and ugly, and now there is no cure for them." "Ah! is that the case?" said the prince, "it is well that I know it; for if people become so ugly thereby, then my bride shall never spin, nor weave, nor work anymore all her life."

RICH PETER THE HUCKSTER.

THERE was once a man who was called Rich Peter, because by travelling about with wares he had amassed so much money that he became a wealthy man. This Rich Peter had a daughter, who was so dear to him that all the suitors who came to offer themselves met with a refusal; for he thought none of them good enough for her. As it fared thus with them all, at length no more came and as time went on, Peter began to fear that his daughter would never be married. "I am surprised," said he to his wife, "that no more suitors come to demand our daughter, who is so rich. It will be a rare thing if no one will have her; for money she has already and will have more; I think I will go to the astrologers and ask them whom she will have, as no one comes here now." "How can the astrologers answer that question?" asked his wife. "Yes, they can, they read everything in the stars," said Rich Peter. Hereupon he took with him a good sum of money and set out to the astrologers and requested them to oblige him by consulting the stars and informing him what person his daughter would get for a husband. The astrologers looked at the stars, and said, that they could not inform him. But Peter begged they would look more carefully and let him know the result; for he would pay them well for it. The astrologers after consulting the stars better, said that his daughter would marry the miller's boy, that was just born at the mill, close by Rich Peter's dwelling. Peter gave the astrologers a hundred dollars and returned home with the answer he had received. He thought it quite absurd that his daughter should marry one who was but just come into the world, and that so poor a man. This he told his wife and added: "I wonder whether they would sell the child to me, and then we could soon get rid of it." "Yes, I should think they would," answered his wife, "for they are but poor people."

Rich Peter then went down to the mill and told the woman that if she would sell him her son, she should have a great deal of money for him. No, she positively would not. "I cannot imagine why you will not," said Peter, "for you have nothing but poverty here and the babe will not make things better, I should think." But she was so happy with her boy that she would not lose him. When the miller came in, Peter said the same to him, and offered to give five hundred dollars for the child, so that they could buy a farm and no longer grind corn for people and starve when there was no water at the mill. This the miller thought a good thing, and consulted with his wife, and so Rich Peter got the babe. The mother cried and was quite in despair; but Peter comforted her by saying, that it should be taken good care of; that they must only promise him one thing, that they would not inquire after the child, as he would send him into distant countries there to learn foreign languages. When Peter brought the babe home, he had a little box made, so nicely contrived that it was a pleasure to look at. He secured it with pitch, laid the child in it, locked it, and sent it down the river; so that the stream soon carried it far away. "Now

I have got rid of him," thought Rich Peter. But when the box had been borne far down the river it came to a watercourse that supplied another mill, through which it passed, and coming in contact with the water-wheel, caused the mill to stand. The man went down to see what had stopped the mill, when he found the box and took it up with him. When he came home at dinner-time, he said to his wife: "I wonder what can be in this box: it came floating down against the water-wheel and stopped the mill for me today." "That we shall presently see," said the woman. "The key is in the lock, open it." When they opened it, there lay the sweetest babe any one could see; they were both delighted, and resolved to keep it, as they had no children of their own, and were both getting into years; so that they could no longer expect to have any. When some time had elapsed, Rich Peter began again to wonder whether any suitor would come after his daughter, who had so much money. But as no one came, he set out again to the astrologers and offered them large sums of money, if they could tell him whom his daughter would marry. "We have already told you that she will have the miller's son down yonder," said the astrologers. "Yes, that is all very fine," answered Peter, "but he is dead; and if I only could know who would be my daughter's husband, I would willingly give you two hundred dollars." The astrologers again consulted the stars, but became angry, and said: "She will have the miller's son, notwithstanding you have cast him into the river to get rid of him; but he is living at the mill that lies farther down the river." Rich Peter gave them the two hundred dollars for this information, and then thought how he should get rid of this miller's boy. So, the first thing he did when he returned home, was to go down to the other mill. Here he found the boy so grown that he was already confirmed, and helped in the mill: he was, in fact, become a fine youth. "Could you not let me have that youth?" said Rich Peter to the miller. "No, that I cannot," answered he; "I have brought him up as my own, and he has conducted himself well, so that I have good use of him in the mill; for I am beginning to be old and weak." "It is the same with me," answered Peter, "and, therefore, I want a youth I can bring up to my trade. If you will let me have him, I will give you six hundred dollars: with that you can buy a house and live in peace and quiet in your old age." When the miller heard this, he let Rich Peter have the youth. They now journeyed together about the country with their wares, till they came to a hostel, which lay on the border of the forest. Here Peter sent the youth home with a letter to his wife—for straight through the forest the distance was not great—and desired him to tell her, that she was to perform, as soon as possible, what was written in the letter. In the letter, she was ordered to make a large fire and throw the miller's boy into it; and if she disobeyed, she herself should be burned when he returned.

The youth set off through the forest with the letter. Towards evening he came to a house in the middle of the wood, into which he entered, but saw no one there. In one room he found a bed, on which he lay down. The letter he had stuck into the band of his hat, and with the hat he had covered his face. When the thieves returned home—for in this house twelve thieves had their retreat and saw the youth lying on the bed, they wondered who he was, and one of them, taking the letter from his hat, broke the seal and read it. "Oh! oh!" said he, "it is Rich Peter who is abroad: now we will play him a trick; for it would be a sin for the old scoundrel to make an end of such a fine young lad." So the thieves wrote another letter to Peter's wife, and placed it under the hatband, in which they said that she should immediately marry her daughter to the miller's son, and give them horses, sheep, and household furniture, and put them into the farm he had up in the mountains, and if all this was not done before he came home she should suffer for it. The next day the thieves let the youth depart, and when he reached home and had delivered the letter, he said, he was to greet her from Peter, and tell her that as soon as possible she was to perform what he had written. "Thou must indeed, have behaved well," said Peter's wife to the miller's son, "that he now writes in this fashion; for when thou went away, he was so exasperated against thee, that he knew not what to do to get rid of thee." She then began directly to prepare for the wedding, and furnished them with horses, sheep, and all kinds of household furniture in the farm up in the mountains.

Not long after this Rich Peter came home, and his first question was, had she done as he had commanded her in the letter? "Yes, I thought it odd, but I was afraid of doing otherwise," said she. Peter then asked, where his daughter was. "You can well imagine where she is," answered his wife. "She is with him at the farm up in the mountains, as you ordered in your letter." When Peter heard what had taken place, and had seen the letter, he was in such a passion that he was ready to burst, and immediately ran up to the farm to see the young couple. "It is all very well, my son," said he, that thou hast got my daughter, but if thou wishest to keep her, thou must go to the dragon of Dybenaa and get me three feathers from his tail; for those who possess them can have whatever they desire." "Where shall I find him?" said his son-in-law. "That I don't know," replied Peter, "that must be thy concern.

The youth set off courageously on his journey, and when he had gone some distance he came to a royal palace. Here I had better go in and inquire my way, thought he for such people know more of the world than others and, perhaps, I can here learn which is the right road. The king asked him whence he came, and on what errand he was going. "I am going to the dragon of Dybenaa, to fetch three feathers from his tail; that is, provided I can find him," said the youth. "There must be good luck for that," thought the king: "for," said he, "I never heard of any one returning from him; but shouldst thou find him, thou mightest as well ask him from me, why I can never get clear water in the well, which I have from time to time sunk deeper and deeper, but can never get clear water in it." "Yes, that I will do," said the youth. At the royal palace he fared well and got both provisions and money when he departed.

Towards evening he approached another royal palace. When he entered the kitchen, the king came in and asked him, whence he came and on what errand he was going. I am going to the dragon of Dybenaa, to fetch three feathers from his tail, said the youth. "There must be good luck for that," thought the king; "for I never heard of any one returning from him. But if thou art successful in getting them, thou mayst ask him from me, where my daughter is, who was lost many years ago. I have both sought her and caused her loss to be published in all the churches; but no one has ever been able to give me any tidings of her." "Yes, that I will do," said the youth. At the royal palace he fared well, and at his departure they gave him provisions and money.

When evening again approached, he came to another palace. Here the queen came into the kitchen and asked him, whence he came, and on what errand he was going. "I am going to the dragon of Dybenaa, to fetch three feathers from his tail," answered the youth. "There must be great luck for that," said the queen; "for I never heard that anybody ever came back from him. But shouldst thou find him, thou canst ask him from me, where I shall find my gold keys which I have lost." "Yes, that I will do," said the youth.

When he had journeyed on some way further, he came to a large, broad river. While he stood thinking how he should cross over, or whether he should walk along its banks, there came an old hunchbacked man, and asked him, whither he was going. "I am going to the dragon of Dybenaa, if any one can tell me where I may find him," said the youth. "That I can do," said the man; "for I am here for the purpose of carrying over those who seek him. He lives just on the other side. When thou comest up the hill thou wilt see his palace; and if thou canst get to talk with him thou canst ask him from me how long I am to remain here, carrying people across." "That I will do," said the youth. The man then took him upon his back, and carried him across the river; and when he got up the hill, he saw the palace, and went in. The princess was at home alone. "Alas!" said she, how can a Christian venture to come hither? No one has been here since I came; and it will be better for you to depart as quickly as you can; for when the dragon comes home, he will smell you out, and devour you in a moment, and you will also make me miserable." "No," replied the youth, "I cannot return before I have got three feathers out of his tail." "Them you will never get," answered the princess. But the youth would not go away; he was determined to wait for the dragon and obtain the feathers and an answer to his questions. "As you are so resolved, I must see how I can help you," said the princess. "Try whether you can lift the sword that hangs there on the wall." No, the youth could not even move it. "Then you must drink a draught from this flask," said the princess. When the youth had sat a little while, he made another trial, and found that he could now move it with ease. "You must take another draught," said the princess, "and then tell me your errand." He drank again, and then informed her that there was a king who had requested him to inquire of the dragon, why he could not get pure water in his well. From another king, he was to ask, what had become of his daughter, who had been stolen away many years ago. From a queen, he was to ask what had become of her gold keys. And lastly, he was to ask the dragon, from the carrier, how long he should continue to carry people over the river. When he now grasped the sword, he could lift it and after taking another draught, he could wield it. "To prevent the dragon from destroying you, you must creep under the bed," said the princess; "for as evening approaches he will soon be home; and then you must lie so still that he does not hear you. When we go to bed I will ask him those questions, and you must listen and pay great attention to his answers; you must remain under the bed till everything is quite quiet and the dragon is asleep; then creep softly out, take the sword with you, and when he rises, you must watch the moment to cut his head off with one stroke. You must at the same instant snatch the three feathers; otherwise he will pluck them out himself, that no one may derive any benefit from them."

Not long after the youth had crept under the bed, the dragon came home. "What a smell there is of a Christian's bones," said the dragon. "Oh, yes, there was a raven came flying with a human bone in its beak, and perched on the roof, answered the princess, that must be what you smell. Is that it?" said the dragon. The princess set the supper on the table, and when they had finished, they went to bed. When they had lain for some time, the princess seemed very uneasy in her sleep, and woke suddenly. "Oh dear!" cried she. "What is the matter with thee?" asked the dragon. "I sleep so uneasily, answered the princess, "and have had such a strange dream." "What didst thou dream?" asked the dragon. I thought there came a king here, who asked you what he should do to procure clear water in his well." "Oh," answered the dragon, "he ought to know that himself. When he digs out the well and takes up the old decayed stick which lies at the bottom, he will soon have clear water again. But now lie still and don't dream any more."

When the princess had lain still a little longer, she began to be very uneasy again, and to toss about in the bed, so that she woke him again "What 's now the matter with thee?" asked the dragon. "Oh, I sleep so uneasily," answered the princess, "and have had such a strange dream." "Well, what didst thou dream?" asked the dragon "I thought a king came and asked you what had become of his daughter, who had been carried away many years ago," said the princess. "That's thyself, replied the dragon; "but he will never see thee more. But now, I beseech thee to let me have a quiet night, and not lie dreaming again, or I will break all thy ribs." And he was so cross and angry that he seemed ready to burst. "Oh! you must not be so cross," said the princess. But she had not lain long before she began to be restless again and started up with a loud cry. "What! again," said the dragon "Oh! I have had such an extraordinary dream," said she. "The foul fiend take thy dreaming; but what didst thou dream about now?" "Oh! I dreamed that a queen came and asked you where she could find her gold keys again, that she had lost." "Let her look for them in the wood where she left them, she very well knows when. She will find them there," answered the dragon. "But now let me rest in peace and have no more dreaming." In a little while the princess started up again and woke the dragon, who exclaimed: "I think thou wilt never be quiet till I have wrung thy neck." And he was in such a passion that his eyes sparkled with rage: "What's now the matter?" he asked. "Oh! you must not be angry with me," answered the princess, "but I have had such a wonderful dream. I never knew the like of your dreaming," said the dragon. "What didst thou now dream?" "I thought that the carrier at the strand came and asked you how long he should go backwards and forwards carrying people across," said the princess. "The simpleton, he could soon get rid of that job," replied the dragon, "for when any one comes who wants to cross, he need only throw him into the river, and say: 'Now you may carry folks across until you are released.' But do let me now go to sleep and hear no more of thy dreams, or it will be the worse for thee."

The princess then let him sleep in peace; but as soon as all was again quiet, and the youth heard the dragon snore, he crept out of his hiding place. Before it was daylight the dragon rose, but no sooner had he put both legs out of bed than the youth struck off his head and snatched the three feathers out of his tail. Now there was great joy; the youth and the princess collected as much gold, silver, and other precious things as they could carry away with them, and when they came down to the water, the carrier was so bewildered with all the things he had to carry over, that be entirely forgot to ask what answer the dragon had given, until the princess, the youth, and all their riches were well across the river. As they were going, he inquired of the youth, whether he had asked the dragon what he had begged of him. "Yes," said the youth; and he answered that when there came a person who wanted to cross, thou must throw him into the middle of the river, and say: "Continue thou to carry across, till thou art released; and then thou wilt be free." "Oh, out upon thee," said the ferryman, "hadst thou told me that sooner, thou shouldst have released me."

When they arrived at the first king's palace, the queen asked the youth about her gold keys. In a whisper he told her to search in the wood. "Hush! hush! don't say another word," said she; and gave him a hundred dollars. When they came to the second palace, the king asked whether he had inquired of the dragon about that which he bade him. "Yes, said the youth, I did, and here is your daughter." At this the king was so rejoiced that he would willingly have given his daughter and the half of his kingdom to the miller-lad; but when he heard that he was already married he gave him two hundred dollars, a carriage and horses, with as much gold and silver as he could carry with him.

When he came to the third royal palace, the king came out and asked him, whether he had inquired of the dragon about that which he bade him. "Yes," answered the youth; "he said, you must empty the well and take up the old rotten stick that lies at the bottom, and then you will get clear water." The king then gave him three hundred dollars.

He then journeyed straight home, and was so laden with gold and silver, and so fine, that no one had ever seen the like before; and was much richer than Peter the huckster. When Peter got the feathers, he had nothing to say against the wedding; and when he saw all the youth's wealth, he asked, whether so much had come from the dragon's. "Yes," replied the youth, "and a great deal more than I could bring with me there is still many horse-loads remaining, and if thou wilt go thither, thou wilt find plenty also."

So, Peter resolved to go. His son-in-law directed him so well that he had no occasion to ask the way as he went on. "But the horses," said he, "thou hadst better leave on this side of the river, for the old carrier will bear thee across." So Peter set out on his journey, taking with him a stock of provisions and many horses, but these he left by the riverside, as the youth had directed him. The carrier then took him upon his back, and when he had gone some way out, he threw him into the middle of the river, saying: "Now you can stay here and carry folks across until thou art released." And if no one has released him, Rich Peter remains there to this day carrying people across the river.

THE THREE GOATS NAMED BRUSE, THAT WENT TO THE MOUNTAIN-PASTURE TO FATTEN.

ONCE on a time there were three goats that were going to the mountain-pasture to fatten, and all of them were called Bruse. On the road there was a bridge across a waterfall, over which they had to pass, and under which lived a great ugly Troll, with eyes as large as tin plates, and a nose as long as a broomstick. The youngest goat came first on the bridge. "Trip trap, trip trap," said the bridge as he went over. "Who trips on my bridge?" cried the Troll. "Oh! it is only the little goat Bruse. I am going to the mountain pasture to get fat," said the goat in a soft voice. "Now I am coming to catch thee," said the Troll. "Oh!

no, pray don't take me, for I am so little; but if you will wait, the second goat Bruse is coming this way, and he is much bigger." "Be it so," said the Troll.

Some time after the second goat came passing over the bridge. "Trip trap, trip trap, trip trap," said the bridge. "Who trips over my bridge?" cried the Troll. "Oh! it is the second goat Bruse, who is going to the mountain-pasture to get fat," said the goat, who was not delicate of speech. "Now I am coming to catch thee", said the Troll. "Oh! no, pray don't take me, but wait a little while, and then the big goat Bruse will come this way: he is much much bigger than I am." "Be it so," answered the Troll.

Just at that moment came the big goat Bruse upon the bridge. "Trip trap, trip trap, trip trap," said the bridge for he was so heavy that the bridge creaked and cracked under him.

"Who goes tramping on my bridge?" screamed the Troll. "It is I, the great goat Bruse!" said the goat, who was very coarse of speech. "Now I am coming to catch thee," cried the Troll.

> "Well come thou then. Two spears I bear,
>   With which thy entrails out I'll tear,"

said the goat, and then rushed upon the Troll, thrust out his eyes, broke his bones, and with his horns thrust him out into the waterfall; and then went on to the pasture.

There the goats grew so fat, so fat, that they were hardly able to go home again; and if they have not lost their fat, they are so still; and snip, snap, snout, now is my story out.

THE YOUTH WHO WENT TO THE NORTH-WIND AND DEMANDED HIS FLOUR AGAIN.

There was once on a time an old woman, who had a son; and as she was very weak and ailing, she desired the youth to go up to the store-room and fetch some flour to make something for dinner; but when he was returning down the stairs, the North-wind came rushing, snatched away his flour and carried it off through the air. The youth returned to the store-room to fetch more, but when he was about to descend the stairs, the North-wind came rushing again and carried away his flour; and thus, it served him a third time. At this the youth became very angry; and, as it seemed to him unreasonable that the North-wind should act in such a manner, he resolved to go in search of him and demand his flour back.

He set off accordingly; but the way was long, and he went, and went, until he at length came to the North-wind. "Good day," said the youth, "and thank you for your kindness." "Good day," answered the North-wind. He was very rough of speech. But what dost thou want added he. "Ah!" answered the youth, "I wish just to ask you if you will be so good as to let me have the flour again which you took from me on the stairs of the store-room for we have but little, and if you are to act so and take the modicum we have, nothing will remain but starvation." "I have no flour," answered the North-wind; "but as thou art so needy, thou shalt have a cloth, which will supply thee with everything thou canst wish for, only by saying: 'Cloth be spread, and be covered with all kinds of costly dishes.'"

With this the youth was well pleased; but as the way was so long, that he could not well reach home in one day, he went into an hostel on the road; and when those who were there were about to take their evening meal, he laid his cloth upon a table which stood in a corner, and said: "Cloth be spread, and be covered with all kinds of costly dishes." Scarcely had he uttered the words, when the cloth did as it was ordered, and everyone thought it a most wonderful thing; but the host's wife especially. So, when the night was far advanced, and everyone was fast asleep, she took the youth's cloth, and laid one in its place that looked exactly like the one he had got from the North-wind, but which could not furnish even dry bread.

When the youth awoke, he took his cloth and continued his journey; and that same day reached home. "Well," said he to his mother, "I have been to the North-wind; he is a gentlemanly person, for he gave me this cloth, which if I only say to it: 'Cloth, be spread out, and covered with all kinds of costly dishes,' I get all the food I wish." "Oh! yes," replied the mother, "I dare say it is very true; though I would rather not believe it till I see it." The youth then in haste set a table out, laid the cloth on it, and said: "Cloth, be spread out, and covered with all kinds of costly dishes." But the cloth would not furnish even so much as a bit of bread.

"Then there is nothing else to be done, but that I go again to the North-wind," said the youth; and instantly set off. Towards the afternoon he came to where the North-wind dwelt. "Good evening," said the youth. "Good evening," answered the North-wind, "I am come to get compensation for the flour you took from me," said the youth; "for the cloth you gave me is worth nothing." "I have got no flour," said the North-wind, "but here is a goat I will give thee, which makes pure gold ducats, if only thou sayest, 'My goat, make money.'" This the youth thought was a fine thing to have; but as he was so far from home that he could not reach it that day, he took up his night's lodging at the hostel. Before he ordered anything, he made trial of the goat, to see if what the North-wind had said was true, and it happened just as he had said; but when the host saw this, he thought it was a most precious goat to have; so when the youth had fallen asleep, he took another, which could not however make ducats, and set it in its place.

The next morning the youth departed, and when he came home to his mother, he said: "The North-wind is an excellent man after all; he has now given me a goat, which can make gold ducats. I need only say, 'My goat, make money.'" "I know all about it," answered his mother "and that it is all fudge; I will believe it when I see it." "My goat, make money," said the youth, but not a penny did the goat make. So he went again to the North-wind, and told him that his goat was of no use, and that he would have compensation for the flour. "Well, I have now nothing to give thee," said the North-wind, "save this old cudgel that stands in the corner; but its nature is such, that if thou sayest, 'My cudgel, hit away!' it will continue striking until thou sayest, 'My cudgel, be still.'"

As the way home was long, the youth went into the hostel again that night. And as he now guessed how matters stood with his cloth, and his goat, he lay down directly on the bench, and began to snore as if asleep. The host, who thought the cudgel was no doubt of some use, went in search of one that resembled it, and was going to put it in the place of the other, as he heard the youth snoring; but at the same moment that the man was about to seize it, the youth cried out, "My cudgel, hit away!" The cudgel then commenced beating away at the host, so that he jumped over benches and tables, and cried, and screamed for help. "Oh! for mercy's sake! Oh, for mercy's sake! Let the cudgel be quiet, or it will beat me to death. You shall have your cloth and goat again." When the youth thought his host had been sufficiently cudgeled, he said: "My cudgel, be still."

He then took the cloth and put it in his pocket, took the cudgel in his hand, tied a cord round the horns of the goat, and led him home. All this was good payment for the flour.

SUCH WOMEN ARE;
OR, THE MAN FROM RINGERIGE AND THE THREE WOMEN.

THERE was once a man and his wife who wanted to sow, but had no seed-corn, nor money to buy it. They had one cow, and this they agreed that the man should drive: to the town and sell, to enable them to buy seed with the money. But when it came to the point, the woman was afraid to let her husband go with the cow, fearing he would spend the money in the town in drinking. "Hear now! father," said she, "I think it will be best for me to go, and then I can sell my old hen at the same time." "As thou wilt," answered the husband, "but act with discretion and remember thou must have ten dollars for the cow." "Oh! that I shall," said the wife, and off she went with the cow and the hen.

Not far from the town she met a butcher "Art thou going to sell thy cow, mother?" asked he. "Yes, that's what I am going to do," answered she. "How much dost thou want for it?" "I want a mark for my cow, and my hen you shall have for ten dollars."[5] "Well that's cheap," said the butcher; "but I am not in want of the hen, and that thou canst always get rid of when thou comest to the town; but for the cow I am willing to give thee a mark." So they settled the bargain, and the woman got her mark; but when she came into the town, there was not a person who would give her ten dollars for an old lean hen. She therefore went back to the butcher and said: "Hear, my good man, I cannot

---

get rid of my hen, so thou must take that also, as thou hast got the cow, and then I can go home with the money."

"Well! Well! I dare say we shall strike a bargain for that also," said he. Hereupon he invited her in, gave her something to eat, and as much brandy as she could drink. "This is a delightful butcher," thought she, and kept on drinking so long that at last she completely lost her senses.

What now did the butcher do? While the woman was sleeping herself sober, he dipped her into a tar barrel, then rolled her in a heap of feathers, and laid her down in a soft place, outside the house. When she awoke and found herself feathered from head to foot, she began to wonder, and said to herself: "What can be the matter with me? Is it I, or is it somebody else? No, this can never be me, this must be some strange, large bird. But what shall I do to know if it is really myself or not? Yes, now I know how I can find out whether it is myself. If the calves lick me and the dog does not bark at me, when I go home, then it is really myself."

The dog had hardly caught a glimpse of the strange animal that was entering the yard, before he set up a terrible barking and the woman felt far from easy. "I begin to think it is not myself," said she; and when she went into the cattle-house, the calves would not lick her, as they smelt the strong tar. "No, I see now it cannot be me, it must be some wonderful strange bird, I may as well fly away." So creeping up on the top of the store-room she began to flap with her arms as if they were wings, and tried to rise in the air. When the man saw this, he seized his rifle, went out into the yard and was just taking aim. "Oh no," exclaimed the woman, "don't shoot me, father, it is I, indeed it is." "Is it thou?" said her husband; then don't stand up there like a fool but come down and give an account of the money. The woman crept down again, but no money could she give him, as she had got none. She looked for the mark the butcher had given her for her cow, but even this she had lost while she was drunk. When the husband heard the whole story, he was so angry that he swore he would leave her and everything, and never return, unless he could find three other women who were as great fools as herself.

He set out accordingly, and had not gone far on the road, before he saw a woman running in and out of a newly built cottage with an empty sieve in her hand. Every time she ran in, she threw her apron over the sieve as if there were something in it. "What is it you are so busy about, mother?" said the man.

"Oh! I am only carrying a little sunshine into my new house; but I know not how it is; when I am out of doors, I have plenty of sun in my sieve, but when I come in it is all away. When I was in my old hut, I had sun enough; although I never carried any in. If I only knew of any one who would bring sunshine into my house, I would willingly give him a hundred dollars." "I think there must be a way for that," answered the man. "If you have got an axe, I will soon procure you sun enough." He got the axe and made a couple of windows in the house, which the carpenter had forgotten to do. Immediately the sun came in, and he got a hundred dollars. "There was ONE," said the man as he again walked on.

Some time after, he came to a house and heard from the outside a terrible bellowing and noise within. He entered and saw a woman beating her husband about the head with a washerwoman's batlet. He had got a new shirt over his head, but could not get it on, because there was no slit made for the neck. "What's the matter here," cried the stranger at the door: "are you killing your husband, mother?" "No, Lord preserve us," said the woman, I am only helping him to put on his new shirt." The man struggled and cried: "The Lord preserve and take pity upon all who put on a new shirt." If any one will only teach my wife to cut a slit in the proper place, I will give him a hundred dollars." I think there must be a way for that; come bring a pair of scissors," said the stranger. The woman gave him the scissors, and he immediately cut a hole in the shirt, and got a hundred dollars. "There is the SECOND," said the man as he went on his way.

After walking on for some time he at length came to a farm-house where he thought of stopping to rest. When he entered the room, the woman of the house asked him "Where he was from?" "I come from Ringerige," answered the man, "Oh, indeed! what, do you say you come from Himmerige (Heaven), then of course you know the second Peter, my poor late husband?" The woman, who was very deaf, had had three husbands, all named Peter. The first husband had used her ill, and therefore she thought that only the second, who had been kind to her, could be in heaven. "Know him, aye, and well too," answered the man from Ringerige. "How does he fare above?" asked the woman further. "Ah! but poorly," said the man. He goes wandering from one farm to another to get a little food and has scarcely clothes to his back; and as to money, that is quite out of the question. "Oh God, be merciful to him!"

exclaimed the poor woman, "I am sure he need not go so miserable, for there was plenty left after him. I have got a whole room full of his clothes, also a box of money, which I have taken care of, that belonged to my late husband. If you will take charge of all this for him, you shall have a cart and a horse to draw it. The horse he can keep up there, and the cart also he then can sit in it and drive from one farm to another for he was never so poor that he was obliged to walk." So the man from Ringerige got a whole cart-load of clothes, and a little box of bright silver-money, with as much provision as he liked to take When he had filled the cart, he got up in it and drove away.

"That was the THIRD," said he. But in the fields was the woman's third husband ploughing, who, when he saw a person, he knew nothing of, coming from the yard with horse and cart, hurried home, and asked his wife who it was that was driving away with the dun horse. "Oh, that was a man from Himmerige (Heaven), said she; "he told me that things went so badly with my second Peter, my poor husband; that he goes begging from one farm to another, and that he had neither food nor clothing, so I sent him a load of old things that were left after him."

But the box of silver-money she said nothing about. The man seeing how matters stood, saddled a horse, and set off at full gallop. It was not long before he was close behind the man in the cart, who, on observing him, turned off with the horse into a little wood, pulled out a handful of the horse's tail, ran up a small hill with it, and tied it to a birch tree; then laid himself down under the tree, and kept staring up at the clouds. "Well!" cried he, as the man on horseback approached him, "never have I seen such a thing before in my life—" Peter the third stood a while staring at him and wondering what he was about. At length he asked: "What art thou lying there for, gazing and gaping? "No, never have I seen anything like it," said the other. "There is a man just gone up to heaven on a dun horse here is some of the tail hanging in the birch, which he left behind, and there up in the clouds you can see the dun horse." Peter the third looked first at the man, then up at the clouds, and said: "I see nothing but some hair of a horse's tail hanging in the birch tree. "No, you cannot see it where you stand," said the other, "but come and lie down here where I am, and look straight up, and you must continue gazing for some time, without turning your eyes from the clouds." While Peter lay quite still staring up at the clouds, the man from

Ringerige sprang upon his horse and galloped off as fast as he could, both with that and the cart. When it began to rattle along the road, Peter jumped up, but he was at first so bewildered by this adventure, that he did not think of pursuing the man who had run off with his horse, until it was too late to overtake him. Peter then returned home to his wife quite chap-fallen. When she asked him what he had done with the other horse, he said: "I gave it to the man that he might take it to Peter the second; for I thought it was not becoming for him to sit in a cart and drive about from one farm to another up in heaven. Now he can sell the cart, buy a carriage, and drive a pair of horses." "How I thank you for that Peter; never did I think you were so reasonable a man," said his wife.

When the man from Ringerige returned home with his two hundred dollars, a cart full of clothes, and a box of money, he saw that his land had been ploughed and sown. The first question he put to his wife was, where she had got the seed from to sow the fields with. "Oh!" exclaimed she, "I have always heard say, 'that what you sow, you shall reap,' so I took the salt we had left from the winter, and sowed that; and if we only get rain soon, I don't doubt but it will come up, and yield many a bushel." "A fool thou art, and a fool thou wilt be as long as thou livest," said her husband; "but there is no help, and others are no wiser than thou."

THE COCK AND THE HEN IN THE NUT-WOOD.

A COCK and a hen went once into a wood to pluck nuts, when the hen got a piece of a nutshell in her throat, and lay gasping, and flapping her wings. The cock ran to fetch some water for her and came to the spring and said: "My dear spring, pray give me some water; the water I will give to Tuppen, my hen, that lies for dead in the nut-wood." The spring answered: "Thou wilt get no water from me till I get leaves from thee." Then the cock ran to the lime tree, and said: "My dear lime-tree, pray give me some leaves; the leaves I will give to the spring, the spring will give me water, the water I will give to Tuppen, my hen that lies for dead in the nut-wood." "Thou wilt get no leaves from me, until I get red gold ribands from thee," answered the lime-tree. So, the cock ran to the

Virgin Mary, and said: "My dear Virgin Mary, pray give me some red gold ribands; the red gold ribands I will give to the lime-tree," etc. "Thou wilt get no red gold ribands from me, until I get shoes from thee," answered the Virgin. So, the cock ran to the shoemaker. "Dear shoemaker, pray give me shoes; the shoes I will give to the Virgin Mary, the Virgin Mary will give me red gold ribands," etc.

"Thou wilt get no shoes from me, till I get bristles from thee," answered the shoemaker. So the cock ran to the sow. "My dear sow, pray give me some bristles; the bristles I will give to the shoemaker, the shoemaker will give me shoes," etc.

"Thou wilt get no bristles from me, until I get corn from thee," answered the sow. So the cock ran to the thrasher, and said: "My dear thrasher, pray give me some corn; the corn; I will give to the sow, the sow will give me bristles," etc.

"Thou wilt get no corn from me, until I get bread from thee," said the thrasher. So, the cock ran to the baker's wife, and said: "My dear baker's wife, give me some bread; the bread I will give to the thrasher, the thrasher will give me corn," etc.

"Thou wilt get no bread from me, until I get wood from thee," said the baker's wife. So, the cock ran to the wood cutter, and said: "My dear wood-cutter, pray give me some wood the wood I will give to the baker's wife, the baker's wife will give me a loaf," etc.

"Thou wilt get no wood from me, until I get an axe from thee," answered the wood-cutter. So, the cock ran to the smith, and said: "My dear smith, pray give me an axe; the axe I will give to the wood-cutter, the wood-cutter will give me wood," etc.

"Thou wilt get no axe from me, until I get coals from thee," answered the smith. So the cock ran to the coal burner, and said: "My dear coal-burner, pray give me some coals; the coals I will give to the smith, the smith will give me an axe, the axe I will give to the wood-cutter, the wood cutter will give me wood, the wood I will give to the baker's wife, the baker's wife will give me a loaf, the loaf I will give to the thrasher, the thrasher will give me corn, the corn I will give to the sow, the sow will give me bristles, the bristles I will give to the shoemaker, the shoemaker will give me shoes, the shoes I will give to the Virgin Mary, the Virgin Mary will give me red gold ribands, the red gold ribands I will give to the lime-tree, the lime-tree will give me leaves, the leaves I will give to the spring, the spring will give me water, the water I will give to Tuppen, my hen, that lies for dead in the nut-wood."

The coal-burner took pity upon the cock and gave him some coal. And now the smith got the coal the wood-cutter got the axe, the baker's wife got the wood, the thrasher got the loaf, the sow got the corn, the shoemaker got the bristles, the Virgin Mary got the shoes, the lime-tree got the red gold ribands, the spring got the leaves, and the cock got the water, which he gave to Tuppen, his hen, which lay for dead in the nut-wood, and so she got well again.

III. DANISH.[1]

SVEND'S EXPLOITS.

ONCE on a time there was a peasant who lived on the Alhede in Jutland. When winter came, he and his wife suffered much; they were starving and knew not what to do to support themselves. At length they determined to leave house and home and beg. Each took a different road, and the woman, laying her child in a basket, carried it on her back.

The man wandered the first few days from one town to another, and at length came to a great wood, where there was a Troll's house, at the door of which he knocked. The Troll came out and asked what he wanted. The man told him how hard it went with him, and begged the Troll to help him, if with ever so little. "Yes, that I can do," said the Troll; "you see here, for instance, a purse, which has the property, that every time you shake it you will find money. If you will give me your son the day, he is fourteen years old, this purse shall be yours but this you must know, that if you deceive me, you will have to come in his place."

The peasant immediately complied with the conditions, received the purse, and went his way. In the meantime, the woman met with another incident. One afternoon she met on the heath with a little man crying and making doleful lamentations. "Why are you so sorrowful?" asked the woman when they had walked some way by the side of each other. "Oh!" answered he, "my wife lies sick and our child I fear will die for I can get no nurse for it. I will help you," said the woman; conduct me to your house. They walked on together, and when they came to a large mound, they crept into it; whence the woman saw immediately that they were mount-folk she had to do with. However, she cared little for that, but nursed the sick woman and her child, and scoured and cleaned the place, so that it was quite a pleasure to see. Before

---

[1] With the exception of "The Girl clad in Mouse-skin," all the Danish tales and traditions are from "Eventyr og Folkesagen fra Jylland, fortalte af Carit Etlar, Kjob." 1847.

long the sick woman recovered, and the child began to thrive under the nurse's care.

The little Man of the Mount was rejoiced to see this change, and one day he asked the peasant woman what she desired in return for her services. "Nothing," answered the woman, "for if I have been of any help to you, you have also fed me and my son during the time we have been here; but as your wife is now well again, I should like to return home, and see how things go on there."

"Yet, I must give you something," said the Man of the Mount, "and we can, I dare say, find some trifle in the cupboard, which can be of service either to you or your son." Hereupon he took a little packet out of a press in the wall and gave it to the woman. "See! here is a bear's hair, a fish's scale, and a bird's feather. Take good care of them; for they have the property, that when you squeeze one in your hand, then will appear before you the king of whichever of those animals you wish and will give you all the help he can."

With regard to her son, the Man of the Mount foretold that he would find favour with God and man and would wed a king's daughter. Having said this, he led the woman out of the mount. Taking, then, her little son by the hand, she wandered towards home, where she found everything changed. Her husband, by the help of the Troll's purse, had become so rich that he had built a fine house and lived in luxury and splendour. The report of the Man of the Mount's prediction was soon spread through the country, and many persons came from a distance to see a poor peasant boy who was destined to be the husband of a princess. At length the report reached the palace; and as the king one day came from Viborg Ting[2], he rode to the peasant's house, and talked with him about taking the boy into his service. At this the parents, and particularly the mother, were delighted, thinking that the prophecy was already about to be fulfilled. They, therefore, immediately gave their consent, and the king took the child. But could these parents only have looked into his heart, they would have found they had but little reason to rejoice; for as soon as the king reached the river Skoldborg, he put the boy into a chest, threw him into the water, and rode away. But Providence had ordained it otherwise than that he should come to such an untimely end in the water. The chest floated

---

[2] Viborg is the oldest city in Jutland, and in which the Danish kings received the homage of their subjects. The great assembly, or *Ting*, was held there from time immemorial.

down to a mill, and when the miller's man went the next morning to open the sluices, he saw the chest floating on the water, dragged it up, and, on opening it, was much surprised to find a little boy in it. He called his master, who, as he had no children and was well to do in the world, resolved on taking care of Svend, as the boy was called, and bringing him up as his own son. About the same time the king's daughter disappeared, and no one could discover what had become of her. The king was sorely afflicted for her loss, regarding it as a punishment for his cruel conduct to Svend.

In the meantime, the boy grew up, promised well, and advanced in courtesy and good manners. When he had attained the age of manhood, he requested the miller to let him go out in the world and seek his parents. The miller gave him much good advice, and a purse well stocked, to take with him, and Svend set out on his travels.

One evening, as he was passing across a heath, he met with an old woman who was crying and lamenting. Upon asking her the cause of her grief, she answered, that the Trolls had carried off her husband. While she was relating her misfortunes, Svend found that chance had brought him to the place where he most desired to be, and that he stood before his mother. He made himself known, and went home with her, and then it was agreed, that the next day Svend should continue his travels, to see if he could not come upon some traces of his father and rescue him. When his mother took leave of him, she gave him the presents from the Man of the Mount and explained to him how he was to act when he needed the help of the animals. Svend then committed himself to God's care and departed.

At noon he came to a thick wood, where he resolved to eat his dinner. While he sat enjoying his meal, there came a swarm of ants, which collected all the crumbs that had fallen, and carried them away. Svend crumbled a morsel of his bread for the little creatures, so that each might have a portion, and no sooner had he clone so, than it seemed to him as if a soft voice rose out of the ant-hill, saying: Thou shalt not have done this for nothing; a time will come when we can requite thee. Svend now continued his journey, and when he entered further into the wood, he met with an old woman, who was staggering under a heavy load of sticks, which she had collected. "I think it will be best for me to give you a helping hand, mother!" said Svend; "if you are willing you may place your wood on my back, I have younger shoulders than you." "Such an offer deserves thanks," answered the old woman, quite pleased. "I am now more than eighty years old, and no one ever yet made me such an offer." While Svend carried the old woman's wood, they conversed together, and Svend confided to her the motive of his journey. "Did I not think right?" said she. "There is not a twig in the wood, be it ever so little, that will not do to burn; now thou hast done me a service and I will repay thee. I serve a Troll, who can give thee information of what thou wishest to know; provided I can get thee well and safely into his house. During the day he changes himself into an owl and sits over the door to take care that no stranger enters his dwelling and robs him of the precious treasure he has hoarded there; but I think we shall find a way. Thou hadst better wait here and let me take the wood on my back. I will soon return and see to smuggle thee in." Svend did as she desired him, and when night came on, the old woman returned to him, tied him fast under the belly of the Troll's cow, and in this manner got him safely past the owl, that sat looking out over the door. When Svend had taken some supper, he crept under the bed, and soon after the Troll came into the room. "Oh!" cried he, "I smell Christian blood. Hast thou dared to bring any one in here to me?" "Oh! no," answered the woman boldly. "It was only a crow that let fall a little bone as he flew over our house at noon." The Troll now sat down to his supper, and then went to bed. In the night, the woman gave a loud scream, and when the Troll woke and asked her what the matter was, she said: "I have had such an unpleasant dream about a Troll that took a poor man instead of his son." "Well, that has happened over at my brother's," answered the Troll; "but now let me be quiet."

A little while after this the woman gave another scream and begged the Troll to tell her where his brother lived. "He lives," said the Troll, "on an island at the other end of the forest. In the daytime he transforms himself into a dragon, and his twelve sons fly about as crows; but every night they become men again. Leave me now in peace; if thou wakest me again, it will be the worse for thee." Svend listened to every word the Troll said and remained quite quiet under the bed till it was daylight. When the Troll had gone out, the old woman gave him something to eat, and then conveyed him out as she had brought him into the house. When they parted, she advised him, before he encountered the dragon, to get a sword made by her brother, who was a smith and understood a little of the black art. So Svend went to the smith's.

The smith made a sword for Svend; but when he learned against whom it was to be used, he doubted whether his art was sufficient, and advised Svend not to engage with the dragon. But his words availed nothing; Svend was bent on the adventure, and he bade the smith farewell, after paying him for his work.

He now wandered about for a long time without being able to find an outlet in the forest. His provisions were all gone, and he knew not what to do, when he suddenly recollected the presents his mother had given him when they parted. He then drew forth the eagle's feather, and no sooner had he pressed it in his hand than an enormously large bird came clattering through the air, and descended at his feet, asking what his commands were. When Svend had somewhat recovered from his fright, he informed the eagle of his undertaking, and asked him if he could convey him over to the dragon's island. "That, I fear, will be a difficult task," said the eagle, "but we can make the attempt; so, spring up on my back and hold fast. The eagle now soared up in the air with Svend, and in a short time began to descend on a small island. But the terrific dragon instantly approached; and every time the eagle would alight on the island, he hissed, and spat a long stream of fire at them. "I see that we shall not succeed" said the bird as he flew back; "but if thou wilt take my advice, try what the fishes can do for thee." Svend then went down to the sea, and drew forth the scale, which he had no sooner pressed than a Merman appeared and asked what he could do to serve him. When the Merman had heard Svends wish, he bound up his mouth and ears, and then plunged under the water with him. In this manner they fortunately reached the island, but no sooner had Svend set his foot on shore, than the dragon came creeping towards him, and it would have fared ill with him, had not all the little birds at the same moment perched upon him, and thus concealed him from head to foot while the dragon crept past. A dragon is a formidable animal to look on it has three crowned heads, and some maintain there are dragons that have six heads. The tail is long and covered with scales, and at the same time so powerful, that a dragon once overthrew the tower of Randböl church with his tail; a dragon can also spit fire out of his mouth. Such a creature as this was Svend going to encounter; and although he saw his own destruction almost certain, he did not lose courage, but only resolved to defer the combat till the following day, when he should have recruited himself with sleep. He, therefore, laid himself down to rest under some elder-trees, making himself a couch of leaves and moss. Just as he was going to sleep, twelve crows came flying and perched in the elder-trees over Svend's head. They began to converse together, and the one told the other what had happened to him that day. When they were about to fly away, one crow said: "I am so hungry, so hungry! where shall I get something to eat? We shall have food enough tomorrow, when father has killed Svend," answered the crow's brother. Dost thou then think that such a miserable fellow dare to fight with our father?" said another. "Yes, it is probable enough that he will; but it will not profit him much, as our father cannot be overcome but with the Man of the Mount's sword, and that hangs in the mound, within seven locked doors before each of which are two fierce dogs that never sleep." Svend here learned that he should only be sacrificing his strength and life in attempting a combat with the dragon, before he had made himself master of the Man of the Mount's sword. As soon, therefore, as it began to dawn, he hastened down to the sea, and called on the Merman. He appeared directly, and Svend begged him to convey him across to the wood again.

When he got into a thick part of the forest, he drew forth the bear's hair, and immediately the king of the beasts came running towards him, asking his commands. When Svend said that he wanted to know where the Man of the Mount was, the bear instantly called all the four-footed animals altogether, and inquired of them one by one as they came, but not one knew the place. At last the bear came running; the bear chided her because she had been so long absent; but the bear excused herself by saying that she had been watching the oddest sight anybody could imagine.

"And what might that be?" asked the bear.

The hare related that while she was skipping and playing outside the cave where the Man of the Mount lives, an old witch came out who had made herself a finger-stall, which had the property of making her invisible every time she put it on.

"That must, indeed, be a strange kind of finger-stall," said the bear; "dost thou know what, Svend, this may be of some service to thee, and we will try to get possession of it."

The bear forthwith sent a little mouse to get it, and let the hare go also to be its guide. Soon after the mouse returned with the finger-stall, and the bear gave it to Svend saying: "Now seat thyself on my back, and in a trice thou shalt be at the cave of the Man of the Mount. Thou art now in possession of a thing which can enable thee to pass securely in and out of the Mount." The hare was now obliged again to go and show the way.

Svend, mounted on the bear's back, soon reached the hill. "Thus far have I helped thee," said the bear, "the rest thou must manage thyself. Take good care of the finger-stall and wait out here till the watchmen come to open the door, then thou wilt have an opportunity of slipping in without being perceived."

When the bear had thus spoken, he ran back to the forest, and soon after Svend saw the watchmen, who every evening went through all the rooms in the Troll's mound, to see that everything was in order by the time their master came home. At the moment they opened the door Svend ran in, and also passed safely by the fierce dogs. The Troll's palace was furnished in the richest manner, with ebony and ivory, and covered with ornaments of pure gold. But the room in which the enchanted sword hung was the most costly of them all. This sword was so heavy that Svend could not lift it from the wall. After making many fruitless attempts he was just going to turn back without accomplishing his object, when his eyes fell on a little flask that hung under the sword, and on which was written, "Seven men's strength." Svend emptied the flask, and now he could almost lift the sword; he then drank from another flask, on which was written, "Twenty men's strength;" then he emptied a third flask, on which stood, "Thirty men's strength." When he had so done, he could swing the sword as easily as a straw.

He then stole quietly away; but as he was going out of the door, he accidentally made a rattling with the sword, and instantly a whole swarm of Trolls came about him screaming and howling; but owing to his having on the finger-stall they could not see him, and he fortunately got out of the Mount unscathed.

"Well how hast thou sped?" asked the bear, that had waited for him a little way in the wood. Svend related to him what had passed, then mounted on the bear's back, and away they went over hill and dale till they came down to the water which ran between the forest and the dragon's island. Here Svend called the Merman, who bound up his mouth and ears as before, and then conveyed him over to the island. The monster came instantly towards him, but Svend was prepared for the combat. He was not only become much stronger from emptying the three small flasks in the Troll's mount, but his courage was greater than it had ever been. As the dragon was now sensible that he could effect nothing by threats, he said: "I will grant thee thy miserable life till tomorrow, and then thou shalt serve me for breakfast." The monster then crept away to his den. He had thus spoken because he thought to himself that his adversary would be sure to make his escape in the night.

But Svend had determined quite differently. He went into the thicket, made himself a couch of moss and leaves, and lay down to sleep, first putting on the finger-stall. This was a good precaution, for when night came the dragon called together the twelve crows and held a council with them what was best to be done. They all agreed that they would fly away and pick Svend's eyes out while he slept. Now the finger-stall had, as we have seen, the property of rendering him invisible, so that the crows could not find him, although their sharp scent brought them directly to the place where he lay.

He rose with the sun and offered up a prayer that he might succeed in delivering his father. He then went forth to fight with the dragon. The monster was already on the spot, lashing the earth with his tail, and appeared so ferocious and grim that it might easily be seen he had resolved on the destruction of Svend. The combat now began with such fury that the earth seemed to thunder under them, and the whole island trembled to its very foundation. Fore noon came, and noon came yet neither of them had the mastery but in the afternoon the dragon was obliged to yield. When he saw that he could no longer stand against Svend, he began to beg for his life, and was desirous of coming to terms but Svend thought on his father and slew the monster. He then went up to the palace. All the doors stood open, and his father came out to meet him, threw his arms round his son's neck and kissed him. Soon after the old man prepared a good meal and while they ate Svend related all the wonderful feats he had achieved. His father answered that he feared there were more adventures in store for him, for as soon as night came on, the dragon's twelve sons would come to avenge his death; "but I will see whether we cannot get rid of them," said the old man. He then went to the spot where the dragon lay and cut off twelve pieces of his flesh. These he roasted and prepared so well that it was impossible for anyone to imagine this dish so poisonous, that whoever ate a mouthful of it must die. When evening came the twelve crows flew into the palace. They did not know of their father's death, and Svend concealed himself from them. They laid aside their feathery garb and called for supper. The old peasant then brought them the dragon's flesh, and they had no sooner eaten a morsel of it than one after another they fell down under the table and died. Svend and his father were now masters over all the palace, and went to rest for the night.

The next morning, they walked all over the palace, and came at length to a cellar in which was a young damsel, who cried and lamented bitterly, for she thought that it was the dragon coming to kill her. When Svend comforted her by telling her that he was the slayer of the dragon, she was greatly rejoiced, and informed him that she had been carried away from her parents, and that she was a Danish princess. Scarcely had Svend heard these words than he remembered the prophecy of the Mount-folk, when with his mother he lived in their mound. He resolved therefore on conducting the princess home to the king.

So one afternoon he took leave of his father, who wished him a happy journey, and be with the princess left the dragon's island, while the old peasant returned to his own house and there lived nobly and happily. To travel from the island to Denmark was, however much sooner said than done, and the truth of this saying Svend soon experienced. When they had wandered about for some days, they lost their way, and could find neither road nor path, and as they had not taken with them any great stock of provisions they were obliged to subsist on such wild fruits and berries as they found in the wood. The princess was very sorrowful, but Svend comforted her as well as he could. He was of good courage himself, thinking that as Providence had assisted him so often and so long, it would not now leave him to perish.

In the evening of the fourth day they saw a light at a great distance glimmering through the trees. They went towards it and came to a little cottage, at the door of which stood an old woman looking out. "Now you must be guided by me," said Svend to the princess, "and say *yes* to all I relate, then I no doubt shall procure you a night's lodging and a good sum of money into the bargain." The princess promised that she would do as he desired her.

Svend then wished the old woman a good evening and asked her whether they could have anything to eat, and shelter for the night. "My accommodations are but scanty," answered the woman, "and my stock of provisions still more so but, nevertheless, come in, it is not the first time I have housed people, and no one has ever made a complaint."

They entered the cottage, and the old woman placed victuals before them. "Where do you come from so late?" said she while they were eating. "I will tell you," said Svend, "if you will promise not to betray us. I and my sister belonged to a band of robbers which in the last few days has been destroyed by the king's men, so that our whole company is exterminated with the exception of us two; and now I am in search of new comrades." "Of what use are girls in your den of thieves?" asked the woman, incredulously. "To dress our meals," answered Svend; and my sister understands the art of cooking as well as anyone. Then that happens luckily enough, said the woman, "for I have twelve sons who are also robbers, and if you are inclined you can stay with them; but since as you say your sister is such a good cook, let her go into the kitchen and make a savory dish for our people by the time they come home in the evening." "Yes, that shall soon be done," answered the princess, upon Svend making a sign to her; and although, as may be well imagined, she possessed no extraordinary knowledge of culinary matters, she, nevertheless, went and boiled and roasted what the old woman had set out. In the meanwhile, Svend whispered to her to make the evening-drink as strong as possible.

When everything was ready, the robbers came home. They immediately sat down to table, and all agreed that the supper that evening was much better than they generally had it. When they had made a hearty meal, they began to drink till the night was far spent. Svend was admitted into the fraternity, but he, nevertheless, saw plainly that they harboured treacherous designs against both him and the princess he was therefore careful not to drink with the robbers, but excused himself by saying that he was tired and sleepy after his perilous flight.

The woman then showed the strangers a sleeping chamber and went back to her sons. But hardly was she gone before Svend crept softly down after her and heard how the old crone agreed with the robbers to murder both him and the princess. In the meantime, the strong drink began to take effect, so that one after another they fell down under the table in a deep sleep. When Svend saw that they were all dead drunk he drew his sword, sprang into the room where they lay, and killed every one of them, together with the old woman. He then went upstairs and lay down outside the door of the princess's sleeping chamber. The next morning, they continued their journey, after having furnished themselves with provisions from the thieves' kitchen. The following afternoon they came to the inhabited part of the country and saw a large mansion, which they entered, and requested a lodging for the night. They were now in the Danish territory. The knight to whom the mansion belonged was called Peter; he received them in the most courteous manner, especially when he heard that it was a Danish princess he should entertain. A great banquet was immediately prepared, and all the chief persons of the neighbourhood came to the mansion, because the king had promised that whoever should bring back his daughter should be richly rewarded and invested with the highest offices.

When they were all assembled at table, Svend related his adventures, greatly to the gratification of the guests. Before their departure on the following morning the knight conducted Svend over the mansion and showed him all its splendour. At length they came to a den of lions and while Svend stood viewing these fierce animals, Peter seized him round the waist, cast him down into the den, and fastened the door upon him. When he had perpetrated this atrocious deed, he went to the princess, and told her the infamous falsehood that Svend, weary of accompanying her any longer, had requested him to conduct her to the king. The princess at once doubted the truth of this story, partly because she already entertained a strong partiality for Svend, for every day as they travelled together, she became more and more attached to him, partly because he had at all times shown her so much devotion.

But as she had no alternative, she was obliged to continue her journey with the knight Peter. At the end of a few days they arrived at the king's palace. There was rejoicing over the whole land when it was known that the princess was restored, and the king was so delighted at having recovered his daughter that he promised her hand to the knight. Thus, Peter rose to great consideration, in consequence of his base conduct to Svend. The noblest among the courtiers considered it an honour to associate with him, and the king overloaded him every day with new proofs of favour. But now let us see how things in the meantime went with Svend.

No sooner had he been thrown into the lions' den than the hungry animals rushed forward to tear him in pieces, and the history would have been ended, had not late events rendered our here so familiar with danger that he stood prepared as soon as a new one presented itself. At the moment he fell into the den, he pressed the bear's hair in his hand, and then it should have been seen how friendly the wild animals became all at once, wagging their tails, licking his hands and feet, and were in all respects devoted to him. He shared in their food, and thereby sustained his life for some months. Nevertheless, the time at length grew tedious, and as he longed to know what was passing in the upper world, he one day summoned the king of the birds, and asked him how things were going on above. The eagle informed him, that the princess had returned to her home, and that the king had resolved on giving her in marriage to the knight Peter, and that on the following day there was to be a great tournament at the palace. Svend thereupon resolved in his mind to be at that entertainment, so taking a friendly farewell of the beasts, he caused the eagle to convey him out of the den. He then entered the palace, and chose a suit of armour, and the king of the beasts gave him a horse, and he rode to the tournament. The journey from the lions' den to the royal city occupied an ordinary traveller more than four days, but Svend was a good rider and his horse could not grow weary it galloped away as if it flew; and thus, Svend reached the palace just as the tournament was about to end. The knight Peter had vanquished all his opponents, and was already declared the victor, as Svend rode into the place. He had concealed his face by drawing down his visor and refused to give his name when asked by Peter. The two new engaged together, and although the contest was only in sport, it could be seen that Svend was in earnest, and that he strove to fell his antagonist. The knight was sorely perplexed, being chased from one side of the place to the other. But what took place Just as he was in the greatest danger, he suddenly recollected the finger-stall which he had taken from Svend on the morning when he cast him into the lions' den, and which from that time he had always carried about with him. This he drew on in an instant, and immediately he came invisible. Svend could now no longer defend himself against him and was wounded. Peter then concealed the finger-stall, and drove Svend close up to the throne, that the king might see how bravely he fought. Thus, by the help of the finger-stall, was Svend overpowered, and obliged to surrender unconditionally.

The knight Peter called his attendants and ordered them to carry the wounded man into the tent, where he was undressed and his wounds were bound up and hardly was this done when there came a messenger from the king, to order him to be conveyed to the palace. When he stood in the king's presence, he threw himself at the foot of the throne and spoke thus: "Most gracious king! you see before you an unhappy youth, whom the treachery and wickedness of one of your courtiers has deprived of his most precious treasure—honour—and nearly of life also, had it not pleased the Almighty, by a wonderful dispensation, to save me." Hereupon he related his exploits and accused the knight Peter as guilty of intending his death, in order to hinder him from bringing back the princess. The king could not believe what he heard, and sent for his daughter, that she might say whether she knew Svend. But since Svend had last seen the princess, he had become pale and emaciated, partly in consequence of his confinement in the lions' den, and partly through the pain of his wounds. The princess, therefore, did not recognise him, and Svend was declared a slanderer and driven out of the palace. But this was not the worst for when Peter's servants had bound up his wounds, they took off his bloody clothes and gave him others in their place. In this manner he had been deprived of his sword, his feather, his hair, and his fish-scale, so that he was more helpless than he had ever been before.

Svend now wandered for many days, hardly knowing what course to take. Little had he to live on, and when that was consumed, he was forced to beg his way, until he reached home. There he found his father in the enjoyment of wealth; because he was still in possession of the Troll's purse, which afforded him money as often as he desired it. The peasant received his son with open arms, and when Svend had related all his adventures, the old man sought to persuade him to remain quietly at home and think no more of the princess. But to this Svend would not accede; for he was not only strongly attached to the king's daughter, but also relied on the Man of the Mount's prediction to his mother. They then took counsel together and agreed that they would shake the purse until it had yielded money enough to last the old man's lifetime, and that Svend should take it, and again set out in search of fresh exploits, and see what fortune had yet in store for him. No sooner said than done so when Svend had remained at home a whole month, and had recovered somewhat of his health and strength, he bade his father farewell, and departed with the Troll's purse. Just as he stood ready to begin his journey, the old man said "Wait a little, my son, I have got a small present for thee, which may, perhaps, prove of use. When I came back from the dragon's island, I found in my pocket an apple-pip, which I set in our garden. It has shot up rapidly, and this year, for the first time, has borne three apples. Take them with thee and take good care of them."

The old man then gave him the apples, two of which were large and red, the third, on the contrary, was small and green. "Thou mayest on no account eat the apples thy self," said his father, "and take especial care of the least, for although it looks the worst, it is far better than the other two, and can cure any injury caused by the others." After having thus spoken, the old man bade him farewell, and gave him his blessing.

Svend now set out a second time on his wanderings, and, on reaching the next town, went to an inn, and remained there for some days, while he ordered new clothes, bought horses, and a carriage so splendid and costly, that the king himself hardly had the like. He also shook the purse so often that at last he got a large sack full of money, and then continued his journey, until he arrived at the town in which was the palace, where the princess resided. There he took up his quarters in the best inn, lived sumptuously, and drove out every day at the same hour as the princess. It could not be very long before the news of the arrival of so rich a man reached the palace, and the king sent to desire his company, and Svend conducted himself so courteously, both in words and manners, that he soon won the heart of everyone. Money be scattered on all sides and sent the most precious gifts to the king and princess, till at length he became almost a daily guest at the palace. One day he drove with them down to the sea-side, and the discourse turned on the beautiful view there, on which occasion, the princess remarked, that she would not exchange that spot for any place in the world, if there were only a wood there, that could screen them from the midday sun. When Svend heard this, he sent for all the gardeners in the place, and gave them large sums of money to plant by the next day the princess's favourite spot with trees. When all was done, he went up to the palace and invited the king and his daughter to ride out with him. The joy of the princess can well be imagined, when she saw that the wish, she had expressed the day before, and which she considered an impossibility, had been accomplished. By such attentions Svend gained favour daily in the eyes of the princess, and there was no one who recognised him, or believed that the wealthy stranger could be the same person whom the king had called an impostor and caused to be driven from the palace.

The knight Peter alone seemed to have some misgivings. The princess had constantly, on some pretence or other, deferred her marriage; and since Svend's arrival, she appeared more indisposed than ever to marry him. "There is certainly some mystery in all this," said he to himself; "either this stranger is Svend or else a Troll; but I can soon find out, if I put on my finger-stall."

When he had put it on, he went up in the evening to the inn where Svend lodged, but notwithstanding all the exertion he made, he could not get inside the door. He tried many times but was always held back by some invisible power. This arose from the three magic apples, which were in Svend's trunk, that stood near the door. Peter was, therefore, obliged to return without being a whit the wiser. When Svend had passed a year in the city, and increased daily in the king's favour, and, as we can easily imagine, still more so in that of his daughter, he began to drop some words indicating his love for the princess, and the king seemed not indisposed to having so rich a son-in-law; but knew not how he could manage matters on account of the promise he had previously made to the knight Peter; although he saw that the princess had but little regard for him, and was always finding excuses to delay her wedding. The king, being thus undecided which of the rivals to choose, went to consult an old courtier, who being well disposed towards Svend, advised the king to fix the condition, that he who could produce as large a sum as would be equal to the amount of all the treasure of the country, should have the princess.

When Svend heard this, he was very glad and begged to be shown into the room in which the king wished the money to be deposited. When the evening came, he went in, and began shaking his purse until he obtained the sum required. He now knew that the princess belonged to him; but what he did not know and least suspected was, that the knight Peter had stolen into the room, snatched up the purse when Svend had laid it down, and disappeared with it as unobserved as when he entered. Peter then went into another room, and as he had watched how Svend got the money, he did the like, and continued shaking the purse until he also had got the desired sum.

As soon as this was done, he went to the king and told him, that Svend was a Troll, and gained his wealth by witchcraft, and to prove the truth of his words, he showed the king the stolen purse, which he promised to give him, if in return the king would give him his daughter. The king was as delighted as surprised at this discovery and consulted with the knight how they should get rid of Svend.

When morning came, the king said to Svend: "It is true thou hast fulfilled thy promise and produced the money; but as the knight Peter has, as thou seest, done the like, I will fix a new condition. In the granary are seven barrels of wheat, and seven barrels of rye, in one heap; these thou must separate by the morning, so that each kind of grain may lie apart. If thou canst do this, then my daughter shall be thine. Upon hearing this, Svend was much troubled, and still more so, when he found that he had lost his purse. He sought after it the whole day in vain, and in the evening, he was conducted up into a granary where the grain lay that he was to sort. While sitting there he heard people underneath talking about the princess's wedding, which was to take place the next day, and how busy they all were in preparing for the entertainment. In his sorrows for the misfortunes which constantly attended him, he began to weep and think of destroying himself, as now everything was lost, and he could not live to see his rival victorious. But Providence always helps the good, and just as Svend was most sorrowful, he thought he heard a little rustling in the heap of grain. The moon was shining in the granary, and by its light he saw that the wheat and the rye were gently separating, each into its own heap. Here were all the ants, for which he once had crumbled his bread, when he first set out on his wanderings, and which had promised they would return his kindness, when the time should come. They had now all crept up into the granary, and each taking a grain on its back went from heap to heap. Some stood and loaded the others, while others received the grains. And thus, they continued working all the night long, until, in the morning, the wheat lay all in one heap, the rye in another. When they had finished their task, the little ant-king placed himself on the top of the heap of wheat, and asked Svend, in a small voice, if he were content now. "No," answered Svend, "I am not quite content until I get my finger-stall back, and that is impossible for you to get." The ants went their way, and Svend, who was very weary with having watched all night to see how the work was going on, fell asleep but when he awoke again, he found the finger-stall by his side. Now he was really glad he paced up and down the room, and sang so merrily, that it echoed again; and when the messenger came from the king, the work was done. While all this was going on the knight Peter as soon as he missed the finger-stall in the morning, went to Svend's lodging to seek for it; but there he found nothing, save the three apples, which the old man had given Svend when he left home. The knight took the two ripe and finest looking apples, and as it was just that time of the year when this fruit was a rarity, he sent them up to the palace, as a present to the king and the princess. The small apple, which was green, and in appearance far from tempting, he left behind.

The king and his daughter ate the apples, and soon after, Peter was sent for, to show before the whole assembled court his wonderful feat with the inexhaustible purse. He drew forth the purse, and let it pass from hand to hand among all those present, but what he was not aware of was, that Svend had in the meanwhile made himself invisible, and snatched up the purse, substituting in its stead another of like appearance the natural consequence was, that Peter could not extract a single skilling, although he shook and shook the purse with all his might; but all to no purpose the king hereupon became highly incensed, and thought he was making a fool of him.

But this was not the worst that was to befall the wretched culprit; for while the king and princess were thus sitting among their courtiers, their noses began to grow, and, in a few moments, had attained such a length that nobody who looked at them could refrain from laughing. This was caused by the bewitched apples that Peter had sent, and which they had eaten that morning.

There was now a general alarm and outcry in the palace, and Peter was threatened with the severest punishment, if he did not immediately confess all that related to the apples and the purse. He was new obliged to make a full confession of everything, and thus the king became quainted with all his villany, and how he had acted towards Svend. A messenger was then instantly despatched after Svend, who in the meantime had returned to the granary, where he sat, thinking he would let the king suffer a little, for all the wrongs and troubles he had endured.

When he appeared before the assembly, he confirmed all that Peter had confessed, adding that it was now his intention to return to the place of his birth, and to resign the princess to any one on whom the king might think proper to bestow her. The unfortunate king wept and begged of him that at least he would be so merciful, before he went away, as to help them to get rid of their long noses. The princess also besought him so piteously that he could resist no longer. He therefore went to fetch the green apple and, cutting it in two, gave the father and daughter each a part; and hardly had they eaten a morsel before their noses began to resume their proper form. To make an end of the story, Svend was married to the princess, as the Troll had foretold, and they lived many years together in happiness and splendour till their deaths.

But the knight Peter was cast into a pen of serpents.

TOLLER'S NEIGHBOURS.

ONCE upon a time a young man and a young girl were in service together at a mansion down near Klode Mill, in the district of Lysgaard. They became attached to each other, and as they both were honest and faithful servants, their master and mistress had a great regard for them and gave them a wedding dinner the day they were married. Their master gave them also a little cottage with a little field, and there they went to live.

This cottage lay in the middle of a wild heath, and the surrounding country was in bad repute; for in the neighbourhood were a number of old grave-mounds, which it was said were inhabited by the Mount-folk; though Teller, so the peasant was called, cared little for that. "When one only trusts in God," thought Teller, "and does what is just and right to all men, one need not be afraid of anything." They had now taken possession of their cottage and moved in all their little property. When the man and his wife, late one evening, were sitting talking together as to how they could best manage to get on in the world, they heard a knock at the door, and on Teller opening it, in walked a little little man, and wished them "Good evening." He had a red cap on his head, a long beard and long hair, a large hump on his back, and a leathern apron before him, in which was stuck a hammer. They immediately knew him to be a Troll; notwithstanding he looked so good-natured and friendly, that they were not at all afraid of him.

"Now hear, Toller," said the little stranger, "I see well enough that you know who I am, and matters stand thus I am a poor little hill-man, to whom people have left no other habitation on earth than the graves of fallen warriors, or mounds, where the rays of the sun never can shine down upon us. We have heard that you are come to live here, and our king is fearful that you will do us harm, and even destroy us. He has, therefore, sent me up to you this evening, that I should beg of you, as amicably as I could, to allow us to hold our dwellings in peace. You shall never be annoyed by us or disturbed by us in your pursuits."

"Be quite at your case, good man," said Teller, "I have never injured any of God's creatures willingly, and the world is large enough for us all, I believe; and I think we can manage to agree, without the one having any need to do mischief to the other."

"Well, thank God!" exclaimed the little man, beginning in his joy to dance about the room, that is excellent, and we will in return do you all the good in our power, and that you will soon discover; but new I must depart."

"Will you not first take a spoonful of supper with us?" asked the wife, setting a dish of porridge down on the stool near the window; for the Man of the Mount was so little that he could not reach up to the table. "No, I thank you," said the mannikin, "our king is impatient for my return and it would be a pity to let him wait for the good news I have to tell him." Hereupon the little man bade them farewell and went his way.

From that day forwards, Teller lived in peace and concord with the little people of the Mount. They could see them go in and out of their mounds in daylight, and no one ever did anything to vex them. At length they became so familiar, that they went in and out of Toller's house, just as if it had been their own. Sometimes it happened that they would borrow a pot or a copper-kettle from the kitchen, but always brought it back again, and set it carefully on the same spot from which they had taken it. They also did all the service they could in return. When the spring came, they would come out of their mounds in the night, gather all the stones off the arable land, and lay them in a heap along the furrows. At harvest time they would pick up all the ears of corn, that nothing might be lost to Teller. All this was observed by the farmer, who, when in bed, or when he read his evening prayer, often thanked the Almighty for having given him the Mount-folk for neighbours. At Easter and Whitsuntide, or in the Christmas holidays, he always set a dish of nice milk-porridge for them, as good as it could be made, out on the mound.

Once, after having given birth to a daughter, his wife was so ill that Teller thought she was near her end. He consulted all the cunning people in the district, but no one knew what to prescribe for her recovery. He sat up every night and watched over the sufferer, that he might be at hand to administer to her wants. Once he fell asleep, and on opening his eyes again towards morning, he saw the room full of the Mount-folk: one sat and rocked the baby, another was busy in cleaning the room, a third stood by the pillow of the sick woman and made a drink of some herbs, which he gave his wife. As soon as they observed that Teller was awake, they all ran out of the room; but from that night the poor woman began to mend, and before a fortnight was past, she was able to leave her bed and go about her household work, well and cheerful as before.

Another time, Teller was in trouble for want of money to get his horses shod before he went to the town. He talked the matter over with his wife, and they knew not well what course to adopt. But when they were in bed his wife said: "Art thou asleep, Toller?" "No," he answered, "what is it?" "I think," said she, "there is something the matter with the horses in the stable, they are making such a disturbance." Toller rose, lighted his lantern, and went to the stable, and, on opening the door, found it full of the little Mount-folk. They had made the horses lie down, because the mannikins could not reach up to them. Some were employed in taking off the old shoes, some were filing the heads of the nails, while others were tacking on the new shoes and the next morning, when Teller took his horses to water, he found them shod so beautifully that the best of smiths could not have shed them better. In this manner the Mount-folk and Teller rendered all the good services they could to each other, and many years passed pleasantly. Toller began to grow an old man, his daughter was grown up, and his circumstances were better every year. Instead of the little cottage in which he began the world, he now owned a large and handsome house, and the naked wild heath was converted into fruitful arable land.

One evening just before bed-time, someone knocked at the door, and the Man of the Mount walked in. Teller and his wife looked at him with surprise; for the mannikin was not in his usual dress. He wore on his head a shaggy cap, a woollen kerchief round his throat, and a great sheep-skin cloak covered his body. In his hand he had a stick, and his countenance was very sorrowful. He brought a greeting to Toller from the king, who requested that lie, his wife, and little Inger would come over to them in the Mount that evening, for the king had a matter of importance, about which he wished to talk with him. The tears ran down the little man's cheeks while he said this, and when Toller tried to comfort him, and inquired into the source of his trouble, the Man of the Mount only wept the more, but would not impart the cause of his grief.

Toller, his wife and daughter, then went over to the Mount. On descending into the cave, they found it decorated with bunches of sweet willow, crowfoots, and other flowers, that were to be found on the heath. A large table was spread from one end of the cave to the other. When the peasant and his family entered, they were placed at the head of the table by the side of the king. The little folk also took their places. and began to eat, but they were far from being as cheerful as usual; they sat and sighed and hung down their heads; and it was easy to see that something had gone amiss with them. When the repast was finished, the king said to Toller: "I invited you to come over to us because we all wished to thank you for having been so kind and friendly to us, during the whole time we have been neighbours. But now there are so many churches built in the land, and all of them have such great bells which ring so loud morning and evening, that we can bear it no longer; we are, therefore, going to leave Jutland and pass over to Norway, as the greater number of our people have done long ago. We now wish you farewell, Teller, as we must part."

When the king had said this, all the Mount-folk came and took Teller by the hand, and bade him farewell, and the same to his wife. When they came to Inger, they said: "To you, dear Inger, we will give a remembrance of us, that you may think of the little Mount-people when they are far away." And as they said this, each took up a stone from the ground and threw it into Inger's apron. They left the Mount one by one, with the king leading the way.

Toller and his family remained standing on the Mount as long as they could discern them. They saw the little Trolls wandering over the heath, each with a wallet on his back and a stick in his hand. When they had gone a good part of the way, to where the road leads down to the sea, they all turned round once more, and waved their hands, to say farewell. Then they disappeared, and Toller saw them no more. Sorrowfully he returned to his home.

The next morning, Inger saw that all the small stones the Mount-folk had thrown into her apron shone and sparkled and were real precious stones. Some were blue, others brown, white, and black, and it was the Trolls who had imparted the colour of their eyes to the stones, that Inger might remember them when they were gone; and all the precious stones which we now see, shine and sparkle only because the Mount-folk have given them the colour of their eyes, and it was some of these beautiful precious stones which they once gave to Inger.

THE TROLL'S HAMMER.

THERE was once a great famine in the country; the poor could not procure the necessaries of life, and even the rich suffered great privation. At that time a poor peasant dwelt out on the heath. One day he said to his son, that he could no longer support him, and that he must go out in the world, and provide for himself. Niels, therefore, left home and wandered forth.

Towards evening he found himself in a large forest, and climbed up into a tree, lest the wild beasts might do him harm during the night. When he had slept at out an hour or perhaps more, a little man came running towards the tree. He was hunch-backed, had crooked legs, a long beard, and a red cap on his head. He was pursued by a werwolf, which attacked him just under the tree in which Niels was sitting. The little man began to scream; he hit and scratched, and defended himself as well as he could, but all to no purpose, the werwolf was his master, and would have torn him in pieces, if Niels had not sprung down from the tree, and come to his assistance. As soon as the werwolf saw that he had two to contend with, he was afraid, and fled back into the forest.

The Troll then said to Niels: "Thou hast preserved my life and done me good service; in return I will also give thee something that will be beneficial to thee. See here is a hammer, with which all the smith's work thou doest, no one shall be able to equal. Continue thy way, and things will go better than thou thinkest." When the Troll had spoken these words, he sank into the ground before Niels.

The next day the boy wandered on, until he came in the neighbourhood of the royal palace, and here he engaged himself to a smith.

Now it just happened, that a few days previously a thief had broken into the king's treasury and stolen a large bag of money. All the smiths in the city were, therefore, sent for to the palace, and the king promised that he who could make the best and securest lock, should be appointed court locksmith, and have a considerable reward into the bargain. But the lock must be finished in eight days, and so constructed that it could not be picked by any one.

When the smith, with whom Niels lived, returned home and related this, the boy thought he should like to try whether his hammer really possessed those qualities which the Troll had said. He therefore begged his master to allow him to make a lock and promised that it should be finished by the appointed time. Although the smith had no great opinion of the boy's ability, he, nevertheless, allowed him to make the trial. Niels then requested to have a separate workshop, locked himself in and then began hammering the iron. One day went, and then another, and the master began to be inquisitive; but Niels let no one come in, and the smith was obliged to remain outside, and peep through the keyhole. The work, however, succeeded far better than the boy himself had expected; and, without his really knowing how it came to pass, the lock was finished on the evening of the third day.

The following morning, he went down to his master and asked him for some money. "Yesterday I worked hard," said he, "and today I will make myself merry." Here upon he went out of the city and did not return to the workshop till late in the evening. The next day he did the same and idled away the rest of the week: His master was, consequently, very angry, and threatened to turn him away, unless he finished his work at the appointed time. But Niels told him to be quite easy and engaged that his lock should be the best. When the day arrived, Niels brought his work forth, and carried it up to the palace, and it appeared that his lock was so ingenious and delicately made, that it far excelled all the others. The consequence was, that Niels' master was acknowledged as the most skillful and received the promised office and reward.

The smith was delighted, but he took good care not to confess to anyone who it was that had made the curious lock. He now received one work after another from the king, and let Niels do them all, and he soon became a wealthy man.

In the meantime, the report spread from place to place of the ingenious lock the king had got for his treasury. Travellers came from a great distance to see it, and it happened that a foreign king came also to the palace. When he had examined the work for a long time, he said, that the man who could make such a lock deserved to be honoured and respected. "But however good a smith he may be," added the king, "I have got his master at home." He continued boasting in this manner, till at length the king offered to wager with him which could execute the most skillful piece of workmanship. The smiths were sent for, and the two kings determined, that each smith should make a knife. He who won was to have a considerable reward. The smith related to Niels what had passed and desired him to try whether he could not make as good a knife as he had a lock. Niels promised that he would, although his last work had not benefited him much. The smith was in truth an avaricious man, and treated him so niggardly, that at times he had not enough to eat and drink.

It happened one day, as Niels was gone out to buy steel to make the knife, that he met a man from his own village, and, in the course of conversation, learnt from him that his father went begging from door to door, and was in great want and misery. When Niels heard this, he asked his master for some money to help his father; but his master answered, that he should not have a shilling, before he had made the knife. Hereupon Niels shut himself up in the workshop, worked a whole day, and, as on the former occasion, the knife was made without his knowing how it happened.

When the day arrived on which the work was to be exhibited, Niels dressed himself in his best clothes, and went with his master up to the palace, where the two kings were expecting them. The strange smith first showed his knife. It was so beautiful, and so curiously wrought, that it was a pleasure to look at it; it was, moreover, so sharp and well tempered, that it could cut through a millstone to the very centre, as if it had been only a cheese, and that without the edge being in the least blunted. Niels' knife, on the contrary, looked very poor and common. The king already began to think he had lost his wager, and spoke harshly to the master-smith, when his boy begged leave to examine the stranger's knife a little more closely. After having looked at it for some time, he said: "This is a beautiful piece of workmanship which you have made, and shame on those who would say otherwise; but my master is nevertheless, your superior, as you shall soon experience." Saying this, he took the stranger's knife and split it lengthwise from the point to the handle with his own knife, as easily as one split a twig of willow. The kings could scarcely believe their eyes and the consequence was, that the Danish smith was declared the victor, and got a large bag of money to carry home with him.

When Niels asked for payment, his master refused to give him anything, although he well knew that the poor boy only wanted the money to help his father. Upon this, Niels grew angry, went up to the king, and related the whole story to him, how it was he who had made both the rock and the knife. The master was now called, but he denied everything, and accused Niels of being an idle boy, whom he had taken into his service out of charity and compassion.

"The truth of this story we shall soon find out," said the king, who sided with the master. "Since thou sayest it is thou who hast made this wonderful knife, and thy master says it is he who has done it, I will adjudge each of you to make a sword for me within eight days. He who can make the most perfect one shall be my master-smith but he who loses, shall forfeit his life."

Neils was well satisfied with this agreement. He went home, packed up all his things, and bade his master farewell. The smith was now in great straits and would gladly have made all good again; but Niels appeared not to understand him, and went his way, and engaged with another master, where he cheerfully began to work on the sword.

When the appointed day arrived, they both met at the palace, and the master produced a sword of the most elaborate workmanship that any one could wish to see, besides being inlaid with gold, and set with precious stones. The king was greatly delighted with it.

"Now, little Niels," said he, "what dost then say to this sword?"

"Certainly," answered the boy, "it is not so badly made as one might expect from such a bungler."

"Canst thou show anything like it?" asked the king.

"I believe I can," answered Niels.

"Well, produce thy sword where is it?" said the king.

"I have it in my waistcoat pocket," replied Niels.

Hereupon there was a general laugh, which was increased when they saw the boy take a little packet out of his waistcoat pocket. Niels opened the paper, in which the blade was rolled up like a watch-spring. "Here is my work," said he, "will you just cut the thread, master?"

The smith did it willingly, and in a moment the blade straightened itself and struck him in the face.

Niels took out of his other pocket a hilt of gold and screwed it fast to the blade; then presented the sword to the king; and all present were obliged to confess that they never before had seen such matchless workmanship.

Niels was unanimously declared the victor, and the master was obliged to acknowledge that the boy had made both the lock and the knife.

The king in his indignation would have had the master executed, if the boy had not begged for mercy on the culprit. Niels received a handsome reward from the king, and from that day all the work from the palace was intrusted to him. He took his old father to reside with him and lived in competence and happiness till his death.

THE MAGICIAN'S PUPIL.

THERE was once a peasant who had a son, whom, when of a proper age, his father apprenticed to a trade but the boy, who had no inclination for work, always ran home again to his parents; at this the father was much troubled, not knowing what course to pursue. One day he entered a church, where, after repeating the Lord's Prayer, he said: "To what trade shall I apprentice my son? He runs away from every place."

The clerk, who happened at that moment to be standing behind the altar, hearing the peasant utter these words, called out in answer: "Teach him witchcraft; teach him witchcraft!"

The peasant, who did not see the clerk, thought it was our Lord who gave him this advice, and determined upon following it.

The next day he said to his son, that he should go with him, and he would find him a new situation. After walking a good way into the country, they met with a shepherd tending his flock.

"Where are you going to, good man?" inquired the shepherd.

"I am in search of a master, who can teach my son the black art," answered the peasant. "You may soon find him," said the shepherd "keep straight on and you will come to the greatest wizard that is to be found in all the land." The peasant thanked him for this information and went on. Soon after, he came to a large forest, in the middle of which stood the Wizard's house. He knocked at the door and asked the Troll-man whether he had any inclination to take a boy as a pupil. "Yes," answered the other; "but not for a less term than four years and we will make this agreement, that at the end of that time, you shall come, and if you can find your son, he shall belong to you, but should you not be able to discover him, he must remain in my house, and serve me for the rest of his life."

The peasant agreed to these conditions and returned home alone. At the end of a week he began to look for his son's return; thinking that in this, as in all former cases, he would run away from his master. But he did not come back, and his mother began to cry, and say her husband had not acted rightly in giving their child into the power of the evil one, and that they should never see him more.

After four years had elapsed the peasant set out on a journey to the magician's, according to their agreement. A little before he reached the forest, he met the same shepherd, who instructed him how to act so as to get his son back. "When you get there," said he, "you must at night keep your eyes constantly turned towards the fireplace, and take care not to fall asleep, for then the Troll-man will convey you back to your own house, and afterwards say you did not come at the appointed time. Tomorrow you will see three dogs in the yard, eating milk-porridge out of a dish. The middle one is your son, and he is the one you must choose."

The peasant thanked the shepherd for his information and bade him farewell.

When he entered the house of the magician, everything took place as the shepherd had said. He was conducted into the yard, where he saw three dogs. Two of them were handsome with smooth skins, but the third was lean and looked ill. When the peasant patted the dogs, the two handsome ones growled at him, but the lean one, on the contrary, wagged his tail. "Canst then now tell me which of these three dogs is thy son?" said the Troll-man; "if so thou canst take him with thee; if not, he belongs to me."

"Well then I will choose the one that appears the most friendly," answered the peasant; "although he looks less handsome than the others." "That is a sensible choice," said the Troll-man; "he knew what he was about who gave thee that advice."

The peasant was then allowed to take his son home with him. So, putting a cord round his neck, he went his way, bewailing that his son was changed into a dog. "Oh! why are you bewailing so?" asked the shepherd as he came out of the forest, "it appears to me you have not been so very unlucky."

When he had gone a little way, the dog said to him: "Now you shall see that my learning has been of some use to me. I will soon change myself into a little tiny dog, and then you must sell me to those who are coming past." The dog did as he said and became a beautiful little creature. Soon after a carriage came rolling along with some great folks in it. When they saw the beautiful little dog that ran playing along the road, and heard that, it was for sale, they bought it of the peasant for a considerable sum, and at the same moment the son changed his father into a hare, which he caused to run across the read, while he was taken up by those who had bought him. When they saw the hare, they set the dog after it, and scarcely had they done so, than both hare and dog ran into the wood and disappeared. Now the boy changed himself again, and this time both he and his father assumed human forms. The old man began cutting twigs and his son helped him. When the people in the carriage missed the little dog, they got out to seek after it, and asked the old man and his son if they had seen anything of a little dog that had run away. The boy directed them further into the wood, and he and his father returned home, and lived well on the money they had received by selling the dog.

When all the money was spent, both father and son resolved upon going out again in search of adventures. "Now I will turn myself into a boar," said the youth, "and you must put a cord round my leg and take me to Horsens market for sale; but remember to throw the cord over my right ear at the moment you sell me, and then I shall be home again as soon as you."

The peasant did as his son directed him and went to market; but he set so high a price on the boar, that no one would buy it, so he continued standing in the market till the afternoon was far advanced. At length there came an old man who bought the boar of him. This was no other than the magician, who, angry that the father had got back his son, had never ceased seeking after them from the time they had left his house. When the peasant had sold his boar, he threw the cord over its right ear as the lad had told him, and in the same moment the animal vanished; and when he reached his own door he again saw his son sitting at the table.

They now lived a pleasant merry life until all the money was spent, and then again set out on fresh adventures. This time the son changed himself into a bull, first reminding his father to throw the rope over his right ear as soon as he was sold. At the market he met with the same old man, and soon came to an agreement with him about the price of the bull. While they were drinking a glass together in the alehouse, the father threw the rope over the bull's right horn, and when the magician went to fetch his purchase it had vanished, and the peasant upon reaching home again found his son sitting by his mother at the table. The third time the lad turned himself into a horse, and the magician was again in the market and bought him. "Thou hast already tricked me twice, said he to the peasant; but it shall not happen again." Before he paid down the money, he hired a stable and fastened the horse in, so that it was impossible for the peasant to throw the rein over the animal's right ear. The old man, nevertheless, returned home, in the hope that this time also he should find his son; but he was disappointed, for no lad was there. The magician in the meantime mounted the horse and rode off. He well knew whom he had bought and determined that the boy should pay with his life the deception he had practised upon him. He led the horse through swamps and pools, and galloped at a pace that, had he long continued it, he must have ridden the animal to death; but the horse was a hard trotter, and the magician being old he at last found he had got his master, and was therefore obliged to ride home.

When he arrived at his house, he put a magic bridle on the horse and shut him in a dark stable without giving him anything either to eat or drink. When some time had elapsed, he said to the servant-maid: "Go out and see how the horse is." When the girl came into the stable the metamorphosed boy (who had been the girl's sweetheart while he was in the Troll's house) began to moan piteously and begged her to give him a pail of water. She did so, and on her return told her master that the horse was well. Some time after he again desired her to go out and see if the horse were not yet dead. When she entered the stable the poor animal begged her to loosen the rein and the girths, which were strapped so tight that he could hardly draw breath. The girl did as she was requested, and no sooner was it done than the boy changed himself into a hare and ran out of the stable. The magician, who was sitting in the window, was immediately aware of what had happened on seeing the hare go springing across the yard, and, instantly changing himself into a dog, went in pursuit of it. When they had run many miles over cornfields and meadows, the boy's strength began to fail, and the magician gained more and more upon him. The hare then changed itself into a dove, but the magician as quickly turned himself into a hawk and pursued him afresh.

In this manner, they flew towards a palace where a princess was sitting at a window. When she saw a hawk in chase of a dove, she opened the window, and immediately the dove flew into the room, and then changed itself into a gold ring. The magician now became a prince and went into the apartment for the purpose of catching the dove. When he could not find it, he asked permission to see her gold rings. The princess showed them to him but let one fall into the fire. The Troll-man instantly drew it out, in doing which be burnt his fingers, and was obliged to let it fall on the floor. The boy now knew of no better course than to change himself into a grain of corn.

At the same moment the magician became a hen, in order to eat the corn, but scarcely had he done so than the boy became a hawk and killed him.

He then went to the forest, fetched all the magician's gold and silver, and from that day lived in wealth and happiness with his parents.

TEMPTATIONS.

IN Vinding, near Veile, lived once a poor cottager, who went out as day labourer; his son was employed by the priest at Skjærup to run on errands, for which he received his board and lodging. One day the boy was sent with a letter for the priest at Veile. It was in the middle of summer, and the weather was very hot; when he had walked some distance, he became tired and drowsy, and lay down to sleep. On awaking he saw a willow, from the roots of which the water had washed away all the earth, whereby the tree was on the point of perishing. "I am but little, it is true," said John, for such was the boy's name, "and can do but little, still I can help thee." He then began to throw mould on the bare roots and ceased not till they were quite covered and protected. When he had finished, he heard a soft voice proceeding from the tree, which said to him: "Thou shalt not have rendered me this good service for nothing; cut a pipe from my branches, and everything for which thou blowest shall befall thee."

Although the boy did not give much credit to this, he, nevertheless, cut off a twig for a pipe. "As such a fine promise has been made me, thought he to himself, I will wish that I could blow myself into a good situation by Michaelmas, that I might be of some use to my poor old father." He blew, but saw nothing, and then, putting his pipe in his pocket, hurried on to make up for the time he had loitered away at the willow-tree. Not long after he found a pocket-book full of money lying in the road. Now John by keeping it, could at once have relieved both his own and his father' s necessities, but such a thought never entered his mind, on the contrary, he ran back to the town, inquired of all that he met, whether they had not lost a pocket-book. At length there came a horseman galloping along the road, and when John also asked him the stranger replied that he had that morning dropped his pocket-book on his way from home, at the same time giving a description of it.

John delivered the pocket-book to him, and the horse man, who was a proprietor from Ostedgaard, near Fredericia, was so gratified, that he immediately gave the boy a handsome reward, and asked him if he would like to enter his service. "Yes, I should indeed," answered John, quite pleased at the thought. He then parted from the gentle man with many thanks for his kindness, after having agreed between them that John should come down to Osted at Michaelmas. He then executed his errand for the priest, and felt convinced, that it was alone owing to the pipe that he had met with such a lucky adventure he therefore concealed it carefully and let no one know anything of the matter.

Now this gentleman was an adept in the black art and had only offered to take the lad into his service that he might see how far his honesty would be proof against the temptations into which he purposed to lead him.

At the appointed time John went to Ostedgaard, and was summoned by the master, who inquired of him what he could do. "I am not fit for much," said John, as I am so little; but I will do my best at all times to perform whatever my good master requires of me. "That is well, with that I am contented," answered the master; I have twelve hares, these thou must take to the wood every morning, and if thou bringest back the full number every evening, I will give thee house and home in remuneration; but if thou allowest them to run away, thou wilt have a reckoning to settle with me." "I will do my best," answered John.

The next morning his master came down to the inclosure and counted the hares. As soon as he opened the door and gave the animals their liberty, away they all ran, one to the east, another to the west, and John remained standing alone; he was not, however, so disheartened as might be imagined; for he had his willow pipe in his pocket. As soon, therefore as he came into a lonely part of the wood, he took out his pipe and began to blow, and no sooner had he put it to his mouth, than all the twelve hares came running and assembled round him. As John now felt he could rely on the virtues of his pipe, he let them all go again, and passed his time in amusing himself. In the evening he took out his pipe again, and as he walked up to the manor continued blowing it. All the hares then came forth and followed him one by one. The master was standing at the gate, to see what would take place. He could not recover from his astonishment, when he saw the little herd-boy blowing his pipe as he approached the house, and all the hares following him as gently and quietly as if it were a flock of sheep he was driving home. "Thou art more clever than thou appearest," said the master; "the number is right, go in and get some food; for today thou hast done a good piece of work: we shall now see whether thou art as fortunate tomorrow."

The next day everything passed in exactly the same manner. As soon as the inclosure was opened, all the hares ran out in different directions, and the boy let them enjoy their liberty, as he now felt certain that he could bring them back whenever he wished. But this time his master had prepared a harder trial for him.

At noon he desired his daughter to disguise herself in a peasant's dress, and to go and ask the boy to give her a bare. The young maiden was so beautiful that he did not think John could refuse her request.

When the daughter had thus disguised herself, she went into the field and began talking to John, asking him what he was doing there. "I am taking care of hares," answered the boy.

"What has become of thy hares?" said the maiden, "I see nothing of them." "Oh, they are only gone a little way into the wood," said he; "but as soon as I call them, they will all come back again." When the young girl pretended to doubt this, he blew on his pipe, and instantly all the twelve came running towards him. She now begged and prayed him to give her one of them. The boy at first refused, but as she was very importunate, he at length told her that she should have a hare for a kiss. In short, the maiden got the bare, and carried it up to the manor: but when John thought she must be near home, he blew on his pipe, and immediately the hare came bounding back to him, and so he brought all the twelve home that evening.

On the third day, the lord of Osted was determined to try whether he could not trick the boy. He therefore dressed himself like a peasant and went in search of John. When they had conversed some time, he requested him to call his hares together, and when they came, he wished to purchase one of them, but the boy answered, that he did not dare to sell what did not belong to him.

As the lord continued to entreat him most urgently, John promised him a bare, if he would give him the ring that was on his finger. The lord, it must be observed, had forgotten to take off his ring when he put on the peasant's dress, and now found that he was known. He, nevertheless, gave the boy the ring and got one of the hares. When he had nearly reached Osted, John blew on his pipe, and, although the master held the hare as firmly as he could, it got away and ran back, just as on the preceding day. When the master found he could not get the better of the boy by fair means, he had recourse to the black art, and ascertained that the willow pipe was the cause of the hares always obeying John.

When the boy returned on the fourth evening, his master gave him plenty of food and strong drink, and being unaccustomed to such things, he soon fell asleep, so that it was no difficult matter to steal his pipe from him. The next day the hares were turned out as usual; but this time John could not bring them back; he, consequently, durst not show himself at Osted, but continued wandering about the wood, crying and sobbing. His master had now gained his point. When it began to grow dark, he went to seek for John, and asked him why he remained away so long that evening. John scarcely ventured to confess his misfortune; but as his master continued urging him to tell him, he at length acknowledged that the hares had run away, and that it was not in his power to get them back again.

The lord took pity on him and told him to return home, for the loss was not very great. "A house and home I see thou wilt not get at present," said he as they walked back, "unless thou canst fulfil a condition, which I will propose tomorrow." John was glad to hear these words; for his sorrow was less at losing what his master had promised him than at forfeiting his benefactor's favour and being turned out of the house. The next day there were guests at Ostedgaard, and when they were all assembled, the lord of the manor, calling John, told him he should have what had been promised him, if he could relate a bagful of untruths. "No," replied John, to untruths I have never been addicted; but, if my good master pleases, I can, perhaps, tell him a bagful of truths."

"Well then," said his master, "here is a bag, and now begin thy story."

John began to recite about his lot as a little boy, how he had passed all his life in indigence and misery. Then he recited about his adventure with the willow-tree, how he had obtained his pipe, and had afterwards found the pocket book, which was the cause of his master taking him into his service. Lastly, he recited how a maiden had come to him and given him a kiss for a hare. As he was continuing, his master called out (as he did not wish his own fruitless attempt should be known): "Stop, John, thou hast kept thy word—the bag is full." He then let the boy go out of the room and told his guests how faithfully and honourably John had always conducted himself, adding, that it was not possible to seduce him to deceive or to tell an untruth."

"Still I think it is to be done," said the proprietor of Nebbegaard. "I will answer for it that he will not be able to withstand, if he is seriously tempted."

His host felt offended by this doubting, and immediately offered to lay as large a wager as his neighbour pleased, that he could not get John either to deceive him or to tell an untruth. The challenge was accepted, and their estates were pledged for and against the boy.

The proprietor of Nebbegaard wrote a letter to his daughter, in which he explained to her what had taken place, and how important it was for him to win the wager. He desired her, therefore, to entertain John in the best manner possible and to appear as affable and friendly towards him as she could, with the view of prevailing on him to give her the horse on which he rode.

The lad was then sent to Nebbegaard with this letter. His master lent him a horse, that he might the more expeditiously perform his errand; but warned him not to ride too fast, or by any means to lose the horse, which was the finest and most valuable animal he had in his stable. John promised to follow his instructions and rode away. When he had ridden a short way from home, he dismounted, and led the horse, in order to comply, as much as possible, with his master's wish. In this manner, he proceeded but slowly, and it was evening before he reached Nebbegaard.

When the young lady had read her father's letter, she sent for John, and behaved in the kindest and most friendly manner towards him. The maiden was very handsome and treated the young lad as her equal in condition and rank. She entertained him sumptuously and said not a word about the horse till he had drunk much more than he could bear. Without knowing what he did, John promised (after she had long entreated him in vain) that he would give her the horse, and the young girl behaved yet more friendly towards him; so, the next morning John finding he had no longer a horse, took the saddle and bridle and wandered back to Ostedgaard. As he walked along it struck him how wrongly he had acted, and he began to repent bitterly of what he had done. "What shall I now say when I reach home, and my master finds that the horse is gone?" said he to himself, as he hung the saddle and bridle on the hedge. "'Well, John,' master will say, 'hast thou executed my errand?' Then I shall answer, 'Yes.' But what then is become of my horse, with which I entrusted thee?' Then I will say, 'that I met a band of robbers on the way, and they took the horse from me.' No, that will never do," continued he, "never have I told a lie yet, and I will not do it now." Not long after another thought rose to his mind: "I can say that the horse fell, and that I buried it in a ditch. That won't do either—Lord knows what I, poor fellow, had best do." When he had gone on a little further, he resolved within himself that he would say that the horse had run away and had shaken off his saddle and bridle.

Long before he reached Ostedgaard, the guests saw him approaching with the saddle on his head and the bridle on his arm.

"Here comes our truthful boy," exclaimed the proprietor of Nebbegaard, "look only how slowly he approaches; who do you now think has won the wager?"

The lord of Osted had already recognised John and was highly incensed at seeing him return without the horse. As soon as the boy entered the house, he was called up where all the guests were assembled, and his master said: "Well, John, hast thou executed my errand?" "Yes, I have, gracious master," answered the boy, trembling with fear. "What then is become of my good horse, which I ordered thee to take such care of?"

John did not dare to meet the look of his master, but cast his eyes on the ground and said, in a whimpering voice:—

> "Dainty the fare, sweet was the mead,
>   The lady's arm was soft and round,
>   The sparkling cup my senses drown'd,
>   And thus I lost my master's steed."

When he had recited this, his master embraced him in his joy, and exclaimed: "See now! I knew well enough that he would speak the truth. Which of us two has won the wager?"

John did not comprehend the meaning of these words, and continued sorrowful, till his master said to him "Be of good heart, my boy! as thou hast always kept to truth and right, I will give thee both house and land, and when thou art old enough, I will give thee my daughter to wife."

The following day John was allowed to fetch his old father to live with him, and some years after he was married to his master's daughter.

THE GIRL CLAD IN MOUSE-SKIN.[3]

THERE was once a nobleman who had an only daughter, whom he placed in a mount, there to remain as long as there was war in the country. The father had secretly caused a room to be built for her in the mount, and had laid in a stock of provisions, and wood enough to last for seven years and she was not to come out until he fetched her; but if at the end of seven years he did not come for her, she might conclude that he was dead, and might then leave the mount. Her little dog was the only companion she was to have. The father kissed her when they parted, and comforted her by saying, that he had lodged her in a secure place, while the dissolute soldiery was spread over the land. He then collected all his retainers and went forth to fight for his country.

The young damsel occupied herself in the mount with spinning, weaving, and sewing; and thus, one year passed after another. She made a great number of fine clothes, some of which were embroidered with gold, and others with silver; but when she had no longer anything to spin or employ her, the time began to be tedious. Her stock of food was also nearly exhausted, and she was fearful that her father would not return. As the time that she was to remain in the mount had nearly expired, and he had not come to fetch her, she concluded that he was dead. She now began to dig her way out of the mount, but this was a very slow work, and no easy task for her.

In the meantime all her provisions were consumed, but the mount was full of mice, and her little dog destroyed a great many every day; these she skinned, roasted, and ate the meat, and gave the bones to her little dog; but she stitched all the skins together, and made herself a cloak or garment, which was so large, that she could quite wrap herself up in it. Every day she laboured at the

---

³ Molbech, Udval te Eventr, etc., Kiob. 1843.

aperture, and at length succeeded so far as to be able once more to see the light of day. When she had made an opening large enough, she went out, accompanied by her little faithful dog. On finding herself on the outside, she knelt down, and returned thanks for her deliverance. She then closed up the opening, and the mouseskins that remained over she hung round the mount upon little sticks, which she stuck in the earth.

She now left the hill with her little dog, and went through the wood, and there was much she found changed in the seven years she had lived underground. She had her silver and her gold dresses on, and over them she wore the mouseskin cloak, which quite covered her, so that she had more the appearance of a poor man's child than a young lady of rank. At the first house she came to, she inquired who lived at the manor. She was told it was the young lord, who had inherited it after the death of the former proprietor. "How then did he die?" asked she, hardly able to conceal her feelings. She received for answer, that he was a brave soldier, and drove the enemy out of the country, but in the last battle that was fought he was killed. That his only child was a daughter who had been carried off before that time, and no one had since ever heard anything of her.

The young maiden then asked, if they could tell her where she could be employed, as she wanted work. "Our young master is soon to be married," said the people; "his bride, with her father and mother, are arrived at the mansion to make preparations for the wedding; if you only go up there, you may be sure they will find something for you to do."

The young girl in the mouseskin dress then went up to her late father's abode, and her little dog was so happy; for it knew the place again; but its mistress wept with grief, as she humbly knocked at the door. When the people heard that she wished to be employed, they gladly engaged her, and set her to sweep the yard, and the steps, and do other menial kinds of work. But she did everything willingly and well, so that everybody was satisfied with her. Many as they passed her were amused at the sight of her mouseskin dress, but no one could get a glimpse of her face for she wore along hood which hung down and completely concealed it, and this she never would throw aside.

The day before the wedding the bride sent for her and told her that she had a great favour to ask: "Thou art of the same height as I am," said she; "thou must tomorrow put on my bridal dress and veil, and drive to the church, and be wedded to the bridegroom, instead of me." The young girl could not imagine why the other objected to be wedded to the handsome young lord. The bride then told her, that there was another lover, to whom she had previously betrothed herself; but that her parents wanted to force her to marry this rich young lord that she was afraid of disobeying them, but that she had agreed with her first beloved, that on the wedding day she would elope with him. This she could not do, if she were wedded at the altar to another; but if she sent someone in her place, everything might end well. The young maiden promised to do all that the bride requested of her.

The next day the bride was attired in the most costly dress, and all the people in the house came into her chamber to look at her; at length she said "Now call that poor young girl that sweeps the yard, and let her also see me." The girl in the mousekin dress came up accordingly, and when they were alone together, the bride locked the door, dressed her in the beautiful clothes, with the bridal veil over her head, and then wrapped herself in the young girl's large mouseskin cloak.

The late lord's daughter was then conducted to a chariot, in which was the bridegroom, and they drove to church together, accompanied by all the bridal guests. On the road they passed the mount, where she had lived so long concealed. She sighed beneath her veil, and said:—

> "Yonder stands yet every pin,
>   With every little mouse's skin,
>   Where seven long years I pined in sadness
>   In the dark mount and knew no gladness."

"What sayest thou, dearest of my heart?" asked the bride groom. "Oh! I am only talking a little to myself," answered the bride.

When she entered the church, she saw the portraits of her parents suspended on each side of the altar; but it appeared to her as if they turned from her, as she wept beneath her veil while gazing on them; she then said:—

> "Turn, turn again, ye pictures dear; dear father and mother, turn again;"

and then the pictures turned again. "What sayest thou, my dear bride?" asked the bridegroom. "Oh! I am only talking a little to myself," answered she again. They were then wedded in the church, the young lord put a ring upon her finger, and they drove home. As soon as the bride alighted from the carriage she hurried up into the lady's chamber, as they had agreed, where they changed dresses once more, but the wedding-ring which she had on her finger she kept. When standing in her mouseskin dress again among all the servants, little did anyone think that she had just before stood at the altar as a bride.

In the evening there was dancing, and the young lord danced with her who he thought was his bride but when he took her hand, he said: "Where is the ring I put on your finger in the church?" The bride was at first embarrassed but said quickly: "I took it off and left it in my chamber, but now I will run and fetch it." She then ran out of the room, called the real bride, and demanded the ring. "No," answered the maiden, "the ring I will not part with, it belongs to the hand that was given away at the altar. But I will go with you to the door, then you can call him, and we will both stand in the passage; when he comes, we will extinguish the light that is there, and I will stretch forth my hand in at the door, so that he can see the ring." Thus, it was arranged.

The bridegroom was standing near the door, when the bride called him into the passage, and said: "See here is the ring." At the same moment as the one damsel extinguished the light, the other stretched forth her hand with the ring.

But the bridegroom was not satisfied with merely seeing the ring, he seized the hand, and drew the young girl into the room, and then, to his astonishment, saw it was the damsel in the mouseskin dress. All the guests flocked round them and were eager to know how it had all happened.

She then threw off her mouseskin dress, and stood clad in her beautiful gold embroidery, and was more lovely to look at than the other bride. Everyone was impatient to hear her story; and she was obliged to relate to them, how long she had remained concealed in the mount, and that her father had been their former lord. The little dog was fetched from her miserable room, and many of the neighbours knew it again.

Hereupon there was great joy and wonder. Everybody revered her father, who had fought so bravely for his country, and all were unanimous that the estate belonged to her. Her sorrow was now turned into joy, and as she wished everyone to be as happy as herself, she bestowed land and money on the other bride, that she might marry the man of her choice, to whom she had secretly given her heart The parents were contented with this arrangement, and now the marriage feast was gay, when the young lord danced with his true bride, to whom he had been wedded in the church, and given the ring.

THE OUTLAW.

AT Palsgaard, in the district of Bjerge, lived once a knight, whose name was Eisten Brink. He was addicted to the belief in supernatural agency, and kept an astrologer in his house, that he might foretell him his fate. As Eisten had been many years a widower, he resolved to marry again, and with that object courted the daughter of Jens Grib of Barritskov. Although the young maiden was not very favourably inclined towards her old suitor, her father forced her to give the consenting "Yes" to his proposals.

Two nights before the wedding was to take place, Eisten went up to the Astrologer's tower, and requested him to foretell what his fate would be in the married state.

The Astrologer took out his instruments, and after having for some time consulted the heavens, he told the knight, "that there always appeared a little black spot upon his star, which signified some secret, and with this he must become acquainted before he could possibly foretell his future."

At first Eisten would divulge nothing; but as the Astrologer refused to proceed before he made a full confession, the knight was at last obliged to acknowledge, that Palsgaard had unjustly come into his possession in the following manner. His brother-in-law, a knight named Palle, had, many years ago, made him the superintendent of the castle, and, at the same time, committed to his care his little son, while he went to join in the war. A few years after this, Eisten received intelligence of Falle's death, and a year later his son also disappeared one day, when he had been seen playing near the lake. The people in the neighbourhood believed that the boy had fallen into the water and been drowned; but the truth was, that Eisten Brink had got an old woman to kidnap the child, and conceal him, so that he might be no impediment in the way of his becoming master of Palsgaard.

When Eisten had related this tale, the Astrologer asked him, if he had never since heard what had become of Palle's son. "Yes," replied the knight, "old

Trude (so the woman was called) sent him first to Sleswig, to live with a sister of hers, but at her death he returned to Trude, and she got him placed as huntsman to my future father-in-law."

"And is be there now?" asked the Astrologer.

"No, that he is not; for a day or two ago, as Grib observed that Abel was paying too much attention to Inger, who is to be my wife tomorrow, he turned him out of doors, and forbade him ever to appear again at Barritskov."

When the Astrologer had heard all he wished to know, he predicted much happiness to Eisten in the married state. The next day the knight, richly attired, and attended by a numerous retinue, rode over to Jens Grib's at Barritskov. Jens immediately told his son-in-law in confidence, that Abel, although forbidden the house and grounds, was still lingering about, and that Inger did not appear to be unfavourably disposed towards him. He therefore advised Eisten to have all his eyes about him when they were married, and to be cautious whom he admitted to Palsgaard Eisten smiled at this warning and thought that he could very well manage matters.

In the afternoon of that day, he rode down to Rosenvold, or Staxesvold, as it was then called. This place belonged at that time to a noted freebooter who roamed about in Middlefart Sound and plundered all the vessels he could master. Eisten, through good words and good pay, got a promise that two of the freebooters would waylay and murder Abel, whom they knew by sight, having often met him, as Jens Grib's wood reached down to theirs. They agreed to do their work the following night, so that the knight should never more be troubled with the hunts man. With regard to Abel, Jens Grib's suspicions were well founded. Inger and he had been attached to each other for some time, long, in fact, before Eisten thought of becoming her suitor. The young lover was therefore much grieved at finding himself suddenly dismissed from Barritskov and knew not how to find an opportunity of speaking to Inger.

In his distress, he went in the evening down to the wood, where old Trude, his foster-mother, lived. He confided to her his secret and asked her what course she thought he had best pursue. After they had had some conversation together, the old woman advised him to accompany her into the wood, to a mount in which lived a Troll, and if he could be brought to interest himself in the matter, Abel need have no fear, either for the father or lover of Inger. The young huntsman felt no great inclination to follow this advice, yet what else could he do? He at length consented, and they set out together, taking the road that led to the Troll's Mount.

The real cause why Trude was desirous of inducing Abel to go with her to the Troll was, that she had sold herself to him, body and soul, after a certain period, unless she could find another willing to enter into the same conditions. This period expire d on the very evening of Abel's visit, and the wicked woman resolved in her evil heart to save herself by the sacrifice of her foster-son. When they came to the spot the old woman began to summon forth the Troll. She made a circle of human bones about the hill, within which she placed herself and Abel. A great noise was then heard around them; the mount rose on four pillars of fire, and the Troll appeared.

The woman made known her errand, and presented Abel to him. The Troll was just laying hold of the young man, when a loud cry was heard in the wood, and the Astrologer from Palsgaard rushed towards Abel, but could not enter the circle which the crone had made. He cried again with all his might: "This boy is mine, take him not from me, he is my only son."

To this appeal the Troll gave little heed, and it would have fared ill with the huntsman, had not the Astrologer again cried with a powerful voice: "In the name of our Lord, I conjure you to spare my son!" No sooner had he uttered these words, than the Troll gave a horrible scream, and, seizing old Trude round the waist, disappeared with her in the mount, which immediately closed upon them and sank down again; but Abel remained behind and was saved.

The Astrologer was no other than the old knight Palle, the brother-in-law of Eisten Brink. He had been outlawed for having joined the king's enemies, hence the reason of his living in concealment at Palsgaard. No sooner had Eisten informed him how he had acted towards his son than he went down to Trude's cottage. Not finding her at home, he wandered into the wood, where he fortunately came to the Troll's Mount, just as Abel was in the greatest danger. When he had made himself known to his son, and they had embraced each other, and thanked God for their happy deliverance, they consulted together as to the course they should pursue, then lay down in the wood to sleep.

That same night the two freebooters left Staxesvold in quest of Abel, as had been agreed between them and Eisten Brink. They first took the road to old

Trude's house, then proceeded further along the same path which the Astrologer had taken just before. On the same day, it happened that the king had been out hunting from a neighbouring manor. He had found a white hind, and pursued it throughout the day, over hill and through dale, until it reached the wood of Palsgaard. He thus became separated from his followers, and as the evening was drawing on, he could neither find his way out of the wood, nor any path through it. He rode about for some time at a venture, when the voices of Abel and his father talking together attracted his attention. He went in the direction of the sound and came to the spot where they had lain down to rest.

Here he was met by the freebooters, who, believing they had found the man they were in search of, entered into discourse with the king, who did not dream of any mischief. Abel looked up on hearing voices and saw one of the miscreants draw forth a knife and steal softly behind the king. He immediately saw that murder was intended, and sprang up, exclaiming: "Defend yourself, sir! for your life is threatened."

Old Palle rushed to the assistance of his son, and it cost them but little trouble to overpower the two freebooters. One was killed in the fray, the other threw away his weapon and begged for mercy. The king ordered him immediately to confess what inducement he had for making this murderous attack; when the assassin, without reserve, acknowledged how Eisten had instigated them to murder Abel.

The king now turned to the Astrologer and asked him who he was. The old man laid his sword at the king's feet, and said: "Kneel down with me, my son, for you stand before Denmark's king." Hereupon he related his history, and also the manner in which Eisten Brink had acted towards him and his son Abel.

The king pardoned him; and when he heard that Eisten's wedding was to be celebrated at Barritskov on the following day, he determined on being present at the festival, taking with him the captured robber. Palle and his son also accompanied him to the castle.

At Barritskov all was mirth and glee; the bridemaids were adorning Inger and twining the bridal wreath in her hair. Jens Grib was busied in receiving the congratulations of his neighbours. But Eisten had not yet made his appearance; he was sitting alone in his chamber, impatiently waiting to hear tidings from the two assassins, who had undertaken to murder Abel.

At once he thought he heard a great and unusual noise in the castle-yard. He approached the door to ascertain the cause, when his future father-in-law burst into the room with the intelligence, that the king had arrived at the castle, in company with Abel, the Astrologer, and a prisoner.

Eisten Brink could scarcely believe his own ears, but still more astounded was he upon finding that the king had suspended all the festivities and commanded everyone to meet him in the knights' hall.

Here the king related to the astonished company how Eisten had acted towards his brother-in-law, the old Palle, and requested the assembled guests to pass judgment upon such a criminal.

Eisten was deprived of his honours. Palle was restored to his power and dignity; but the best of all was, that Abel was wedded to Inger, and lived with her many years in splendour and felicity.

KIELD;
OR, THE FOUNDING OF THE CHURCH AT VARDE.

TO the south of Varde, in the direction of Ribe, are to be seen two half-ruined barrows, called the Robbers' Cellars where it was supposed a band of robbers once had their resort. At that time, it was hardly possible for travellers to pass the road without being attacked and plundered. Carriers and hucksters in particular were the greatest sufferers; and it was the more difficult for the authorities to track out the gang, as they had lurking places in Gellerup and other villages in the neighbourhood.

Late one evening, a young man arrived at Endrupholm, an old manor-house near Varde. He begged permission to remain there the night, as he had been pursued by robbers who were lying in wait for him, so that he thought it would not be advisable to continue his journey that night. He related that he had been attacked on the heath, and that his horse had fallen over a rope stretched across the road. When the horse had fallen, he had escaped on foot, and had, with the greatest difficulty, reached Endrupholm.

The proprietor and his daughter received the stranger with much courtesy, and endeavoured, by every attention in their power, to efface the unpleasant impression which this rencontre with the robbers had occasioned. This was rendered the more easy on the father's part, as the stranger, in the course of conversation, displayed the delicacy and tact of a cultivated and refined mind; and on that of the daughter, because he was handsome, and at the very first moment of his addressing her, had done his best to express the admiration her youth and beauty excited in him. He related that he was the son of a gentleman named Kield, who lived on the other side of Kolding, and that he had been travelling all the summer about the country for amusement. The following day passed, but the stranger still remained at Endrupholm, the inmates of which found more and more pleasure in his society. He was a willing participator in the knight's hunting and card-parties, and his presence gave a variety to the daughter's monotonous life: she listened with eager attention to all be related of the different towns and countries he had visited and blushed at the praises and flattery he whispered in her ear.

A month was thus passed by Kield at the mansion; each day he fixed for his departure, yet was his journey as constantly postponed, through the persuasions and entreaties of his host. When he at length departed, he was betrothed with the young maiden. He quitted the mansion, to the great regret of its master and his daughter; but on taking leave, promised soon to return. He would in the meantime inform his family of the engagement he had made, and, if possible, persuade his father to accompany him back. His absence appeared to the inmates of Endrupholm both long and tedious. When he at length returned, he was received with open arms. He brought not only his father's consent, but many kind messages from his whole family, and excuses from his father, who was suffering from an illness that prevented him from accompanying his son to Endrupholm.

The wedding of the young people was settled to take place in the spring. In the meantime, Kield remained at the mansion, and daily became dearer both to the father and the daughter. The father acknowledged that he had never seen his equal in all that related to the chase, although he himself was an able huntsman. Kield appeared to have a strong inclination for field sports and passed more of his time either down in the moors, or in the forest, than was agreeable to his bride, and was not to be withheld either by her entreaties or the fear of the robbers, who had never before committed such depredations as at that time.

One day Kield, as usual, went to the chase, and the twilight had set in before his return. The young damsel's fears increased every minute. She at length prevailed on her father, who had not for some time been able to indulge in his favourite amusement, owing to a fall from his horse, to go out in search of him.

The old man went, and long wandered about in the forest, but saw nothing of the object of his search. On a sudden he heard his name mentioned by some person not far from him. He listened and saw two figures approach from a copse which had till that moment screened them from him. Cautiously be concealed himself behind a bush to be unobserved by the strangers, who continued talking. What the old man overheard made his hair stand on end. He did not doubt that he was in the neighbourhood of the robbers' lurking place but determined quietly to await the result.

In a few minutes the speakers separated. The one disappeared behind a bank on the high road; the other, who, as far as the light allowed him to see, was an old woman, passed the spot where he stood, and entered the copse. On reaching a thickly-wooded grave-mound, she stood for a moment still, as if to look on all sides. She then, apparently with little exertion, removed a large stone that lay at the foot of the mound and crept in through a hole which it had served to conceal, then from within drew back the stone to its former place.

The old man instantly formed his resolution; he drew his sword, lifted the stone, and followed the woman. On passing through the hole his foot struck against a narrow steep staircase, down which he crept as softly as possible. The hole became wider by degrees, and when he again stood on the earth, he found himself in a capacious cellar formed of large unhewn blocks of stone, the gray walls of which were lighted up by two torches. Scattered about the cave lay a quantity of clothes and weapons. A long table was covered with provisions and full bottles. Under the ceiling or roof hung a large bell, which was so contrived that it sounded whenever anyone drove or rode on the road above. At the time the master from Endrupholm visited the cave there was, fortunately for him, no one there but the old woman, who, without suspecting it, had been his guide. She was busy in the passage that led under the road to the other grave-mound on the opposite side of the road, and had, therefore, not heard anything of the noise which his entrance must have occasioned. When she came back, he saw, by the slow and cautious manner in which she walked, and by the way in which she stretched out her hands before her, that she was blind.

After he had for a few minutes surveyed with fear and curiosity what he saw before him, he heard on a sudden a noise over his head. The bell in the roof rang, and the old woman gave a laugh of satisfaction, and mumbled to herself, "Here they come. I wonder what they will bring with them tonight."

In the greatest alarm at being discovered, the old man looked about for a place of concealment, and, in the same moment that the stone above was being raised, crept under a large bed which stood in one corner of the cave. He had scarcely done so when he heard the noise of many voices, and eight or ten persons came down the stairs. One of them carried in his arms the body of a young female. "Here, old mother," cried he, "I bring thee our prize for tonight. It is the handsomest woman I ever beheld; I could have broken Jacob's head for stabbing her. If I had only been in time, she should have lived and been my wife; now all that is left to do is to strip her and bury her by the side of the others."

While the robber thus spoke some of the gang stripped the corpse of its jewels. They had already despoiled it of all save a massive gold ring, which, in spite of their exertions, they could not draw from the finger. One of the men thereupon took a hatchet, and, laying the hand on the edge of the bed under which the old man lay concealed, chopped off the finger. From the violence of the blow the finger flew under the bed, and he was within a hair's breadth of being discovered while the robbers were in search for their prize. Fortunately for him, one of the men said he could find it at any time, and it would be better to bury the body in the other mound, and then go to supper. This advice was followed.

Soon after the robbers took their places round the table and began to eat and drink. The old man from underneath the bed was witness to all that was going on. The more they drank the higher rose his hope of an opportunity to escape. The night was, however, far advanced before the robbers left the table and betook themselves to rest, stupified by their deep potations. As soon as they had extinguished the lights, the old man attempted to leave his hiding place. Gently and noiselessly he crept from under the bed when all was quiet and succeeded in reaching the stairs; but in the act of ascending in the dark, he made a false step and fell heavily on the ground. This noise awoke one of the sleepers; he started up and asked what was the matter. Receiving no answer, he sprang to the stairs, and at the same moment saw the old man above moving the stone and creeping through the hole.

In one moment, all the robbers were on the alert, and hurried up the stairs, unable to conceive who this nocturnal disturber could be. On seeing the old man hastening across the heath, they instantly went in pursuit of him; but the night was so dark that at only a short distance it was not possible to discern what direction he had taken; and on emerging from the thicket he had found a horse belonging no doubt to one of the gang, which he mounted, and rode off at full speed, without recollecting that the road he was taking led him farther and farther from Endrupholm.

The robbers, nevertheless, continued their pursuit, notwithstanding the start the old man had gained over them in being mounted; but he was obliged to keep the road, which traversed the heath in innumerable turns and windings, while his pursuers, acquainted with every path, constantly took short cuts, and in a few minutes one of them overtook him, and, seizing his horse's tail, twisted it tightly round his hand and called to his comrades.

The old man looking round, saw that his life depended on immediate action he drew his sword and made a stroke at the robber. The thick darkness that enveloped them, prevented his seeing where he struck; but he heard his pursuer utter a piercing cry and fall.

He was again free, struck his horse's sides with his heels, and galloped towards the town of Varde. When he approached the Vase, an extensive meadow, a causeway across which led to the south gate of the town, the water from the river had so overflowed the road, that it was impassable. After a moment's consideration, the old man thought the most prudent course would be to ride to Gellerup, and main there till the next morning; for although he had for the last few minutes heard nothing more of his pursuers, he durst not return by the same path, from fear of meeting them near the grave-mounds, which he would be obliged to pass, in order to reach his own house. He therefore turned his horse and soon after arrived at Gellerup.

Here he found all the doors shut; even in the inn every light was extinguished, and the unfortunate man was again about leaving the town, when he saw a light glimmering in the window of a little solitary cottage.

Quickly he turned his jaded horse towards it and knocked. A young woman and a boy received him and accorded him most cheerfully the night's lodging he desired. The girl got a lantern, that he might see to lead his horse into the stable. When it was secured for the night, and they were leaving the stable, the little boy, who had followed them, exclaimed: "Oh, see! only look at what is hanging in the horse's tail." Saying these words, the boy pulled out from the tangled hair a human hand, that had been struck off, and held it up to the lantern. The girl gave a scream, and the old man was not a little surprised at the sight of it; he knew that it must belong to the robber he had struck on the road. "See, Jane," continued the boy, who, with an inquisitive astonishment, had examined the hand, "it is my brother's hand, I know it by the scar on the thumb. And this is his gold ring."

The girl cast an angry look at the boy and winked at him to be silent. A deadly fear now seized the old man. There could be no doubt that the inmates of this cottage stood in very close connection with the robbers. Therefore, without saying a word, he led his horse out of the stable, mounted and rode back to Varde, fearing every moment to be over taken by the robbers.

When not far from the Vase, he made a vow to heaven that he would find a church at Varde, if he should safely pass through the waters. He then let his horse take its course and reached the opposite side in safety.

The following day, as he was returning home, he met Kield, in the early morn, going to Endrupholm. He related that his horse while hunting had fallen with him into a ditch; there he had lain insensible and dreadfully hurt, until some peasants passing by found him, and conveyed him to a surgeon, where his wounds were dressed. His betrothed had passed a night full of fear and anxiety on his account, as well as on that of her father. The old man seemed to have banished from his mind all unpleasant recollections of the night's adventure he was good-humoured and cheerful as usual and gave, as an excuse for being absent all night, that in his search for Kield, he had met a neighbour, who with a party of friends was returning from the chase that he had gone home with them and there passed the night.

The day after all these adventures was the birthday of the young lady, which, according to old custom at Endrupholm, was to be celebrated with great festivity. Early in the afternoon the guests assembled at the mansion. Mirth and glee prevailed everywhere. Kield alone, contrary to his usual custom, was pensive and taciturn; but his pale countenance sufficiently showed that it was the pain arising from the accident which had caused the change. Towards his betrothed he was as affectionate and tender as before. At table many a glass was emptied to the future happiness of the young couple; and after dinner the time was pleasantly passed in relating stories and humorous anecdotes.

When everyone appeared to have exhausted his stock of mirth, and the conversation began to flag, the host took up the theme, and, turning to his guests, said: "I must now tell you a wonderful dream I had last night. It is the most extraordinary one I ever had." After this introduction, he began to relate the events of the preceding night; how he came to the thicket by the grave-mounds, heard his name mentioned, had followed an old woman down into a cave, and had concealed himself under the bed on the arrival of the robbers. "I could not see the corpse they brought with them," said he, "but when they struck off the finger on which was the gold ring, it appeared to me, that it flew under the bed where I lay; and although the whole is but a dream, yet, nevertheless,—here is the finger." At these words he drew forth the finger and placed it before him on the table.

An exclamation of surprise burst from all his hearers. But on no one did the story make so deep an impression as on Kield; he became deadly pale, and rose from his seat, for the purpose of leaving the room but the old man held him back.

"You must remain here with us, my dear son-in-law," said he, in a friendly tone, "and hear my story to the end the best yet remains to be told."

He then related how he had fled from the place, had mounted a horse, had been pursued, and, lastly, the difficulties he had encountered at the Vase, which obliged him to ride up to Gellerup. "The child recognised the severed hand," continued the knight, "and exclaimed that it was his brother's. It appeared to me as if I took the hand with me, when I rode away; and although all this, as you can well imagine, is only a dream, yet I can lay the hand here before you." With these words he drew forth a human hand, that had been severed just above the wrist, and laid it on the table.

Without heeding the unspeakable surprise that seized all present, the reciter continued: "It appeared to me also that I should know it by the ring on one of the fingers, and on a nearer inspection I found that it belonged to one of my acquaintances." The old man then rising from his seat, took up the hand and threw it at Kield, who, more dead than alive, had listened to the recital. "There, Kield," exclaimed the knight, "take back your ring, and try if the hand will fit the stump you have bound up there."

All the guests rose. All eyes were fixed on Kield; his arm was in a sling, the old man sprang forward, tore the bandage away, and all saw that the hand had been struck off. "At this moment," continued be, "your den is sur rounded by the police of Varde, your comrades are prisoners, and I hear those approaching who will conduct you to a place more suitable to you than this." Kield was the chief of the banditti; he had courted the acquaintance of the lord of the manor, that he might have a better opportunity of leading his men into the mansion and robbing the old man of his wealth. He and his comrades were broken on the wheel and beheaded on the same mound that had so long been then retreat.

The old man, according to his vow, built the so-called "Little Church," in Varde; and it is related, that on laying the first stone, he declared that that man should be accursed to all eternity who first attempted to demolish it.

When the church was to be pulled down a few years ago, no labourer would begin the work, before the priest had taken out the first stone from the wall.

THE AMBER-SEEKER.

MANY years before the birth of Christ, Denmark was divided into three states, namely, the Cimbric, which included Jutland; the Gothic, comprising Scania, Halland, and Bleking; and the Baltic, consisting of the islands. The rulers of these states were called judges. In the eighth century of the Christian era, in the time of Sivart Ring, the Cimbric state was the most powerful, and subdued the other two, and at length Regnar Lodbrok united the whole land under his dominion.

It is related of Sivart Ring, that he lived in a town which he had himself built on the coast of the Western ocean, and named after him Ringkjöbing, or Ring's trading town; though some are of opinion that it derives its name from its insignificance (ringe signifying little): but be that as it may, suffice it to say, that the whole of Holmsland, which is separated from the mainland by the fiords of Stavning and Stadil, was under Sivart Ring, and that he had power over life and limb of those who lived on the island. Everything which the sea cast on shore of goods and floating wreck belonged to Sivart Ring, and it was strictly forbidden to everyone to take any part of such property. In like manner, be derived a large revenue from the amber which at that time was washed ashore in much greater quantities than it is at the present day. At every ebb, after a south-west wind, Ring sent out his men to the narrow ridge or sand-bank, for the purpose of searching the beach. All that they collected was his, and the punishment was death to whomsoever carried away the smallest particle of his property.

Above this sand-bank, not far from the sea, there lived a fisherman, who had come into the neighbourhood only a few years before as a poor man, but in a short time had accumulated considerable property, without any one being able to discover by what means. Some thought he had found a treasure, which was not unlikely, as the country had formerly belonged to a powerful sea-king, who lived by plundering all the vessels which came in his way and died on Holmsland without leaving any great property behind him; whence his relatives felt positive that he had buried his treasures. Others believed that Sam (so the fisherman was called) was in compact with the evil one; his company therefore was not much sought after, nor was he ever invited to join in his neighbours' guilds, or festive meetings. The fisherman was quite indifferent about the matter, he lived quiet and unnoticed in his cottage, with a pretty grown-up daughter, and let the world take its course.

As there was constantly a great talk about the fisherman's riches, it at length came to the ears of Ring. He, therefore, sent for him, and questioned him; but Sam's answers must have been satisfactory, as Ring let him go again in peace, and from that time appeared to think no more about him.

Some time after this event, it happened, one winter's evening, that many people were standing on the Klit, or sand-bank, without Holmsland, looking at a strange vessel, which seemed on the point of perishing, as the wind blew strong in shore, and the people on board appeared ignorant of the dangerous shoal. The ship continued labouring amid the towering billows, as long as daylight lasted, and the sea-faring men, who watched her from the height, separated in the belief that the following morning they should find her a shattered wreck upon the coast.

In the night, when all were gone to rest, there was a knock at Sam's door. The fisherman rose and opened it, and saw there a young man, who begged for shelter. When Sam asked what brought him so late, he answered, that he belonged to the vessel which had stranded during the night and sunk; all on board excepting himself having perished. He was received into the house, and all possible care taken of him.

The rest of the winter the young man remained with Sam and appeared to attach himself daily more and more to the family; till at length, one evening in the spring, he confessed to the fisherman his love for his daughter and asked his consent to make her his wife. Sam had nothing against this proposal, although Jonas, which was the name of the stranger, had nothing on which to support a wife. When talking this matter over, the fisherman said: "That shall not stand in the way; for I have enough for both You and Maria can remain living with me, and the field I plough will yield to you also as much as you require."

Thus was everything arranged between them, and the young people began already to talk about their wedding, when Sam one evening called Jonas to him, and said: "Listen to me, Jonas: as you will so soon be my son-in-law, it is but right that I make you a little acquainted with my circumstances, and, therefore, you can go out with me tonight, if you are so inclined."

Jonas was quite willing, and when it became dark, he and the fisherman set out together. It blew a gale, and the night was so black, that not a star was to be seen in the heavens, nevertheless Sam pushed his beat out to sea, and sailed away with Jonas. He at first stood out at some distance from the land, and, making a sign to Jonas to keep quiet, he began to listen. Immediately afterwards they heard a low whistle from the shore. "Ah, now I hear from Maria's signal," said the fisherman, "that everything is safe on the coast, so we can go back again."

He turned the boat, and when he had approached the shore so near that he grounded, he stepped out and dragged up a number of fine nets which had been placed aslant against the stream, so that the amber which was driven into them remained among the meshes. When he had drawn the nets up into the boat, he picked out the amber, and then set them again. This work proceeded without a word being spoken in the boat, and not until the approach of morning did the fisherman return to his house; but he brought as much amber home with him as would have taken Ring and all his people a month, perhaps even longer, to collect.

When they had again reached the cottage in safety, they concealed the amber in a deep cellar, which was so ingeniously contrived, that it was impossible for any stranger to discover it.

"Now," said Sam, "I have confided to you how I have acquired my wealth. My life is in your hands, Jonas; and although I am far from thinking you so base that you would betray me, especially as Maria will soon be your wife, yet you must swear to me that you will never disclose to any one what you have witnessed tonight."

Jonas took the required oath, and no more was said on the subject. When the summer was come and the wedding day was fixed, it seemed to the fisherman and his daughter that Jonas was more silent and reserved than he used to be. They asked him, many times, the cause of this change, but he only gave evasive answers, and appeared to be brooding over some secret he feared to divulge.

One afternoon he went over to Holmsland, and as he did not return at the usual hour, Maria walked out to meet him. She wandered on among the sand-hills, so busied with her thoughts that she was not aware how far she had gone. On a sudden she heard voices near her, and being frightened, hid herself. In a moment Jonas appeared in company with a person, who was no other than Sivart Ring. They were talking together in an earnest tone, and Maria heard Ring say: "It shall be as I have said; tonight, I will come with all my men and seize that thief, whether thou art in love with his daughter or not." When Jonas now began to beg hard for Sam, Ring answered in an angry and threatening tone: "Silence, boy! thou art my son, and shalt obey me. Go back and behave as usual; set a light in the window which looks out to the road, that I may know when all is quiet in the house." When the father and son had thus arranged, they separated.

Maria was ready to sink on the earth in consequence of what she had overheard. She found that Jonas had betrayed her father, and although she felt as if her heart would burst, she, nevertheless, composed herself, and thought only of the danger which threatened her parent.

As soon as Jonas was gone, she ran across a by-path as quickly as she could, to reach home and tell her father all she had heard. Night came. It was stormy and dark, not a star was to be seen; it was such weather as when Sam and Jonas first went out together to seek for amber.

Soon after Holmsland church clock had struck twelve, a number of men crossed the fiord to the sand-bank on the opposite side. They stole along unobserved towards Sam's house. The band was well armed, and led by Ring himself, who went first with a drawn sword in his hand and exhorted them to keep silence. In Sam's house all was still and quiet, at the top window burnt a faint light, the preconcerted signal between father and son in parting at the Klit. When Ring saw the light gleaming in the dark night, he smiled with satisfaction, and, turning to his people, said "There's the signal, I knew I could depend upon my son; everything is as it ought to be; you must know, that I have long suspected that this Sam was growing rich at my expense, yet without being able to discover how it was effected, till I caused my son, who had just come back from his long voyages, to go to him and gain admission to his house, by representing himself as having escaped from shipwreck. He has related to me the manner in which Sam contrives to fish up the amber and will conduct us to the place where he conceals it. Only follow me in silence and we shall catch the mouse in the trap." And it proved as he had said, the mouse was caught in the trap.

When Ring opened Sam's door he saw his own son hanging by a cord from the ceiling but the fisherman, his daughter, and all their treasure, had disappeared, leaving not a trace behind; and they were never heard of again in Holmsland.

THE NESS KING.

ABOUT four miles from Fredericia, where the village of Egeskov now is, there once stood a castle of the same name. Its last owner was Lars Brokhuus; but before the castle fell into his hands, it belonged to a knight named Börre, who dwelt there with his daughter Mette. The knight being far from wealthy, was desirous of seeing his child provided for before his death, and therefore determined upon making a "Brudeskue" (bride-show).

This, in former times, was a fete at which all the nobles, knights, and esquires assembled, tilted with each other, rode at the ring, and lastly, paid their court to the fair daughter of the house with costly presents. In consequence of Mette's great beauty and amiable character, many were the knights assembled at the fete. For several days previous to the festivities, every room at Egeskov was occupied by the guests, while fresh ones still continued to arrive, so that Börre at length knew not where to find room for all the strangers.

The last day, just before the running at the ring commenced, a young knight with a numerous retinue arrived at Egeskov. He was splendidly armed, and bore himself so proudly and arrogantly, that he looked with scorn on all those who were riding to the castle at the same time. Among these was an esquire, named Ebbe, from a manor which lay a little westward of the creek of Veile-fiord, which on the other side of Rosenvold runs in between Veilby and the parish of Gaarslev. The poverty of this esquire was become proverbial among the people of that time; they had made a lampoon on him, in which it was said:—

> "Ebbe from Nebbe, with all his men good,
>   Has neither food nor firewood."

He was mounted on a horse, which in its younger days had been a noble animal but was new old and worn out. His armour was riven and mended in many places, as were also his kirtle and mantle. When Ebbe and Sir Olaf (such was the name of the haughty knight) met, the latter immediately began to jeer and taunt the other; and when they both arrived at the castle-gate, Ebbe fell back while Olaf with all his retinue pressed forward, in order to enter first. Ebbe, however, took but little heed of Sir Olaf's jeers: "Ride on," cried he to the knight, "when the lord enters his castle the lowest servants are always accustomed to go first to prepare the way."

They rode immediately up to the race-course, where the eyes of all the dames and damsels were directed to Olaf, on account of his handsome figure and costly equipment. Ebbe, on the contrary, excited no notice, and remained a little behind the others; as if he were too bashful to come forward and expose his poverty. But when it came to the running at the ring, he was the foremost of all, and Sir Olaf, let him strive and manage his horse as he might, was unable to carry off more than one ring on his spear, while Ebbe bore away three. When all the assembled knights had ridden at the ring, they began to try their skill at tilting. At this game Ebbe was for a long time the most successful candidate, and challenged Olaf, who had already unhorsed many knights but he at length began to tire, and his worn out horse tottered under him. Olaf, on the contrary, rode a noble steed, and had, moreover, changed his horse after riding at the ring. Ebbe, nevertheless, ventured to encounter him, and fought bravely as long as he was able; but in a short time, Olaf overpowered him. Ebbe fell, and left the tilting ground, and as there were no other competitors, Olaf was declared victor, and received the prize from the hand of Mette.

In the evening all the guests assembled in the knight's hall, where the different suitors entered, according to their rank and condition, bringing with them presents to Mette. The greater number brought costly gifts; but herein also, Olaf surpassed all the others. Besides the costly present which he brought for Mette, he gave to the knight Börre two small castles of embossed gold, saying: "These two castles, of which you here see a representation, belong to me, and I will share them with your daughter, if you will bestow her on me."

Last of all came Ebbe. The knights smiled on seeing him, poor and meanly clad, without a gift, appear before Börre. Ebbe was not unconscious of their contempt, but without deigning to notice them, he bent his knee before Mette, and said in a loud and audible voice: "I approach you last, as is befitting a poor man, who is so far beneath the other suitors in condition and wealth. I here lay at your feet the most precious thing I own;" with these words he placed his sword on the ground before Mette.

"That's no great thing to give away," observed Olaf contemptuously, "seeing you have been so recently overpowered, while you bore this sword in your hand."

"God grant, Sir Olaf," answered Ebbe, "that Mette may receive my poor gift as surely as thou shouldst have suffered a mischance under this sword, had our conditions been more equally matched."

Several of the guests here interfered between the speakers, in order to make peace, and the two rivals separated. It was now agreed among those assembled that Mette should be allowed a month for consideration, before she fixed her choice.

The following day there was a great hunt at Egeskov. From early dawn, the huntsman's horn resounded through the forest, and here, as at the tilting, everyone was eager to show his skill. The ladies, according to the fashion of the times, partook in the amusement of the chase, and followed the deer with all the ardour of the bolder sex. Most of them gathered round Mette, but foremost rode Sir Olaf, and to judge from the friendly looks with which the lady regarded him, it seemed as if he would be the object of her choice. Ebbe was last of all. His horse had not yet recovered from the fatigues of the preceding day. He would not, therefore force it on, as he cared but little at being left far behind the others. Thus, passed the greater part of the forenoon, and the hunt took its course farther and farther down towards Trelde, when Ebbe, just as he was turning his horse into a cross path, saw Mette returning and coming towards him. After riding together a short way, Mette said "I am tired of the pursuit after hares and deer, and will accompany you among these green trees. Why are you so far behind the others? Are you not fond of hunting?" "Yes, undoubtedly I am," replied Ebbe, "but my poor horse is old and tired, and I must spare him." "I think," said Mette, "it would be better to part with him than always to be the last in jousts and other manly games." "That I would not do willingly," answered Ebbe; "this horse is all my father had to leave me many years it carried him and has done good service in its better days; in reward for which, I will cherish him out of my slender means, new that he is old."

"Do you know what I am thinking of, Ebbe?" said Mette. "I will make an exchange with you. Give me your horse, and you shall have mine instead; it is young and strong, and then you need no longer remain in the background, when there is a striving who shall be foremost."

"That bargain," replied Ebbe, "you would hardly stand to, and my horse must be where I am; he is my greatest treasure."

"Then," said Mette, "your words yesterday were but empty sounds, when you told me, you gave me the most valuable thing you owned."

Before Ebbe had time to answer, Mette urged on her horse, and rode from him into the wood. The following day all the knights took their departure from Egeskov and were invited to return when a month had elapsed, in order that they might know whose gift Mette preferred, and, consequently, whom she chose for her husband. Mette stood on the balcony and courteously greeted them as they passed; but when Ebbe, the last of all, rode through the gate, she turned her head away and would not greet him. Dejected at the unlucky result of his visit, he took the road back to Nebbegaard. When he reached that part of the wood where the shepherd from Egeskov was sitting tending his flock, he called to him and said: "Go and greet the lady Mette from Ebbe, and tell her, that when she offered to exchange horses with him yesterday, he refused, because he would not barter his steed; but that she may know he spoke only the truth, when he said he offered her the dearest thing of all that he possessed, relate what thou hast seen him do." Ebbe caressed his horse, and when the animal bent down his head on his master's shoulder and neighed with joy, he exclaimed: "I offer thee to Mette's beauty." At the same moment he drew his sword and killed the horse. Thus, closed the "Brudeskue" at Egeskov.

Almost all the knights that had been present felt convinced that Olaf would be the fortunate suitor with Mette and her father, on account of his youth, beauty, and manly accomplishments, and also because he was related to a man of whom Börre would not willingly make an enemy.

On the point of Trelde, surrounded and concealed by a thick forest, there was at that time a castle belonging to a rich and powerful Ness king (or sea king), named Trolle. His reputation was so great and wide-spread, that there was not a tract of land in the whole country where he was not known, at least by name. From the beginning of spring until late in the winter he sailed along the coasts of Jutland, Eyen, and Seeland, with his well-manned vessels (Snekker), in order to plunder all the merchantmen, he found and not unfrequently landed on the coasts, wherever he saw there was an opportunity of carrying off any booty. Trolle was a man of such extraordinary strength and courage, that he had no need to rely on the number of his companions. He had frequently engaged single-handed against four, and always come off victorious. Although the Danish kings, even at that early period, sought to check these lawless men, who disturbed the peaceable inhabitants of the kingdom, and destroyed all confidence in commerce; yet there was no one bold enough to encounter Trolle. He laughed at the king's laws and cared but little for being proclaimed an outlaw. On the ocean he was master wherever his vessels appeared, and his castle at the Ness of Trelde was so well fortified and guarded that he never needed to fear a surprise.

The knight Börre, who was Trelle's nearest neighbour, was not well pleased with the proximity, especially as it often happened that he was aggrieved by the many wanton annoyances he was compelled to submit to during the winter months, at which time the Ness king remained at his castle of Trelde. After enduring many vexations, be resolved on forming a plan to rid himself of his adversary, and just before Christmas sent a secret message to all his neighbours. They came, and it was settled among them that each should quietly assemble as many of his followers as possible, and attack Trolle on the following New Year's eve. When this was arranged, as well as the best method they could adopt for making the attack, they separated, and each returned home.

But the evening after, when all the confederates were assembled at a Yule festivity in the neighbourhood, the Ness king and his men suddenly burst into the apartment, extinguished the lights, made prisoners of five of the knights, and bore them off to Trelde, where they were kept in durance, until they had paid a very large ransom. No one could imagine how Trolle became acquainted with their plan; but certain it is, that from that time none of his neighbours thought any more of attacking him, considering it more prudent to bear patiently with the annoyances to which he subjected them.

Ebbe's father had been one of the confederates, and his poverty was partly in consequence of the heavy ransom he had been obliged to pay for the recovery of his liberty. One day, just before the festivities took place at Egeskov, Börre went out to hunt and returned towards evening loaded with game. On coming to the boundary between Egeskov and Trelde he met Trolle, who also had been out hunting on that day. "Thanks for the past, Sir Börre," said Trolle with a scornful laugh. "You ride about here killing game in our woods, so that at last I must put a stop to it." "I have not been hunting on your domain, Trolle," answered Börre; "and the right of hunting here belongs to me." "It matters little to whom the right of hunting belongs," answered Trolle; "for when you have destroyed all the game in your own woods, the deer will go from mine over to yours; but I think I shall be able to find a remedy for that, when I am so inclined. 'Those who stretch out furthest can embrace the most,' says an old proverb; but this time I will not be so particular, as I hear that Olaf looks with a favourable eye on your daughter." With these words the Ness king rode back to Trelde. Olaf was the son of the Ness king.

To resume our story. After slaying his horse, Ebbe returned home to Nebbegaard.

A week after this event, his servant came early one morning to tell him that a beautiful horse, ready saddled, stood fastened at the castle gate, and no one knew to whom it belonged. Greatly surprised, Ebbe went out to look at the horse, which stood proudly and impatiently stamping on the ground. The rein was of crimson silk, on which was embroidered the old proverb:—

"A straightforward difference is easiest settled."

No sooner had Ebbe read these words than he understood their meaning and felt pleased and happy in the thought that the horse came from Mette, and in the hope that her present raised in him. He led the horse into the castle and passed the remainder of the time that Mette had required in riding and exercising it.

At the expiration of the month, the knights again assembled at Egeskov to learn their fate. They were received with equal kindness by Börre and his daughter; and after their repast, the old knight conducted them into the great hall, where all the presents which they had brought on their former visits were displayed on a table. Mette walked at her father's side into the apartment. To the surprise of all, she took up the sword of the poor esquire, kissed the hilt, and said: "As Ebbe has given me all that he owned; I will return gift for gift, and call him my husband." No one present expected this. Ebbe fell on his knee before Mette, kissed her hand, and said: "May heaven bless you, Mette, and grant that you may never repent those words, or of the happiness you bestow on so poor a man."

Olaf could hardly control his anger at finding himself supplanted and eclipsed by an obscure esquire. Börre then came forward, and said to Mette: "My daughter, as thou hast chosen him thou thinkest best of, I will now say a word which shall be carried into effect. The last time we were all assembled here, Ebbe had but little luck either in the tournament or the chase; tomorrow, therefore, at break of day, we will meet in the forest and afford him an opportunity of proving his manhood."

"It is well," said Ebbe, "be it as you say; and when the chase is over, I will challenge each of Mette's knightly suitors to single combat with sharp or blunt lances, or with any weapon they may choose."

"That challenge I accept," answered Olaf angrily. "Tomorrow we shall hunt, but the day after you shall do battle with me for life or death; and I will advise the lady Mette, while we are away, to pray that heaven may grant her betrothed better luck than he had the last time our swords met."

"Good luck will come when I stand in need of it," answered Ebbe, "and Mette can spare her prayers until she knows which of us two most requires them."

The next morning at sunrise, all the knights rode out into the forest, to strive which could bring home the largest quantity of game. This time Mette and the other ladies at the castle did not join in the hunt. Towards evening they came back, one after another, and showed Börre the result of their day's sport. They had all assembled, with the exception of Olaf and Ebbe. Mette began to be very uneasy; she wished most anxiously that Ebbe might bring the greatest share and could not imagine what detained him so long. At length she began to fear that he and Olaf had met each other in the forest and had fought together; but her father calmed her by saying, that before they left in the morning for the chase, each had pledged his word, that they would not engage in combat at the hunt.

At length, just as it was growing late Olaf returned, and that day, as on the former occasion, his success had been greater than that of the others, and everyone was now anxious to see what Ebbe would bring home with him. But hour passed after hour, and there were no tidings of him, and Börre gave the signal for the guests to go to table. At the same moment the watchman's horn was heard, and Ebbe came riding into the castleyard, and greeted the company. "Well, Sir Ebbe," cried Olaf, in a sarcastic tone, "where is your booty? It appears you have been as fortunate this time as you were at the last hunt. "Much game I certainly do not bring," answered Ebbe, coolly, "and what I have was hardly worth the trouble of bringing home; but at the chase things go by chance, and one must take what one can get."

"Well! but let us see what you bring," cried Börre, impatiently. "Here it is," said Ebbe, throwing aside his cloak, and casting a human head across the table to Olaf. "Do you know that head? The crews in the forest are feeding on the carcass."

A cry of surprise was uttered by all the knights present, for in the distorted features each recognised the formidable sea-robber, the Ness king Trolle,

Olaf's father. Before the knights had recovered from their astonishment, Ebbe continued: "I have slain that lawless man, Sir Börre, in order to rid you of a troublesome neighbour, and in retribution for the wrong he did to my father. Tomorrow I will defend my deed against the knight Olaf, in whatever way he chooses."

But no combat took place between Ebbe and Olaf; for with the father's death, the son's courage departed, and he thought it not advisable to meet an adversary who had pre vailed over the far-dreaded Ness king.

Olaf immediately departed from Egeskov and returned to Trelde. The following day, he, together with all Trolle's men, left their castle, and from that time were never seen or heard of more. Some said that Olaf had gone more northward, and settled in Sallingland[4] with his followers, while others thought he had quitted Denmark altogether.

Ebbe's valour gained him great consideration in Börre's family; he and Mette lived happily together for many years.

GLOB AND ALGER.

BEFORE Jutland was united under one sovereign there were many petty kings there, each of whom had his portion of land to rule over, who were almost always engaged in quarrels and warfare with one another. One of these kings was named Alger; he ruled over Sallingland. His neighbour was Glob of Fuur, an isle also in the Limfiord, about a mile from Salling. Glob had come from Thy[5] with a great army, and warred with the king of Fuurland, until he at length slew him, drove away his son, and made himself king over the people of Fuur. Alger was thus king in Salling, and Glob in Fuur.

The fugitive prince fled from place to place, without having any fixed abode; for Glob had declared him an outlaw and set a price upon his head. At the time these events took place, he lived in a small dwelling in the neighbourhood of Alger's castle at Salling. When Glob had gained a firm

---

[4] In the Limfiord on the west coast of Jutland.
[5] Also in the Limfiord.

footing in Fuurland he resolved on extending his power and flying whether he could not also become king over Salling. For this purpose, he assembled a large army and crossed the "fiord;" but his attempt ended by his being driven back with great loss, and it subsequently appeared that he had given up all hostile designs against Alger. In the meantime, Alger, placing but little reliance on Glob's pacific policy, entered into a secret alliance with some of his neighbours, by which they bound themselves to come to his aid with all the force they could bring, as soon as Alger should light the beacons outside his castle, as a sign that the enemy was in the neighbourhood.

When Glob made his attack on Salling, it happened that one of his courtiers, named Birke, saw Alger's daughter Helvig, and became enamoured of her. When the two kings had settled their quarrel, Birke crossed over to Salling and visited Alger. Glob saw this with pleasure, because, when he asked permission of the king to go, he promised to avail himself of the opportunity to spy out all he could. Alger, on his part, was also glad to see Birke, knowing how high he stood in Glob's favour, and that no one could give, better information of the king's intentions and feelings than he.

But it was impossible for Birke to preserve the favour of both princes. When he had been for some time at Alger's, and had nearly obtained the promise of Helvig's hand, his love triumphed, and made him a traitor to Glob, so that he revealed to Alger all the kings plans, informing him that he only waited for an opportunity to make an attack on Salling. This soon reached the ear of Glob, who was bitterly enraged at the conduct of his emissary.

He immediately sent a messenger over to Alger, demanding that he should give up the traitor Birke, also the fugitive prince Eiler, who had found shelter in his land. Alger refused to comply with either of these demands and laughed at the threats uttered by the king's messenger.

With regard to Alger's daughter Helvig, her beauty had already called forth a host of suitors who, to gain her favour, vied with each other in knightly games and song, long before Glob came to Fuurland. But Helvig was indifferent to them all; she had secretly engaged herself to the fugitive Eiler, who lived in the neighbourhood of Alger's castle, and was their daily guest. At first, she only viewed with pity the unfortunate prince; but this feeling soon turned to fervent love, and Helvig called Heaven to witness, that she would rather sink into the grave than choose any other for her husband.

Alger was attached to Eiler, but his interest bade him favour Birke; he therefore commanded Helvig to give her promise to Birke and forget Eiler. But the maiden was not to be persuaded.

Two years had nearly passed, and Glob had taken no hostile steps against Alger. The latter had sent many spies over to Fuur, in order to find out whether Glob had any warlike intentions against him: but the king seemed occupied only in chivalrous games and the chase. He even once sent a messenger over to Sallingland to invite Alger to visit him. Birke advised the king not to go, adding, that he knew Glob too well not to feel certain that it was only a stratagem to get him into his power. Alger followed his counsel and remained at home.

It was in the winter, just before Yule, that this invitation was sent from Fuurland to the king. A few days after, Alger had a great banquet, and drank Yule-ale with his guests. Birke in the meanwhile was growing impatient at the long procrastination of his wishes and obtained Alger's promise that he should have his daughter's consent before the New Year's festivities were over.

In the evening, when all the guests were assembled at the castle and just as the mirth was at its height, the watchman's horn sounded from the tower. At the same moment a retainer rushed into the hall, announcing that he had seen a number of boats from Fuurland coming in the direction of Salling. Immediately after, another messenger arrived, who related that King Glob had landed with his men and was burning and destroying everything as he advanced. The guests were paralyzed at these unlooked-for tidings. Alger alone retained his self-possession.

"I thought rightly enough," said he, "that Glob would invite himself to our festivity, since I refused to go over to him. It concerns all when the wolf is at the door. Our business is now to receive him in a fitting manner, and that that may take place, I beseech you, my friends, to lend me your aid."

The guests were silent and looked at each other: they had assembled at the castle to drink Yule-ale, but not to fight, and Alger plainly saw that their silence signified no less than a refusal. His embarrassment was the greater as, in consequence of the mildness of the winter, many of his men were gone to sea to plunder along the coast of Norway.

Before Alger's guests had come to any determination, Helvig entered the hall, and thus addressed them: "Be it known to all here assembled, that I am the betrothed of Eiler, the son of the late king of Fuurland, and that I would rather endure the greatest sufferings than break my word, were not my father's life and fortune now threatened; but as I see among his guests men who have been suitors for my hand, I say to them, that to him who is able to free us from this danger, I will give myself and be his dutiful wife, so may God help me, as I will keep my promise."

These words had a powerful effect on all. The young were inflamed to daring deeds in the hope of possessing the lovely Helvig, the older were moved by her devotion to her father; and thus, they left the castle, firmly resolved to exert all their power to save Alger, and drive Glob from Salling.

The same night, some hours after the guests had de parted, while Glob was making preparations to invest the castle on the following day, Helvig left her chamber, and, accompanied by an attendant, glided silently through a secret passage that led into a copse, at the opposite side of which Eiler abode. He was greatly surprised at seeing them enter his dwelling.

"Rise, Eiler," said Helvig, "it is not fitting that thou shouldst sleep when Alger's enemies are awake." She now related to the prince the promise that, urged by necessity, she had been obliged to make to her father's guests, and prayed of him to devise some means of anticipating the others. "Take thy sword," added she, "for tonight thy part will be to save thyself, my father, and our youthful love." She then took leave of him, and the two females returned home.

But Eiler remained motionless and mute long after Helvig's departure. He felt how much depended on immediate action, he wished so heartily to save Alger, but he seemed destitute of all the means necessary for that object. After reflecting some time, he rose, threw a dark cloak over his weapons, and stole into the thicket, towards the spot where Glob had pitched his camp.

There all was life and activity; for the king had resolved upon attempting a storm as soon as daylight appeared, fearing, if he delayed longer, he should be attacked by Alger's friends.

Eiler crept as near as he could to the camp, so that he heard the enemy's men conversing together; but he was concealed from their sight, by the rushes on the bank of a deep ditch, which conveyed the water from the Limfiord into the fosses surrounding Alger's castle. Towards morning, Glob had completed his preparations. He had caused a small but to be raised for himself of turf and hides, in which he hoped to take some rest before the dawn gave the signal for the attack.

All was quiet in the camp.

When the men had lain down to sleep where they best could, Eiler approached softly, and crept along the edge of the ditch, concealed among the rushes, until he had passed the watch. He then walked fearlessly forward. The camp fires were nearly burnt out, and the darkness veiled his features, so that those of the enemy, who were not yet asleep, took him for one of their comrades, and let him pass where he pleased.

When he came to the spot where Glob slept, he gently raised the hide which hung before the entrance and crept into the hut.

The king lay on a bench, wrapped in his scarlet cloak. A torch was burning on a sod, which threw a red glare over the sleeper's countenance. Eiler drew a dagger from his belt, held his breath, and glided noiselessly as a snake towards the bench.

He thought of his father, whom Glob had dethroned and slain he thought of the injury he had himself suffered, how his youth had been passed amid dangers and want, during the many years Glob had hunted him as an outlaw from place to place; he thought also that Glob's death would free Alger from a dangerous foe, and gain for him Helvig, the dear object of all his thoughts; but yet he hesitated to plunge the dagger in Glob's breast.

The king lay still and motionless in a deep sleep, his hands folded, as if he had fallen asleep while repeating his evening prayer. The longer Eiler looked on him, the more incapable he became of killing the unarmed. He fixed the dagger into the couch close to the king's head; then left the hut, and stole softly out of the camp, as unobserved and silently as he had entered it.

When he had reached the copse, he continued along the secret path that led up to Alger's castle. He went to the king, informed him of what he had overheard in the enemy's camp, and what he had done. Alger praised Eiler's daring, and, although he might have been freed from a dangerous enemy, who threatened him with destruction, he could not withhold his admiration of the youth's exploit and would rather live and die with honour than owe his deliverance to treachery and crime. Eiler remained in the castle, resolved to meet his death with the rest of the warriors.

As the morning sun rose over the wood, the horns were sounded in Glob's camp and the king moved forwards towards the castle with all his men, and the strife began. All went as Alger had predicted; his force was' too weak and small to prevent his enemy from ascending the ram parts, and when the bells over in Fuur sounded formations, Glob was master of the castle. Alger ordered his men to lay down their arms, and no longer fight against such overwhelming numbers. He then descended into the courtyard, took the royal crown from his head, and laid it at the feet of Glob.

"God's peace, and a kindly greeting to you, my brother," cried Fuurland's king to him, at the same time smilingly lifting off his helmet and wiping his forehead. "You see how anxious I am to enjoy your company by coming to invite you myself; although you refused to be my guest. But why take off your crown; I think such a greeting too lowly."

"I give you my crown," answered Alger, "that you may take it as you have taken my castle and my kingdom."

"Take back your crown, brother," replied Glob, "it is shaped to your head, and is much better there than at my feet. And know that I am come today with the intention of giving, not of taking." In saying these words, he drew from his belt the dagger which Eiler the previous night had stuck in his couch.

"Look here," said he, "I bring you a knife which one of your people, whoever he may be, left behind him in my tent last night and we have been obliged to creep over the wall to get in, as you had barred your gates against us. Let me now have a few words with the man who owns this knife."

"The knife is mine," said Eiler, advancing towards the king. God delivered thy life into my hands, and I spared it, although I have suffered wrongs and bitter misery from thee.

"And was my life really in thy hand, Eiler?" answered Glob. "Then, as thou hast spared me, I will reward thee in the best way I can; and if I have not enough to give, Alger shall help me. What thinkest thou, my brother? If thou wilt give Eiler thy daughter, I will give them their outfit. I think that my kingdom of Fuurland will suffice for them. I am an old and childless man, and if Eiler will take reparation for blood, he and Helvig shall be my children."

Alger could hardly believe what he heard, so great was his surprise. He shed tears for joy, as he threw his arms round Glob and pressed him to his breast;

and as the horn in the morning sounded for battle, so did the music in the evening resound to the dance; for that same night the marriage of Helvig and Eiler was celebrated.

All Helvig's suitors, who had promised to help Alger against his enemy, arrived at the castle just in time to be present at the wedding.

THE LUCKY PENNY.

TWO young herdsmen, Peter and Paul, tended jointly all the sheep belonging to the town. One day as they were sitting together upon a hill, from which they had a view of all the pasture-lands around, a dealer passed with a drove of fat oxen. They knew the man, and Peter said: "That man may be called happy who is as rich as he is."

"Certainly," answered Paul; "it would not be amiss to have some of his money in one's old age.

"For one's old age?" cried Peter; "no, never mind that time: if I am to have money, let it be while I am young, that I can enjoy it, and live a merry and pleasant life."

While they were thus talking together, there came a little man up the hill with a red cap on his head. Going up to Peter, he presented him with a little purse, and said: This purse I will give to thee; there is only one silver penny in it, but every time thou art in need of money, thou hast only to thrust thy finger into the purse, and thou mayst take out as much as thou pleasest, either silver or gold; but beware thou never give the little penny away. Hereupon he showed Peter the silver penny and gave him the purse. "But to thee," said he to Paul, "I will give good advice. Learn some useful handiwork, *that* will best promote thy fortune." The little man then left them and disappeared in the mount.

Soon after this event Paul bound himself to a smith; but Peter began to trade. He bought all kinds of goods, went from city to city, always made a good business, and took so much money that he was known all over Jutland under the name of Rich Peter the Huckster. He then thought it was not worthwhile to travel longer about the country, for he had wealth enough, and could, moreover, take daily from his purse as much as he desired. He therefore bought a fine manor, called Lanting, surrounded by woods; and near the mansion flowed a river, in which there were excellent eels. Here Peter established an eel-fishery, the like of which had never before been seen, and everything in his household was on the most costly scale. Here he lived in splendour and luxury and married a young maiden of rank.

Every day there were guests at the mansion, and Rich Peter the Huckster had no other thought than to enjoy himself. His wife, however, thought it impossible that he had money enough to continue such a life, and talked to him on the subject. But he only laughed, and said, she might be quite easy on that score, for there was no end to his riches.

But his wife secretly hoarded the gold and silver which he gave her to buy fine clothes, and this money she was desirous to conceal in some safe place. Now, down near the eel-pond she had noticed a large piece of timber, that had in it a hole, into which a wedge had been driven, but which no one could see, save those who knew it was there. Here, thought she, must be a secure hiding-place; so, stealing one day down to the spot, she drew the wedge out and put in all her money; then replaced the wedge, so that no one could perceive it had been touched. This money she thought she would have as a reserve, in case her husband ever came to want it.

But it happened some time after this that the lady became ill and died, without telling any one of her treasure. She died childless, and after her death Rich Peter became still more dissipated than ever. At his house there was always a swarm of boon companions, who hunted with him drank and gambled when they returned home, from the evening till the dawn of day, and led such a dissolute life that no respectable man would be seen there, much less any respectable woman.

Once, when Peter was sitting with his gambling comrades, and they had all drank too much, he was going to pay one of them what he had lost to him in play, but he was so bewildered with drinking that he knew not what he was doing. Instead, therefore, of counting his money piece by piece, as he took it out of his purse, he shook the whole contents out upon the table, and threw the purse into a corner of the room.

The next morning, when he became sober again, he picked up the purse, but the lucky penny was gone, and it was now only like all other purses, it would give no more money out than what had been put into it. "Never mind," thought he, "I am rich enough as it is." But all the rich woods and fisheries were insufficient to pay for the extravagant life he led. Nothing was managed with order; therefore everything fell into decay for he was never inclined to look after things himself. Thus matters went on, so that from year to year his property decreased, till he was obliged to sell house and land, and at last to take a wallet on his back and beg from door to door: he was, at the same time, sick and miserable; his spirit was broken and his appearance was so wretched, that none of his former companions could have known him again.

The other herd-boy, Paul, had in the meanwhile become an able smith; he worked from morning to night, yet he could never become rich. He married a young girl as poor as himself, and they had many children. It required much bread to feed so many mouths, but yet they never knew want, although what one day brought in was consumed the next. In the meantime, the children grew up, behaved well, and were healthy and industrious; and Paul, the smith, felt well pleased every time he looked at them. His smithy lay near the same river which ran past Peter the Huckster's mansion, but from which it was many miles distant. One day a large piece of timber came driven down by the stream and ran aground close to Paul's workshop. He went out, examined it, and finding it was very hard wood, he thought it might serve to make a new block for his anvil. He and his sons drew it on shore and set it up against a wall, that it might dry.

Some time after, it happened that a poor miserable beggar came to his door and begged for a bit of bread. The smith's wife gave him both beer and food, and he chanced to hear that the smith's name was Paul. They entered into conversation, and it appeared that the beggar was the same person who had once been called Rich Peter the Huckster, and who in his youth had been a herd-boy together with Paul. The smith now made him welcome, and they related to each other their adventures. Peter talked about his great mansion, his woods, and his fine fisheries, all of which he had lost, in consequence of parting with his lucky penny and Paul showed him his children and his little property. When they had thus talked together for some time, the smith said that he must go out to his work; he was going to chop a piece of wood to make a block for his anvil.

When Peter soon after went into the yard and looked at the piece of timber lying outside the house, which had floated down the river, he said: "I am much mistaken if this has not belonged to my eel-pond." And this proved to be true;

for there was his name cut on the end of the log, and he told them why it was so chopped. At length his eyes fell on the wedge, which was so rotten that it came out as soon as it was touched, when to their great astonishment out rolled the gold and silver. Peter thought that the money must be his but knew not how it came there. Paul wished him to take it, saying, that by right it belonged to him. But Peter cared nothing about it. Money, he said, was the cause of all his misfortunes, and that he had neither courage nor strength to begin any new trade. It was the same to him how he dragged out the last days of his miserable life.

The smith wished at least to share the money with him, or he offered to keep him in his house and take care of him; but to this he would not consent. It suited him best, he said, to wander from place to place for he never fell at rest or at peace with himself; but he would once more are long come again and see the old companion of his youth.

They were unable to persuade him to remain with them, and the next morning he again set out on his wanderings. As he would not take a single piece of the money which was found, the smith's wife consulted with her husband, and they agreed that they would bake a good part of the money in a loaf which she would give to the beggar to take with him on his journey. They thought, "When he finds the money, he will find a use for it." She then filled his bag with provisions and put the loaf in at the bottom.

Peter bade them farewell, promised to come seen again, and set forth on his wanderings with his beggar's staff. The bag upon his back soon felt too heavy, he took it off, examined it, and found that it was the loaf which weighed the most. He then went to the nearest cottage and said, that some kind friends had given him a loaf to take on his journey, but it was too heavy for him to carry, and asked whether they would buy it of him. The people said they would and gave him as much for it as they thought it was worth; he then continued on his way.

The woman who had bought the bread said to her husband: "The other day I borrowed a loaf from the smith, this looks a well-baked one, let us send it him in its place."

The man was afraid the loaf was too small, but when they weighed it, they found it had the right weight, which was caused by the money baked in it. It was therefore sent to the smiths, with their thanks for the loaf they had lent.

Paul and his wife were not a little astonished to see the money come back to them in such a strange manner. But they would not use it and determined to keep it till Peter should come again. But this never happened; for a few days after, he was found dead in a field, with his bag of provisions and his staff by his side.

Paul now considered that he could with justice use the money as his own property and thus he passed his old age in wealth and happiness.

THE WILL.

IN ancient times Varde was only a village. It always kept a beacon (Varde) upon the hill, which is now called the Arnebierg. This beacon was lighted as a warning, whenever pirates were to be seen, who swarmed on the west coast of Jutland, plundering wherever they saw an opportunity. Eight miles from the village, the river runs out into the Western Ocean, and at that time is said to have been navigable the whole way, and to have served as a winter shelter for the small craft, which in the summer traded to Norway with corn and other provisions As the place thus lay rather advantageously for commerce, it gradually became the residence of many families, and at length King Christopher, in 1440, granted it the privileges of a market town.

A long time before this took place, a royal castle was built on the south, or opposite, side of the river for the protection of the surrounding country and the trading vessels, which in old documents is called Varde Castle, ruins of which may still be seen. There are yet visible traces of ditches arid rampaits, also two hills or mounds out in the river, which are still called "the sconces."

The arms of the town, a lion rampant crowned, over a river, have reference to this castle, which was erected for the protection of the river.

The last owner of the castle was Godske Lembek. He was a widower with two daughters, whom he dearly loved. He procured a monk from the monastery of Tvisel to undertake their education, who apparently executed his task with great solicitude. When the two young maidens were grown up, their father lived wholly for them he gratified all their wishes and had no higher aim than to secure their future happiness, as far as lay in his power.

The monk continued to visit at the castle, he was Lembek's constant companion, and spent more of his time with him than he did at the convent of Tvisel.

Thus, passed many years. Lembek was now growing old. He lived in amity with his neighbours, was respected and beloved by all, and so contented with his lot, that his happiness became almost a proverb among the people.

One day, upon returning from the Ting or Diet held in Viborg, where he had staid for a short time, he was received by his sorrowing household with the news that both his daughters had disappeared, and that all endeavours to discover what had become of them had proved fruitless. Lembek could not at first believe his own ears, but when the monk, to whom the domestics had applied in their master's absence, confirmed the sorrowful tidings, he sank into a state of unconsciousness, so that for many days they knew not whether he was alive or dead. When he recovered, he was as a raving maniac; he cried and lamented, cursed his lot, and ridiculed all the sympathy and comfort which the monk offered him.

After that day a great change took place in Lembek. His hair became white, his gait slow and faltering, his whole frame bore marks of the grief under which he was labouring. He avoided all intercourse with his former friends, even with the monk, and spent whole days on those spots which had been dear to his lost children; he sought solitude, and his mind dwelt only on what he had possessed and lost.

Many years after this event, a poor woman came to the castle and demanded to speak with its lord. When she entered his apartments, she begged of him to go with her down into the town, where her husband, who was sick and bed-ridden, had a weighty matter to communicate to him.

At first Lembek refused her request; but when the woman, who was prepared for a refusal, added, that the sick man was on his death-bed, and had said, he could find no peace in death until he had imparted a secret to the lord, which had long lain heavy on his conscience, he allowed himself to be persuaded, and went with the woman.

The dying man was longing to see him. When they were alone together, he related, that, tempted by a large sum of money, he had been induced, by a rich and powerful man, to carry off Lembek's daughters one evening as they walked together on the Arnebierg. The man had bound him by a fearful oath never to reveal this transaction; but now that he was near death he would, for the bone of salvation, confess everything to the knight, and implore his forgiveness. The place to which the two young damsels were conveyed was not famed for its morality, nor were Lembek's daughters the only victims who had met with a similar fate. The place was Tvisel Convent, and it was the monk, the friend of Lembek, who had done this deed. When the sick man had related all that he knew about the two damsels, he sank back on his couch and expired.

Although this information made a powerful impression on the old knight, his actions and whole conduct from that day bore a character of great determination. He seemed as if he again had an object in view, a plan to live for. What the dying man had confided to him he never divulged to any one, and whether he placed any reliance on it or not, he continued his intimacy with the monk, who had now become abbot of Tvisel.

Lembek was an old man and appeared to have not many years to live; and, therefore, thought of making his will before he died. On this subject he consulted with the abbot, and informed him, at the same time, that he had resolved on bestowing upon him and the monks of Tvisel all that he possessed, on this condition, that all the brotherhood should come to the castle and perform a mass for the souls of his daughters.

Although this was against the rules of the Cistertian order, to which the monks of Tvisel belonged, yet the thoughts of Lembek's great wealth at length triumphed over all obstacles. The abbot promised to come with the whole fraternity to the castle at the appointed time.

The mass for the dead was celebrated, and in the evening Lembek executed his last will. When he had finished, he said, "As we have now settled everything which I had at heart, we will go and see the treasures which I have bequeathed to you. They are all preserved in one room. When you have taken a view of them, I will deliver the key to your custody, and after my death you can send for the treasure."

The monks were well pleased with this arrangement, and followed Lembek down into the cellar, to a small square room which he had shortly before caused to be constructed. All the walls in this apartment, as well as the roof, were composed of huge blocks of stone, such as may still be seen in old grave-mounds. There was no other ingress than through an aperture, which appeared upon removing a flag-stone in the roof. It had no windows, but only two small air-holes which looked towards the river. One lamp illumined the vault, and the descent to it was by a ladder made fast to the roof.

To this place Lembek conducted his future heirs and let them descend one by one. The last to go down was the abbot. Just as he came to the bottom, the ladder was drawn up, and Lembek, stooping over the aperture, called down to the monks. "Now you can take payment for your mass as well as for all the villany you have perpetrated against my poor daughters."

He then called a servant, and, at the same time, ordered a quantity of fine hay to be brought tied in small bundles, which they continued throwing down through the opening, until the space above the monks was nearly filled. He then set the hay on fire, and when assured that it burnt well, he replaced the stone over the aperture, that the smoke might escape only through the two small holes in the thick wall, which also supplied the fire with air enough to keep it burning. In this manner Lembek destroyed nearly all the monks of Tvisel.

The following day the news of this event reached the town. Some few of the monks that had remained in the convent induced the peasants from Skærn, Felling and Quistrup, who were vassals of the convent, to avenge the deed. The castle was stormed, and burnt on the 2nd of April, 1434.

The nobles in the neighbourhood could not come to the help of Lembek before it was too late; they, however, assembled together, pursued the peasants, and obliged them to take shelter in Varde when, not only the town, but the newly-built church of St. Ib, into which the fugitives had fled for safety, were laid in ashes.

THE LITTLE CHICKEN KLUK AND HIS COMPANIONS.[6,][7]

THERE was once a little chicken called Kluk. A nut fell on his back and gave him such a blow that he fell down and rolled on the ground. So, he ran to the hen, and said: "Henny Penny[8], run, I think all the world is falling!" "Who has told thee that, little chicken Kluk?" "Oh, a nut fell on my back, and struck me so that I rolled on the ground." "Then let us run," said the hen.

So, they ran to the cock, and said "Cocky Locky[9], run, I think all the world is falling." "Who has told thee that, Henny Penny?" "Little chicken Kluk." "Who told thee that, little chicken Kluk?" "Oh, a nut fell on my back, and struck me so that I rolled on the ground." "Then let us run," said the cock.

So, they ran to the duck, and said: "Ducky Lucky[10], run, I think all the world is falling." "Who told thee that, Cocky Locky?" "Henny Penny." "Who has told thee that, Henny Penny?" "Little chicken Kluk." "Who has told thee that, little chicken Kluk?" "Oh, a nut fell on my back, and struck me so that I rolled on the ground." "Then let us run," said the duck.

So, they ran to the goose. "Goosy Poosy[11], run, I think all the world is falling." "Who has told thee that, Ducky Lucky?" "Cocky Locky." "Who has told thee that, Cocky Locky?" "Henny Penny." "Who has told thee that, Henny Penny?" "Little chicken Kluk." "Who has told thee that, little chicken Kluk?" "Oh, a nut fell on my back, and struck me so, that I rolled on the ground." "Then let us run," said the goose.

Then they ran to the fox, and said; "Foxy Coxy[12], run, I think all the world is falling." "Who has told thee that, Goosy Poosy?" "Ducky Lucky." Who has told thee that, Ducky Lucky?" "Cocky Locky." "Who has told thee that, Cocky Locky?" "Henny Penny." "Who has told thee that, Henny Penny?"

---

[6] Thiele, Danske Folkesagn: Kiob. 1823.

[7] The above is a pendant to the Scottish story, "The Hen and her Fellow Travellers," printed in Chambers' Popular Rhymes, etc., of Scotland, p. 51.

[8] Dan. Höne Pöne.

[9] Dan. Hane Pane.

[10] Dan. And. Svand.

[11] Dan. Gaase Paase.

[12] Dan. Ræv Skræv.

"Little chicken Kluk." "Who has told thee that, little chicken Kluk?" "Oh, a nut fell on my back, and struck me so, that I rolled on the ground." "Then let us run," said the fox.

So they all ran into the wood. Then the fox said: "I must now count and see if I have got you all here. I, Foxy Coxy, one; Goosy Poosy, two; Ducky Lucky, three, Cocky Locky, four; Henny Penny, five; and little chicken Kluk, six; Hei! That one I'll snap up." He then said: "Let us run."

So they ran further into the wood. Then said he: "Now I must count and see if I have got you all here. I, Foxy Coxy, one; Goosy Poosy, two; Ducky Lucky, three; Cocky Locky, four; Henny Penny, five; Hei! That one I'll snap up." And so, he went on till he had eaten them all up.

IV. NORTH GERMAN.

STRONG FRANK.[1]

From Frestede in Ditmarschen.

A PEASANT had two sons, the elder of whom was named Christian, and the younger Frank. But Frank was much taller than his brother, and stronger than his father and brother together, although so much younger. One day the father said to his sons: "Come, let us go to the forest, and fetch some firewood." They went, but could find no good firewood, whereupon Frank, seizing one of the largest trees by the trunk, wrenched it root and all out of the earth and laid it on his shoulder. He did the like with seven or eight trees besides and said to his father: "We will at any rate take home a load of wood and not come out for nothing." So, he took all the trees home with him. But the father said: "Thou wilt spoil the whole forest another time thou must not root up so many." So, the next time they were about to fetch firewood, Frank said: "I must seek either for another forest or another master; for with you I will not go out again." Frank then started off alone and penetrated far into the forest. While wandering about, he was met by a little man, named Hermanni, who asked him whether he was in search of employment, and whether he would enter his service. "Yes," answered Frank, why not, if you will give me good wages Hermanni replied: "Thou shalt have four hundred marks wages, and two hundred marks as a gift; thou wilt have nothing more to do than to take care of my brown horse; with anything besides thou needst not trouble thyself." Frank was satisfied with the wages, and the master showed him his castle, which stood on a high mountain. There Frank had to take care of the horse, which he curried daily, and fed, and performed his duty faithfully.

When a year had passed, the master came to Frank and asked him whether he wished to stay another year with him. "Yes," answered Frank, "but I would

---

gladly have more wages." The master said: "This year I will give thee eight hundred marks wages, and four hundred marks as a gift." Frank at once agreed to the bargain, but requested permission to go once to see his father and brother. The master said: "That could be, were it not that during thy absence there will be no one to attend to the horse." To this Frank answered: "If there is no other obstacle than that, I can go for I can make the journey in a day and be back here at night." So, Frank went to see his father and brother, who rejoiced much at seeing him once again, after so long an absence. To his father's inquiry where he had been, Frank answered: "That I may not say." When evening came, and Frank was about to return to the castle, his brother Christian begged to accompany him, but Frank said: "Whither I go thou canst not follow me." He then returned alone to his master's castle. On the following morning his master said to him: "Frank, dost thou see a door there in the north side of the castle? That thou mayest never open, otherwise evil will befall thee. If thou art obedient to me, thou shalt receive further good of me." Frank promised accordingly, performed his duty faithfully, and the year passed so quickly, that it seemed to him only a few days.

At the end of the second year Hermanni came again to Frank and asked him whether he would still continue with him. Frank answered, that he was well content to continue with him, provided only he could have more wages. His master said: "For this third year I will give thee sixteen hundred marks wages, and eight hundred marks as a gift." So, Frank entered upon his third year. When it was nearly expired, his master departed on a journey. Frank now thought he might venture to open the north door of the castle, to see what was there to be seen. "It can do no harm," said he to himself, "and my master will know nothing about it, as he is not at home." Frank went and opened the door accordingly, and in an instant found himself in a garden of indescribable beauty, full of the most wonderful flowers; all the shrubs that grew in it being of diamonds, gold, and silver. From every plant that he saw, Frank gathered a little nosegay, wrapped it in his handkerchief, and put it into his pocket. He then left the garden and returned to the stable, where, to his great astonishment, he found that the horse could speak, and thus addressed him: "Frank, what hast then done! Saddle me instantly, and leap on me; flight alone can save us; otherwise our lives are forfeited." In a moment Frank did as the horse had enjoined him, sprang on it, and rode off at full speed.

They had already travelled many miles, when the horse said to Frank Just look back; it seems to me that someone is behind us. Frank looked round, and said: "Yes, it is our master, and he has nearly overtaken us." "Then cast thy riding whip behind thee," said the horse; and when Frank had done so, a high thick hedge rose up, that the master must long labour at before he could make a way through it. In the meanwhile, Frank and the horse had got greatly ahead. Again, the horse said: "Look once more round; it seems to me that someone is behind." Frank looked round and said: "Yes, our master is close at our heels." "Cast, then, thy cloak-bag behind thee," said the horse; and when Frank had so done, there arose a great mountain behind them, many thousand feet high. To clamber over this was a work of difficulty, and employed the master for some time nevertheless, he at length again nearly overtook the fugitives. The horse then a third time said: "Look back once again; I think there is something coming." "Yes," answered Frank, our master is quite near. "Then cast off the saddlecloth," said the horse and in an instant a great water arose between them and Hermanni, who, being unable either to pass over or wade through it, laid himself down to drink it up. But the quantity was so great, that in his attempt he burst and died. They now proceeded some way farther and came to a pleasant green wood. Here Frank, letting his horse graze, laid himself down in the shade, and consumed such provisions as he had taken with him. After having finished his meal, he fell asleep, fatigued with his toilsome journey.

On awaking, he saw standing before him a table, on which lay a sword. Then said the horse to him: "With this sword cut off my head." "That," said Frank, "would be the basest ingratitude. Thou hast rendered me inestimable service, and shall I requite thee by taking thy life?" "Only do so," said the horse; "it will be for your happiness as well as mine." As the horse prayed so earnestly, Frank at length took up the sword and struck off his head; when in an instant a beautiful lady stood before him, and said: "Fear not, dear Frank; I am a princess of Russia; I was carried off by the base Hermanni and transformed into a horse. Thou hast now released me, and hast always treated me kindly; I will, therefore, always be grateful to thee. Here hast thou a little stick; strike with it on this hollow tree whenever thou art in difficulties, and I will help thee out of thy trouble." Frank took the little stick, and having thanked her, they bade farewell to each other. He then continued his journey on foot, and soon arrived in a royal city. Here he resolved to remain and made inquiry whether any gardener there needed an assistant. The people directed him to a gardener, whose garden was near to the king's palace. To this man Frank offered his services as a journeyman, who, liking the young man's appearance, at once engaged him.

The gardener now pointed out to him several works to be performed; but Frank, who knew nothing about gardening, did everything badly. One day he was ordered to clear all the weeds out of a patch of turnips. The gardener said: "The plants with the curled leaves thou must leave standing, for they are the turnips, but all the rest are weeds, and must be plucked up." Frank pulled up a plant with curled leaves, but finding no turnips on it, he thought: "These are no turnips," and so plucked the turnips up together with the weeds. When the master came and saw that the whole patch was destroyed, he was excessively angry, and said: "If the like happens again, I will turn thee adrift." He then ordered him to hoe some potatoes and showed him how to work so as not to injure the tubers, and that the plants should stand in rows with furrows between them. But when the master's back was turned, and Frank was left to continue the work alone, he hoed all smooth and level alike. Now was the master more angry than before, and said: "If thou dost so again, I will surely turn thee away."

One day the gardener sent Frank to the garden to see how the cabbages stood. Franz thought they stood well, but that they would look still better if they were like the shrubs in Hermanni's garden. So, feeling in his pocket, he drew forth the sprigs which he had formerly gathered there, and rubbed them over the cabbages, so that they shone like diamonds, gold and silver. All this was observed by the king's daughter from a window of the palace, who immediately sent to the gardener, desiring him to send some vegetables to the palace, and to let his man be the bearer of them. Thereupon the gardener put some young peas and turnips into a basket, and Frank carried them to the palace. "Good morning, lass!" said he, as he entered. She thanked him. "I have brought you here some vegetables, some peas, and young turnips." "'T is well, said she; come in for a moment, sit down and eat something." "That I 'll do most willingly," answered Frank, entering the apartment and seating himself at a table, which was well furnished with wine and delicate viands, of which he partook as liberally as one who had not tasted food or drink for the three preceding days. The princess was pleased with him, and when he had eaten his fill and was about to depart, asked him how much she was indebted to him for the vegetables. "A hundred dollars," answered Frank. The princess paid him the sum named, and when he reached home, and his master asked him how much he had received, Frank threw the hundred dollars on the table. On seeing them the master said: "Young fellow, thou hast taken too much by far." "Not at all," answered Frank, "the princess gave them to me."

After some days had passed, the princess sent a second time to the gardener, ordering more vegetables, and that his man should bring them. So, the master again packed some young peas and turnips in a basket and sent Frank with them. "Good day, lass!" said he on entering, "I have brought you some more peas and turnips." The princes; then invited him into her apartment, as on the previous occasion, and Frank again ate and drank, so that at length, he fell asleep on his chair. The princess then drew clandestinely from his pocket the bouquets of diamonds, gold and silver. When he woke, he demanded two hundred dollars for the vegetables. The princess paid him his demand, and he returned home quite contented. On entering the garden, he chanced to feel in his pocket, when lo! the bouquets were no longer there. He searched and searched, but could find them nowhere, and was quite unhappy and disconsolate. His master noticed his tribulation and inquired the cause of it; but Frank answered: "That I neither can nor will tell you."

Not long after, the princess ordered more vegetables to be brought to the palace, and Frank must again be the bearer. When he entered, he said in a depressed tone: "Here, I have brought you the vegetables." The princess desired him to sit and eat something, but he would not. She asked him what ailed him, and why he was so churlish. "What should ail me, indeed! why, my nosegays are gone." "If that's all," said the princess, "make thyself easy; for I have them. When thou wast last here, I took them out of thy pocket while thou wast sleeping, and will now return them, on condition that thou wilt go with me to my father and exhibit thy art to us." To this proposal Frank readily acceded; the princess conducted him to her father and said: "I here bring thee the greatest and most extraordinary painter in all Europe." "That's saying something," answered the king; "let him give us a specimen of his art." Frank thereupon took his bouquets and painted the king's table all over so that it resembled pure diamonds, gold, and silver. The king was astonished, rewarded Frank liberally, and was about to dismiss him, when the princess prayed her father that she might be permitted to marry the young man. At first the king refused his consent, but the princess said, that if she might not marry Frank, she would marry no other man. The king ultimately consented. Frank was sent for and questioned on the subject, and as he did not say no, the betrothal was celebrated. "My son," said the king then to Frank, "thou must now see about getting a palace how wilt then set about it? Until then thy marriage cannot take place." Frank answered: "I desire of you nothing more than the great heath of four hundred acres." "That thou shalt have," said the king, "but what besides?" "For that let me provide, dear father," answered Frank.

On the following morning early Frank rode to the hollow tree in the forest, which the enchanted princess had pointed out to him. He struck it with the stick she had given him, and instantly she was at his side, and asked him what he desired. "I have to build myself a palace," said Frank, "but want money for the purpose." Thereupon the princess gave him a small purse, saying: "Only take from it and disburse; it will never be empty." Frank then returned to the king, and said: "I have now got money, so we will begin to build." But the old king answered: "My good son, that will not go far towards building a palace for *that*, sums of a very different kind will be required." But Frank said: "I believe this will suffice, and that in this purse there is more money than in all your treasury." The king now ordered the money to be counted, and the longer they counted the more there was in the purse. At last the king was forced to acknowledge that his son-in-law was richer than himself; and now the building proceeded and proved a structure more beautiful and splendid than any other in the world.

When the palace was ready, Frank invited his father-in-law and his betrothed to view it. They were perfectly astounded at the magnificence and splendour everywhere displayed. But the old king said: "All this is, indeed, noble and sumptuous; but, my son, I am apprehensive that we shall soon be afflicted by war. Until that is ended no marriage can be thought of." The old king appeared troubled and sad; his foreboding did not deceive him; for within a few days certain powerful foes declared war against him. But Frank was, nevertheless, of good courage, and said: "We have nothing to fear, although we are unprepared and less numerous than our adversaries. Leave all to me, dear father, I will soon be in readiness." He then rode again to the forest, knocked on the hollow tree, and when the princess of Russia appeared, he said: "I am now again in difficulty; our country is being devastated by war, the number of our people is too small to resist the enemy; I pray thee, help me, if thou canst." The princess there upon gave him a sword, saying: "When thou strikest with this on a tree, soldiers will march out of it in multitudes, as many as thou requirest."

On his return Frank found that during his absence the king had raised the whole male population of the country, and that old and young, rich and poor, cripples and sound, married and unmarried, were all ready to march. But Frank asked what it all meant. "It means," answered the king, "that we have not yet enough by many." But Frank answered: "We have already by far too many; let, therefore, all who have wives and children bewailing their absence return home; the aged and the lame we will also leave behind." But to this proposal the king would not assent. Frank then said: "These neither can nor should fight. Only allow me to act, and we will soon overcome the enemy."

The army now broke up, and after a short march, came in sight of the enemy, whose number was so great, that as far as the eye could reach nothing but soldiers could be seen. The whole field glittered and shone with arms, and the air resounded with the sounds of military music. "Now," said Frank, "it is time for us also to make preparations and fetch more soldiers. "Whence are they to be obtained?" inquired the king. Frank answered: "Step aside for a moment, dear father; they shall march up instantly. How many do we require?" The king thought he was joking, and paid no attention to his words, but Frank cried out: "I pray you to step aside, that my soldiers may not tread you under foot." He then struck with his sword on an oak, and instantly there came forth, first six regiments of foot, then eight regiments of cavalry, next ten regiments of heavy-armed troops. The battle now began; but as the enemy did not immediately give ground, Frank again struck on the tree, and out came twelve regiments more. The enemy would now have fled but were annihilated by the soldiers of Frank to the last man.

The old king had now no objection to the celebration of the marriage, but rather rejoiced at having such a son-in-law as Frank. So, the marriage took place accordingly with great pomp and splendour. It may be added, that they always lived happily together, and that the princess was not deceived in Frank.

THE BLUE RIBAND.

From Marne.

THERE was once a man, who was very poor, and sick into the bargain. When he felt that his end was drawing nigh, be summoned his wife to his bedside, and said to her: "My dear wife, I feel that my end approaches, but I should die tranquil and free from solicitude, if I only knew that all would go well with thee and our Hans, when I shall be no more. I can leave you nothing to protect you from want; but when I am dead, go with our son to my brother, who dwells in a village on the other side of the great forest. He is wealthy and has always cherished brotherly feelings towards me, and will, I doubt not, provide for you." He then died. After his burial, the widow and her son set out on their way to her brother-in-law, as her husband had recommended. Now it must be observed that the mother hated her son, and was hostile to him in eve way possible, though Hans was a good youth and approaching to manhood. When they had been journeying for some time, they observed a blue riband lying in the path. Hans stooped to take it up, but his mother said: "Let the old riband lie; what dost thou want with it?" But Hans thought within himself: "Who knows what it may be good for? It would be a real pity to let so pretty a riband lie here;" so he took it up, and bound it, without his mother's knowledge, under his jacket round his arm. He now became so strong, that no one, as long as he were that riband, could prevail against him, and everyone must stand in awe of him.

When they had proceeded some way further, and had entered the large forest, after having wandered about for a long time, they came to a cave, in which stood a covered table, loaded with a profusion of the daintiest viands in silver dishes. Hans said: "We are come just in the right moment. I have been hungry a long while; I will now make a hearty meal." So, they sat down and ate and drank to their hearts' content. They had scarcely finished when the giant to whom the cave belonged, returned home but he was quite friendly, and said: "You were right to help yourselves and not wait for me; if you find it pleasant, you can remain always here in the cave with me." To the woman he said that she might be his wife. To his proposal they both agreed, and now for a while lived content in the cave with the giant.

From day to day the giant became more and more attached to Hans but his mother's hatred to him increased every hour, and when she observed how strong he was become, she was still more embittered, and said one day to the giant: "Dost thou notice how strong Hans is? He may become dangerous to us the older he grows and the more he increases in strength, and may one day easily strike us both dead, that he may possess the cave alone; or he may drive us from it. It would be well and prudent on thy part, if thou wert to provide in time, and take an opportunity of getting rid of him." But the giant answered: "Never again speak to me in that strain. Hans is a good youth and will do us no harm; I will not hurt a hair of his head."

When the woman found that the giant would not lend himself to her purpose, she lay in bed on the following day and pretended to be ill. She then called her son, and said: "My dear Hans, I am so ill that I shall certainly die. There is, nevertheless, one remedy that may save me. I dreamed that if I could get a draught of the milk of the lioness that has her den not far from here, I should surely recover. If thou lovest me, thou canst help me; thou art so strong and fearest nothing; thou couldst go and fetch me some of the milk." "Certainly, dear mother," answered Hans; "that I will most readily do, if I only knew that it would do you good." So, he took a bowl and went to the den of the lioness. There she lay suckling her young ones; but Hans, laying the young ones aside, began to milk, which the lioness allowed quite quietly; but then in came the old lion roaring, and attacked Hans from behind, who, turning round, took the lion's neck under his arm and squeezed him so firmly that he began to whine most piteously, and became quite tame. Hans then released him, and he went and lay in the corner, and Hans proceeded with his milking, until the basin was full. When he left the den, the lioness sprang after him with her young ones, and were soon followed by the old lion. Hans then carried the milk to his mother, who was so terrified at the sight of the lions that she cried: "Hans, send the savage beasts away, or I shall die of fright." The lions thereupon went away of their own accord and lay down before the door, and when Hans came out, they ran to him and appeared glad.

When this attempt of the wicked mother had thus failed, she again said to the giant: "If thou hadst directly followed my counsel, we should now have nothing more to fear; but now it is worse than before, and as he has got the wild beasts, we cannot so easily do anything to harm him." The giant answered: "I know not why we should do anything to injure him. Hans is a good youth, and the animals are tame. I would on no account lay a hand on him." To this the mother replied: "It may, notwithstanding, easily enter his mind either to drive us from the cave, or even destroy us outright, in order to become its master. I cannot feel happy so long as I must live in fear."

After a time, the woman again lay in bed, saying she was sick, and again called to her son and said: "I have had another dream, that if I could get a few of the apples that grow in the garden of the three giants, I should again be well; otherwise I feel that I must die." Hans said: "My dear mother, as you have such great need of them, I will go to the giants and fetch you some." So, taking a sack, he was instantly on his way, and the lions after him. But the wicked mother thought that this time he would surely never return. Hans went straight into the garden and gathered a sackful of apples; and having so done, ate a few himself; immediately after which he fell into a deep sleep and sank down under one of the trees. This was caused by the apples, which possessed that property. Had the faithful lions now not been with him, he must have perished; for instantly there rushed a huge giant through the garden, crying: "Who has stolen our apples?" But Hans slept on and answered not. On perceiving Hans, the giant ran fiercely at him, and would have finished him, but then up sprang the lions, fell upon the giant, and in a short time tore him in pieces. Now came the second giant, also crying out: "Who has stolen our apples?" and when he was about to rush on Hans, the lions again sprang up, and in like manner despatched him. Lastly came the third giant and cried: "Who is stealing our apples here?" Hans slept on, but the lions seized this giant also and killed him. Hans then opened his eyes and went wandering about the garden. When he came near the castle, in which the giants had dwelt, he heard, from a deep underground chamber, a voice of lamentation. He descended and found a princess of exquisite beauty, whom the giants had carried away from her father, and here confined, loaded with heavy Chains. But Hans had scarcely touched the chains, when they flew in fragments, and he conducted the beautiful princess up into the most magnificent apartment of the castle, that she might recover herself, and wait until he returned. She entreated him to accompany her to her father's court, but he answered: "I must first go and carry the apples to my mother, who is sick to death." He then left the princess in the castle, took his sack of apples, and returned to the cave to his mother.

When she saw him coming, she could scarcely believe her eyesight, so great was her astonishment at seeing him unscathed and bearing a sackful of apples she instantly asked him how he had been able to accomplish his errand. "My dear mother," said he, "since I wear the blue riband, that you would not have had me take with me, I am so strong that nothing can prevail against on this occasion my lions killed all the giants, and now you shall go with me and leave this old den. Henceforth we will live at the castle in joy and splendour; I have found there a most beautiful princess, who shall remain with us." The mother and the giant now went with Hans to the castle; but when the former saw all the magnificence there, and how beautiful the princess was, she grudged Hans his good fortune more than ever, and was constantly on the watch for an opportunity to destroy him; for she now knew whence he derived his strength. So, one day, as Hans was lying at rest on his bed, with his riband hanging by him on a nail, she stole softly in, and, before he was aware, pierced out both his eyes; then took the riband, and as Hans was now blind and helpless, thrust him out of the castle and said, that thenceforward she would be sole mistress there. Poor Hans would soon have perished, had not the faithful lions conducted the princess to him. She attended him and led him; for she would proceed to her father's kingdom, hoping there to find a cure for her deliverer. But the way was long, and long they wandered about at length, however, they arrived in the neighbourhood of the city in which the father of the princess resided. Here she observed a blind hare running in the read before her, which, on coming to a brook that flowed by, dived thrice under the water, and ran, with its sight restored, away. She then led Hans to the water, who, when he had plunged into it three times, could see as before.

Full of joy they now entered the city, and when the old king was informed that Hans was the deliverer of his daughter, he would have no other son-in-law but him, nor could the princess have chosen a husband more agreeable to her than Hans. But when his mother had learned that Hans was restored to sight and had married the princess, she became suddenly ill through spite, and this time in earnest, and she died. Shortly after the giant also died. When looking under their pillow, Hans found the blue riband, which he wore as long as he lived, never laying it aside. He afterwards succeeded his father-in-law in the kingdom, and as king was feared by all his enemies far and near and regarded as a true protector of his people.

THE MAN WITHOUT A HEART.

From Meldorf.

THERE were once seven brothers, who had neither father nor mother. They lived together in one house, and had to do all the household work themselves, to wash, cook, sweep and whatever else was to be done; for they had no sisters. Of this kind of housekeeping they soon grew tired, and one of them said: "Let us set out, and each of us get a wife." This idea pleased the other brothers, and they made themselves ready for travelling, all excepting the youngest, who preferred to remain at home and keep house, his six brothers promising to bring him a wife with them. The brothers then set out, and all six went forth merrily in the wide world. They soon came into a large, wild forest, where, after wandering about for some time, they found a small house, at the door of which an old man was standing. On seeing the brothers passing by and appearing so gay, he called to them: "For what place are you bound that you pass my door so merrily?" "We are going each of us to fetch a handsome young bride," answered they, "and therefore are we so merry. We are all brothers, but have left one at home, for whom we are also to bring a bride." "I wish you then success in your undertaking," replied the old man; "you see, however, very plainly that I am so lonely that I too have need of a wife, and so I advise you to bring me one also with you." To this the brothers made no answer, but continued their way, thinking the old man spoke only in jest, and that he could have no occasion for a wife.

They soon arrived in a city, where they found seven young and handsome sisters, of whom each of the brothers chose one, and took the seventh with them for their youngest brother.

When they again arrived in the forest, there stood the old man at his door, apparently awaiting their coming. He even called to them at a distance: "Well, have you brought me a wife with you as I desired you?" "No," answered they, "we could not find one for thee, old man; we have only brought brides for ourselves, and one for our youngest brother." "You must leave her for me," said the old man, "for you must keep to your promise." This the brothers refused to do. The old man then took a little white staff from a shelf over the door, with which when he had touched the six brothers and their brides, they

"

were all turned into gray stones. These, together with the staff, he laid on the shelf above the door, but kept the seventh young bride for himself.

The young woman had now to attend to all that was to be done in the house; and she did it all cheerfully, for what would resistance have availed her? She had, moreover, every comfort with him, the only thought that gave her easiness being that he might soon die; for what was she then to do alone in the great wild forest, and how was she to release her six poor enchanted sisters and their betrothed husbands? The longer she lived with him the more dreadful did this thought become; she wept and wailed the whole livelong day, and was incessantly crying in the old man's ear: "Thou art old, and mayest die suddenly, and what am I then to do? I shall be left alone here in this great forest." The old man would then appear sad, and at length said: "Thou hast no cause to be uneasy; I cannot die, for I have no heart in my breast; but even if I should die, the twelve gray stones lie over the house-door, and with them a little white staff. If thou strikest the stones with that staff, thy sisters and their betrothed will again be living." The young woman now appeared contented, and asked him, that as his heart was not in his breast, where he kept it. "My child," answered the old man, "be not so inquisitive; thou canst not know everything." But she never ceased her importunities, until he at last said somewhat peevishly, "Well, in order to make you easy, I tell thee that my heart lies in the coverlet."

Now it was the old man's custom to go every morning into the forest and not return till the evening, when his young housekeeper had to prepare supper for him. One evening on his return, finding his coverlet adorned with all kinds of beautiful feathers and flowers, he asked the young woman the meaning of it. "Oh, father," answered she, "I sit here the whole day alone and can do nothing for thy gratification, and so thought I would do something for the delight of thy heart, which, as thou sayest, is in the cover let!" "My child," said the old man, laughing, "that was only a joke of mine; my heart is not in the coverlet, it is in a very different place." She then began again to weep and lament, and said: "Thou hast then a heart in thy breast and canst die; what am I then to do, and how shall I recover my friends when thou art dead?" "I tell thee," answered the old man, "that I cannot die, and have positively no heart in my breast; but even if I should die, which is not possible, there lie the gray stones over the door together with a little white stick, with which thou hast only, as I have already told thee, to strike the stones, and thou wilt have all thy friends again!" She then prayed and implored him so long to inform her where he kept his heart, that he at length said: "It is in the room-door."

On the following day she decorated the room-door with variegated feathers and flowers from top to bottom, and when the old man came home in the evening and inquired the cause, she answered: "Oh, father, I sit here the whole day, and can do nothing for thy pleasure, and wished therefore to give some delight to thy heart." But the old man answered as before: "My heart is not in the room-door; it is in a very different place." Then, as on the previous day, she began to weep and implore, and said: "Thou hast then a heart and canst die; thou wilt only deceive me." The old man answered: "Die I cannot; but as thou wilt positively know where my heart is, I will tell thee, that thou mayest be at ease. Far, very far, from here, in a wholly unknown solitary place, there is a large church; this church is well secured by thick iron doors; around it there runs a wide, deep moat; within the church there flies a bird, and in that bird is my heart. So long as that bird lives, I also live. Of itself it will not die, and no one can catch it. Hence, I cannot die, and thou mayest be without apprehension."

In the meantime, the youngest brother had waited and waited at home; but as his brothers did not return, he supposed that some mishap had befallen them, and therefore set out in quest of them. After travelling for some days, he arrived at the house of the old man. He was not at home, but the young woman, his bride, received him. He related to her how he had six brothers, who had all left home to get themselves wives, but that some mischance must have befallen them, as they had never returned. He had, therefore, set out in search of them. The young woman then instantly knew him for her bridegroom, and informed him who she was, and what had become of his brothers and their brides. Both were overjoyed at having thus met; she gave him to eat, and when he had recruited his strength he said: "Tell me now, my dear bride, how I can release my brothers." She then related to him all about the old man, whose heart was not in his breast, but in a far distant church, of which she gave him every particular, according to the old man's own narrative. "I will at all events try," said the young man, "whether I cannot get hold of the bird. It is true that the way is long and unknown to me, and the church is well secured; but by God's help I may succeed." "Do so," said the young woman, "seek the bird; for as long as that lives thy brothers cannot be released. This night thou must hide thyself under the bedstead, that the old man may not find thee: tomorrow thou canst continue thy journey." Accordingly, he crept under the bed just before the old man's return, and on the following morning, as soon as the old man was gone out, the young woman drew her bridegroom forth from his hiding-place, gave him a whole basketful of provisions, and after a tender farewell, he resumed his journey. He had proceeded a considerable way, when feeling hungry he sat down, placed his basket before him and opened it. While in the act of taking forth some bread and meat, he said: "Let come now everyone that desires to eat with me!" At the instant there came a huge red ox and said: "If thou didst say that everyone should come that desires to eat with thee, I would gladly eat with thee." "Very well," said the young man, "I did say so, and thou shalt partake with me." They then began to eat, and when they were satisfied, the red ox, when about to depart, said: "If at any time thou art in difficulty and requirest my aid, thou hast only to utter the wish, and I will come and help thee." He then disappeared among the trees, and the young man recommended his journey.

When he had proceeded a considerable way farther, he was again hungry, so sat down, opened his basket, and said as before: "Let those come that desire to eat with me!" In a moment there came from the thicket a large wild boar and said: "Thou hast said that whoever desired to eat with thee should come; now I would gladly eat with thee." The bridegroom answered: "Thou art quite right, comrade; so just fall to." When they had eaten, the boar said: "If thou art ever in difficulty and needest my aid, thou hast only to utter the wish, and I will help thee." He then disappeared in the forest, and the young man pursued his journey.

On the third day, when about to eat, he said again: "Let all that desire to eat with me come!" At the instant a rattling was heard among the trees and a large griffon descended and placed himself by the side of the traveller, saying: "If thou didst say that all who desired to eat with thee might come, I would gladly eat with thee." "With all my heart," answered the bridegroom; "'t is far more pleasant to eat in company than alone; so just fall to." Both then began to eat. When their hunger was satisfied, the griffon said: "If ever thou art in difficulty, thou hast only to call me and I will aid thee." He then disappeared in the air, and the young man went his way.

After travelling a while longer, he perceived the church at a distance; so redoubling his pace, he was soon close by it. But now there was the moat in his way, which was too deep for him to wade through, and he could not swim. Now the red ox occurred to his recollection: "He could help thee," thought he, "if he were to drink a green path through the water. Oh, that he was here!" Hardly had he expressed the wish when the red ox was there, laid himself on his knees and drank until there was a dry green path through the water. The young man now passed through the moat and stood before the church, the iron doors of which were so strong that he could not force one open, and the walls many feet thick, without an opening in any part. Knowing no other means, he endeavoured to break some stones, one by one out of the wall, and after great labour succeeded in extracting a few. It then occurred to him that the wild boar could help him, and he cried: "Oh, if the wild boar were here!" In an instant it came rushing up, and ran with such force against the wall, that in one moment a large hole was broken through it, and the young man entered the church. Here he saw the bird flying about. "Thou canst not catch it thyself," thought he, "but if the griffon were here—!" Scarcely had he uttered the thought, when the griffon was there; but it cost even the griffon a great deal of trouble to catch the little bird; at last, however, he seized it, gave it into the young man's hand and flew away. Overjoyed, he placed his prize in the basket, and set forth on his way back to the house in which his bride was.

When he reached the house and informed her that he had the bird in his basket, she was overjoyed, and said: "Now thou shalt first eat something in haste, and then creep again under the bed with the bird, so that the old man may know nothing of the matter." This was done, and just as he had crept under the bed, the old man returned home, but felt ill and complained. The young woman then again began to weep, and said: "Ah, now father will die, that I can well see, and he has a heart in his breast!" "Ah, my child," answered the old man, "be still only; I cannot die; it will soon pass over." The bridegroom under the bed now gave the bird a little pinch, and the old man felt quite ill and sat down, and when the young man squeezed it yet harder, he fell to the earth in a swoon. The bride then cried out: "Squeeze it quite to death." The young man did so, and the old man lay dead on the ground. The young woman then drew her bridegroom from under the bed, and afterwards went and took the stones and the little white staff from the shelf over the door, struck every stone with the staff, and in one instant there stood all her sisters and the brothers before her. "Now," said she, "we will set out for home, and celebrate our marriage and be happy for the old man is dead, and there is nothing more to fear from him." They did so and lived many years in harmony and happily together.

GOLDMARIA AND GOLDFEATHER.

From Puttgarden on the Isle of Femeru.

THERE was once a nobleman who had a daughter of wondrous beauty named Goldmaria. Her parents one day resolved on making an excursion, and Goldmaria would fain have accompanied them, but they would not allow her; so Goldmaria remained at home. At night, on their return, they lost their way in a vast forest, and were unable to find it, when they were met by a large poodle. "I will lead you into the right path," said the poodle, "if you will give that which first meets you from your house." The parents instantly thought of their dear Goldmaria, and feared that she might be the first to meet them; but as the weather from bad became worse and worse, and they had totally lost their way, they at last consented, and promised the poodle what he required, thinking that the house-dog might probably be the first to come to their carriage. They now soon reached home; but the first that came to their carriage was no other than Goldmaria. Thereupon said the poodle: "She now belongs to me and not to you." The parents earnestly besought him to take everything else, only to leave them their dear Goldmaria but the poodle was inexorable and would have Goldmaria, and no prayers were of any avail. A respite of three days only would he grant them, and then return and fetch her away.

Goldmaria now employed her time in taking leave of her friends and relations. Amid all their lamentations she was quite calm and content. On the last evening she said to her mother: "I will now bid farewell to our old neighbour." My daughter, said the mother, what hast thou to do at the old woman's?" "I must and will go," answered the daughter. She went accordingly, and when she came, the old woman said to her: "Fear nothing, my child; if thou wilt sleep with me tonight, I will teach thee *to wish*, and that will be highly useful to thee." Goldmaria was quite rejoiced at this and went back to her mother to tell her she would pass the night with her neighbour. When Goldmaria rose on the following morning she could conjure forth anything that she *wished*; and, having heartily thanked the old woman, took leave, hoping that, by means of her art, she might be able to see her parents as often as she desired.

When she returned home, the poodle was already there to fetch her away. Goldmaria then bade farewell to her disconsolate parents but made no mention of her having learned to *wish*. On coming to the open country, the poodle said to her: "Set thyself on my back, and I will soon bring thee to our journey's end." Goldmaria did so, and in a short time they came to a house, in which were two young maidens. When they entered, the poodle immediately transformed himself into an old woman, and was the mother of the two maidens. "Now," said she, "I have three lasses in whom I can find pleasure. Thou, Goldmaria, wilt be very happy with me, if thou wilt be obedient." Goldmaria promised to be so, and whenever the old woman said: "Goldmaria, do this, or do that, she would always do it quickly," as she had only to *wish* it.

One day when the old woman, in the likeness of a poodle, went again into the forest, she met with a comely young man who had lost his way, and was named Goldfeather. The poodle said to him: "I will conduct thee out of the forest, if thou wilt promise to return and abide with me." Goldfeather answered that he could make no promise, for that he was a king's son, and must speak with his father. At length, however, when he found himself quite unable to recover his path, he was obliged to say *yes*, and promise to belong to the poodle, who then conducted him out of the forest to his father's court. But at the expiration of three days he returned to fetch away Goldfeather. The father at first would not deliver him up, but was at length forced to comply, when the poodle said: "Goldfeather has himself promised, and he must keep his word." So Goldfeather was obliged to go and came to the place where Goldmaria already was. Goldmaria said to Goldfeather: "Be on thy guard against the old woman, for she is a bad one, and can do more than eat bread: tomorrow thou wilt certainly have to mow the grass." "But," answered Goldfeather, "I cannot; I don't know how I am to do it." And so, it proved;

for in the evening the old woman said to him: Goldfeather, thou must get a sithe ready, for tomorrow thou shalt mow the grass. Goldfeather then went to Goldmaria and said: "I am to get a sithe ready, and don't know how." "Oh," said she, "just knock a little on the sithe, then it will soon be ready." Goldfeather did so, and the sithe was instantly fit for use. On the following morning the old woman said: "Goldfeather, go and mow the grass." He went, however, first to Goldmaria, and asked her: "How am I to do it? I know nothing of the matter." Goldmaria answered: "Only strike the sithe so that it rings about the time when the old woman brings thee food." Goldfeather then went to the meadow and laid himself down to sleep; but at the time when his food was to be brought, he struck the sithe so that it rang, and in one moment all the grass fell down at once. Now came the old woman, who, seeing that all was done praised him for his diligence, and promised that he should be rewarded for it.

On the day following, the old woman again said to Gold feather: "My son, go today and sharpen an axe, for thou shalt cut wood. But he did not know how to sharpen an axe, and so went to Goldmaria for her instruction. She said to him: "Take a stone and only rub it twice or thrice up and down the axe, and it will instantly be sharp." Goldfeather did so. Shortly after, the old woman said to him: "Now go into the forest and hew wood." He went but could accomplish nothing. At length came Goldmaria and brought him his breakfast. "Ah," said he, "thou must help me again, for I know nothing about wood-cutting." "So," answered she, "it seems, then, that I am always to help thee and thou never helpest me." "Oh, dearest Goldmaria," answered Goldfeather, "I will ever love thee and never forsake thee as long as there is a drop of warm blood within me. Help me but this time out of difficulty." "Well then" said she, only turn the axe round and strike the tree. He did so, and in a moment all the wood was hewed. When the old mother came at noon, she was astonished at his diligence, praised him, and promised that it should be for his advantage. When Goldfeather returned home in the evening, he threw himself on his bed, thought much on his parents, but much more on Goldmaria.

The next day the old woman said: "Thou must get some rakes ready, for today thou shalt all turn the hay and carry it in." "Mother," said the daughters, "how can we carry in the hay? It is not possible." "It shall be done, and you must do it," answered the mother. Goldfeather then went, and with the aid of Goldmaria, prepared the rakes. When both the daughters, together with Goldfeather, were out in the field, where they were joined by Goldmaria, Goldfeather said to her: "How are we now to carry in the hay?" "Just do as I do," answered she; "only lay a stick on the nape of thy neck, and the hay will be soon got in." So, when the two daughters were foremost with a small quantity of hay, Goldmaria and Goldfeather placed sticks on the nape of their necks, and all the hay came after them, and they soon had it all together in the place where it was to lie. When the old woman came, she praised Goldfeather and the others for their diligence.

On the following day, he was ordered to bring wood home; but when he went for the purpose, he could bring only a very small quantity and was soon weary, so was obliged again to have recourse to Goldmaria, who said to him: "Do as thou didst with the hay;" and when Goldfeather had so done, all the wood was soon in the house. Then said the old woman: "Now get some spades in readiness, for tomorrow thou shalt dig clay. Make also some moulds for bricks; for thou shalt also make me some bricks." Now must Goldmaria again give her aid, so that the spades and moulds were soon ready, and when Goldfeather set about digging clay and could extract none, Goldmaria again came to his assistance, and told him he had only to thrust vigorously with the spade, and there would fly out clay enough. When Goldfeather had finished his task, the eldest daughter came and praised him to the skies; where upon Goldmaria said: "You praise him too much, for I have shared in the work." But the daughter still thought that Goldfeather deserved the greatest praise. "It bodes no good to me," said Goldmaria to Goldfeather, when the daughter had left them, "that she praised thee so warmly." But Goldfeather answered: "I will surely be true to thee, dear Goldmaria, as long as I live."

When the old woman came, she ordered the bricks to be made. Goldfeather made them, and when they were dry, would carry them to the house, but found them too heavy recourse must now again be had to Goldmaria. "Thou art truly a dolt," said she. "How often have I not told thee that thou hadst only to take a stick and lay it on thy neck, and that then all would be easy." Goldfeather then laid a stick across the nape of his neck, and all the bricks followed him. The old woman next asked him: "Dost thou know how to build an oven?" "No," answered he, "but I will do my best." So

Goldfeather set to work but could neither prepare the mortar nor lay the bricks and must therefore again apply to Goldmaria to help him out of his trouble. "Oh, thou canst do nothing," said she; "take a stick and beat the mortar with it, then it will be fit for use; and for the walls thou canst hammer a bit on a brick, and the oven will be ready." While the work was going on, the old woman came to look after it; and on his asking her if she were satisfied, she answered in the affirmative. But when he had finished, Goldmaria came to him and said: "We must now prepare for travelling; for I heard the old woman say we were too clever, and that when the oven was ready, we should be baked in it. Now I tell thee, Goldfeather, that, if thy life is dear to thee, thou must not leave me; for thou alone canst effect nothing against the old beldam. Tomorrow she will allow thee to rest and will bake thee the day after, be therefore on thy guard. Goldfeather was greatly alarmed, and it proved exactly as Goldmaria had said. "Tomorrow," said the old woman to him, "thou canst rest." But quite early, just at the break of day, Goldmaria rose and waked Goldfeather. They soon made themselves ready, and when about to set out Goldmaria spat on each side of her chamber-door and said: "When the old woman calls me the first time, do thou answer, *I am coming*, and if she calls a second time, answer, *I am coming directly*." In the morning the old woman screamed out for Goldmaria, and the door answered from the chamber, "I am coming." But when she called a second time, the door answered from the kitchen, "I am coming directly." But no one came. The old woman at length rose, looked into the chamber and into the kitchen, but no one was in either place. She then waked both her daughters and said: "Rise up quickly; Goldmaria and Goldfeather are away, and you must go after them. Go thou first," said she to the younger: on the declivity of the Blue Mountain there stands a rose-bush with a withered rose; that thou must on no account fail to pluck and bring to me." The daughter went in all haste after the fugitives, who had already proceeded a considerable distance, when Goldmaria said to Goldfeather: "Tread on my left foot and look over my right shoulder whether any one is coming." Goldfeather did so and said: "The younger daughter is coming in all haste after us." Goldmaria thereupon said: "I will then turn myself into a rose-bush and thee into a withered rose; but let not thyself be plucked and prick her smartly; for if she plucks; thee, we are both lost." When the girl now came to the rose, she was about to pluck it, but it pricked her so severely that she was forced to desist. She then returned home and was well scolded by her mother for her stupidity. The old woman then said to the elder daughter: "Do thou now go, and when thou art over the Blue Mountain, thou wilt see a white church, in which there is a preacher in the pulpit: take him by the hand and bring him with thee." Goldmaria and Goldfeather had in the meanwhile proceeded farther; but Goldmaria soon said again: "Tread on my left foot and look over my right shoulder whether any one is coming." "Yes," answered Goldfeather, the elder daughter is coming. "Then," said Goldmaria, "I will turn myself into a church and thee into a priest; but let her not lay hold of thee for else we are lost." Now came the daughter and entered the church; but was unable to ascend the pulpit and obliged to return home. At seeing her the old woman's rage exceeded all bounds, and she ran forth herself. "Then" said Goldmaria again to Goldfeather: "Tread on my left foot and look over my right shoulder whether any one is coming after us." "Yes," answered Goldfeather, "the old woman herself is now coming." "Then I will turn myself into a pond and thee into a duck; but I beseech thee, Goldfeather, let not thyself be enticed to the edge, so that she may take hold of thee but take the gold rings, which she will cast in for the purpose of catching thee, if thou canst get them without danger." Now came the old woman to the pond and would decoy the duck, which continued swimming about. She threw in her gold rings, one after another, but the duck was not to be so tempted; and when she had thrown in the last was so angry that she resolved to drink up the pond, and, laying herself down for the purpose, drank so long that she burst. Goldmaria and Goldfeather now resumed their natural forms, and swore eternal fidelity to each other, and that they would never part. From the old woman there was now nothing more to fear.

After a tedious journey, they at length reached the city in which the king, Goldfeather's father, resided. When they came before the palace, and Goldfeather was about to enter, Goldmaria said to him: "Hear me, Goldfeather, I have only one request to make thee, that thou mayest not forget me when thou art in thy father's house, and leave me here without, standing on the broad stone: beware that no one kisses thee; for then thou wilt instantly forget me." Goldfeather promised to observe her injunction and recollected the warning on entering the house; and when his father and mother hastened to welcome him, he did not kiss them. But when he entered an apartment, there sat his old betrothed, whose name was Menne, who, the instant she saw him, sprang up for joy and kissed him before he was aware of her design. In one moment, all remembrance of Goldmaria was banished from his mind. She stood long without on the broad stone, expecting that he would send for her; but finding that no one came, she wept for a long time, and then took her departure, hired a neat little cottage opposite the palace, and gave herself out as a seamstress. There she lived alone, a pair of doves being her only companions; and on the grassplot behind the house she had a little calf which she fed and found great delight in seeing it grow from day to day. Being admirably skilled in needlework, she soon got an abundance of work; no young person in the city, it was said, being able to sew more curiously and beautifully.

The young sparks of the court had in the meantime dis covered what a handsome maiden Goldmaria was and were desirous of making her acquaintance. But Goldmaria paid no heed to them, and never looked off from her work, when they passed to and fro before her window. Among these young courtiers there were three brothers, all of whom were deeply in love with Goldmaria. They one day begged some fine linen of their mother, saying that Goldmaria worked so delicately, they wished her to make them some collars. The eldest was the first that went to Goldmaria, wished her a good day, and sat down to converse with her. "Tomorrow evening you can fetch your collars," said Goldmaria. When the time came for fetching the collars, she invited him to stay awhile, and he remained till bedtime. When he was about to take leave, she said to him that he was welcome to stay there that night, which the young man was perfectly ready to do. When Goldmaria was retiring to rest, she requested him to go and lock the door of the house, and when he touched the lock, she cried out:—

> "Man to lock and lock to man,
> Then go to rest I calmly can."

There sat be fast at the door, where he was obliged to remain the whole night. In the morning, when Goldmaria rose, she recollected that he was yet standing there and said:—

> "Man from lock and lock from man,
> Then give thanks for his soothing sleep he can."

He then entered, returned thanks for his tranquil sleep, took his collars, with which he was much pleased, and went away. At home he made no mention of his adventure. His younger brother then said: "This evening I must away to the seamstress."

In the evening he went accordingly to Goldmaria and said: "I wish to have some collars made like my brother's." "Those you can easily have," said Goldmaria; "sit down and stay a little." They then entered into conversation, while Goldmaria sewed, and so passed the evening. When it was time for him to depart, she told, as she had told his brother, that he was welcome to stay there that night; but before she withdrew, she said to him: "I have quite forgotten to fasten the garden door; would you have the kindness to fasten it for me?" "Most willingly," answered he, and hastened away for the purpose; but the instant he touched the ring of the door, she cried out:—

> "Man to ring and ring to man,
>   Then go to rest I calmly can."

He was then unable to get loose and had to remain standing the whole night until morning, when Goldmaria rose and said:—

> "Man from ring and ring from man,
>   Then give thanks for his soothing sleep he can."

Being thus released, he entered and thanked her for his comfortable sleep.

On his return home with the collars, his elder brother instantly asked him where he had been standing all night. "What?" answered he, "Why, I have been sleeping?" "That's not true," said the other; "so tell me where thou hast been standing, and I'll tell thee where I was standing." He then said I have been standing by the garden door. "And I by the house door," said the other. They then agreed not to say a word of what had befallen them to their youngest brother, that he might also be tricked.

In the evening, the youngest brother went. "Good evening, Goldmaria," said he; "wilt thou make me two or three collars like those of my brothers, but prettier, if possible?" "Most willingly," answered Goldmaria; "just sit down a little while and stay." When evening was over, she also requested him to remain there all night; but just as she was about to retire, she said to him: "Oh, my calf is not yet tethered, and is running about the yard do me the kindness."

"With pleasure," answered he, running out but on his touching the rope, she cried:—

> "Man to rope and rope to man,
> Then go to rest I calmly can."

The calf then began running with him over stock and stone and through thick and thin the whole night long. In the morning Goldmaria recollected that the young man was still running about with the calf, and said:—

> "Man from rope and rope from man,
> Then give thanks for his soothing sleep he can."

He then entered, thanked her for his comfortable sleep, and was exceedingly delighted with his collars, which were much handsomer than those she had made for his brothers. On his return home, and his brothers asking him how he had passed the night, he would not confess that he had been running about with the calf.

Matters had in the meantime proceeded so far with Goldfeather and Menne, that the day was fixed for their marriage. When the carriage with the bridal pair came down from the palace and was passing by Goldmaria's window, she *wished* that it might sink in a deep swamp that was exactly before her door. The carriage stuck fast accordingly, so that neither horses nor men could draw it from the spot. At this mishap the old king was sorely vexed, and ordered more horses to be put to, and that more men should assist; but all to no purpose. Among the retinue, which attended the bridegroom to church, were the three brothers before mentioned, the eldest of whom said to the king: "Sir king, here in this small house there dwells a maiden that can *wish* whatever she desires; and she has surely wished the carriage to stick fast in this place." "How dost thou know that she can do so?" asked the old king. The young man answered: "She lately wished me to the house door, and there I was obliged to stand all night." "Yes," said the second brother, "but when she has wished any one fast, she can also wish him loose." "And how dost thou know that?" inquired the king. "I was lately obliged to stand the whole night at her garden door; but in the morning she released me." The old king would then instantly send to Goldmaria, but the youngest brother said: "Sir king, the young woman has also a calf that has the strength of ten horses. Let the bridegroom go to her and beg her to lend us the calf; the carriage will then be soon set free." "That I'll do most readily," said the bridegroom, at the same time alighting from the vehicle and going to Goldmaria, whom he besought to lend him her calf, which, as he had heard, possessed such wonderful power. "The calf you can have and welcome," answered she, "but you must first promise that I shall be invited to the wedding, together with my doves." This the bridegroom promised, and as soon as the calf was harnessed to the vehicle, it drew it forth with perfect ease.

After the ceremony, when the young couple had returned home and many guests were assembled, Goldmaria also made her appearance with her two doves. She met with a most friendly reception, and was conducted into the saloon, having a dove perched on each shoulder. At table the most costly dishes were served up, portions of which were set before Goldmaria; but she touched nothing, and sat sad and silent. At seeing so fair a damsel sitting so sad and tasting nothing, the guests were astonished, and on asking her the cause, the doves answered:—

> "No food can the little dove eat,
>   For Goldfeather his bride has forgotten,
>   And left on the stone in the street."

The bridegroom hearing this, ordered the servants to place before her viands yet more costly; but Goldmaria touched nothing, and the doves repeated:—

> "No food can the little dove eat,
>   For Goldfeather his bride has forgotten,
>   And left on the stone in the street."

At this the bridegroom became lost in thought, looked stedfastly at Goldmaria, and recognised her. He then addressed his bride: "My dear bride, I pray thee answer me one question. I have a cabinet to which there are two keys, an old one, which I once lost, but have now found again, and a new one, which I procured in place of the old one, when that was lost. Tell me now which of the two I ought to use first, the old one or the new?" She answered: "Thou shouldst first use the old one. Thou hast now," replied he, "pronounced thy own sentence; for this is my dear Goldmaria, with whom I have shared joy and sorrow at the old witch's in the forest, who at all times aided me, who saved me, and to whom I have sworn eternal fidelity." Menne then, having no alternative, renounced Goldfeather, and all the people and his and her parents declared there was no one that so well deserved to be his wife as Goldmaria. They were then married and lived happily together for very many years.

THE KING OF SPAIN AND HIS QUEEN.

AN OLD king of Spain had seven sons. He once fell sick, and, to amuse him, his eldest son related a tale. When he had finished, the king said: "My son that thou hast read from some book, thou hast not thyself experienced it." This vexed the young man, and day and night he pondered the matter over how he himself might achieve something in the world. He therefore caused a ship to be built and resolved on making a voyage; but just as the ship was finished, and everything ready for his departure, the old king died. The son then became king. He now took to wife a very prudent and sagacious lady. The day after the marriage, his bride presented him with a shirt of snowy whiteness, but which, as she said. would turn black when she was dead; and should she not conduct herself in all respects as a wife ought to do, would become all over stained.

The king could not rest from his desire to see the world; he therefore went on board his ship and put to sea. A violent storm soon arose, which drove the vessel as far as Turkey, where he was made a captive. The Sultan was quite delighted when he heard that his prisoner was the king of Spain, and immediately despatched a ship to Spain, with his minister, to fetch the queen, as he wished to make her his wife. But the queen returned for answer that she must be faithful to her husband and could not marry so long as she was ignorant whether he was living or dead. So, the minister was obliged to return to his ship.

Now the queen did not know what had become of her husband, for she had not been informed of his mishap. She therefore set out in search of him, and came to a large forest, where she met with a hermit. She asked him whether he knew where her husband was, as she was going in search of him. The hermit said to her: "You have royal clothes still on, with them you cannot travel, you must lay them aside and put on mine." This the queen did, and the hermit then directed her to proceed through the forest, when she would come to the great ocean, and there would find a ship, in which she should sail. When the queen came on board the vessel, she found in it a person of rank, whom she immediately recognised to be the Sultan's minister, who had been sent to fetch her. She asked him whether she might accompany him to Turkey, for she could both play and sing sweetly. The minister consented willingly to take her with him.

They now sailed to Turkey; and when the minister appeared before the Sultan, he said: "The queen of Spain we have not been able to bring with us; but we have brought a Spanish hermit, who was well worth the trouble of going for, as he plays and sings so sweetly."

The Sultan answered: "Let the queen of Spain remain where it pleases her best, but let the hermit play before me. As a reward, you shall both of you always dine at my table." When the Sultan had heard the hermit sing, he said again to his minister: "I cannot part with the hermit, he is too dear to me, you must therefore let me retain him I will give you a ton of gold for him." The Sultan then ordered an instrument to be brought, that the hermit might play upon it; and calling on the captive king of Spain, he said: "The king of Spain shall be your footstool." Then the king was obliged to lie down on the ground, and his wife placed her foot on his neck, but he did not recognise her; and the same took place every time the hermit played before the Sultan. The hermit continued to play and sing every day, and the Sultan became more and more attached to him; he also walked every day with the Sultan in his rose-garden. He once said to the Sultan: "My revered Sultan, is it permitted to pluck a beautiful rose in your garden?"

"Yes, my dear hermit," answered the Sultan, "ask from me whatever thou wilt, and it shall be granted thee."

"Then," replied the hermit, "I will pray that I may conduct the king of Spain back to his own country."

To this the Sultan assented; but the hermit must first swear that he would return as soon as he had conducted the king of Spain home. The hermit now took the king back to his own land and was about to return immediately; but the king said: "My dear hermit, I cannot let thee go back to Turkey; thou must remain with me, I cannot part with thee." The king would on no account suffer him to depart, and so the hermit was obliged to remain.

When the chief minister appeared before his sovereign, the king asked him what had become of his queen. The minister answered, that she had conducted herself unbecomingly, and had fled with her coachman.

"That I am surprised to hear," replied the king; "for the shirt my wife gave me at our marriage is quite white."

The minister answered: "Of that I know nothing; I only know that she is fled, and no one knows whither."

At this the king was bitterly grieved. Now the minister's plan was that the king should marry his daughter, and the king himself seemed at times inclined to enter into it. At table the minister's daughter sat by the side of the king, who joked and toyed with her; but immediately after he would relapse into sadness, and sigh mournfully at the remembrance of his lost wife. The hermit he had always with him to sing while he sat at table with his minister. One day the king said to him: "Come, my dear hermit, sing me a beautiful song, with thy fine clear voice, to comfort me." The hermit sang:—

> "Ah, why must I so sad
>   From out this garden wander;
> And what I've ever loved,
>   Renounce through cruel slander?"

Upon this the king said: "My dear hermit, thou surely hast known my wife." The hermit answered: "But the minister has told you she had fled." "Certainly, he did say so," replied the king; but my shirt is still quite white. He then said to him, confidentially: "If thou knowest my wife, tell me."

"Yes, I know her well," answered the hermit; "but even if I were to tell you so, you would not believe me. I brought you out of Turkey, and you have been my foot stool every day, and I have been so long with you and you have not known me but have believed the words of the minister."

The king thereupon looked attentively at the hermit and felt convinced that he was his wife. But now his anger was turned upon the wicked minister.

He caused a great banquet to be announced, and invited all his ministers and his governors, and when they were all assembled, asked them what ought to be the punishment of him who slandered the absent. Then the chief minister answered: "He deserves to have his tongue torn out."

At this moment the queen entered the hall in her royal robes, and the king said: "There stands one whom thou hast slandered! He then ordered the executioner to be summoned, to fulfil the judgment the minister had passed upon himself[2].

MILLET-THIEF.[3]

THERE was once a very rich merchant who had a fine house and a large and beautiful garden, in which was a piece of land sown with millet. As the merchant was one day walking in his garden—it was in the spring of the year, and the seed had sprung up fast and strong—he saw to his great vexation that, during the night, a part of the millet had been shorn away by some bold thief; and just that part of the garden in which every year he was in the habit of sowing millet, was that in which he took the greatest delight. He determined to capture the thief, and then either punish him severely himself, or give him over to justice. For this purpose, he called his three sons, Michael, George, and John, and said to them: "This night a thief has been in our garden, and cut a part of the millet, which vexes me exceedingly. The offender must be caught and punished. You, my sons, must now keep watch during the night, one after another, and whoever catches the thief shall receive from me a handsome reward."

The eldest son Michael kept watch the first night. He took with him a brace of loaded pistols and a sharp sabre, with plenty to eat and drink, wrapped himself up in a warm cloak, and seated himself under an elder, where he soon fell into a sound sleep. When he awoke in the bright morning, there was a still larger piece of the millet cut away than on the preceding night; and

---

² This tale agrees in substance with the ballad of the "Graf von Rom" in Uhland, ii. 784; and with the Flemish story of "Ritter Alexan der aus Metz und seiner Frau Florentina." See Grimm, "Deutsche Sagen," No. 531.

³ This and the four following tales are from Bechstein, Deutsches Marchenbuch, Leipsig, 1848.

when the merchant came into the garden, and saw this, and found that his son, instead of keeping watch and catching the thief, had slept, he was yet more angry, reprimanded and jeered him as a model of a watchman, from whom his very sword and pistols might have been stolen.

The next night George watched. Besides the weapons his brother had had with him, he took a strong cord and a stout cudgel. But the good watchman, George, likewise fell asleep, and the next morning found that the millet had been shorn off much more than on the preceding nights. The father now became quite furious, and said: "If the third watchman sleeps, there will be an end of the millet, and we shall require no more watching."

The third night it was John's watch. He, notwithstanding all their persuasions, would not take any weapons with him, but secretly armed himself against sleep. He collected thorns and thistles, which, when he went into the garden to the place where he was to keep watch, he made into a heap; so that whenever he began to nod, he pricked his nose with the thorns which woke him up again instantly. At midnight he heard a tramping which came nearer and nearer, and at length reached the millet; he then heard a most diligent munching. "Oho!" thought he, "I have caught thee now," and, taking a cord from his pocket, pushed the thorns gently aside and crept a little nearer to the thief; when—who could have thought it—the thief proved to be a most beautiful little colt! John was highly delighted and had no trouble in catching it; the little animal followed him quietly to the stable, which John securely fastened. And now he went to bed quite contented. Early in the morning, when his brothers rose and were going down into the garden, what was their astonishment at seeing their brother in bed and fast asleep. They awoke and jeered him as being such an excellent watchman, who could not stay out even for one night to watch. But John answered: "Only be quiet, and, I will show you the millet thief." And his brothers and father then followed him to the stable, where the wonderful colt stood, of which no one was able to say whence it came or to whom it belonged. It was most beautiful of aspect, of slender and elegant form, and of snowy whiteness.

The merchant was overjoyed and gave his vigilant son the colt as a reward. John received it with delight and named it MILLET-THIEF.

Soon after this, the brothers heard that a princess was enchanted in a palace that stood on the top of a glass mountain, which no one, on account of its being so slippery, could ascend; but whoever should be so fortunate as to reach the summit and ride three times round the palace, would disenchant the princess and have her to wife. Numbers had already endeavoured to ride up the mountain but were all precipitated to its foot and lay dead around. This wonderful story was re-echoed through the whole country, and among others the three brothers thought that they should also like to try their luck in riding up the glass mountain, and, if possible, win the princess. Michael and George bought powerful young horses and had their shoes well sharpened; but John saddled his little Millet-Thief, and they set out on their adventure. They soon reached the glass mountain. The eldest rode first, but alas! his horse slipped, fell down with him, and both horse and rider forgot to get up again. The second then attempted to ride up, but his horse also slipped, fell down with him, and both man and horse forgot to get up again. Now John rode up, and it went trap, trap, trap, trap, trap, and up they were, and again trap, trap, trap, trap, trap, and they had gone three times round the palace as if Millet-Thief had been the same road a hundred times before. Now they stood in front of the palace gates, which opened spontaneously, and the lovely princess stepped forth clad in silk and gold, and extended her arms joyfully towards John, who instantly alighting from Millet-Thief, hastened towards her and embraced her with the greatest delight.

The princess then turning to the colt, caressed it fondly, and said: "Ah! thou little rogue, why didst thou run away from me, so that I could no longer enjoy the only indulgence granted me, that of riding by night below on the green earth, as thou didst not return to bear me up and down the glass mountain? But now thou must never leave me again."

Then John became aware that his Millet-Thief belonged to the lovely princess. His brothers recovered from their fall, but John never saw them again. He lived happily and far removed from all earthly cares with his beautiful consort in the enchanted palace on the glass mountain. But to this mountain no other child of man has since found the way; because the enchantment was dissolved, and the princess released from the spell, by the sagacity of her little horse, which had conducted to her her liberator and consort.

THE SEVEN RAVENS.

As many strange things come to pass in the world, so there was a poor woman who had seven sons at a birth, all of whom lived and throve. After some years, the same woman had a daughter. Her husband was a very industrious and active man, on which account people in want of a handicraftsman were very willing to take him into their service, so that he could not only support his numerous family in an honest manner, but earned so much that, by prudent economy, his wife was enabled to lay by a little money for a rainy day. But this good father died in the prime of life, and the poor widow soon fell into poverty; for she could not earn enough to support and clothe her eight children. Her seven boys grew bigger, and daily required more and more, besides which they were a great grief to their mother, for they were wild and wicked. The poor woman could hardly stand against all the afflictions that weighed so heavily upon her. She wished to bring up her children in the paths of virtue, but neither mildness nor severity availed anything: the boys' hearts were hardened. One day, when her patience was quite exhausted, she spoke thus to them: "Oh, you wicked young ravens! would that you were seven black ravens, and would fly away, so that I might never see you again!" and the seven boys immediately became seven ravens, flew out of the window, and disappeared.

The mother now lived with her little daughter in peace and contentment and was able to earn more than she spent. And the young girl grew up handsome, modest, and good. But after some years had passed, both mother and daughter began to long after the seven boys; they often talked about them and wept; they thought, that could only the seven brothers return and be good lads, how well they could all live by their work and have so much pleasure in one another. And as this longing in the heart of the young maiden increased daily, she one day said to her mother: "Dear mother, let me wander in the world in quest of my brothers, that I may turn them from their wicked ways, and make them a comfort and a blessing to you in your old age." The mother answered: "Thou good girl! I will not restrain thee from accomplishing this pious deed. Go, my child! and may God guide thee." She then gave her a small gold ring which she had formerly worn when a child, at the time the brothers were changed into ravens.

The young girl set out, and wandered far, very far away, and for a very long time found no traces of her brothers; but at length she came to the foot of a very high mountain, on the top of which stood a small dwelling. At the mountain's foot she sat down to rest, all the while looking up in deep thought at the little habitation. It appeared at first to her like a bird's nest, for it was of a grayish hue, as if built of small stones and mud then it looked like a human dwelling. She thought within herself: "Can that be my brothers' habitation?" And when she at length saw seven ravens flying out of the house, she was confirmed in her conjecture. Full of joy, she began to ascend the mountain, but the road that led to the summit was paved with such curious glass-like stones, that every time she had with the greatest caution proceeded but a few paces, her feet slipped, and she fell down to the bottom. At this she was sadly disheartened and felt completely at a loss how to get up, when she chanced to see a beautiful white goose, and thought: "If I had only thy wings, I could soon be at the top." She then thought again. "But can I not cut thy wings off? yes, they would help me." So she caught the beautiful goose, and cut off its wings, also its legs, and sewed them on to herself; and see! when she attempted to fly, she succeeded to perfection and when she was tired of flying, she walked a little on the goose's feet, and did not slip down again. She arrived at length safely at the desired spot. When at the top of the mountain, she entered the little dwelling it was very small; within stood seven tiny tables, seven little chairs, seven little beds, and in the room were seven little windows, and in the oven seven little dishes, in which were little baked birds and seven eggs. The good sister was weary after her long journey and rejoiced that she could once again take some rest and appease her hunger. So, she took the seven little dishes out of the oven and ate a little from each and sat down for a while on each of the seven little chairs, and lay down on each of the little beds, but on the last she fell fast asleep, and there remained until the seven brothers came back. They flew through the seven windows into the room, took their dishes out of the oven, and began to eat; but instantly saw that a part of their fare had disappeared. They then went to lie down, and found their beds rumpled, when one of the brothers uttered a loud cry, and said: "Oh what a beautiful young girl there is on my bed!" The other brothers flew quickly to see, and with amazement beheld the sleeping maiden. Then the one said to the other: "Oh, if only she were our sister." Then they again cried out to each other with joy: "Yes, it is our sister; oh yes, it is, just such hair she had, and just such a mouth, and just such a little gold ring she wore on her middle finger as she now has on her little one." And they all danced for joy, and all kissed their sister, but she continued to sleep so soundly, that it was a long time before she awoke.

At length the maiden opened her eyes and saw her seven black brothers standing about the bed. She then said: "Oh happy meeting, my dear brothers; God be praised that I have at length found you! I have had a long and tedious journey on your account, in the hope of fetching you back from your banishment, provided your hearts are inclined never more to vex and trouble your good mother; that you will work with us diligently, and be the honour and comfort of your old affectionate parent." During this discourse the brothers wept bitterly, and answered: "Yes, dearest sister, we will be better, never will we offend our mother again. Alas! as ravens we have led a miserable life, and before we built this, but we almost perished with hunger and cold. Then came repentance, which racked us day and night; for we were obliged to live on the bodies of poor executed criminals and were thereby always reminded of the sinner's end."

The sister shed tears of joy at her brothers' repentance, and on hearing them utter such pious sentiments: "Oh!" exclaimed she, "all will be well. When you return home, and your mother sees how penitent you are, she will forgive you from her heart, and restore you to your human form."

When the brothers were about to return home with their sister, they said, while opening a small box: "Dear sister, take these beautiful gold rings and shining stones, which we have from time to time found abroad: put them in your apron and carry them home with you, for with them we shall be rich as men. As ravens we collected them only on account of their brilliancy." The sister did as her brothers requested her and was pleased with the beautiful ornaments. As they journeyed home, first one of the ravens and then another bore their sister on their pinions, until they reached their mother's dwelling, when they flew in at the window and implored her forgiveness and promised that in future, they would be dutiful children. Their sister also prayed and supplicated for them, and the mother was full of joy and love, and forgave her seven sons. They then became human beings again, and were fine blooming youths, each one as large and graceful as the other. With heartfelt gratitude they kissed their dear mother and darling sister; and soon after, all the seven brothers married young discreet maidens, built themselves a large beautiful house (for they had sold their jewels for a considerable sum of money), and the house-warming was the wedding of all the seven brothers. Their sister was also married to an excellent man, and, at the earnest desire of her brothers, she and her husband took up their abode with them.

The good mother had great joy and pleasure in her children in her old age, and as long as she lived was loved and honoured by them.

THE LITTLE CUP OF TEARS.

THERE was once a mother and a child, and the mother loved this her only child with her whole heart and thought she could not live without it; but the Almighty sent a great sickness among children, which also seized this little one, who lay on its bed sick even to death. Three days and three nights the mother watched, and wept, and prayed by the side of her darling child; but it died. The mother, now left alone in the wide world, gave way to the most violent and unspeakable grief; she ate nothing and drank nothing, and wept, wept, wept three long days and three long nights without ceasing, calling constantly upon her child. The third night, as she thus sat overcome with suffering in the place where her child had died, her eyes bathed in tears, and faint from grief, the door softly opened, and the mother started, for before her stood her departed child. It had become a heavenly angel, and smiled sweetly as innocence, and was beautiful like the blessed. It had in its hand a small cup, that was almost running over, so full it was. And the child spoke: "O! dearest mother, weep no more for me; the angel of mourning has collected in this little cup the tears which you have shed for me. If for me you shed but one tear more, it will overflow, and I shall have no more rest in the grave, and no joy in heaven. Therefore, O dearest mother! Weep no more for your child; for it is well and happy, and angels are its companions." It then vanished.

The mother shed no more tears, that she might not disturb her child's rest in the grave and its joys in heaven. For the sake of her infant's happiness, she controlled the anguish of her heart. So strong and self-sacrificing is a mother's love.

THE THREE GIFTS.

THERE was once a poor weaver who became known to three rich students, who, seeing that the man was very poor, gave him for his housekeeping a hundred dollars. The weaver was overjoyed at the gift, and resolved on employing it to the greatest advantage, but would first for a time feast his eyes on the shining money. He would not tell his wife of his good fortune, who happened just then to be from home, and concealed the money where no one would think of looking for it, namely, among some old rags. One day, while he was out, a rag-collector came to the house, and his wife sold him the whole bundle of rags for a few pence. Now there was grief of heart when the weaver returned, and his wife, full of joy, showed him the trifle of money she had got for her old rags.

When a year had passed, the three students came again, hoping to find the weaver in comfortable circumstances instead of which they found him poorer than ever, and on their expressing wonder at this, he informed them of his misfortune. After warning him to be more careful in future, they gave him another hundred dollars. Now he thought he would be very prudent, so, without saying a word to his wife, he hid the money in the dust-tub; and this time it fell out just as on the former occasion. His wife exchanged the ashes with a dustman for two or three pieces of soap, while her husband was just gone out to carry some work to a customer. When he returned, and was told of the bargain with the ashes, he was so enraged that he gave his wife a beating.

When another year had passed, the three students came for the third time, and found the weaver in rags and misery. They said, throwing at the same time a piece of lead at his feet: "Of what use is a nutmeg to a cow? To give thee money again would prove us to be greater fools than thou art. We will never come to thee again." Thereupon they went away in anger, and the weaver picked up the piece of lead and laid it on the window-sill. Soon after his neighbour entered the room—he was a fisherman—bade him good day, and said: "My friend, have you perchance a piece of lead, or anything heavy, that I can use for my net? for I have just now nothing of the kind at hand." The weaver gave him the piece of lead which the students had left, for which the fisherman thanked him, and promised that he should have in return the first large fish he caught. "Very well," replied the weaver, "but it is not worth speaking about." Soon after, the fisherman actually brought a fine fish, weighing four or five pounds, and obliged his neighbour to accept it. He immediately cut up the fish and found a great stone in its belly. This stone the weaver also laid in the window-sill. In the evening, when it he came dark, the stone began to shine, and the darker it grew the brighter the stone became, and just like a candle. "That's a cheap lamp," said the weaver to his wife; "wouldst thou not like to dispose of it as thou didst the two hundred dollars?" and he placed the stone so that it illumined the whole room.

The next evening a merchant chanced to ride past the house, who, on seeing the brilliant stone, alighted, and entered the room, looked at it, and offered ten dollars for it. The weaver answered: "The stone is not for sale." "What, not for twenty dollars?" said the stranger. "Not even for that," replied the weaver. The merchant, however, kept on bidding and bidding for the stone, till at last he offered a thousand dollars; for the stone was a precious diamond, and really worth much more. Now the weaver struck the bargain and was the richest man in the village.

His wife would have the last word, and took much credit to herself, saying: "See, husband, how well it was that I threw away the money twice; for thou hast me to thank for this good luck."

THE MAN IN THE MOON.[4]

VERY, very long ago there was a man who went into the forest one Sunday to cut wood. Having chopped a large quantity of brushwood, be tied it together, thrust a stick through the bundle, threw it over his shoulder, and was on his way home, when there met him on the road a comely man, dressed in his Sunday clothes, who was going to church. He stopped, and, accosting the wood-cutter, said: "Dost thou not know that on earth this is Sunday, the day on which God rested from his works, after he had created the world, with all the beasts of the field, and also man? Dost thou not know what is written in the fourth commandment, 'Thou shalt keep holy the Sabbath-day?'" The

---

[4] See Chaucer, Testament of Cresseide, 260-263, Shakspeare, Tempest, ii. 2. Mids. Night's Dream, i. 3; also Grimm, Deutsche Mythologie, p. 679.

questioner was our Lord himself. The wood-cutter was hardened, and answered: "Whether it is Sunday on earth or Monday (Monday) in heaven, what does it concern thee or me?"

"For this thou shalt forever bear thy bundle of wood," said the Lord; and because the Sunday on earth is profaned by thee, thou shalt have an everlasting Monday, and stand in the moon, a warning to all such as break the Sunday by work."

From that time the man stands in the moon, with his faggot of brushwood, and will stand there to all eternity.

LORA, THE GODDESS OF LOVE.[5]

THE mountain-fortress of Lora is so called from a goddess of that name. Before Charles, the conqueror of Saxony, and his missionary, Winfrid[6], had baptized the subjugated inhabitants of the Harz, Lora was held in great veneration by the Saxons of those parts. To her was consecrated a large awe-inspiring forest, the remains of which, even at the present day, almost involuntarily, and as it were by enchantment, transport our thoughts back to ages long passed away. The only memorial of it, at the present day, is a wood of small extent, the abode of numberless flocks of birds, called the Ruhensburg, between the Reinhartsberg, Bleicherode, and the fortress of Lora, together with some detached woods, among which well-built villages, watered by the Wipper, now enliven the delightful land scape, to which the distant Brocken serves as a background.

From this forest the youths, in time of old, offered to the goddess Lora, in the autumn, the first-fruits of the chase; and in the spring, the young maidens,

---

[5] This and the twelve following are from Otmar, Volcks—Sagen (Traditions of the Harz), Bremen, 1800.

[6] The apostle of Germany, better known by his ecclesiastical name of Boniface. He was born at Crediton in the year 680 and was murdered by the pagan Frisians in 755. Boniface placed the crown on the head of Pepin, the first monarch of the Carlovingian race, and, besides many monasteries in Germany, founded the sees of Erfurt, Buraburg, Eichstädt, and Würzburg. He died archbishop of Mentz.

singing joyful songs, brought wreaths of flowers to the goddess. With the finest wreath the high priest of Lora solemnly adorned the head of that maiden who had most distinguished herself by the feminine virtues: by constancy in love, and by unshaken fidelity to her beloved.

In the middle of the mountain on which Lora was principally worshiped there gushed forth a spring, to which a pilgrimage was made by unhappy lovers, especially young maidens, whom death had bereft of their beloved, in the hope that, by drinking of those waters, they might obtain peace and forgetfulness. On the summit of this mountain a noble Saxon lady, whose lover had fallen in a battle with the Franks, built the Ruhensburg[7], from which the wood derives its present name. She called the spot the Ruhensburg, because in the wood the goddess sent her a new lover worthy of her, whose love comforted the mourner, and gave back to her heart its long-lost peace.

But terrible was this sacred forest to the faithless lover. There Hermtrud expiated her crime with her life. She was betrothed to Eilgern, a noble Saxon youth. The defence of his country tore him from her. At parting, she swore to him, with hypocritical tears, eternal fidelity; but in a few days after, Lora saw the violator of faith and duty in the arms of Herrman. The culprits had concealed themselves in the Buchen, a wood not far from the Ruhensburg. Here Lora startled them by a deer that came rushing through the thicket; and Hermtrud fled, and entered, without reflection, Lora's sacred grove. The mountain trembled, and the earth darted forth flames, which consumed the false-hearted fair one. The priests hastened to the spot, collected Hermtrud's ashes, and buried them in a little valley at the foot of the mountain. Here may still be heard at twilight the mournful wail of the false one, a warning to all faithless lovers not to enter the sacred grove.

Winfrid, the terror of the Saxon gods, together with his companions, destroyed the Ruhensburg for Lora's might had then fled. The following act of revenge exhausted her last remaining powers. Not far from the Reinhartsberg she overtook Winfrid, exulting in his spiritual victories. His carriage and horses suddenly stuck fast in the mire; and he would have been instantly swallowed up, had not his prayers to the Holy Virgin saved him. In memory of this danger he erected three crosses, which are yet to be seen, on

---

[7] From ruhe, *peace of mind, quiet,* and burg, *castle.*

the spot where the abyss opened its jaws to receive him, and in his misery dedicated, in Lora's wood, a chapel to the Virgin. From this event the place is still called Elend (Misery).

THE HORSESHOES ON THE CHURCH-DOOR.

COUNT ERNEST, of Klettenberg[8], rode once, on a Sunday morning, to a great drinking match at Ehich. Many knights were invited thither to drink for a prize; the reward offered was a gold chain.

The old, well-proved knights continued drinking for many hours, until the victory should be decided; and one here, another there, fell under the influence of the monstrous bumpers, and were laid on the floor as poor weaklings, amid the loud scornful laugh of their companions. At length four only of the so-called noblemen remained on the battlefield; and of these, three leaned against the wall, exulting with stammering tongues and trembling hands that they could still hold the huge beaker. Only Ernest von Klettenberg could keep on his feet; who, seizing triumphantly the gold chain, which lay on the table, hung it round his neck.

That he might show himself to the people as victor, he tottered out of the hall, and ordered his horse to be brought. Four esquires lifted him into the saddle, and he rode, amid the cries of the rushing multitude, through the town, on his way home to Klettenberg. As he passed through the suburb, he heard vespers being sung in the church which was dedicated to St. Nicholas. Count Ernest, in his drunken frenzy, rode through the open door, in the midst of the assembled congregation, straight up to the altar. The song of devotion passed first into dumb astonishment, and then into a wild scream.

But not long did Count Ernest enjoy his outrage. For as the spurred horse trod on the steps of the altar, behold! oh, wonderful! its four shoes fell off, and it sank down together with its rider. In perpetual remembrance of this event,

---

[8] The same Count probably whose monument is to be seen in the conventual church at Walkenried, where he appears kneeling, as if praying for forgiveness for similar juvenile sins to that here related.

the four horseshoes were nailed to the church-door, where they remained for ages, an object of wonder, on account of their size and of that awful catastrophe.

THE WREATH.

OF the Quästenburg, once a very celebrated fortress at the extremity of the Harz, the terror of the surrounding plains and of the itinerant trader, only a ruin and a popular tradition, kept in remembrance by an annual public festival, have been preserved. Coarse grass now covers the castle yard; and in the halls where high-spirited knights held their carousals, where the scornful laugh of the robbers' feast resounded, now hardly a trace is to be found. Instead of retainers on the look-out for prey, a cowering screech owl is to be seen sitting on the moss-covered openings of the walls. Of all the once vast buildings nothing remains but here and there some ruined walls, or some cellars, the entrance to which snakes and toads and wild plants (which also deck the walls) dispute with the inquisitive wanderer; some ruins of the former gate-tower and the castle dungeons.

The hill on which the robbers' castle rose is surrounded by high mountains as with a wreath, which in former times served both to conceal and protect it. These are in some parts covered with wood, in others heaped up like rugged masses of rock in the most fantastic groups. On one side only a pass, which opens between the mountains, gives to the scarcely perceived castle a freer prospect across a narrow valley, which at the present time is occupied by the peaceful village of Questenberg, and thence, across a somewhat confined tract of land, over the golden meadows, which at the extremity of the horizon is bounded by the Kyffhäuser Mountains and the Rothenburg.

Craftily enough had a knight of the middle ages selected this lurking place for deeds that shunned the light; for not easily could the wagons laden with goods, which passed through this much frequented part of Thuringia, escape the vigilant eyes of the owner of the castle, who, concealed in the fortress, lay in wait for his prey, like the ant-eater by his sandy crater. The following tradition explains the origin of the name of the Quästenburg, and shows that, even in times of lawless rapine, nature asserts her rights.

One of the old lords of this castle had an only daughter. When this child was about four or five years old, she one day lost herself in the forest which encircled it. In the evening of that day a charcoal-burner, living at some distance, found the little girl quietly sitting by his hut, and busied in plaiting a wreath of wild flowers. He asked her whence she came, who her father and mother were, and what she came there for. To all these questions the little girl could only answer that her mother was dead, and that her father's name was Kurt. At that time a hundred different persons thereabouts owned the name of Kurt; so that all the charcoal-burner could do was to carry the child home to his hut, and take care of her, until he obtained further information.

The lord of the castle, inconsolable for the loss of his child, had despatched all his followers and serving-men in every direction, in quest of her. After a long, fruitless search, and after many days passed in sorrow, some of the villagers of Rota found the child sitting in a meadow, busied in plaiting a wreath of wild flowers. She led them to the hut of the charcoal-burner, who had taken such care of her, and soon after they carried her with great rejoicings back to the castle. The charcoal-burner, who had also accompanied her thither, took the wreath, which the child had plaited while sitting at the door of his hut, and presented it to her father, who joyfully clasped his little daughter in his arms.

A wreath was in those days called Quäste. In commemoration of this event he named his castle the Quästenburg (which had previously borne the name of Finsterberg), from the wreath, which he ever after religiously preserved. In gratitude for having recovered his daughter, he gave to the charcoal-burner, and the villagers of Rota, the meadow forever, in which his child was found, and appointed a public festival for all his serving-men, at which a wreath, or Quäste, was to be fastened on the largest oak on the highest mountain in the neighbourhood, that it might be seen far and wide.

This festival is still held and is perhaps unique of its kind. On the third day of Whitsuntide, the young men from the valley of Questenberg bring the largest oak which they have been able to find in the neighbouring forest, amidst a countless multitude of shouting spectators from the adjacent places; and accompanied by horns and trumpets, ascend the mountain which looks down on the ruins of the old Quästenburg. But they must, conformably to the custom, use only their hands in rolling or in dragging the huge tree to the mountain. On the summit of the mountain, which overlooks the neighbouring country, the tree is then set up, and to a pole laid crosswise a large wreath, formed of boughs, and resembling a carriage wheel, is fastened, when all exclaim: "The wreath hangs! The wreath hangs!" Dancing on the mountain follows, in which consists the principal amusement.

After some hours thus passed, the whole assembled multitude, accompanied by loud music, descend the mountain, and proceed to the house of the clergyman of Questenberg, whom they fetch to a solemn service in the church, which terminates the holyday. The oak remains erect on the mountain for a year and is afterwards sold to defray the expenses of the festival. The great wreath is by the inhabitants of the neighbourhood called the "QUÄSTE."

THE KNIGHTS' CELLAR IN THE KYFFHÄUSER.

A POOR, though honest and very merry man in Tilleda, once invited some friends to a christening; it was already the eighth he had had; and, according to custom, he was obliged to give a treat to the gossips. The wine of the country, which he had set before his guests, was soon drunk out, and they called for more. "Go," said the merry host to his daughter Ilsabe, a handsome girl of sixteen, go, and fetch some better wine out of the cellar." "Out of what cellar?" asked the girl. "Oh!" replied her father jokingly, "out of the great wine cellar belonging to the knights in the Kyffhäuser. The maiden, in her simplicity, went out, with a jug in her hand, to the mountain. About midway she found a venerable matron sitting at the ruined entrance of a large cellar in a strange garb, and with a huge bunch of keys at her side. The young girl was dumb with astonishment; but the old woman, in a friendly tone, said to her: "You, no doubt, wish to fetch some wine from the knights' cellar?" Yes," answered the girl timidly, "but I have no money." "Come with me, said the woman, and you shall have wine for nothing and better than your father has ever yet tasted." They both then passed through a half-ruinous passage, and

446

the young maiden had to tell how things were going on in Tilleda. "Once," said the old woman, "I was as young and fair as you, when the knights stole me away by night, through a passage underground from the house in Tilleda which now belongs to your father. Not long before this, they carried off by force from Kelbra, as they were coming out of church in broad daylight, the four fair damsels, who still at times ride about here on their richly-caparisoned horses, and then vanish. When I grew old, they made me the overseer of their wine-cellar, and that I am still." They had now arrived at the cellar-door, which the old woman opened. It was a large, roomy vault, on both sides of which lay huge casks of wine. She tapped on the casks, the greater number of which were half, or entirely full. She then took the small pitcher, filled it with most excellent wine, and said: "There, take that to your father, and as often as you have a merry-making in your house, you can return; but tell no one save your father whence you get the wine. Nor may you sell any of it; for as you get it for nothing, you must give it for nothing. If any one comes here to fetch wine to make a profit by it, his last loaf is baked."

The young girl brought the wine to her father, which the guests found most excellent, without being able to guess whence it came, and whenever there was a little merry-making in the house, Ilsabe fetched wine from the Kyffhäuser in her little pitcher. But this pleasure did not last long. The neighbours wondered whence the poor man procured such excellent wine, as the like of it was not to be found in the whole country. But the father told no one, neither did Ilsabe. Opposite to them lived a vintner, who adulterated all that he sold. He had once tasted the knights' wine and thought: "That wine thou couldst dilute with ten times the quantity of water, and yet sell it with profit." He therefore allowed the young maiden when she was going with her little pitcher for the fourth time to the Kyffhäuser, hid himself among the bushes when she stopped, and after some time saw her come out of the passage which led to the cellar, with her pitcher filled.

The next evening, he went himself up the mountain, and wheeled on a barrow the largest empty cask he could find. This he hoped to fill with the excellent wine, to wheel it down the mountain in the night-time, and then return every day as long as any wine remained in the cellar. When he came to the place where he had on the previous day seen an opening to the cellar, everything became dark before his eyes; the wind began to howl awfully, and the storm dashed him, his barrow, and his empty barrel from one crag to another. He continued falling deeper and deeper, and at length fell into—a grave. Here he saw borne before him a coffin covered with black, and his wife with four mourning neighbours, whom by their dress and figure he well recognised, following the bier. With terror he fell into a swoon.

After some hours, consciousness returned; he looked around, and to his horror found himself still in the dimly lighted grave and heard just above his head the well-known sound of the church-clock in Tilleda striking twelve.

Now he knew that it was midnight, and that he was lying in the vaults under the village church. He was more dead than alive, and hardly dared to breathe. See! a monk approaches, and carries him up a long, long flight of steps, opens a door, silently places some money in his hand, and lays him down at the foot of the mountain. It was a cold, fine, frosty night.

By degrees the wine-dealer was sufficiently recovered to crawl home, but without either cask or wine. It struck one just as he reached his door. He was obliged to go to bed immediately, and in three days he died. The money which the necromantic monk had given him was just enough to pay for the expenses of his funeral.

THE WONDERFUL FLOWER.

A SHEPHERD from the village of Sittendorf was once driving his flock at the foot of the Kyffhäuser. He was a comely youth and betrothed to a good but poor girl. Neither he nor she owned a hut, or any money to begin housekeeping with.

Sorrowful he ascended the mountain, and the higher he went—it was a lovely day—the lighter was his heart. He soon reached its summit, where he found a wonderfully beautiful flower, the like of which he had never before seen. He plucked it, and stuck it in his hat, in order to carry it to his betrothed.

On the summit of the mountain he found an open vault, the entrance to which was somewhat ruinous. He went in, and there saw several small shining stones lying on the ground, of which he put as many into his pocket as it would hold. He was about to return into the open air, when a hollow voice called to him: "Forget not the best." This so terrified him that he knew not how he got out of the vault. No sooner did he see the sun and his flock again, than the door, which he had not before perceived, was shut behind him. He put his hand to his hat, and the wonderful flower was gone; it had fallen out when he stumbled. Suddenly a dwarf stood before him. "Where is the wonderful flower, thou didst find?" said he. "Lost!" answered the shepherd, mournfully. "It was not for thee," answered the dwarf. "It is of more value than all Rothenburg!" Sorrowful the shepherd went in the evening to his betrothed and told her the history of the lost flower; they both wept, for all hopes of a cottage and a wedding again vanished.

At length the shepherd recollected the stones, and playfully threw them into the lap of his beloved. Behold, they were all gold pieces. Now they bought a cottage, and a piece of land to it, and in less than a month they were man and wife.

And the wonderful flower? That has vanished but is at the present day sought for by the dwellers on the mountain, not alone in the vaults of the Kyffhäuser, but also (as hidden treasures are not stationary) on the Quästenburg, and even on the north side of the Harz; but the lucky one, for whom it is destined, is yet to come.

THE GOATHERD.

PETER CLAUS, a goatherd from Sittendorf, who led his herd to pasture on the Kyffhäuser, was accustomed in the evening to stop and let them rest in a place inclosed by old walls, and there to count them.

He had observed for several days that one of his finest goats, as soon as they came to this place, disappeared, and did not follow the herd till quite late. He watched it more closely and saw that it crept through a rent in the wall. He followed and found it in a cave comfortably enjoying some oats which were falling from the roof. He looked up at seeing the rain of oats, but with all his peering, was unable to solve the mystery. At length he heard the neighing and stamping of horses overhead, from whose cribs the oats must have fallen.

While the goatherd was thus standing, lost in astonishment at hearing the sound of horses in such an uninhabited mountain, a young man suddenly appeared, who silently beckoned Peter to follow him. The goatherd ascended some steps and came through a walled courtyard to a deep dell, inclosed by steep craggy precipices, down into which a dim light penetrated through the dense foliage of the overhanging branches. Here he found, on a well-levelled, cool grass-plot, twelve grave knightly personages playing at skittles, not one of them uttering a word. Peter was silently directed to set up the fallen skittles.

He began his task with trembling knees, when with a stolen glance he viewed the long beards and slashed doublets of the noble knights. By degrees, however, use made him bolder; he gazed around him with a more observing eye, and at length ventured to drink from a can that stood near him, the wine in which exhaled towards him a delicious fragrance. He felt as if inspired with new life, and as often as he was fatigued, he drew fresh strength from the inexhaustible wine-can. But at length he was overpowered by sleep.

When he awoke, he found himself again on the inclosed plain, where his goats had been accustomed to rest. He rubbed his eyes but could see neither dog nor goats; he was astonished at the height of the grass, and at the sight of shrubs and trees which he had never before observed. Shaking his head, he walked on through all the ways and paths, along which he had been in the daily habit of wandering with his herd; but nowhere could he find a trace of his goats. At his feet he saw Sittendorf, and with quickened steps began to descend the mountain, for the purpose of inquiring in the village after his herd. The people he met coming from the village were all strangers to him, and differently clad, and did not even speak like his acquaintances; everyone stared at him, when he inquired after his goats, and stroked their chins; he unconsciously did the same, and found, to his astonishment, that his beard was more than a foot long. He began to think that both himself and all around were bewitched; nevertheless, he recognised the mountain he had just descended as the Kyffhäuser; the houses also with their gardens were familiar to him some boys, too, when asked by a traveller the name of the place, answered: "Sittendorf."

He now walked up the village towards his own hut. He found it in a very ruinous condition: before it lay a strange herd-boy, in a ragged jacket, and by him a half-famished dog, which showed its teeth and snarled when he called to it.

He passed through an opening where once had been a door; when he entered, he found all void and desolate. Like a drunken man he reeled out at the back-door, calling on wife and children by name. But no one heard—no voice answered him. Soon many women and children collected round the old graybeard, all eagerly asking him what he sought. To ask before his own house after his wife and children, or after himself, appeared to him so extraordinary, that, in order to get rid of his questioners, he named the first one that recurred to his memory, "Kurt Steffen! All were now silent and looked at each other. At length an aged woman said: "For more than twelve years he has dwelt under the Sachsenburg, but you will not get so far today." "Where is Velter Meier?" "God be merciful to him, answered an old crone, leaning on her crutches, "for more than fifteen years he has lain in that house, which he will never leave." Shuddering, he now recognised a neighbour, though, as it seemed to him, grown suddenly old; but he had lost all desire to make further inquiries. There now pressed forward through the inquisitive crowd, a young comely woman with a boy in her arms about a year old, and a little fellow of four years holding by her hand; they were all three the image of his wife. "What is your name?" asked he with astonishment. "Maria." "And your father's?" "God be merciful to him, Peter Claus. It is now twenty years and more that we searched for him a whole day and night upon the Kyffhäuser, the herd having come back without him. I was then seven years old."

No longer could the goatherd dissemble: "I am Peter Claus," he exclaimed, "and no other," taking the boy out of his daughter's arms. Everyone stood as if petrified, until first one voice and then another exclaimed: "Yes, that is Peter Claus! Welcome, neighbour, welcome after twenty years!"

THE DWELLER IN THE ILSENSTEIN.

HAST thou never seen the beautiful maiden sitting on the Ilsenstein? Every morning with the first beams of the sun, she opens the rock and goes down to the Ilse to bathe in its clear cold waters. True, the power of seeing her is not granted to everyone, but those who have seen her, praise her beauty and benevolence. She often dispenses the treasures contained in the Ilsenstein; and many families owe their prosperity to the lovely maiden.

Once, very early in the morning, a charcoal-burner, proceeding to the forest, saw the maiden sitting on the Ilsenstein. He greeted her in a friendly tone, and she beckoned to him to follow her. He went, and they soon stood before the great rock. She knocked thrice, and the Ilsenstein opened. She entered, and brought him back his wallet filled, but strictly enjoined him not to open it till he reached his hut. He took it with thanks. As he proceeded, he was struck by the weight of the wallet, and would gladly have seen what it contained. At length, when he came to the bridge across the Ilse, he could no longer withstand his curiosity. He opened it and saw in it acorns and fir-cones. Indignant he shook the cones and acorns from the bridge down into the swollen stream, when he instantly heard a loud jingling as the acorns and cones touched the stones of the Ilse and found to his dismay that he had shaken out gold. He then very prudently wrapped up the little remnant that he found in the corners of the wallet and carried them carefully home and even this was enough to enable him to purchase a small house and garden.

But who is this maiden? Listen to what our fathers and mothers have told us. At the Deluge, when the waters of the North Sea overflowed the valleys and plains of Lower Saxony, a youth and a maiden, who had been long attached to each other, fled from the North country towards the Harz mountains, in the hope of saving their lives. As the waters rose, they also mounted higher and higher, continually approaching the Brocken, which in the distance appeared to offer them a safe retreat. At length they stood upon a vast rock, which reared its head far above the raging waters. From this spot they saw the whole surrounding country covered by the flood, and houses, and animals, and men had disappeared. Here they stood alone and gazed on the foaming waves, which dashed against the foot of the rock.

The waters rose still higher, and already they thought of fleeing farther over a yet uncovered ridge of rock, and climbing to the summit of the Brocken, which appeared like a large island rising above the billowy sea.

At this moment the rock on which they stood trembled under their feet and split asunder, threatening every instant to separate the lovers. On the left side towards the Brocken stood the maiden, on the right the youth their hands were firmly clasped in each other's the precipice inclined right and left outwards; the maiden and the youth sank into the flood.

The maiden was called Ilse, and she gave her name to the beautiful Ilsenthal, to the river which flows through it, and to the Ilsenstein, in which she still dwells.

THE ROSSTRAPPE; OR, HORSE'S FOOT-MARK.

THE Rosstrappe, or Horse's Foot-mark, is the name of a rock in the lofty projection of the Harz behind Thale, with an oval cavity bearing some resemblance to the impression of a gigantic horse's hoof, which many passengers ascend, on account of the beautiful romantic Swiss-like view from its summit.

Popular tradition gives the following account of the cavity.

More than a thousand years ago, before the robber knights had erected the surrounding castles of Hoymburg, Leuenburg, Steckelnburg, and Winzenburg, the whole country round the Harz was inhabited by giants, who were heathens and sorcerers. They knew no other pleasure than murder, rapine, and violence. If in want of weapons, they tore up the nearest sexagenarian oak, and fought with it. Whatever stood in their way they beat down with their clubs, and the women who pleased them they carried off by force, to be either their servants or wives.

In the Bohemian forest there lived at that time a giant named Bohdo, of vast stature and strength, and the terror of the whole country; every giant in Bohemia and Franconia crouched before him; but he could not prevail on Emma, the daughter of the king of the Riesengebirge[9], to return his love. Here neither strength nor stratagem availed him aught; for she stood in compact with a mighty spirit. One day Bohdo caught sight of his beloved as she was hunting on the Schneekoppe, and instantly saddled his horse, which could spring over the plains at the rate of five miles a minute and swore by all the

---

[9] Or Giant-mountains, a chain of mountains which separate Silesia from Bohemia, the highest of which is the Schneekoppe.

powers of darkness to obtain Emma this time or perish in the attempt. Quicker than the hawk flies he darted forward and had almost overtaken her before she was aware that her enemy was so near. But when she saw him only nine miles behind and knew him by the gates of a destroyed town, which served him as a shield, she hastily urged on her horse. And it flew, impelled by her spurs, from mountain to mountain, from cliff to cliff, through valleys, morasses and forests, so that the beeches and oaks were scattered like so much stubble by the force of her horse's hoofs. Thus, she fled through the country of Thuringia, and came to the mountains of the Harz. From time to time she heard behind her the snorting of Bohdo's horse, and then pushed on her yet unwearied steed to new exertions.

Her horse now stood snorting and panting on the frightful rock which, from the evil one holding his revels there, is called the Devil's Dancing-place. Emma cast a fearful glance around, her horse trembled as it looked into the abyss, for the precipice was perpendicular as a tower, and more than a thousand feet down to the yawning gulf below. She heard the hollow rushing of the water under her feet, which here formed a frightful whirlpool. The opposite rock, on the other side of the precipice, appeared to her even more distant than the abyss, and hardly to afford space enough for one of her horse's fore-feet.

Here she stood, anxious and doubtful. Behind her was an enemy whom she dreaded more than death itself. Before her was the abyss, which opened its jaws towards her. Emma now again heard the snorting of Bohdo's panting horse. In her terror she called upon the spirits of her fathers for help, and without reflection pressed the ell-long spurs into the sides of her steed; and she sprang! sprang across over the abyss, and happily reached the opposite rock; but it struck its hoofs four feet deep into the hard stone, so that the flying sparks illumined the whole country around like lightning. This is the horse's footmark. Time has made the hollow less, but no rains can entirely efface it.

Emma was saved! but the gold crown which she wore, and which weighed a hundred pounds, fell into the abyss as the horse sprang across it. Bohdo, who saw only Emma and not the abyss, sprang after the fugitive, and fell with his horse into the vertex of the stream, to which he gave its name[10].

---

[10] The Bode, which, with the Emme and the Saale, flows into the Elbe.

Here, changed into a black dog, he guards the princess's golden crown, that no thirster after gold may raise it up from the foaming gulf. A diver once, induced by large promises, tried to obtain it. He descended into the abyss, found the crown, and raised it so high, that all the assembled people could see the rays of it. Twice it fell from his hands, and the spectators called to him to descend a third time. He did so, and a stream of blood rose high up in the air. The diver never appeared again.

With fear and horror, the traveller now approaches the gulf, which is covered with the darkness of night. The stillness of the grave reigns over the abyss. No birds fly over it, and, in the dead of the night, may often be heard in the distance the hollow dog-like howl of the heathen.

At the present day the whirlpool where the dog guards the golden crown is called the Kreetpfuhl[11], and the rock where Emma implored the aid of the spirits of her fathers, the Devil's Dancing-place.

THE DUMMBURG.

WITH dread the wanderer approaches the ruins of the Dummburg. Terror seizes him if night overtakes him in its vicinity; for when the sun goes down and he treads on the site of the castle, he hears from beneath hollow means and the clank of chains. At midnight he sees in the moonlight the spectres of knights of former days, who ruled the land with an iron sceptre. In solemn procession twelve tall white figures rise from amid the rocky fragments, bearing a large open coffin, which they place on the top of the hill, and then vanish. The Skulls also move about, that lie scattered under the rock.

For many years the Dummburg was the abode of robbers, who slew the passing travellers and merchants, whom they perceived on the road from Leipsig to Brunswick and heaped together the treasures of the plundered churches and the surrounding country, which they concealed in subterranean caverns. Deep wells were choked up with their murdered victims; and in the frightful castle-dungeon, many miserable beings perished by the slower death

---

[11] That is, the devil's pool. So Kreetkind, the devil's child, in the dialect of those parts.

of hunger. Long did this lurking-place of banditti continue undiscovered. At length the vengeance of the confederated princes reached them. The boards of gold, silver, and precious stones still remain piled up in the ruined cellars and vaults of the Dununburg; but it is seldom granted to the wanderer to find the doors, even if here and there he may discover ruined entrances. Spectres in the form of monks, and also living monks, are often seen descending into the rock.

A poor wood-cutter, who was about to fell a beech at the back of the scattered ruins, seeing a monk approach slowly through the forest, hid himself behind a tree. The monk passed by and went among the rocks. The wood-cutter stole cautiously after him, and saw that he stopped at a small door, which had never been discovered by any of the villagers. The monk knocked gently and cried: "Little door, open!"—and the door sprang open. "Little door, shut!" he also heard him cry, and the door was closed. Trembling in every limb, the wood-cutter marked the crooked path with twigs and heaps of stones. But from that time, he could neither eat nor drink, nor sleep, so anxious was he to know what was contained in the cellars to which this wonderful door gave entrance.

The following Saturday evening he fasted, and on the Sunday, rising with the sun, he took his rosary and proceeded to the rock. He now stood before the door, and his teeth chattered with fear, as he expected to see a spectre in the form of a monk—but no spectre appeared. Trembling he approached the door; he listened long and—heard nothing. In the anxiety of his heart he prayed to all the saints and to the Virgin, and then, without reflecting, tapped on the door, at the same time saying in a low tremulous voice: "Little door, open!" and the door opened, when he saw before him a narrow dim passage. He entered tottering and found that it led into a spacious and rather light vault. "Little door, shut!" said he, almost unconsciously, and the door closed behind him.

With fear he now walked forward and found large open vessels and sacks full of old dollars and fine guilders, together with heavy gold pieces. Here were also many beautiful caskets filled with jewels and pearls, costly shrines, and decorated images of saints, which lay about or stood on tables of silver in the corners of the vault. The wood-cutter crossed himself and wished himself a thousand miles from the enchanted spot yet could not withstand the desire of taking some of the useless treasures, to enable him to clothe his wife and eight children more comfortably, as they had long been in rags.

Shuddering, and with averted eyes, he stretched out his hand towards the sack that stood nearest to him and took out a few guilders. Feeling now somewhat more composed, with less tremor and half closing his eyes he then took a few dollars, also a handful or two of the small copper coins, and again crossing himself, tottered back to the door,

"Come again!" cried a hollow voice from the depth of the vault. As everything about him seemed to whirl round, he could scarcely stammer out: "Little door, open!" The door sprang open. In a livelier and louder voice, he now cried out: "Little door, shut!" and it closed behind him.

He ran home with the utmost speed but uttered not a syllable about the treasures he had found; then went into the conventual church and offered up, for the church and for the poor, two-tenths of all that he had taken in the vault. The next day he went to the town and bought some clothes for his wife and children. He had, he said, found an old dollar and a few guilders under the roots of the beech that he had felled. The following Sunday he went with firmer steps to the door in the rock, did as he had done the first time, and supplied himself better than on the former occasion; still with moderation and discretion. "Come again!" cried the same hollow voice. And he went on the third Sunday and filled his pockets as before. He was now in his own estimation a rich man, but what could he do with his riches? He gave to the church and to the poor two-tenths of all he had, the rest he resolved to bury in his cellar, and from time to time fetch some as he required it. Yet he could not resist the desire first to measure his money; for as to counting it, that was an art he had never learned.

He accordingly went to his neighbour, a very rich man, but who starved himself in the midst of his wealth. He hoarded up corn, deprived the labourer of his hire, extorted from the widow and orphan, and lent money on pledges. He had no children. From this man the wood-cutter borrowed a measure, measured his money, buried it, and returned the measure to its owner. The measure had some long cracks in it, through which the corn-dealer, when selling to the poor labourer, always shook some grains back to his own heap. In one of these cracks two or three of the small copper coins had lodged, which the wood-cutter, in throwing out the money, had not observed. But they did not so easily escape the vulture-eyes of his rich neighbour. He went in search of the wood-cutter and asked him what he had been measuring. "Pine-cones and beans," answered he confusedly. The usurer shook his head, and showed him the copper coins, threatened him with the law, the torture, and, lastly, promised to give him all he could possibly wish for, if he would tell him the truth. Thus, he extorted the secret out of the poor man, and learned from him the powerful words.

The whole week the rich usurer employed in forming plans how he might at once get possession of all the treasures in the vault, as well as of those he thought might be concealed in the neighbouring vaults or buried under the earth. He reckoned beforehand, that if he could get together all this money, he could by degrees, either purchase at a cheap rate from his neighbours, or extort from them, by false accusations and false witnesses, one acre and one hide of land after another, and thus make himself lord of the whole village, and, perhaps, of several of the neighbouring villages; then get ennobled by the emperor; and, as a robber-knight, lay the country around under contribution.

It did not please the wood-cutter that his evil-disposed neighbour should visit the castle-vaults. He prayed him to desist from his purpose and represented to him the fate of many luckless treasure-seekers. But who ever held back a miser from an open sack of gold?

By threats and entreaties, the wood-cutter was at length prevailed on to accompany him to the door; he was only to receive the sacks, which the miser would himself drag out, and conceal them among the bushes. For this service he was to have the half of all the treasure, and the church a tenth: all the poor also in the village should be newly clothed. So spake the usurer. In his heart he had resolved, when he no longer required his aid, to throw the wood-cutter headlong into a deep well which was near the castle, to give nothing to the poor, and to the church only a few copper coins.

The following Sunday the extortioner, accompanied by the wood-cutter, set off before sunrise to the Dummburg. On his shoulder he carried a sack, which contained three bushels, into which he put twenty smaller ones, and in his hand a spade and a large axe. The wood-cutter warned him most strongly against covetousness, but in vain; he recommended him to offer up prayers to the saints for protection, but he would not. Muttering and gnashing his teeth, he walked on.

They now arrived at the door. The wood-cutter, who did not feel very easy in the affair, but was held back by the fear of the torture, stood at some distance to receive the sacks. "Little door, open!" cried the miser in a hurried tone and trembling with eagerness. The door then opened, and he entered. "Little door, shut!" cried he, and it closed after him. No sooner was he in the vault and saw all the vessels and sacks full of gold, and caskets of precious stones and pearls, and shining money, than he devoured them all with his eyes then with trembling hands pulled the twenty sacks out of the large one, and began filling them. At this moment there came slowly from the depth of the vault a great black dog with fire-darting eyes, and laid himself on all the full sacks, and then on the money. "Away with thee, miser!" cried the dog, grinning fiercely at him. Trembling, the usurer fell to the ground, and crept on hands and knees to the door; but in his fear he forgot the words, "Little door, open," and continued calling out, "Little door, shut," and the door continued closed.

The wood-cutter waited long with beating heart; at length he approached the door. It seemed to him that he heard groans and moaning and the hollow howl of a dog, and then all was silent.

He now heard the sound of the mass-bell at the convent and counted his beads; then gently knocked at the door, saying: "Little door, open!" The door opened, and there lay the bleeding body of his wicked neighbour stretched on his sacks; but the vessels of gold and silver, and diamonds and pearls, sank deeper and deeper before his eyes into the earth, till all had completely vanished.

HACKELNBERG AND THE SCREECH-OWL.

FAR and wide in the Harz Mountains and the Thuringian Forest rides the wild huntsman Hackelnberg, although he prefers abiding in the Hakel, whence he has his name, particularly in the neighbourhood of the Dummburg. With his dogs he is often to be heard at midnight riding in storm and rain, or in moonlight when the sky is partially covered with fleeting clouds, following in the air the shades of the game he slaughtered in his lifetime. His usual course is from the Dummburg across the Hakel, to the present desolate village of Ammendorf. But only to a few Sunday's children[12] is granted the power of seeing him. To them he appears at times as a solitary huntsman with a dog; at other times, they see him in a carriage drawn by four horses and accompanied by six hunting dogs. But everyone may hear his terrific rushing through the air, the hollow baying of his dogs, and the plashing of his horse's hoofs, as if they were passing through water; they hear his wild "Hu! Hu!" and see his companion and horn-blower, the Screech-owl.

Three travellers were once sitting in the neighbourhood of the Dummburg. The night was far advanced; the moon peeped forth between the fleeting clouds, and all around was still. Suddenly a rushing noise was heard above their heads; they looked up, and a large screech-owl flew before them. "Oh!" exclaimed one of the travellers, "that is the *Tut-Osel,* then the wild huntsman Hackelnberg is not far off." "Let us run," said the second in a tremulous tone, "before the spectre overtakes us." "Escape we can not," said the third; but you have nothing to fear, if you do not provoke him; lie flat down, quite still, on your faces, while he passes over us, but you must not speak to him, or it may be with us as it was with that shepherd. The travellers laid themselves down in the underwood, and soon heard around them a great noise as of a pack of hounds forcing their way through the thicket, and above them a hollow sound as of game when pursued, intermingled with the wild huntsman's appalling "Hu! Hu!" Two of the travellers lay close to the ground, but the third could not resist his curiosity; he cast a sideward glance through the branches, and saw the shadow of a huntsman, who with his dogs hurried over them. Everything was again still around. The travellers raised themselves slowly, and timidly they gazed after Hackelnberg, but he was gone, and did not again appear.

After a long pause, one of them asked: "Who or what is the Tut-Osel?" His companion answered: "In a remote convent in Thuringia there once lived a nun of the name of Ursel. In her lifetime she was wont to annoy the sisterhood with her howling voice, and frequently disturbed the singing, on which account they called her the Tut-Ursel. But it was much worse after her death;

---

[12] Children born on a Sunday were by the Germanic nations believed to possess the faculty of seeing spectres. See Northern Mythology, ii. 203, 275. The superstition probably still exists among the rural population of Denmark and the north of Germany.

then every night, at eleven o'clock, she put her head through a hole in the tower that opened into the choir of the church and screamed mournfully: and every morning at four o'clock she joined in the choral song."

For a day or two the sisters endured this with beating hearts and trembling knees; but on the fourth morning, when she joined in the chant, one of the sisters whispered in a tremulous voice to her neighbour: "Oh, that is certainly Ursel!" The chanting was suddenly stopped, their hair stood on end, and all the nuns ran out of the church screaming: "Oh, the Tut-Ursel! Tut-Ursel!" and all the threats of punishment and penance were insufficient to induce them again to enter the sacred edifice, until Ursel had been exercised from within the convent walls. The most famous exorcist of his time, who resided in a Capuchin convent on the banks of the Danube, was sent for, who by fasting and prayer banished Ursel, in the form of a screech owl, to the distant Dummburg.

Here she met with Hackelnberg and found in his wild cry of "Hu! Hu!" as much pleasure as he did in her "U! hu!" and now, united for ever, they go forth on their aerial hunt, he pleased at having found a being to his mind, she not less delighted at being no longer confined within the convent-walls listening to the echo of the nuns' chant.

"Now we have heard the story of the Tut-Osel," said one of the travellers, "tell us what happened to the shepherd who spoke to Hackelnberg." "Listen to the wonderful tale," answered his companion. "A shepherd once heard the wild huntsman riding just over his pens, and set his dogs after him, calling out: 'Good luck, Hackelnberg!' Hackelnberg instantly turned and cried with a hollow thundering voice: 'As thou hast helped me to hunt, thou shalt have some of the game.' The Shepherd crouched down trembling; but Hackelnberg threw a putrid haunch of a horse down into his hutch[13], so that he could neither move backwards nor forwards."

What probably gave rise to these traditions of the middle ages was a hunter, like Nimrod, of the noble house of Hakelberg or Hackelnberg. The last known hunter of this race was Hans von Hakelberg, in the sixteenth century, who died in a hospital on the road not far from the village of Wulperode, near

---

[13] The word thus rendered is Schäferkarren, which signifies a sort of cart or barrow on which there is a small sort of cabin, in which the shepherds can rest occasionally.

to Hornburg, on the confines of Brunswick. In the churchyard there his ashes are covered by a stone, on which is represented a knight in complete armour on a mule. Formerly, the traveller who passed through Wulperode was astonished at the heavy knightly armour to be seen hanging in the church, belonging to Hans of Hackelnberg. At the present time the helmet only is to be seen there; all the rest of the armour is although one knows not why—in Deersheim. Of his singular death the following tradition is preserved.

Hans von Hackelnberg, chief huntsman to the duke of Brunswick, lived only for the chase. To gratify his passion, he either bought or farmed several hunting districts, and traversed, with his followers and his large pack of dogs, fields and forests, and the mountains of the Harz, year after year, by day and by night.

He once passed the night in Harzeburg, and there dreamed that he saw a formidable wild boar, which, after a long conflict, overpowered him. When he awoke, the frightful image was ever before his eyes, and no remonstrances could divert his thoughts from the monster, although he affected to laugh at his dream. Some days after, he actually met in the Harz with a powerful boar, exactly resembling the one he had seen in his dream, in colour, in the erecting of his bristles, in size, and in the great length of his tusks. With ferocity, courage, and strength, the strife began on both sides, and long continued doubtful. To his dexterity Hans von Hackelnberg was indebted for his victory, and he ultimately stretched his formidable enemy at his feet. When he saw him at length extended on the earth, he feasted his eyes for some time on the sight, and then struck with his foot against the animal's tusks, exclaiming: "Thou canst do nothing with them now!" But he struck with such force, that one of the sharp teeth penetrated his boot and wounded his foot.

At first, he thought but little of the wound, and continued the chase till night came on. On his return home, his foot was so swollen, that it was found necessary to cut off the boot. From want of proper bandages and care, the wound became so bad in a few days, that he was obliged to hasten to Wolfenbüttel to procure help. But every motion of the carriage was intolerable to him, and it was with great difficulty he could reach the hospital of Wulperode, in which he soon after expired[14].

---

[14] For other traditions of Hackelnberg, see Northern Mythology, iii. 91-95.

HONESTY IS THE BEST POLICY.

IN the court of the castle of Grüningen on the Bode, sat, one fine summer evening, Henry, bishop of Halberstadt, and with him another bishop, who for some months had been his guest. Before them stood, in two capacious goblets, their evening potation. From ten o'clock in the morning, when they dined, until sunset, they had been sitting talking about a great wine-tun, which some bishop on the Rhine had had constructed, such as in their opinion every ecclesiastical prince, who was desirous of imparting a proper degree of splendour to his court, ought to have. The plan was at length settled, and only waited for execution; and the conversation was beginning to be very dull and monosyllabic, and interrupted by frequent gapings on both sides, when luckily Conrad the shepherd drove his beautiful white flock across the castleyard, where every evening they were counted by Bishop Henry. "May God protect you, Lord Bishop," said the Shepherd. "Good evening, Conrad," answered the prelate. But where is Harm?"

Conrad whistled, and a beautiful large ram sprang forth, first to the shepherd, and then to the bishop, who caressed it and fed it with pieces of bread which he had purposely reserved from the dinner table. The bishop then spoke a few words to his shepherd, and jokingly asked him, when he was to be married? Conrad shrugged his shoulders and drove on his flock.

The bishop now launched out in praise of the beautiful ram, which he would not lose for the world; then be com mended his good Conrad, who, he said, was honesty itself. At this his guest laughed aloud; for much travelling and long residence at many princely courts had inspired him with mistrust towards all mankind. He maintained, that to find perfectly honest servants was a downright impossibility, at least in an ecclesiastical court; they all deceived and cheated their masters; all of them were rogues, only some more, others less. Bishop Henry contradicted him with warmth, praised the general good character of all who lived under the protection of his pastoral staff, but more particularly his shepherd, Conrad, who never told him an untruth, nor had ever deceived him. "Has Conrad then never lied? Has he never deceived others? Never wronged his master?" asked the bishop ironically. "No," an wered Henry emphatically, "Conrad has never done so, nor will he ever do so."

"Never?" repeated his guest. "What will you wager?"

After many proposals, the bishops wagered a wine-cask that should contain a hundred and fifty hogsheads. And in three days Conrad, without his knowledge, was to be put to the proof. The bishops then parted for the night, rejoiced at having found for the next few days some new excitement, and each sure of the victory.

The stranger bishop, before he retired to rest, entered as usual into conference with his man Peter. This Peter was a servant in name only and occasionally was also the court-fool; he was in fact the bishop's privy councillor more than many who bore titles and orders. In all spiritual and secular matters, Peter was always the adviser and helper. He was accustomed to see, to hear, and often to think for his master, without letting it be perceived; and he had so done in the present instance.

But this evening Peter was in no very loquacious humour, for the epithet of *rogue*, which his master just before had allowed to escape him, vexed him at heart, and not until he was promised a new scarlet cloak, in the event of the wager being won, would he open his mouth. But after many sarcastic remarks on the cost of the wine-cask, that was to contain a hundred and fifty hogsheads, which would be more than the half of the yearly revenue yielded by the bishopric, he undertook to find out how this Conrad, the pattern, quintessence, and phoenix of honesty, as both master and man deridingly called him, was to be acted upon.

Peter by sunrise put the night's reflections into immediate practice, and already, before the hour of dinner, he was enabled to inform his master that Conrad entertained a passion for a young girl named Lise, who, however, would not listen to him until he had a cottage to offer her, as both of them were very poor. Peter had already spoken to Lise and found her quite ready and willing to cooperate with him in a scheme he had projected. He requested of his master a handful or two of shining batzen[15], to enable him to win the wine-tun. The bishop let him take as much as be pleased, in order that he might sit down to table so much the freer from care.

Peter now went again to the pretty Lise, and showed her the bright money, which quite covered her small table: they settled about a cottage, which a poor

---

[15] A small coin.

widow had long wished to sell, and Peter engaged to pay the price for Lise, as soon as she had brought him what he required.

The following morning Lise went to weed in the field through which Conrad was accustomed to drive his flock to pasture. Hardly had he caught a glimpse of her in the distance, than he flew towards her, accompanied by his ram Harm, seated himself by her side, and repeated to her all that he had so often said before, in the hope of obtaining his wishes. But Lise answered him very coldly, saying, she had heard it all a thousand times, that if he had nothing to tell her about a cottage of his own, he already knew her determination.

Conrad was going sorrowful away, when a half-friendly look from Lise encouraged him to ask her, why she dismissed him so prudishly, and if there were anything, he could do for her. "Well, then, by way of trial, let us see whether you really will do something for me," answered Lise. (The bishop's pet ram had in the meantime thrust himself between Conrad and herself and was eating some bread out of her hand.) "Suppose I were now to beg of you to give me your Harm, that I might sell him?" Conrad's heart sank within him. He answered sorrowfully: "Everything in the world save this. If the bishop could not feed my Harm every evening, I would not be witness to his distress. Take ten of the best sheep out of the whole flock, take all the fifty that belong to me, only leave me the one poor ram." "See!" exclaimed Lise, "you are like all men. Away with your fifty sheep! Can you refuse me such a trifle for a marriage-present? You would make a nice husband when the honey-moon was over. Go to your bishop, and let him feed his ram, while you kiss his slipper." They thus continued jarring for some time. Conrad wept for sheer vexation. Lise at length confessed to him that she had already sold the ram, to get the little cottage which they had both so often longed for, and that she must deliver it on that day, cost what it might; as she had given her word for it and would not be called a liar. She then let fall a few tears, said that all the fond hopes she had cherished of being able to purchase a cottage, in which they might live happily together with their children, were now blighted and then asked him whether sheep did not die every day, whether he never lost one, whether none were ever stolen, whether the wolf never ate up one of the counted sheep.

Love triumphed. Conrad gave her his hand and promised that before noon he would deliver the ram to her, and Lise gave Conrad hers, and engaged to be his wife within a month and perhaps something besides into the bargain.

Lise quickly returned to the town, and Conrad gazed long after her. But the joy of his betrothal was much clouded by the thoughts of the trial he had to undergo before his august and gracious master, in whose service he had until then been so happy, and who took such great pleasure in the ram.

He now stood alone in the field where Lise had been weeding, his thoughts turned inwards, and his eyes fixed on the ground. At length he struck his shepherd's staff into the earth, hung his coat upon it, and placed his hat on the top; and now a dialogue or rather a monologue ensued, during which Harm from time to time made an accompanying movement. "God's blessing, my Lord Bishop." "Good evening, Conrad; but where is Harm?" "Harm! my Lord Bishop; he is lost! he has run away!" As Conrad was thus speaking, Harm thrust himself between his feet to gaze on the strange object before which his master was making so many obeisances—"Conrad! Conrad! (with a shake of the head) he is too much accustomed to his bread. Harm could not run away, that will not pass." "Conrad tried another dialogue, in which he represented to the bishop that the ram had been stolen, when Harm interrupted him by a violent push, just as he was going to repeat his obeisances:—"He is not to be deceived so easily," cried Conrad, "that will never do."

Thus he continued for some time talking to himself, and always ending with a shake of his head, and "Conrad, Conrad! that will never do;" "and yet," he added, "I must deliver up the ram before noon; for if Lise, who has already sold it, does not keep her word, she will be a deceiver and cannot be my wife."

At length he gave a high spring in the air for joy and cried out: "Honesty is the best policy! That will do, that will do." Then, putting on his coat and hat, he drove his flock further. And before noon, with a deep sigh, he delivered to Lise his favourite Harm, which she exchanged for the money to purchase the cottage, without bestowing a thought on the dilemma in which her lover was placed.

The evening of that day was fixed for the proof of Conrad's honesty without his having any suspicion of it. Both the bishops were sitting in the courtyard over their evening cup, expecting the shepherd with his flock, who was to decide their wager. The heart of each beat high, and they spoke but little, as each would rather yield to the other the honour of constructing the great wine-tun. But Peter, the privy councillor, felt quite at ease, and, laughing in his sleeve, was rejoicing in victory, and his well-laid plans beforehand; for he had got the bishop's pet ram safe in the stable; and how could Conrad venture to disclose the real truth, which would bring down upon him the displeasure of his master, and deprive him for ever of his livelihood?

Thus, thought Peter, the privy councillor. In the meantime, Conrad drove his flock across the castleyard, and just before the bishops. Peter chuckled, for he thought he could read anxiety and trepidation in Conrad's countenance. This time no ram sprang joyfully towards Bishop Henry to be fed. "Where is Harm?" asked the prelate with a significant look. Conrad answered with a firm voice: "I have sold him—that is the truth—Honesty is the best Policy, is my maxim, my Lord Bishop, as you know, and, please God, it shall ever be so."

Peter's face visibly grew longer. The bishop exclaimed with darkened countenance and trembling voice: "Why hast thou sold the ram without informing me? I would have given thee tenfold for it. Dost thou not know"—"Hear me, my Lord Bishop," said Conrad; "Lise tempted me, as Eve once tempted Adam, and some knave tempted Lise, as the evil one tempted Eve. If he will give me back my Harm, I will not name him." (Peter turned aside full of rage, for away were his shining batzens, and his scarlet cloak, and even the ram, which must else have paid the reckoning.) "Lise," continued he, "had sold the ram without informing me beforehand; otherwise it never would have happened. I was therefore obliged to give it to her, much as it grieved me; if I had not, she would have been a liar, and now she is my wife! This is the real truth, my Lord Bishop. You can now do what you please with me. Done is done only do not punish Lise—a weak creature is soon seduced by a serpent."

Bishop Henry was about to chide, but the other bishop interrupted him, saying, with an angry side-glance at Peter, who skulked away: "I have lost the wager; for this was the trial."

And Bishop Henry did not chide. Winning the wager gave him pleasure, but more than all the casks of wine he rejoiced over the integrity of his servant and felt also what love is capable of.

Both the bishops exclaimed: "Honesty is indeed the best policy." Bishop Henry added: "As a reward for thy honesty, I will be at the expense of the wedding, and half of the flock shall be thine." "And," continued the stranger bishop, "thy favourite Harm thou shalt have again, and shalt keep the cottage as a christening gift for thy first-born."

And the bishop who lost the wager had the great wine-tun constructed, which formerly drew so many travellers to Grüningen, and which still lies, on the Spiegelsberg near Halberstadt.

THE DEVIL'S MILL.

THE summit of the Rammberg, a mountain in the Harz, which rises about two thousand feet above the level or the sea, offers to the traveller an unexpected splendid prospect. The whole rounded summit is covered with large blocks of granite, partly heaped upon each other, partly strewed around. On its highest point a group of these masses is particularly conspicuous. Here are numerous layers of such granite blocks of considerable circuit, piled one on another, partly rounded and smoothed, as if by the hand of man; these form a kind of pyramid, standing quite isolated, and rising about thirty feet above the flat summit of the mountain: round about them lie dispersed thousands of greater and smaller blocks of granite. About the middle of the last century, a tower was built on the summit of the mountain, the view from which is, perhaps, unique in North Germany, as it commands both sides of the Harz. These masses of rock are known in the neighbourhood under the name of the Devil's Mill, concerning which people relate the following tradition.

Rammberg derives its name from the god Ramm, whom the Old Saxons worshipped here. On the point of the rock which is now called the Devil's Mill once stood a statue of the god; and the inhabitants of the most beautiful and populous part of Old Saxony might see the fires which the priests here kindled for their sacrifices. The ascending columns of smoke announced to the inhabitants of the Harz, far and near, when new victims were required. Then the worshippers of Ramm flocked from every part of the Hartingau and rejoiced at seeing the bright towering flame.

When Charles and Winfrid[16] abolished German heathenism, Ramm's fire was also gradually quenched; but instead of the god, the devil, for a time, played a part on the inhospitable mountain.

---

[16] See page 441, *note.*

A miller had built himself a mill on the declivity of the Rammberg, but which at times lacked wind. The wish, therefore, soon rose within him of having a mill standing quite free on the highest point of the mountain, which would then always be in motion, let the wind blow from the east or the west, the north or the south. But it appeared to him a difficult task for men to build a large mill on such a height; and more difficult still to secure it against the storms which scattered all ordinary structures like stubble. This ever-recurring wish, and the apparent impossibility of satisfying it, deprived him of all rest both by day and night, but, all on a sudden, the devil made his appearance, and offered his services. After bargaining and haggling for a long while, the miller at last signed a contract to become the property of the evil one at the expiration of thirty years; and the devil, on his part, promised to build him a faultless mill, with six sets of stones, on the top of the Rammberg, and that it should be completed in the following night before cock-crowing.

The infernal architect heaped the rocks one upon another and built a mill, the like of which had never been seen. Soon after midnight, he went to the miller's house on the declivity of the mountain, to fetch him, for the purpose of trying the new mill, and taking possession of it.

With a beating heart the miller followed the fiend and found everything even beyond his expectations. Gladly would he have given the half of his life away could he but have found a single fault. But everything appeared perfect.

Trembling he was now going to receive the mill under the terrible conditions, when he discovered that there was a stone wanting, which to a miller was indispensable. The builder long denied the asserted fault but was at length obliged to confess it. Immediately he set about supplying the deficiency; but just as he came flying through the air with the stone, lo! the cock, at the mill below, crowed.

Frantic with rage at the failure of his plan, the fiend grasped the building, tore down the sails, and wheels, and stones, and flung them about in all directions. He then hurled about the rocks which he had heaped up to the clouds, so that they covered the whole of the Rammberg, and only a small portion of the foundation remained, as an everlasting memorial of the DEVIL'S MILL.

THE DAMBECK BELLS IN ROBEL.[17]

THE church at Dambeck, the walls of which are yet standing, is of the remotest antiquity; it was, in fact, built before the flood; but the bell-tower has sunk into the lake; and, therefore, in former times, the bells were sometimes on St John's day seen to rise out of the water, and place themselves in the sun at noon-tide.

Once some children, who had been taking their parents' dinner to them in the field, on their return sat down on the borders of the lake to wash their handkerchiefs, when they saw the bells rise up so high that one of the little girls hung her handkerchief upon one of them to dry. After a while, two of the bells began to sink down into the water again; but the third could not move from the spot. Here upon the children ran into the town and related what they had seen. Now the whole town of Röbel came running out; and the wealthy, who wished to get the hell for themselves, attached eight, sixteen, and even more horses to it, but still they were unable to move it from the spot.

Then came a poor man driving by with two oxen, who, seeing what was going on, instantly yoked his two oxen to the bell, saying: "With God go poor as well as rich, all alike," and conveyed the bell, without difficulty, to Röbel.

There they hung it in the Neustadt church; and every time a poor person dies, whose relations cannot afford to pay for the tolling of the other bells, this hell is rung, and its sound is ever, "Dambeck, Dambeck."

THE WITCHES' HORN.

IN the neighbourhood of Rönneby lived a landowner whose fields and farm-yards the witches on every Walpurgis[18] night so damaged that at length a faithful domestic resolved to put a stop to their mischief. In order to carry out

---

[17] This and the following are from Kuhn und Schwartz, Norddeutsche Sagen, &c., Leipsig, 1848.

[18] The eve of the 1st of May, when the witches are said to ride to the Brocken. See Northern Mythology, iii. *passim*.

his project, he rode on May-day eve to the spot where they all were accustomed to assemble and found them collected round a large marble slab, which rested on four golden pillars; on the slab lay a golden horn of beautiful form and workmanship. The witches were eating and drinking and invited him to partake of their refection; but one of his fellow-servants, whom he found there, warned him against drinking, saying they only wished to poison him. He therefore threw the proffered beverage away, seized the horn, and rode off in full gallop towards his master's house, where all the gates and doors had been left open, in order to remove all hindrances; so that, however quickly the witches were after him, they were unable to overtake him.

The next day, when he had just brought the horn to his master, an elegantly-dressed gentleman was announced, and, on being introduced, requested him to restore the golden horn, and promised, in return, to inclose his property with a wall seven feet high; but in case of his refusal, he threatened him with the destruction of his farms three times by fire, and that just at the moment when he was most priding himself in his wealth. The stranger then departed, giving the owner three days for reflection. He would not, however, restore the horn.

But hardly had he got the next harvest well housed, when all his barns stood in flames, and the same disaster happened a second and a third time, till he was quite reduced to poverty. The king, however, who had heard of his misfortunes, bestowed on him such a liberal donation that he was enabled to rebuild his farms.

And now the horn was sent about in every direction, in the hope of discovering whence it came; it was even sent to Constantinople, to ascertain whether it belonged to the Turks, but no owner could be found. Where it now is, the narrator of the above, who was a Swede, but settled in Swinemünde, knows not.

PETER MUGGEL.[19]

IN the period when Hamburg and Lübeck were powerful cities, the bold robber Peter Muggel was master of the village and castle of Schwienkuhlen near Arensbök. From this place he plundered the surrounding country, and particularly kept a strict look-out for travellers or wagons laden with merchandise, on their way between the two cities. His depredations soon became intolerable, and a party of soldiers was sent against him, who reduced both the village and castle to a heap of ruins. The hill on which the castle stood is still called Muggelberg. Peter had long been expecting an attack, and had, consequently, removed his most precious treasures and ready money into a cave, which he had prepared for the purpose in the Klenzauer Weide, a wood near the village of Klenzau. When the soldiers had destroyed his nest, he rode away on his white horse, and soon resumed his old profession, even more zealously than before. All attempts made by the two cities to discover his new lurking-place were for a long time fruitless. At length it was found; but with his desperate companions he succeeded in destroying those who were sent to take him; but the citizens were constantly sending more troops against him, so that Peter before long had lost nearly all his men and had good reason to fear that he himself should fall into the hands of his enemies. But rather than they should get possession of his treasures he had recourse to the last expedient. In a dark stormy night, he called upon the evil one for help. Soon he made his appearance, in the form of a black goat, and commanded Peter to dig a hole and deposit his treasures in it. When he cast up the first spadeful of earth, all around became as light as day; for before him stood the black goat, with a lamp burning under his tail. When the hole was finished, the treasures were counted and deposited. The evil one then set his seal upon the spot, which is yet to be seen as a broad flat stone. "Now," said he, "your treasure is safe; should you, or any other, require it again, then you must come in such a night as this, with just such a black goat as I am, and also with exactly the same kind of light to fetch it; for if the goat has a single white hair, or you bring any other light, your work will be in vain." And the seal remains to this day untouched on the same spot, so that the treasure has not yet been raised; for Peter Muggel's days were numbered.

---

[19] This and the three following traditions are from Müllenhoff, ut sup.

The Lübeckers were soon again in quest of him. To deceive his pursuers, he rode in the twilight to a smith's, had his horse's shoes reversed, and rode to his hiding-place, flattering himself that his enemies would believe he had ridden away. They came upon his traces, and believed such to be the case; but, in the hope of finding treasure, they went into the cave and found the robber sleeping. One of the party fell upon him and stabbed him. Had he been awake they certainly would not have overcome him.

Since that time, Peter Muggel often hunts in the night, on his three-legged white horse, through the village of Gieselrade with a frightful noise and rattling. He then rides to a large pond in the neighbourhood of the village, swims his horse across, and then rides back to his hiding place. Everyone must beware of meeting him[20].

BLACK MARGARET.

THERE once reigned over Denmark a queen, who was called Black Margaret[21]; she caused the Elbe to be blockaded with long stakes and a strong chain, so that no vessel could either leave or enter the river. In like manner, she' obstructed the ports of Kiel and Flensborg, and ruined the navigation of the Schlei. She besieged Itzehoe, and on the feast of the Nativity of the Virgin (Sept. 8), she caused a great wall and a bridge to be built across the Stör, for the purpose of driving the waters into the town, and the burghers have ever since kept the day as a festival and call it the *Borgerdag.*

Black Margaret also caused the Dannewerk[22] to be constructed, as a barrier against the Germans. Before it was quite finished, being attacked by the

---

[20] In the year 1470, Frau Abel, Peter Muggel's widow, sold the village and manor of Schwienkuhlen to the convent of Arensbök. Schröder, Topogr. von Holstein, ii. 340.

[21] She was the wife of Christopher L; she died A.D. 1283. The nickname of Sprenghest was given her from her agility in horsemanship.

[22] The celebrated rampart of earth and stones extending from the Eider or Treen to the Schlei. It was originally constructed by the Danish king Godefrid, at the beginning of the ninth century, as a defence against the Germans. Considerable remains of it still exist. This legend about Queen Margaret is a complete fiction.

enemy, she placed a row of cows in the outer ditch, from which it is named the Cow-ditch. On these her assailants expended all their ammunition, mistaking the cattle for helmed warriors. In the meantime, she completed the work.

She was very crafty, and always rode through the country with her horse's shoes reversed, so that no one should know where she was. In this manner she once escaped from the Oldenburgers. She had sent her son to Oldenburg to receive the contributions; but the Oldenburg shoemakers seized him, cut him in pieces, and sent him back to his mother in a barrel of salt. Frantic with rage and grief at this atrocity, she laid siege to the town, and threw up intrenchments, which may still be seen at Weissenhaus on the Baltic. The Russians, however, came to the succour of the town, and it was only by the above-mentioned stratagem that Margaret escaped. From that time, the Oldenburg shoemakers have not dared to leave the town, and, even to this day, attend no annual fair.

Near Börnhoved she fought a great battle and as she mounted her horse, trod on a large stone, which long her the marks of her footstep. Others say that it was the mark of her horse's hoof, and that a similar stone lies on the boundaries of the estates of Depenau and Bockhorn. This queen was a witch, and still wanders about: many tales are related of her.

In the neighbourhood of Lohheide, in Schleswig, there is a small hill called Dronningshöi (the Queen's Mount). It was thrown up by her soldiers, who carried the earth in their helmets. On this spot Black Margaret overcame and killed a prince with whom she was engaged in war. When she saw that fortune was turning against her, the crafty woman sent a messenger to him to say, that it was unrighteous to sacrifice so many lives in their quarrel; far better would it be, if they alone settled the strife. The prince thinking himself a match for a woman, accepted the challenge. While they were fighting together, the queen begged for a few moments' respite, while she fastened her helmet a little tighter. The prince acceded to her request. She then said, she durst not trust him, unless he stuck his sword up to the hilt into the earth. This he accordingly did when she immediately assailed him and cut his head off.

He is buried in the Queen's Mount, and the people who live in the neighbourhood have often seen him sitting before a silver table, on which stood a silver teapot, a silver cream-jug, and a silver cup.

KING WALDEMAR.[23]

NOT far from Bau there stood formerly the hunting-seat of Waldemarstoft, where King Waldemar was accustomed to pass the summer and autumn, that he might enjoy his favourite diversion of the chase. The king once, accompanied by many huntsmen and dogs, rode early in the morning to the forest. The hunt was good, but the more game they found, the stronger grew his desire to continue the chase. The day ended, the sun went down, yet still he did not give in. But when dark night set in, and it was no longer possible to continue the sport, the king exclaimed "Oh! that I could hunt forever!" A voice was then heard in the air, saying: "Thy wish shall be granted, King Waldemar, from this hour thou shalt hunt forever." Soon after the king died, and from the day of his death he rides every night, on a snow-white horse, through the air, in furious chase, surrounded by his huntsmen and dogs. It is only on St. John's night that he is to be heard but in the city-ditch at Flensborg he has been also heard in the autumn. The air then resounds with the echo of the horn and the baying of dogs, with whistling and calling, as if a whole party were in motion. People then say, "There goes King Waldemar!"

The old hunting-palace is now converted into an inn but one of the rooms still remains in the same state it was in when inhabited by King Waldemar. The walls are covered with old pictures in one corner is a canopy-bed over which is a dark red velvet coverlet, bordered with gold fringe, in very tolerable preservation. There is also an old organ, on which the king was in the habit of playing. In this room he was once shot at. The murderer fired through the door, but missed his aim, and hit the wall where the king's picture hung. There is a hole in the picture through which the bullet passed before it entered the wall, where the mark is still visible.

---

[23] This was Waldemar IV., king of Denmark. He reigned from 1334 to 1375. He is distinguished by the sobriquet of Atterdag, given him, it is said, in consequence of a phrase he was constantly using: "Morgen er *atter* en *dag,*" *Tomorrow is* again *a* day. For other traditions of his hunt, see Northern Mythology. ii.

THE WONDERFUL TREE IN DITMARSCHEN.

NEAR the bridge at Süderheistede, where in ancient times the chief fortress and vast intrenchments, for the protection of the country, were constructed, there stood in those times of freedom a linden-tree, on a beautiful circular spot, surrounded by a ditch, which was known throughout the land as the Wonderful Tree. It was much higher than all the other trees far and near, and its branches all grew cross wise, so that no one had ever seen its like.

Until the conquest of the country, it was always fresh and green. But there was an old prophecy, that as soon as the Ditmarschers lost their freedom, the tree would wither. And so, it came to pass. But a magpie will one day build its nest in its branches, and batch five white young ones, and then the tree will begin to sprout out anew, and again be green, and the country recover its ancient freedom.